J.K. ROWLING
A BIBLIOGRAPHY 1997–2013

J.K. ROWLING
A BIBLIOGRAPHY 1997–2013

PHILIP W. ERRINGTON

Bloomsbury Academic
An imprint of Bloomsbury Publishing Plc

BLOOMSBURY

LONDON · NEW DELHI · NEW YORK · SYDNEY

Bloomsbury Academic

An imprint of Bloomsbury Publishing Plc

50 Bedford Square	1385 Broadway
London	New York
WC1B 3DP	NY 10018
UK	USA

www.bloomsbury.com

**BLOOMSBURY and the Diana logo are trademarks of Bloomsbury
Publishing Plc**

First published 2015
Reprinted 2015

British Library Cataloguing-in-Publication Data

A catalogue record for this book is available from the British Library.

ISBN: HB: 978-1-8496-6974-0
ePDF: 978-1-8496-6976-4
ePUB: 978-1-8496-6977-1

Library of Congress Cataloging-in-Publication Data

Errington, Philip W.
J.K. Rowling: a bibliography 1997–2013/Philip W. Errington.
pages cm
Includes bibliographical references and index.
ISBN 978-1-84966-974-0 (hardback: alk. paper) 1. Rowling,
J. K.–Bibliography. I. Title.
Z8763.65.E88 2015
[PR6068.O93]
016.823'914–dc23
2014025489

Typeset by Fakenham Prepress Solutions, Fakenham, Norfolk NR21 8NN
Printed and bound in Great Britain

THE DEDICATION OF THIS BOOK IS SPLIT SEVEN WAYS:

to Liz Errington
to Sophie Errington
to Caroline Errington
to Angus Henderson, who first suggested I read a *Harry Potter* book,
to Henry Woudhuysen, who first introduced me to descriptive bibliography,
to my colleagues at Sotheby's
and, finally, to J.K. Rowling

CONTENTS

A.   BOOKS AND PAMPHLETS BY J.K. ROWLING

A8   The Daily Prophet - 1 October 1999 (1999)

A9   Harry Potter and the Goblet of Fire (2000)

A10   Fantastic Beasts & Where to Find Them (2001)

A14   Harry Potter and the Deathly Hallows (2007)

A15   The Tales of Beedle the Bard (2008)

A16   The Casual Vacancy (2012)

ACKNOWLEDGEMENTS

I am grateful to Jo Rowling for responding positively to my suggestion of a bibliography.

Nigel Newton has supported the project from the beginning and permitted access to Bloomsbury's archives. He also allowed me to interview him and hearing his perspective was hugely valuable. His staff have also been extremely helpful and I thank Emma Matthewson for guiding me through much material, Polly Whybrow for her unfailing patience in answering questions, Jyoti Basuita, James Tupper, Natalie Hamilton, Louise Cameron and Laura McCarthy for their help, Terry Woodley for his design expertise and, especially, Caroline Wintersgill who has been unfailing in her assistance and enthusiasm.

Neil Blair of the Blair Partnership has illuminated many dark areas. Rachel Pronger has been exceptionally efficient and Joanne Warren has conducted some valuable research in the Blair Partnership archives.

Arthur A. Levine allowed me to interview him and provided much useful information. His staff, including Emily Clement and Nick Thomas, have been helpful.

Fiddy Henderson, the author's personal assistant until 2014, has been unfailing in her help.

I enjoyed a most entertaining lunch with Barry Cunningham and he later read a draft of part of the notes for the first Harry Potter book. He corrected a number of mistakes. I would also like to thank David Shelley of Little, Brown for his assistance.

There are a number of people who have aided my research into newspapers and periodicals. Nicky Stonehill of StonehillSalt PR, Nick Mays of News UK, Tim Dale of News UK, Christine McGilly of Newsquest Media Group, Ruth Marsh of the Telegraph media group and Jean Martin of *Harvard Magazine* have been most helpful.

Others who have answered annoying questions include Melissa Anelli (also known as the webmistress of The Leaky Cauldron website) and Christine Robinson of Scottish Language Dictionaries.

I am hugely grateful to the numerous bookdealers who have answered questions or given access to their stock. David Cornell deserves special mention for his generosity and trust. Others include Donald Algeo, Pat Cramer, Dennis M. V. David, Brian LeMasters, Pom Harrington, David Oyerly, Taney Reynolds and Justin G. Schiller.

My colleagues at Sotheby's deserve special mention. The photography in this volume is by Paul Brickell. He has taken all shots with limitless good humour and skill. I would also like to thank Heath Cooper and Steve Curley for their assistance with digital images. My colleagues in the book and manuscript department have been kind in feigning interest from the beginning to the conclusion of the project. Leah Delany, from Sotheby's book and manuscript department in New York, has been more than helpful in sending books across the Atlantic.

I am deeply indebted to Prof. Henry Woudhuysen who first introduced me to the discipline of descriptive bibliography and, many years ago, supervised my first bibliography as a PhD dissertation. Others who have taken an interest in bibliographical endeavours include Prof. Warwick Gould, Colin Smythe and Wayne G. Hammond.

I would also like to thank Lawrence Drizen, Angus Henderson, Sarah Howard, Sarah Hyde, Kathy Thompson and Phil Thompson for raiding their shelves and lending volumes. Bill Zachs kindly provided an article from the *Journal of the Edinburgh Bibliographical Society*. Angus Henderson deserves a second mention for urging me, time and again, to read a Harry Potter.

I am grateful to Kim Storry, Dawn Booth and others at Fakenham Prepress Solutions for all their help doing proof stages.

Finally, my thanks to my long-suffering family: Liz, Sophie and Caroline. Will Sophie and Caroline prefer the adventures of Harry Potter or those of Kay Harker? Time alone will tell.

As someone who respects comprehensive research, I am in awe of the level of detail and amount of time Philip Errington has dedicated to this slavishly thorough and somewhat mind-boggling bibliography. Even in my most deluded moments, I could never have anticipated that an idea that occurred to me on a train to Manchester could have spawned this amount of verbiage and prose in every language under the sun. I am humbled and deeply flattered.

J.K. Rowling
Edinburgh,
November 2014

INTRODUCTION

This is a book about books. A descriptive bibliography looks at books as objects and describes them as such (often in painstaking detail). It can also tell some of the story behind the books themselves.

Whether you originally encountered Harry Potter as a book, film, e-book or audio book, the series was first presented to the world in a traditional printed paper format. That the publishing world responded to demand and supplied the growing phenomenon is unique in the history of publishing. Never has a series sold so well, required such large print-runs and been marketed in such a carefully planned and successful manner. Never before did a series start with 500 copies in hardback and conclude with a matching edition of over eight million copies.

Of course, these original books are merely the carriers of information: the physical form in which readers first experienced the imaginary world of J.K. Rowling. Yet, the features of those books provide some detail behind one of the defining moments in late twentieth- and early twenty-first-century culture. From the first edition of the first Harry Potter book (in which the publisher's blurb seized upon a comparison with Roald Dahl) to the desire of the author to publish adult crime fiction under a pseudonym, these books chart a development of an author and a brand.

Inevitably, a bibliography also provides the answer to one basic question: 'is my copy a first edition?' This, of course, leads to the great chestnut of the book world: 'what is a first edition?' Within John Carter's 1952 Bible for bibliophiles, *ABC for Book Collectors*, the term is defined as

> Very, very roughly speaking… the first appearance of the work in question, independently, between its own covers. But, like many other household words, this apparently simple term is not always as simple as it appears…

One problem is that technology and book production change, and a set of terms appropriate to one era may be outdated in another. As noted by Carter:

> … an edition comprises all copies of a book printed at any time or times from one setting-up of type without substantial change… while an impression or printing comprises the whole number of copies of that edition printed at one time…

In the strictest bibliographical terms, one might claim that the recent 2013 Andrew Davidson artwork series edition of *Harry Potter and the Philosopher's Stone* is a first edition since the setting of text is (almost) identical to the original book released on 26 June 1997. Yet this is obviously nonsense.

But, potentially, lucrative nonsense. The auction record, to date, for a copy of *Harry Potter and the Philosopher's Stone* (excluding an annotated copy) is £23,000. A market has developed in which the unscrupulous offer (and sometimes sell) common reprints as collectable first editions. For our purposes, a first edition is a first impression of a new edition and this volume will provide a guide to those apparently affected by a confundus charm. In the simplest terms, unless your copy includes a strike-line of numbers (usually '10 9 8 7 6 5 4 3 2 1') or notes 'First Edition', it is a reprint. Surprisingly even some librarians get these simple facts wrong.

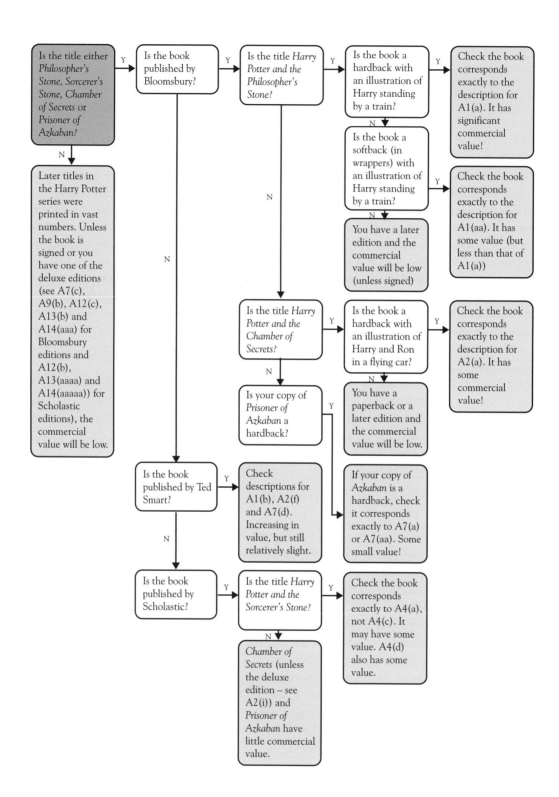

Is the title either *Philosopher's Stone*, *Sorcerer's Stone*, *Chamber of Secrets* or *Prisoner of Azkaban*?

N → Later titles in the Harry Potter series were printed in vast numbers. Unless the book is signed or you have one of the deluxe editions (see A7(c), A9(b), A12(c), A13(b) and A14(aaa) for Bloomsbury editions and A12(b), A13(aaaa) and A14(aaaaa)) for Scholastic editions), the commercial value will be low.

Y → Is the book published by Bloomsbury?

Y → Is the title *Harry Potter and the Philosopher's Stone?*

Y → Is the book a hardback with an illustration of Harry standing by a train?

Y → Check the book corresponds exactly to the description for A1(a). It has significant commercial value!

N → Is the book a softback (in wrappers) with an illustration of Harry standing by a train?

Y → Check the book corresponds exactly to the description for A1(aa). It has some value (but less than that of A1(a))

N → You have a later edition and the commercial value will be low (unless signed)

N → Is the title *Harry Potter and the Chamber of Secrets?*

Y → Is the book a hardback with an illustration of Harry and Ron in a flying car?

Y → Check the book corresponds exactly to the description for A2(a). It has some commercial value!

N → You have a paperback or a later edition and the commercial value will be low.

N → Is your copy of *Prisoner of Azkaban* a hardback?

Y → If your copy of *Azkaban* is a hardback, check it corresponds exactly to A7(a) or A7(aa). Some small value!

N → Is the book published by Ted Smart?

Y → Check descriptions for A1(b), A2(f) and A7(d). Increasing in value, but still relatively slight.

N → Is the book published by Scholastic?

Y → Is the title *Harry Potter and the Sorcerer's Stone?*

Y → Check the book corresponds exactly to A4(a), not A4(c). It may have some value. A4(d) also has some value.

N → *Chamber of Secrets* (unless the deluxe edition – see A2(i)) and *Prisoner of Azkaban* have little commercial value.

In June 2010 I was in the New York Public Library and tried to see a first American edition of *Harry Potter and the Chamber of Secrets*. One copy (formerly known as 'JFE 03-7277') had been given special status. It had been re-classified as '***Rowling, J.K.' This was going to something quite special, I thought. When it arrived it had a library bookmark noting it was 'to be read under supervision'. All very curious treatment for a fiftieth impression with a commercial value, I'd suggest, of a few dollars.

Whilst on the subject of value, now is a good opportunity to mention the hologram stickers produced by J.K. Rowling's office from around 2007. Given the number of forged signatures, the author's office had hologram stickers produced that provide authentication of the genuine article. Rolls of stickers therefore accompanied the author when attending signing sessions. To date there have been two versions of the stickers.

Many readers will cherish their own copy of a book simply because it was their first exposure to a much-loved work. Between these boards (or wrappers) unfolded a text which consumed, entertained, distracted, educated, intrigued or captivated them. (The choice of verb is as varied as the reader.) However, there are also other people known as collectors for whom there is a desire to construct an accumulation of material – perhaps a small library – which reflects and becomes a passion. For these people, the first impression of a new edition is important.

There are others who may seek to understand, perhaps, the development of Harry Potter from a marketing perspective, or seek to work out an order of books, chart the development of writer or understand the chronology of textual changes, etc. There are many uses of a bibliography and I hope that the present work will help answer some popular questions.

The most common question, connected to commercial value, is 'have I got a *valuable* first edition?' This is a relatively basic question and can be answered most simply with the aid of a flowchart. I encourage anyone wishing to receive an answer to this question to work their way through the opposite diagram. If, at any point, you find that the diagram abandons you without a choice, the chances are you do *not* have a valuable first edition.

Here, then, is a descriptive bibliography, in chronological order of title, of the works of J.K. Rowling from 1997 until the end of 2013. I regret that I was unable to include paperback editions of *The Cuckoo's Calling*, the new editions of the seven Harry Potter books with artwork by Jonny Duddle or *The Silkworm*. The bibliography comprises four sections.

A. Books and Pamphlets

The largest portion of this book is the 'A' section, which lists and describes books and pamphlets by Rowling published in English in the UK and US. Large print and Braille editions are excluded. Within each title different editions are presented in date order (and given sequential letters of the alphabet). When two (or more) editions were published on the same date, double letters are used. 'New' editions comprise changes in livery or design, rather than re-setting of text. It is convenient, here, to categorize the different series of Harry Potter novels which have been published. To this listing may be added the one-off editions. In the UK, therefore, we can classify as follows:

- Original children's artwork series in hardback
  see A1(a), A2(a), A7(a), A7(aa), A7(aaa), A9(a), A12(a), A13(a) and A14(a)
- Original children's artwork series in paperback
  see A1(aa), A2(b), A7(e), A9(e), A12(d), A13(c) and A14(b)
- Ted Smart/'The Book People' children's artwork series in hardback
  see A1(b), A2(f), A7(d) and A9(c)
- Adult artwork series in paperback
  see A1(c), A2(d), A7(ee) and A9(d)
- Children's artwork series in deluxe hardback
  see A1(d), A2(e), A7(c), A9(b), A12(c), A13(b) and A14(aaa)
- 'Celebratory' children's artwork series in paperback
  see A1(e), A2(j), A7(h), A9(j), A12(g), A13(f) and A14(e)
- Adult Michael Wildsmith photography artwork series in paperback
  see A1(f), A2(l), A7(i), A9(h), A12(dd), A13(cc) and A14(bb)
- Adult Michael Wildsmith photography artwork series in hardback
  see A1(g), A2(m), A7(j), A9(i), A12(aa), A13(aa) and A14(aa)
- 'Bloomsbury 21' series in paperback
  see A1(h)
- 'Signature' Claire Melinsky artwork series in paperback
  see A1(i), A2(n), A7(k), A9(k), A12(h), A13(g) and A14(f)
- 'Signature' Claire Melinsky artwork series in hardback
  see A1(j), A2(o), A7(l), A9(l), A12(i), A13(h) and A14(g)
- 'Spineless Classics' poster
  see A1(k)
- Adult Andrew Davidson artwork series in paperback
  see A1(l), A2(p), A7(m), A9(m), A12(j), A13(j) and A14(i)
- Later children's artwork series in paperback
  see A1(m), A2(r) and A7(o)

In the US there have been fewer groups, as follows:

- Original children's artwork series in hardback
  see A4(a), A2(c), A7(b), A9(aa), A12(aaa), A13(aaa) and A14(aaaa)
- Original children's artwork series in paperback
  see A4(b), A2(g), A7(f), A9(f), A12(e), A13(d) and A14(c)
- Book Club children's artwork series in hardback
  see A4(c), A2(h), A7(g), A9(g), A12(f), A13(e) and A14(d)
- Children's artwork series in deluxe hardback
  see A4(d) and A2(i)
- Mass market adult artwork series in paperback
  see A4(e) and A2(k)
- Children's artwork series in deluxe hardback and slipcase
  see A12(b), A13(aaaa) and A14(aaaaa)

- School market children's artwork in paperback
    see A4(f)
- 'Anniversary' children's artwork in hardback
    see A4(g)
- Later children's artwork series in paperback
    see A4(h), A2(q), A7(n), A9(n), A12(k), A13(i) and A14(h)

Restricting the bibliography to UK and US editions regrettably excludes the Canadian editions first distributed by Raincoast Books. Although the Canadian editions comprise the Bloomsbury settings, the first edition of *Harry Potter and the Order of the Phoenix* was published on 100 per cent recycled paper and carried an ecologically worded paragraph written by Rowling on the half-title. This bibliographical oddity is excluded, but noted here.

The decision to separate the English *Harry Potter and the Philosopher's Stone* from the American *Harry Potter and the Sorcerer's Stone* is correct within the strictest bibliographical rules since the two titles are different (and so, in occasional places, is the text). Nobody will need reminding that both titles are the first in the Harry Potter series.

We start each description with a transcription of the title-page before providing details of collation. The construction of the book is noted here.

Modern binding techniques or methods of mass publication have made traditional gatherings and signatures largely redundant. Most books described within these pages are constructed from unsigned leaves and bound by 'perfect binding' using a strong adhesive. Few are constructed in the traditional manner of gatherings sewn together. Although noted as 'indeterminate gatherings', *some* sense of more traditional book imposition can be gathered. With the current method of book production a collation *might* be discerned by dissecting the book, but this is too drastic an action. Moreover, beyond indicating whether a volume is complete or not, collation is less important to the modern bibliophile than to a collector of books printed in an earlier era.

A measurement of page size is provided in addition to a register of page numbers. Numbers noted within square brackets are not printed but may be inferred.

Details of the page contents are then given. Full transcriptions are, mostly, provided. There are many little details which vary: the change in Bloomsbury's office address or the appearance (and wording) of Warner Bros' copyright line, for example. Note, also, the lack of space between the name of the illustrator and copyright date in A1(a) and A1(aa). These minute details can only be shown in full transcriptions. Although a bibliographer might feel justified in noting, for example: 'seven lines of copyright information', this can hide considerable detail. I have chosen, therefore, to provide exhaustive detail hoping that these transcriptions of text will find a variety of uses. Ultimately, the insomniac may find soporific comfort too. My own additions are provided within square brackets. Naturally, when transcribing text that includes square brackets, an additional system is required. Therefore, the words 'square bracket' within printed square brackets correspond to the printed symbol in the original source text. Please note that my transcriptions of text do not reproduce small caps or bold text.

Traditional areas of bibliographical description continue with a note of paper stock used (although, to date, no laid paper has been used for English or American publications). A brief note of running titles is then provided (noted as being on the verso or recto of a leaf). In the book world the leaf is important, not the page. One leaf presents two pages: the verso and the recto. When viewing an open book the verso is on the left and the recto on the right.

A note about illustrations within the volume is then given. When no note is provided, it can be assumed that the volume is not illustrated. It will be immediately seen that the English editions of the Harry Potter novels are not illustrated, whereas the American editions contain vignettes at the beginning of each chapter. There is also some variation in typographical features and these are listed in the description at this point.

A description of the book's binding is then provided. The term 'pictorial boards' describes the familiar English hardback sporting a printed design. 'Boards', together with a note of a colour, describes a hardback book bound with a paper-like finish. This is in contrast to coloured 'cloth'. A combination of boards and cloth can be found on several American editions which comprise cloth-backed spines with boards. The term 'wrappers' describes paperback editions. If the insides of wrappers are not described, it can be assumed that they are blank. When describing colours, I have avoided the use of complicated colour chart terminology. With the colourful printing of children's books (in particular), a vast pallet of colours has been used. There is, however, usually one colour that predominates for printing text on the binding. A statement such as 'all in yellow' can be taken to mean 'all text printed in yellow, unless otherwise noted'. I have omitted ISBN information when it appears printed as part of the barcode. Presence or omission of an ISBN as part of a barcode is never an issue point and, I assume, of little interest.

If a dust-jacket was issued this will then be described, together with a transcription of all text. The terms 'spine', 'upper cover', 'lower cover', 'upper inside flap' and 'lower inside flap' are used for different sections. As one would expect, no paperback editions have been issued with dust-jackets.

A bibliography records facts and one obvious detail is the accurate publication date for a volume. This has not been easy to uncover, however. I have been assisted by staff at Bloomsbury, Scholastic and the Blair Partnership, but when doubt remains this is noted. The original publication price is also cited.

A note of contents provides a basic transcription of the opening of the text, or sections of text (in the case of the four issues of *The Daily Prophet*).

The 'notes' section seeks to record any interesting background including, for the English editions, details of textual changes for reprints (or new editions).

A register of consulted copies is of some limited use and records the surprising lack of first edition copies in the British Library (BL). For many traditional bibliographers, the date stamped within the copy from the national collection provides interesting detail to their work. Not so here. The British Library has a thiry-third reprint of A1(a) (stamped May 2005) and a fourth reprint of A1(aa) (stamped 8 December 1997). It seems to have bought a twenty-fifth reprint of A2(c) in April 2000. This is slightly interesting, but not particularly noteworthy.

Private collectors have been most generous in providing copies for me to describe. Where no identification of source is provided, the collector wished to remain completely anonymous.

Some very limited reprint information concludes this section. Such detail is far from comprehensive, due to the quantity of reprints published. For English editions, reprints usually include a strike-line ('10 9 8 7 6 5') or a single figure ('22'), for example. These correspond to the fifth impression and twenty-second impressions respectively. American editions also tend to include a year strike-line ('9/9 0/0 1 2 3 4') in addition to place of publication and a plant code. These additional pieces of information have been included. I have generally omitted providing a register of where reprint copies have been consulted. If any readers would care to send me details of the reprints I have failed to include, I would be most grateful.

AA. Proof Copies/Advance Reader's Copies of Books

The same rules of description are employed to record proof copies or, as named by Scholastic, 'Advance Reader's Copies'. It is a strange circumstance that book collectors generally rate a first edition more highly than a proof copy.

However, for the textual scholar, for example, the English proof of *Prisoner of Azkaban* exists in two states and rewards investigation.

B. Books and Pamphlets with Contributions

The next portion of this book provides some detail about the books and pamphlets published in the UK and US to which Rowling has contributed original material. It is of interest to note that her first contribution appears before publication of *Philosopher's Stone* and formed part of Bloomsbury's marketing campaign for the book. The majority of contributions result from support for charities and other organizations.

A less thorough description is adopted for this section (as with most bibliographies). Following a title-page transcription, significant information is transcribed from the publisher's imprint page.

A measurement of page size starts the core of the description of the book itself. This includes a register of page numbers, details of paper stock, a brief note about binding (printed wrappers, pictorial wrappers or boards), publication date (usually as cited by the Nielsen BookData online database) and price.

The Rowling contribution is then listed, with the opening quoted and details of how it is headed or signed.

C. Contributions to Newspapers and Periodicals

Contributions to newspapers and periodicals form the penultimate section. I have chosen to omit pieces that appear to be based entirely on interviews or are obviously written by a reporter or journalist. The pieces included here are original contributions written by the author: a diary entry (C02), a piece in support of a charity (C13, C14 or C15), a book review (C18) or the written version of speeches (C08 and C19), for example. The only piece of fiction is the first chapter from *Goblet of Fire* (C05), published a few days after the book was released. Occasionally the distinction between interview or report and original contribution becomes blurred. Items C03 and C04, for example, appear to derive from BBC Radio Four's *With Great Pleasure* series. For those seeking pieces based on interviews and filtered by a journalist there are a number of admirable websites which seek to record every statement and slight utterance by the author. It's an endeavour best suited outside the restrictions of a printed book.

In descriptions, the title of the article or contribution is given before the title of the publication. If the piece appeared in a specific section or supplement of a newspaper, this is noted. Page references are usually included.

D. Items Created Specifically for Sale at Auction

The final section presents items created by the author specifically for sale at auction. For over a decade the allure of unique pieces by J.K. Rowling has benefitted a number of charities. These are, with one exception, part of the author's cannon of written work and deserve to be recorded as such. The major exception is item D8 but it seems appropriate to record it here as evidence of a versatile author.

Some bibliographies include recordings, TV or radio broadcasts. With a few exceptions (a 2005 recording by HNP Limited of Rowling in conversation with Stephen Fry, released at the time as a bonus to several of the English audio book versions, for example), there have been few commercially issued items of the author herself. There have been, of course, a vast number of broadcast items and, as with newspaper or magazine interviews, the detail of these is probably best excluded from this record of printed items.

I have also excluded contributions to video games (the 2012 *Book of Spells* for the Sony PlayStation) and websites (Pottermore and www.jkrowling.co.uk of particular note).

As with any book of this nature, there will be errors and inconsistencies. Producing the first map of the territory allows others to navigate more easily and invites participants to test the data. I apologize in advance for any short-comings but if I have omitted an item or incorrectly (or inconsistently) recorded something I would be grateful if you could bring it to my attention. As the bibliography of a living writer, this is, above all, a work in progress.

When Robin Ellacott, working for Cormoran Stike in *The Cuckoo's Calling*, starts some research she is rewarded with 'loads of information… including a bibliography…' Lucky old Robin.

Dr Philip W. Errington
April 2014

A. BOOKS AND PAMPHLETS BY J.K. ROWLING

HARRY POTTER AND THE PHILOSOPHER'S STONE

A1(a)   **FIRST ENGLISH EDITION**   **(1997)**
(children's artwork series in hardback)

Harry Potter and the | Philosopher's Stone | J. K. Rowling | [publisher's device of a dog, 11 by 18mm] | BLOOMSBURY (All width centred)

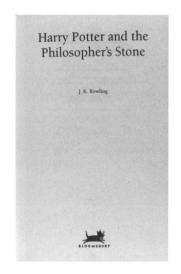

Collation: 112 unsigned leaves bound in indeterminate gatherings; 197 by 128mm; [1-7] 8-18 [19] 20-27 [28] 29-38 [39] 40-48 [49] 50-66 [67] 68-84 [85] 86-97 [98] 99-106 [107] 108-120 [121] 122-32 [133] 134-42 [143] 144-57 [158] 159-66 [167] 168-76 [177] 178-90 [191] 192-208 [209] 210-23 [224]

Page contents: [1] half-title: 'Harry Potter and the | Philosopher's Stone'; [2] blank; [3] title-page; [4] 'All rights reserved; no part of this publication may be reproduced or | transmitted by any means, electronic, mechanical, photocopying or otherwise, | without the prior permission of the publisher | [new paragraph] First published in Great Britain in 1997 | Bloomsbury Publishing Plc, 38 Soho Square, London W1V 5DF | [new paragraph] Copyright © Text Joanne Rowling 1997 | Copyright © Cover illustration Thomas Taylor1997 [*sic*] | [new paragraph] The moral right of the author has been asserted | A CIP catalogue record of this book is available from the | British Library | [new paragraph] ISBN 0 7475 3274 5 Paperback | 0 7475 3269 9 Hardback | [new paragraph] Printed and bound in Great Britain by Clays Ltd, St Ives plc | [new paragraph] 10 9 8 7 6 5 4 3 2 1'; [5] '*for Jessica, who loves stories,* | *for Anne, who loved them too,* | *and for Di, who heard this one first.*'; [6] blank; [7]-223 text; [224] blank

Paper: wove paper

Running title: 'HARRY POTTER' (24mm) on verso, recto title comprises chapter title, pp. 8-223

Binding: pictorial boards.

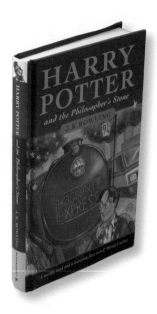

On spine: '[colour illustration of head of a wizard on white panel, 18 by 18mm] HARRY POTTER [in white on crimson panel, 18 by 47mm] *and the Philosopher's Stone* [in light yellow] J. K. ROWLING [in dark yellow, both title conclusion and author on blue panel, 18 by 102mm] BLOOMSBURY [publisher's device of the head of a dog, 3 by 4mm] [both in black on dark yellow panel, 18 by 37mm]' (reading lengthways down spine).

On upper cover: 'HARRY | POTTER | *and the Philosopher's Stone* [lines 1 and 2 in dark yellow, line 3 in white, all on crimson panel, 65 by 133mm] | [green rule, 133mm intersected by orange panel with 'J.K.ROWLING' in brown] | [colour illustration of Harry Potter and the Hogwarts Express at Platform 9¾, 122 by 133mm with two stars touching or intersecting first green rule] | [green rule, 133mm] | "A terrific read and a stunning first novel" *Wendy Cooling* [in dark yellow on black panel, 13 by 133mm]' (all width centred).

On lower cover: 'Harry Potter thinks he is an ordinary | boy – until he is rescued by an owl, taken | to Hogwarts School of Wizardry and | Witchcraft, learns to play | Quidditch and does battle in | a deadly duel. The Reason: | HARRY POTTER IS A WIZARD! | [new paragraph] *Acclaim for Harry Potter | and the Philosopher's Stone:* | [new paragraph] "Splendid stuff! It's got just the | right mix of normal life vs. magic to | make it extra-ordinary and hugely | readable." *David Morton – Daisy & Tom* | [new paragraph] "I just loved this book, it is full of | pace and interest and so very funny. | There is something about Harry Potter that | reminds me of Charlie Buckett in Charlie and | the Chocolate Factory…" | *Fiona Waters – Fiona Waters Associates* | [new paragraph] "Mystery, magic, a spectacular cast of | characters and a splendid plot – this is a bold | and confident debut from a splendid writer | and storyteller." | *Lindsay Fraser – Book Trust Scotland* | [barcode in black on white panel, 21 by 61mm together with '[publisher's device of a dog, 6 by 10mm] | BLOOMSBURY | £10.99' in black on left side of panel] | http://www.bloomsbury.com'. All in white with the exception of the first 'H' in 'Harry' which is in green and the final line printed in dark yellow and all on a blue background with colour illustration on left-hand side of a wizard smoking a pipe, together with ten stars. The initial capital 'H' of 'Harry' is a drop capital and is printed in green.

All edges trimmed. Binding measurements: 205 by 133mm (covers), 205 by 18mm (spine). End-papers: wove paper.

Dust-jacket: none

Publication: 26 June 1997 (simultaneous with A1(aa)) in an edition of 500 copies (confirmed by Bloomsbury)

Price: £10.99

Contents:
Harry Potter and the Philosopher's Stone
('Mr and Mrs Dursley, of number four, Privet Drive, were proud to say...')

Notes:
The genesis of Harry Potter is now the stuff of legend: the idea of Harry Potter 'slid' into the mind of Joanne Rowling on a train journey from Manchester to London during the summer of 1990. The manuscript was completed early in 1996 and sent to a literary agent who rejected it. The second approach was to the Christopher Little Literary Agency where it was read by Bryony Evans. She and a freelance reader, Fleur Howle, convinced Christopher Little to sign up the unknown author. The agency sent the manuscript to eight publishers and there was interest from both HarperCollins and Bloomsbury. HarperCollins was slow in making a definite offer and the UK rights to the title therefore went to Bloomsbury for an advance of around £1,500.

Bloomsbury had recently launched a children's booklist following the company's floatation on the stock market. Barry Cunningham, a former children's marketing director for Puffin Books, had written a business plan for Bloomsbury as a consultant but was then taken on by Bloomsbury. In an interview with me in September 2013, Nigel Newton, the founder and Chief Executive of Bloomsbury Publishing Plc, recalled that 'the following Frankfurt [Book Fair], Christopher Little, who I knew well, was there and I introduced him to Barry. Following that introduction, Christopher made a submission of *Harry Potter* to Barry. Subsequent folklore indicates that this was, by that stage, a much-rejected book. So Barry and his new children's publishing team received what Christopher submitted – my recollection is that it was about three chapters. They became extremely excited by it and our children's marketing manager, Rosamund de la Hey, photocopied it for the ten or so members of the editorial committee. Ros was trying to say this book was something unusual. So she rolled the photocopy of the three chapters into a scroll, sellotaped one end, filled it with Smarties, sellotaped the other end and put a red ribbon around this scroll. That was their way of saying to us that they thought this book would win the Smarties prize... which funnily enough it did. The fact that they did that is a sure sign that they did think they were onto something big or good, rather than something that we didn't notice either. The next day at the meeting Barry proposed that we make an offer for it – £1,500 as an advance – and I cast my vote (as chairman of the meeting) in favour as did everybody else with alacrity. My confidence came from the fact that my then eight-year-old daughter, Alice, had read it for me the night before and came down the stairs glowing about it. But there is some kind of media manipulation of that story saying that it was all about Alice and me. That's not true: Barry Cunningham was the children's publishing director and it was he who 'steered it through.' Newton noted that he had always assumed that 'as the novel was the work of a first-time author and it was being offered by a literary agency, other publishers would be considering the work.'

Newton recalls that the children's division at Bloomsbury became excited about the novel very quickly. He noted that between accepting the book and publishing it 'something called email had been invented. So we all had computers on our desks and these new things called emails started to be sent around internally. I remember that Ros de la Hey sent us emails almost every day saying "no, no, no, no – I know you all think that *Harry Potter* is great but you don't understand... *Harry Potter* is really, really, really great." So she and Barry Cunningham and his editor, Elinor Bagenal, and their marketing colleague, Janet Hogarth, sat around on beanbags in our office at the top of the

Twentieth-Century Fox building in Soho Square and when Barry got the full typescript he started circulating the pages around the room to the other three and they read the same text simultaneously. They were all really humming about this book and our sales force and marketing and publicity departments went out crusading on its behalf... I remember Ottaker's bookshop chain chose it as one of their books of the month for publication in July 1997.'

Rowling accepted the publisher's criticism that the novel was 'overlong' and the text was pruned by Bloomsbury's editorial process. Barry Cunningham has noted that the freelance editor for the book was Susan Dickinson. Rowling also allowed her name to appear as a gender-free 'J.K. Rowling'.

A publication figure of 500 hardback copies is confirmed by Bloomsbury. Many of these copies were destined for libraries (the book trade suggests a figure of around 300 copies). Newton noted that '... I think the assumption in 1997 would have been that you would sell 500 hardcovers of any good book to public libraries so that edition would be aimed at them. The general edition for the market would be a paperback.' This explains the lack of a dust-jacket for the first edition: it was simply not required by libraries. Note that both hardback and paperback were published on the same date and neither has bibliographical priority. The print-run for the paperback was significantly larger, however. A story has arisen that, beyond copies sold to libraries, a large number were shipped to Australia. There appears no evidence within the archives at Bloomsbury that this is correct.

A report compiled by the printers, Clays Ltd, notes that the initial print run was 'followed quickly by a reprint of 1,000 copies and three reprints of 500 copies'. These figures confirm the widely-held view that the book was an instant success.

For years the book trade has claimed that the *total* edition of A1(a) and A1(aa) was 500 copies. The usual statement has been that there were 300 copies of A1(a) and 200 copies of A1(aa). With confirmation from the publisher that there were 500 copies of A1(a) and 5,150 copies of A1(aa), the old statement is exposed as woefully inaccurate.

Note that the seventh line of the publisher's imprint page does not include a space between 'Taylor' and '1997'. On page 53, under the heading, 'Other Equipment', '1 wand' is listed twice. These errors were retained from the proof (see note to AA1(a)). See also note to A1(aa).

The original manuscript was exhibited at the British Library in its 'Writing Britain – Wastelands to Wonderlands' exhibition from 11 May to 25 September 2012.

In the EnglishPEN charity auction entitled 'First Editions, Second Thoughts' (Sotheby's, 21 May 2013) a first edition was offered which included the author's annotations or illustrations on 43 pages. The author freely added comments on the process of writing, editorial decisions and sources of inspiration together with references to the series as a whole and the film adaptations:

> I wrote the book... in snatched hours, in clattering cafes or in the dead of night. For me, the story of how I wrote Harry Potter and the Philosopher's Stone is written invisibly on every page, legible only to me. Sixteen years after it was published, the memories are as vivid as ever as I turn these pages...

With approximately 22 illustrations and 1,100 words, the copy sold for £150,000 to a private collector. It was immediately loaned to the Bodleian library for its exhibition 'Magical Books: From the Middle Ages to Middle-earth' (23 May–27 October 2013).

The illustrator Thomas Taylor, in a blog on his website entitled 'Harry Potter and the Missing Artist' (dated 1 September 2009), stated that the artwork for this volume had been his first professional commission. In 1996 he 'noticed that Bloomsbury were creating a children's list' and he therefore left his portfolio with them. Taylor notes 'they must have seen something they liked because they gave me a book jacket to do... There was an incomplete manuscript to read, roughs to do, and then the painting. The final image – a faint pencil sketch, painted with concentrated watercolour (Doc Martins, I think) and then outlined with a black Karisma pencil – took two days, and all things considered I was quite pleased with it. I think I delivered it by hand. This was the only Harry Potter cover I did. Quite understandably, once the books took off... Bloomsbury turned to more experienced illustrators with a track record of art for this age range. By then I was working on my first picture books anyway, alienating myself from Harry's readers. So I don't have any great regrets about losing out to Cliff Wright, *et al.*, or about the briefness of my very brief involvement with HP.'

A further blog, entitled 'Harry Potter and the Mysterious Wizard' (dated 20 June 2011) discusses the lower cover illustration of a wizard. The original picture was quickly replaced by a clearly recognizable illustration of Dumbledore, probably appearing first on the eighteenth impression. Taylor notes that 'when I was commissioned by Barry Cunningham to produce the cover art for a debut middle grade novel by an unknown author... I was asked to provide "a wizard to decorate the back cover". So I did. The books are full of magical characters and sorcerers, so it wasn't difficult to conjure up one of my own. It never even crossed my mind to depict Dumbledore.' The publisher, however, was challenged repeatedly about the identity of the wizard and Bloomsbury therefore asked Taylor to provide a replacement.

The original pencil and watercolour illustration by Thomas Taylor of Harry Potter standing by the Hogwarts Express, measuring 401 by 282mm, was offered for sale at auction by Sotheby's on 10 July 2001. There was additional detail present in the original that was not reproduced when printed. Platform 10, for example, was shown in the original but cropped for publication. Estimated at £20,000 to £25,000 it sold for a total of £85,750 (including buyer's premium). The purchaser was a private collector in the United States.

The original pencil and watercolour illustration of the lower cover wizard by Thomas Taylor was offered for sale at auction by Sotheby's on 10 July 2013. The illustration measured 250 by 105mm. Estimated at £8,000 to £12,000 it sold for a total of £9,750 (including buyer's premium). The purchaser was a London bookdealer. Included with the piece was a letter, dated 1999, from the illustrator explaining that the image was scanned by the publisher and printed in an elongated state, which accounted for 'the small difference in proportion from original to reproduction'.

The original pencil and watercolour illustration by Thomas Taylor of Albus Dumbledore (that replaced the pipe-smoking wizard), measuring 442 by 285mm, was offered for sale at auction by Sotheby's on 10 July 2001. Estimated at £4,000 to £6,000 it sold for a total of £3,525 (including buyer's premium). The purchaser was a London bookdealer.

To celebrate the fifteenth anniversary of the publication of *Harry Potter and the Philosopher's Stone*, Bloomsbury printed a circular commemorative device on the upper cover (and dust-jacket) of the fifyfifth reprint (and later reprints) of this edition. The device featured Harry from the Thomas Taylor illustration used in A1(a) together with '15 | YEARS OF | HARRY | POTTER | MAGIC'.

The English audiobook version, read by Stephen Fry, has a duration of approximately eight and a half hours. In a unique broadcasting event, BBC Radio 4 entirely cleared its schedule on the FM frequency for 26 December 2000 and from 12 noon the complete text was broadcast. Fry apparently stated that '… reading Harry Potter books out loud is more fun than I feel a single human being could ever deserve. It's like swimming in chocolate.'

Reprints (and subsequent new editions) include a number of corrections to the text. These comprise:

Page 15, line 3	'he tried to kill the Potter's son' to 'he tried to kill the Potters' son'
Page 17, lines 31-32	'I'll be takin' Sirius his bike back' to 'I'd best get this bike away'
Page 31, line 34	deletion of single inverted comma at the beginning of the line
Page 52, line 35	'A Beginners' Guide' to 'A Beginner's Guide'
Page 53, line 9	deletion of second '1 wand' from list
Page 56, lines 17-18	'seventeen Sickles an ounce' to 'sixteen Sickles an ounce'
Page 72, line 25	'a shiny silver badge' to 'a shiny red and gold badge'
Page 87, line 31	'*Hogwarts, a History*' to '*Hogwarts: A History*'
Page 92, line 22	'four hundred years' to 'five hundred years'
Page 101, line 4	'head of Gryffindor House' to 'Head of Gryffindor House'
Page 147, line 7-8	'looking forward to next day' to 'looking forward to the next day'
Page 168, lines 9-10	'*One Hundred Magical Herbs*' to '*One Thousand Magical Herbs*'
Page 193, line 27	'that's the pub' to 'that's one of the pubs'
Page 205, line 3	'you go next to him' to 'you go there'
Page 205, line 32	'I take one step forward and she'll take me' to 'I'll make my move and she'll take me'

Copies: Sotheby's, 15 December 2011, lot 149; Sotheby's, 21 May 2013, lot 39

Reprints include:

20 19 18 17 16 15 14 13 12 11		[wizard on lower cover]
20 19 18 17 16 15		[wizard on lower cover]
20 19 18		[Dumbledore on lower cover]
26 27 28 29 30		[Dumbledore on lower cover]
33	BL (RF.2005.a.359) stamped May 2005	[Dumbledore on lower cover]
32		[Dumbledore on lower cover]
29		[Dumbledore on lower cover]

A report compiled by the printers, Clays Ltd, in October 2013 noted that 'to date we have produced a minimum of 11.6 million paperbacks and 1.3 million hardbacks across 337 printings'.

FIRST ENGLISH EDITION
(children's artwork series in paperback)

Harry Potter and the | Philosopher's Stone | J. K. Rowling | [publisher's device of a dog, 11 by 18mm] | BLOOMSBURY (All width centred)

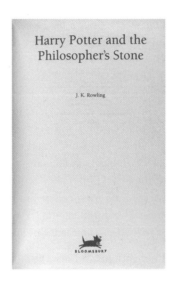

Collation: 112 unsigned leaves bound in indeterminate gatherings; 197 by 128mm; [1-7] 8-18 [19] 20-27 [28] 29-38 [39] 40-48 [49] 50-66 [67] 68-84 [85] 86-97 [98] 99-106 [107] 108-120 [121] 122-32 [133] 134-42 [143] 144-57 [158] 159-66 [167] 168-76 [177] 178-90 [191] 192-208 [209] 210-23 [224]

Page contents: [1] half-title: 'Harry Potter and the | Philosopher's Stone'; [2] blank; [3] title-page; [4] 'All rights reserved; no part of this publication may be reproduced or | transmitted by any means, electronic, mechanical, photocopying or otherwise, | without the prior permission of the publisher | [new paragraph] First published in Great Britain in 1997 | Bloomsbury Publishing Plc, 38 Soho Square, London W1V 5DF | [new paragraph] Copyright © Text Joanne Rowling 1997 | Copyright © Cover illustration Thomas Taylor1997 [*sic*] | [new paragraph] The moral right of the author has been asserted | A CIP catalogue record of this book is available from the | British Library | [new paragraph] ISBN 0 7475 3274 5 Paperback | 0 7475 3269 9 Hardback | [new paragraph] Printed and bound in Great Britain by Clays Ltd, St Ives plc | [new paragraph] 10 9 8 7 6 5 4 3 2 1'; [5] '*for Jessica, who loves stories,* | *for Anne, who loved them too,* | *and for Di, who heard this one first.*'; [6] blank; [7]-223 text; [224] blank

Paper: wove paper

Running title: 'HARRY POTTER' (24mm) on verso, recto title comprises chapter title, pp. 8-223

Binding: pictorial wrappers.

    On spine: '[colour illustration of head of a wizard on white panel, 13 by 14mm] HARRY POTTER [in white on crimson panel, 13 by 47mm] *and the Philosopher's Stone* [in light yellow] J. K. ROWLING [in dark yellow, both title conclusion and author on blue panel, 13 by 102mm] BLOOMSBURY [publisher's device of the head of a dog, 3 by 4mm] [both in black on dark yellow panel, 13 by 32mm] (reading lengthways down spine).

    On upper wrapper: 'HARRY | POTTER | *and the Philosopher's Stone* [lines 1 and 2 in dark yellow, line 3 in white, all on crimson panel, 61 by

128mm] | [light blue rule, 128mm intersected by orange panel with 'J. K. ROWLING' in brown] | [colour illustration of Harry Potter and the Hogwarts Express at Platform 9¾, 122 by 128mm with two stars touching or intersecting first light blue rule] | [light blue rule, 128mm] | "A terrific read and a stunning first novel" *Wendy Cooling* [in dark yellow on black panel, 10 by 128mm]' (all width centred).

On lower wrapper: 'Harry Potter thinks he is an ordinary | boy – until he is rescued by an owl, taken | to Hogwarts School of Wizardry and | Witchcraft, learns to play | Quidditch and does battle in | a deadly duel. The Reason: | HARRY POTTER IS A WIZARD! | [new paragraph] *Acclaim for Harry Potter* | *and the Philosopher's Stone:* | [new paragraph] "Splendid stuff! It's got just the | right mix of normal life vs. magic to | make it extra-ordinary and hugely | readable." *David Morton – Daisy & Tom* | [new paragraph] "I just loved this book, it is full of | pace and interest and so very funny. | There is something about Harry Potter that | reminds me of Charlie Buckett in Charlie and | the Chocolate Factory…" | *Fiona Waters – Fiona Waters Associates* | [new paragraph] "Mystery, magic, a spectacular cast of | characters and a splendid plot – this is a bold | and confident debut from a splendid writer | and storyteller." | *Lindsay Fraser – Book Trust Scotland* | [barcode in black on white panel, 21 by 61mm together with '[publisher's device of a dog, 6 by 10mm] | BLOOMSBURY | £4.99' in black on left side of panel] | http://www.bloomsbury.com'. All in white with the exception of the first 'H' in 'Harry' which is in green and the final line printed in dark yellow and all on a blue background with colour illustration on left-hand side of a wizard smoking a pipe, together with ten stars. The initial capital 'H' of 'Harry' is a drop capital and is printed in green.

All edges trimmed. Binding measurements: 197 by 128mm (wrappers), 197 by 14mm (spine).

Publication: 26 June 1997 (simultaneous with A1(a)) in an edition of 5,150 copies (confirmed by Bloomsbury)

Price: £4.99

Contents:
Harry Potter and the Philosopher's Stone
('Mr and Mrs Dursley, of number four, Privet Drive, were proud to say…')

Notes:
Both hardback (A1(a)) and paperback (A1(aa)) were published on the same date and neither has bibliographical priority. For years the book trade has claimed that the *total* edition of A1(a) and A1(aa) was 500 copies. The usual statement has been that there were 300 copies of A1(a) and 200 copies of A1(aa). With confirmation from the publisher that there were 500 copies of A1(a) and 5,150 copies of A1(aa), the old statement is exposed as woefully inaccurate.

As in A1(a), the seventh line of the publisher's imprint page does not include a space between 'Taylor' and '1997'. On page 53, under the heading, 'Other Equipment', '1 wand' is listed twice. A copy of this First English edition (children's artwork series in paperback) was sold at Christie's South Kensington (30 November 2010, lot 208) which included a handwritten note by the author. Next to the final '1 wand', Rowling drew an arrow and stated 'this was taken out in the next print of the book (a mistake). Keep this copy, it might be valuable one day!'

A copy sold at Sotheby's on 12 December 2012, which included an inscription dated 25 June 1997. The author had evidently received a number of copies before the publication date. The copy inscribed by the author to her father and stepmother, for example, was dated 11 June 1997. This copy was offered at auction at Sotheby's New York on 10 December 2003. It was inscribed on the half-title '11-6-97 | To Dad and Jan, | with lots of love | Jo.' Estimated at $10,000/15,000, it sold for $8,000 to a member of the London book trade.

Copies: Sotheby's, 14 July 2010, lot 201; Sotheby's, 12 December 2012, lot 178

Reprints include:

10 9 8 7 6 5 4 3		[wizard on lower wrapper]
10 9 8 7 6 5 4	BL (H.98/557) stamped 8 Dec 1997	[wizard on lower wrapper]
40 39 38 37		[wizard on lower wrapper]
58 59 60		[Dumbledore on lower wrapper]

A1(b)   TED SMART/'THE BOOK PEOPLE' EDITION   (1998)
(children's artwork series in hardback)

Harry Potter and the | Philosopher's Stone | J. K. Rowling | [publisher's device of a rule, 39mm | 'TED SMART' | rule, 39mm, all within single ruled border, 7 by 40mm] (Lines 1 and 2 justified on left and right margins, and all width centred)

Collation: 112 unsigned leaves bound in indeterminate gatherings; 197 by 128mm; [1-7] 8-18 [19] 20-27 [28] 29-38 [39] 40-48 [49] 50-66 [67] 68-84 [85] 86-97 [98] 99-106 [107] 108-120 [121] 122-32 [133] 134-42 [143] 144-57 [158] 159-66 [167] 168-76 [177] 178-90 [191] 192-208 [209] 210-23 [224]

Page contents: [1] half-title: 'Harry Potter and the | Philosopher's Stone'; [2] blank; [3] title-page; [4] 'First published in Great Britain in 1997 | This edition produced for The Book People Ltd 1998 | Hall Wood Avenue | Haydock | St Helens WA11 9UL | [new paragraph] Copyright © Text Joanne Rowling 1997 | Copyright © Cover illustration Thomas Taylor 1997 | [new paragraph] The moral right of the author has been asserted | A CIP catalogue record of this book is available from the | British Library | [new paragraph] ISBN 1 85613 403 2 | [new paragraph] Printed and bound in Great Britain by Clays Ltd, St Ives plc | [new paragraph] 10 9 8 7 6 5 4 3 2 1'; [5] 'for Jessica, who loves stories, | for Anne, who loved them too, | and for Di, who heard this one first.'; [6] blank; [7]-223 text; [224] blank

Paper: wove paper

Running title: 'HARRY POTTER' (24mm) on verso, recto title comprises chapter title, pp. 8-223

Binding: pictorial boards.

On spine: '[colour illustration of head of a wizard on white panel, 18 by 18mm] HARRY POTTER [in white on crimson panel, 18 by 47mm] *and the Philosopher's Stone* [in light yellow] J. K. ROWLING [in dark yellow, both title conclusion and author on blue panel, 18 by 102mm] [publisher's device of a rule, 26mm | 'TED SMART' | rule, 26mm, all within single ruled border, 5 by 27mm] [in black on yellow panel, 18 by 38mm]' (reading lengthways down spine).

On upper cover: 'HARRY | POTTER | *and the Philosopher's Stone* [lines 1 and 2 in dark yellow, line 3 in white, all on crimson panel, 65 by 133mm] | [green rule, 133mm intersected by orange panel with 'J.K.ROWLING' in brown] | [colour illustration of Harry Potter and the Hogwarts Express at Platform 9¾, 122 by 133mm with one star touching or intersecting first green rule] | [green rule, 133mm] | WINNER OF THE 1997 SMARTIES GOLD AWARD [in dark yellow on black panel, 13 by 133mm]' (all width centred).

On lower cover: 'Harry Potter thinks he | is an ordinary boy – | until he is rescued by an | owl, taken to Hogwarts | School of Witchcraft and | Wizardry, learns to play | Quidditch and does | battle in a deadly duel. | The Reason… | HARRY POTTER IS | A WIZARD! | [new paragraph] [barcode in black on white panel, 21 by 61mm]'. All in white on a blue background with colour illustration on left-hand side of a wizard smoking a pipe, together with seven stars.

All edges trimmed. Binding measurements: 205 by 133mm (covers), 205 by 18mm (spine). End-papers: wove paper.

Dust-jacket: present, but not consulted

Publication: May 1998 (see notes)

Price: no exact price is recorded (see notes)

Contents:
Harry Potter and the Philosopher's Stone
('Mr and Mrs Dursley, of number four, Privet Drive, were proud to say…')

Notes:
The Book People is an independent bookselling company founded in 1988 by Ted Smart. It operates by using self-employed distributors to visit customers in workplaces and other similar locations. The company orders and stocks a restricted range of titles in bulk without the right of return to the publisher. Bulk purchasing for this method of distribution brings savings in cost which are reflected in the purchase price for the buyer. To reduce the risk of these books being sold through any means other than The Book People they frequently carry the company's own imprint (as with the Ted Smart editions of *Harry Potter*).

Note the slight differences on the upper cover between this edition and the first English edition (see A1(a) and A1(aa)). The Bloomsbury editions show two stars touching or intersecting the first rule (an orange star on the left and a yellow star on the right). In the Ted Smart edition the orange star is omitted. The quotation from Wendy Cooling has been replaced in the Ted Smart edition with a statement about the 1997 Smarties Gold Award. The initial capital 'H' of 'Harry' is a drop capital for A1(a) and A1(aa). In the Ted Smart edition it is a regular capital.

Neither Ted Smart nor Bloomsbury were able to provide any detail about the Ted Smart/'The Book People' editions. Information was provided by the Blair Partnership who noted that this edition was available from May 1998. Production of the Ted Smart/'The Book People' editions ceased in April 2001.

In an interview with me in September 2013, Nigel Newton noted that the Ted Smart edition 'just happened because it was the norm in supplying The Book People'. He reflected that 'later we decided perhaps that that wasn't the right way…' Noting the appearance of the Ted Smart edition so early in the chronology of editions, Newton exclaimed 'oh, good for us – we *were* on the ball… good.'

No exact price has been recorded for this edition. A1(b) was, presumably, sold by itself. A slipcase containing the three volumes A1(b), A2(f) and A7(d) was, probably, available from November 1999 and a slipcase containing the four volumes A1(b), A2(f), A7(d) and A9(c) was, presumably, available from November 2000. In each case the price would have been lower than the single (or combined) prices of the Bloomsbury version.

Copies: private collection

Reprints include:
10 9 8 7 6 5 4 3 2   [wizard on lower cover]
10 9 8 7 6 5 4 3   [wizard on lower cover]
10 9 8 7 6 5 4   [wizard on lower cover]
10 9 8 7 6 5   [wizard on lower cover]
10 9 8 7 6   [wizard on lower cover]

A1(c)   ENGLISH ADULT EDITION   (1998)
(original adult artwork series in paperback)

Harry Potter and the | Philosopher's Stone | J. K. Rowling | BLOOMSBURY (All width centred)

Collation: 112 unsigned leaves bound in indeterminate gatherings; 197 by 128mm; [1-7] 8-18 [19] 20-27 [28] 29-38 [39] 40-48 [49] 50-66 [67] 68-84 [85] 86-97 [98] 99-106 [107] 108-120 [121] 122-32 [133] 134-42 [143] 144-57 [158] 159-66 [167] 168-76 [177] 178-90 [191] 192-208 [209] 210-23 [224]

Page contents: [1] half-title: 'Harry Potter and the | Philosopher's Stone'; [2] blank; [3] title-page; [4] 'All rights reserved; no part of this publication may be reproduced or | transmitted by any means, electronic, mechanical, photocopying or otherwise, | without the prior permission of the publisher | [new paragraph] First published in Great Britain in 1997 | Bloomsbury Publishing Plc, 38 Soho Square, London, W1V 5DF | [new paragraph] This edition published in 1998 | [new paragraph] Copyright © Text Joanne Rowling 1997 | [new paragraph] The moral right of the author has been asserted | A CIP catalogue record for this book is available from the | British Library | [new paragraph] ISBN 0 7475 4298 8 | [new paragraph] Printed in Great Britain by Clays Ltd, St Ives plc | [new paragraph] 10 9 8 7 6 5 4 3 2 1'; [5] *'for Jessica, who loves stories, | for Anne, who loved them too, | and for Di, who heard this one first.';* [6] blank; [7]-223 text; [224] blank

Paper: wove paper

Running title: 'HARRY POTTER' (24mm) on verso, recto title comprises chapter title, pp. 8-223

Binding: pictorial wrappers.

On spine: 'HARRY POTTER [in orange] | *and the Philosopher's Stone* [in white] [black and white photographic illustration of steam train, 14 by 21mm] J. K. ROWLING [in orange within white rectangle with rounded ends, 9 by 46mm] [publisher's device of a figure with a bow, 7 by 7mm] [in white]' (reading lengthways down spine). All on black.

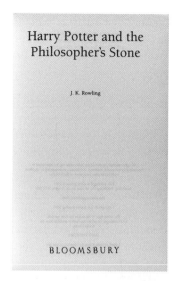

On upper wrapper: 'HARRY POTTER | *and the Philosopher's Stone* [line 1 in black and line 2 in grey, all on orange panel, 26 by 128mm] | J. K. ROWLING [in orange on black within double grey and black rectangle with rounded ends, 14 by 74mm] | *'FUNNY, IMAGINATIVE, MAGICAL'* – [in grey] THE TIMES [in orange] [lines 3 and 4 on black and white photographic illustration of steam train, 171 by 128mm]' (all width centred with the exception of line 2 which is off-set to the right).

On lower wrapper: 'HARRY POTTER [in orange] | *and the Philosopher's Stone* [in black] | [new paragraph] *Harry Potter and the Philosopher's Stone* has all the makings | of a classic...Rowling uses classic narrative devices with flair | and originality and delivers a complex and demanding plot in | the form of a hugely entertaining thriller.' *The Scotsman* | [new paragraph] 'A richly textured first novel given lift-off by an inventive wit.' | *The Guardian* | [new paragraph] 'This is a terrific book.' *The Sunday Telegraph* | [new paragraph] 'J. K. Rowling has woken up a whole generation to reading. | In the 2020s, thirty something book-lovers will know each other | by smug references to Diagon Alley and Quidditch.' *The Times* | [new paragraph] 'And you thought wizardry was for children. Harry Potter will | make you think again. He casts his spell on grown-ups too.' | *James Naughtie* | [new paragraph] 'Full of surprises and jokes; comparisons with Dahl are, this | time, justified.' *The Sunday Times* | ['BLOOMSBURY [in white on black panel, 6 by 40mm] | *paperbacks* [in black on orange panel, 10 by 40mm]' (all on left side)] [£6.99 [in black] | [barcode in black on white panel, 19 by 39mm] | http://www.bloomsbury.com [in black] (all on orange panel, 32 by 40mm and on right side)]'. Reading lengthways down right side next to foot of spine 'COVER DESIGN WILLIAM WEBB PHOTOGRAPH © O. WINSTON LINK'. All in black with the exception of sources which are in orange and all on photographic illustration of clouds of steam, 198 by 128mm.

All edges trimmed. Binding measurements: 197 by 128mm (wrappers), 197 by 14mm (spine).

Publication: 11 September 1998 (confirmed by Bloomsbury)

Price: £6.99

Contents:
Harry Potter and the Philosopher's Stone
('Mr and Mrs Dursley, of number four, Privet Drive, were proud to say…')

Notes:
Interviewed in September 2013, Nigel Newton recalls that inspiration for the adult editions came from a member of staff at Bloomsbury. Apparently the staff member saw a commuter reading Harry Potter on the train whilst holding a copy of *The Economist* to block the book from the view of other passengers. Newton notes '… then one of us – it might even have been me – repeated this to a journalist, possibly from the *Independent*, who made a thing of it. And we thought, well why *don't* we produce an adult edition? It was quite clear that this book was being read just as much by adults. So we created this new edition and it got a lot of coverage. The jackets were photographic rather than line drawings to indicate that they were more adult. I thought they looked really great. They sold hugely well… So that created a great surge in the readership.'

Newton is quick to recall that there was already a tradition of books published by the same publisher sporting different bindings or jackets. The specific example he remembers was the 1987 English publication of Edward Rutherfurd's *Sarum* by Anthony Cheetham's Century Hutchinson firm.

Noting the higher price of the adult edition, Newton stated that the book was 'brought into line with adult prices… The truth is you end up making children's books almost too cheap to price to the market.'

The number of copies printed of this edition is not recorded in the Bloomsbury archives.

A copy of this editon inscribed by the author to her stepmother was offered at auction at Sotheby's New York on 10 December 2003. It was inscribed on the dedication page 'To Jan | with lots of love | Jo.' Estimated at $8,000/12,000, it failed to sell.

Each occurrence of the title on the spine, upper and lower wrappers shows '*and the Philosopher's Stone*' off-set to the right of 'HARRY POTTER'.

Later reprints would provide more information about the photograph:

The publishers gratefully acknowledge the following permission to reproduce the cover image Norfolk & Western Railway's Train, 'The Cavalier', Leaves Williamson, West Virginia, on a Rainy Day, 1958. Photograph (© [*sic*] by O Winston Link. Reproduced by kind permission of O Winston Link.

Ogle Winston Link (1914-2001) was an American photographer remembered, chiefly, for his photographs of the last days of steam locomotives on the Norfolk and Western line in America. The line was the last American railway to convert from steam to diesel in the late 1950s and early 1960s.

Reprints include:
22
23

A1(d)   ENGLISH DELUXE EDITION   (1999)
(children's artwork series in deluxe hardback)

HARRY | POTTER | *and the Philosopher's Stone* | [illustration of Hogwarts crest with legend 'DRACO DORMIENS NUNQUAM TITILLANDUS' on banner, 70 by 86mm] | J.K.ROWLING | [publisher's device of a dog, 12 by 19mm] | BLOOMSBURY (All width centred)

Collation: 112 unsigned leaves bound in indeterminate gatherings; 233 by 151mm; [1-7] 8-18 [19] 20-27 [28] 29-38 [39] 40-48 [49] 50-66 [67] 68-84 [85] 86-97 [98] 99-106 [107] 108-120 [121] 122-32 [133] 134-42 [143] 144-57 [158] 159-66 [167] 168-76 [177] 178-90 [191] 192-208 [209] 210-23 [224]

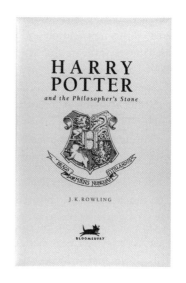

Page contents: [1] half-title: 'HARRY | POTTER | *and the Philosopher's Stone* | [illustration of Hogwarts crest with legend 'DRACO DORMIENS NUNQUAM TITILLANDUS' on banner, 49 by 60mm]'; [2] '*Also available:* | Harry Potter and the Chamber of Secrets'; [3] title-page; [4] 'All rights reserved; no part of this publication may be reproduced or | transmitted by any means, electronic, mechanical, photocopying or otherwise, | without the prior permission of the publisher | [new paragraph] This edition first published in Great Britain in 1999 | Bloomsbury Publishing Plc, 38 Soho Square, London, W1V 5DF | [new paragraph] Copyright © J. K. Rowling 1997 | Copyright © Cover illustration Thomas Taylor 1997 | [new paragraph] The moral right of the author has been asserted | A CIP catalogue record of this book is available from the | British Library | [new paragraph] ISBN 0 7475 4572 3 | [new paragraph] Printed in Great Britain by Clays Ltd, St Ives plc | [new paragraph] 10 9 8 7 6 5 4 3 2 1'; [5] '*for Jessica, who loves stories,* | *for Anne, who loved them too,* | *and for Di, who heard this one first.*'; [6] blank; [7]-223 text; [224] blank

Paper: wove paper

Running title: 'HARRY POTTER' (24mm) on verso, recto title comprises chapter title, pp. 8-223

Binding: red cloth.

On spine: 'HARRY POTTER *and the Philosopher's Stone* J.K.ROWLING' (reading lengthways down spine) with '[publisher's device of a dog, 10 by 17mm] | BLOOMSBURY' (horizontally at foot). All in gilt.

On upper cover: 'HARRY | POTTER | *and the Philosopher's Stone* | [double ruled border, 104 by 104mm with the outer border thicker than the inner and colour illustration by Thomas Taylor laid down] | JKRowling [facsimile signature]' (all width centred). All in gilt.

Lower cover: blank.

All edges gilt. Blue sewn bands at head and foot of spine together with blue marker ribbon. Binding measurements: 241 by 152mm (covers), 241 by 30mm (spine). End-papers: red wove paper.

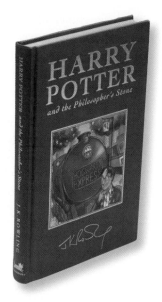

Dust-jacket: none

Publication: 27 September 1999 in an edition of 4869 copies (confirmed by Bloomsbury)

Price: £18

Contents:

Harry Potter and the Philosopher's Stone

　('Mr and Mrs Dursley, of number four, Privet Drive, were proud to say...')

Notes:

Interviewed in September 2013, Nigel Newton recalled that this edition was specifically created for the gift market. He explained, '... if you think of any of the great children's classics, there would tend to be a really nice edition. Harry Potter deserves it more than anything we've ever published.' He suggested that people buy books either to read themselves or to give away and that '... if you are going to give something away you probably want to give away a hardcover, not a paperback. And if you want to give away a hardcover of something that is a classic then you probably want it to look like – or better than – other classics.'

　This focus on the gift market explains the numerous box sets published by Bloomsbury. As each new novel came out, Bloomsbury would release a new box set 'widening each time', as Newton observed. He remarked 'now that the series is complete it's very much in demand and one of our biggest Harry Potter offerings'.

It is thought that the first English deluxe editions of *Philosopher's Stone*, *Chamber of Secrets* and *Prisoner of Azkaban* were published on the same date (see note to A7(c)).

In December 2011 Sotheby's offered a unique copy of this edition with twelve full-colour illustrations by Thomas Taylor. In 2002 the consignor of the book commissioned Taylor to paint a series of colour illustrations for *Harry Potter and the Philosopher's Stone*. These comprise a frontispiece of the Hogwarts Crest together with Harry, a small vignette noting 'The End' and eight full-page illustrations. The scenes were chosen due to their significance to the story and to provide an even spread of illustrations throughout the narrative.

The original intention had been to bind the original illustrations into a copy of the book for the ultimate personal copy, but the thickness of the paper prevented this. Consequently, and with Taylor's permission, the ten original watercolours, together with two separate reproductions of Taylor's work, were reproduced on fine wove paper and sumptuously bound by Asprey in 2004 within a copy of A1(d), signed by the author. A handwritten limitation note stated 'This book is specially | illustrated by | Thomas Taylor, and is | limited to one copy | only | Thomas Taylor | 2002'.

The ten original watercolours were included with the book. Offered as lot 150 in Sotheby's 'English Literature, History, Private Press, Children's Books and Illustrations' auction on 15 December 2011 at £30,000/50,000, it failed to sell.

Copies: Sotheby's, 17 December 2009, lot 169

A1(e)   ENGLISH 'CELEBRATORY' EDITION   (2001)
(children's artwork series in paperback)

HARRY | POTTER | *and the Philosopher's Stone* | [illustration of Hogwarts crest with legend 'DRAGO DORMIENS NUNQUAM TITILLANDUS' on banner, 67 by 82mm] | J.K.ROWLING | [publisher's device of a dog, 11 by 18mm] | BLOOMSBURY (Lines 1 and 2 justified on left and right margins, and all width centred)

Collation: 112 unsigned leaves bound in indeterminate gatherings; 197 by 128mm; [1-7] 8-18 [19] 20-27 [28] 29-38 [39] 40-48 [49] 50-66 [67] 68-84 [85] 86-97 [98] 99-106 [107] 108-120 [121] 122-32 [133] 134-42 [143] 144-57 [158] 159-66 [167] 168-76 [177] 178-90 [191] 192-208 [209] 210-23 [224]

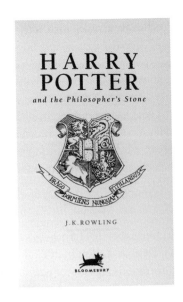

Page contents: [1] half-title: 'HARRY | POTTER | *and the Philosopher's Stone* | [illustration of Hogwarts crest with legend 'DRAGO DORMIENS NUNQUAM TITILLANDUS' on banner, 47 by 57mm]'; [2] '*Also available:* | Harry Potter and the Chamber of Secrets'; [3] title-page; [4] 'All rights reserved; no part of this publication may be reproduced or | transmitted by any means, electronic, mechanical, photocopying or otherwise, | without the prior permission of the publisher | [new paragraph] First published in Great Britain in 1997 | Bloomsbury Publishing Plc, 38 Soho Square, | London W1D 3HB | [new paragraph] This edition first published in 2001 | [new paragraph] Copyright © 1997 J.K. Rowling | Cover illustrations copyright © by Thomas Taylor 1997

| [new paragraph] Harry Potter, names, characters and related indicia are | copyright and trademark Warner Bros., 2000™ | [new paragraph] The moral right of the author has been asserted | A CIP catalogue record of this book is available from the | British Library | [new paragraph] ISBN 0 7475 5819 1 | [new paragraph] Printed and bound in Great Britain by Clays Ltd, St Ives plc | Typeset by Dorchester Typesetting | [new paragraph] 10 9 8 7 6 5 4 3 2 1 | [new paragraph] www.bloomsbury.com/harrypotter'; [5] '*for Jessica, who loves stories,* | *for Anne, who loved them too,* | *and for Di, who heard this one first.*'; [6] blank; [7]-223 text; [224] blank

Paper: wove paper

Running title: 'HARRY POTTER' (24mm) on verso, recto title comprises chapter title, pp. 8-223

Binding: pictorial wrappers.

On spine: '[colour illustration of head of Professor Dumbledore on white panel, 13 by 16mm] HARRY POTTER [in red on gilt panel, 13 by 46mm] *and the Philosopher's Stone* [in white] J.K.ROWLING [in gilt, both title conclusion and author on red panel, 13 by 103mm] BLOOMSBURY [publisher's device of the head of a dog, 3 by 4mm] [both in white on purple panel, 13 by 31mm]' (reading lengthways down spine).

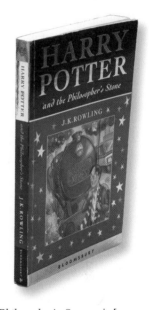

On upper wrapper: 'HARRY | POTTER | *and the Philosopher's Stone* [lines 1 and 2 in gilt, line 3 in white, all on purple panel, 61 by 128mm] | [gilt rule, 128mm] | ['J.K. ROWLING' [in gilt] with colour illustration of Harry Potter and the Hogwarts Express at Platform 9¾, within single gilt ruled border, 91 by 86mm, all on red panel with orange, yellow and gilt stars, 124 by 128mm] | [purple rule, 128mm] | BLOOMSBURY [in purple on gilt panel, 11 by 128mm]' (all width centred).

On lower wrapper: 'Harry Potter thinks he is an | ordinary boy – until he is rescued by | a beetle-eyed giant of a man, enrols at | Hogwarts School of Witchcraft and | Wizardry, learns to play Quidditch and | does battle in a deadly duel. The Reason: | HARRY POTTER IS A WIZARD! | [new paragraph] *Acclaim for Harry Potter and* | *the Philosopher's Stone:* | [new paragraph] 'Like Gameboys, Teletubbies | and films by George Lucas, | Harry Potter has permeated | the national child consciousness.' | *The Independent on Sunday* | [new paragraph] 'The Harry Potter books are that rare | thing, a series of stories adored by | children and parents alike.' | *The Daily Telegraph* | [new paragraph] 'JK Rowling has woken up a whole | generation to reading.' *The Times* | [new paragraph] 'The Harry Potter stories will join that | small group of children's books which | are read and re-read into adulthood. | I imagine that the number of readers | waiting patiently for the next | instalment grows by the | day.' *TLS* | [barcode in black on white panel, 21 by 61mm together with '£5.99 | [publisher's device of a dog, 6 by 10mm] | BLOOMSBURY' in black] | http://www.bloomsbury.com | Cover Illustrations by Thomas Taylor'. All in white with the exception of the penultimate line which is in black and the first 'H' in 'Harry' which is in purple and all on a red background with colour illustration on left-hand side of Professor Dumbledore with a Put-Outer in his left hand, together with nine stars. The initial capital 'H' of 'Harry' is a drop capital and is printed in blue.

All edges trimmed. Binding measurements: 197 by 128mm (wrappers), 197 by 13mm (spine).

Publication: 8 October 2001 in an edition of 400,200 copies (confirmed by Bloomsbury)

Price: £5.99

Contents:
Harry Potter and the Philosopher's Stone
   ('Mr and Mrs Dursley, of number four, Privet Drive, were proud to say…')

Notes:
Dumbledore's left foot and one star intersect the white barcode panel on the lower wrapper.

The individual titles in the 'celebratory' edition were each published to celebrate the release of the film version. The UK premiere of *Harry Potter and the Philosopher's Stone* took place on 4 November 2001.

To celebrate the fifteenth anniversary of the publication of *Harry Potter and the Philosopher's Stone*, Bloomsbury printed a circular commemorative device on the upper wrapper of the thirty-third reprint (and later reprints) of this edition. The device featured Harry from the Thomas Taylor illustration used in A1(a) together with '15 | YEARS OF | HARRY | POTTER | MAGIC'.

Copies: private collection (PWE)

Reprints include:
3
16 15 14 13 12 11
19

A1(f)   ENGLISH ADULT EDITION   (2004)
(Michael Wildsmith photography adult artwork series in paperback)

Harry Potter and the | Philosopher's Stone | J. K. Rowling | BLOOMSBURY (All width centred)

Collation: 168 unsigned leaves bound in one gathering of six leaves, thirteen gatherings of twelve leaves and one gathering of six leaves; 177 by 110mm; [1-7] 8-24 [25] 26-38 [39] 40-54 [55] 56-70 [71] 72-98 [99] 100-124 [125] 126-43 [144] 145-56 [157] 158-77 [178] 179-95 [196] 197-209 [210] 211-32 [233] 234-46 [247] 248-61 [262] 263-82 [283] 284-309 [310] 311-32 [333-36]

Page contents: [1] half-title: 'Harry Potter and the | Philosopher's Stone'; [2] *'Titles available in the Harry Potter series | (in reading order):* | Harry Potter and the Philosopher's Stone | Harry Potter and the Chamber of Secrets | Harry Potter and the Prisoner of Azkaban | Harry Potter and the Goblet of Fire | Harry Potter and the Order of the Phoenix'; [3] title-page; [4] 'All rights reserved; no part of this publication may be reproduced or | transmitted by any means, electronic, mechanical, photocopying or otherwise, | without the prior permission of the publisher | [new paragraph] First published in Great Britain in 1997 | Bloomsbury Publishing Plc, 38 Soho Square, London, W1D 3HB | [new paragraph] This paperback edition first published in 2004 | [new paragraph] Copyright © J. K. Rowling 1997 | [new paragraph] Harry Potter, names, characters and related indicia are | copyright and trademark Warner Bros., 2000™ | [new paragraph] The moral right of the author has been asserted | A CIP catalogue record of this book is available | from the British Library | [new paragraph] ISBN 0 7475 7447 2 | [new paragraph] 1 3 5 7 9 10 8 6 4 2 | [new paragraph] Typeset by Dorchester Typesetting | Printed in Great Britain by Clays Ltd, St Ives plc | [new paragraph] All papers used by Bloomsbury Publishing are natural, | recyclable products made from wood grown in well-managed forests. | The paper used in this book contains 20% post consumer waste material | which was de-inked using chlorine free methods. The | manufacturing processes conform to the environmental | regulations of the country of origin. | [new paragraph] www.bloomsbury.com/ harrypotter'; [5] '*for Jessica, who loves stories, | for Anne, who loved them too, | and for Di, who heard this one first.*'; [6] blank; [7]-332 text; [333-36] blank

Paper: wove paper

Running title: 'HARRY POTTER' (24mm) on verso, recto title comprises chapter title, pp. 8-332 (excluding pages on which new chapters commence)

Binding: pictorial wrappers.
   On spine: 'HARRY POTTER AND THE [colour photograph of a shining red stone, 19 by 18mm] | J.K. ROWLING [publisher's device of a figure with a bow, 10 by 10mm] | PHILOSOPHER'S STONE' (reading lengthways down spine). All in white with the exception of last line which is in gilt and all on black.
   On upper wrapper: 'HARRY POTTER AND THE [in white] | PHILOSOPHER'S [embossed in gilt] | STONE [embossed in gilt] | J. K. ROWLING [in white] | BLOOMSBURY [in white]' (all width centred). All on colour photograph of a shining red stone.
   On lower wrapper: '[colour photograph of a shining red stone, all within single white border, 22 by 22mm] 'Funny, imaginative, magical … Rowling | has woken up a whole generation to | reading. In the 2020s, thirty-something | book-lovers will know each other by smug | references to Diagon Alley and Quidditch' | *The Times* | [new paragraph] When a letter arrives for unhappy but ordinary Harry | Potter, a decade-old secret is revealed to him. His parents | were wizards, killed by a Dark Lord's curse when Harry was | just a baby, and which he somehow survived. Escaping from | his unbearable Muggle guardians to Hogwarts, a wizarding | school brimming with ghosts and enchantments, Harry | stumbles into a sinister adventure when he finds a three- | headed dog guarding a room on the third floor. Then he | hears of a missing stone with astonishing powers which | could be valuable, dangerous, or both. | [new paragraph] 'This is a terrific book' *Sunday Telegraph* | [new paragraph] 'Has all the makings of a classic … Rowling uses classic | narrative devices with flair and originality and delivers | a complex and demanding plot in the form of a hugely | entertaining thriller' *Scotsman*

| [new paragraph] 'And you thought wizardry was for children. Harry Potter | will make you think again. He casts his spells on grown- | ups too' James Naughtie | [new paragraph] 'Full of surprises and jokes; comparisons with Dahl are, | this time, justified' *Sunday Times* | [new paragraph] [barcode in black on white panel, 24 by 39mm together with 'bloomsbury[in black]pbk[in white]s[in black] | £6.99 [in black] | www.bloomsbury.com [in black]' and all on red panel, 25 by 75mm] | Cover image: Michael Wildsmith Design: William Webb Author Photograph: © Bill de la HEY'. All in white on black with colour photograph to the left of lines 1-6.

On inside upper wrapper: black and white photograph of J.K. Rowling standing against bookshelves.

On inside lower wrapper: 'Other titles available in the | HARRY POTTER series | [colour illustrations in two columns of four book designs]'. All in white on black.

All edges trimmed. Binding measurements: 177 by 110mm (wrappers), 177 by 19mm (spine).

Publication: 10 July 2004 in an edition of 110,200 copies (confirmed by Bloomsbury)

Price: £6.99

Contents:

Harry Potter and the Philosopher's Stone

('Mr and Mrs Dursley, of number four, Privet Drive, were proud to say…')

Notes:

This edition marks a significant stage in the publication of Bloomsbury's editions. Beyond the standard hardback and paperback editions and the series aimed at specific markets (adults for the original adult edition, bookclub editions, the gift market for the deluxe editions, the movie-going public for the 'celebratory' edition), this volume marks the first time an existing look (the original adult edition) was changed to refresh the image. Bloomsbury would redesign and rebrand the series many times.

Interviewed in September 2013, Nigel Newton remarked that the strategy was one 'to keep the series looking fresh' and that '… this is what publishers do. This is what brands do. To be honest, the book trade is quite short-termist and if you release something new, with a new ISBN, it is treated like a new publication even if the words are the same. So you have a chance of getting back at the front of the shop again. Not that Harry Potter has ever malingered for lack of support from the book trade.'

Questioned whether new editions are run past the author, Newton responded that 'we would never publish any edition without her full approval and input' and noted that Rowling had been 'very helpful and giving over the years'.

Copies: BL (H.2005/1621) stamped 10 May 2004

Reprints include:

5 7 9 10 6

10

A1(g)   ENGLISH ADULT EDITION   (2004)
(Michael Wildsmith photography adult artwork series in hardback)

Harry Potter and the | Philosopher's Stone | J. K. Rowling | BLOOMSBURY (All width centred)

Collation: 112 unsigned leaves bound in indeterminate gatherings; 197 by 125mm; [1-7] 8-18 [19] 20-27 [28] 29-38 [39] 40-48 [49] 50-66 [67] 68-84 [85] 86-97 [98] 99-106 [107] 108-120 [121] 122-32 [133] 134-42 [143] 144-57 [158] 159-66 [167] 168-76 [177] 178-90 [191] 192-208 [209] 210-23 [224]

Page contents: [1] half-title: 'Harry Potter and the | Philosopher's Stone'; [2] *Titles available in the Harry Potter series | (in reading order):* | Harry Potter and the Philosopher's Stone | Harry Potter and the Chamber of Secrets | Harry Potter and the Prisoner of Azkaban | Harry Potter and the Goblet of Fire | Harry Potter and the Order of the Phoenix | [new paragraph] *Harry Potter and the Philosopher's Stone | also available in Latin, Ancient Greek, Welsh and Irish:* | Harrius Potter et Philosophi Lapis (Latin) | Ἄρειος Ποτήρ καί ἡ τοῦ ψιλοσόψον λίθος (Ancient Greek) | Harri Potter a Maen yr Anthronydd (Welsh) | Harry Potter agus an Órchloch (Irish)'; [3] title-page; [4] 'All rights reserved; no part of this publication may be reproduced or | transmitted by any means, electronic, mechanical, photocopying | or otherwise, without the prior permission of the publisher | [new paragraph] First published in Great Britain in 1997 | Bloomsbury Publishing Plc, 38 Soho Square, London, W1D 3HB | [new paragraph] This edition first published in 2004 | [new paragraph] Copyright © 1997 J. K. Rowling | [new paragraph] Harry Potter, names, characters and related indicia are | copyright and trademark Warner Bros., 2000™ | [new paragraph] The moral right of the author has been asserted | A CIP catalogue record of this book is available from the British Library | [new paragraph] ISBN 0 7475 7360 3 | [new paragraph] Typeset by Dorchester Typesetting | [new paragraph] All papers used by Bloomsbury Publishing are natural, recyclable products made | from wood grown in well-managed forests. The manufacturing processes | conform to the environmental regulations of the country of origin. | [new paragraph] Printed in Great Britain by Clays Ltd, St Ives plc | [new paragraph] 1 3 5 7 9 10 8 6 4 2 | [new paragraph] www.bloomsbury. com/harrypotter'; [5] '*for Jessica, who loves stories, | for Anne, who loved them too, | and for Di, who heard this one first.*'; [6] blank; [7]-223 text; [224] blank

Paper: wove paper

Running title: 'HARRY POTTER' (24mm) on verso, recto title comprises chapter title, pp. 8-223 (excluding pages on which new chapters commence)

Binding: black boards.
   On spine: 'HARRY POTTER | J. K. ROWLING | AND THE PHILOSOPHER'S STONE [publisher's device of a figure with a bow, 14 by 14mm]' (reading lengthways down spine). All in gilt.
   Upper and lower covers: blank.
   All edges trimmed. Binding measurements: 204 by 128mm (covers), 204 by 31mm (spine). End-papers: wove paper.

Dust-jacket: coated wove paper, 204 by 485mm

On spine: '[colour photograph of a shining red stone, all within single white ruled border, 20 by 20mm] HARRY POTTER [in gilt] | J. K. ROWLING [in white] | AND THE PHILOSOPHER'S STONE [in white]' (reading lengthways down spine) together with publisher's device of a figure with a bow, 14 by 14mm [in olive beige] (at foot).

On upper cover: 'J. K. ROWLING [in white] | HARRY [embossed in gilt] | POTTER [embossed in gilt] | AND THE PHILOSOPHER'S STONE [in white] | BLOOMSBURY [in white]' (all width centred). All on colour photograph of a shining red stone.

On lower cover: black and white photograph of J.K. Rowling standing against bookshelves with 'www.bloomsbury.com/harrypotter [in black on olive beige panel, 5 by 40mm] | [barcode in black on white panel, 20 by 39mm] | BLOOMSBURY [in black on olive beige panel, 7 by 40mm]' (lower right).

On upper inside flap: 'When a letter arrives for unhappy but | ordinary Harry Potter, a decade-old secret | is revealed to him. His parents were | wizards, killed by a Dark Lord's curse | when Harry was just a baby, and which he | somehow survived. Escaping from his | unbearable Muggle guardians to Hogwarts, | a wizarding school brimming with ghosts | and enchantments, Harry stumbles into a | sinister adventure when he finds a three- | headed dog guarding a room on the third | floor. Then he hears of a missing stone | with astonishing powers which could be | valuable, dangerous, or both. | [new paragraph] 'Funny, imaginative, magical … Rowling has | woken up a whole generation to reading. In | the 2020s, thirty-something book-lovers | will know each other by smug references | to Diagon Alley and Quidditch' *The Times* | [new paragraph] 'This is a terrific book' *Sunday Telegraph* | [new paragraph] 'Has all the makings of a classic … Rowling | uses classic narrative devices with flair and | originality and delivers a complex and | demanding plot in the form of a hugely | entertaining thriller' *Scotsman* | [new paragraph] 'And you thought wizardry was for | children. Harry Potter will make you think | again. He casts his spell on grown- | ups too' James Naughtie | [new paragraph] 'Full of surprises and jokes; comparisons | with Dahl are, this time, justified' | *Sunday Times* | [new paragraph] £11.99'. All in white on black.

On lower inside flap: 'J. K. (JOANNE KATHLEEN) ROWLING | has written fiction since she was a child. | Born in 1965, she grew up in Chepstow | and wrote her first 'book' at the age of six | – a story about a rabbit called Rabbit. | She studied French and Classics at Exeter | University, then moved to London to | work at Amnesty International, and then | to Portugal to teach English as a foreign | language, before settling in Edinburgh. | [new paragraph] The idea for Harry Potter occurred to her | on the train from Manchester to London, | where she says Harry Potter 'just strolled | into my head fully formed', and by the | time she had arrived at King's Cross, | many of the characters had taken shape. | During the next five years she outlined | the plots for each book and began writing | the first in the series, *Harry Potter and* | *the Philosopher's Stone*, which was first | published by Bloomsbury in 1997. The | other Harry Potter titles: *Harry Potter and* | *the Chamber of Secrets, Harry Potter and the* | *Prisoner of Azkaban, Harry Potter and the* | *Goblet of Fire*, and *Harry Potter and the* | *Order of the Phoenix*, followed. | J. K. Rowling has also written two other | companion books, *Quidditch Through the* | *Ages* and *Fantastic Beasts and Where to* | *Find Them*, in aid of Comic Relief. | [new paragraph] Jacket Design: William Webb | Jacket Image: Michael Wildsmith | Author Photograph: © Bill de la HEY'. All in white on black.

Publication: 4 October 2004 in an edition of 12,500 copies (confirmed by Bloomsbury)

Price: £11.99

Contents:
Harry Potter and the Philosopher's Stone
('Mr and Mrs Dursley, of number four, Privet Drive, were proud to say…')

Notes:
Having rebranded the look of the adult artwork edition to feature photography by Michael Wildsmith, it was perhaps inevitable that a hardback version would become available. A1(g), A2(m) and A7(j) were all published on 4 October 2004 with A9(i) following a few days later on 10 October 2004. As the series progressed, later titles published in this livery (see A12(aa), A13(aa) and A14(aa)) would also comprise the simultaneous first edition issues.

Copies: Bloomsbury Archives

Reprints include:
3 5 7 9 10 8 6 4
5 7 9 10 8 6
13 15 17 19 20 18 16 14 12

A1(h) ENGLISH 'BLOOMSBURY 21' EDITION (2007)
(adapted children's artwork series in paperback)

HARRY POTTER | AND THE | PHILOSOPHER'S | STONE | J. K. Rowling | BLOOM21SBURY (All width centred)

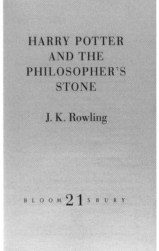

Collation: 120 unsigned leaves bound in indeterminate gatherings; 197 by 128mm; [i-iv] [1-7] 8-18 [19] 20-27 [28] 29-38 [39] 40-48 [49] 50-66 [67] 68-84 [85] 86-97 [98] 99-106 [107] 108-120 [121] 122-32 [133] 134-42 [143] 144-57 [158] 159-66 [167] 168-76 [177] 178-90 [191] 192-208 [209] 210-23 [224-36]

Page contents: [i] half-title: 'HARRY POTTER | AND THE PHILOSOPHER'S STONE'; [ii] blank; [iii] title-page; [iv] 'All rights reserved; no part of this publication may be reproduced or | transmitted by any means, electronic, mechanical, photocopying or otherwise, | without the prior permission of the publisher | [new paragraph] First published in Great Britain in 1997 | Bloomsbury Publishing Plc, 36 Soho Square, London W1D 3QY | [new paragraph] This edition first published in 2007 | [new paragraph] Copyright © J. K. Rowling 1997 | Cover illustrations copyright © Thomas Taylor 1997 | Introduction copyright © Alexander McCall Smith 2007 | [new paragraph] Harry Potter, names, characters and related indicia are | copyright and trademark Warner Bros., 2000™ | [new paragraph] The moral right of the author has been asserted | A CIP catalogue record for this book is available from | the British Library | [new paragraph] ISBN 978 0 7475 8994 5 | [new paragraph] Printed and bound in Great Britain by Clays Ltd, St Ives plc | Typeset by Dorchester Typesetting | [new paragraph] 10 9 8 7 6 5 4 3 2 1 | [new paragraph] | www.bloomsbury.com/harrypotter | [new paragraph] The paper this book is printed on is certified by the © Forest Stewardship | Council 1996 A.C. (FSC). It is ancient-forest friendly. | The printer holds FSC chain of custody SGS-COC-2061 | [new paragraph] [Forest Stewardship Council logo, 8 by 9mm together with ® symbol and text: 'FSC | Mixed Sources | Product group from well-managed | forests and other controlled sources | [new paragraph] Cert no. SGS-COC-2061 | www.fsc.org | © 1996 Forest Stewardship Council']'; [1-3] 'Introduction' ('In 1990, Joanne Rowling was travelling on a train from Manchester to London…') (headed 'Alexander McCall Smith'); [4] blank; [5] *'for Jessica, who loves stories, | for Anne, who loved them too, | and for Di, who heard this one first.'*; [6] blank; [7]-223 text; [224] blank; [225-26] 'J. K. ROWLING'S | FAVOURITE BOOKS' (four sections); [227] 'OTHER BOOKS IN THE | HARRY POTTER SERIES | BY J. K. ROWLING'; [228] blank; [229-33] five books described with press comments; [234] blank; [235] 'BLOOM21SBURY' (21 titles listed with their authors in two columns); [236] blank

Paper: wove paper

Running title: 'HARRY POTTER' (24mm) on verso, recto title comprises chapter title, pp. 8-223

Binding: pictorial wrappers.

On spine: 'J.K. ROWLING [vertical line] *Harry Potter and the Philosopher's Stone*' (reading lengthways down spine) together with '6 | [rule, 8mm] 21' (horizontally at head) and publisher's device of a figure with a bow, 11 by 9mm (horizontally at foot). All in white on red.

On upper wrapper: '[colour photographic illustration, at an angle, of a hardback edition, in dust-jacket (with shadow), of *Harry Potter and the Philosopher's Stone* (original children's artwork series), the corners of the book at the spine and upper right corner are not shown, 145 by 128mm] | *With a new introduction* | *by Alexander McCall Smith* | J.K. ROWLING | Harry Potter and the | Philosopher's Stone' (all on left margin with 'B | L | O | O | M | 21 | S | B | U | R | Y' reading lengthways down right side next to fore-edge). All in black on white with the exception of the title which is in red.

On lower wrapper: 'BLOOM21SBURY | THE INTERNATIONAL PHENOMENON | [new paragraph] Is there anybody left in the Muggle world who hasn't heard of Harry Potter, | or read his extraordinary and exciting adventures? In this first book in the | series which catapulted J.K. Rowling to the very heights of literary fame, | Harry discovers that he is no ordinary boy but a wizard of great renown and | that he is expected at Hogwarts School of Witchcraft and Wizardry. Moreover, | at Hogwarts he encounters He Who Must Not Be Named, a master of magic | whose ambition is more dark and terrifying than Harry can possibly imagine. | [new paragraph] 'Funny, imaginative, magical … Rowling has woken up a whole generation | to reading' *The Times* | [new paragraph] 'Has all the makings of a classic … Rowling uses narrative devices with | flair and originality and delivers a complex and demanding plot in the | form of a hugely entertaining thrilled' *Scotsman* | [new paragraph] 'A richly textured first novel given lift-off by an inventive wit' *Guardian* | [new paragraph] 'And you thought wizardry was for children. Harry Potter will make you | think again. He casts his spells on grown-ups too' James Naughtie | [new paragraph] 'Full of surprises and jokes; comparisons with Dahl, are, | this time, justified' *Sunday Times* | [new paragraph] [barcode in black on white panel, 24 by 39mm together with 'bloomsburypbks | [new paragraph] £5.99 | www.bloomsbury.com' all in white on red panel, 25 by 35mm and all enclosed by single red ruled border, 25 by 74mm] | [new paragraph] Cover photograph © Michael Wildsmith, featuring the cover illustration for | *Harry Potter and the Philosopher's Stone* © Thomas Taylor 1997'. All in black and red on white.

All edges trimmed. Binding measurements: 197 by 128mm (wrappers), 197 by 17mm (spine).

Publication: 2 January 2007 in an edition of 19,550 copies (confirmed by Bloomsbury)

Price: £5.99

Contents:
Harry Potter and the Philosopher's Stone
('Mr and Mrs Dursley, of number four, Privet Drive, were proud to say…')
J.K. Rowling's Favourite Books
('Children's book | It's a three-way tie between *The Story of the Treasure Seekers* by…')

Notes:
The sixth of twenty-one titles in the series released by the publisher to celebrate its twenty-first anniversary in 2007. The setting of text was the standard A1(a) version, with an additional introduction by Alexander McCall Smith and new material entitled 'J.K. Rowling's Favourite Books' at the end.

There are four sections to 'J.K. Rowling's Favourite Books'
'Children's book'
('It's a three-way tie between *The Story of the Treasure Seekers* by Edith Nesbit…')
'Classic'
('*Emma* by Jane Austen, for the incomparable characterisation…')
'Contemporary book'
('It changes monthly, but the last novel I fell in love with was *Arthur and George*…')
'Top 10'
('*Emma* by Jane Austen…')

Copies: private collection (PWE)

ENGLISH 'SIGNATURE' EDITION
(Clare Melinsky artwork series in paperback)

Harry Potter ['signature' above 'z' rule with numerous stars] | *and the* | *Philosopher's Stone* | [illustration of Hogwarts crest with legend 'DRAGO DORMIENS NUNQUAM TITILLANDUS' on banner, 68 by 84mm] | J.K.ROWLING | [publisher's device of a dog, 8 by 13mm] | BLOOMSBURY | LONDON BERLIN NEW YORK SYDNEY (All width centred)

Collation: 112 unsigned leaves bound in indeterminate gatherings; 197 by 128mm; [1-7] 8-18 [19] 20-27 [28] 29-38 [39] 40-48 [49] 50-66 [67] 68-84 [85] 86-97 [98] 99-106 [107] 108-120 [121] 122-32 [133] 134-42 [143] 144-57 [158] 159-66 [167] 168-76 [177] 178-90 [191] 192-208 [209] 210-23 [224]

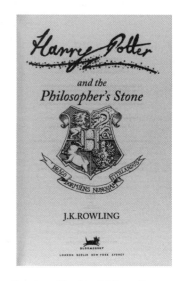

Page contents: [1] half-title: 'Harry Potter ['signature' above 'z' rule with numerous stars] | *and the* | *Philosopher's Stone* | [illustration of Hogwarts crest with legend 'DRAGO DORMIENS NUNQUAM TITILLANDUS' on banner, 60 by 75mm]'; [2] '*Titles available in the Harry Potter series* | *(in reading order):* | Harry Potter and the Philosopher's Stone | Harry Potter and the Chamber of Secrets | Harry Potter and the Prisoner of Azkaban | Harry Potter and the Goblet of Fire | Harry Potter and the Order of the Phoenix | Harry Potter and the Half-Blood Prince | Harry Potter and the Deathly Hallows | [new paragraph] *Titles available in the Harry Potter series* | *(in Latin):* | Harry Potter and the Philosopher's Stone | Harry Potter and the Chamber of Secrets | *(in Welsh, Ancient Greek and Irish):* | Harry Potter and the Philosopher's Stone'; [3] title-page; [4] 'All rights reserved; no part of this publication may be reproduced or | transmitted by any means, electronic, mechanical, photocopying | or otherwise, without the prior permission of the publisher | [new paragraph] First published in Great Britain in 1997 by Bloomsbury Publishing Plc | 36 Soho Square, London, W1D 3QY | [new paragraph] Bloomsbury Publishing, London, Berlin, New York and Sydney | [new paragraph] This paperback edition first published in November 2010 | [new paragraph] Copyright © J.K.Rowling 1997 | Cover illustrations by Clare Melinsky copyright © Bloomsbury Publishing Plc 2010 | [new paragraph] Harry Potter, names, characters and related indicia are | copyright and trademark Warner Bros., 2000™ | [new paragraph] The moral right of the author has been asserted | A CIP catalogue record of this book is available from the British Library | [new paragraph] ISBN 978 1 4088 1054 5 | [new paragraph] [Forest Stewardship Council logo, 8 by 9mm together with ® symbol and text: 'FSC | www.fsc.org | MIX | Paper from | responsible sources | FSC® C018072'] | [new paragraph] Typeset by Dorchester Typesetting | Printed in Great Britain by Clays Ltd, St Ives plc | [new paragraph] 1 3 5 7 9 10 8 6 4 2 | [new paragraph] | www.bloomsbury.com/harrypotter'; [5] '*for Jessica, who loves stories,* | *for Anne, who loved them too,* | *and for Di, who heard this one first.*'; [6] blank; [7]-223 text; [224] blank

Paper: wove paper

Running title: 'HARRY POTTER' (24mm) on verso, recto title comprises chapter title, pp. 8-223

Binding: pictorial wrappers.

On spine: 'Harry Potter ['signature' above 'z' rule with numerous stars] [in gilt] *and* | *the Philosopher's Stone* [orange, yellow and blue illustration of key-bird, 11 by 16mm] J.K.ROWLING BLOOMSBURY [publisher's device of the head of a dog, 3 by 4mm]' (reading lengthways down spine). All in white on blue.

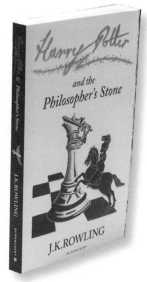

On upper wrapper: 'Harry Potter ['signature' above 'z' rule with numerous stars] [embossed in gilt] | *and the* | *Philosopher's Stone* | [blue, yellow and light green illustration of white queen chess piece swinging sword at black knight chess piece, 95 by 111mm] | J.K.ROWLING | BLOOMSBURY' (all width centred). All in blue with deckle-edge effect of white leaf on blue background at fore-edge.

On lower wrapper: 'Harry Potter thinks he is an ordinary boy. He lives with | Uncle Vernon, Aunt Petunia and cousin Dudley, who | make him sleep in a cupboard under the stairs. Then Harry | starts receiving mysterious letters and his life is changed | for ever. He is whisked away by a beetle-eyed giant of a | man and enrolled in Hogwarts School of Witchcraft and | Wizardry. The reason: Harry Potter is a wizard! | [new paragraph] 'J.K. Rowling has woken up a whole generation to reading.' | *The Times* | [new paragraph] 'The Harry Potter books are that rare thing, a series of | stories adored by parents and children alike.' | *Daily Telegraph* | [new paragraph] 'Hooray for Harry Potter … as funny as Roald Dahl's | stories and as vivid as the Narnia books.' | *Daily Mail* | [new paragraph] 'A richly textured first novel given lift-off by an | inventive wit.' | *Guardian* | Designed by Webb & Webb Design | Cover illustrations by Clare Melinsky | Author photograph © J.P.Masclet | [barcode together with publisher's device of a dog, 6 by 10mm and 'BLOOMSBURY' together with Forest Stewardship Council logo, 7 by 8mm together with © symbol and text: 'FSC | Mixed Sources | Product group from well-managed | forests and other controlled sources | [new paragraph] Cert no. SGS-COC-2061 | www.fsc.org | © 1996 Forest Stewardship Council'] | www.bloomsbury. com/harrypotter £6.99'. Lines 1-18 in blue with all other text in black with brown, blue, yellow and light green illustration of ornate railway station pillar and sign '9¾' together with deckle-edge effect of green and brown leaf on blue background at fore-edge. The initial capital 'H' of 'Harry' is a drop capital.

On inside upper wrapper: 'The magical world of … | Harry Potter ['signature' above 'z' rule with numerous stars] | [colour illustrations in three columns of seven book designs] | The internationally bestselling series | [new paragraph] For more from Harry Potter, visit | www.bloomsbury.com/ harrypotter'. All in blue with the exception of line 2 which is in gold, together with deckle-edge effect of white leaf on blue background at fore-edge.

On inside lower wrapper: colour photograph of J.K. Rowling seated by a window.

All edges trimmed. Binding measurements: 197 by 128mm (wrappers), 197 by 14mm (spine).

Publication: 1 November 2010 in an edition of 63,586 copies (confirmed by Bloomsbury)

Price: £6.99

Contents:
Harry Potter and the Philosopher's Stone
    ('Mr and Mrs Dursley, of number four, Privet Drive, were proud to say…')

Notes:
Bloomsbury announced a 'new look' for the Harry Potter series in a news release on 30 March 2010. The publisher noted that 'the newly designed "Signature" livery will appeal to the next generation of readers who did not "grow up" with Harry Potter…' The new illustrations were by the illustrator and linocut artist Clare Melinsky (born 1953) with the design created by Webb and Webb Design Limited. The artist's website noted that 'all the covers have been approved by J.K. Rowling herself'. Bloomsbury's news release noted that 'the "Signature" livery will be exclusively available in paperback format…' It took a year before Bloomsbury released a hardback edition.

Published as a boxed set of seven volumes comprising A1(i), A2(n), A7(k), A9(k), A12(h), A13(g) and A14(f). Individual volumes were also available separately.

To celebrate the fifteenth anniversary of the publication of *Harry Potter and the Philosopher's Stone*, Bloomsbury printed a circular commemorative device on the upper wrapper of the twelfth reprint (and later reprints) of this edition. The device featured Harry from the Thomas Taylor illustration used in A1(a) together with '15 | YEARS OF | HARRY | POTTER | MAGIC'.

Copies: private collection (PWE)

A1(j)   ENGLISH 'SIGNATURE' EDITION   (2011)
(Clare Melinsky artwork series in hardback)

Harry Potter ['signature' above 'z' rule with numerous stars] | *and the* | *Philosopher's Stone* | [illustration of Hogwarts crest with legend 'DRAGO DORMIENS NUNQUAM TITILLANDUS' on banner, 68 by 84mm] | J.K.ROWLING | [publisher's device of a dog, 8 by 13mm] | BLOOMSBURY | LONDON BERLIN NEW YORK SYDNEY (All width centred)

Collation: 112 unsigned leaves bound in indeterminate gatherings; 197 by 124mm; [1-7] 8-18 [19] 20-27 [28] 29-38 [39] 40-48 [49] 50-66 [67] 68-84 [85] 86-97 [98] 99-106 [107] 108-120 [121] 122-32 [133] 134-42 [143] 144-57 [158] 159-66 [167] 168-76 [177] 178-90 [191] 192-208 [209] 210-23 [224]

Page contents: [1] half-title: 'Harry Potter ['signature' above 'z' rule with numerous stars] | *and the* | *Philosopher's Stone* | [illustration of Hogwarts crest with legend 'DRAGO DORMIENS NUNQUAM TITILLANDUS' on banner, 60 by 75mm]'; [2] '*Titles available in the Harry Potter series* | (*in reading* *order*): | Harry Potter and the Philosopher's Stone | Harry Potter and the Chamber of Secrets | Harry Potter and the Prisoner of Azkaban | Harry Potter and the Goblet of Fire | Harry Potter and the Order of the Phoenix | Harry Potter and the Half-Blood Prince | Harry Potter and the Deathly Hallows | [new paragraph] *Titles available in the Harry Potter series* | *(in Latin)*: | Harry Potter and the Philosopher's Stone | Harry Potter and the Chamber of Secrets | *(in Welsh, Ancient Greek and Irish)*: | Harry Potter and the Philosopher's Stone | [new paragraph] *Also available* | *(in aid of Comic Relief)*: | Fantastic Beasts and Where to Find Them | Quidditch Through the Ages | *(in aid of Lumos)*: | The Tales of Beedle the Bard'; [3] title-page; [4] 'All rights reserved; no part of this publication may be reproduced or | transmitted by any means, electronic, mechanical, photocopying | or otherwise, without the prior permission of the publisher | [new paragraph] First published in Great Britain in 1997 by Bloomsbury Publishing Plc | 49-51

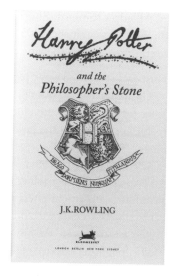

Bedford Square, London, WC1B 3DP | [new paragraph] Bloomsbury Publishing, London, Berlin, New York and Sydney | [new paragraph] This hardback edition first published in November 2011 | [new paragraph] Copyright © J.K.Rowling 1997 | Cover and endpaper illustrations by Clare Melinsky copyright © J.K.Rowling 2010 | [new paragraph] Harry Potter, names, characters and related indicia are | copyright and trademark Warner Bros., 2000™ | [new paragraph] The moral right of the author has been asserted | A CIP catalogue record of this book is available from the British Library | [new paragraph] ISBN 978 1 4088 2586 0 | [new paragraph] [Forest Stewardship Council logo, 8 by 9mm together with ® symbol and text: 'FSC | www.fsc.org | MIX | Paper from | responsible sources | FSC® C018072'] | [new paragraph] Typeset by Dorchester Typesetting | Printed in Great Britain by Clays Ltd, St Ives plc | [new paragraph] 1 3 5 7 9 10 8 6 4 2 | [new paragraph] | www.bloomsbury. com/harrypotter'; [5] '*for Jessica, who loves stories,* | *for Anne, who loved them too,* | *and for Di, who heard this one first.*'; [6] blank; [7]-223 text; [224] blank

Paper: wove paper

Running title: 'HARRY POTTER' (24mm) on verso, recto title comprises chapter title, pp. 8-223

Binding: blue boards.

    On spine: 'Harry Potter ['signature' above 'z' rule with numerous stars] *and* | *the Philosopher's Stone* [illustration of key-bird, 11 by 16mm] J.K.ROWLING BLOOMSBURY [publisher's device of the head of a dog, 3 by 4mm]' (reading lengthways down spine). All in gilt.

    Upper and lower covers: blank.

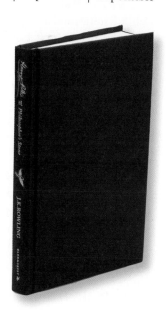

All edges trimmed. Blue sewn bands at head and foot of spine together with blue marker ribbon. Binding measurements: 205 by 128mm (covers), 205 by 27mm (spine). End-papers: wove paper overprinted in blue showing design, in white, of spine motifs from the series (see notes).

Dust-jacket: coated wove paper, 205 by 484mm

On spine: 'Harry Potter ['signature' above 'z' rule with numerous stars] [in gilt] *and* | *the Philosopher's Stone* [orange, yellow and blue illustration of key-bird, 11 by 16mm] J.K.ROWLING BLOOMSBURY [publisher's device of the head of a dog, 3 by 4mm]' (reading lengthways down spine). All in white on blue.

On upper cover: 'Harry Potter ['signature' above 'z' rule with numerous stars] [in gilt] | *and the* | *Philosopher's Stone* | [blue, yellow and light green illustration of white queen chess piece swinging sword at black knight chess piece, 95 by 111mm] | J.K.ROWLING | BLOOMSBURY' (all width centred). All in blue with deckle-edge effect of white leaf on blue background at fore-edge.

On lower cover: "As funny as Roald Dahl's stories | and as vivid as the Narnia books.' | *Daily Mail* | [publisher's device of a dog, 6 by 10mm and 'BLOOMSBURY'] [barcode and 'www.bloomsbury. com/harrypotter' in black on white panel, 24 by 38mm]'. All in blue, with brown, blue, yellow and light green illustration of ornate railway station pillar and sign '9¾' together with deckle-edge effect of green and brown leaf on blue background at fore-edge. The initial capital 'A' of 'As' is a drop capital.

On upper inside flap: 'Harry Potter thinks he is an ordinary | boy. He lives with Uncle Vernon, | Aunt Petunia and his cousin, Dudley, | who make him sleep in a cupboard under | the stairs. Then Harry starts receiving | mysterious letters and his life is changed | for ever. He is whisked away by a beetle-| eyed giant of a man and enrolled in | Hogwarts School of Witchcraft and | Wizardry. The reason: Harry Potter is | a wizard! [new paragraph] 'J. K. Rowling has woken up a whole | generation to reading.' | *The Times* [new paragraph] 'Hooray for Harry Potter ... as funny as | Roald Dahl's | stories and as vivid as the | Narnia books.' | *Daily Mail* [new paragraph] 'A richly textured first novel given lift-off | by an inventive wit.' | *Guardian* | [new paragraph] [orange, yellow and blue illustration of key-bird, 14 by 21mm]'. All in white on blue. The initial capital 'H' of 'Harry' is a drop capital.

On lower inside flap: 'J. K. Rowling has written fiction since she was a child, | and she always wanted to be an author. Her parents loved | reading and their house in Chepstow was full of books. | In fact, J. K. Rowling wrote her first 'book' at the age | of six – a story about a rabbit called Rabbit. She studied | French and Classics at Exeter University, then moved to | Edinburgh – via London and Portugal. In 2000 she was | awarded an OBE for services to children's literature. | [new paragraph] The idea for Harry Potter occurred to her on the | train from Manchester to London, where she says | Harry Potter 'just strolled into my head fully formed', | and by the time she had arrived at King's Cross, many | of the characters had taken shape. During the next | five years she outlined the plots for each book and | began writing the first in the series, *Harry Potter and* | *the Philosopher's Stone*, which was first published by | Bloomsbury in 1997. The other Harry Potter titles: | *Harry Potter and the Chamber of Secrets, Harry Potter* | *and the Prisoner of Azkaban, Harry Potter and the* | *Goblet of Fire, Harry Potter and the Order of the Phoenix,* | *Harry Potter and the Half-Blood Prince* and *Harry* | *Potter and the Deathly Hallows* followed. J. K. Rowling | has also written three companion books: *Quidditch*

| *Through the Ages* and *Fantastic Beasts and Where to Find* | *Them*, in aid of Comic Relief, and *The Tales of Beedle* | *the Bard*, in aid of Lumos. | [new paragraph] THE COMPLETE HARRY POTTER SERIES: | [colour illustrations in two rows of seven book designs] | Designed by Webb & Webb Design | Cover illustrations by Clare Melinsky | copyright © J. K. Rowling 2010'. All in white on blue with white panel, 19 by 12mm, to right on which in black: '[Forest Stewardship Council logo, 6 by 7mm together with ® symbol] | FSC | www.fsc.org | MIX | Paper from | responsible sources | FSC® C018072'.

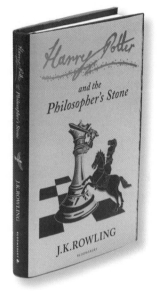

Publication: 7 November 2011 in an edition of 9,200 copies (confirmed by Bloomsbury)

Price: £115 [together with A2(o), A7(l), A9(l), A12(i), A13(h) and A14(g)]

Contents:

Harry Potter and the Philosopher's Stone

('Mr and Mrs Dursley, of number four, Privet Drive, were proud to say…')

Notes:

The end-papers carry a design of eight miniature illustrations. Seven of these reproduce the spine motifs from the series and an eighth comprises a variant of the key-bird from the first book.

Published as a boxed set of seven volumes comprising A1(j), A2(o), A7(l), A9(l), A12(i), A13(h) and A14(g). Individual volumes were not available separately. The ISBN for the boxed set was ISBN 978 1 4088 2594 5.

Copies: private collection (PWE)

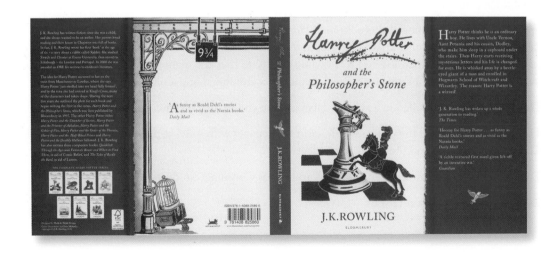

A1(k)   ENGLISH 'SPINELESS CLASSICS' EDITION   (2012)
(broadside poster)

J.K. Rowling | Harry Potter | and the | Philosopher's Stone (Lines 1, 2 and 4 with similar right margin, line 3 ranged towards left margin and all within blank space in the shape of a letter carried by an owl)

Collation: single leaf; 1000 by 700mm, [i-ii]

Page contents: [i] full text of *Harry Potter and the Philosopher's Stone* in 17 columns featuring design in white of Harry's round glasses held together with a lot of Sellotape (left lens and part of right) across columns 1-16 (lower left) and design in white of a letter carried by an owl across columns 11-16 (upper right), at foot of column 17 'HARRY POTTER: TM & © Warner Bros. Entertainment Inc. | Publishing Rights © J.K. Rowling 1997 (s13) | spinelessclassics.com'; [ii] blank

Paper: wove paper

Publication: 26 November 2012 (see notes)

Price: £44.99

Notes:
Spineless Classics provide the complete text of a book printed on a poster. The company's website notes '… no text is lost and all paragraphs and formatting are preserved. Where there are shapes in the design the words merely wrap to the edges. As the font size used is four point, the text is fully legible to the naked eye or with light magnification…' The concept behind Spineless Classics was devised by Carl Pappenheim in 2003. To date there are over 80 designs in the range.

Spineless Classics announced this edition of *Harry Potter and the Philosopher's Stone* in a blog on their website dated 26 November 2012. They noted that 'all author royalties from the print will be donated to Lumos, the charity founded by J.K. Rowling to ensure that the eight million children worldwide living in large institutions are given a real chance of a childhood and a future…'

The poster was issued rolled in a tube. A label on one end includes a barcode and the code 'SP131'.

The publisher described the paper as 'lush, satin finish paper with state-of-the-art printing technology. The text is pin-sharp and the paper non-reflective'.

The poster was issued under licence from Warner Bros Consumer Products.

Copies: private collection (PWE)

ENGLISH ADULT EDITION
(Andrew Davidson artwork series in paperback)

J.K. [in grey] | ROWLING [in grey] [reading lengthways down title-page] | HARRY | POTTER | &THE [reading lengthways up title-page] PHILOSOPHER'S STONE | BLOOMSBURY | LONDON [point] NEW DELHI [point] NEW YORK [point] SYDNEY (Author and final part of title justified on right margin, first part of title justified on left margin, publisher with publisher's offices width centred)

Collation: 112 unsigned leaves bound in indeterminate gatherings; 198 by 128mm; [1-7] 8-18 [19] 20-27 [28] 29-38 [39] 40-48 [49] 50-66 [67] 68-84 [85] 86-97 [98] 99-106 [107] 108-120 [121] 122-32 [133] 134-42 [143] 144-57 [158] 159-66 [167] 168-76 [177] 178-90 [191] 192-208 [209] 210-23 [224]

Page contents: [1] half-title: 'HARRY | POTTER | &THE [reading lengthways up title-page] PHILOSOPHER'S STONE'; [2] '*Titles available in the Harry Potter series* | *(in reading order):* | Harry Potter and the Philosopher's Stone | Harry Potter and the Chamber of Secrets | Harry Potter and the Prisoner of Azkaban | Harry Potter and the Goblet of Fire | Harry Potter and the Order of the Phoenix | Harry Potter and the Half-Blood Prince | Harry Potter and the Deathly Hallows | [new paragraph] *Titles available in the Harry Potter series* | *(in Latin):* | Harry Potter and the Philosopher's Stone | Harry Potter and the Chamber of Secrets | *(in Welsh, Ancient Greek and Irish):* | Harry Potter and the Philosopher's Stone | [new paragraph] *Also available* | *(in aid of Comic Relief):* | Fantastic Beasts and Where to Find Them | Quidditch Through the Ages | *(in aid of Lumos):* | The Tales of Beedle the Bard'; [3] title-page; [4] 'All rights reserved; no part of this publication may be reproduced or | transmitted by any means, electronic, mechanical, photocopying | or otherwise, without the prior permission of the publisher | [new paragraph] First published in Great Britain in 1997 by Bloomsbury Publishing Plc | 50 Bedford Square, London WC1B 3DP | [new paragraph] Bloomsbury Publishing, London, New Delhi, New York and Sydney | [new paragraph] This paperback edition first published in 2013 | [new paragraph] Copyright © J.K. Rowling 1997 | Cover illustrations by Andrew Davidson copyright © J.K. Rowling 2013 | [new paragraph] Harry Potter, names, characters and related indicia are | copyright and trademark Warner Bros., 2000™ | [new paragraph] The moral right of the author has been asserted | A CIP catalogue record for this book is available from the British Library | [new paragraph] ISBN 978 1 4088 3496 1 | [new paragraph] [Forest Stewardship Council logo, 6 by 7mm together with ® symbol and text: 'FSC | www.fsc.org' with 'MIX | Paper from | responsible sources | FSC® C020471' to the right and all within single ruled border with rounded corners, 12 by 26mm] | [new paragraph] Typeset by Dorchester Typesetting | Printed and bound in Great Britain by CPI

Group (UK) Ltd, Croydon CR0 4YY | [new paragraph] 1 3 5 7 9 10 8 6 4 2 | [new paragraph] | www.bloomsbury.com/harrypotter'; [5] 'for Jessica, who loves stories, | for Anne, who loved them too, | and for Di, who heard this one first.'; [6] blank; [7]-223 text; [224] blank

Paper: wove paper

Running title: 'HARRY POTTER' (24mm) on verso, recto title comprises chapter title, pp. 8-223

Binding: pictorial wrappers.

    On spine: 'J.K. ROWLING [in white] HARRY POTTER [in blue] &THE [in white] PHILOSOPHER'S STONE [in blue] [publisher's device of a figure with a bow, 8 by 6mm] [in white]' (reading lengthways down spine with the exception of '&THE' and the publisher's device which are horizontal). All on pink.

    On upper wrapper: 'J.K. [in white] | ROWLING [in white] [reading lengthways down upper wrapper] | HARRY [in pink] | POTTER [in pink] | &THE [in white] [reading lengthways up upper wrapper] PHILOSOPHER'S STONE [in pink] | BLOOMSBURY [in white]' (author and final part of title justified on right margin, first part of title justified on left margin, publisher with publisher's offices width centred). All on light and dark blue illustration of the Hogwarts Express, train tracks, lake and Hogwarts castle.

    On lower wrapper: 'Strange things always seem to happen when Harry Potter | is around. Things that unsettle his guardians, the Dursleys. | They strongly disapprove of strangeness. It's only when a letter | arrives, delivered by a shaggy giant of a man called Hagrid, | that Harry learns the truth that will transform his entire future: | his parents were killed by the evil Lord Voldemort, and he, | Harry, is a wizard. | [new paragraph] Whisked away to Hogwarts School of Witchcraft and Wizardry, | Harry discovers a world of enchantments, ghosts, Quidditch, | and friends who will stand, throughout everything, by his side. | But when Harry hears of a stone with great powers, he finds | that his school has its own dark secrets – and an adventure that | will become the stuff of legend begins … | [new paragraph] [section of white illustration of Hogwarts castle, 54 by 110mm] | BLOOMSBURY www.bloomsbury.com/harrypotter www.pottermore.com £7.99 [in black] | [section of white illustration of Hogwarts castle, 27 by 110mm upon which: Forest Stewardship Council logo, 5 by 6mm together with ® symbol and text: 'FSC | www.fsc.org | MIX | Paper from | responsible sources | FSC® C020471' all in black on white panel with rounded corners, 19 by 12mm, with barcode in black on white panel, 18 by 38mm, with 'Designed by Webb & Webb Design | Cover illustrations by Andrew Davidson | copyright © J.K. Rowling 2013' in black on pink panel, 9 by 38mm]'. Lines 1-13 in white and all on pink. The initial capital 'S' of 'Strange' is a drop capital and is printed in blue.

    On inside upper wrapper: pink and white illustration of the Hogwarts Express, train tracks, lake and Hogwarts castle.

    On inside lower wrapper: pink and white illustration of train tracks.

    All edges trimmed. Binding measurements: 198 by 128mm (wrappers), 198 by 13mm (spine).

Publication: 18 July 2013 in an edition of 65,200 copies (confirmed by Bloomsbury) (see notes)

Price: £7.99

Contents:
Harry Potter and the Philosopher's Stone
('Mr and Mrs Dursley, of number four, Privet Drive, were proud to say…')

Notes:
The illustrations by Andrew Davidson derive from a single wood engraving. A single illustration is presented on both the upper wrapper and inside upper wrapper. A section (including part not previously reproduced) is printed on the lower wrapper. A detail from the upper wrapper is shown on the inside lower wrapper.

The original source of the illustration was a wood-engraving on nine by seven inch English boxwood. This was then printed on Japanese paper. Davidson noted 'I wanted them to look as if they had come straight from the library at Hogwarts… Each image aims to capture the spirit and setting of each book – as the stories become darker, so do the engravings. There are also hidden clues in each of the illustrations to look out for…' The project took approximately two and a half months to complete.

As part of the contract with the artist, Andrew Davidson was permitted to produce a limited edition of seven prints printed directly from the original engraved woodblocks. The edition was limited to twenty copies.

James Webb of Webb & Webb Design noted that 'the brief was to create a set of covers that would stand out on the shelves of any shop and to make the author's name a key focus, which is why we've used large type and bold colours… we wanted to steer clear of using photographs of the characters, or the black and white imagery used on a lot of teen fiction, so we presented the idea of using Andrew's illustrations to Bloomsbury. We had originally approached Andrew to work on a set of Harry Potter covers three years ago…' This suggests that the 'signature' edition (see A1(i)) may have originally have been conceived with work by Davidson.

A boxed set containing all seven novels was issued by the publisher on 7 November 2013. All the novels had previously been available separately.

Although Bloomsbury's 'official' publication date was 18 July 2013, copies were available from amazon.co.uk at the beginning of July.

Copies: private collection (PWE)

A1(m) ENGLISH 'THE MAGICAL ADVENTURE
BEGINS…' EDITION (2013)
(line drawn artwork in paperback)

HARRY | POTTER | AND THE | PHILOSOPHER'S | STONE | J.K. ROWLING | [publisher's device of a figure with a bow, 10 by 9mm] | BLOOMSBURY | LONDON NEW DELHI NEW YORK SYDNEY (All width centred and within broken single ruled border, 183 by 114mm)

Collation: 112 unsigned leaves bound in indeterminate gatherings; 198 by 128mm; [1-7] 8-18 [19] 20-27 [28] 29-38 [39] 40-48 [49] 50-66 [67] 68-84 [85] 86-97 [98] 99-106 [107] 108-120 [121] 122-32 [133] 134-42 [143] 144-57 [158] 159-66 [167] 168-76 [177] 178-90 [191] 192-208 [209] 210-23 [224]

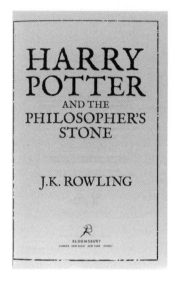

Page contents: [1] half-title: 'HARRY | POTTER | AND THE | PHILOSOPHER'S | STONE' (all within broken single ruled border, 183 by 114mm); [2] *Titles available in the Harry Potter series | (in reading order):* | Harry Potter and the Philosopher's Stone | Harry Potter and the Chamber of Secrets | Harry Potter and the Prisoner of Azkaban | Harry Potter and the Goblet of Fire | Harry Potter and the Order of the Phoenix | Harry Potter and the Half-Blood Prince | Harry Potter and the Deathly Hallows | [new paragraph] *Titles available in the Harry Potter series | (in Latin):* | Harry Potter and the Philosopher's Stone | Harry Potter and the Chamber of Secrets | *(in Welsh, Ancient Greek and Irish):* | Harry Potter and the Philosopher's Stone | [new paragraph] *Also available | (in aid of Comic Relief):* | Fantastic Beasts and Where to Find Them | Quidditch Through the Ages | *(in aid of Lumos):* | The Tales of Beedle the Bard'; [3] title-page; [4] 'All rights reserved; no part of this publication may be reproduced or | transmitted by any means, electronic, mechanical, photocopying | or otherwise, without the prior permission of the publisher | [new paragraph] First published in Great Britain in 1997 by Bloomsbury Publishing Plc | 50 Bedford Square, London WC1B 3DP | [new paragraph] Bloomsbury Publishing, London, New Delhi, New York and Sydney | [new paragraph] This paperback edition first published in 2013 | [new paragraph] Copyright © J.K. Rowling 1997 | [new paragraph] Harry Potter, names, characters and related indicia are | copyright and trademark Warner Bros., 2000™ | [new paragraph] The moral right of the author has been asserted | A CIP catalogue record for this book is available from the British Library | [new paragraph] ISBN 978 1 4088 4992 7 | [new paragraph] [Forest Stewardship Council logo, 6 by 7mm together with ® symbol and text: 'FSC | www.fsc.org' with 'MIX | Paper from | responsible sources | FSC® C020471' to the right and all within single ruled border with rounded corners, 12 by 26mm] | [new paragraph] Typeset by Dorchester Typesetting | Printed and bound in Great Britain by CPI Group (UK) Ltd, Croydon CR0 4YY | [new paragraph] 1 3 5 7 9 10 8 6 4 2 | [new paragraph] | www.

bloomsbury.com/harrypotter | www.pottermore.com'; [5] '*for Jessica, who loves stories,* | *for Anne, who loved them too,* | *and for Di, who heard this one first.*'; [6] blank; [7]-223 text; [224] blank

Paper: wove paper

Running title: 'HARRY POTTER' (24mm) on verso, recto title comprises chapter title, pp. 8-223

Binding: pictorial wrappers.

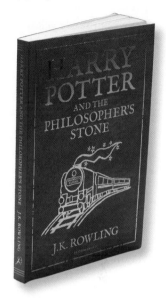

On spine: '[triple rule] HARRY POTTER AND THE PHILOSOPHER'S STONE J.K. ROWLING [publisher's device of a figure with a bow, 9 by 8mm] [triple rule]' (reading lengthways down spine with rules and publisher's device horizontally at head or foot of spine). All in gilt on red.

On upper wrapper: 'HARRY | POTTER | AND THE | PHILOSOPHER'S | STONE | [illustration of the Hogwarts Express] | J.K. ROWLING | BLOOMSBURY' all width centred and within broken single ruled border, 183 by 114mm. All in gilt on red.

On lower wrapper: '[illustration of Hogwarts Express] | [new paragraph] Strange things always seem to happen when Harry Potter | is around. Things that unsettle his guardians, the Dursleys. | They strongly disapprove of strangeness. It's only when a | letter arrives, delivered by a shaggy giant of a man called | Hagrid, that Harry learns the truth that will transform | his entire future: his parents were killed by the evil | Lord Voldemort, and he, Harry, is a wizard. | [new paragraph] Whisked away to Hogwarts School of Witchcraft | and Wizardry, Harry discovers a world of enchantments, | ghosts, Quidditch, and friends who will stand, throughout | everything, by his side. But when Harry hears of a stone | with great powers, he finds that his school has its own | dark secrets – and an adventure that will become | the stuff of legend begins … | [new paragraph] [barcodes together with '[Forest Stewardship Council logo, 5 by 6mm together with ® symbol] | FSC | www.fsc.org | MIX | Paper from | responsible sources | FSC® C020471' within single ruled border with rounded corners, 18 by 12mm together with '[publisher's device of a figure with a bow, 8 by 7mm] | BLOOMSBURY | www.bloomsbury.com/harrypotter | www.pottermore.com', all in black on white panel, 23 by 84mm]' all within broken single ruled border, 183 by 114mm. All in yellow on red.

All edges trimmed. Binding measurements: 198 by 128mm (wrappers), 198 by 14mm (spine).

Slipcase: card slipcase covered in blue paper.

On spine: 'HARRY | POTTER | The magical adventure | begins … | [new paragraph] HARRY POTTER | AND THE | PHILOSOPHER'S STONE | [new paragraph] HARRY POTTER | AND THE | CHAMBER OF | SECRETS | [new paragraph] HARRY POTTER | AND THE | PRISONER OF | AZKABAN | [new paragraph] JKRowling [facsimile signature] | [publisher's device of a figure with a bow, 12 by 11mm]'. All in gilt.

On upper and lower sides: '[illustration of the Hogwarts Express] | J.K. ROWLING | HARRY | POTTER | The magical adventure | begins …' all width centred and within broken single ruled border, 183 by 114mm. All in gilt.

Top and lower edges: blank.

The slipcase was shrink-wrapped with a label attached. This measures 103 by 127mm, with text in yellow on blue: 'The magical adventure begins … | [colour illustrations of three book designs each within single yellow ruled borders] | The perfect way for any young Muggle to discover | the irresistible, magical world of Harry Potter. | ['[publisher's device of a figure with a bow, 6 by 5mm] | BLOOMSBURY | £21' together with barcodes all in black on white panel within single yellow ruled border, 18 by 48mm] Contains: | *Harry Potter and the Philosopher's Stone* | *Harry Potter and the Chamber of Secrets* | *Harry Potter and the Prisoner of Azkaban* | www.bloomsbury.com/harrypotter www.pottermore.com' all within broken single yellow ruled border, 93 by 117mm.

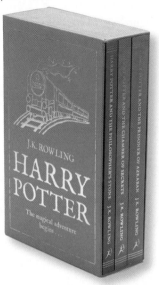

Publication: 10 October 2013 in an edition of 42,700 copies (confirmed by Bloomsbury)

Price: £21 [together with A2(r) and A7(o)]

Contents:
Harry Potter and the Philosopher's Stone
('Mr and Mrs Dursley, of number four, Privet Drive, were proud to say…')

Notes:
Published as a boxed set of three volumes comprising A1(m), A2(r) and A7(o). Individual volumes were not available separately. Bloomsbury announced the set stating 'Every great story has a great beginning – and this is where Harry Potter's extraordinary, magical adventure starts... Harry Potter is a milestone in every child's reading life and this gorgeous, collectable boxed set is the perfect introduction for new readers, wizard and Muggle alike.'

Although the second and third volumes note 'Cover illustration by Joe McLaren', there is no such statement on the first volume. Bloomsbury has confirmed that the image of the Hogwarts Express was created many years previously by an in-house designer.

Copies: private collection (PWE)

HARRY POTTER AND THE CHAMBER OF SECRETS

A2(a)   **FIRST ENGLISH EDITION**   **(1998)**
(children's artwork series in hardback)

HARRY | POTTER | *and the Chamber of Secrets* | J.K.ROWLING | [publisher's device of a dog, 11 by 18mm] | BLOOMSBURY (Lines 1 and 2 justified on left and right margins, and all width centred)

Collation: 128 unsigned leaves bound in indeterminate gatherings; 197 by 128mm; [1-7] 8-14 [15] 16-23 [24] 25-36 [37] 38-52 [53] 54-67 [68] 69-80 [81] 82-93 [94] 95-106 [107] 108-121 [122] 123-36 [137] 138-53 [154] 155-69 [170] 171-84 [185] 186-96 [197] 198-209 [210] 211-25 [226] 227-40 [241] 242-51 [252-56]

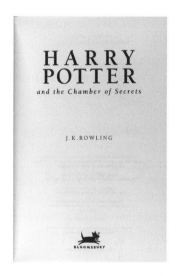

Page contents: [1] half-title: 'HARRY | POTTER | *and the Chamber of Secrets*'; [2] blank; [3] title-page; [4] 'All rights reserved; no part of this publication may be reproduced or | transmitted by any means, electronic, mechanical, photocopying or otherwise, | without the prior permission of the publisher | [new paragraph] First published in Great Britain in 1998 | Bloomsbury Publishing Plc, 38 Soho Square, London W1V 5DF | [new paragraph] Copyright © Text J.K. Rowling 1998 | Copyright © Cover Illustration Cliff Wright 1997 | [new paragraph] The moral right of the author has been asserted | A CIP catalogue record of this book is available from the | British Library | [new paragraph] ISBN 0 7475 3849 2 | [new paragraph] Printed and bound in Great Britain by Clays Ltd, St Ives plc | Typeset by Dorchester Typesetting | [new paragraph] 10 9 8 7 6 5 4 3 2 1 | [new paragraph] Cover design by Michelle Radford'; [5] '*For Séan P. F. Harris, | getaway driver and foulweather friend*'; [6] blank; [7]-251 text; [252] blank; [253] 'Acclaim for: | Harry Potter and the Philosopher's Stone by J.K. Rowling | [10 reviews]'; [254-55] six facsimile letters to the author; [256] publisher's advertisement: upper cover design of *Harry Potter and the Philosopher's Stone*

Paper: wove paper

Running title: 'HARRY POTTER' (25mm) on verso, recto title comprises chapter title, pp. 8-251

Binding: pictorial boards.
    On spine: '[colour illustration of head of owl in cage on coloured panel, 20 by 13mm] HARRY POTTER [in green on blue panel, 20 by 51mm] *and the Chamber of Secrets* [in black] J.K.ROWLING

[in blue, both title conclusion and author on green panel, 20 by 109mm] BLOOMSBURY [publisher's device of the head of a dog, 3 by 4mm] [both in black on red panel, 20 by 33mm]' (reading lengthways down spine).

On upper cover: 'J.K. ROWLING [in white on red panel (with rounded edges), 8 by 52mm] | HARRY | POTTER | *and the Chamber of Secrets* [lines 2-3 in green, line 4 in red, all on blue panel, 62 by 128mm] | [red rule, 128mm] | [colour illustration of Harry Potter, Ron Weasley and Hedwig the Owl in a flying car, 129 by 128mm (the top of the car is printed over the red rule and encroaches on the blue panel)] | [red rule, 128mm] | 'Inventive and action-packed' *The Bookseller* [in white on black panel, 10 by 128mm]' (all width centred). A blue prize 'sticker' is printed over the lower left corner of the illustration with 'J.K. ROWLING | 1997 SMARTIES AWARD WINNER | Shortlisted for the | 1997 CARNEGIE MEDAL | [publisher's device of the head of a dog, 4 by 3mm]' in white.

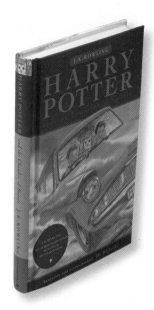

On lower cover: 'Harry Potter is a wizard. He is in his second year at | Hogwarts School of Witchcraft and Wizardry. Little does he | know that this year will be just as eventful as the last… | [new paragraph] Acclaim for HARRY POTTER AND THE PHILOSOPHER'S STONE | 'An absolutely must-have read of the year' *The Sunday Times* | [new paragraph] 'I've yet to meet a ten-year-old who hasn't been entranced by | its witty, complex plot and the character of the eponymous | Harry.' *The Independent on Saturday* | [new paragraph] [barcode in black on white panel, 22 by 40mm together with '[publisher's device of a dog, 8 by 14mm] | BLOOMSBURY | Cover Illustrations by Cliff Wright' in black on left side of panel and 'www.bloomsbury.com' below panel, in black on green panel, 8 by 40mm]'. All in black on colour illustration of Hogwarts castle and clouds. The barcode and web address panels are enclosed by a single black rule.

All edges trimmed. Binding measurements: 204 by 128mm (covers), 204 by 40mm (spine). End-papers: wove paper.

Dust-jacket: coated wove paper, 204 by 484mm

Spine, upper and lower covers replicate the binding.

On upper inside flap: 'Harry, Ron and Hermione have | returned to Hogwarts School of | Witchcraft and Wizardry for their second | year. (But Harry and Ron only just made | it – they missed the Hogwarts Express | and had to get there in a flying car …!) | Soon the threesome are immersed in the | daily round of Potions, Herbology, | Charms, Defence Against the Dark Arts, | and Quidditch. | [new paragraph] But then horrible things start happening. | Harry hears evil voices. Sinister messages | appear on the wall. But nothing can prepare | the three friends for what

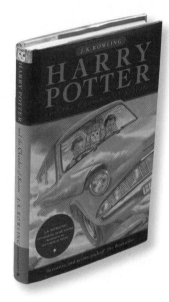

happens next … | [new paragraph] A brilliant sequel to the award-winning | *Harry Potter and the Philosopher's Stone.* | [new paragraph] REVIEWS FROM SMARTIES YOUNG JUDGES, | PUPILS FROM COALWAY JUNIOR SCHOOL: | [new paragraph] | 'I think Harry Potter and the Philosopher's | Stone is a great book – it's excellent. You | have to just unlock the key and the story | goes straight into your head. It is very | funny. I would love to be Harry and make | up some magic spell to play on my | teachers.' Tom El-Shawk Age 11 | [new paragraph] 'Harry Potter is a spectacular book. You start | it and you can not put it down. I know, | because my mum kept telling me off because | every night I was using up the electricity | very LATE! I showed Harry to my dad and | he's reading it now. It's for all ages and it's | BRILLIANT.' Katrina Farrant Age 10 | [new paragraph] £10.99'. All in black on red. The initial capital 'H' of 'Harry' is a drop capital.

On lower inside flap: '[illustration of test tube and six stars, 26 by 26mm] | Dear Joanne Rowling, | [new paragraph] My name is Gail Williams and | I am 10 years old. | [new paragraph] I am writing to tell you how absolut- | ely astonished I was when I read | your book, "Harry Potter and the | Philosiphers Stone" It was just | amazing! I literally loved it. | I was totally hooked!! You described | All of the characters perfectly, I had | a picture of each of them in my | mind. I could just emajine Snape, | with an evil, sly face, and an | extremly snappy personality. | [new paragraph] I don't think you could improve | it in anyway. | [new paragraph] The story is so magical, and | thrilling. | [new paragraph] Harry's brave, Rons wise, Hermaine |is very brainy, but think my | favouroute has to be proffecer | Dumbledor. He seems so kind, | and magical. | [new paragraph] I would be very grateful if you could | in your spare time, (because I'm sure | you are very busy), you could write | back to me, maybe tell what the | next book in the Harry Potter story, (I | can't wait for it to come out), and | give me a couple of hints, about | the plot. | Yours | Sinceerly, | Gail Williams.' All in black facsimile of child's handwriting on red panel.

Publication: 2 July 1998 in an edition of 706 copies (confirmed by Bloomsbury)

Price: £10.99

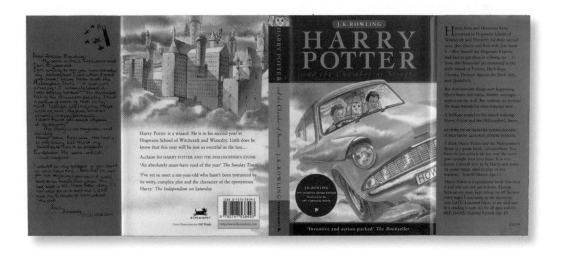

Contents:

Harry Potter and the Chamber of Secrets

('Not for the first time, an argument had broken out over breakfast at number four...')

Notes:

Interviewed in September 2013, Nigel Newton noted that '... it's unusual for a series *not* to stay in one place, for obvious reasons... uniformity of editions and so on'. Moreover, Newton proposed that Bloomsbury had done 'quite a reasonable job' in publishing *Philosopher's Stone*. His recollection of when each book was signed up is that '... we signed up one book and then the second book, and then we signed up the next three, and then we bought the last two together'.

Less than a couple of months after the publication of *Philosopher's Stone*, the manuscript of *Chamber of Secrets* was at Bloomsbury. Barry Cunningham had, by this stage, passed on the role of editor to Emma Matthewson. Cunningham would later found the children's book publishing company Chicken House. As Nigel Newton, in an interview with me in September 2013, stated '... it's a shame that Barry wasn't around to see what he spawned. I cannot tell you how exciting publishing this series was to become...'

A copy of a letter from Emma Matthewson to J.K. Rowling, preserved in the Bloomsbury archives, is dated 6 August 1997:

> ... I am writing now with my thoughts on HARRY POTTER AND THE CHAMBER OF SECRETS. My first thought I should say right now is that it is going to be absolutely brilliant! There is no doubt about that – and no danger of the sequel not coming up to the expectations of the first... ... enclosed is the manuscript where I have written on various comments and suggestions... generally, as we've discussed, the manuscript is over-long. I have suggested some possible places for cuts...

There was also a suggestion made, at this time, for an 'information/glossary/history' at the end of the book for readers who hadn't read *Philosopher's Stone*. This idea, evidently, was abandoned.

The editorial files suggest that Matthewson and Rowling met in Edinburgh during the afternoon of 20 August 1997. It appears that the author took back the manuscript for some revision. It was returned to Bloomsbury on 25 October 1997 with a letter which stated:

> ... here, finally, is the manuscript... I've done more to it that you suggested, but I am very happy with it now, which wasn't the case before, The hard work, the significant rewrites I wanted to do, are over, so if it needs more cuts after this, I'm ready to make them, *speedily*...

One casualty in the rewritten manuscript was a song for Nearly Headless Nick. The author noted this was 'a wrench' but admitted that it was 'superfluous to requirements'. The author posted the text on her website and has also written out the text on at least two occasions, including an auction during March 2005 to raise funds for a Scottish language dictionary (see D3). The song commences 'It was a mistake any wizard could make'.

The facsimile fan letters to the author, reproduced on pages 254-55, are by Fiona Chadwick, Valerie Rutt, Emily Booth, Daniel Hougham, Thomas New and Alexander Benno. The facsimile letter on the lower inside flap is by Gail Williams. It appears that permission to reproduce letters was sought at the end of March 1998. One request, dated 31 March 1998 from Pippa le Quesne, an editorial assistant at Bloomsbury, states:

… We have a few spare, blank pages in the back of the book and so we would like to include some of the fan letters Jo has received. Yours (or part of your letter) is one of the ones we would like to use, and so I am writing to ask for your permission to publish it.

The upper cover design was composed of two individual pieces by Cliff Wright. The first piece comprises a pencil and watercolour illustration, 354 by 223mm, showing a landscape with most of a flying Ford Anglia. The second piece comprises a pencil and watercolour illustration, 356 by 438mm of an entire Ford Anglia (without landscape). This second piece is annotated by the artist 'for: Harry Potter – shop display'. It appears that Bloomsbury took the landscape from the first piece and superimposed the car from the second to produce the upper cover design. Both illustrations were offered for sale at auction by Christie's South Kensington on 6 December 2001. The first piece, estimated at £20,000 to £30,000, failed to sell. The second piece, estimated at £12,000 to £18,000, sold for £14,100 (including buyer's premium). It was later sold again at auction at Sotheby's on 10 July 2012 for £12,500 (including buyer's premium).

The original lower cover design by Cliff Wright, measuring 355 by 229mm, was also offered for sale at auction by Christie's South Kensington on 6 December 2001. The original shows that Bloomsbury reversed the image from left to right for publication. Estimated at £4,000 to £6,000 it sold for a total of £4,700 (including buyer's premium).

In *Harry Potter and Me* (BBC television, 28 December 2001) the dedicatee of the book, Séan P.F. Harris, was revealed as a schoolfriend of Rowling's and owner of a turquoise Ford Anglia. On one occasion the author sent a package containing around thirteen inscribed volumes of foreign translations of *Chamber of Secrets* to Harris. The parcel went astray and several of the missing volumes were offered for sale (although seven or eight copies were later recovered). Any copies offered for sale, therefore, appearing to be foreign dedication copies are likely to derive from this source.

A copy of this edition inscribed by the author to her father and stepmother was offered at auction at Sotheby's New York on 10 December 2003. It was inscribed on the title-page 'To Dad and Jan | with lots of love | from Jo x'. On the imprint page the author circled the number one in the strike-line and wrote, with a pointing arrow, '1st edition – I got one!' Estimated at $10,000/15,000, it sold for $9,000.

The story that this edition was bought by Americans in advance of the American publication by Scholastic is confirmed by a report in the *Wall Street Journal* (dated 26 March 1999). The report states that 'a dispute' between Amazon and Scholastic had been 'ignited' as copies of the book were sent from Amazon in the UK to the US. The publication of the series and the emergence of significant levels of buying books on the internet are, of course, inextricably linked.

The English audiobook version, read by Stephen Fry, has a duration of approximately nine and three-quarter hours.

Reprints (and subsequent new editions) include a number of corrections to the text. These comprise:

Page 28, line 5	'his family were rolling' to 'his family was rolling'
Page 28, line 33	'Muggle Artifacts Office' to 'Muggle Artefacts Office'
Page 29, line 2	'The teapot went beserk' to 'The teapot went berserk'
Page 31, line 40	'yawned George' to 'yawned Fred'
Page 32, line 6	'glaring at Ron and Fred' to 'glaring at Ron and George'

Page 32, line 14	'Geoge groaned' to 'George groaned'
Page 40, line 13	'working for the wizard's bank' to 'working for the wizards' bank'
Page 77, line 24	'Honourary Member' to 'Honorary Member'
Page 78, line 8	*'Weekend with a Werewolf'* to *'Wanderings with Werewolves'*
Page 88, line 37	'plate of treacle fudge' to 'plate of treacle toffee'
Page 90, line 30	'Hagid' to 'Hagrid'
Page 91, line 6	'treacle fudge since dawn' to 'treacle toffee since dawn'
Page 98, line 18	'into the envelope. Harry threw' to 'into the envelope, Harry threw'
Page 102, line 12	'walk though it' to 'walk through it'
Page 110, line 9	'Madam Sprout' to 'Professor Sproat'
Page 115, lines 12-13	'can only opened' to 'can only be opened'
Page 125, line 31	'checking the coast was clear' to 'checking that the coast was clear'
Page 128, line 12	'flies up my sleeve,' said Harry. 'Go back' to 'flies up my sleeve. Go back'
Page 140, line 33	'Deflating Draft' to 'Deflating Draught'
Page 141, line 21	'around the notice-board' to 'around the noticeboard'
Page 161, line 3	'Crabbe, and Goyle-sized feet' to 'Crabbe- and Goyle-sized feet'
Page 170, line 31	'Honourary Member' to 'Honorary Member'
Page 176, line 7	'morale-booster become clear' to 'morale-booster became clear'
Page 180, line 33	'miniscule television screen' to 'minuscule television screen'
Page 187, line 2	'the study of Ancient Runes' to 'the Study of Ancient Runes'
Page 189, line 29	'Madam Hooch releasd' to 'Madam Hooch released'
Page 190, line 25	'fifth-year girl' to 'sixth-year girl'
Page 199, line 35	'Professor Snape escorted' to 'Professor Sprout escorted'
Page 203, lines 9-10	'It's already heard. Fang!' to 'It's already heard Fang!'
Page 211, line 3	'he'd been just been told' to 'he'd just been told'
Page 216, line 3	*'The crowing of the rooster is fatal'* to *'The Basilisk flees only from the crowing of the rooster, which is fatal'*
Page 216, lines 5-6	*'Spiders flee before it!'* to *'Spiders flee before the Basilisk!'*
Page 220, line 20	'had a hare lip' to 'had a hairy chin'
Page 224, line 27	*'Obliviate!'* to *'Obliviate!'*
Page 239, line 34	'Moaning Myrtle's floor' to 'Moaning Myrtle's bathroom'
Page 245, line 5	'last remaining ancestor' to 'last remaining descendant'

Copies: Sotheby's, 10 July 2013, lot 367

Reprints include:
10 9 8 7 6 5 4
10 9 8 7 6

A report compiled by the printers, Clays Ltd, in October 2013 noted that, following the first edition, the second impression comprised 200 copies on 29 June 1998 and a third impression comprised 5,000 copies on 7 July 1998. Clays also noted that, to date, they had produced a minimum of 19.1 million paperbacks and 2 million hardbacks across 248 printings.

A2(b)   ENGLISH CHILDREN'S EDITION   (1998 [1999])
(children's artwork series in paperback)

HARRY | POTTER | *and the Chamber of Secrets* | [illustration of Hogwarts crest with legend 'DRAGO DORMIENS NUNQUAM TITILLANDUS' on banner, 67 by 81mm] | J.K.ROWLING | [publisher's device of a dog, 11 by 18mm] | BLOOMSBURY (Lines 1 and 2 justified on left and right margins, and all width centred)

Collation: 128 unsigned leaves bound in indeterminate gatherings; 197 by 128mm; [1-7] 8-14 [15] 16-23 [24] 25-36 [37] 38-52 [53] 54-67 [68] 69-80 [81] 82-93 [94] 95-106 [107] 108-121 [122] 123-36 [137] 138-53 [154] 155-69 [170] 171-84 [185] 186-96 [197] 198-209 [210] 211-25 [226] 227-40 [241] 242-51 [252-56]

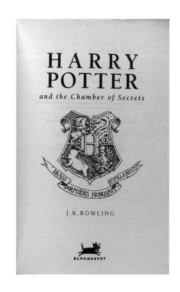

Page contents: [1] half-title: 'HARRY | POTTER | *and the Chamber of Secrets* | [illustration of Hogwarts crest with legend 'DRAGO DORMIENS NUNQUAM TITILLANDUS' on banner, 47 by 57mm]'; [2] '*Also available:* | Harry Potter and the Philosopher's Stone'; [3] title-page; [4] 'All rights reserved; no part of this publication may be reproduced or | transmitted by any means, electronic, mechanical, photocopying or otherwise, | without the prior permission of the publisher | [new paragraph] First published in Great Britain in 1998 | Bloomsbury Publishing Plc, 38 Soho Square, London W1V 5DF | [new paragraph] Copyright © Text J. K. Rowling 1998 | Copyright © Cover Illustration Cliff Wright 1997 | [new paragraph] The moral right of the author has been asserted | A CIP catalogue record of this book is available from the | British Library | [new paragraph] ISBN 0 7475 3848 4 | [new paragraph] Printed and bound in Great Britain by Clays Ltd, St Ives plc | Typeset by Dorchester Typesetting | [new paragraph] 10 9 8 7 6 5 4 3 2 1 | [new paragraph] Cover design by Michelle Radford'; [5] '*For Séan P. F. Harris,* | *getaway driver and foulweather friend*'; [6] blank; [7]-251 text; [252] blank; [253] 'Acclaim for: | Harry Potter and the Philosopher's Stone by J.K. Rowling | [10 reviews]'; [254-55] six facsimile letters to the author; [256] publisher's advertisement: upper cover design of *Harry Potter and the Philosopher's Stone*

Paper: wove paper

Running title: 'HARRY POTTER' (25mm) on verso, recto title comprises chapter title, pp. 8-251

Binding: pictorial wrappers.
   On spine: '[colour illustration of head of owl in cage on coloured panel, 16 by 11mm] HARRY POTTER [in green on blue panel, 16 by 49mm] *and the Chamber of Secrets* [in black] J.K.ROWLING [in blue, both title conclusion and author on green panel, 16 by 102mm] BLOOMSBURY [publisher's

device of the head of a dog, 3 by 4mm] [both in black on red panel, 16 by 34mm]' (reading lengthways down spine).

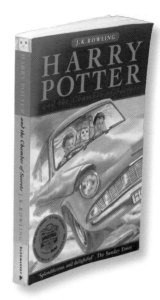

On upper wrapper: 'J.K. ROWLING [in white on red panel (with rounded edges), 8 by 52mm] | HARRY | POTTER | *and the Chamber of Secrets* [lines 2-3 in green, line 4 in red, all on blue panel, 60 by 128mm] | [red rule, 128mm] | [colour illustration of Harry Potter, Ron Weasley and Hedwig the Owl in a flying car, 129 by 128mm (the top of the car is printed over the red rule and encroaches on the blue panel)] | [red rule, 128mm] | 'Splendiferous and delightful' *The Sunday Times* [in white on black panel, 8 by 128mm]' (all width centred). A 1998 Smarties Book prize 'sticker' is printed over the lower left corner of the illustration. This includes the text '1998 Gold Award 9-11 Age Category'.

On lower wrapper: 'Harry Potter is a wizard. He is in his second year at | Hogwarts School of Witchcraft and Wizardry. Little does | he know that this year will be just as eventful as the last... | [new paragraph] 'Joanne Rowling's second book is just as funny, | frightening and unexpected as her first.' *The Daily Mail* | [new paragraph] '*Harry Potter and the Chamber of Secrets* is as good as | its predecessor ... Hogwarts is a creation of genius.' | *The Times Literary Supplement* | [new paragraph] [barcode in black on white panel, 23 by 40mm together with '[publisher's device of a dog, 8 by 14mm] | BLOOMSBURY | £4.99' in black on left side of panel and 'www.bloomsburymagazine.com' below panel, in white on green panel, 8 by 40mm]'. In lower left: 'Cover Illustrations by Cliff Wright'. All in black on colour illustration of Hogwarts castle and clouds.

All edges trimmed. Binding measurements: 197 by 128mm (wrappers), 197 by 16mm (spine).

Publication: 28 January 1999 (see notes)

Price: £4.99

Contents:
Harry Potter and the Chamber of Secrets
   ('Not for the first time, an argument had broken out over breakfast at number four...')

Notes:
The publisher's imprint page does not provide the publication date of this edition. Bloomsbury has stated that it was published ten months after the first trade edition on 28 May 1999. Evidence within the press, however, suggests publication on 28 January 1999. Because this edition was launched at King's Cross Station (platform one), there was extensive press coverage. Press reports note that a green steam locomotive and a television crew from *Blue Peter* were in attendance, accompanied by cups of pumpkin soup and a dry-ice machine.

Copies: private collection (PWE)

Reprints include:
20 19 18 17 16 15 14 13 12 11   BL (H.99/1867) stamped 2 Aug 1999

20 19 18 17 16
30 29 28 27 26 25 24 23 22 21
30 29 28 27 26 25 24
40 39 38 37 36 35
40 39 38 37
30 29

A2(c)   FIRST AMERICAN EDITION   (1999)
(children's artwork series in hardback)

HARRY POTTER | AND THE CHAMBER OF SECRETS | [black and white illustration of doorway with carved snakes on surrounding pillars, 55 by 74mm] | BY | J.K. ROWLING | ILLUSTRATIONS BY MARY GRANDPRÉ | [publisher's device of a lantern, 12 by 9mm] | ARTHUR A. LEVINE BOOKS | AN IMPRINT OF SCHOLASTIC PRESS (All width centred on a diamond pattern background)

Collation: 176 unsigned leaves bound in eleven gatherings of sixteen leaves; 228 by 150mm; [I-VI] VII-VIII [IX-X] 1-341 [342]

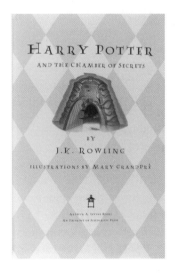

Page contents: [I] 'HARRY POTTER | AND THE CHAMBER OF SECRETS' (all on diamond pattern background); [II] 'ALSO BY J. K. ROWLING | *Harry Potter and the Sorceror's* [*sic*] *Stone*'; [III] title-page; [IV] '[device of twelve stars] | Text copyright © 1999 by J.K. Rowling. | Illustrations copyright © 1999 by Mary GrandPré. | All rights reserved. Published by Scholastic Press, a division of Scholastic Inc., | *Publishers since 1920.* | SCHOLASTIC, SCHOLASTIC PRESS, ARTHUR A. LEVINE BOOKS, and associated logos | are trademarks and/or registered trademarks of Scholastic Inc. | [new paragraph] No part of this publication may be reproduced, or stored in a retrieval system, or transmitted | in any form or by any means, electronic, mechanical, photocopying, recording, or otherwise, | without written permission of the publisher. For information regarding permission, write | to Scholastic Inc., Attention: Permissions Department, 555 Broadway, New York, NY 10012. | [new paragraph] Library of Congress Cataloging-in-Publication Data | [new paragraph] Rowling, J. K. | Harry Potter and the Chamber of Secrets / by J. K. Rowling. | p. cm. | Summary: When the Chamber of Secrets is opened again at the Hogwarts School | for Witchcraft and Wizardry, second-year student Harry Potter finds himself in danger | from a dark power that has once more been released on the school. | ISBN 0-439-06486-4 | [square bracket]1. Wizards — Fiction.

2. Magic — Fiction. 3. Schools — Fiction. | 4. England — Fiction.[square bracket] I. Title. | PZ7.R7968Har 1999 | [square bracket]Fic[square bracket] — dc21 98-46370 | [new paragraph] 10 9 8 7 6 5 4 3 2 1   9/9 0/0 1 2 3 4 | Printed in the U.S.A. 37 | First American edition, June 1999'; [V] 'FOR SEÁN P. F. HARRIS, | GETAWAY DRIVER AND FOUL-WEATHER FRIEND'; [VI] blank; VII-VIII 'CONTENTS' (eighteen chapters listed with titles and page references); [IX] half-title: 'HARRY POTTER | AND THE CHAMBER OF SECRETS' (all on diamond pattern background); [X] blank; 1-341 text; [342] colophon: '[publisher's device of a lantern, 13 by 10mm] | *This | book was art | directed by David Saylor. The | art for both the jacket and the interior was | created using pastels on toned printmaking paper. The | text was set in 12-point Adobe Garamond, a typeface based on the | sixteenth-century type designs of Claude Garamond, redrawn by Robert | Slimbach in 1989. The book was printed and bound at | Berryville Graphics in Berryville, Virginia. The | production was supervised by | Angela Biola and Mike | Derevjanik.*'

Paper: wove paper

Running title: 'CHAPTER' and chapter number on verso, recto title comprises chapter title, pp. 1-341. Each running title (excluding pages on which new chapters commence) includes a three-star design to left and right of both running-titles on verso and recto. On pages on which a new chapter commences, the three-star design is omitted.

Illustrations: title-page vignette, together with eighteen vignettes at the beginning of each chapter (after chapter and chapter number but before chapter title). In addition to standard typographical changes (including italics, capitals and small capitals) there are other typographical features, comprising:

    p. 21 facsimile of Mafalda Hopkirk's signature

    p. 127 course description and students' endorsements

    p. 221 newspaper headline

Binding: green cloth-backed spine with purple boards (with diamond pattern in blind).

    On spine: 'ROWLING | [rule]' (horizontally at head) with 'HARRY POTTER | AND THE CHAMBER OF SECRETS' (reading lengthways down spine) and '[publisher's device of a lantern, 17 by 13mm] | ARTHUR A. | LEVINE BOOKS | [rule] | SCHOLASTIC | PRESS' (horizontally at foot). All in silver.

    Upper and lower covers: blank.

    All edges trimmed. Binding measurements: 235 by 149mm (covers), 235 by 40mm (spine). The green cloth continues onto the covers by 38mm. End-papers: red wove paper.

Dust-jacket: uncoated wove paper, 235 by 559mm. A single illustration spans the entire dust-jacket.

    On spine: 'ROWLING | [rule]' (horizontally at head) with 'HARRY POTTER | AND THE CHAMBER OF SECRETS' (reading

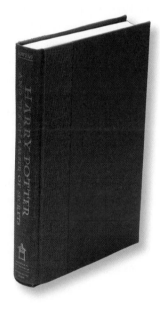

lengthways down spine) and '[publisher's device of a lantern, 19 by 14mm] | ARTHUR A. | LEVINE BOOKS | [rule] | SCHOLASTIC | PRESS' (horizontally at foot). All embossed in silver on colour illustration of pillar.

On upper cover: 'Harry Potter [hand-drawn lettering] [embossed in silver] | AND THE [hand-drawn lettering in red of illustration] | CHAMBER [hand-drawn lettering in red of illustration] | OF SECRETS [hand-drawn lettering in red of illustration] | J. K. ROWLING [embossed in silver]' (all width centred); all on colour illustration of Harry Potter holding onto tail of a flying phoenix.

On lower cover: 'Praise for the *New York Times* Bestseller | HARRY POTTER AND THE SORCERER'S STONE | [new paragraph] "You don't have to be a wizard or a kid to appreciate | the spell cast by Harry Potter." —*USA Today* | [new paragraph] "A charming, imaginative, magical | confection of a novel." —*Boston Globe* | [new paragraph] "Harry is destined for greatness." | —*The New York Times* | [barcode with smaller barcode to the right (51795) all in black on orange panel, 51 by 21mm]'. All in black and all on colour illustration of cat, snake, Hermione Granger and Ron Weasley.

On upper inside flap: '$17.95 US | THE DURSLEYS | were so mean and hideous that summer that all | Harry Potter wanted was to get back to the | Hogwarts School for Witchcraft and Wizardry. | But just as he's packing his bags, Harry receives a | warning from a strange, impish creature named | Dobby who says that if Harry Potter returns to | Hogwarts, disaster will strike. | [new paragraph] And strike it does. For in Harry's second year | at Hogwarts, fresh torments and horrors arise, | including an outrageously stuck-up profes- | sor, Gilderoy Lockheart, a spirit named Moaning | Myrtle who haunts the girls' bathroom, and the | unwanted attentions of Ron Weasley's younger | sister, Ginny. | [new paragraph] But each of these seem minor annoyances | when the real trouble begins, and someone—or | something—starts turning Hogwarts students to | stone. Could it be Draco Malfoy, a more poison- | ous rival than ever? Could it possibly be Hagrid, | whose mysterious past is finally told? Or could it | be the one everyone at Hogwarts most sus- | pects … Harry Potter himself!' All in black and all on colour illustration of a pillar and wall.

On lower inside flap: 'Awards and Accolades for | HARRY POTTER | AND THE SORCERER'S STONE | [new paragraph] [five-pointed star] "A delightful romp. Rowling leaves the door wide open | for a sequel; bedazzled readers will surely clamor for | one."—*Publishers Weekly*, starred review | [new paragraph] [five-pointed star] "Surely the vilest household in children's literature since | the family Roald Dahl created for *Matilda*. Harry himself | is the perfect confused and unassuming hero." | —*School Library Journal*, starred review | [new paragraph] [five-pointed star] "A brilliantly imagined and beautifully written fantasy." | —*Booklist*, starred review | [new paragraph] [four-sided device] Winner of the National Book Award (UK) | [four-sided device] Winner of the Gold Medal Smarties Prize (UK) | [four-sided device] *Publishers Weekly* Best Book of 1998 | [four-sided device] *School Library Journal* Best Book of 1998 | [four-sided device] *Parenting* Book of the Year Award 1998 | [four-sided device] New York Public Library Best Book of the Year 1998 | [four-sided device] An

ALA Notable Book | [publisher's device of a lantern, 15 by 11mm] ARTHUR A. LEVINE BOOKS | *An Imprint of Scholastic Press* | 555 Broadway, New York, New York 10012 | [new paragraph] *Jacket art © 1999 by Mary GrandPré* | *Jacket design by Mary GrandPré and David Saylor*'. All in black and all on colour illustration of a wall, pillar and flaming torch.

Publication: June 1999 (see notes)

Price: $17.95

Contents:
Harry Potter and the Chamber of Secrets
  ('Not for the first time, an argument had broken out over breakfast at number four…')

Notes:
Although Arthur A. Levine had been the successful highest bidder for the American rights for the first Harry Potter book, he had not secured the rights to the series. He recalled, in an interview with me in March 2012, that 'right away, from the start, we were only sold book one, book two, book three, etc.'

The first American edition omits 'Year | 2' on the spine and the spine of the dust-jacket. The dust-jacket also notes a price of $17.95. It is widely reported that the first edition exists in three different states:
  State 1 – described above with 'Year 2' omitted from spine and dust-jacket priced at $17.95
  State 2 – 'Year 2' added to spine and dust-jacket priced at $17.95
  State 3 – 'Year 2' added to spine and dust-jacket priced at $19.95
Only copies of the first state have been consulted and later 'states' presumably correspond to later impressions.

Although no publication day is recorded, 1 June 1999 is assumed (some newspaper reports suggest publication on 2 June). In an email to me from January 2013 Arthur A. Levine noted that 'I'm fairly

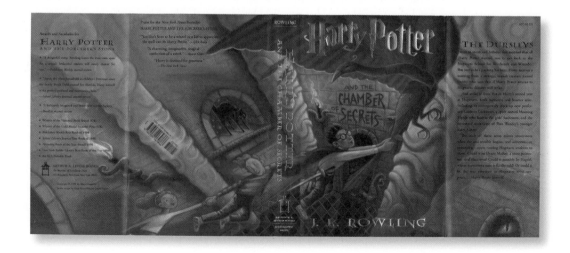

certain that we didn't have strict "on sale" dates… the publication "day" would simply be the first of the month listed.'

A publication figure of 250,000 copies is widely accepted throughout the book world. This is unconfirmed by Scholastic.

Scholastic released a 'dumpbin' display case for this edition at the beginning of July 1999 (Nielsen BookData provides a date of 1 July 1999). The case was filled with 20 copies of the book. Alternatively, Scholastic made a multiple copy pack available on the same date containing 20 copies of this edition.

The publication date for this edition was brought forward from September to June 1999 according to a number of press reports. Enterprising fans had ordered the Bloomsbury edition from websites (and a report in the *Wall Street Journal*, dated 26 March 1999, cited 'a dispute' between Amazon and Scholastic). The publisher issued a statement at the end of March in which Barbara Marcus, Executive Vice President of Scholastic, commented '… we have received so many requests to publish the sequel, *Harry Potter and the Chamber of Secrets*, from both bookstores and consumers, that we felt we had to release the book early in order to satisfy that demand. People simply cannot wait for more adventures of Harry Potter…'

Each chapter commences with a drop capital.

The American audiobook version, read by Jim Dale, has a duration of approximately nine hours.

Copies: New York Public Library (J FIC R); private collection (PWE)

Reprints include:

10 9 8 7 6 5 4 3 2	9/9 0/0 1 2 3 4	Printed in the U.S.A. 37	
10 9 8 7	9/9 0/0 1 2 3 4	Printed in the U.S.A. 37	
10	9/9 0/0 1 2 3 4	Printed in the U.S.A. 37	
20 19 18 17 16 15 14 13 12	9/9 0/0 1 2 3 4	Printed in the U.S.A. 45	
20 19 18 17 16 15 14	9/9 0/0 1 2 3 4	Printed in the U.S.A. 45	
30 29 28 27 26 25	0/0 1 2 3 4	Printed in the U.S.A. 37	BL (YA.2000.a.15899) stamped 6 Apr 2000
40 39 38 37 36 35 34	0/0 1 2 3 4	Printed in the U.S.A. 37	
60 59 58 57 56 55 54 53	02 03 04 05 06	Printed in the U.S.A. 23	

A2(d) ENGLISH ADULT EDITION (1999)
(original adult artwork series in paperback)

Harry Potter and the | Chamber of Secrets | J. K. Rowling | BLOOMSBURY (All width centred)

Collation: 128 unsigned leaves bound in indeterminate gatherings; 198 by 128mm; [1-7] 8-14 [15] 16-23 [24] 25-36 [37] 38-52 [53] 54-67 [68] 69-80 [81] 82-93 [94] 95-106 [107] 108-121 [122] 123-36

[137] 138-53 [154] 155-69 [170] 171-84 [185] 186-96 [197] 198-209 [210] 211-25 [226] 227-40 [241] 242-51 [252-56]

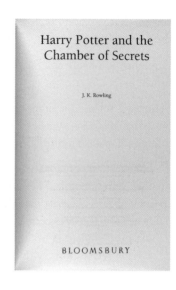

Page contents: [1] half-title: 'Harry Potter and the | Chamber of Secrets'; [2] '*Also available:* | Harry Potter and the Philosopher's Stone'; [3] title-page; [4] 'All rights reserved; no part of this publication may be reproduced or | transmitted by any means, electronic, mechanical, photocopying or otherwise, | without the prior permission of the publisher | [new paragraph] First published in Great Britain in 1998 | Bloomsbury Publishing Plc, 38 Soho Square, London, W1V 5DF | [new paragraph] This edition first published in 1999 | [new paragraph] Copyright © Text Joanne Rowling 1998 | [new paragraph] The moral right of the author has been asserted | A CIP catalogue record of this book is available from the | British Library | [new paragraph] ISBN 0 7475 4407 7 | [new paragraph] Printed in Great Britain by Clays Ltd, St Ives plc | [new paragraph] 10 9 8 7 6 5 4 3 2 1'; [5] '*For Séan P. F. Harris,* | *getaway driver and foulweather friend*'; [6] blank; [7]-251 text; [252] blank; [253] 'Acclaim for: | Harry Potter and the Philosopher's Stone by J.K. Rowling | [10 reviews]'; [254-55] six facsimile letters to the author; [256] blank

Paper: wove paper

Running title: 'HARRY POTTER' (25mm) on verso, recto title comprises chapter title, pp. 8-251

Binding: pictorial wrappers.

   On spine: 'HARRY POTTER [in white] | *and the Chamber of Secrets* [in blue] [black and white photographic illustration of car in clouds, 16 by 21mm] J. K. ROWLING [in white within blue rectangle with rounded ends, 9 by 46mm] [publisher's device of a figure with a bow, 7 by 7mm] [in white]' (reading lengthways down spine). All on black.

   On upper wrapper: 'HARRY POTTER | *and the Chamber of Secrets* [line 1 in white and line 2 in black, all on blue panel, 27 by 128mm] | J. K. ROWLING [in white on black within double blue rectangle with rounded ends, 15 by 74mm] | 'A WONDERFUL CREATION' – [in white] IAN HISLOP [in blue] [lines 3 and 4 on black and white photographic illustration of car in clouds, 171 by 128mm]' (all width centred with the exception of line 2 which is off-set to the right).

   On lower wrapper: 'HARRY POTTER [in blue] | *and the Chamber of Secrets* [in black] | [new paragraph] '*Harry Potter and the Chamber of Secrets*, unlike many sequels, | is as good as its predecessor... Hogwarts is a creation of | genius.' *The Times Literary Supplement* | [new paragraph] 'When Joanne Rowling blithely said she had enough unworked ideas | from *Harry Potter and the Philosopher's Stone* for

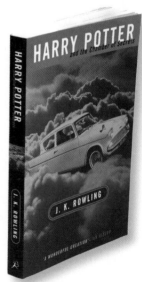

six sequels, it | seemed so unlikely that she could replicate the imaginative power, | emotional intensity and entrancing complexity of the prototype, that | I received the draft of volume two with trepidation. It's good to be | wrong sometimes.' Anne Johnstone, *The Herald* | [new paragraph] '*Harry Potter* is an intricately woven, highly imaginative | tale…cleverly textured, sophisticated fiction.' | *Scotland on Sunday* | [new paragraph] 'The *Harry Potter* books by JK Rowling have turned out to be | one of publishing's great success stories…readers have been | evangelical about its merits…the comic handling of the material | and the insight into the child's world are fresh and magical in | every sense…the new *Harry Potter* is in my suitcase ready for | my holiday.' Ian Hislop, *The Sunday Telegraph* | ['BLOOMSBURY [in white on black panel, 6 by 40mm] | *paperbacks* [in black on blue panel, 10 by 40mm]' (all on left side)] [£6.99 [in black] | [barcode in black on white panel, 19 by 39mm] | http://www.bloomsbury.com [in black] (all on blue panel, 32 by 40mm and on right side)]'. Reading lengthways down right side next to foot of spine 'COVER PHOTOGRAPH Ford Anglia – ©National Motor Museum Clouds – John Turner/©Tony Stone Images'. All in black with the exception of sources which are in blue and all on photographic illustration of clouds, 198 by 128mm.

All edges trimmed. Binding measurements: 198 by 128mm (wrappers), 198 by 16mm (spine)

Publication: 17 June 1999 (confirmed by Bloomsbury)

Price: £6.99

Contents:
Harry Potter and the Chamber of Secrets
  ('Not for the first time, an argument had broken out over breakfast at number four…')

Notes:
The registration plate on the Ford Anglia car shown on the upper wrapper is '100 MWC'.

Each occurrence of the title on the spine, upper and lower wrappers shows '*and the Chamber of Secrets*' off-set to the right of 'HARRY POTTER'.

Copies: private collection (AJH); private collection (SJH)

Reprints include:
10 9 8 7 6 5 4   BL (H.2000/1727) stamped 20 Apr 2000
20 19

A2(e) ENGLISH DELUXE EDITION (1999)
(children's artwork series in deluxe hardback)

HARRY | POTTER | *and the Chamber of Secrets* | [illustration of Hogwarts crest with legend 'DRACO DORMIENS NUNQUAM TITILLANDUS' on banner, 70 by 86mm] | J.K.ROWLING | [publisher's device of a dog, 12 by 19mm] | BLOOMSBURY (All width centred)

Collation: 128 unsigned leaves bound in sixteen gatherings of eight leaves; 233 by 151mm; [1-7] 8-14 [15] 16-23 [24] 25-36 [37] 38-52 [53] 54-67 [68] 69-80 [81] 82-93 [94] 95-106 [107] 108-121 [122] 123-36 [137] 138-53 [154] 155-69 [170] 171-84 [185] 186-96 [197] 198-209 [210] 211-25 [226] 227-40 [241] 242-51 [252-56]

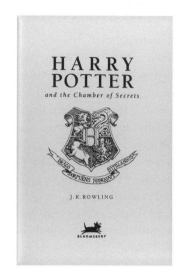

Page contents: [1] half-title: 'HARRY | POTTER | *and the Chamber of Secrets* | [illustration of Hogwarts crest with legend 'DRACO DORMIENS NUNQUAM TITILLANDUS' on banner, 49 by 60mm]'; [2] '*Also available:* | Harry Potter and the Philosopher's Stone | Harry Potter and the Prisoner of Azkaban'; [3] title-page; [4] 'All rights reserved; no part of this publication may be reproduced or | transmitted by any means, electronic, mechanical, photocopying or otherwise, without | the prior permission of the publisher | [new paragraph] This edition first published in Great Britain in 1999 | Bloomsbury Publishing Plc, 38 Soho Square, London, W1V 5DF | [new paragraph] Copyright © J. K. Rowling 1998 | Cover illustration based upon original art by Cliff Wright | [new paragraph] The moral right of the author has been asserted | A CIP catalogue record of this book is available from the | British Library | [new paragraph] ISBN 0 7475 4577 4 | [new paragraph] Printed in Great Britain by Clays Ltd, St Ives plc | [new paragraph] 10 9 8 7 6 5 4 3 2 1'; [5] '*for Séan P. F. Harris,* | *getaway driver and foulweather friend*'; [6] blank; [7]-251 text; [252] blank; [253] 'Acclaim for: | *Harry Potter and the Philosopher's Stone* by J. K. Rowling | [9 reviews]; [254-55] six facsimile letters to the author; [256] publisher's advertisement: upper cover design of *Harry Potter and the Philosopher's Stone*

Paper: wove paper

Running title: 'HARRY POTTER' (25mm) on verso, recto title comprises chapter title, pp. 8-251

Binding: light blue cloth.

On spine: 'HARRY POTTER *and the Chamber of Secrets* J.K.ROWLING' (reading lengthways down spine) with '[publisher's device of a dog, 10 by 17mm] | BLOOMSBURY' (horizontally at foot). All in gilt.

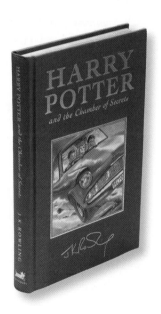

On upper cover: 'HARRY | POTTER | *and the Chamber of Secrets* | [double ruled border, 104 by 104mm with the outer border thicker than the inner and colour illustration by Cliff Wright laid down] | JKRowling [facsimile signature]' (all width centred). All in gilt.

Lower cover: blank.

All edges gilt. Green sewn bands at head and foot of spine together with green marker ribbon. Binding measurements: 241 by 151mm (covers), 241 by 35mm (spine). End-papers: dark blue wove paper.

Dust-jacket: none

Publication: 27 September 1999 in an edition of 7,500 copies (confirmed by Bloomsbury)

Price: £18

Contents:

Harry Potter and the Chamber of Secrets
  ('Not for the first time, an argument had broken out over breakfast at number four…')

Notes:

It is thought that the first English deluxe editions of *Philosopher's Stone*, *Chamber of Secrets* and *Prisoner of Azkaban* were published on the same date (see note to A7(c)).

Copies: Sotheby's, 17 December 2009, lot 169

Reprints include:

10 9 8 7 6 5 4
10 9 8 7
10 9

A2(f) TED SMART/'THE BOOK PEOPLE' EDITION   (1998 [1999])
(children's artwork series in hardback)

HARRY | POTTER | *and the Chamber of Secrets* | [illustration of Hogwarts crest with legend 'DRAGO DORMIENS NUNQUAM TITILLANDUS' on banner, 67 by 82mm] | J.K.ROWLING | [publisher's device of a rule, 39mm | 'TED SMART' | rule, 39mm, all within single ruled border, 7 by 40mm] (Lines 1 and 2 justified on left and right margins, and all width centred)

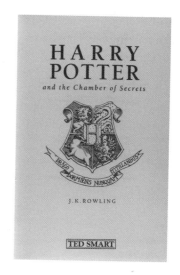

Collation: 128 unsigned leaves bound in indeterminate gatherings; 197 by 128mm; [1-7] 8-14 [15] 16-23 [24] 25-36 [37] 38-52 [53] 54-67 [68] 69-80 [81] 82-93 [94] 95-106 [107] 108-121 [122] 123-36 [137] 138-53 [154] 155-69 [170] 171-84 [185] 186-96 [197] 198-209 [210] 211-25 [226] 227-40 [241] 242-51 [252-56]

Page contents: [1] half-title: 'HARRY | POTTER | *and the Chamber of Secrets* | [illustration of Hogwarts crest with legend 'DRAGO DORMIENS NUNQUAM TITILLANDUS' on banner, 47 by 57mm]'; [2] blank; [3] title-page; [4] 'All rights reserved; no part of this publication may be reproduced or | transmitted by any means, electronic, mechanical, photocopying or otherwise, | without the prior permission of the publisher | [new paragraph] First published in Great Britain in 1998 | Bloomsbury Publishing Plc, 38 Soho Square, London W1V 5DF | [new paragraph] This edition produced for | The Book People Ltd, | Hall Wood Avenue, | Haydock, St. Helens WA11 9UL | [new paragraph] Copyright © 1998 J.K. Rowling | Cover illustration copyright © Cliff Wright 1998 | Cover illustration from original artwork by Cliff Wright | [new paragraph] The moral right of the author has been asserted | A CIP catalogue record of this book is available from the | British Library | [new paragraph] ISBN 1-85613-612-4 | [new paragraph] Printed and bound in Great Britain by Clays Ltd, St Ives plc | Typeset by Dorchester Typesetting | [new paragraph] 10 9 8 7 6 5 4 3 2 1 | Cover design by Michelle Radford'; [5] 'For Séan P. F. Harris, | getaway driver and foulweather friend'; [6] blank; [7]-251 text; [252] blank; [253] 'Acclaim for: | Harry Potter and the Philosopher's Stone by J.K. Rowling | [10 reviews]'; [254-55] six facsimile letters to the author; [256] publisher's advertisement: upper cover design of *Harry Potter and the Philosopher's Stone*

Paper: wove paper

Running title: 'HARRY POTTER' (24mm) on verso, recto title comprises chapter title, pp. 8-251

Binding: pictorial boards.

On spine: '[colour illustration of head of owl in cage on coloured panel, 20 by 12mm] HARRY POTTER [in green on blue panel, 20 by 51mm] *and the Chamber of Secrets* [in black] J.K.ROWLING [in blue, both title conclusion and author on green panel, 20 by 109mm] [publisher's device of a rule, 26mm | 'TED SMART' | rule, 26mm, all within single ruled border, 5 by 27mm] [in black on red panel, 20 by 33mm]' (reading lengthways down spine).

On upper cover: 'J.K.ROWLING [in white within red panel, 9 by 52mm] | HARRY | POTTER | *and the Chamber of Secrets* [lines 2-3 in green, line 4 in red, all on blue panel, 62 by 132mm] | [red rule, 132mm] | [colour illustration of Harry Potter, Ron Weasley and Hedwig the Owl in a flying car, 132 by 132mm] | [red rule, 132mm] 'Inventive and action-packed' *The Bookseller* [in white on black panel, 11 by 132mm]' (all width centred). There is a circular blue panel in the lower left corner of the illustration with 'J.K.ROWLING | 1997 SMARTIES AWARD WINNER | Shortlisted for the | 1997 CARNEGIE MEDAL | [publisher's device of the head of a dog, 4 by 3mm]' in white.

On lower cover: 'Harry Potter is a wizard. He is in his second year at | Hogwarts School of Witchcraft and Wizardry. Little does he | know that this year will be just as eventful as the last... | [new paragraph] Acclaim for HARRY POTTER AND THE PHILOSOPHER'S STONE | 'An absolutely must-have read of the year' *The Sunday Times* | [new paragraph] 'I've yet to meet a ten-year-old who hasn't been entranced by | its witty, complex plot and the character of the eponymous | Harry.' *The Independent on Saturday* | ['*TO ORDER FURTHER COPIES &* | *SEE OUR FULL RANGE OF TITLES* | [rule, 38mm] | [telephone symbol] 01942 724444 | Lines are open 7 days a week 8am-8pm | [rule, 38mm] | *CALL US NOW FOR YOUR* | *FREE COLOUR BROCHURE!* | Cover Illustrations by Cliff Wright' (with the exception of final line, all within single ruled border, 20 by 40mm) at centre, with barcode in black on white panel, 13 by 40mm together with 'http://www.bloomsbury.com' below panel, in black on green panel, 8 by 40mm all to right]'. All in black and all on colour illustration of Hogwarts castle and clouds.

All edges trimmed. Binding measurements: 204 by 132mm (covers), 204 by 24mm (spine). End-papers: wove paper.

Dust-jacket: coated wove paper, 204 by 483mm

Spine, upper and lower covers replicate the binding.

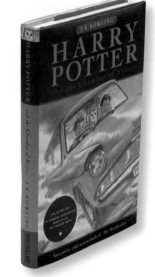

On upper inside flap: 'Harry, Ron and Hermione have | returned to Hogwarts School of | Witchcraft and Wizardry for their second | year. (But Harry and Ron only just made | it – they missed the Hogwarts Express | and had to get there in a flying car …!) | Soon the threesome are immersed in the | daily round of Potions, Herbology, | Charms, Defence Against the Dark Arts, | and Quidditch. | [new paragraph] But then horrible things start happening. | Harry hears evil voices. Sinister messages | appear on the wall. But nothing can prepare | the three friends for what happens next … | [new paragraph] A brilliant sequel to the award-winning | *Harry Potter and the Philosopher's Stone.* | [new paragraph] REVIEWS FROM SMARTIES YOUNG JUDGES, | PUPILS FROM COALWAY JUNIOR SCHOOL: | [new paragraph] 'I think *Harry Potter and the Philosopher's* | *Stone* is a great book – it's excellent. You | have to just unlock the key and the story | goes straight into your head. It is very | funny. I would love to be Harry and make | up some magic spell to play on my | teachers.' Tom El-Shawk, age 11 | [new paragraph] 'Harry Potter* is a spectacular book. You start | it and you cannot put it down. I know, | because my mum kept telling me off because | every night I was using up the electricity | very LATE! I showed *Harry* to my dad and | he's reading it now. It's for all ages and it's | BRILLIANT.' Katrina Farrant, age 10 | [new paragraph] £10.99'. All in black on red panel.

On lower inside flap: '[illustration of test tube and six stars, 26 by 26mm] | Dear Joanne Rowling, | [new paragraph] My name is Gail Williams and | I am 10 years old. | [new paragraph] I am writing to tell you how absolut- | ely astonished I was when I read | your book, "Harry Potter and the | Philosiphers Stone" It was just | amazing! I literally loved it. | I was totally hooked!! You described | All of the characters perfectly, I had | a picture of each of them in my | mind. I could just emajine Snape, | with an evil, sly face, and an | extremly snappy personality. | [new paragraph] I don't think you could improve | it in anyway. | [new paragraph] The story is so magical, and | thrilling. | [new paragraph] Harry's brave, Rons wise, Hermaine | is very brainy, but think my | favouroute has to be proffecer | Dumbledor. He seems so kind, | and magical. | [new paragraph] I would be very grateful if you could | in your spare time, (because I'm sure | you are very busy), you could write | back to me, maybe tell what the | next book in the Harry Potter story, (I | can't wait for it to come out), and | give me a couple of hints, about | the plot. | Yours | Sinceerly, | Gail Williams.' All in black facsimile of child's handwriting on red panel.

Publication: November 1999 (see notes)

Price: no exact price is recorded (see notes)

Contents:
Harry Potter and the Chamber of Secrets
    ('Not for the first time, an argument had broken out over breakfast at number four…')

Notes:
Neither Ted Smart nor Bloomsbury were able to provide any detail about the Ted Smart/'The Book People' editions. Information was provided by the Blair Partnership who noted that this edition was available from November 1999 (presumably at the same time as A7(d)). Production of the Ted Smart/'The Book People' editions ceased in April 2001.

No exact price has been recorded for this edition. A1(b) was, presumably, sold by itself. A slipcase containing the three volumes A1(b), A2(f) and A7(d) was probably available from November 1999 and a slipcase containing the four volumes A1(b), A2(f), A7(d) and A9(c) was, presumably, available from November 2000. In each case the price would have been lower than the single (or combined) prices of the Bloomsbury version.

Copies: private collection (PWE)

Reprints include:
10 9 8 7 6 5 4 3 2
10 9 8 7 6 5
10 9 8 7

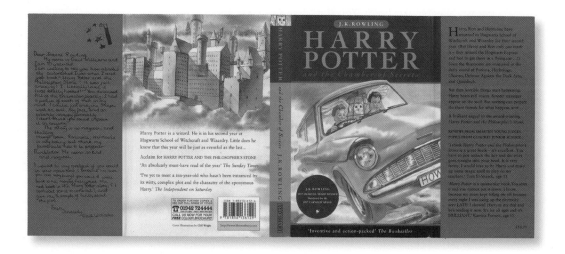

AMERICAN CHILDREN'S EDITION (2000)
(children's artwork series in paperback)

HARRY POTTER | AND THE CHAMBER OF SECRETS | [black and white illustration of doorway with carved snakes on surrounding pillars, 49 by 66mm] | BY | J. K. ROWLING | ILLUSTRATIONS BY MARY GRANDPRÉ | SCHOLASTIC INC. | NEW YORK [four-sided device] TORONTO [four-sided device] AUCKLAND [four-sided device] SYDNEY | MEXICO CITY [four-sided device] NEW DELHI [four-sided device] HONG KONG (All width centred on a diamond pattern background)

Collation: 176 unsigned leaves bound in indeterminate gatherings; 193 by 133mm; [I-IV] V-VI [VII-VIII] 1-341 [342-44]

Page contents: [I-II] 'PRAISE FOR J. K. ROWLING'S | HARRY POTTER | AND THE CHAMBER OF SECRETS | [device of nine stars] | [7 reviews and a listing of 7 statements] | ALSO BY J. K. ROWLING | *Harry Potter and the Sorcerer's Stone* | Year One at Hogwarts'; [III] title-page; [IV] 'FOR SEÁN P. F. HARRIS, | GETAWAY DRIVER AND FOUL-WEATHER FRIEND | [device of twelve stars] | Text copyright © 1999 by J. K. Rowling. | Illustrations copyright © 1999 by Mary GrandPré. | [new paragraph] All rights reserved. Published by Scholastic Inc. SCHOLASTIC, | the LANTERN DESIGN, and associated logos are trademarks | and/or registered trademarks of Scholastic Inc. | [new paragraph] If you purchased this book without a cover, you should be aware that this book is | stolen property. It was reported as "unsold and destroyed" to the publisher, and | neither

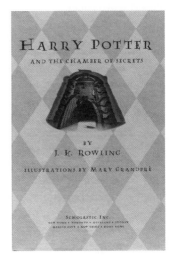

the author nor the publisher has received any payment for this "stripped book." | [new paragraph] No part of this publication may be reproduced in whole or in part, or stored in a | retrieval system, or transmitted in any form or by any means, electronic, mechanical, | photocopying, recording, or otherwise, without written permission | of the publisher. For information regarding permission, write to Scholastic Inc., | Attention: Permissions Department, 555 Broadway, New York, NY 10012. | [new paragraph] [publisher's device of a lantern, 7 by 5mm] | Arthur A. Levine Books hardcover edition | art directed by David Saylor, published by | Arthur A. Levine Books, an imprint | of Scholastic Press, June 1999. | [new paragraph] ISBN 0-439-06487-2 | Library of Congress number 98-46370 | 12 11 10 9 8 7 6 5 4 3 2 1 0 1 2 3 4 5/0 | [new paragraph] Printed in the U.S.A. 40 | First Scholastic Trade paperback printing, September 2000'; VI-VII 'CONTENTS' (eighteen chapters listed with titles and page references); [VII] half-title: 'HARRY POTTER | AND THE CHAMBER OF SECRETS' (all on diamond pattern background); [VIII] blank; 1-341 text; [342] publisher's advertisement: 'THE ADVENTURE CONTINUES…' (advert for *Harry Potter and the Prisoner of Azkaban*); [343] 'HARRY POTTER | AND THE PRISONER OF AZKABAN | [device of nine stars]

Harry Potter has to sneak back to his third year at | Hogwarts after accidentally inflating his horrible Aunt | Petunia. But returning to Hogwarts means facing Sirius Black, a | twelve-year prisoner in the dreaded fortress of Azkaban. | Convicted of killing thirteen people with a single curse, Black was | said to be the heir apparent to the Dark Lord, Voldemort. | [new paragraph] Now Black has escaped, leaving only clues as to where he | might be headed: Black lost everything the night Harry defeated | You-Know-Who, and the Azkaban guards heard Black muttering | in his sleep, "He's at Hogwarts… he's at Hogwarts." | [new paragraph] Harry Potter isn't safe, not even within the walls of his magi- | cal school, surrounded by his friends. Because on top of it all, | there may well be a traitor in their midst….'; [344] '[device of three stars] ABOUT THE AUTHOR [device of three stars] | J.K. ROWLING grew up in England in the Forest of Dean | and is a graduate of Exeter University. She lives in Edinburgh.'

Paper: wove paper

Running title: 'CHAPTER' and chapter number on verso, recto title comprises chapter title, pp. 1-341 except for pages on which a new chapter commences. On these pages, the running title comprises 'CHAPTER' and chapter number. Each running title (excluding pages on which new chapters commence) begins and ends with a three star device (in mirror image)

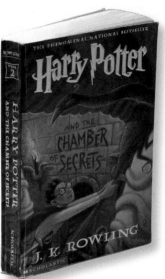

Illustrations: title-page vignette, together with eighteen vignettes at the beginning of each chapter (after chapter and chapter number but before chapter title). In addition to standard typographical changes (including italics, capitals and small capitals) there are other typographical features, comprising:

p. 21 facsimile of Mafalda Hopkirk's signature

p. 127 course description and students' endorsements

p. 221 newspaper headline

Binding: pictorial wrappers.

On spine: 'ROWLING | [rule] | ['YEAR | 2' within concave square]' (horizontally at head) with 'HARRY POTTER | SCHOLASTIC | AND THE CHAMBER OF SECRETS' (reading lengthways down spine). All in silver on green and burgundy diamond pattern background.

On upper wrapper: 'THE PHENOMENAL NATIONAL BESTSELLER [in silver] | Harry Potter [hand-drawn lettering] [embossed in silver] | AND THE [hand-drawn lettering in red of illustration] | CHAMBER [hand-drawn lettering in red of illustration] | OF SECRETS [hand-drawn lettering in red of illustration] | J. K. ROWLING [embossed in silver]' (all width centred). All on colour illustration of Harry Potter holding onto tail of a flying phoenix. In lower left: '[publisher's book device] SCHOLASTIC' in white on red panel, 9 by 47mm.

On lower wrapper: 'Ever since Harry Potter had come home for the summer, the | Dursleys had been so mean and hideous that all Harry wanted was | to get back to the Hogwarts School for Witchcraft and Wizardry. But | just as he's packing his bags, Harry receives a warning from a strange, | impish creature who says that if Harry returns to Hogwarts, disaster will | strike. | [new paragraph]

And strike it does. For in Harry's second year at Hogwarts, fresh tor- | ments and horrors arise, including an outrageously stuck-up new profes- | sor and a spirit who haunts the girls' bathroom. But then the real trouble | begins—someone is turning Hogwarts students to stone. Could it be | Draco Malfoy, a more poisonous rival than ever? Could it possibly be | Hagrid, whose mysterious past is finally told? Or could it be the one | everyone at Hogwarts most suspects…Harry Potter himself! | [new paragraph] [four-sided diamond device] The #1 *New York Times* Bestseller [four-sided diamond device] | [new paragraph] *Booklist* 1999 Editor's Choice [four-sided diamond device] Winner of the 1999 National Book Award (UK) | [four-sided diamond device] An ALA Notable Book [four-sided diamond device] An ALA Best Book for Young Adults 1999 [four-sided diamond device] Winner | of the 1999 Gold Medal Smarties Prize [four-sided diamond device] *School Library Journal*, 1999 Best | Book of the Year | [new paragraph] COVER ART BY MARY GRANDPRÉ'. All in black on colour illustration of a wall, pillar and flaming torch. In lower right: 'SCHOLASTIC INC. $6.99 US | [rule, 51mm] | [barcode with smaller barcode to the right (06487)]' all in black on white panel within single black ruled border, 26 by 51mm. The initial capital 'E' of 'Ever' is a drop capital.

On inside upper wrapper: barcode with smaller barcode below (5069) all in black.

All edges trimmed. Binding measurements: 193 by 133mm (wrappers), 193 by 20mm (spine).

Publication: September 2000 (see notes)

Price: $6.99

Contents:
Harry Potter and the Chamber of Secrets
  ('Not for the first time, an argument had broken out over breakfast at number four…')

Notes:
Although no publication day is recorded, 1 September 2000 is assumed. In an email to me from January 2013 Arthur A. Levine noted that 'I'm fairly certain that we didn't have strict "on sale" dates… the publication "day" would simply be the first of the month listed. None of the paperbacks were given a strict "on sale" date either.' Nielsen BookData provides a publication date of August 2000.

Scholastic released a 'dumpbin' display case for this edition at the end of August 2000 (Nielsen BookData provides a date of 28 August 2000). The case was filled with 36 copies of this edition. Alternatively, Scholastic made a multiple copy pack available on the same date containing 36 copies of this edition.

Note the incorrect Aunt identified on page [343] in the publisher's blurb for *Harry Potter and the Prisoner of Azkaban*. It is Aunt Marge, not Aunt Petunia, who is inflated.

Each chapter commences with a drop capital.

Copies: private collection (PWE)

Reprints include:

12 11 10 9 8 7 6 5 4	0 1 2 3 4 5/0	Printed in the U.S.A. 40
54 53 52 51	11 12 13/0	Printed in the U.S.A. 40
54	11 12 13/0	Printed in the U.S.A. 40

AMERICAN BOOK CLUB EDITION (1999 [2000])
(children's artwork series in hardback)

HARRY POTTER | AND THE CHAMBER OF SECRETS | [black and white illustration of doorway with carved snakes on surrounding pillars, 55 by 74mm] | BY | J.K. ROWLING | ILLUSTRATIONS BY MARY GRANDPRÉ | [publisher's device of a lantern, 12 by 9mm] | ARTHUR A. LEVINE BOOKS | AN IMPRINT OF SCHOLASTIC PRESS (All width centred on a diamond pattern background)

Collation: 176 unsigned leaves bound in eleven gatherings of sixteen leaves; 226 by 149mm; [I-VI] VII-VIII [IX-X] 1-341 [342]

Page contents: [I] 'HARRY POTTER | AND THE CHAMBER OF SECRETS' (all on diamond pattern background); [II] 'ALSO BY J. K. ROWLING | *Harry Potter and the Sorceror's* [sic] *Stone*'; [III] title-page; [IV] '[device of twelve stars] | Text copyright © 1999 by J.K. Rowling. | Illustrations copyright © 1999 by Mary GrandPré. | All rights reserved. Published by Scholastic Press, a division of Scholastic Inc., | *Publishers since 1920.* | SCHOLASTIC, SCHOLASTIC PRESS, ARTHUR A. LEVINE BOOKS, and associated logos | are trademarks and/or registered trademarks of Scholastic Inc. | [new paragraph] No part of this publication may be reproduced, or stored in a retrieval system, or transmitted | in any form or by any means, electronic, mechanical, photocopying, recording, or otherwise, | without written permission of the publisher. For information regarding permission, write | to Scholastic Inc., Attention: Permissions Department, 555 Broadway, New York, NY 10012. | [new paragraph] Library of Congress Cataloging-in-Publication Data |

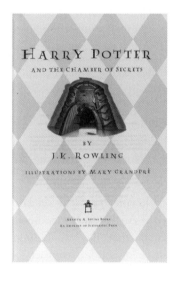

[new paragraph] Rowling, J. K. | Harry Potter and the Chamber of Secrets / by J. K. Rowling. | p. cm. | Summary: When the Chamber of Secrets is opened again at the Hogwarts School | for Witchcraft and Wizardry, second-year student Harry Potter finds himself in danger | from a dark power that has once more been released on the school. | ISBN 0-439-06486-4 | [square bracket]1. Wizards — Fiction. 2. Magic — Fiction. 3. Schools — Fiction. | 4. England — Fiction.[square bracket] I. Title. | PZ7.R7968Har 1999 | [square bracket]Fic[square bracket] — dc21 98-46370 | [new paragraph] 10 9 8 7 6 5 4 3 2 1   9/9 0/0 1 2 3 4 | Printed in the U.S.A. 37 | First American edition, June 1999'; [V] 'FOR SEÁN P. F. HARRIS, | GETAWAY DRIVER AND FOUL-WEATHER FRIEND'; [VI] blank; VII-VIII 'CONTENTS' (eighteen chapters listed with titles and page references); [IX] half-title: 'HARRY POTTER | AND THE CHAMBER OF SECRETS' (all on diamond pattern background); [X] blank; 1-341 text; [342] colophon: '[publisher's device of a lantern, 13 by 10mm] | *This* | *book was art* | *directed by David Saylor. The* | *art for both the jacket and the interior was* | *created using pastels on toned printmaking paper. The | text was set in 12-point Adobe Garamond, a typeface based on the | sixteenth-century type designs of Claude Garamond, redrawn by Robert | Slimbach in 1989. The book was printed and bound at | Berryville Graphics in Berryville, Virginia. The | production was supervised by | Angela Biola and Mike | Derevjanik.'*

Paper: wove paper

Running title: 'CHAPTER' and chapter number on verso, recto title comprises chapter title, pp. 1-341. Each running title (excluding pages on which new chapters commence) includes a three-star design to left and right of both running-titles on verso and recto. On pages on which a new chapter commences, the three-star design is omitted.

Illustrations: title-page vignette, together with eighteen vignettes at the beginning of each chapter (after chapter and chapter number but before chapter title). In addition to standard typographical changes (including italics, capitals and small capitals) there are other typographical features, comprising:

    p. 21 facsimile of Mafalda Hopkirk's signature
    p. 127 course description and students' endorsements
    p. 221 newspaper headline

Binding: black boards.

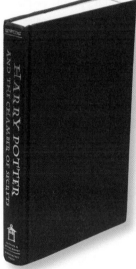

    On spine: 'ROWLING | [rule]' (horizontally at head) with 'HARRY POTTER | AND THE CHAMBER OF SECRETS' (reading lengthways down spine) and '[publisher's device of a lantern, 18 by 13mm] | ARTHUR A. | LEVINE BOOKS | [rule] | SCHOLASTIC | PRESS' (horizontally at foot). All in silver.

    Upper and lower covers: blank.

    All edges trimmed. Binding measurements: 233 by 149mm (covers), 233 by 40mm (spine). End-papers: white wove paper.

Dust-jacket: uncoated wove paper, 232 by 564mm. A single illustration spans the entire dust-jacket.

    On spine: 'ROWLING | [rule] | ['YEAR | 2' within concave square]' (horizontally at head) with 'HARRY POTTER | AND THE CHAMBER OF SECRETS' (reading lengthways down spine) and '[publisher's device of a lantern, 19 by 14mm] | ARTHUR A. | LEVINE BOOKS | [rule] | SCHOLASTIC | PRESS' (horizontally at foot). All in silver on colour illustration of pillar.

    On upper cover: 'Harry Potter [hand-drawn lettering] [in silver] | AND THE [hand-drawn lettering in red of illustration] | CHAMBER [hand-drawn lettering in red of illustration] | OF SECRETS [hand-drawn lettering in red of illustration] | J. K. ROWLING [in silver]' (all width centred). All on colour illustration of Harry Potter holding onto tail of a flying phoenix.

    On lower cover: 'Praise for the *New York Times* Bestseller | <u>HARRY POTTER AND THE SORCERER'S STONE</u> | [new paragraph] "You don't have to be a wizard or a kid to appreciate | the spell cast by Harry Potter." —*USA Today* | [new paragraph] "A charming, imaginative, magical |

confection of a novel." —*Boston Globe* | [new paragraph] "Harry is destined for greatness." | —*The New York Times* | [barcode with smaller barcode to the right (un-numbered) all in black on orange panel, 51 by 21mm]'. All in black and all on colour illustration of cat, snake, Hermione Granger and Ron Weasley.

On upper inside flap: 'PRINTED IN U.S.A. [on white panel, 5 by 24mm] | THE DURSLEYS | were so mean and hideous that summer that all | Harry Potter wanted was to get back to the | Hogwarts School for Witchcraft and Wizardry. | But just as he's packing his bags, Harry receives a | warning from a strange, impish creature named | Dobby who says that if Harry Potter returns to | Hogwarts, disaster will strike. | [new paragraph] And strike it does. For in Harry's second year | at Hogwarts, fresh torments and horrors arise, | including an outrageously stuck-up profes- | sor, Gilderoy Lockheart, a spirit named Moaning | Myrtle who haunts the girls' bathroom, and the | unwanted attentions of Ron Weasley's younger | sister, Ginny. | [new paragraph] But each of these seem minor annoyances | when the real trouble begins, and someone—or | something—starts turning Hogwarts students to | stone. Could it be Draco Malfoy, a more poison- | ous rival than ever? Could it possibly be Hagrid, | whose mysterious past is finally told? Or could it | be the one everyone at Hogwarts most sus- | pects… Harry Potter himself!' All in black and all on colour illustration of a pillar and wall.

On lower inside flap: 'Awards and Accolades for | HARRY POTTER | AND THE SORCERER'S STONE | [new paragraph] [five-pointed star] "A delightful romp. Rowling leaves the door wide open | for a sequel; bedazzled readers will surely clamor for | one." —*Publishers Weekly*, starred review | [new paragraph] [five-pointed star] "Surely the vilest household in children's literature since | the family Roald Dahl created for *Matilda*. Harry himself | is the perfect confused and unassuming hero." | —*School Library Journal*, starred review | [new paragraph] [five-pointed star] "A brilliantly imagined and beautifully written fantasy." | —*Booklist*, starred review | [new paragraph] [four-sided device] Winner of the National Book Award (UK) | [four-sided device] Winner of the Gold Medal Smarties Prize (UK) | [four-sided device] *Publishers Weekly* Best Book of 1998 | [four-sided device] *School Library Journal* Best Book of 1998 | [four-sided device] *Parenting* Book of the Year Award 1998 | [four-sided device] New York Public Library Best Book of the Year 1998 | [four-sided device] An ALA Notable Book | [publisher's device of a lantern, 15 by 11mm] ARTHUR A. LEVINE BOOKS | *An Imprint of Scholastic Press* | 555 Broadway, New York, New York 10012 | [new paragraph] *Jacket art by Mary GrandPré* | *Jacket design by Mary GrandPré and David Saylor*'. All in black and all on colour illustration of a wall, pillar and flaming torch.

Publication: between July and December 2000 (see notes)

Price: see notes

Contents:
Harry Potter and the Chamber of Secrets
    ('Not for the first time, an argument had broken out over breakfast at number four…')

Notes:

As with A4(a) and A4(c), the American book club edition differs very slightly from the true American first edition. The contents of the book, including the publisher's imprint page, is exactly the same. The binding, however, is different and slightly shorter. There are some minor differences on the dust-jacket: there is no embossing present, 'YEAR | 2' has been added to the spine, the second bar code lacks the numbers '51795', the price has been replaced with printing information on the upper inside flap and the jacket art copyright line is different on the lower inside flap.

Given that the true American first and the book club editions share a single ISBN, the Blair Partnership noted that book club editions could only be dated to within a half-year period end in their files. This edition was, therefore, published within the period July to December 1999. The Blair Partnership Royalties Manager noted that the American book club editions did not have 'a set price'.

Each chapter commences with a drop capital.

Copies: private collection (PWE)

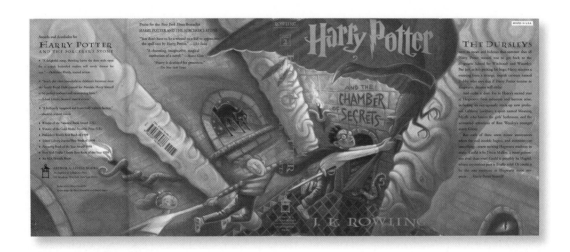

A2(i) AMERICAN DELUXE EDITION (2002)
(children's artwork series in deluxe hardback)

HARRY POTTER | AND THE CHAMBER OF SECRETS | [black and white illustration of doorway with carved snakes on surrounding pillars, 53 by 73mm] | BY | J.K. ROWLING | ILLUSTRATIONS BY MARY GRANDPRÉ | [publisher's device of a lantern, 12 by 9mm] |

ARTHUR A. LEVINE BOOKS | AN IMPRINT OF SCHOLASTIC PRESS (All width centred on a diamond pattern background)

Collation: 176 unsigned leaves bound in eleven gatherings of sixteen leaves; 227 by 150mm; [I-VI] VII-VIII [IX-X] 1-341 [342]

Page contents: [I] 'HARRY POTTER | AND THE CHAMBER OF SECRETS' (all on diamond pattern background); [II] 'ALSO BY J. K. ROWLING | *Harry Potter and the Sorcerer's Stone* | *Harry Potter and the Prisoner of Azkaban* | *Harry Potter and the Goblet of Fire*'; [III] title-page; [IV] '[device of twelve stars] | Text copyright © 1999 by J.K. Rowling. | Illustrations by Mary GrandPré copyright © 1999 Warner Bros. | All rights reserved. Published by Scholastic Press, a division of Scholastic Inc., | *Publishers since 1920.* | SCHOLASTIC, SCHOLASTIC PRESS, and the LANTERN LOGO | are trademarks and/or registered trademarks of Scholastic Inc. | HARRY POTTER, characters, names, and related indicia are trademarks of and © Warner Bros. | [new paragraph] No part of this publication may be reproduced, or stored in a retrieval system, or transmitted | in any form or by any means, electronic, mechanical, photocopying, recording, or otherwise, | without written permission of the publisher. For information

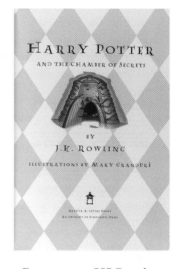

regarding permission, write | to Scholastic Inc., Attention: Permissions Department, 557 Broadway, New York, NY 10012. | [new paragraph] Library of Congress Cataloging-in-Publication Data | Rowling, J. K. | Harry Potter and the Chamber of Secrets / by J. K. Rowling. | p. cm. | Summary: When the Chamber of Secrets is opened again at the Hogwarts School | for Witchcraft and Wizardry, second-year student Harry Potter finds himself in danger | from a dark power that has once more been released on the school. | ISBN 0-439-20353-8 | [square bracket]1. Wizards — Fiction. 2. Magic — Fiction. 3. Schools — Fiction. | 4. England — Fiction.[square bracket] I. Title. | PZ7.R7968Har 1999 | [square bracket]Fic[square bracket] — dc21 98-46370 | [new paragraph] 10 9 8 7 6 5 4 3 2 1   02 03 04 05 | Printed in the U.S.A. 24 | Collector's Edition, October 2002'; [V] 'FOR SEÁN P. F. HARRIS, | GETAWAY DRIVER AND FOUL-WEATHER FRIEND'; [VI] blank; VII-VIII 'CONTENTS' (eighteen chapters listed with titles and page references); [IX] half-title: 'HARRY POTTER | AND THE CHAMBER OF SECRETS' (all on diamond pattern background); [X] blank; 1-341 text; [342] colophon: '[publisher's device of a lantern, 19 by 14mm] | *This Collector's Edition* | *was art directed and designed* | *by David Saylor. Mary GrandPré's* | *artwork for both the case inset and the interior* | *was created using pastels on toned printmaking paper.* | *The text was set in 12-point Adobe Garamond, a typeface* | *based on the sixteenth-century type designs of Claude Garamond,* | *redrawn by Robert Slimbach in 1989. The book is printed on acid-free 70-* | *pound Potter Offset paper, specially manufactured for Scholastic by Weyerhauser* | *Co. in Johnsonburg, Pennsylvania. The case is wrapped in Taratan Bonded* | *Leather produced at Corium Corporation in Seabrook, New* | *Hampshire, a division of Cromwell Leather Group. The* | *book was printed and bound at Quebecor World in* | *Kingsport, Tennessee. The Managing Editor* | *was Manuela Soares and the* | *Manufacturing Director was* | *Angela Biola.* | [device of six stars]'

Paper: wove paper

Running title: 'CHAPTER' and chapter number on verso, recto title comprises chapter title, pp. 1-341. Each running title (excluding pages on which new chapters commence) includes a three-star design to left and right of both running-titles on verso and recto. On pages on which a new chapter commences, the three-star design is omitted.

Illustrations: title-page vignette, together with eighteen vignettes at the beginning of each chapter (after chapter and chapter number but before chapter title). The original dust-jacket art is present on an inserted sheet fixed with a glue dot to the rear fixed endpaper. This sheet measures 146 by 222mm. On the textured front there is a colour illustration of Hermione Granger, Ron Weasley and Harry Potter holding onto tail of a flying phoenix. On the glossy back, at the foot, in black: 'HARRY POTTER AND THE CHAMBER OF SECRETS jacket illustration by Mary GrandPré copyright © 1999 by Warner Bros. and published by | Arthur A. Levine Books, An Imprint of Scholastic Press, 557 Broadway, New York, NY 10012. Printed in the U.S.A. All rights reserved.' In addition to standard typographical changes (including italics, capitals and small capitals) there are other typographical features, comprising:

p. 21 facsimile of Mafalda Hopkirk's signature

p. 127 course description and students' endorsements

p. 221 newspaper headline

Binding: red morocco.

On spine: 'J. K. | ROWLING | [raised band] | Harry [hand-drawn lettering] | Potter [hand-drawn lettering] | AND THE | CHAMBER | OF | SECRETS | [bolt of lightning, 26 by 12mm] | YEAR | TWO | [raised band] | [publisher's device of a lantern, 19 by 14mm] | ARTHUR A. | LEVINE BOOKS | [rule, 23mm] | SCHOLASTIC'. All in gilt.

On upper cover: 'J. K. | ROWLING | Harry Potter [hand-drawn lettering] | [colour illustration of Harry Potter holding onto tail of a flying phoenix, 70 by 94mm laid down to blind panel, 71 by 95mm] | AND THE | CHAMBER OF | SECRETS' (within ornate decorative border in ten sections together with ten stars, 215 by 134mm) (all width centred). All in gilt.

On lower cover: ornate decorative border in ten sections, 215 by 134mm. All in gilt.

All edges gilt. Red and yellow sewn bands at head and foot of spine. Binding measurements: 234 by 152mm (covers), 234 by 42mm (spine). End-papers: wove paper printed with diamond pattern in green and purple.

Dust-jacket: clear acetate, 234 by 616mm
Spine: blank.

*On **upper cover**:* 'COLLECTOR'S EDITION'. All in white.

*On **lower cover**:* '*This Collector's Edition of* | HARRY POTTER | AND THE | CHAMBER OF SECRETS | *is a specially produced,* | *leather-bound gift volume* | *that includes the complete* | *text of the original novel.* | [new paragraph] *This edition is available for a* | *limited time only* | —$75.00— | [new paragraph] [barcode with smaller barcode to the right (57500) all in black on white panel, 26 by 51mm]' (within ornate decorative border, 148 by 91mm) (all width centred). All in white

There is a circular gold sticker on the upper cover, diameter 38mm, on which, in black: 'FULL-COLOR | FRAMEABLE | JACKET ART | INSIDE!'

Publication: October 2002 (see notes)

Price: $75

Contents:

Harry Potter and the Chamber of Secrets

('Not for the first time, an argument had broken out over breakfast at number four…')

Notes:

The 'frameable jacket art' comprises the inserted sheet fixed with a glue dot to the rear fixed endpaper (see previous section on illustrations).

Although no publication day is recorded, 1 October 2002 is assumed. In an email to me from January 2013 Arthur A. Levine noted that 'I'm fairly certain that we didn't have strict "on sale" dates… the publication "day" would simply be the first of the month listed.' Nielsen BookData provides a publication date of 1 November 2002.

In March 2012 the publisher's New York flagship store was still selling copies of this edition. They were no longer available by November 2013.

Each chapter commences with a drop capital.

Copies: private collection (PWE)

A2(j)   ENGLISH 'CELEBRATORY' EDITION   (2002)
(children's artwork series in paperback)

HARRY | POTTER | *and the Chamber of Secrets* | [illustration of Hogwarts crest with legend 'DRAGO DORMIENS NUNQUAM TITILLANDUS' on banner, 67 by 82mm] | J.K.ROWLING | [publisher's device of a dog, 11 by 18mm] | BLOOMSBURY (Lines 1 and 2 justified on left and right margins, and all width centred)

Collation: 128 unsigned leaves bound in indeterminate gatherings; 197 by 128mm; [1-7] 8-14 [15] 16-23 [24] 25-36 [37] 38-52 [53] 54-67 [68] 69-80 [81] 82-93 [94] 95-106 [107] 108-121 [122] 123-36 [137] 138-53 [154] 155-69 [170] 171-84 [185] 186-96 [197] 198-209 [210] 211-25 [226] 227-40 [241] 242-51 [252-56]

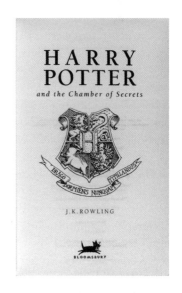

Page contents: [1] half-title: 'HARRY | POTTER | *and the Chamber of Secrets* | [illustration of Hogwarts crest with legend 'DRAGO DORMIENS NUNQUAM TITILLANDUS' on banner, 47 by 57mm]'; [2] '*Also available:* | Harry Potter and the Philosopher's Stone | Harry Potter and the Prisoner of Azkaban'; [3] title-page; [4] 'All rights reserved; no part of this publication may be reproduced or | transmitted by any means, electronic, mechanical, photocopying or otherwise, | without the prior permission of the publisher | [new paragraph] First published in Great Britain in 1998 | [new paragraph] Bloomsbury Publishing Plc, 38 Soho Square, | London W1D 3HB | [new paragraph] This edition first published in 2002 | [new paragraph] Copyright © 1998 J.K. Rowling | Cover illustrations copyright © by Cliff Wright 1998 | [new paragraph] Harry Potter, names, characters and related indicia are | copyright and trademark Warner Bros., 2000™ | [new paragraph] The moral right of the author has been asserted | [new paragraph] A CIP catalogue record for this book is | available from the British Library | [new paragraph] ISBN 0 7475 6218 0 | [new paragraph] 10 9 8 7 6 5 4 3 2 1 | [new paragraph] Typeset by Dorchester Typesetting | Printed in Great Britain by Clays Ltd, St Ives plc | [new paragraph] www.bloomsbury. com/harrypotter'; [5] '*For Séan P. F. Harris,* | *getaway driver and foulweather friend*'; [6] blank; [7]-251 text; [252-53] publisher's advertisement: '*Wondrous editions available | in the celebrated Harry Potter series:*' within illustration of scrolls; [254] '*Also by* | J.K. ROWLING | [new paragraph] *Read these books packed with fantastic wizarding | facts and amaze your friends with your knowledge | of Harry Potter's magical world ...* | [upper wrappers of *Quidditch Through the Ages* and *Fantastic Beasts* together with 'COMIC | RELIEF^UK' logo] | *Available from* | *www.bloomsburymagazine.com and retail outlets* | [new paragraph] *A percentage of the proceeds from the sale of these books will be donated to Comic Relief*'; [255-56] blank

Paper: wove paper

Running title: 'HARRY POTTER' (25mm) on verso, recto title comprises chapter title, pp. 8-251

Binding: pictorial wrappers.

On spine: '[colour illustration of head of owl in cage on coloured panel, 16 by 16mm] HARRY POTTER [in blue on silver panel, 16 by 46mm] *and the Chamber of Secrets* [in white] J.K.ROWLING [in silver, both title conclusion and author on blue panel, 16 by 103mm] BLOOMSBURY [publisher's device of the head of a dog, 3 by 4mm] [both in white on dark blue panel, 16 by 32mm]' (reading lengthways down spine).

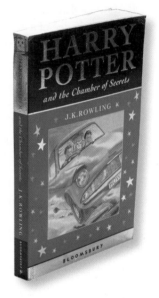

On upper wrapper: 'HARRY | POTTER | *and the Chamber of Secrets* [lines 1 and 2 in silver, line 3 in white, all on dark blue panel, 61 by 128mm] | [silver rule, 128mm] | ['J.K. ROWLING' [in silver] with colour illustration of Harry Potter, Ron Weasley and Hedwig the Owl in a flying car, within single silver ruled border, 91 by 86mm, all on light blue panel with orange, yellow and silver stars, 123 by 128mm] | [dark blue rule, 128mm] | BLOOMSBURY [in dark blue on silver panel, 11 by 128mm]' (all width centred).

On lower wrapper: 'Harry Potter is a wizard. He is in his second year at | Hogwarts School of Witchcraft and Wizardry. Little does | he know that this year will be just as eventful as the last... | [new paragraph] 'Joanne Rowling's second book is just as funny, | frightening and unexpected as her first.' *The Daily Mail* | [new paragraph] '*Harry Potter and the Chamber of Secrets* is as good as | its predecessor ... Hogwarts is a creation of genius.' | *The Times Literary Supplement* | [new paragraph] [barcode in black on white panel, 23 by 40mm together with '[publisher's device of a dog, 8 by 14mm] | BLOOMSBURY | £5.99' in black on left side of panel and 'www.bloomsburymagazine. com' below panel, in white on dark blue panel, 8 by 40mm]'. In lower left: 'Cover illustration from | original artwork by Cliff Wright'. All in black on colour illustration of Hogwarts castle and clouds.

All edges trimmed. Binding measurements: 197 by 128mm (wrappers), 197 by 16mm (spine).

Publication: 7 October 2002 in an edition of 700,200 copies (confirmed by Bloomsbury)

Price: £5.99

Contents:
Harry Potter and the Chamber of Secrets
  ('Not for the first time, an argument had broken out over breakfast at number four…')

Notes:
The individual titles in the 'celebratory' edition were each published to celebrate the release of the film version. The UK premiere of *Harry Potter and the Chamber of Secrets* took place on 3 November 2002.

Copies: private collection (PWE)

Reprints include:
10 9 8
11

A2(k)   AMERICAN MASS MARKET EDITION   (2002)
(adult artwork series in paperback)

Harry Potter [hand-drawn lettering] | AND THE | CHAMBER | OF SECRETS | J. K. ROWLING | SCHOLASTIC INC. | New York Toronto London Auckland Sydney | Mexico City New Delhi Hong Kong Buenos Aires (All width centred)

Collation: 224 unsigned leaves bound in indeterminate gatherings; 171 by 105mm; [I-XII] 1-433 [434-36]

Page contents: [I-II] 'PRAISE FOR J. K. ROWLING'S | HARRY POTTER | AND THE CHAMBER OF SECRETS | [6 reviews and a listing of 6 statements]'; [III] 'ALSO BY J. K. ROWLING | [new paragraph] HARRY POTTER | AND THE SORCERER'S STONE | *Year One at Hogwarts* | [new paragraph] HARRY POTTER | AND THE PRISONER OF AZKABAN | *Year Three at Hogwarts* | [new paragraph] HARRY POTTER | AND THE GOBLET OF FIRE | *Year Four at Hogwarts*'; [IV] blank; [V] title-page; [VI] 'FOR SÉAN P. F. HARRIS, | GETAWAY DRIVER AND FOUL-WEATHER FRIEND | [new paragraph] If you purchased this book without a cover, you should be aware that | this book is stolen property. It was reported as "unsold and destroyed" | to the publisher, and neither the author nor the publisher has received | any payment for this "stripped book." | [new paragraph] No part of this publication may be reproduced in whole or in part, or | stored in a retrieval system, or transmitted in

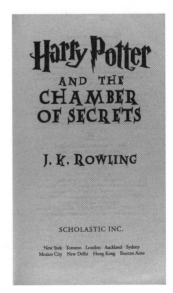

any form or by any | means, electronic, mechanical, photocopying, recording, or otherwise, | without written permission of the publisher. For information regarding | permission, write to Scholastic Inc., Attention: Permissions | Department, 557 Broadway, New York, NY 10012. | [new paragraph] [publisher's device of a lantern, 6 by 5mm] | Arthur A. Levine Books hardcover edition | published by Arthur A. Levine Books, | an imprint of Scholastic Press, July 1999 | [new paragraph] ISBN 0-439-42010-5 | [new paragraph] Text copyright © 1999 by J. K. Rowling | Illustrations by Mary GrandPré copyright © 1999 by Warner Bros. | All rights reserved. Published by Scholastic Inc. | HARRY POTTER, characters, names, and related indicia are | trademarks of and © Warner Bros. | SCHOLASTIC, the LANTERN LOGO, and associated logos are | trademarks and/or registered trademarks of Scholastic Inc. | [new paragraph] | 12 11 10 9 8 7 6 5 4 3 2 1   2 3 4 5 6 7/0 | [new paragraph] Printed in the U.S.A. 01 | First mass market paperback printing, November 2002'; [VII-IX] 'CONTENTS' (eighteen chapters listed with titles and page references); [X] blank; [XI] half-title: 'Harry Potter [hand-drawn lettering] | AND THE | CHAMBER | OF SECRETS'; [XII] blank; 1-433 text; [434] blank; [435] 'J. K. ROWLING | grew up in England in the Forest of Dean and is a | graduate of Exeter University. She lives in Edinburgh'; [436] publisher's advertisement: 'Harry Potter [hand-drawn lettering] | THE MAGICAL BOOKS THAT STARTED IT ALL!'

Paper: wove paper

Running title: none

Illustrations:

In addition to standard typographical changes (including italics, capitals and small capitals) there are other typographical features, comprising:

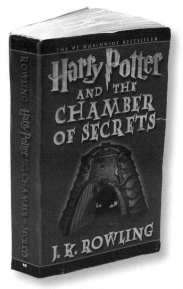

    p. 26 facsimile of Mafalda Hopkirk's signature

    p. 160-61 course description and students' endorsements

    p. 282 newspaper headline

Binding: pictorial wrappers.

    On spine: '[black panel, 10 by 27mm] | [orange rule, 27mm]' (horizontally at head) with 'ROWLING Harry Potter [hand-drawn lettering] AND THE CHAMBER OF SECRETS' (reading lengthways down spine) and '[orange rule, 27mm] | [black panel, 8 by 27mm with publisher's book device in black and white at centre]' (horizontally at foot). The 'ND' of 'AND' is positioned above the 'TH' of 'THE'. All in orange with white highlights on dark red.

    On upper wrapper: 'THE #1 WORLDWIDE BESTSELLER [in white on black panel, 10 by 105mm] | [orange rule, 105mm] | Harry Potter [hand-drawn lettering] | AND THE | CHAMBER | OF SECRETS | [black, grey and white illustration of open doorway to a chamber with two eyes peering from darkness, 63 by 77mm] | J. K. ROWLING | [orange, rule, 105mm] | [black panel, 8 by 105mm]' (all width centred). Title and author in embossed gilt and all on dark red.

    On lower wrapper: '[black panel, 10 by 105mm] | [orange rule, 105mm] | HARRY'S | SECOND YEAR | AT HOGWARTS [together with black, brown and grey illustration of an unfurled scroll positioned to the right, 29 by 46mm] | [new paragraph] *Strange warnings.* | *New challenges.* | *Deadly surprises.* | [new paragraph] *Harry Potter and the Chamber of Secrets* | is the haunting, thrilling second book | in J. K. Rowling's phenomenal saga. | [new paragraph] "Those needing a bit of magic, morality and mystical | worlds can do no better than opening *Harry Potter* | *and the Chamber of Secrets.*" — *USA Today* | [new paragraph] "Harry's enchanted world is a refreshing break." | — *The Wall Street Journal* | [new paragraph] "A wonderful sequel, as suspenseful, charming and | ultimately satisfying as its predecessor." | — *The Los Angeles Times* | [new paragraph] Visit Harry Potter on the Web at | www.scholastic.com/harrypotter'. In lower left: barcode with smaller barcode to the right (42010) together with 'S' within triangle, all in black on white panel within single orange ruled border, 20 by 58mm. In lower right: 'SCHOLASTIC INC. | *Cover art by Mary GrandPré* | *Cover design by Steve Scott* | $6.99 US [this line in black on white panel within single orange ruled border, 7 by 17mm]'. At foot, '[orange rule, 105mm (intersected by barcode panel and price panel)] | [black panel, 8 by 105mm]'. Lines 1-3 in orange with white highlights, lines 4-6 in white, lines 7-9 in orange, lines 10-17 in white, lines 18-19 in orange and lines 20-22 in white and all on dark red.

On inside upper wrapper: barcode with smaller barcode (50699) together with 'S' within triangle below, all in black.

All edges trimmed. Binding measurements: 171 by 105mm (wrappers), 171 by 27mm (spine).

Publication: November 2002 (see notes)

Price: $6.99

Contents:
Harry Potter and the Chamber of Secrets
  ('Not for the first time, an argument had broken out over breakfast at number four…')

Notes:
Presumably this edition was the Scholastic equivalent of Bloomsbury's 'celebratory' edition in that it was primarily aimed at a movie-going audience. See also A4(e).

Although no publication day is recorded, 1 November 2002 is assumed. In an email to me from January 2013 Arthur A. Levine noted that 'I'm fairly certain that we didn't have strict "on sale" dates… the publication "day" would simply be the first of the month listed. None of the paperbacks were given a strict "on sale" date either.' Nielsen BookData does not provide a publication date.

Scholastic released two sizes of 'dumpbin' display cases for this edition at the end of October 2002 (Nielsen BookData provides a date of 22 October 2002). The larger display case was filled with 24 copies of the edition. The smaller display case was filled with 18 copies.

Each chapter commences with a drop capital.

Copies: private collection (PWE)

ENGLISH ADULT EDITION
(Michael Wildsmith photography adult artwork series in paperback)

Harry Potter and the | Chamber of Secrets | J. K. Rowling | BLOOMSBURY (All width centred)

Collation: 184 unsigned leaves bound in indeterminate gatherings; 177 by 110mm; [1-7] 8-17 [18] 19-30 [31] 32-49 [50] 51-73 [74] 75-95 [96] 97-114 [115] 116-33 [134] 135-53 [154] 155-75 [176] 177-97 [198] 199-222 [223] 224-45 [246] 247-68 [269] 270-85 [286] 287-304 [305] 306-328 [329] 330-50 [351] 352-66 [367-68]

Page contents: [1] half-title: 'Harry Potter and the | Chamber of Secrets'; [2] *'Titles available in the Harry Potter series | (in reading order):* | Harry Potter and the Philosopher's Stone | Harry Potter and the Chamber of Secrets | Harry Potter and the Prisoner of Azkaban | Harry Potter and the Goblet of Fire | Harry Potter and the Order of the Phoenix'; [3] title-page; [4] 'All rights reserved; no part of this publication may be reproduced or | transmitted by any means, electronic, mechanical, photocopying or otherwise, | without the prior permission of the publisher | [new paragraph] First published in Great Britain in 1998 | Bloomsbury Publishing Plc, 38 Soho Square, London, W1D 3HB | [new paragraph] This paperback edition first published in 2004 | [new paragraph] Copyright © J. K. Rowling 1998 | [new paragraph] Harry Potter, names, characters and related indicia are | copyright and trademark Warner Bros., 2000™ | [new paragraph] With thanks to the Natural History Museum, London, for permission | to photograph the snake stone carving for use on the cover image | [new paragraph] The moral right of the author has been asserted | A CIP catalogue record of this book is available from the British Library | [new paragraph] ISBN 0 7475 7448 0 | [new paragraph] 1 3 5 7 9 10 8 6 4 2 | [new paragraph] Typeset by Dorchester Typesetting | Printed in Great Britain by Clays Ltd, St Ives plc | [new paragraph] All papers used by Bloomsbury Publishing are natural, | recyclable products made from wood grown in well-managed forests. | The paper used in this book contains 20% post consumer waste material | which was de-inked using chlorine free methods. The | manufacturing processes conform to the environmental | regulations of the country of origin. | [new paragraph] www.bloomsbury.com/harrypotter'; [5] 'For Séan P. F. Harris, | *getaway driver and foulweather friend*'; [6] blank; [7]-366 text; [367-68] blank

Paper: wove paper

Running title: 'HARRY POTTER' (24mm) on verso, recto title comprises chapter title, pp. 8-366 (excluding pages on which new chapters commence)

Binding: pictorial wrappers.
   On spine: 'HARRY POTTER AND THE [colour photograph of a shining green stone eye within a carved snake, 23 by 18mm | J.K. ROWLING [publisher's device of a figure with a bow, 10 by 10mm] | CHAMBER OF SECRETS' (reading lengthways down spine). All in white with the exception of last line which is in gilt and all on black.
   On upper wrapper: 'HARRY POTTER AND THE [in white] | CHAMBER OF [embossed in gilt] | SECRETS [embossed in gilt] | J. K. ROWLING [in white] | BLOOMSBURY [in white]' (all width

centred). All on colour photograph of a wall above two entwined carved snakes with shining green stone eyes.

On lower wrapper: '[colour photograph of two entwined carved snakes with shining green stone eyes, all within single white border, 22 by 22mm] 'A wonderful creation … The comic | handling of the material and the insight into | the child's world are fresh and magical in | every sense … the new Harry Potter is in | my suitcase ready for my holiday' | Ian Hislop, *Sunday Telegraph* | [new paragraph] Harry can't wait for his holidays with the dire Dursleys to | end. But a small, self-punishing house-elf warns Harry of | mortal danger awaiting him at Hogwarts School. Returning | to the castle nevertheless, Harry hears a rumour about a | chamber of secrets, holding unknown horrors for wizards | of Muggle parentage. Now someone is casting spells that | paralyse people, making them seem dead, and a terrible | warning is found painted on the wall. The chief suspect – | and always in the wrong place – is Harry. But something | much darker has yet to be unleashed. | [new paragraph] '*Harry Potter and the Chamber of Secrets*, unlike many | sequels, is as good as its predecessor … Hogwarts is a | creation of genius' *Times Literary Supplement* | [new paragraph] 'An intricately woven, highly imaginative tale … cleverly | textured, sophisticated fiction' *Scotland on Sunday* | [new paragraph] 'It seemed so unlikely that she could replicate the imaginative | power, emotional intensity and entrancing complexity of | the prototype, that I received the draft of volume two with | trepidation. It's good to be wrong sometimes' | *Glasgow Herald* | [new paragraph] [barcode in black on white panel, 24 by 39mm together with 'bloomsbury[in black]pbk[in white]s[in black] | £6.99 [in black] | www.bloomsbury.com [in black]' and all on red panel, 25 by 75mm] | Cover image: Michael Wildsmith Design: William Webb Author Photograph: © Bill de la HEY'. All in white on black with colour photograph to the left of lines 1-6.

On inside upper wrapper: black and white photograph of J.K. Rowling standing against bookshelves.

On inside lower wrapper: 'Other titles available in the | HARRY POTTER series | [colour illustrations in two columns of four book designs]'. All in white on black.

All edges trimmed. Binding measurements: 177 by 110mm (wrappers), 177 by 23mm (spine).

Publication: 10 July 2004 in an edition of 110,200 copies (confirmed by Bloomsbury)

Price: £6.99

Contents:
Harry Potter and the Chamber of Secrets
   ('Not for the first time, an argument had broken out over breakfast at number four…')

Notes:
See note to A1(f) about this series replacing an existing livery. This volume, A2(l), can be seen as the successor to A2(d).

Copies: BL (H.2005/1669) stamped 4 May 2004

Reprints include:
3 5 7 9 10 8 6 4 2
9 10

ENGLISH ADULT EDITION
(Michael Wildsmith photography adult artwork series in hardback)

Harry Potter and the | Chamber of Secrets | J. K. Rowling | BLOOMSBURY (All width centred)

Collation: 128 unsigned leaves bound in indeterminate gatherings; 197 by 125mm; [1-7] 8-14 [15] 16-23 [24] 25-36 [37] 38-52 [53] 54-67 [68] 69-80 [81] 82-93 [94] 95-106 [107] 108-121 [122] 123-36 [137] 138-53 [154] 155-69 [170] 171-84 [185] 186-96 [197] 198-209 [210] 211-25 [226] 227-40 [241] 242-51 [252-56]

Page contents: [1] half-title: 'Harry Potter and the | Chamber of Secrets'; [2] *'Titles available in the Harry Potter series | (in reading order)*: | Harry Potter and the Philosopher's Stone | Harry Potter and the Chamber of Secrets | Harry Potter and the Prisoner of Azkaban | Harry Potter and the Goblet of Fire | Harry Potter and the Order of the Phoenix | [new paragraph] *Harry Potter and the Philosopher's Stone* | *also available in Latin, Ancient Greek, Welsh and Irish:* | Harrius Potter et Philosophi Lapis (Latin) | Ἄρειος Ποτὴρ καί ἡ τοῦ ψιλοσόψου λίθος (Ancient Greek) | Harri Potter a Maen yr Anthronydd (Welsh) | Harry Potter agus an Órchloch (Irish)'; [3] title-page; [4] 'All rights reserved; no part of this publication may be reproduced or | transmitted by any means, electronic, mechanical, photocopying | or otherwise, without the prior permission of the publisher | [new paragraph] First published in Great Britain in 1998 | Bloomsbury Publishing Plc, 38 Soho Square, London, W1D 3HB | [new paragraph] This edition first published in 2004 | [new paragraph] Copyright © 1998 J. K. Rowling | [new paragraph] Harry Potter, names, characters and related indicia are | copyright and trademark Warner Bros., 2000™ | [new paragraph] With thanks to the Natural History Museum, London, for permission to | photograph the snake stone carving for use on the cover image | [new paragraph] The moral right of the author has been asserted | A CIP catalogue record of this book is available from the British Library | [new paragraph] ISBN 0 7475 7361 1 | [new paragraph] Typeset by Dorchester Typesetting | [new paragraph] All papers used by Bloomsbury Publishing are natural, recyclable products made | from wood grown in well-managed forests. The manufacturing processes | conform to the environmental regulations of the country of origin. | [new paragraph] Printed in Great Britain by Clays Ltd, St Ives plc | [new paragraph] 1 3 5 7 9 10 8 6 4 2 | [new paragraph] www.bloomsbury.com/harrypotter'; [5] *'For Séan P. F. Harris,* | *getaway driver and foulweather friend*'; [6] blank; [7]-251 text; [252-56] blank

Paper: wove paper

Running title: 'HARRY POTTER' (24mm) on verso, recto title comprises chapter title, pp. 8-251 (excluding pages on which new chapters commence)

Binding: black boards.
   On spine: 'HARRY POTTER | J. K. ROWLING | AND THE CHAMBER OF SECRETS [publisher's device of a figure with a bow, 14 by 14mm]' (reading lengthways down spine). All in gilt.
   Upper and lower covers: blank.

All edges trimmed. Binding measurements: 204 by 128mm (covers), 204 by 36mm (spine). End-papers: wove paper.

Dust-jacket: coated wove paper, 204 by 490mm

On spine: '[colour photograph of two entwined carved snakes with shining green stone eyes, all within single white ruled border, 20 by 20mm] HARRY POTTER [in gilt] | J. K. ROWLING [in white] | AND THE CHAMBER OF SECRETS [in white]' (reading lengthways down spine) together with publisher's device of a figure with a bow, 14 by 14mm [in olive beige] (at foot).

On upper cover: 'J. K. ROWLING [in white] | HARRY [embossed in gilt] | POTTER [embossed in gilt] | AND THE CHAMBER OF SECRETS [in white] | BLOOMSBURY [in white]' (all width centred). All on colour photograph of a wall above two entwined carved snakes with shining green stone eyes.

On lower cover: black and white photograph of J.K. Rowling standing against bookshelves with 'www.bloomsbury.com/harrypotter [in black on olive beige panel, 5 by 40mm] | [barcode in black on white panel, 20 by 39mm] | BLOOMSBURY [in black on olive beige panel, 7 by 40mm]' (lower right).

On upper inside flap: 'Harry can't wait for his holidays with the | dire Dursleys to end. But a small, self- | punishing house-elf warns Harry of mortal | danger awaiting him at Hogwarts School. | Returning to the castle nevertheless, Harry | hears a rumour about a chamber of | secrets, holding unknown horrors for | wizards of Muggle parentage. Now | someone is casting spells that paralyse | people, making them seem dead, and a | terrible warning is found painted on the | wall. The chief suspect – and always in the | wrong place – is Harry. But something | much darker has yet to be unleashed. | [new paragraph] 'A wonderful creation … The comic | handling of the material and the insight | into the child's world are fresh and magical | in every sense … the new Harry Potter is in | my suitcase ready for my holiday' | Ian Hislop, *Sunday Telegraph* | [new paragraph] '*Harry Potter and the Chamber of Secrets,* | unlike many sequels, is as good as its | predecessor … Hogwarts is a creation of | genius' *Times Literary Supplement* | [new paragraph] 'An intricately woven, highly imaginative | tale … cleverly textured, sophisticated | fiction' *Scotland on Sunday* | [new paragraph] 'It seemed so unlikely that she could | replicate the imaginative power, emotional | intensity and entrancing complexity of | the prototype, that I received the draft of | volume two with trepidation. It's good to | be wrong sometimes' | *Glasgow Herald* | [new paragraph] £11.99'. All in white on black.

On lower inside flap: 'J. K. (JOANNE KATHLEEN) ROWLING | has written fiction since she was a child. | Born in 1965, she grew up in Chepstow | and wrote her first 'book' at the age of six | – a story about a rabbit called Rabbit. | She studied French and Classics at Exeter | University, then moved to London to | work at Amnesty International, and then | to Portugal to teach English as a foreign | language, before settling in Edinburgh. | [new paragraph] The idea for Harry Potter occurred to her | on the train from Manchester to London, | where she says Harry Potter 'just strolled | into my head fully formed', and by the | time she had arrived at King's Cross, | many of the characters had taken shape. | During the next five years she outlined | the plots for each book and began writing | the first in the series, *Harry Potter and* | *the Philosopher's Stone,* which was first | published by Bloomsbury in 1997. The | other Harry Potter titles: *Harry Potter and* | *the Chamber of Secrets, Harry Potter and the* | *Prisoner of Azkaban, Harry Potter and the* | *Goblet of Fire,* and *Harry*

Potter and the | *Order of the Phoenix*, followed. | J. K. Rowling has also written two other | companion books, *Quidditch Through the* | *Ages* and *Fantastic Beasts and Where to* | *Find Them*, in aid of Comic Relief. | [new paragraph] Jacket Design: William Webb | Jacket Image: Michael Wildsmith | Author Photograph: © Bill de la HEY'. All in white on black.

Publication: 4 October 2004 in an edition of 12,500 copies (confirmed by Bloomsbury)

Price: £11.99

Contents:
Harry Potter and the Chamber of Secrets
   ('Not for the first time, an argument had broken out over breakfast at number four…')

Notes:
Having rebranded the look of the adult artwork edition to feature photography by Michael Wildsmith, it was perhaps inevitable that a hardback version would become available. A1(g), A2(m) and A7(j) were all published on 4 October 2004 with A9(i) following a few days later on 10 October 2004. As the series progressed, later titles published in this livery (see A12(aa), A13(aa) and A14(aa)) would also comprise the simultaneous first edition issues.

Copies: Bloomsbury Archives

Reprints include:
3 5 7 9 10 8 6 4
7 9 10 8 6
13 15 17 19 20 18 16 14 12

A2(n) ENGLISH 'SIGNATURE' EDITION (2010)
(Clare Melinsky artwork series in paperback)

Harry Potter ['signature' above 'z' rule with numerous stars] | *and the* | *Chamber of Secrets* | [illustration of Hogwarts crest with legend 'DRAGO DORMIENS NUNQUAM TITILLANDUS' on banner, 68 by 84mm] | J.K.ROWLING | [publisher's device of a dog, 8 by 13mm] | BLOOMSBURY | LONDON BERLIN NEW YORK SYDNEY (All width centred)

Collation: 128 unsigned leaves bound in indeterminate gatherings; 197 by 128mm; [1-7] 8-14 [15] 16-23 [24] 25-36 [37] 38-52 [53] 54-67 [68] 69-80 [81] 82-93 [94] 95-106 [107] 108-121 [122] 123-36 [137] 138-53 [154] 155-69 [170] 171-84 [185] 186-96 [197] 198-209 [210] 211-25 [226] 227-40 [241] 242-51 [252-56]

Page contents: [1] half-title: 'Harry Potter ['signature' above 'z' rule with numerous stars] | *and the* | *Chamber of Secrets* | [illustration of Hogwarts crest with legend 'DRAGO DORMIENS NUNQUAM

TITILLANDUS' on banner, 60 by 75mm]'; [2] *Titles available in the Harry Potter series | (in reading order):* | Harry Potter and the Philosopher's Stone | Harry Potter and the Chamber of Secrets | Harry Potter and the Prisoner of Azkaban | Harry Potter and the Goblet of Fire | Harry Potter, and the Order of the Phoenix | Harry Potter and the Half-Blood Prince | Harry Potter and the Deathly Hallows | [new paragraph] *Titles available in the Harry Potter series | (in Latin):* | Harry Potter and the Philosopher's Stone | Harry Potter and the Chamber of Secrets | *(in Welsh, Ancient Greek and Irish):* | Harry Potter and the Philosopher's Stone'; [3] title-page; [4] 'All rights reserved; no part of this publication may be reproduced or | transmitted by any means, electronic, mechanical, photocopying | or otherwise, without the prior permission of the publisher | [new paragraph] First published in Great Britain in 1998 by Bloomsbury Publishing Plc | 36 Soho Square, London, W1D 3QY | [new paragraph] Bloomsbury Publishing, London, Berlin,

New York and Sydney | [new paragraph] This paperback edition first published in November 2010 | [new paragraph] Copyright © J.K.Rowling 1998 | Cover illustrations by Clare Melinsky copyright © Bloomsbury Publishing Plc 2010 | [new paragraph] Harry Potter, names, characters and related indicia are | copyright and trademark Warner Bros., 2000™ | [new paragraph] The moral right of the author has been asserted | A CIP catalogue record of this book is available from the British Library | [new paragraph] ISBN 978 1 4088 1055 2 | [new paragraph] [Forest Stewardship Council logo, 8 by 9mm together with ® symbol and text: 'FSC | www.fsc.org | MIX | Paper from | responsible sources | FSC® C018072'] | [new paragraph] Typeset by Dorchester Typesetting | Printed in Great Britain by Clays Ltd, St Ives plc | [new paragraph] 1 3 5 7 9 10 8 6 4 2 | [new paragraph] | www.bloomsbury.com/harrypotter'; [5] *'For Séan P. F. Harris, | getaway driver and foulweather friend'*; [6] blank; [7]-251 text; [252-56] blank

Paper: wove paper

Running title: 'HARRY POTTER' (25mm) on verso, recto title comprises chapter title, pp. 8-251

Binding: pictorial wrappers.

On spine: 'Harry Potter ['signature' above 'z' rule with numerous stars] [in gilt] *and* | *the Chamber of Secrets* [black, yellow and blue illustration of a spider, 13 by 8mm] J.K.ROWLING BLOOMSBURY [publisher's device of the head of a dog, 3 by 4mm]' (reading lengthways down spine). All in white on red.

On upper wrapper: 'Harry Potter ['signature' above 'z' rule with numerous stars] [embossed in gilt] | *and the* | *Chamber of Secrets* | [blue, yellow, green, brown and red illustration of snake, phoenix and hat, 100 by 110mm] | J.K.ROWLING | BLOOMSBURY' (all width centred). All in red with deckle-edge effect of white leaf on red background at fore-edge.

On lower wrapper: 'Harry Potter is a wizard. He is in his second year at Hogwarts | School of Witchcraft and Wizardry. The three friends, Harry, | Ron and Hermione, are soon immersed in the daily round of Potions, | Herbology, Charms, Defence Against the Dark Arts and Quidditch. | Then mysterious and scary things start happening. First Harry hears | strange voices, and then Ron's sister, Ginny, disappears … | [new paragraph] 'Joanne Rowling's second book is just as funny, frightening and | unexpected as her first.' | *Daily Mail* | [new paragraph] 'The Harry Potter books are that rare thing, a series of | stories adored by parents and children alike.' | *Daily Telegraph* | [new paragraph] '*Harry Potter and the Chamber of Secrets* is as | good as its predecessor … Hogwarts is a | creation of genius.' | *TLS* | [blue, yellow and green illustration of a tree, 122 by 107mm] | [barcode together with publisher's device of a dog, 6 by 10mm and 'BLOOMSBURY' together with Forest Stewardship Council logo, 7 by 8mm together with © symbol and text: 'FSC | Mixed Sources | Product group from well-managed | forests and other controlled sources | [new paragraph] Cert no. SGS-COC-2061 | www.fsc.org | © 1996 Forest Stewardship Council'] | Designed by Webb & Webb Design | Cover illustrations by Clare Melinsky www.bloomsbury.com/harrypotter £6.99 | Author photograph © J.P.Masclet'. Lines 1-16 in red with all other text in black, together with deckle-edge effect of white leaf on red background at fore-edge. The initial capital 'H' of 'Harry' is a drop capital.

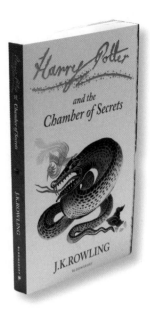

On inside upper wrapper: 'The magical world of … | Harry Potter ['signature' above 'z' rule with numerous stars] | [colour illustrations in three columns of seven book designs] | The internationally bestselling series | [new paragraph] For more from Harry Potter, visit | www.bloomsbury.com/harrypotter'. All in red with the exception of line 2 which is in gold, together with deckle-edge effect of white leaf on red background at fore-edge.

On inside lower wrapper: colour photograph of J.K. Rowling seated by a window.

All edges trimmed. Binding measurements: 197 by 128mm (wrappers), 197 by 15mm (spine).

Publication: 1 November 2010 in an edition of 63,102 copies (confirmed by Bloomsbury)

Price: £6.99

Contents:
Harry Potter and the Chamber of Secrets
    ('Not for the first time, an argument had broken out over breakfast at number four…')

Notes:
Published as a boxed set of seven volumes comprising A1(i), A2(n), A7(k), A9(k), A12(h), A13(g) and A14(f). Individual volumes were also available separately.

Copies: BL (YK.2011.a.21128) stamped 9 Aug 2010; private collection (PWE)

ENGLISH 'SIGNATURE' EDITION   (2011)
(Clare Melinsky artwork series in hardback)

Harry Potter ['signature' above 'z' rule with numerous stars] | *and the* | *Chamber of Secrets* | [illustration of Hogwarts crest with legend 'DRAGO DORMIENS NUNQUAM TITILLANDUS' on banner, 68 by 84mm] | J.K.ROWLING | [publisher's device of a dog, 8 by 13mm] | BLOOMSBURY | LONDON BERLIN NEW YORK SYDNEY (All width centred)

Collation: 128 unsigned leaves bound in indeterminate gatherings; 197 by 124mm; [1-7] 8-14 [15] 16-23 [24] 25-36 [37] 38-52 [53] 54-67 [68] 69-80 [81] 82-93 [94] 95-106 [107] 108-121 [122] 123-36 [137] 138-53 [154] 155-69 [170] 171-84 [185] 186-96 [197] 198-209 [210] 211-25 [226] 227-40 [241] 242-51 [252-56]

Page contents: [1] half-title: 'Harry Potter ['signature' above 'z' rule with numerous stars] | *and the* | *Chamber of Secrets* | [illustration of Hogwarts crest with legend 'DRAGO DORMIENS NUNQUAM TITILLANDUS' on banner, 60 by 75mm]'; [2] '*Titles available in the Harry Potter series* | *(in reading order):* | Harry Potter and the Philosopher's Stone | Harry Potter and the Chamber of Secrets | Harry Potter and the Prisoner of Azkaban | Harry Potter and the Goblet of Fire | Harry Potter and the Order of the Phoenix | Harry Potter and the Half-Blood Prince | Harry Potter and the Deathly Hallows | [new paragraph] *Titles available in the Harry Potter series* | *(in Latin):* | Harry Potter and the Philosopher's

Stone | Harry Potter and the Chamber of Secrets | *(in Welsh, Ancient Greek and Irish):* | Harry Potter and the Philosopher's Stone | [new paragraph] *Also available* | *(in aid of Comic Relief):* | Fantastic Beasts and Where to Find Them | Quidditch Through the Ages | *(in aid of Lumos):* | The Tales of Beedle the Bard'; [3] title-page; [4] 'All rights reserved; no part of this publication may be reproduced or | transmitted by any means, electronic, mechanical, photocopying | or otherwise, without the prior permission of the publisher | [new paragraph] First published in Great Britain in 1998 by Bloomsbury Publishing Plc | 49-51 Bedford Square, London, WC1B 3DP | [new paragraph] Bloomsbury Publishing, London, Berlin, New York and Sydney | [new paragraph] This hardback edition first published in November 2011 | [new paragraph] Copyright © J.K.Rowling 1998 | Cover and endpaper illustrations by Clare Melinsky copyright © J.K.Rowling 2010 | [new paragraph] Harry Potter, names, characters and related indicia are | copyright and trademark Warner Bros., 2000™ | [new paragraph] The moral right of the author has been asserted | A CIP catalogue record of this book is available from the British Library | [new paragraph] ISBN 978 1 4088 2581 5 | [new paragraph] [Forest Stewardship Council logo, 8 by 9mm together with ® symbol and text: 'FSC | www.fsc.org | MIX | Paper from | responsible sources | FSC® C018072'] | [new paragraph] Typeset by Dorchester Typesetting | Printed in Great Britain by Clays Ltd, St Ives plc | [new paragraph]

1 3 5 7 9 10 8 6 4 2 | [new paragraph] | www.bloomsbury.com/harrypotter'; [5] 'For Seán P. F. Harris, | getaway driver and foulweather friend'; [6] blank; [7]-251 text; [252-56] blank

Paper: wove paper

Running title: 'HARRY POTTER' (24mm) on verso, recto title comprises chapter title, pp. 8-251

Binding: red boards.

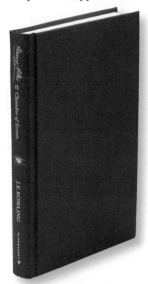

On spine: 'Harry Potter ['signature' above 'z' rule with numerous stars] *and* | *the Chamber of Secrets* [illustration of a spider, 13 by 8mm] J.K.ROWLING BLOOMSBURY [publisher's device of the head of a dog, 3 by 4mm]' (reading lengthways down spine). All in gilt.

Upper and lower covers: blank.

All edges trimmed. Red sewn bands at head and foot of spine together with red marker ribbon. Binding measurements: 205 by 128mm (covers), 205 by 31mm (spine). End-papers: wove paper overprinted in red showing design, in white, of spine motifs from the series (see notes).

Dust-jacket: coated wove paper, 205 by 487mm

On spine: 'Harry Potter ['signature' above 'z' rule with numerous stars] [in gilt] *and* | *the Chamber of Secrets* [black, yellow and blue illustration of a spider, 13 by 8mm] J.K.ROWLING BLOOMSBURY [publisher's device of the head of a dog, 3 by 4mm]' (reading lengthways down spine). All in white on red.

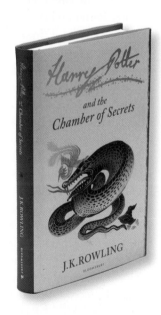

On upper cover: 'Harry Potter ['signature' above 'z' rule with numerous stars] [in gilt] | *and the* | *Chamber of Secrets* | [blue, yellow, green, brown and red illustration of snake, phoenix and hat, 100 by 110mm] | J.K.ROWLING | BLOOMSBURY' (all width centred). All in red with deckle-edge effect of white leaf on red background at fore-edge.

On lower cover: "Hogwarts is a creation of genius.' | *Times Literary Supplement* | [blue, yellow and green illustration of a tree, 101 by 91mm] | [publisher's device of a dog, 6 by 10mm and 'BLOOMSBURY'] [barcode and 'www.bloomsbury.com/harrypotter' in black on white panel, 24 by 39mm]'. All in red, with deckle-edge effect of white leaf on red background at fore-edge. The initial capital 'H' of 'Hogwarts' is a drop capital.

On upper inside flap: 'Harry Potter is a wizard. He is | in his second year at Hogwarts | School of Witchcraft and Wizardry. | The three friends, Harry, Ron and | Hermione, are soon immersed in the | daily round of Potions, Herbology, | Charms, Defence Against the Dark | Arts and Quidditch. Then mysterious | and scary things start happening. First | Harry hears strange voices, and then | Ron's sister, Ginny, disappears … | [new paragraph] 'Joanne Rowling's second book is just | as funny, frightening and unexpected as |

her first.' | *Daily Mail* | [new paragraph] 'The Harry Potter books are that rare thing, | a series of stories adored by parents and | children alike.' | *Daily Telegraph* | [new paragraph] '*Harry Potter and the Chamber of Secrets* is | as good as its predecessor … Hogwarts | is a creation of genius.' | *Times Literary Supplement* | [black, yellow and blue illustration of a spider, 12 by 21mm]'. All in white on red. The initial 'H' of 'Harry' is a drop capital.

On lower inside flap: 'J. K. Rowling has written fiction since she was a child, | and she always wanted to be an author. Her parents loved | reading and their house in Chepstow was full of books. | In fact, J. K. Rowling wrote her first 'book' at the age | of six – a story about a rabbit called Rabbit. She studied | French and Classics at Exeter University, then moved to | Edinburgh – via London and Portugal. In 2000 she was | awarded an OBE for services to children's literature. | [new paragraph] The idea for Harry Potter occurred to her on the | train from Manchester to London, where she says | Harry Potter 'just strolled into my head fully formed', | and by the time she had arrived at King's Cross, many | of the characters had taken shape. During the next | five years she outlined the plots for each book and | began writing the first in the series, *Harry Potter and* | *the Philosopher's Stone*, which was first published by | Bloomsbury in 1997. The other Harry Potter titles: | *Harry Potter and the Chamber of Secrets, Harry Potter* | *and the Prisoner of Azkaban, Harry Potter and the* | *Goblet of Fire, Harry Potter and the Order of the Phoenix,* | *Harry Potter and the Half-Blood Prince* and *Harry* | *Potter and the Deathly Hallows* followed. J. K. Rowling | has also written three companion books: *Quidditch* | *Through the Ages* and *Fantastic Beasts and Where to Find* | *Them*, in aid of Comic Relief, and *The Tales of Beedle* | *the Bard*, in aid of Lumos. | [new paragraph] THE COMPLETE HARRY POTTER SERIES: | [colour illustrations in two rows of seven book designs] | Designed by Webb & Webb Design | Cover illustrations by Clare Melinsky | copyright © J. K. Rowling 2010'. All in white on red with white panel, 19 by 12mm, to right on which in black: '[Forest Stewardship Council logo, 6 by 7mm together with ® symbol] | FSC | www.fsc.org | MIX | Paper from | responsible sources | FSC® C018072'

Publication: 7 November 2011 in an edition of 9,200 copies (confirmed by Bloomsbury)

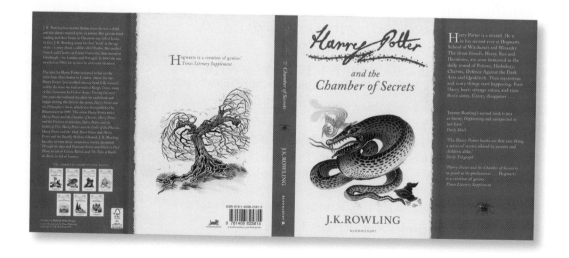

Price: £115 [together with A1(j), A7(l), A9(l), A12(i), A13(h) and A14(g)]

Contents:

Harry Potter and the Chamber of Secrets

('Not for the first time, an argument had broken out over breakfast at number four...')

Notes:

The end-papers carry a design of eight miniature illustrations. Seven of these reproduce the spine motifs from the series and an eighth comprises a variant of the key-bird from the first book.

Published as a boxed set of seven volumes comprising A1(j), A2(o), A7(l), A9(l), A12(i), A13(h) and A14(g). Individual volumes were not available separately. The ISBN for the boxed set was ISBN 978 1 4088 2594 5.

Copies: private collection (PWE)

A2(p)   ENGLISH ADULT EDITION   (2013)
(Andrew Davidson artwork series in paperback)

J.K. [in grey] | ROWLING [in grey] [reading lengthways down title-page] | HARRY | POTTER | &THE [reading lengthways up title-page] CHAMBER OF SECRETS | BLOOMSBURY | LONDON [point] NEW DELHI [point] NEW YORK [point] SYDNEY (Author and final part of title justified on right margin, first part of title justified on left margin, publisher with publisher's offices width centred)

Collation: 128 unsigned leaves bound in indeterminate gatherings; 198 by 128mm; [1-7] 8-14 [15] 16-23 [24] 25-36 [37] 38-52 [53] 54-67 [68] 69-80 [81] 82-93 [94] 95-106 [107] 108-121 [122] 123-36 [137] 138-53 [154] 155-69 [170] 171-84 [185] 186-96 [197] 198-209 [210] 211-25 [226] 227-40 [241] 242-51 [252-56]

Page contents: [1] half-title: 'HARRY | POTTER | &THE [reading lengthways up title-page] CHAMBER OF SECRETS'; [2] *'Titles available in the Harry Potter series | (in reading order):* | Harry Potter and the Philosopher's Stone | Harry Potter and the Chamber of Secrets | Harry Potter and the Prisoner of Azkaban | Harry Potter and the Goblet of Fire | Harry Potter and the Order of the Phoenix | Harry Potter and the Half-Blood Prince | Harry Potter and the Deathly Hallows | [new paragraph] *Titles available in the Harry Potter series | (in Latin):* | Harry Potter and the Philosopher's Stone | Harry Potter and the Chamber of Secrets |

(in Welsh, Ancient Greek and Irish): | Harry Potter and the Philosopher's Stone | [new paragraph] *Also available* | *(in aid of Comic Relief):* | Fantastic Beasts and Where to Find Them | Quidditch Through the Ages | *(in aid of Lumos):* | The Tales of Beedle the Bard'; [3] title-page; [4] 'All rights reserved; no part of this publication may be reproduced or | transmitted by any means, electronic, mechanical, photocopying | or otherwise, without the prior permission of the publisher | [new paragraph] First published in Great Britain in 1998 by Bloomsbury Publishing Plc | 50 Bedford Square, London WC1B 3DP | [new paragraph] Bloomsbury Publishing, London, New Delhi, New York and Sydney | [new paragraph] This paperback edition first published in 2013 | [new paragraph] Copyright © J.K. Rowling 1998 | Cover illustrations by Andrew Davidson copyright © J.K. Rowling 2013 | [new paragraph] Harry Potter, names, characters and related indicia are | copyright and trademark Warner Bros., 2000™ | [new paragraph] The moral right of the author has been asserted | A CIP catalogue record for this book is available from the British Library | [new paragraph] ISBN 978 1 4088 3497 8 | [new paragraph] [Forest Stewardship Council logo, 6 by 7mm together with ® symbol and text: 'FSC | www.fsc.org' with 'MIX | Paper from | responsible sources | FSC® C020471' to the right and all within single ruled border with rounded corners, 12 by 26mm] | [new paragraph] Typeset by Dorchester Typesetting | Printed and bound in Great Britain by CPI Group (UK) Ltd, Croydon CR0 4YY | [new paragraph] 1 3 5 7 9 10 8 6 4 2 | [new paragraph] | www.bloomsbury.com/harrypotter'; [5] 'For Séan P. F. Harris, | *getaway driver and foulweather friend*'; [6] blank; [7]-251 text; [252-56] blank

Paper: wove paper

Running title: 'HARRY POTTER' (24mm) on verso, recto title comprises chapter title, pp. 8-251

Binding: pictorial wrappers.

   On spine: 'J.K. ROWLING [in white] HARRY POTTER [in burgundy] &THE [in white] CHAMBER OF SECRETS [in burgundy] [publisher's device of a figure with a bow, 8 by 6mm] [in white]' (reading lengthways down spine with the exception of '&THE' and the publisher's device which are horizontal). All on green.

   On upper wrapper: 'J.K. [in white] | ROWLING [in white] [reading lengthways down upper wrapper] | HARRY [in green] | POTTER [in green] | &THE [in white] [reading lengthways up upper wrapper] CHAMBER OF SECRETS [in green] | BLOOMSBURY [in white]' (author and final part of title justified on right margin, first part of title justified on left margin, publisher with publisher's offices width centred). All on light and dark red illustration of Hogwarts castle viewed through forest foliage.

   On lower wrapper: 'Harry Potter receives an ominous warning from a house-elf | at Hogwarts School of Witchcraft and Wizardry: if he | returns to the school at the end of the summer, terrible things | will happen. But return Harry must. | [new paragraph] His second year begins with a new Defence Against the Dark | Arts teacher, Quidditch training and the intensification of old | rivalries. Then the warning starts to ring true, as mysterious | words are daubed on a wall, students are attached and Ron's | sister, Ginny, disappears. And so the search for Salazar | Slytherin's heir begins, with the mystery pointing Harry to a | clandestine chamber and a deadly creature at its heart… | [new paragraph] [section of white illustration of Hogwarts castle and foliage, 55 by 111mm] | BLOOMSBURY www. bloomsbury.com/harrypotter www.pottermore.com £7.99 [in black] | [section of white illustration of Hogwarts castle and foliage, 26 by 111mm upon which: Forest Stewardship Council logo, 5 by 6mm together with ® symbol and text: 'FSC | www.fsc.org | MIX | Paper from | responsible sources | FSC® C020471' all in black on white panel with rounded corners, 19 by 12mm, with barcode in black on white panel, 18 by 38mm, with 'Designed by Webb & Webb Design | Cover illustrations by Andrew Davidson | copyright © J.K. Rowling 2013' in black on green panel, 9 by 38mm]'. Lines 1-11 in white and all on green. The initial capital 'H' of 'Harry' is a drop capital and is printed in burgundy.

On inside upper wrapper: green and white illustration of Hogwarts castle viewed through forest foliage.

On inside lower wrapper: green and white illustration of foliage and tree trunk.

All edges trimmed. Binding measurements: 198 by 128mm (wrappers), 198 by 15mm (spine).

Publication: 18 July 2013 in an edition of 57,200 copies (confirmed by Bloomsbury) (see notes)

Price: £7.99

Contents:
Harry Potter and the Chamber of Secrets
('Not for the first time, an argument had broken out over breakfast at number four…')

Notes:
The illustrations by Andrew Davidson derive from a single wood engraving. A single illustration is presented on both the upper wrapper and inside upper wrapper. A section is printed on the lower wrapper. A detail from the upper wrapper is shown on the inside lower wrapper.

Although Bloomsbury's 'official' publication date was 18 July 2013, copies were available from amazon.co.uk at the beginning of July.

Copies: private collection (PWE)

A2(q)   AMERICAN CHILDREN'S EDITION   (2013)
(Kazu Kibuishi artwork in paperback)

HARRY POTTER | AND THE CHAMBER OF SECRETS | [black and white illustration of doorway with carved snakes on surrounding pillars, 49 by 66mm] | BY | J. K. ROWLING | ILLUSTRATIONS BY MARY GRANDPRÉ | SCHOLASTIC INC. (All width centred on a diamond pattern background)

Collation: 184 unsigned leaves bound in indeterminate gatherings; 204 by 134mm; [I-IV] V-VI [VII-VIII] 1-341 [342-60]

Page contents: [I-II] 'PRAISE FOR J. K. ROWLING'S | HARRY POTTER | AND THE CHAMBER OF SECRETS | [device of nine stars] | [7 reviews and a listing of 7 statements]'; [III] title-page; [IV] 'FOR SEÁN P. F. HARRIS, | GETAWAY DRIVER AND FOUL-WEATHER FRIEND | [device of twelve stars] | Text © 1998 by J. K. Rowling | Interior illustrations by Mary GrandPré © 1999 by Warner Bros. | Excerpt from *Harry Potter and the Prisoner of Azkaban*, text © 1999 by J. K. Rowling; | illustration by Mary GrandPré © 1999 by Warner Bros. | Cover illustration by Kazu Kibuishi © 2013 by Scholastic Inc. | HARRY POTTER and all related characters and elements are TM of and © WBEI. | Harry Potter Publishing Rights © J. K. Rowling | All rights reserved. Published by Scholastic Inc. SCHOLASTIC, the LANTERN LOGO, and associated | logos are trademarks and/or registered trademarks of Scholastic Inc. | [new paragraph] If you purchased this book without a cover, you should be aware that this

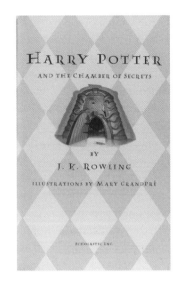

book is stolen property. | It was reported as "unsold and destroyed" to the publisher, and neither the author nor the | publisher has received any payment for this "stripped book." | [new paragraph] No part of this publication may be reproduced, stored in a retrieval system, or transmitted in any | form or by any means, electronic, mechanical, photocopying, recording, or otherwise, without | written permission of the publisher. For information regarding permission, write to Scholastic Inc., | Attention: Permissions Department, 557 Broadway, New York, NY 10012. | [new paragraph] [publisher's device of a lantern, 6 by 4mm] | Arthur A. Levine Books hardcover edition art directed by David Saylor, | published by Arthur A. Levine Books, an imprint of Scholastic Inc., June 1999. | [new paragraph] ISBN 978-0-545-58292-6 | [new paragraph] Library of Congress Control Number: 98-46370 | [new paragraph] 12 11 10 9 8 7 6 5 4 3 2 1   13 14 15 16 17 | [new paragraph] Printed in the U.S.A. 40 | This edition first printing, September 2013 | [new paragraph] We try to produce the most beautiful books possible, and we are extremely concerned about the impact of our | manufacturing process on the forests of the world and the environment as a whole. Accordingly, we made sure | that the text paper contains a minimum of 30% post-consumer waste, and that all the paper has been certified as | coming from forests that are managed to insure the protection of the people and wildlife dependent upon them.'; V-VI 'CONTENTS' (eighteen chapters listed with titles and page references); [VII] half-title: 'HARRY POTTER | AND THE CHAMBER OF SECRETS' (all on diamond pattern background); [VIII] blank; 1-341 text; [342] blank; [343] 'HARRY POTTER'S | ADVENTURES CONTINUE IN | [new paragraph] HARRY POTTER | AND THE PRISONER OF AZKABAN | [new paragraph] TURN THE PAGE FOR | A SNEAK PREVIEW!' (all on diamond pattern background); [344] blank; [345-55] text; [356] advertisement for Pottermore; [357] '[black and white photograph of J.K. Rowling seated by curtains, credited 'ANDREW MONTGOMERY' reading lengthways up right margin] | [new paragraph] J. K. ROWLING is the author of the beloved, | bestselling, record-breaking Harry Potter series. She started writing | the series during a delayed Manchester to London King's Cross | train journey, and during the next five years, outlined the plots for | each book and began writing the first novel. *Harry Potter and the | Sorcerer's Stone* was published in the United States by Arthur A. | Levine Books in 1998, and the series concluded nearly ten years | later with *Harry Potter and the Deathly Hallows*, published in 2007. | J. K. Rowling is the recipient of numerous awards and honorary | degrees, including an OBE for services to children's literature, | France's Légion d'honneur, and the Hans Christian Andersen | Literature Award. She supports a wide number of causes through | her charitable trust, Volant, and is the founder of Lumos, a charity | working to transform the lives of disadvantaged children. J. K. | Rowling lives in Edinburgh with her husband and three children.'; [358] blank; [359] 'MARY GRANDPRÉ has illustrated more than twenty | beautiful books for children, including the American editions of | the Harry Potter novels. Her work has also appeared in the *New* | *Yorker*, the *Atlantic Monthly*, and the *Wall Street Journal*, and her | paintings and pastels have been shown in galleries across the United | States. Ms. GrandPré lives in Sarasota, Florida, with her family. | [new paragraph] KAZU KIBUISHI is the creator of the *New York Times* | bestselling Amulet series and *Copper*, a collection of his popular | webcomic. He is also the founder and editor of the acclaimed | Flight anthologies. *Daisy Kutter: The Last Train*, his first graphic | novel, was listed as one of the Best Books for Young Adults by | YALSA, and *Amulet, Book One: The Stonekeeper* was an ALA Best | Book for Young Adults and a Children's Choice Book Award | finalist. Kazu lives and works in Alhambra, California, with his | wife and fellow comics artist, Amy Kim Kibuishi, and their two | children. Visit Kazu online at www.boltcity.com.'; [360] blank

Paper: wove paper

Running title: 'CHAPTER' and chapter number on verso, recto title comprises chapter title, pp. 1-341 and pp. [345-55]. Each running title (excluding pages on which new chapters commence) includes a three-star design to left and right of both running-titles on verso and recto. On pages on which a new chapter commences, the three-star design is omitted.

Illustrations: title-page vignette, together with eighteen vignettes at the beginning of each chapter (after chapter and chapter number but before chapter title). The 'sneak preview' also includes a vignette. In addition to standard typographical changes (including italics, capitals and small capitals) there are other typographical features, comprising:

   p. 21 facsimile of Mafalda Hopkirk's signature
   p. 127 course description and students' endorsements
   p. 221 newspaper headline
   p. [352] newspaper headline
   p. [354] facsimile of Ron's signature (repeated twice)
   p. [355] facsimile of Hermione's signature

Binding: pictorial wrappers.
   On spine: 'ROWLING | Harry Potter and the Chamber of Secrets [reading lengthways down spine] | 2' and '[publisher's book device] | [rule] | S' in white on red panel, 14 by 6mm. All in white on colour illustration (see notes).
   On upper wrapper: 'J. K. ROWLING | Harry Potter [hand-drawn lettering] [embossed in white] | and the | Chamber of Secrets' (all width centred). All in white on colour illustration of Harry Potter with Ron Weasley in a flying Ford Anglia, driven by Fred Weasley, approaching the Weasleys' house. In centre at foot: '[publisher's book device] SCHOLASTIC' in white on red panel, 5 by 45mm.

On lower wrapper: "'This diary holds memories of terrible things. Things | that were covered up. Things that happened at Hogwarts | School of Witchcraft and Wizardry." | — Tom Marvolo Riddle | [new paragraph] Harry's second year at Hogwarts is rife with fresh torments and horrors, | including an outrageously stuck-up new professor, Gilderoy Lockhart, | a spirit named Moaning Myrtle who haunts the girls' bathroom, and the | unwanted attentions of Ron Weasley's younger sister, Ginny. | [new paragraph] But these seem minor when the real trouble begins, and someone — or | something — starts turning Hogwarts students to stone. Could it be | Draco Malfoy, a more poisonous rival than ever? Could it possibly be Hagrid, | whose mysterious past is finally revealed? Or could it be the one everyone at | Hogwarts most suspects ... Harry Potter himself! | [new paragraph] $12.99 US | [new paragraph] [publisher's book device with 'SCHOLASTIC' in white on red panel, 5 by 45mm] | www.scholastic.com | COVER DESIGN BY KAZU KIBUISHI AND JASON CAFFOE | COVER ART BY KAZU KIBUISHI © 2013 BY SCHOLASTIC INC.' Lines 1-4 in white with other lines in light blue and all on colour illustration of Harry standing before a giant statue flanked by serpentine columns. In lower right: barcode with smaller barcode to the right (51299) together with 'S' within triangle, all in black on white panel, 21 by 53mm.

On inside upper wrapper: barcode with smaller barcode (51299) together with 'S' within triangle below, all in black on white panel, 53 by 21mm. All on orange brown.

On inside lower wrapper: '[colour illustration of book design] Harry Potter [hand-drawn lettering] [in white] | The Complete Series [in white] | Read All of Harry's [in white] | Magical Adventures! [in white] | [publisher's device of a lantern, 10 by 7mm] [in black] | ARTHUR A. LEVINE BOOKS [in black] | [publisher's book device with 'SCHOLASTIC' in white on red panel, 5 by 45mm] | scholastic.com/harrypotter [in white] | [colour illustrations in three columns of six book designs]'. All on lavender blue.

All edges trimmed. Binding measurements: 204 by 134mm (wrappers), 204 by 17mm (spine).

Publication: 27 August 2013

Price: $12.99

Contents:

Harry Potter and the Chamber of Secrets

('Not for the first time, an argument had broken out over breakfast at number four...')

Notes:

See notes to A4(h) about this series.

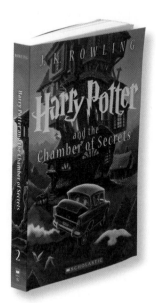

The seven volumes in this edition were available individually or as a set issued in a slipcase. The set, presented in order, reveals a single illustration of Hogwarts castle across the seven spines. Scholastic released images of the new illustrations in a careful marketing campaign: the upper wrapper illustration for *Chamber of Secrets* was unveiled on 30 May 2013 at the Book Expo America in New York.

The 'sneak preview' of *Prisoner of Azkaban* comprises only the first 11 (of 15) pages of chapter one. This, therefore, fails to provide the conclusion of Hermione's letter to Harry.

Each chapter commences with a drop capital.

Copies: private collection (PWE)

A2(r) ENGLISH 'THE MAGICAL ADVENTURE BEGINS…' EDITION (2013)
(line drawn artwork in paperback)

HARRY | POTTER | AND THE | CHAMBER OF | SECRETS | J.K. ROWLING | [publisher's device of a figure with a bow, 10 by 9mm] | BLOOMSBURY | LONDON NEW DELHI NEW YORK SYDNEY (All width centred and within broken single ruled border, 183 by 114mm)

Collation: 128 unsigned leaves bound in indeterminate gatherings; 198 by 128mm; [1-7] 8-14 [15] 16-23 [24] 25-36 [37] 38-52 [53] 54-67 [68] 69-80 [81] 82-93 [94] 95-106 [107] 108-121 [122] 123-36 [137] 138-53 [154] 155-69 [170] 171-84 [185] 186-96 [197] 198-209 [210] 211-25 [226] 227-40 [241] 242-51 [252-56]

Page contents: [1] half-title: 'HARRY | POTTER | AND THE | CHAMBER OF | SECRETS' (all within broken single ruled border, 183 by 114mm); [2] *Titles available in the Harry Potter series* | *(in reading order):* | Harry Potter and the Philosopher's Stone | Harry Potter and the Chamber of Secrets | Harry Potter and the Prisoner of Azkaban | Harry Potter and the Goblet of Fire | Harry Potter and the Order of the Phoenix | Harry Potter and the Half-Blood Prince | Harry Potter and the Deathly Hallows | [new paragraph] *Titles available in the Harry Potter series* | *(in Latin):* | Harry Potter and the Philosopher's Stone | Harry Potter and the Chamber of Secrets | *(in Welsh, Ancient Greek and Irish):* | Harry Potter and the Philosopher's Stone | [new paragraph] *Also available* | *(in aid of Comic Relief):* | Fantastic Beasts and Where to Find Them | Quidditch Through the Ages | *(in aid of Lumos):* | The Tales of Beedle the Bard'; [3] title-page; [4] 'All rights reserved; no part of this publication may be reproduced or | transmitted by any means, electronic, mechanical, photocopying | or otherwise, without the prior permission of the publisher | [new paragraph] First published in Great Britain in 1998 by Bloomsbury Publishing Plc | 50 Bedford Square, London WC1B 3DP | [new paragraph] Bloomsbury Publishing, London, New Delhi, New York and Sydney | [new paragraph] This paperback edition first published in 2013 | [new paragraph] Copyright © J.K. Rowling 1998 | [new paragraph] Harry Potter, names, characters and related indicia are | copyright and trademark Warner Bros., 2000™ | [new paragraph] The moral right of the author has been asserted | A CIP catalogue record for this book is available from the British Library | [new paragraph] ISBN 978 1 4088 4993 4 | [new paragraph] [Forest Stewardship Council logo, 6 by 7mm together with ® symbol and text: 'FSC | www.fsc.org' with 'MIX | Paper from | responsible sources | FSC® C020471' to the right and all within single ruled border with rounded corners, 12 by 26mm] | [new paragraph] Typeset by Dorchester Typesetting | Printed and bound in Great Britain by CPI Group (UK) Ltd, Croydon CR0 4YY | [new paragraph] 1 3 5 7 9 10 8 6 4 2 | [new paragraph] | www.bloomsbury.com/harrypotter | www.pottermore.com'; [5] 'For Séan P. F. Harris, | *getaway driver and foulweather friend*'; [6] blank; [7]-251 text; [252-56] blank

Paper: wove paper

Running title: 'HARRY POTTER' (24mm) on verso, recto title comprises chapter title, pp. 8-251

Binding: pictorial wrappers.
   On spine: '[triple rule] HARRY POTTER AND THE CHAMBER OF SECRETS J.K. ROWLING [publisher's device of a figure with a bow, 9 by 8mm] [triple rule]' (reading lengthways down spine with rules and publisher's device horizontally at head or foot of spine). All in gilt on blue.
   On upper wrapper: 'HARRY | POTTER | AND THE | CHAMBER OF | SECRETS | [illustration of a snake] | J.K. ROWLING | BLOOMSBURY' all width centred and within broken single ruled border, 183 by 114mm. All in gilt on blue.
   On lower wrapper: '[illustration of a snake] | [new paragraph] Harry Potter receives an ominous warning from | a house-elf at Hogwarts School of Witchcraft and | Wizardry: if he returns to the school at the end | of the summer, terrible things will happen. | But return Harry must. | [new paragraph] His second year begins with a new Defence Against | the Dark Arts teacher, Quidditch training and | the intensification of old rivalries. Then the warning | starts to ring true, as mysterious words are daubed | on a wall, students are attached and Ron's sister, | Ginny, disappears. And so the search for Salazar | Slytherin's heir begins, with the mystery pointing | Harry to a clandestine chamber and a deadly | creature at its heart ... | [new paragraph] [barcodes together with '[Forest Stewardship Council logo, 5 by 6mm together with ® symbol] | FSC | www.fsc.org | MIX | Paper from | responsible sources | FSC® C020471' within single ruled border with rounded corners, 18 by 12mm together with '[publisher's device of a figure with a bow, 8 by 7mm] | BLOOMSBURY | www.bloomsbury.com/ harrypotter | www.pottermore.com', all in black on white panel, 23 by 84mm] | [new paragraph] Cover illustration by Joe McLaren' all within broken single ruled border, 183 by 114mm. All in yellow on blue.

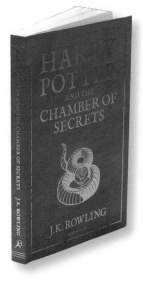

   All edges trimmed. Binding measurements: 198 by 128mm (wrappers), 198 by 15mm (spine).

Slipcase: card slipcase covered in blue paper (see A1(m))

Publication: 10 October 2013 in an edition of 42,700 copies (confirmed by Bloomsbury)

Price: £21 [together with A1(m) and A7(o)]

Contents:
Harry Potter and the Chamber of Secrets
   ('Not for the first time, an argument had broken out over breakfast at number four...')

Notes:
Published as a boxed set of three volumes comprising A1(m), A2(r) and A7(o). Individual volumes were not available separately. Bloomsbury announced the set stating: 'Every great story has a great beginning – and this is where Harry Potter's extraordinary, magical adventure starts... Harry Potter is a milestone in every child's reading life and this gorgeous, collectable boxed set is the perfect introduction for new readers, wizard and Muggle alike.'

Copies: private collection (PWE)

THE DAILY PROPHET – 31 JULY 1998

A3(a)   **FIRST ENGLISH EDITION**   **(1998)**

Banner:
July 31ˢᵗ 1998 The Daily Prophet Price: 7 Knuts
(All within single ruled border, 15 by 157mm)

Collation: 3 single leaves with staple upper left corner; 297 by 211mm; [1] 2-3

Page contents: [1] Headlines section; 2 Quidditch section; 3 Letters page

Paper: wove paper

Running title: *'The Daily Prophet'* (33mm) and *'July 31ˢᵗ 1998'* (23mm); the page number occurs in the middle of this running title on p. 3 only

Publication: 31 July 1998

Price: issued as part of membership of the Harry Potter Fan Club (membership fee: £4.25 per year)

Contents:
[Headlines section, p. 1]
Muggles Not as Stupid as We Think, Says Ministry Report
('A long-awaited Ministry for Magic report made public today warns…')
Faulty Wands Recalled
('The Department of Magical Equipment Control has issued a warning…')
[Advert]
('Madam Malkin's Robes for All Occasions…')

[Quidditch section, p. 2]
Quidditch League Table & Match Information
('1. Tutshill Tornados…')
Cannons Go Down in a Shower of Arrows
('The Chudley Cannons, who have been having their worst season…')
Magpie Chaser "Only Tried Football for a Laugh"
('Embarrassed Alasdair Maddock, Chaser for the Montrose Magpies, admitted…')
Puddlemere United
('United will be changing the design of their robes…')
Holyhead Harpies Draw Record Crowd
('The only all-witch team currently playing in the Quidditch league…')

[Letters page, p. 3]
Star Letter
    ('Dear Sir, | As a law-abiding member of the magical community...')
Gripe with Gringott's Bank
    ('Dear Sir, | Am I alone in wondering why Gringott's Bank has recently...')
Gobstones Tournament Overlooked (together with 'Our editor writes')
    ('Dear Sir, | As a member of the Welsh National Gobstones Team...')
A Word in Support of Hags
    ('Dear Sir, | I am sick and tired of reading what horrible creatures hags are...')
Merlin Remembrance Day Suggestion (together with 'Our editor writes')
    ('Dear Sir, | Is it not time that the wizarding community set aside a day...')
[Notice]
    ('Please send your letters by owl to: The Daily Prophet...')

Notes:
A copyright note at the foot of page 2 ascribes copyright to J.K. Rowling.

There are six sections presented within ruled borders: 'Madam Malkin's Robes for all Occasions' advert (64 by 48mm), contents banner (4 by 62mm), 'Quidditch League Table & Match Information' (65 by 157mm), 'Letters Page' banner (13 by 67mm), 'Star Letter' (122 by 71mm) and 'Please send your letters by owl...' (15 by 36mm).

There were four issues of *The Daily Prophet*, dated as follows:
    31 July 1998 – A3(a)
    8 February 1998 – A5(a)
    1 June 1999 – A6(a)
    1 October 1999 – A6(a)

Copies: private collection

HARRY POTTER AND THE SORCERER'S STONE

A4(a)   **FIRST AMERICAN EDITION**   (1998)
               (children's artwork series in hardback)

HARRY POTTER | AND THE SORCERER'S STONE | [black and white illustration of Hogwarts castle, in oval, 52 by 87mm] | BY | J.K. ROWLING | ILLUSTRATIONS BY MARY GRANDPRÉ | [publisher's device of a lantern, 12 by 9mm] | ARTHUR A. LEVINE BOOKS | AN IMPRINT OF SCHOLASTIC PRESS (All width centred on a diamond pattern background)

Collation: 160 unsigned leaves bound in ten gatherings of sixteen leaves; 228 by 148mm; [I-IV] V-VI [VII-VIIII] 1-309 [310-312]

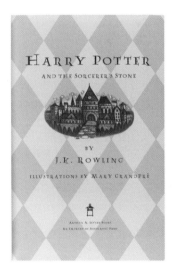

Page contents: [I] half-title: 'HARRY POTTER | AND THE SORCERER'S STONE' (all on diamond pattern background); [II] blank; [III] title-page; [IV] 'FOR JESSICA, WHO LOVES STORIES, | FOR ANNE, WHO LOVED THEM TOO; | AND FOR DI, WHO HEARD THIS ONE FIRST. | [device of twelve stars] | Text copyright © 1997 by J.K. Rowling | Illustrations copyright © 1998 by Mary GrandPré | All rights reserved. Published by Scholastic Press, a division of Scholastic Inc., | *Publishers since 1920* | by arrangement with Bloomsbury Publishing Plc. | SCHOLASTIC, SCHOLASTIC PRESS, ARTHUR A. LEVINE BOOKS, and associated logos | are trademarks and/or registered trademarks of Scholastic Inc. | [new paragraph] No part of this publication may be reproduced, or stored in a retrieval system, or transmitted | in any form or by any means, electronic, mechanical, photocopying, recording, or otherwise, | without written permission of the publisher. For information regarding permissions, write | to Scholastic Inc., Attention: Permissions Department, 555 Broadway, New York, NY 10012. | [new paragraph] Library of Congress Cataloging-in-Publication Data | [new paragraph] Rowling, J.K. | Harry Potter and the Sorcerer's Stone / by J.K. Rowling | p. cm. | Summary: Rescued from the outrageous neglect of his aunt and uncle, a young boy | with a great destiny proves his worth while attending Hogwarts School | of Witchcraft and Wizardry. | ISBN 0-590-35340-3 | [square bracket]1. Fantasy — Fiction. 2. Witches — Fiction. 3. Wizards — Fiction. | 4. Schools — Fiction. 5. England — Fiction.[square bracket] I. Title. | PZ7.R79835Har 1998 | [square bracket]Fic[square bracket] — dc21 97-39059 | [new paragraph] 1 3 5 7 9 10 8 6 4 2   8 9/9 0/0 01 02 | Printed in the U.S.A. 23 | First American edition, October 1998'; V-VI 'CONTENTS' (seventeen chapters listed with titles and page references); [VII] half-title: 'HARRY

POTTER | AND THE SORCERER'S STONE' (all on diamond pattern background); [VIII] blank; 1-309 text; [310] blank; [311] colophon: '[publisher's device of a lantern, 17 by 13mm] | *This book* | *was art directed by* | *David Saylor and designed by Becky* | *Terhune. The art for both the jacket and interior was* | *created using pastels on toned printmaking paper. The text was* | *set in 12-point Adobe Garamond, a typeface based on the sixteenth-* | *century type designs of Claude Garamond, redrawn by Robert* | *Slimbach in 1989. The book was printed and bound* | *at Berryville Graphics in Berryville, Virginia.* | *The production was supervised by* | *Angela Biola and Mike* | *Derevjanik.*'; [312] blank

Paper: wove paper

Running title: 'CHAPTER' and chapter number on verso, recto title comprises chapter title, pp. 1-309. Each running title (excluding pages on which new chapters commence) includes a three-star design to left and right of both running-titles on verso and recto. On pages on which a new chapter commences, the three-star design is omitted.

Illustrations: title-page vignette, together with seventeen vignettes at the beginning of each chapter (after chapter and chapter number but before chapter title). In addition to standard typographical changes (including italics, capitals and small capitals) there are other typographical features, comprising:

- p. 34 'handwritten' envelope address
- p. 42 'handwritten' envelope address
- p. 51 facsimile of Minerva McGonagall's signature
- p. 52 'handwritten' letter
- pp. 135-36 'handwritten' letter
- p. 141 newspaper headline
- p. 164 facsimile of Minerva McGonagall's signature [different from that above]
- p. 202 'handwritten' letter
- p. 247 facsimile of Minerva McGonagall's signature [as on p. 164]
- p. 261 'handwritten' note

Binding: red cloth-backed spine with purple boards (with diamond pattern in blind).

On spine: 'J. K. | ROWLING | [rule]' (horizontally at head) with 'HARRY POTTER | AND THE SORCERER'S STONE' (reading lengthways down spine) and '[publisher's device of a lantern, 17 by 13mm] | ARTHUR A. | LEVINE BOOKS | [rule] | SCHOLASTIC | PRESS' (horizontally at foot). All in gilt.

Upper and lower covers: blank.

All edges trimmed. Binding measurements: 235 by 150mm (covers), 235 by 40mm (spine). The red cloth continues onto the covers by 39mm. End-papers: green wove paper.

Dust-jacket: uncoated wove paper, 235 by 555mm. A single illustration spans the entire dust-jacket.

On spine: 'J. K. | ROWLING | [rule]' (horizontally at head) with 'HARRY POTTER | AND THE SORCERER'S STONE' (reading lengthways down spine) and '[publisher's device of a lantern, 19 by 15mm] | ARTHUR A. | LEVINE BOOKS | [rule] | SCHOLASTIC | PRESS' (horizontally at foot). All in gilt on colour illustration of archway.

On upper cover: 'Harry Potter [hand-drawn lettering] [embossed in gilt] | AND THE [hand-drawn lettering in brown of illustration] | SORCERER'S STONE [hand-drawn lettering in brown of illustration] | J. K. ROWLING [in gilt]' (all width centred); all on colour illustration of Harry Potter playing Quidditch.

On lower cover: '"HARRY POTTER | could assume the same near-legendary status as | Roald Dahl's Charlie, of chocolate factory fame." | — *The Guardian*, London | [barcode with smaller barcode to the right (51695) all in black on cream panel, 22 by 51mm]'. All in black on colour illustration of owl, key and shrouded wizard hiding behind column.

On upper inside flap: '$16.95 | HARRY POTTER | has never been the star of a Quidditch team, | scoring points while riding a broom far above | the ground. He knows no spells, has never | helped to hatch a dragon, and has never worn a | cloak of invisibility. | [new paragraph] All he knows is a miserable life with the | Dursleys, his horrible aunt and uncle, and | their abominable son, Dudley—a great big | swollen spoiled bully. Harry's room is a | tiny closet at the foot of the stairs, and he | hasn't had a birthday party in eleven | years. | [new paragraph] But all that is about to change when | a mysterious letter arrives by owl mes- | senger: a letter with an invitation to | an incredible place that Harry— | and anyone who reads about | him—will find un- | forgettable. | [new paragraph] For it's there that he | finds not only friends, | aerial sports, and magic in | everything from classes to | meals, but a great destiny | that's been waiting for him… | if Harry can survive the | encounter.' All in black on colour illustration of a curtain with hand holding a lit candle.

On lower inside flap: 'J.K. ROWLING | was a struggling single mother when she wrote | the beginnings of *Harry Potter and the Sorcerer's* | *Stone* on scraps of paper at a local café. But her | efforts soon paid off, as she received an unprece- | dented award from the Scottish Arts Council | enabling her to finish the book. Since then, the | debut novel has become an international phe- | nomenon, garnering rave reviews and major | awards, including the British Book Awards | Children's Book of the Year, and the Smarties | Prize. | [new paragraph] Ms. Rowling lives in Edinburgh with her | daughter. | [new paragraph] *Jacket art © 1998 by Mary GrandPré* | *Jacket design by Mary GrandPré and David Saylor* | [new paragraph] | [publisher's device of a lantern, 12 by 9mm] | ARTHUR A. LEVINE BOOKS | *An Imprint of Scholastic Press* | 555 Broadway, New York, | New York 10012'. All in black on colour illustration of a curtain.

Publication: October 1998 (see notes)

Price: $16.95

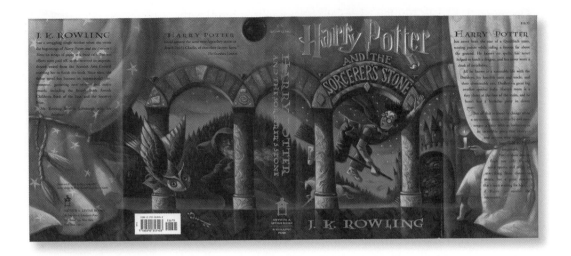

Contents:

Harry Potter and the Sorcerer's Stone

   ('Mr. and Mrs. Dursley, of number four, Privet Drive, were proud to say…')

Notes:

In an interview with me in March 2012, the publisher Arthur A. Levine explained that he had first heard about Harry Potter at the Bologna book fair in March 1997. He stated 'I was just starting my imprint – so this was my first Bologna as Arthur A. Levine Books – and this was going to be a literary imprint and so I was meeting with all of my pals in the literary world seeing what I could draw from them. In particular I wanted my imprint to be the best of the world's literature for American readers. So I met with Bloomsbury, which at that point was a tiny literary start-up, and I met with their rights director. She talked to me about a bunch of projects which didn't seem right at all. Then she said, "so what is it that you are looking for if none of those things are quite right?" And I said, "I just really want one of those books that would be a classic: the kind of book you would look back on from your adulthood and say 'that was the book that I loved – I still have it on my shelf'." And she said, "I think we have one of those coming up, but it hasn't been published and we don't have the rights".'

   Levine finds it significant that he was told about the book even though Bloomsbury didn't have the rights to sell themselves: '… that is what happens at a book fair like Bologna. People who have overlapping tastes will tell each other about books which they think are wonderful or authors who they think are exciting'. A set of galley proofs of the book was provided which Levine devoured.

   Having returned to the United States, Levine contacted the Christopher Little Agency. He was told that there were other publishers interested and an auction for the American rights would be forthcoming. This was sometime in the Spring of 1997 before publication of the English edition. An auction was held, with Christopher Little talking to interested publishers on the phone. Levine states 'I believe there were seven other publishers and after a few rounds it was just me and one other… I know that, in the end, my bid was only $5,000 more than the other publisher at $105,000…' Asked (once again) why he was the highest bidder, Levine stated quite simply that 'I knew that I loved that book'. Levine notes that he did not know that he would make back his money right away and felt that this was a long-term investment.

The publication of *Sorcerer's Stone* in the US, compared to the English title *Philosopher's Stone*, 'confuses people' in the words of Arthur A. Levine. He states '… what confuses people is that people think I bought it'. The reality is that Levine identified the book, loved it and bought the US rights long before the Harry Potter craze took off in the UK. Levine does note, however, that Bloomsbury's enthusiasm for the book was infectious.

Early criticism was directed at Levine for changes that were made to the author's English prose. There were around 80 word changes and some significant alteration in the placing of commas. When questioned, in March 2012, he responded that 'I did not *do* anything to the text. Every change was something that I discussed with Jo. In fact, Jo came up with the alternative title of *Sorcerer's Stone*… It's one of the most common conversations that you have in a publishing company with a writer. The conversation goes something like this: "I presented this to the sales and marketing department and they feel that the title doesn't do *this*… So let's consider alternatives". Of course if the author says "no absolutely not – that's my title" then that's the title that goes on the book. It's a simple matter. But authors are professional people and sometimes just changing the title gives the sales and marketing department a degree of confidence that helps your book.' Levine noted that he needed a title that said 'magic' more overtly to American readers. He continued, 'I certainly did not mind *Harry Potter and the Philosopher's Stone* but I can see, if you forget now what happened after, …why a book that is titled *Philosopher's Stone* might seem more arcane or something. So the title that I had suggested to me and which I then turned to Jo was *Harry Potter and the School of Magic*. Jo very thoughtfully said "No – that doesn't feel right to me… there are objects that I would like. What if we called it the *Sorcerer's Stone?*" And that completely does it. But I would like to point you to the French title of the first book which is *Harry Potter et l'ecole de Sorcerer*.'

Levine noted that the print-run was exceptional: 'I think initially we printed 35,000 copies of the first book. We went into our sales conference with a proposed print run of 15,000 which, in itself, would have been a confident run. Memory runs short and people don't remember that in 1997 there was a notion that you couldn't sell hardcover fiction and especially British fantasy. I didn't go into it thinking this is a blockbuster. I thought this is something of such special and unique quality that people will love it. I was right. Going into the sales conference there was such passion among our sales reps… The enthusiasm from within our sales force was so great that it immediately pushed it up into this very, very large print-run.'

Although no publication day is recorded, 1 October 1998 is assumed. In an email to me from January 2013 Arthur A. Levine noted that 'I'm fairly certain that we didn't have strict "on sale" dates… the publication "day" would simply be the first of the month listed.' Nielsen BookData provides a publication date of 1 October 1998.

In contrast to the first English editions, Scholastic used the artwork of a single illustrator across the series: Mary GrandPré. To Levine this is part of the image and branding of the series. He noted '… I have always said this is a classic book. This is a book that you remember when you're thirty-five and you remember when you were ten. And that was the book that changed your life. There's continuity there – when you see that on your shelf you think, wow this is that book …'

The first American edition omits 'Year | 1' on the spine and the spine of the dust-jacket. The dust-jacket also notes a price of $16.95. There are two states of the dust-jacket reported. The first state includes a quote from *The Guardian* on the lower cover. The second state (not seen) replaces this with a quote from *Publishers Weekly*. This may be a confusion with the book club edition (see A4(c)). The only embossed gilt on the dust-jacket is for the hand-drawn lettering of 'Harry Potter' on the upper cover. Other gilt lettering is not raised.

The facsimile of Minerva McGonagall's signature on page 247 is first printed here. It is missing in the American proof where the 'signature' is rendered in standard type. Note, also, that the colophon is different from that in the American proof (see AA3(a)).

A presentation copy inscribed by the author to her father and stepmother was offered at auction at Sotheby's New York on 10 December 2003. It was inscribed on the half-title 'To Jan and Dad | with lots of love | Jo x'. Estimated at $25,000/35,000, it failed to sell.

During January 1999, the *New York Times* listed the book in their best-sellers lists with the description 'a Scottish boy, neglected by his relatives, finds his fortune attending a school of witchcraft' and also 'a Scottish boy attends witchcraft school'. A slight improvement on accuracy saw this changed quickly to 'a British boy'.

Each chapter commences with a drop capital.

The American audiobook version, read by Jim Dale, has a duration of approximately eight and a quarter hours.

Copies: New York Public Library (J FIC R); private collection

Reprints include:

30 29 28 27 26 25 24 23 22 21	9/9 0/0 01 02	Printed in the U.S.A.	37
35 34 33 32 31 30 29 28 27 26	9/9 0/0 01 02	Printed in the U.S.A.	45
35 34 33 32 31	9/9 0/0 01 02	Printed in the U.S.A.	45
40 39	0/0 01 02	Printed in the U.S.A.	12
45 44 43 42 41 40	0/0 01 02	Printed in the U.S.A.	56
50 49 48 47 46 45 44 43 42 41	00 01 02 03 04	Printed in Mexico	59
54 53 52 51 50 49 48 47	0/0 01 02 03 04	Printed in Mexico	49

A4(b) AMERICAN CHILDREN'S EDITION (1999)
(children's artwork series in paperback)

HARRY POTTER | AND THE SORCERER'S STONE | [black and white illustration of Hogwarts castle, in oval, 47 by 83mm] | BY | J. K. ROWLING | ILLUSTRATIONS BY MARY GRANDPRÉ | SCHOLASTIC INC. | NEW YORK [four-sided device] TORONTO [four-sided device] AUCKLAND [four-sided device] SYDNEY | MEXICO CITY [four-sided device] NEW DELHI [four-sided device] HONG KONG (All width centred on a diamond pattern background)

Collation: 159 unsigned leaves bound in indeterminate gatherings; 193 by 133mm; [I-IV] V-VI 1-309 [310-11] 312

Page contents: [I-II] 'PRAISE FOR J. K. ROWLING'S | HARRY POTTER | AND THE SORCERER'S STONE | [device of nine stars] | [9 reviews and a listing of 8 statements]'; [III] title-page; [IV] 'FOR JESSICA, WHO LOVES STORIES, | FOR ANN, [*sic*] WHO LOVED THEM TOO; | AND FOR DI, WHO HEARD THIS ONE FIRST. | [device of twelve stars] | Text copyright © 1997 by J. K. Rowling. | Illustrations copyright © 1998 by Mary GrandPré | [new paragraph] All rights reserved. Published by Scholastic Inc. SCHOLASTIC, | ARTHUR A. LEVINE BOOKS, and associated logos are trademarks | and/or registered trademarks of Scholastic Inc. | [new paragraph] If you purchased this book without a cover, you should be aware that this book is | stolen property. It was reported as "unsold and destroyed" to the publisher,

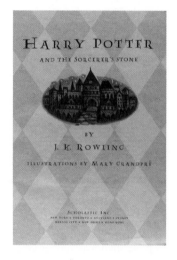

and | neither the author nor the publisher has received any payment for this "stripped | book." No part of this publication may be reproduced in whole or in part, or stored | in a retrieval system, or transmitted in any form or by any means, electronic, | mechanical, photocopying, recording, or otherwise, without written permission | of the publisher. For information regarding permission, write to Scholastic Inc., | Attention: Permissions Department, 555 Broadway, New York, NY 10012. | [new paragraph] [publisher's device of a lantern, 7 by 5mm] | Arthur A. Levine Books hardcover edition | art directed by David Saylor and designed by Becky Terhune, | published by Arthur A. Levine Books, an imprint | of Scholastic Press, October 1998. | [new paragraph] ISBN 0-590-35342-X | Library of Congress number 97-39059 | 12 11 10 9 8 7 6 5 4 3 2 1   9/9 0 1 2 3 4/0 | [new paragraph] Printed in the U.S.A. 40 | First Scholastic trade paperback printing, September 1999'; V-VI 'CONTENTS' (seventeen chapters listed with titles and page references); 1-309 text; [310] publisher's advertisement: 'HOGWARTS IS BACK IN SESSION!' including upper cover design of *Harry Potter and the Chamber of Secrets*; [311] 'HARRY POTTER | AND THE CHAMBER OF SECRETS | [device of nine stars] The summer after his first year at Hogwarts' is worse than | ever for Harry Potter. The Dursleys of Privet Drive reach | new lows of malevolent prissiness. And just when Harry thinks | the endless vacation is over, a neurotic house-elf named Dobby | shows up to warn him against going back to school. Of course, | Harry doesn't listen. But Hogwarts isn't the cure he expects it to | be. Almost immediately a student is found turned to stone, and | then another. And somehow Harry stands accused. Could Harry | Potter be the long-feared heir of Slytherin? | [new paragraph] Harry and friends are stretched to their limits dealing with the likes of Moaning Myrtle, a spirit who haunts the girls' bathroom; | the outrageously conceited new professor Gilderoy Lockheart; | and the diary of Tom Riddle (a boy from Hogwarts' past) which | gives terrifying new meaning to the phrase, "a compelling read."'; 312 '[device of three stars] ABOUT THE AUTHOR [device of three stars] | J.K. ROWLING was a struggling single mother when she | wrote the beginnings of *Harry Potter and the Sorcerer's Stone* on | scraps of paper at a local café. But her efforts soon paid off, as she | received an unprecedented award from the Scottish Arts Council | enabling her to finish the book. Since then, the debut novel has | become an international phenomenon, garnering rave reviews | and major awards, including the British Book Awards Children's | Book of the Year, and the Smarties prize. | [new paragraph] Ms. Rowling lives in Edinburgh with her daughter.'

Paper: wove paper

Running title: 'CHAPTER' and chapter number on verso, recto title comprises chapter title, pp. 1-309. Each running title (excluding pages on which new chapters commence) includes a three-star design to left and right of both running-titles on verso and recto. On pages on which a new chapter commences, the three-star design is omitted.

Illustrations: title-page vignette, together with seventeen vignettes at the beginning of each chapter (after chapter and chapter number but before chapter title). In addition to standard typographical changes (including italics, capitals and small capitals) there are other typographical features, comprising:

    p. 34 'handwritten' envelope address
    p. 42 'handwritten' envelope address
    p. 51 facsimile of Minerva McGonagall's signature
    p. 52 'handwritten' letter
    pp. 135-36 'handwritten' letter
    p. 141 newspaper headline
    p. 164 facsimile of Minerva McGonagall's signature [different from that above]
    p. 202 'handwritten' letter
    p. 247 facsimile of Minerva McGonagall's signature [as on p.164]
    p. 261 'handwritten' note

Binding: pictorial wrappers.
    On spine: 'HARRY POTTER | ROWLING SCHOLASTIC | AND THE SORCERER'S STONE' (reading lengthways down spine). All in gilt on blue and red diamond pattern background.
    On upper wrapper: 'THE EXTRAORDINARY NEW YORK TIMES BESTSELLER [in gilt] | Harry Potter [hand-drawn lettering] [embossed in gilt] | AND THE [hand-drawn lettering in brown of illustration] | SORCERER'S STONE [hand-drawn lettering in brown of illustration] | J. K. ROWLING [embossed in gilt]' (all width centred). All on colour illustration of Harry Potter playing Quidditch with author on blue and red diamond pattern background panel, 15 by 133mm.

On lower wrapper: 'HARRY POTTER has never played a sport while flying on a | broomstick. He's never worn a cloak of invisibility, befriended a giant, or | helped hatch a dragon. All Harry knows is a miserable life with the | Dursleys, his horrible aunt and uncle, and their abominable son, | Dudley. Harry's room is a tiny closet at the foot of the stairs, and he | hasn't had a birthday party in eleven years. | [new paragraph] But all that is about to change when a mysterious letter arrives by | owl messenger: a letter with an invitation to a wonderful place he | never dreamed existed. There he finds not only friends, aerial | sports, and magic around every corner, but a great destiny that's | been waiting for him…if Harry can survive the encounter. | [new paragraph] A *New York Times* Bestseller [four-sided diamond device] A *Publishers Weekly* Best Book of 1998 | [four-sided diamond device] *Booklist* Editor's Choice [four-sided diamond device] Winner of the 1997 National Book | Award (UK) [four-sided diamond device] an ALA Notable Book [four-sided diamond device] Winner of the 1997 Gold | Medal Smarties Prize [four-sided diamond device] A New York Public Library Best Book | of the Year 1998 [four-sided diamond device] *Parenting* Book of the Year Award 1998 | COVER ART BY ['[publisher's book device] SCHOLASTIC' in white on red panel, 4 by 25mm] | MARY GRANDPRÉ'. All in black on colour illustration of a curtain with hand holding a lit candle. In lower right: 'SCHOLASTIC INC. $5.99 US | [rule, 50mm] | [barcode with smaller barcode to the right (35342)]' all in black on white panel within single black ruled border, 26 by 50mm.

On inside upper wrapper: barcode with smaller barcode below (50599) all in black.

All edges trimmed. Binding measurements: 193 by 133mm (wrappers), 193 by 18mm (spine).

Publication: September 1999 (see notes)

Price: $5.99

Contents:

Harry Potter and the Sorcerer's Stone

('Mr. and Mrs. Dursley, of number four, Privet Drive, were proud to say…')

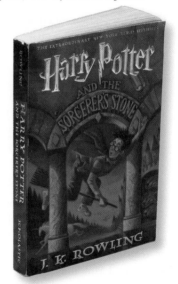

Notes:

Both half-titles from A4(a) are excluded in this edition. The title would be the only one in the original paperback series to exclude all half-titles. A single half-title is found in A4(h).

Although no publication day is recorded, 1 September 1999 is assumed. In an email to me from January 2013 Arthur A. Levine noted that 'I'm fairly certain that we didn't have strict "on sale" dates… the publication "day" would simply be the first of the month listed. None of the paperbacks were given a strict "on sale" date either.'

Note the incorrect spelling of Anne in the dedication on page [IV].

Each chapter commences with a drop capital.

Copies: private collection (PWE)

Reprints include:

32 31 30 29 28 27 26	0 1 2 3 4 5/0	Printed in the U.S.A. 40
32 31 30 29 28 27	0 1 2 3 4 5/0	Printed in the U.S.A. 40
33	1 2 3 4 5/0	Printed in the U.S.A. 40
35	1 2 3 4 5/0	Printed in the U.S.A. 40
100 99 98 97 96 95 94 93 92 91	12 13/0	Printed in the U.S.A. 40
100 99 98 96 95 94 93 92	12 13/0	Printed in the U.S.A. 40
105 104 103 102 101 100 99 98	13 14 15 16 17 18/0	Printed in the U.S.A. 40

A4(c) AMERICAN BOOK CLUB EDITION (1998 [1999])
(children's artwork series in hardback)

HARRY POTTER | AND THE SORCERER'S STONE | [black and white illustration of Hogwarts castle, in oval, 52 by 87mm] | BY | J.K. ROWLING | ILLUSTRATIONS BY MARY GRANDPRÉ | [publisher's device of a lantern, 12 by 9mm] | ARTHUR A. LEVINE BOOKS | AN IMPRINT OF SCHOLASTIC PRESS (All width centred on a diamond pattern background)

Collation: 160 unsigned leaves bound in ten gatherings of sixteen leaves; 226 by 150mm; [I-IV] V-VI [VII-VIII] 1-309 [310-312]

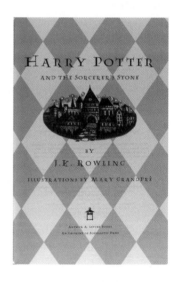

Page contents: [I] half-title: 'HARRY POTTER | AND THE SORCERER'S STONE' (all on diamond pattern background); [II] blank; [III] title-page; [IV] 'FOR JESSICA, WHO LOVES STORIES, | FOR ANNE, WHO LOVED THEM TOO; | AND FOR DI, WHO HEARD THIS ONE FIRST. | [device of twelve stars] | Text copyright © 1997 by J.K. Rowling | Illustrations copyright © 1998 by Mary GrandPré | All rights reserved. Published by Scholastic Press, a division of Scholastic Inc., | *Publishers since 1920* | by arrangement with Bloomsbury Publishing Plc. | SCHOLASTIC, SCHOLASTIC PRESS, ARTHUR A. LEVINE BOOKS, and associated logos | are trademarks and/ or registered trademarks of Scholastic Inc. | [new paragraph] No part of this publication may be reproduced, or stored in a retrieval system, or transmitted | in any form or by any means, electronic, mechanical, photocopying, recording, or otherwise, | without written permission of the publisher. For information regarding permissions, write | to Scholastic Inc., Attention: Permissions Department, 555 Broadway, New York, NY 10012. | [new paragraph] Library of Congress Cataloging-in-Publication Data | [new paragraph] Rowling, J.K. | Harry Potter and the Sorcerer's Stone / by J.K. Rowling | p. cm. | Summary: Rescued from the outrageous neglect of his aunt and uncle, a young boy | with a great destiny proves his worth while attending Hogwarts School | of Witchcraft and Wizardry. | ISBN 0-590-35340-3 | [square bracket]1. Fantasy — Fiction. 2. Witches — Fiction. 3. Wizards — Fiction. | 4. Schools — Fiction. 5. England — Fiction.[square bracket] I. Title. | PZ7. R79835Har 1998 | [square bracket]Fic[square bracket] — dc21 97-39059 | [new paragraph] 1 3 5 7 9 10 8 6 4 2 8 9/9 0/0 01 02 | Printed in the U.S.A. 23 | First American edition, October 1998'; V-VI 'CONTENTS' (seventeen chapters listed with titles and page references); [VII] half-title: 'HARRY POTTER | AND THE SORCERER'S STONE' (all on diamond pattern background); [VIII] blank; 1-309 text; [310] blank; [311] colophon: '[publisher's device of a lantern, 17 by 13mm] | *This book* | *was art directed by* | *David Saylor and designed by Becky* | *Terhune. The art for both the jacket and interior was* | *created using pastels on toned printmaking paper. The text was* | *set in 12-point Adobe Garamond, a typeface based on the sixteenth-* | *century type designs of Claude Garamond, redrawn by Robert* | *Slimbach in 1989. The book was printed and bound* | *at Berryville Graphics in Berryville, Virginia.* | *The production was supervised by* | *Angela Biola and Mike* | *Derevjanik.*'; [312] 'MP7EE'

Paper: wove paper

Running title: 'CHAPTER' and chapter number on verso, recto title comprises chapter title, pp. 1-309. Each running title (excluding pages on which new chapters commence) includes a three-star design to left and right of both running-titles on verso and recto. On pages on which a new chapter commences, the three-star design is omitted.

Illustrations: title-page vignette, together with seventeen vignettes at the beginning of each chapter (after chapter and chapter number but before chapter title). In addition to standard typographical changes (including italics, capitals and small capitals) there are other typographical features, comprising:

- p. 34 'handwritten' envelope address
- p. 42 'handwritten' envelope address
- p. 51 facsimile of Minerva McGonagall's signature
- p. 52 'handwritten' letter
- pp. 135-36 'handwritten' letter
- p. 141 newspaper headline
- p. 164 facsimile of Minerva McGonagall's signature [different from that above]
- p. 202 'handwritten' letter
- p. 247 facsimile of Minerva McGonagall's signature [as on p. 164]
- p. 261 'handwritten' note

Binding: burgundy board-backed spine with black boards.

On spine: 'J. K. | ROWLING | [rule]' (horizontally at head) with 'HARRY POTTER | AND THE SORCERER'S STONE' (reading lengthways down spine) and '[publisher's device of a lantern, 17 by 13mm] | ARTHUR A. | LEVINE BOOKS | [rule] | SCHOLASTIC | PRESS' (horizontally at foot). All in gilt.

Upper and lower covers: blank.

All edges trimmed. Binding measurements: 233 by 150mm (covers), 233 by 37mm (spine). The burgundy paper board continues onto the covers by 30mm. End-papers: white wove paper.

Dust-jacket: uncoated wove paper, 233 by 560mm. A single illustration spans the entire dust-jacket.

On spine: 'J. K. | ROWLING | [rule]' (horizontally at head) with 'HARRY POTTER | AND THE SORCERER'S STONE' (reading lengthways down spine) and '[publisher's device of a lantern, 19 by 11mm] | ARTHUR A. | LEVINE BOOKS | [rule] | SCHOLASTIC | PRESS' (horizontally at foot). All in dark yellow on colour illustration of archway.

On upper cover: 'Harry Potter [hand-drawn lettering] [in dark yellow] | AND THE [hand-drawn lettering in brown of illustration] | SORCERER'S STONE [hand-drawn lettering in brown of illustration] | J. K. ROWLING [in dark yellow]' (all width centred); all on colour illustration of Harry Potter playing Quidditch.

On lower cover, in black: '[five point star] "A DELIGHTFUL | award-winning debut from an author who dances | in the footsteps of P.L. Travers and Roald Dahl." | —*Publishers Weekly*, starred review | [barcode with smaller barcode to the right (un-numbered) all in black on cream panel, 22 by 51mm]'; all on colour illustration of owl, key and shrouded wizard hiding behind column.

On upper inside flap, in black: '$17.95 | HARRY POTTER | has never been the star of a Quidditch team, | scoring points while riding a broom far above | the ground. He knows no spells, has never | helped to hatch a dragon, and has never worn a | cloak of invisibility. | [new paragraph] All he knows is a miserable life with the | Dursleys, his horrible aunt and uncle, and | their abominable son, Dudley—a great big | swollen spoiled bully. Harry's room is a | tiny closet at the foot of the stairs, and he | hasn't had a birthday party in eleven | years. | [new paragraph] But all that is about to change when | a mysterious letter arrives by owl mes- | senger: a letter with an invitation to | an incredible place that Harry— | and anyone who reads about | him—will find un- | forgettable. | [new paragraph] For it's there that he | finds not only friends, | aerial sports, and magic in | everything from classes to | meals, but a great destiny | that's been waiting for him... | if Harry can survive the | encounter.'; all on colour illustration of a curtain with hand holding a lit candle.

On lower inside flap, in black: 'J.K. ROWLING | was a struggling single mother when she wrote | the beginnings of *Harry Potter and the Sorcerer's* | *Stone* on scraps of paper at a local café. But her | efforts soon paid off, as she received an unprece- | dented award from the Scottish Arts Council | enabling her to finish the book. Since then, the | debut novel has become an international phe- | nomenon, garnering rave reviews and major | awards, including the British Book Awards | Children's Book of the Year, and the Smarties | Prize. | [new paragraph] Ms. Rowling lives in Edinburgh with her | daughter. | [new paragraph] *Jacket art © 1998 by Mary GrandPré* | *Jacket design by Mary GrandPré and David Saylor* | [new paragraph] | [publisher's device of a lantern, 12 by 8mm]

| ARTHUR A. LEVINE BOOKS | *An Imprint of Scholastic Press* | 555 Broadway, New York, | New York 10012'; all on colour illustration of a curtain.

Publication: between July and December 1999 (see notes)

Price: $17.95

Contents:
Harry Potter and the Sorcerer's Stone
   ('Mr. and Mrs. Dursley, of number four, Privet Drive, were proud to say...')

Notes:
The American book club edition differs very slightly from the true American first edition. The contents of the book, including the publisher's imprint page, is exactly the same. The binding, however, is different. The dust-jacket also shows two differences: a price of $17.95 and a different quote on the lower wrapper.

Given that the true American first and the book club editions share a single ISBN, the Blair Partnership noted that book club editions could only be dated to within a half-year period end in their files. This edition was, therefore, published within the period July to December 1999. The Blair Partnership Royalties Manager noted that the American book club editions did not have 'a set price'. This one appears, however, to cite a price of $17.95 on the dust-jacket. This was, presumably, the price of the standard retail edition.

Each chapter commences with a drop capital.

Copies: private collection (PWE)

AMERICAN DELUXE EDITION
(children's artwork series in deluxe hardback)

HARRY POTTER | AND THE SORCERER'S STONE | [black and white illustration of Hogwarts castle, in oval, 52 by 88mm] | BY | J.K. ROWLING | ILLUSTRATIONS BY MARY GRANDPRÉ | [publisher's device of a lantern, 12 by 9mm] | ARTHUR A. LEVINE BOOKS | AN IMPRINT OF SCHOLASTIC PRESS (All width centred on a diamond pattern background)

Collation: 160 unsigned leaves bound in ten gatherings of sixteen leaves; 228 by 150mm; [I-IV] V-VI [VII-VIII] 1-309 [310-312]

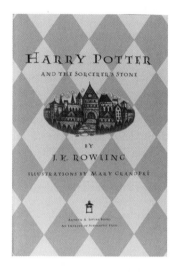

Page contents: [I] '[illustration, 146 by 98mm] | INK PORTRAIT OF HARRY POTTER AT NO. 4, PRIVET DRIVE | By J. K. Rowling, August 1995 | *Note the vase on the mantelpiece. I copied a real one which had been* | *left in my apartment by the previous occupant, and which I thought* | *was horrible enough to belong to the Dursleys.* | JKRowling [facsimile signature]'; [II] blank; [III] title-page; [IV] 'FOR JESSICA, WHO LOVES STORIES, | FOR ANNE, WHO LOVED THEM TOO; | AND FOR DI, WHO HEARD THIS ONE FIRST. | [device of twelve stars] | Text copyright © 1997 by J. K. Rowling | Frontispiece copyright © 1995 by J. K. Rowling | Illustrations by Mary GrandPré copyright © 1998 Scholastic Inc. | All rights reserved. Published by Scholastic Press, a division of Scholastic Inc., | *Publishers since 1920.* | SCHOLASTIC, SCHOLASTIC PRESS, and the LANTERN LOGO | are trademarks and/or registered trademarks of Scholastic Inc. | [new paragraph] No part of this publication may be reproduced, or stored in a retrieval system, | or transmitted in any form or by any means, electronic, mechanical, photocopying, recording, | or otherwise, without written permission of the publisher. For information regarding | permissions write to Scholastic Inc., Attention: Permissions Department, | 555 Broadway, New York, NY 10012. | [new paragraph] ISBN 0-439-20352-X | [new paragraph] LIBRARY OF CONGRESS CATALOGING-IN-PUBLICATION DATA | Rowling, J. K. | Harry Potter and the Sorcerer's Stone / by J. K. Rowling | p. cm. | Summary: Rescued from the outrageous neglect of his aunt and uncle, a young boy | with a great destiny proves his worth while attending Hogwarts School | of Witchcraft and Wizardry. | [square bracket]1. Fantasy — Fiction. 2. Witches — Fiction. 3. Wizards — Fiction. | 4. Schools — Fiction. 5. England — Fiction.[square bracket] I. Title. | PZ7.R79835Har 1998 | [square bracket]Fic[square bracket] — dc21 97-39059 | [new paragraph] 10 9 8 7 6 5 4 3 2 1 0/0 01 02 03 04 | Printed in the U.S.A. 24 | Collector's Edition, November 2000'; V-VI 'CONTENTS' (seventeen chapters listed with titles and page references); [VII] half-title: 'HARRY POTTER | AND THE SORCERER'S STONE' (all on diamond pattern background); [VIII] blank; 1-309 text; [310] blank; [311] colophon: '[publisher's device of a lantern, 17 by 13mm] | *This Collector's* | *Edition was art directed* | *and designed*

by David Saylor. | *Mary GrandPré's artwork for both the* | *case inset and interior was created using* | *pastels on toned printmaking paper. The text was* | *set in 12-point Adobe Garamond, a typeface based on the* | *sixteenth-century type designs of Claude Garamond, redrawn by* | *Robert Slimbach in 1989. The book is printed on 70-pound acid-free* | *offset paper, specially manufactured for Scholastic by Fraser Papers in West* | *Carrollton, Ohio. The case is wrapped in Taratan Bonded Leather* | *produced at Corium Corporation in Seabrook, New Hampshire,* | *a division of Cromwell Leather Group. The book was* | *printed and bound at Quebecor World-Hawkins* | *in Kingsport, Tennessee. The Managing* | *Editor was Manuela Soares and the* | *Manufacturing Director was* | *Angela Biola.* | [device of seven stars]'; [312] blank

Paper: wove paper

Running title: 'CHAPTER' and chapter number on verso, recto title comprises chapter title, pp. 1-309. Each running title (excluding pages on which new chapters commence) includes a three-star design to left and right of both running-titles on verso and recto. On pages on which a new chapter commences, the three-star design is omitted.

Illustrations: three-quarter page illustration by the author, title-page vignette, together with seventeen vignettes at the beginning of each chapter (after chapter and chapter number but before chapter title). In addition to standard typographical changes (including italics, capitals and small capitals) there are other typographical features, comprising:

p. 34 'handwritten' envelope address

p. 42 'handwritten' envelope address

p. 51 facsimile of Minerva McGonagall's signature

p. 52 'handwritten' letter

pp. 135-36 'handwritten' letter

p. 141 newspaper headline

p. 164 facsimile of Minerva McGonagall's signature [different from that above]

p. 202 'handwritten' letter

p. 247 facsimile of Minerva McGonagall's signature [as on p. 164]

p. 261 'handwritten' note

Binding: green morocco.

On spine: 'J. K. | ROWLING | [raised band] | Harry [hand-drawn lettering] | Potter [hand-drawn lettering] | AND | THE | SORCERER'S | STONE | [bolt of lightning, 26 by 12mm] | YEAR | ONE | [raised band] | [publisher's device of a lantern, 19 by 14mm] | ARTHUR A. | LEVINE BOOKS | [rule, 23mm] | SCHOLASTIC'. All in gilt.

On upper cover: 'J. K. | ROWLING | Harry Potter [hand-drawn lettering] | [colour illustration of Harry Potter playing Quidditch, 70 by 92mm laid down to blind panel, 72 by 94mm] | AND THE | SORCERER'S | STONE' (within ornate decorative border in ten sections together with ten stars, 215 by 134mm) (all width centred). All in gilt.

On lower cover: ornate decorative border in ten sections, 215 by 134mm. All in gilt.

All edges gilt. Green and yellow sewn bands at head and foot of spine. Binding measurements: 234 by 151mm (covers), 234 by 40mm (spine). End-papers: wove paper printed with diamond pattern in indigo and burgundy.

Dust-jacket: clear acetate, 234 by 530mm

Spine: blank

On upper cover, in white: 'COLLECTOR'S EDITION' (all width centred).

On lower cover, in white: '*This Collector's Edition of* | HARRY POTTER | AND THE | SORCERER'S STONE | *is a specially produced, leather-* | *bound gift volume that includes the* | *complete text of the original novel* | *as well as a unique pen-and-ink* | *drawing by the author,* | *J. K. Rowling* | [new paragraph] *This edition is available for a* | *limited time only* | — $75.00 — | [new paragraph] [barcode with smaller barcode to the right (57500) all in black on white panel, 25 by 51mm]' (within ornate decorative border, 147 by 91mm)

Inside flaps: blank.

Publication: November 2000 (see notes)

Price: $75

Contents:
Ink portrait of Harry Potter at no. 4, Privet Drive
('Note the vase on the mantelpiece…') (headed, 'By J. K. Rowling, August 1995')
Harry Potter and the Sorcerer's Stone
('Mr. and Mrs. Dursley, of number four, Privet Drive, were proud to say…')

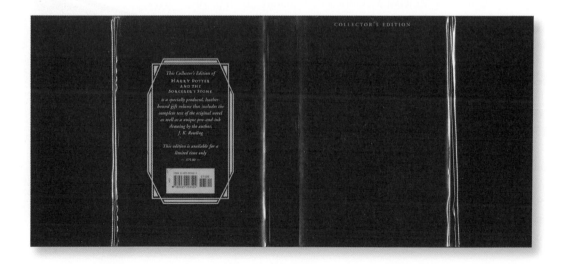

Notes:

In an interview with me conducted in March 2012, the publisher Arthur A. Levine was keen to note that the collector's edition was not marketed as a limited edition, '… I think that was a way of allowing us, if we wanted, to reprint…'

Although no publication day is recorded, 1 November 2000 is assumed. In an email to me from January 2013 Arthur A. Levine noted that 'I'm fairly certain that we didn't have strict "on sale" dates… the publication "day" would simply be the first of the month listed.' Nielsen BookData provides a publication date of 1 October 2000 and a number of contemporary press reports suggest publication during October.

A publication figure of 100,000 copies is widely accepted throughout the book world. This is unconfirmed by Scholastic.

In March 2012 the publisher's New York flagship store was still selling copies of this edition. They were no longer available by November 2013.

Each chapter commences with a drop capital.

Copies: private collection (PWE)

A4(e)   AMERICAN MASS MARKET EDITION   (2001)
(adult artwork series in paperback)

Harry Potter [hand-drawn lettering] | AND THE | SORCERER'S | STONE | J. K. ROWLING | SCHOLASTIC INC. | New York Toronto London Auckland Sydney | Mexico City New Delhi Hong Kong Buenos Aires (All width centred)

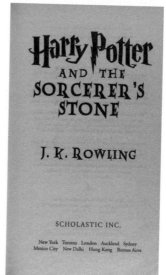

Collation: 200 unsigned leaves bound in indeterminate gatherings; 169 by 103mm; [I-XIV] 1-384 [385-86]

Page contents: [I-III] 'PRAISE FOR J. K. ROWLING'S | HARRY POTTER | AND THE SORCERER'S STONE | [9 reviews and a listing of 5 statements]'; [IV] blank; [V] half-title: 'Harry Potter [hand-drawn lettering] | AND THE | SORCERER'S | STONE'; [VI] 'ALSO BY J. K. ROWLING | [new paragraph] HARRY POTTER | AND THE CHAMBER OF SECRETS | *Year Two at Hogwarts* | [new paragraph] HARRY POTTER | AND THE PRISONER OF AZKABAN | *Year Three at Hogwarts* | [new paragraph] HARRY POTTER | AND THE GOBLET OF FIRE | *Year Four at Hogwarts*'; [VII] title-page; [VIII] 'FOR JESSICA, WHO LOVES STORIES, | FOR ANN, [*sic*] WHO

LOVED THEM TOO; | AND FOR DI, WHO HEARD THIS ONE FIRST. | [new paragraph] Text copyright © 1997 by J. K. Rowling | Illustration by Mary GrandPré copyright © 1998 by Warner Bros. | [new paragraph] All rights reserved. Published by Scholastic Inc. SCHOLASTIC, | the LANTERN LOGO, and associated logos are trademarks and/or | registered trademarks of Scholastic Inc. HARRY POTTER, characters, | names and all related indicia are trademarks of and © Warner Bros. | [new paragraph] If you purchased this book without a cover, you should be aware | that this book is stolen property. It was reported as "unsold and | destroyed" to the publisher, and neither the author nor the | publisher has received any payment for this "stripped book." | [new paragraph] No part of this publication may be reproduced in whole or in part, | or stored in a retrieval system, or transmitted in any form or | by any means, electronic, mechanical, photocopying, recording, | or otherwise, without written permission of the publisher. | For information regarding permissions, write to Scholastic Inc., | Attention: Permissions Department, 555 Broadway, | New York, NY 10012. | [new paragraph] [publisher's device of a lantern, 6 by 5mm] | Arthur A. Levine Books hardcover edition | published by Arthur A. Levine Books, an imprint of | Scholastic Press, October 1998. | [new paragraph] ISBN 0-439-36213-X | Library of Congress number 97-39059 | 12 11 10 9 8 7 6 5 4 3 2 1   1 2 3 4 5 6/0 | [new paragraph] Printed in the U.S.A. 01 | First Scholastic mass market paperback printing, November 2001'; [IX-XI] 'CONTENTS' (seventeen chapters listed with titles and page references); [XII] blank; [XIII] half-title: 'Harry Potter [hand-drawn lettering] | AND THE | SORCERER'S | STONE'; [XIV] blank; 1-384 text; [385] 'J. K. ROWLING | was a struggling single mother when she wrote the | beginnings of Harry Potter and the Sorcerer's Stone | on scraps of paper at a local cafe. But her efforts | soon paid off, as she received an unprecedented | award from the Scottish Arts Council enabling her | to finish the book. Since then, the debut novel | has become an international phenomenon, garnering | rave reviews and major awards, including the British | Book Awards Children's Book of the Year, and the | Smarties prize. | [new paragraph] Ms. Rowling lives in Edinburgh with her | daughter.'; [386] publisher's advertisement: 'J.K. ROWLING'S | Harry Potter [hand-drawn lettering]'

Paper: wove paper

Running title: none

Illustrations: In addition to standard typographical changes (including italics, capitals and small capitals) there are other typographical features, comprising:

p. 42 'handwritten' envelope address

p. 52 'handwritten' envelope address

p. 64 facsimile of Minerva McGonagall's signature

pp. 64-65 'handwritten' letter

pp. 168-69 'handwritten' letter

p. 175 newspaper headline

p. 204 facsimile of Minerva McGonagall's signature [different from that above]

p. 250 'handwritten' letter

p. 308 facsimile of Minerva McGonagall's signature [as on p. 204]

p. 325 'handwritten' note

Binding: pictorial wrappers.

On spine: '[black panel, 4 by 25mm] | [orange rule, 25mm]' (horizontally at head) with 'ROWLING Harry Potter [hand-drawn lettering] AND THE SORCERER'S STONE' (reading lengthways down spine) and '[orange rule, 25mm] | [black panel, 7 by 25mm with publisher's book device in black and white at centre]' (horizontally at foot). The 'ND' of 'AND' is positioned above the 'TH' of 'THE'. All in orange with white highlights on dark blue.

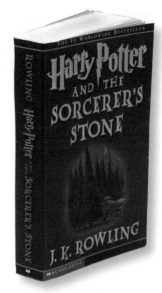

On upper wrapper: 'THE #1 WORLDWIDE BESTSELLER [in white on black panel, 4 by 103mm] | [orange rule, 103mm] | Harry Potter [hand-drawn lettering]| AND THE | SORCERER'S | STONE | [black, grey and white illustration of hooded and cloaked figure running into woods at night, 68 by 63mm] | J. K. ROWLING | [orange, rule, 103mm] | [publisher's book device] SCHOLASTIC [in white on red panel, 7 by 40mm] [black panel, 7 by 63mm]' (all width centred). Title and author in embossed gilt and all on dark blue.

On lower wrapper: '[black panel, 4 by 103mm] | [orange rule, 103mm] | THE BOOK | THAT STARTED | IT ALL ... [together with black, grey and white illustration of a book positioned to the right, 30 by 34mm] | [new paragraph] *A destiny to discover.* | *A magic to behold.* | *An evil to overcome.* | [new paragraph] *Harry Potter and the Sorcerer's Stone* has | already thrilled and inspired millions of | readers. Read it to find out why. | [new paragraph] "The fantasy writer's job is to conduct the willing | reader from mundanity to magic. This is a feat of | which only a superior imagination is capable, and | Rowling possesses such equipment." — *Stephen King* | [new paragraph] "A wonderful first novel ... something quite special." | — *The New York Times Book Review* | [new paragraph] "You don't have to be a wizard or a kid to appreciate | the spell cast by Harry Potter." — *USA Today*'. In lower left: barcode with smaller barcode to the right (36213) together with 'S' within triangle, all in black on white panel within single orange ruled border, 20 by 58mm. In lower right: 'SCHOLASTIC INC. | *Cover art by Mary GrandPré* | *Cover design by Steve Scott* | $6.99 US [this line in black on white panel within single orange ruled border, 7 by 17mm]'. At foot, '[orange rule, 103mm (intersected by barcode panel and price panel)] | [black panel, 7 by 103mm]'. Lines 1-3 in orange with white highlights, lines 4-6 in white, lines 7-9 in orange and lines 10-20 in white and all on dark blue.

On inside upper wrapper: barcode with smaller barcode (50699) together with 'S' within triangle below, all in black.

All edges trimmed. Binding measurements: 169 by 103mm (wrappers), 169 by 25mm (spine).

Publication: November 2001 (see notes)

Price: $6.99

Contents:
Harry Potter and the Sorcerer's Stone
   ('Mr. and Mrs. Dursley, of number four, Privet Drive, were proud to say...')

Notes:

In an interview with me in March 2012, the publisher Arthur A. Levine noted that '… at a certain point in American publishing, some outlets would only carry a mass-market edition. So we made one. But that changed and the mass-marketers were using the trade paperback, so it didn't seem necessary anymore…' There was some sense, initially, that the mass-market edition would cater for the adult market, '… but it also became quite clear that adults had no problem reading our original edition. There was a point that I couldn't go anywhere without seeing people reading the book. I would get on a plane and walk down the aisle and in every aisle someone would be reading the book. And let me tell you it wasn't just ten-year-olds…'

Presumably this edition was the Scholastic equivalent of Bloomsbury's 'celebratory' edition in that it was primarily aimed at a movie-going audience. See also A2(k).

Although no publication day is recorded, 1 November 2001 is assumed. In an email to me from January 2013 Arthur A. Levine noted that 'I'm fairly certain that we didn't have strict "on sale" dates… the publication "day" would simply be the first of the month listed. None of the paperbacks were given a strict "on sale" date either.' Nielsen BookData provides a publication date of 1 November 2001.

Note the incorrect spelling of Anne in the dedication on page [VIII].

Each chapter commences with a drop capital.

Copies: private collection (PWE)

A4(f) AMERICAN 'SCHOOL MARKET' EDITION (2008)
(later children's artwork in paperback)

HARRY POTTER | AND THE SORCERER'S STONE | [black and white illustration of Hogwarts castle, in oval, 47 by 82mm] | BY | J.K. ROWLING | ILLUSTRATIONS BY MARY GRANDPRÉ | SCHOLASTIC INC. | NEW YORK [four-sided device] TORONTO [four-sided device] AUCKLAND [four-sided device] SYDNEY | MEXICO CITY [four-sided device] NEW DELHI [four-sided device] HONG KONG (All width centred on a diamond pattern background)

Collation: 160 unsigned leaves bound in indeterminate gatherings; 192 by 134mm; [I-IV] V-VI [VII-VIII] 1-309 [310-12]

Page contents: [I-II] 'PRAISE FOR J. K. ROWLING'S | HARRY POTTER | AND THE SORCERER'S STONE | [device of nine stars] | [9 reviews and a listing of 8 statements]'; [III] title-page; [IV] 'FOR JESSICA, WHO LOVES STORIES, | FOR ANN, [sic] WHO LOVED THEM TOO; | AND FOR DI, WHO HEARD THIS ONE FIRST. | [device of twelve stars] | Text copyright © 1997 by J. K. Rowling | Interior illustrations by Mary GrandPré copyright ©

1998 by Warner Bros. | Cover illustration by Mary GrandPré copyright © 2008 by Warner Bros. | HARRY POTTER and all related characters and elements are TM of and © WBEI. | Harry Potter Publishing Rights © J. K. Rowling. | All rights reserved. Published by Scholastic Inc. Scholastic, the Lantern Logo and | associated logos are trademarks and/or registered trademarks of Scholastic Inc. | [new paragraph] No part of this publication may be reproduced, stored in a retrieval system, | or transmitted in any form or by any means, electronic, mechanical, photocopying, | recording, or otherwise, without written permission of the publisher. For information | regarding permission, write to Scholastic Inc., Attention: Permissions Department, | 557 Broadway, New York, NY 10012. | [new paragraph] ISBN-13: 978-0-545-12450-8 | ISBN:10: 0-545-12450-6 | [new paragraph] [publisher's device of a lantern, 6 by 4mm] | Arthur A. Levine Books hardcover edition published by Arthur A. Levine Books, | an imprint of Scholastic Inc., October 1998. | [new paragraph] 12 11 10 9 8 7 6 5 4 3 2 1   8 9 10 11 12/0 | [new paragraph] Printed in the U.S.A. | First Scholastic Book Clubs paperback printing, September 2008 | Art directed by David Saylor'; V-VI 'CONTENTS' (seventeen chapters listed with titles and page references); [VII] half-title: 'HARRY POTTER | AND THE SORCERER'S STONE' (all on diamond pattern background); [VIII] blank; 1-309 text; [310] publisher's advertisement: 'HOGWARTS IS BACK IN SESSION!' (advert for *Harry Potter and the Chamber of Secrets*); [311] 'HARRY POTTER | AND THE CHAMBER OF SECRETS | [device of nine stars] The summer after his first year at Hogwarts is worse than | ever for Harry Potter. The Dursleys of Privet Drive reach | new lows of malevolent prissiness. And just when Harry thinks | the endless vacation is over, a neurotic house-elf named Dobby | shows up to warn him against going back to school. Of course, | Harry doesn't listen. But Hogwarts isn't the cure he expects it to | be. Almost immediately a student is found turned to stone, and | then another. And somehow Harry stands accused. Could Harry | Potter be the long-feared heir of Slytherin? | [new paragraph] Harry and friends are stretched to their limits dealing with the | likes of Moaning Myrtle, a spirit who haunts the girls' bathroom; | the outrageously conceited new professor Gilderoy Lockheart; | and the diary of Tom Riddle (a boy from Hogwarts's past), which | gives terrifying new meaning to the phrase "a compelling read."'; [312] '[device of three stars] | ABOUT THE AUTHOR [device of three stars] | J.K. ROWLING began writing stories when she was six years | old. She started working on the Harry Potter sequence in 1990, | when, she says, "the idea ... simply fell into my head." This first | book, *Harry Potter and the Sorcerer's Stone*, was published in the | United Kingdom in 1997 and the United States in 1998. Since | then, books in the Harry Potter series have been honored with | many prizes, including the Anthony Award, the Hugo Award, the | Nebula Award, the Bram Stoker Award, the Whitbread Children's | Book Award, the Nestlé Smarties Book Prize, and the British | Book Awards Children's Book of the Year, as well as *New York | Times* Notable Book, ALA Notable Children's Book, and ALA | Best Book for Young Adults citations. | [new paragraph] Ms. Rowling has also been named an Officer of the Order of | the British Empire. She lives in Scotland with her family.'

Paper: wove paper

Running title: 'CHAPTER' and chapter number on verso, recto title comprises chapter title, pp. 1-309. Each running title (excluding pages on which new chapters commence) includes a three-star design to left and right of both running-titles on verso and recto. On pages on which a new chapter commences, the three-star design is omitted.

Illustrations: seventeen vignettes at the beginning of each chapter (after chapter and chapter number but before chapter title). In addition to standard typographical changes (including italics, capitals and small capitals) there are other typographical features, comprising:

p. 34 'handwritten' envelope address

p. 42 'handwritten' envelope address

p. 51 facsimile of Minerva McGonagall's signature

p. 52 'handwritten' letter

pp. 135-36 'handwritten' letter

p. 141 newspaper headline

p. 164 facsimile of Minerva McGonagall's signature [different from that above]

p. 202 'handwritten' letter

p. 247 facsimile of Minerva McGonagall's signature [as on p. 164]

p. 261 'handwritten' note

Binding: pictorial wrappers.

On spine: 'ROWLING | [rule] | ['YEAR | 1' within concave square]' (horizontally at head) with 'HARRY POTTER | SCHOLASTIC | AND THE SORCERER'S STONE' (reading lengthways down spine). All in dark yellow on dark purple background with a device of three stars in light purple on each side of the title. The concave square has a dark yellow ruled border and a red background.

On upper wrapper: 'EXCLUSIVE SCHOLASTIC SCHOOL MARKET EDITION [in white] | Harry Potter [hand-drawn lettering] [embossed in gilt] | AND [embossed in red] | THE [embossed in red] | SORCERER'S [embossed in red] | STONE [embossed in red] | J. K. ROWLING [embossed in gilt] | [publisher's book device] SCHOLASTIC [in white on red panel, 5 by 45mm]' (all width centred with the exception of lines 3-6 which are set towards the left); all on colour illustration of Harry Potter testing a wand watched by Mr Ollivander and Hagrid.

On lower wrapper: 'FOLLOW ALL OF THE [in dark yellow] | Harry Potter [hand-drawn lettering] [in brown] | ADVENTURES! [in dark yellow] | [colour illustrations of three book designs, each in an single dark yellow ruled border] | YEAR 2 YEAR 3 YEAR 4 [in dark yellow] | [colour illustrations of three book designs, each in a single dark yellow ruled border] | YEAR 5 YEAR 6 YEAR 7 [in dark yellow] | This edition is available for distribution [in white] | only through the school market. [in white] | [publisher's book device] SCHOLASTIC [in white on red panel, 6 by 45mm] | www.scholastic.com/harrypotter [in white] | COVER ART BY MARY GRANDPRÉ [in white]'. In lower right: barcode in black on white panel, 13 by 39mm]. All on dark purple background with a device of seven stars in top left corner in light purple and a device of six stars in lower right.

All edges trimmed. Binding measurements: 192 by 134mm (wrappers), 192 by 19mm (spine).

Publication: September 2008 (see notes)

Price: $8.99 (see notes)

Contents:

Harry Potter and the Sorcerer's Stone

('Mr. and Mrs. Dursley, of number four, Privet Drive, were proud to say...')

Notes:

As noted on the wrappers, this edition was available exclusively through the Scholastic book club. Contemporary marketing material for the club offers this edition as a 'special limited collector's edition' and notes 'exclusive new Mary GrandPré cover artwork'. A price of $8.99 is cited, reduced to $6. It is unclear whether the volume was published at the higher price and was available on special offer for a limited time or whether the $6 price represented the book club price for this volume in contrast to the standard American paperback edition.

During the course of an interview with the publisher Arthur A. Levine in March 2012 I asked about the school edition. Mr Levine replied that he wondered what made it 'exclusive' and concluded that '… it might have been exclusive purely by dint of it having a different cover…'

Although no publication day is recorded, 1 September 2008 is assumed. In an email to me from January 2013 Arthur A. Levine noted that 'I'm fairly certain that we didn't have strict "on sale" dates… the publication "day" would simply be the first of the month listed. None of the paperbacks were given a strict "on sale" date either.'

Note the incorrect spelling of Anne in the dedication on page [IV].

Each chapter commences with a drop capital.

Copies: private collection (AAL)

A4(g)   AMERICAN 'ANNIVERSARY' EDITION   (2008)
(later children's artwork in hardback)

HARRY POTTER | AND THE SORCERER'S STONE | [black and white illustration of Hogwarts castle, in oval, 52 by 87mm] | BY | J.K. ROWLING | ILLUSTRATIONS BY MARY GRANDPRÉ | [publisher's device of a lantern, 12 by 9mm] | ARTHUR A. LEVINE BOOKS | AN IMPRINT OF SCHOLASTIC INC. (All width centred on a diamond pattern background)

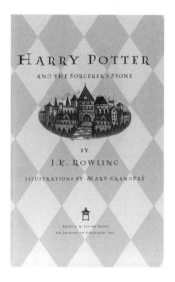

Collation: 160 unsigned leaves bound in indeterminate gatherings together with an additional plate leaf inserted between leaves one and two; 228 by 150mm; [I-II] [additional illustration leaf] [III-VI] VII-VIII [IX-X] 1-309 [310]

Page contents: [I] half-title: 'HARRY POTTER | AND THE SORCERER'S STONE' (all on diamond pattern background); [II] 'ALSO BY J. K. ROWLING | [new paragraph] *Harry Potter and the Chamber of Secrets* | Year Two at Hogwarts | [new paragraph]

Harry Potter and the Prisoner of Azkaban | Year Three at Hogwarts | [new paragraph] | *Harry Potter and the Goblet of Fire* | Year Four at Hogwarts | [new paragraph] *Harry Potter and the Order of the Phoenix* | Year Five at Hogwarts | [new paragraph] *Harry Potter and the Half-Blood Prince* | Year Six at Hogwarts | [new paragraph] *Harry Potter and the Deathly Hallows* | Year Seven' (with additional leaf inserted on the verso of which is the frontispiece, 209 by 133mm); [III] title-page; [IV] illustration, 168 by 112mm; [V] '*Snape, as I always saw him.* | *This was scribbled back in 1992 or 3. Although I have* | *spent years denying that Snape is a vampire (one of the more* | *outlandish and persistent fan theories), I must say he does* | *look a little Count Dracula-ish in that cloak.* | *— J. K. Rowling*'; [VI] 'FOR JESSICA, WHO LOVES STORIES, | FOR ANNE, WHO LOVED THEM TOO; | AND FOR DI, WHO HEARD THIS ONE FIRST. | [device of twelve stars] | Text copyright © 1997 by J. K. Rowling | Sketch of Snape © 2008 by J. K. Rowling | Cover illustration and frontispiece by Mary GrandPré © 2008 by Warner Bros. | Interior illustrations by Mary GrandPré © 1998 by Warner Bros. | HARRY POTTER and all related characters and elements are TM of and © WBEI. | Harry Potter Publishing Rights © J. K. Rowling. | All rights reserved. Published by Arthur A. Levine Books, an imprint of Scholastic Inc., | *Publishers since 1920.* SCHOLASTIC and the LANTERN LOGO are | trademarks and/or registered trademarks of Scholastic Inc. | [new paragraph] No part of this publication may be reproduced, stored in a retrieval system, or transmitted | in any form or by any means, electronic, mechanical, photocopying, recording, or otherwise, | without written permission of the publisher. For information regarding permission, write | to Scholastic Inc., Attention: Permissions Department, 557 Broadway, New York, NY 10012. | [new paragraph] Library of Congress Cataloging-in-Publication Data | Rowling, J.K. | Harry Potter and the Sorcerer's Stone / by J.K. Rowling / p. cm. | Summary: Rescued from the outrageous neglect of his aunt and uncle, a young boy | with a great destiny proves his worth while attending Hogwarts School | of Witchcraft and Wizardry. | ISBN-13: 978-0-590-35340-3 [round point] ISBN-10: 0-590-35340-3 | [square bracket]1. Fantasy — Fiction. 2. Witches — Fiction. 3. Wizards — Fiction. | 4. Schools — Fiction. 5. England — Fiction.[square bracket] I. Title. | PZ7.R79835Har 1998 [square bracket]Fic[square bracket] — dc21 97-39059 | [new paragraph] Special Anniversary Edition | ISBN-13: 978-0-545-06967-0 | ISBN-10: 0-545-06967-X | 10 9 8 7 6 5 4 3 2 1   08 09 10 11 12 | Printed in the U.S.A. 12 | October 2008 | [Forest Stewardship Council logo, 6 by 8mm together with © symbol and 'FSC' to the right is the text: 'Mixed Sources | Cert no. SW-COC-002550 | © 1996 FSC'] | [new paragraph] We try to produce the most beautiful books possible, and we are extremely concerned about | the impact of our manufacturing process on the forests of the world and the environment as a | whole. Accordingly, we make sure that all of the paper we used contains 30% post-consumer | recycled fiber, and has been certified as coming from forests that are managed to insure the | protection of the people and wildlife dependent upon them.'; VII-VIII 'CONTENTS' (seventeen chapters listed with titles and page references); [IX] half-title: 'HARRY POTTER | AND THE SORCERER'S STONE' (all on diamond pattern background); [X] blank; 1-309 text; [310] colophon: '[publisher's device of a lantern, 17 by 13mm] | *This* | *book was* | *art directed by David* | *Saylor. The art for both the jacket* | *and interior was created using pastels on* | *toned printmaking paper. The text was set in 12-* | *point Adobe Garamond, a typeface based on the sixteenth-* | *century type designs of Claude Garamond, redrawn by Robert* | *Slimbach in 1989. The book was typeset by* | *Brad Walrod* | *and was printed and bound at Quebecor World* | *Fairfield in Fairfield, Pennsylvania.* | *The* | *manufacturing was super-* | *vised by Jaime* | *Capifali.*'

Paper: wove paper

Running title: 'CHAPTER' and chapter number on verso, recto title comprises chapter title, pp. 1-309. Each running title (excluding pages on which new chapters commence) includes a three-star design to left and right of both running-titles on verso and recto. On pages on which a new chapter commences, the three-star design is omitted.

Illustrations: colour frontispiece, title-page vignette, full-page illustration by the author, together with seventeen vignettes at the beginning of each chapter (after chapter and chapter number but before chapter title). In addition to standard typographical changes (including italics, capitals and small capitals) there are other typographical features, comprising:

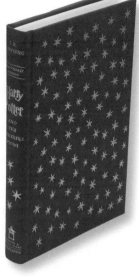

- p. 34 'handwritten' envelope address
- p. 42 'handwritten' envelope address
- p. 51 facsimile of Minerva McGonagall's signature
- p. 52 'handwritten' letter
- pp. 135-36 'handwritten' letter
- p. 141 newspaper headline
- p. 164 facsimile of Minerva McGonagall's signature [different from that above]
- p. 202 'handwritten' letter
- p. 247 facsimile of Minerva McGonagall's signature [as on p.164]
- p. 261 'handwritten' note

Binding: red cloth.

On spine: 'J. K. | ROWLING | [rule, 29mm] | ANNIVERSARY | EDITION | [rule, 29mm] | Harry [hand-drawn lettering] | Potter [hand-drawn lettering] | AND | THE | SORCERER'S | STONE | [four stars] | [publisher's device of a lantern, 15 by 11mm] | ARTHUR A. | LEVINE BOOKS | [rule, 23mm] | SCHOLASTIC'. All in gilt.

On upper and lower covers: pattern of 100 stars. All in gilt.

All edges trimmed. Red and yellow sewn bands at head and foot of spine. Binding measurements: 234 by 149mm (covers), 234 by 40mm (spine). End-papers: purple wove paper.

Dust-jacket: uncoated wove paper, 234 by 561mm

On spine: 'J. K. | ROWLING | ANNIVERSARY | EDITION | Harry [hand-drawn lettering] | Potter [hand-drawn lettering] | AND | THE | SORCERER'S | STONE | [publisher's device of a lantern, 15 by 11mm] | ARTHUR A. | LEVINE BOOKS | [rule, 23mm] | SCHOLASTIC'. All embossed in gilt on navy blue, light blue and purple diamond pattern background with lines 3-4 on red panel, 11 by 28mm.

On upper cover: 'Harry Potter [hand-drawn lettering] [embossed in gilt] | AND THE [in red] | SORCERER'S [in red] | STONE [in red] | J. K. ROWLING [embossed in gilt] | SPECIAL ANNIVERSARY EDITION [embossed in gilt]' (lines 1, 5 and 6 all width centred); lines 1-4 on detail of colour illustration of Harry Potter gazing into the Mirror of Erised, line 5 on a navy blue, light blue and purple diamond pattern background.

On lower cover: colour illustration of Harry Potter gazing into the Mirror of Erised together with barcode with smaller barcode to the right (53000) all in black on yellow panel, 22 by 47mm.

On upper inside flap: '$30.00 US | [new paragraph] A SPECIAL | ANNIVERSARY | EDITION OF | ONE OF THE | BEST-LOVED BOOKS | IN HISTORY! | [new paragraph] HARRY POTTER | has never been the star | of a Quidditch team, | scoring points on a broom far above | the ground. He knows no spells, has | never helped to hatch a dragon, and | has never worn a cloak of invisibility. | [new paragraph] All he knows is a miserable life | with the Dursleys, his horrible aunt | and uncle, and their abominable son, | Dudley—a great big swollen spoiled | bully. Harry's room is a tiny closet at | the foot of the stairs, and he hasn't had | a birthday party in eleven years. | [new paragraph] But all that is about to change | when a mysterious letter arrives by owl | messenger: a letter with an invitation | to an incredible place that Harry—and | anyone who reads about him—will | find unforgettable. | [new paragraph] This special anniversary edition | celebrates the delightful beginning of a | story that has held millions of readers | in its spell.' (line 1 in black, lines 2-7 in blue, line 8 in red and lines 9-31 in black and all on an orange, dark yellow and light yellow diamond pattern background panel, 216 by 76mm which is on a navy blue, light blue and purple diamond pattern background). The initial 'H' of 'HARRY' is a drop capital and is printed in red.

On lower inside flap: 'WHAT THE CRITICS SAID | [new paragraph] "A wonderful first novel. Much like Roald Dahl, | J. K. Rowling has a gift for keeping the emotions, | fears, and triumphs of her characters on a human | scale, even while the supernatural is popping out all | over. The book is full of wonderful, sly humor [square bracket]and[square bracket] | the characters are impressively three-dimensional | (occasionally, four-dimensional!) and move along | seamlessly through the narrative. *Harry Potter and the | Sorcerer's Stone* is as funny, moving and impressive as | the story behind its writing. Like Harry Potter, [square bracket]J. K. | Rowling[square bracket] has wizardry inside, and has soared beyond | her modest Muggle surroundings to achieve something | quite special." —*The New York Times Book Review* | [new paragraph] "A charming, magical confection of a novel ... A | glorious debut, a book of wonderful comic pleasures | and dizzying imaginative flights. There is no cause | to doubt Rowling's abilities and promise, and every | reason to expect great things, truly great things, from | her in the future." —*The Boston Sunday Globe* | [new paragraph] "You don't have to be a wizard or a kid to appreciate | the spell cast by Harry Potter." —*USA Today* | [new paragraph] "Readers are in for a delightful romp with this award- | winning debut from a British author who dances in | the footsteps of P. L. Travers and Roald Dahl. Rowling | leaves the door wide open for a sequel; bedazzled | readers will surely clamor for one." | — *Publishers Weekly*, starred review | [new paragraph] *Jacket art by Mary GrandPré © 2008 Warner Bros.* | *Jacket design by Mary GrandPré and David Saylor* | [new paragraph] [publisher's device of a lantern, 12 by 9mm] | ARTHUR A. LEVINE BOOKS | www.arthuralevinebooks.com | An Imprint of | [publisher's book device] SCHOLASTIC | www.scholastic.com | 557 Broadway, New York, NY 10012 | [new paragraph] PRINTED IN THE U.S.A.'

(line 1 in blue, lines 2-34 in black, line 35 in white on red panel, 4 by 36mm, lines 36-37 in black and line 38 in blue and all on an orange, dark yellow and light yellow diamond pattern background panel, 216 by 76mm which is on a navy blue, light blue and purple diamond pattern background).

Publication: October 2008 (see notes)

Price: $30

Contents:
[Portrait of Professor Snape and author's note]
    ('Snape, as I always saw him. This was scribbled back in 1992 or 3...')
Harry Potter and the Sorcerer's Stone
    ('Mr. and Mrs. Dursley, of number four, Privet Drive, were proud to say...')

Notes:
The 'Special Anniversary Edition' was published to mark a decade since the first American edition. The setting of the text was the same as the regular edition but this anniversary edition featured a colour frontispiece (showing boats arriving at Hogwarts) by Mary GrandPré in addition to an illustration (and explanatory note) of Professor Snape by the author. The binding and dust-jacket were also changed for this edition.

Note the omission of 'at Hogwarts' after 'Year Seven' on page [II] since the majority of the final book does not take place at Hogwarts castle.

Although no publication day is recorded, 1 October 2008 is assumed. In an email to me from January 2013 Arthur A. Levine noted that 'I'm fairly certain that we didn't have strict "on sale" dates... the publication "day" would simply be the first of the month listed.'

In March 2012 the publisher's New York flagship store was still selling copies of this edition. They were no longer available by November 2013.

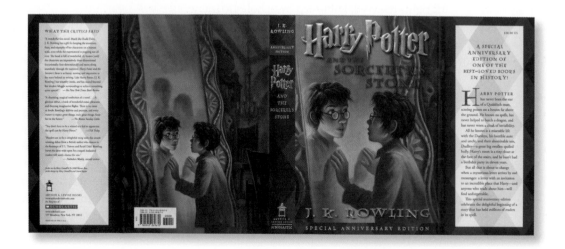

Each chapter commences with a drop capital.

Copies: private collection (PWE)

A4(h)   AMERICAN CHILDREN'S EDITION   (2013)
(Kazu Kibuishi artwork in paperback)

HARRY POTTER | AND THE SORCERER'S STONE | [black and white illustration of Hogwarts castle, in oval, 46 by 80mm] | BY | J. K. ROWLING | ILLUSTRATIONS BY MARY GRANDPRÉ | SCHOLASTIC INC. (All width centred on a diamond pattern background)

Collation: 168 unsigned leaves bound in indeterminate gatherings; 204 by 134mm; [I-IV] V-VI [VII-VIII] 1-309 [310-28]

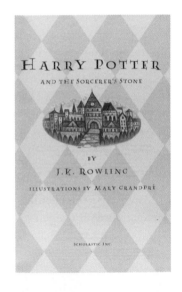

Page contents: [I-II] 'PRAISE FOR J. K. ROWLING'S | HARRY POTTER | AND THE SORCERER'S STONE | [device of nine stars] | [9 reviews and a listing of 8 statements]'; [III] title-page; [IV] 'FOR JESSICA, WHO LOVES STORIES, | FOR ANNE, WHO LOVED THEM TOO; | AND FOR DI, WHO HEARD THIS ONE FIRST. | [device of twelve stars] | Text © 1997 by J. K. Rowling | Interior illustrations by Mary GrandPré © 1998 by Warner Bros. | Excerpt from *Harry Potter and the Chamber of Secrets*, text © 1998 by J. K. Rowling; | illustration by Mary GrandPré © 1999 by Warner Bros. | Cover illustration by Kazu Kibuishi © 2013 by Scholastic Inc. | HARRY POTTER and all related characters and elements are TM of and © WBEI. | Harry Potter Publishing Rights © J. K. Rowling | All rights reserved. Published by Scholastic Inc. SCHOLASTIC, the LANTERN LOGO, and associated | logos are trademarks and/or registered trademarks of Scholastic Inc. | [new paragraph] If you purchased this book without a cover, you should be aware that this book is stolen property. | It was reported as "unsold and destroyed" to the publisher, and neither the author nor the | publisher has received any payment for this "stripped book." | [new paragraph] No part of this publication may be reproduced, stored in a retrieval system, or transmitted in any | form or by any means, electronic, mechanical, photocopying, recording, or otherwise, without | written permission of the publisher. For information regarding permission, write to Scholastic Inc., | Attention: Permissions Department, 557 Broadway, New York, NY 10012. | [new paragraph] [publisher's device of a lantern, 6 by 4mm] | Arthur A. Levine Books hardcover edition | art directed by David Saylor and designed by Becky Terhune, | published by Arthur A. Levine Books, an imprint of Scholastic Inc., October 1998. | [new paragraph] ISBN 978-0-545-58288-9 | [new paragraph] Library of Congress Control Number: 97-39059 | [new paragraph] 12 11 10 9 8 7 6 5 4 3 2 1   13 14 15 16 17 | [new paragraph]

Printed in the U.S.A. 40 | This edition first printing, September 2013 | [new paragraph] We try to produce the most beautiful books possible, and we are extremely concerned about the impact of our | manufacturing process on the forests of the world and the environment as a whole. Accordingly, we made sure | that the text paper contains a minimum of 30% post-consumer waste, and that all the paper has been certified as | coming from forests that are managed to insure the protection of the people and wildlife dependent upon them.'; V-VI 'CONTENTS' (seventeen chapters listed with titles and page references); [VII] half-title: 'HARRY POTTER | AND THE SORCERER'S STONE' (all on diamond pattern background); [VIII] blank; 1-309 text; [310] blank; [311] 'HARRY POTTER'S | ADVENTURES CONTINUE IN | [new paragraph] HARRY POTTER | AND THE CHAMBER OF SECRETS | [new paragraph] TURN THE PAGE FOR | A SNEAK PREVIEW!' (all on diamond pattern background); [312] blank; [313-23] text; [324] advertisement for Pottermore; [325] '[black and white photograph of J.K. Rowling seated by curtains, credited 'ANDREW MONTGOMERY' reading lengthways up right margin] | [new paragraph] J. K. ROWLING is the author of the beloved, | bestselling, record-breaking Harry Potter series. She started writing | the series during a delayed Manchester to London King's Cross | train journey, and during the next five years, outlined the plots for | each book and began writing the first novel. *Harry Potter and the* | *Sorcerer's Stone* was published in the United States by Arthur A. | Levine Books in 1998, and the series concluded nearly ten years | later with *Harry Potter and the Deathly Hallows*, published in 2007. | J. K. Rowling is the recipient of numerous awards and honorary | degrees, including an OBE for services to children's literature, | France's Légion d'honneur, and the Hans Christian Andersen | Literature Award. She supports a wide number of causes through | her charitable trust, Volant, and is the founder of Lumos, a charity | working to transform the lives of disadvantaged children. J. K. | Rowling lives in Edinburgh with her husband and three children.'; [326] blank; [327] 'MARY GRANDPRÉ has illustrated more than twenty | beautiful books for children, including the American editions of | the Harry Potter novels. Her work has also appeared in the *New* | *Yorker*, the *Atlantic Monthly*, and the *Wall Street Journal*, and her | paintings and pastels have been shown in galleries across the United | States. Ms. GrandPré lives in Sarasota, Florida, with her family. | [new paragraph] KAZU KIBUISHI is the creator of the *New York Times* | bestselling Amulet series and *Copper*, a collection of his popular | webcomic. He is also the founder and editor of the acclaimed | Flight anthologies. *Daisy Kutter: The Last Train*, his first graphic | novel, was listed as one of the Best Books for Young Adults by | YALSA, and *Amulet, Book One: The Stonekeeper* was an ALA Best | Book for Young Adults and a Children's Choice Book Award | finalist. Kazu lives and works in Alhambra, California, with his | wife and fellow comics artist, Amy Kim Kibuishi, and their two | children. Visit Kazu online at www.boltcity.com.'; [328] blank

Paper: wove paper

Running title: 'CHAPTER' and chapter number on verso, recto title comprises chapter title, pp. 1-309 and pp. [313-23]. Each running title (excluding pages on which new chapters commence) includes a three-star design to left and right of both running-titles on verso and recto. On pages on which a new chapter commences, the three-star design is omitted.

Illustrations: title-page vignette, together with seventeen vignettes at the beginning of each chapter (after chapter and chapter number but before chapter title). The 'sneak preview' also includes a vignette. In addition to standard typographical changes (including italics, capitals and small capitals) there are other typographical features, comprising:

p. 34 'handwritten' envelope address

p. 42 'handwritten' envelope address

p. 51 facsimile of Minerva McGonagall's signature

p. 52 'handwritten' letter

pp. 135-36 'handwritten' letter

p. 141 newspaper headline

p. 164 facsimile of Minerva McGonagall's signature [different from that above]

p. 202 'handwritten' letter

p. 247 facsimile of Minerva McGonagall's signature [as on p.164]

p. 261 'handwritten' note

Binding: pictorial wrappers.

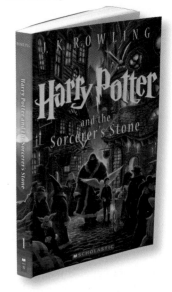

On spine: 'ROWLING | Harry Potter and the Sorcerer's Stone [reading lengthways down spine] | 1' and '[publisher's book device] | [rule] | S' in white on red panel, 14 by 6mm. All in white on colour illustration (see notes).

On upper wrapper: 'J. K. ROWLING | Harry Potter [hand-drawn lettering] [embossed in white] | and the | Sorcerer's Stone' (all width centred). All in white on colour illustration of Harry Potter with Hagrid visiting Diagon Alley. In centre at foot: '[publisher's book device] SCHOLASTIC' in white on red panel, 5 by 45mm.

On lower wrapper: '"It does not do to dwell on dreams and | forget to live, remember that." | — Albus Dumbledore | [new paragraph] Till now there's been no magic for Harry Potter. He lives with the miserable | Dursleys and their abominable son, Dudley. Harry's room is a tiny closet | beneath the stairs, and he hasn't had a birthday party in eleven years. | [new paragraph] But then a mysterious letter arrives by owl messenger: a letter with an | invitation to an incredible place called Hogwarts School of Witchcraft and | Wizardry. And there he finds not only friends, flying sports on broomsticks, | and magic in *everything* from classes to meals, but a great destiny that's | been waiting for him … if Harry can survive the encounter. | [new paragraph] $12.99 US | [new paragraph] [publisher's book device with 'SCHOLASTIC' in white on red panel, 5 by 45mm] | www.scholastic.com | COVER DESIGN BY KAZU KIBUISHI AND JASON CAFFOE | COVER ART BY KAZU KIBUISHI © 2013 BY SCHOLASTIC INC.' Lines 1-3 in white with other lines in light blue and all on colour illustration of Harry staring into the mirror of erised. In lower right: barcode with smaller barcode to the right (51299) together with 'S' within triangle, all in black on white panel, 21 by 53mm.

On inside upper wrapper: barcode with smaller barcode (51299) together with 'S' within triangle below, all in black on white panel, 53 by 21mm. All on lavender blue.

On inside lower wrapper: '[colour illustration of book design] Harry Potter [hand-drawn lettering] [in white] | The Complete Series [in white] | Read All of Harry's [in white] | Magical Adventures!

[in white] | [publisher's device of a lantern, 10 by 7mm] [in black] | ARTHUR A. LEVINE BOOKS [in black] | [publisher's book device with 'SCHOLASTIC' in white on red panel, 5 by 45mm] | scholastic.com/harrypotter [in white] | [colour illustrations in three columns of six book designs]'. All on lavender blue.

All edges trimmed. Binding measurements: 204 by 134mm. (wrappers), 204 by 16mm. (spine).

Slipcase: card slipcase covered in paper.

On spine: 'J. K. R O W L I N G | Harry Potter [hand-drawn lettering] | The Complete Series' (all width centred). All in white on colour illustration of Harry Potter, Ron Weasley, Hermione Granger and others standing outside Honeydukes sweet shop.

On upper side: 'J. K. R O W L I N G | Harry Potter [hand-drawn lettering] | The Complete Series' (all width centred). All in white on colour of Dumbledore and Hagrid walking past Zonko's joke shop.

On lower side: 'J. K. R O W L I N G | Harry Potter [hand-drawn lettering] | The Complete Series' (all width centred). All in white on colour illustration of Professor McGonagall with six students and with the Hogwarts Express and Hogwarts castle behind.

Top edge: 'J. K. R O W L I N G | Harry Potter [hand-drawn lettering] | The Complete Series' (all width centred). All in white on colour illustration of a sky in various colours.

Lower edge: 'The Complete Series | [colour illustrations in two rows of seven book designs] | [three columns with 'BOX ART BY KAZU KIBUISHI © 2013 BY SCHOLASTIC INC. | BOX DESIGN BY KAZU KIBUISHI AND JASON CAFFOE | PRINTED IN THE U.S.A. 71' in first column, '['[publisher's book device] SCHOLASTIC' in white on red panel, 5 by 45mm] | www.scholastic.com | 557 BROADWAY | NEW YORK, NY 10012' in second column and '$100.00 US | [barcodes in black on white panel, 19 by 52mm.]' in third column]. All in light blue on black.

Publication: 27 August 2013

Price: $12.99

Contents:
Harry Potter and the Sorcerer's Stone
  ('Mr. and Mrs. Dursley, of number four, Privet Drive, were proud to say…')

Notes:
Despite the new wrapper illustrations, the text was not re-set for this edition and Mary GrandPré's original vignette illustrations are, therefore, present with the text. A new feature for this series, however, is the inclusion of the first chapter (or opening of first chapter) from the next book in the sequence.

The seven volumes in this edition were available individually or as a set issued in a slipcase. The set, presented in order, reveals a single illustration of Hogwarts castle across the seven spines. Scholastic released images of the new illustrations in a careful marketing campaign: the upper wrapper illustration for *Sorcerer's Stone* was unveiled on 13 February 2013 on the Scholastic website and *Good Morning America*.

Purchase of the complete set in slipcase was 93 cents cheaper than buying the individual volumes.

The publisher's press release on 13 February 2013 noted that the illustrator found the commission 'more than a little surreal'. Kazu Kibuishi stated that 'the Harry Potter covers by Mary GrandPré are so fantastic and iconic, when I was asked to submit samples, I initially hesitated because I didn't want to see them reinterpreted! However, I felt that if I were to handle the project, I could bring something to it that many other designers and illustrators probably couldn't, and that was that I was also a writer of my own series of middle grade fiction. As an author myself, I tried to answer the question, "If I were the author of the books – and they were like my own children – how would I want them to be seen years from now?" When illustrating the covers, I tried to think of classic perennial paperback editions of famous novels and how those illustrations tend to feel. In a way, the project became a tribute to both Harry Potter and the literary classics.'

Note that the lower side, spine, upper side and top edge of the slipcase show panels of a single illustration of part of the village of Hogsmeade.

Each chapter commences with a drop capital.

Copies: private collection (PWE)

Reprints include:
12 11 10 9 8 7 6 5 4 3   13 14 15 16 17   Printed in the U.S.A. 40

THE DAILY PROPHET – 8 FEBRUARY 1999

A5(a)   **FIRST ENGLISH EDITION**   **(1999)**

Banner:
Feb 8*th* 1999 *The Daily Prophet Price: 7 Knuts*
(All within single ruled border, 15 by 157mm.)

Collation: 3 single leaves with staple upper left corner; 297 by 211mm.; [1-3]

Page contents: [1] Headlines section; [2] Quidditch section; [3] Classified advertisements

Paper: wove paper

Running title: '*The Daily Prophet*' (21mm.) and '8*th* *Feb 1999*' (18mm.); the page heading occurs in the middle of this running title on p. [3] only

Publication: 8 February 1999

Price: issued as part of membership of the Harry Potter Fan Club (membership fee: £4.25 per year)

Contents:
[Headlines section, p. 1]
Enquiry at the Improper Use of Magic Office (together with reference to editorial comment)
    ('Scandal hit the Improper Use of Magic Office yesterday, as an enquiry was...')
Celestina Warbeck Concert Causes Broom Smash Over Liverpool
    ('Last night's concert by popular singing sorceress Celestina Warbeck was overshadowed...')
'Troll Rights Movement Out of Control'
    ('In an outspoken speech last night, Artemius Lawson, notorious campaigner...')

[Quidditch section, p. 2]
Quidditch League Table & Match Information
    ('1. Ballycastle Bats...')
Bats Survive the Tornados
    ('To the jubilation of a packed crowd of black-clad Bat fans last night...')
Maddock blamed for Kestrel's win
    ('Alasdair Maddock, Chaser for the Montrose Magpies, bore the brunt...')
Chaos Reigns on Exmoor for Falcons & Pride of Portree
    ('Despite repeated announcements from the Department of Magical Sports and Games...')
Wilda Wallops the Wigs
    ('Puddlemere United wearing their new team robes of kingfisher blue...')
Cannons Didn't Lose Shock
    ('After a disappointing match on Wednesday night...')

[Classified advertisements, p. 3]
Jobs
   [five entries]
For Sale
   [nine entries]
Lonely Hearts
   [four entries]
Births
   [two entries]
Deaths
   [two entries]
[Advert]
   ('S*P*E*C*I*A*L**O*F*F*E*R | Transfiguration | Today...')

Notes:

After each story on pages 1 and 2 there is a large circular point. There are two exceptions: the 'Quidditch League Table & Match Information' (which is in a single ruled border, 65 by 157mm.) and the story 'Wilda Wallops the Wigs'.

There are thirteen sections presented within ruled borders: the reference to editorial comment banner (19 by 47mm.), 'Quidditch League Table & Match Information' (65 by 157mm.) and eleven sections on page 3 including the final one, an advert for *Transfiguration Today*, which appears within a single broken ruled border (54 by 47mm).

Copyright notes at the foot of each page ascribe copyright to J.K. Rowling.

Copies: private collection

THE DAILY PROPHET – 1 JUNE 1999

A6(a)   FIRST ENGLISH EDITION   (1999)

Banner:
June 1ˢᵗ 1999 The Daily Prophet Price: 7 Knuts
(All within single ruled border, 15 by 157mm)

Collation: 4 single leaves with staple upper left corner; 297 by 211mm; [1-4] (pages 2 and 3 both mis-numbered 'page 12')

Page contents: [1] Headlines section; [2-3] Problem pages; [4] Quidditch section

Paper: wove paper

Running title: '*June 1ˢᵗ 1999*' (20mm), '*The Daily Prophet*' (33mm) and '*page 12*' (12mm), pp. [2-3] only

Publication: 1 June 1999

Price: issued as part of membership of the Harry Potter Fan Club (membership fee: £4.25 per year)

Contents:
[Headlines section, p.1]
Goblin Riots Erupt in Chipping Clodbury
   ('Goblin resentment towards the Department for the Regulation and Control...')
[Advert]
   ('Terrortours - action holidays for the wizard family with a sense of adventure...')

[Problem page, p. 2]
[Introduction]
   ('As ever, we have assembled a team of experts...')
How Much Revenge is Safe?
   ('Dear Problem Page, | I have been having a feud with my brother for many years...')
Making it Stick
   ('Dear Problem Page, | No matter how hard I try, I find I am unable to make...')

[Problem page, p. 3]
I'm Turning Purple
   ('Dear Problem Page | I have recently noticed a nasty green and purple rash...')
He Says He Hates Me
   ('Dear Problem Page | I am in love with a wizard who says he is not ready to...')

[Quidditch section, p. 4]
Quidditch League Table & Match Information
    ('1. Ballycastle Bats…')
Mugglemaniac Maddock Must Quit Magpies, Says McLeod
    ('In a shock move just before the Magpies' game against the Caerphilly Catapults…')
Seekers Jinxed as Pride of Portree Fall to the Arrows
    ('A hard-fought match against Pride of Portree resulted in a controversial victory…')
Brand New Harpy Saves the Day
    ('Replacement for Wilda Griffiths, Valmai Morgan, scored a total of ten goals…')
Chudley Canons Win Stuns Fans
    ('"I still can't believe it - pinch me,' said shocked Cannons fan…')

Notes:

After the first story on page 1 only is there is a large circular point. Compare with A5(a).

There are four sections presented within single ruled borders: 'Terrortours' advert (60 by 157mm), 'How Much Revenge is Safe?' (78 by 157mm), 'He Says He Hates Me' (69 by 157mm) and 'Quidditch League Table & Match Information' (59 by 157mm).

Note the presence of commas on the first page of the 'Problem Page' ('Dear Problem Page,') compared to their absence on the second page of the 'Problem Page' ('Dear Problem Page'). Commas after 'Yours sincerely' are inconsistent.

Copyright notes at the foot of pages [1] and [4] ascribe copyright to J.K. Rowling.

Copies: private collection

HARRY POTTER AND THE
PRISONER OF AZKABAN

A7(a) FIRST ENGLISH EDITION, FIRST STATE (1999)
(children's artwork series in hardback)

HARRY | POTTER | *and the Prisoner of Azkaban* | [illustration of Hogwarts crest with legend 'DRAGO DORMIENS NUNQUAM TITILLANDUS' on banner, 67 by 82mm] | J.K.ROWLING | [publisher's device of a dog, 11 by 18mm] | BLOOMSBURY (Lines 1 and 2 justified on left and right margins, and all width centred)

Collation: 160 unsigned leaves bound in indeterminate gatherings; 197 by 127mm; [1-7] 8-17 [18] 19-28 [29] 30-41 [42] 43-55 [56] 57-74 [75] 76-93 [94] 95-106 [107] 108-121 [122] 123-36 [137] 138-56 [157] 158-72 [173] 174-86 [187] 188-98 [199] 200-214 [215] 216-30 [231] 232-43 [244] 245-55 [256] 257-62 [263] 264-76 [277] 278-82 [283] 284-303 [304] 305-317 [318-20]

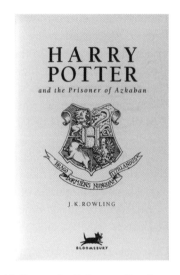

Page contents: [1] half-title: 'HARRY | POTTER | *and the Prisoner of Azkaban* | [illustration of Hogwarts crest with legend 'DRAGO DORMIENS NUNQUAM TITILLANDUS' on banner, 47 by 57mm]'; [2] '*Also available:* | Harry Potter and the Philosopher's Stone | Harry Potter and the Chamber of Secrets'; [3] title-page; [4] 'All rights reserved; no part of this publication may be reproduced or | transmitted by any means, electronic, mechanical, photocopying or otherwise, | without the prior permission of the publisher | [new paragraph] First published in Great Britain in 1999 | Bloomsbury Publishing Plc, 38 Soho Square, London, W1V 5DF | [new paragraph] Copyright © Joanne Rowling 1999 | [new paragraph] The moral right of the author has been asserted | A CIP catalogue record of this book is available from the | British Library | [new paragraph] ISBN 0 7475 4215 5 | [new paragraph] Printed in Great Britain by Clays Ltd, St Ives plc | [new paragraph] 10 9 8 7 6 5 4 3 2 1'; [5] '*To Jill Prewett and Aine Kiely,* | *the Godmothers of Swing*'; [6] blank; [7]-317 text; [318-20] blank

Paper: wove paper

Running title: 'HARRY POTTER' (24mm) on verso, recto title comprises chapter title, pp. 8-317

Binding: pictorial boards.
   On *spine:* '[colour illustration of head of werewolf on coloured panel, 26 by 17mm] HARRY POTTER [in light orange on purple panel, 26 by 47mm] *and the Prisoner of Azkaban* J.K.ROWLING

[both title conclusion and author in purple on red panel, 26 by 107mm] BLOOMSBURY [publisher's device of the head of a dog, 3 by 4mm] [both in light orange on black panel, 26 by 33mm]' (reading lengthways down spine).

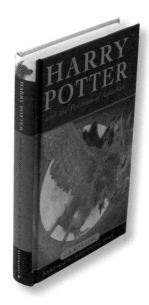

On upper cover: 'HARRY | POTTER | *and the Prisoner of Azkaban* [lines 1 and 2 in light orange, line 3 in green, all on purple panel, 63 by 132mm] | [green rule, 132mm] | [colour illustration of Harry Potter and Hermione Granger riding the back of Buckbeak the Hippogriff, 125 by 132mm] | [green rule, 132mm intersected by light orange panel with 'J.K.ROWLING' in purple] | DOUBLE SMARTIES AWARD-WINNING AUTHOR [in light orange on black panel, 13 by 132mm]' (all width centred)

On lower cover: "*Harry Potter and the Philosopher's Stone* started a cult | last year, the emergence of each of the remaining books in | the series of seven deserves to become a major annual | event. Rowling creates a complete and perfect story.' | *The Times* | [new paragraph] 'The Harry Potter books have become a phenomenon … | parents squabble over who gets to read them to the kids, | and teachers say a chapter can silence the most rowdy of | classes.' *The Guardian* | [new paragraph] HARRY POTTER is a | wizard! Along with Ron | and Hermione, his best | friends, Harry is in his | third year at Hogwarts | School of Witchcraft | and Wizardry. Who | knows what will happen | this year? Read on to find | out and immerse yourself | in the magical world of | Hogwarts … | [barcode in black on white panel, 20 by 37mm together with '[publisher's device of a dog, 6 by 10mm] | BLOOMSBURY' in black on left side of panel and 'http://www.bloomsbury.com' below panel, in black on purple panel, 7 by 37mm]'. Reading lengthways down right side next to foot of spine 'Cover illustrations based upon original art by Cliff Wright'. All in black on an illustration of a werewolf in swirling mists.

All edges trimmed. Binding measurements: 204 by 128mm (covers), 204 by 35mm (spine). End-papers: wove paper.

Dust-jacket: coated wove paper, 204 by 485mm
  Spine, upper and lower covers replicate the binding.
  On upper inside flap: 'HARRY POTTER is a very unusual boy. He | can't wait to get back to school after the | summer holidays! But that's not the only | unusual thing about Harry; Harry's school is | Hogwarts School of Witchcraft and | Wizardry, and Harry is a wizard! | [new paragraph] When Harry, along with his best friends | Ron and Hermione, go back for their third | year at Hogwarts, the atmosphere is tense. | There's an escaped mass murderer on the | loose, and the sinister prison guards of | Azkaban have been called in to guard the | school … | [new paragraph] | A brilliant new story featuring Harry and | his friends, sequel to the award-winning | *Harry Potter and the Philosopher's Stone* and | *Harry Potter and the Chamber of Secrets.* | [new paragraph] HARRY POTTER AND | THE PHILOSOPHER'S STONE | [new paragraph] 'I've yet to meet a 10 year old who hasn't been | entranced by its witty, complex plot and the | character of the eponymous Harry.' | Carolyn Hart, *The Independent* | [new paragraph] [round point] Gold Award Winner of the 1997

Smarties Nestle | Book Prize | [round point] Winner of the Children's Book Award 1998 | [round point] Winner of the Young Telegraph Book Award 1998 | [round point] Winner of the Sheffield Children's Book Award | 1997 | [round point] Winner of the Birmingham Cable Book Award 1997 | [new paragraph] HARRY POTTER AND | THE CHAMBER OF SECRETS | [new paragraph] 'Such a marriage of good writing, inventiveness, | and sheer child-appeal has not been seen since | Roald Dahl, perhaps even since Tolkien, Lewis, | and Ransome. J. K. Rowling has woken a whole | generation to reading.' *The Times* | £10.99'. All in blue, with the exception of the price which is in black, and all on light orange panel.

On lower inside flap: '[three stars, in yellow] | Dear Joanne Rowling, | [new paragraph] I really, really, really liked "Harry Potter | and the philosopher's stone" and "Harry Potter and | the Chamber of Secrets" was <u>FANTASTIC</u>!!!! I | thought it was <u>very</u> funny when the Memory | Charm backfired and it was driving me mad | when I was trying to think who the bodyless | voice belonged to. | [new paragraph] Please can you write another book, because | I'm dying to read more of Harry's adventures. | [new paragraph] Yours sincerely, | Jamie | Patton | Age eight. | [five stars, in yellow]'. All in light orange facsimile of child's handwriting and all on blue panel.

Publication: 8 July 1999 (simultaneous with A7(aa) and A7(aaa)) in an edition of 5,150 copies (confirmed by Bloomsbury) (see notes)

Price: £10.99

Contents:
Harry Potter and the Prisoner of Azkaban
 ('Harry Potter was a highly unusual boy in many ways…')

Notes:

An undated letter from J.K. Rowling to Emma Matthewson is preserved in the Bloomsbury archives:

> Finally! I've read this book so much I'm sick of it, I never read either of the others over and over again when editing them, but I really had to this time… If you think it needs more work, I'm willing and able, but I do think this draft represents an improvement on the first; the dementors are much more of a presence this time round, I think…

The response was an encouraging letter from Matthewson, dated 18 August 1998:

> It's just great Jo – quite a huge, teetering tottering plot that never quite falls down! What a feat! And so moving – when Harry thinks that he has seen his father… it raises the prickles all down my back! I will send the manuscript separately with my comments on once I've had it photocopied – as usual you will find reams of story which I haven't touched as it seems so perfect/funny/brilliant…

The editorial process continued for at least three months. A letter from Rowling to Matthewson is dated 17 November and notes:

> An annoying little speech bubble has just popped onto my screen saying 'looks like you're writing a letter. Would you like some help?' This laptop is too clever for its own good… I am so sick of re-reading this one that I'll be hard put to smile when it comes to doing public readings from it. But perhaps the feeling will have worn off by next summer…

The Bloomsbury archives include a print-out of the text labelled 'Final Final Draft Azkaban 23.12.' This suggests that, at this stage in the series, both author and publisher were well ahead of proposed publishing schedules.

A further set of proofs is dated 5 January 1999. As with the earlier set, the dedication is still lacking and the text includes 'being burned' on page 7.

The title was published on 8 July 1999 and released at the precise time of 3.45 pm. In an interview with me in September 2013, Nigel Newton recalled 'I think I can claim credit for that particular idea. The idea was that children wouldn't play truant and leave school to go and buy it. We were very lucky that the *Daily Telegraph* – perhaps they were tipped off by our publicity department – took a photograph of a queue of children outside the Lion and Unicorn bookshop in Richmond at 3.30pm.' The picture acted as a catalyst as it was published on the front page of the *Daily Telegraph*. Readers of that newspaper were 'core market' but other newpapers started regarding Harry Potter as front page news from this point.

The first state of the first edition is identified by the copyright line 'Copyright © Joanne Rowling 1999' and the incorrect text block on page [7] which appears 'Wendelin the Weird enjoyed being | burnt | so much that she allowed herself to be caught no fewer than | forty-seven times in various disguises.' The error was, seemingly, introduced in correcting the text from the proof setting which read 'Wendelin the Weird enjoyed being | burned so much that she allowed herself to be caught no fewer | than forty-seven times in various disguises.' The second state (see A7(aa)) ascribes copyright to 'J.K. Rowling' and corrects the text block. The third state (see A7(aaa)) matches the second state but lacks the name of the printer and has two publisher's advertisements at the end of the book.

The three states can be compared as follows:

A7(a)
first state

Non-magic people (more commonly known as Muggles) were particularly afraid of magic in medieval times, but not very good at recognising it. On the rare occasion that they did catch a real witch or wizard, burning had no effect whatsoever. The witch or wizard would perform a basic Flame-Freezing Charm and then pretend to shriek with pain while enjoying a gentle, tickling sensation. Indeed, Wendelin the Weird enjoyed being burnt
  so much that she allowed herself to be caught no fewer than forty-seven times in various disguises.

A7(aa)
second state

Non-magic people (more commonly known as Muggles) were particularly afraid of magic in medieval times, but not very good at recognising it. On the rare occasion that they did catch a real witch or wizard, burning had no effect whatsoever. The witch or wizard would perform a basic Flame-Freezing Charm and then pretend to shriek with pain while enjoying a gentle, tickling sensation. Indeed, Wendelin the Weird enjoyed being burnt so much that she allowed herself to be caught no fewer than forty-seven times in various disguises.

A7(aaa)
third state

Non-magic people (more commonly known as Muggles) were particularly afraid of magic in medieval times, but not very good at recognising it. On the rare occasion that they did catch a real witch or wizard, burning had no effect whatsoever. The witch or wizard would perform a basic Flame-Freezing Charm and then pretend to shriek with pain while enjoying a gentle, tickling sensation. Indeed, Wendelin the Weird enjoyed being burnt so much that she allowed herself to be caught no fewer than forty-seven times in various disguises.

The book trade has generally thought that there were 2,500 copies of the first issue. The *total* edition consisting of all three states is 5,150 copies based on figures provided by the publisher.

In the issue following publication of this title, the *Bookseller* reported that 'there are many disappointed customers who have not been able to get hold of first editions of *The Prisoner of Azkaban*' (see *Bookseller*, 16 July 1999, p. 20). Demand for copies evidently led the publishers to order and distribute reprints in advance of the day of publication. A report compiled by Clays Ltd, in October 2013, noted a first edition printing of 5,150 copies in May 1999 with a reprint of 101,800 copies in June 1999.

Note that the title conclusion and the author on the spine (and the spine of the dust-jacket) are in the same colour. This is the only title in the series in this design where this is the case.

The English audiobook version, read by Stephen Fry, has a duration of approximately twelve hours.

The first, second and third states contain the same textual mistakes. Reprints (and subsequent new editions) include a number of corrections to the text. These comprise:

Page 7, line 9	'Adalbert Waffling' to 'Bathilda Bagshot'
Page 35, line 34	'spend' to 'spent'
Page 36, line 3	'Anglesea' to 'Anglesey'
Page 36, line 12	'BANG' to 'BANG!'
Page 37, line 38	'a table betwen Fudge and Harry' to 'a table between Fudge and Harry'
Page 38, line 9	'Magic Reversal Department' to 'Magic Reversal Squad'
Page 38, lines 33-34	'last two weeks of your holidays' to 'last three weeks of your holidays'
Page 40, line 30	'clicked her break' to 'clicked her beak'
Page 41, line 1	'two completely Dursley-free weeks' to 'three completely Dursley-free weeks'
Page 47, line 28	'the Study of Ancient Runes' to 'Study of Ancient Runes'
Page 53, lines 20-21	'they've ended up in the Forbidden Forest twice!' to 'they've even ended up in the Forbidden Forest!'
Page 53, line 29	'It's been three weeks' to 'It's been a month now'
Page 61, line 35	'massive sherbert balls' to 'massive sherbet balls'
Page 63, line 9	'stack of cauldron cakes' to 'stack of Cauldron Cakes'
Page 63, lines 13-14	'taking the cauldron cake' to 'taking the Cauldron Cake'
Page 73, line 31	'a crime he had not commited' to 'a crime he had not committed'
Page 78, line 23	'the murmer of voices' to 'the murmur of voices'
Page 82, line 8	'Profesor Trelawney was staring' to 'Professor Trelawney was staring'
Page 85, line 36	'everywere' to 'everywhere'
Page 92, line 12	'almost as a big as a bucket' to 'almost as big as a bucket'
Page 145, line 31	'Dissendium!' to '*Dissendium!*'
Page 145, line 38	'Lumos!' to '*Lumos!*'
Page 147, line 12	'Droobles Best Blowing Gum' to 'Drooble's Best Blowing Gum'
Page 152, line 36	'or Secret-Keeper' to 'or Secret Keeper'
Page 152, lines 37-38	'the Secret-Keeper chooses' to 'the Secret Keeper chooses'
Page 152, line 38	'the Secret-Keeper refused' to 'the Secret Keeper refused'
Page 153, line 2	'the Potters' Secret-Keeper' to 'the Potters' Secret Keeper'
Page 153, line 8	'Secret-Keeper himself' to 'Secret Keeper himself'
Page 154, line 13	'the Potters' Secret-Keeper' to 'the Potters' Secret Keeper'
Page 154, line 26	'the Potters' Secret-Keeper' to 'the Potters' Secret Keeper'
Page 158, line 25	'their Secret-Keeper' to 'their Secret Keeper'
Page 168, line 25	'examing the Firebolt' to 'examining the Firebolt'
Page 173, line 20	'After last match' to 'After the last match'
Page 175, line 24	'Professor Binn's desk' to 'Professor Binns' desk'
Page 178, line 16	'*It's Him! Go! Run! I'll hold him off -*' to '*It's him! Go! Run! I'll hold him off -*'

Page 180, line 7	'than took a detour' to 'then took a detour'
Page 198, line 7	'baited breath' to 'bated breath'
Page 251, line 31	'breathing came from near the bed' to 'breathing came from the bed'
Page 260, line 39	'self-digust' to 'self-disgust'
Page 268, lines 3-4	'THEIR SECRET-KEEPER' to 'THEIR SECRET KEEPER'
Page 268, line 10	'Secret-Keeper instead of me' to 'Secret Keeper instead of me'
Page 271, line 10	'made you Secret-Keeper' to 'made you Secret Keeper'
Page 278, line 28	'they'd seen on television!' to 'they'd seen on television?'
Page 287, line 19	'the Potters' Secret-Keeper' to 'the Potters' Secret Keeper'
Page 298, lines 23-26	'They saw Lupin, Ron and Pettigrew clambering awkwardly out of the hole in the roots. Then came Hermione … then the unconscious Snape, drifting weirdly upwards. Next came Harry and Black.' to 'They saw Lupin, Ron and Pettigrew clambering awkwardly out of the hole in the roots, followed by the unconscious Snape, drifting weirdly upwards. Next came Harry, Hermione and Black.'

Copies: Peter Harrington Books (bookseller inventory #36818); Sotheby's, 10 July 2013, lot 368

A7(aa)   FIRST ENGLISH EDITION, SECOND STATE   (1999)
(children's artwork series in hardback)

HARRY | POTTER | *and the Prisoner of Azkaban* | [illustration of Hogwarts crest with legend 'DRAGO DORMIENS NUNQUAM TITILLANDUS' on banner, 67 by 82mm] | J.K.ROWLING | [publisher's device of a dog, 11 by 18mm] | BLOOMSBURY (Lines 1 and 2 justified on left and right margins, and all width centred)

Collation: 160 unsigned leaves bound in indeterminate gatherings; 197 by 127mm; [1-7] 8-17 [18] 19-28 [29] 30-41 [42] 43-55 [56] 57-74 [75] 76-93 [94] 95-106 [107] 108-121 [122] 123-36 [137] 138-56 [157] 158-72 [173] 174-86 [187] 188-98 [199] 200-214 [215] 216-30 [231] 232-43 [244] 245-55 [256] 257-62 [263] 264-76 [277] 278-82 [283] 284-303 [304] 305-317 [318-20]

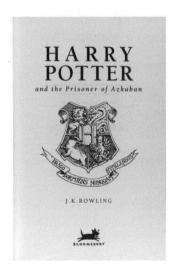

Page contents: [1] half-title: 'HARRY | POTTER | *and the Prisoner of Azkaban* | [illustration of Hogwarts crest with legend 'DRAGO DORMIENS NUNQUAM TITILLANDUS' on banner, 47 by 57mm]'; [2] '*Also available:* | Harry Potter and the Philosopher's Stone | Harry Potter and the Chamber of Secrets'; [3] title-page; [4] 'All rights reserved; no part of this publication may be reproduced or | transmitted by any means, electronic, mechanical, photocopying or otherwise, | without the prior permission of the publisher | [new paragraph] First published in Great Britain in 1999 | Bloomsbury Publishing Plc, 38 Soho Square, London, W1V 5DF | [new paragraph] Copyright © J.K. Rowling 1999 | [new paragraph] The moral right of the author has been asserted | A CIP catalogue record of this book is available from the | British Library | [new paragraph] ISBN 0 7475 4215 5 | [new paragraph] Printed in Great Britain by Clays Ltd, St Ives plc | [new paragraph] 10 9 8 7 6 5 4 3 2 1'; [5] *'To Jill Prewett and Aine Kiely,* | *the Godmothers of Swing*'; [6] blank; [7]-317 text; [318-20] blank

Paper: wove paper

Running title: 'HARRY POTTER' (24mm) on verso, recto title comprises chapter title, pp. 8-317

Binding: as for A7(a)

Dust-jacket: as for A7(a)

Publication: 8 July 1999 (simultaneous with A7(a) and A7(aaa)) (confirmed by Bloomsbury)

Price: £10.99

Contents:
Harry Potter and the Prisoner of Azkaban
('Harry Potter was a highly unusual boy in many ways…')

Notes:
The second issue of the first edition is identified by the copyright line 'Copyright © J.K. Rowling 1999' and the corrected text block on page [7]. See A7(a) for a comparison.

Neither first or second states (see also A7(a)) include publisher's advertisements in the blank pages at the end of the book. Publisher's advertisements have been claimed as a difference between the first and second states (with adverts apparently included in the first state). However, I have found no copies to support this. Compare, however, with the third state (A7(aaa)) which does contain publisher's advertisements at the end of the volume.

Copies: Sotheby's, 17 December 2008, lot 216

Reprints include:
10   BL (Nov 1999/940) stamped 2 Aug 1999
20 19
20 19 18 17
30 29 28 27 26

A report compiled by the printers, Clays Ltd, in October 2013 noted that, to date, they had produced a minimum of 7.7 million paperbacks and 1.9 million hardbacks across 216 printings.

A7(aaa)   FIRST ENGLISH EDITION, THIRD STATE   (1999)
(children's artwork series in hardback)

HARRY | POTTER | *and the Prisoner of Azkaban* | [illustration of Hogwarts crest with legend 'DRAGO DORMIENS NUNQUAM TITILLANDUS' on banner, 67 by 82mm] | J.K.ROWLING | [publisher's device of a dog, 11 by 18mm] | BLOOMSBURY (Lines 1 and 2 justified on left and right margins, and all width centred)

Collation: 162 unsigned leaves bound in indeterminate gatherings; 195 by 124mm; [1-7] 8-17 [18] 19-28 [29] 30-41 [42] 43-55 [56] 57-74 [75] 76-93 [94] 95-106 [107] 108-121 [122] 123-36 [137] 138-56 [157] 158-72 [173] 174-86 [187] 188-98 [199] 200-214 [215] 216-30 [231] 232-43 [244] 245-55 [256] 257-62 [263] 264-76 [277] 278-82 [283] 284-303 [304] 305-317 [318-24]

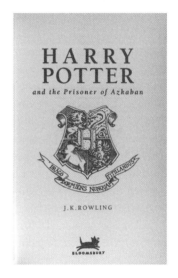

Page contents: [1] half-title: 'HARRY | POTTER | *and the Prisoner of Azkaban* | [illustration of Hogwarts crest with legend 'DRAGO DORMIENS NUNQUAM TITILLANDUS' on banner, 47 by 57mm]'; [2] '*Also available:* | Harry Potter and the Philosopher's Stone | Harry Potter and the Chamber of Secrets'; [3] title-page; [4] 'All rights reserved; no part of this publication may be reproduced or | transmitted by any means, electronic, mechanical, photocopying or otherwise, | without the prior permission of the publisher | [new paragraph] First published in Great Britain in 1999 | Bloomsbury Publishing Plc, 38 Soho Square, London, W1V 5DF | [new paragraph] Copyright © J.K. Rowling 1999 | [new paragraph] The moral right of the author has been asserted | A CIP catalogue record of this book is available from the | British Library | [new paragraph] ISBN 0 7475 4215 5 | [new paragraph] 10 9 8 7 6 5 4 3 2 1'; [5] '*To Jill Prewett and Aine Kiely,* | *the Godmothers of Swing*'; [6] blank; [7]-317 text; [318] blank; [319] publisher's advertisement: upper cover design of *Harry Potter and the Philosopher's Stone*; [320] blank; [321] publisher's advertisement: upper cover design of *Harry Potter and the Chamber of Secrets*; [322-24] blank

Paper: wove paper

Running title: 'HARRY POTTER' (24mm) on verso, recto title comprises chapter title, pp. 8-317

Binding: pictorial boards.
   On spine: '[colour illustration of head of werewolf on coloured panel, 27 by 18mm] HARRY POTTER [in light orange on purple panel, 27 by 47mm] *and the Prisoner of Azkaban* J.K.ROWLING [both title conclusion and author in purple on red panel, 27 by 107mm] BLOOMSBURY [publisher's device of the head of a dog, 3 by 4mm] [both in light orange on black panel, 27 by 33mm]' (reading lengthways down spine).

On upper cover: 'HARRY | POTTER | *and the Prisoner of Azkaban* [lines 1 and 2 in light orange, line 3 in green, all on purple panel, 63 by 134mm] | [green rule, 134mm] | [colour illustration of Harry Potter and Hermione Granger riding the back of Buckbeak the Hippogriff, 125 by 134mm] | [green rule, 134mm intersected by light orange panel with 'J.K.ROWLING' in purple] | DOUBLE SMARTIES AWARD-WINNING AUTHOR [in light orange on black panel, 13 by 134mm]' (all width centred).

On lower cover: "*Harry Potter and the Philosopher's Stone* started a cult | last year, the emergence of each of the remaining books in | the series of seven deserves to become a major annual | event. Rowling creates a complete and perfect story.' | *The Times* | [new paragraph] 'The Harry Potter books have become a phenomenon ... | parents squabble over who gets to read them to the kids, | and teachers say a chapter can silence the most rowdy of | classes.' *The Guardian* | [new paragraph] HARRY POTTER is a | wizard! Along with Ron | and Hermione, his best | friends, Harry is in his | third year at Hogwarts | School of Witchcraft | and Wizardry. Who | knows what will happen | this year? Read on to find | out and immerse yourself | in the magical world of | Hogwarts ... | [barcode in black on white panel, 20 by 37mm together with '[publisher's device of a dog, 6 by 10mm] | BLOOMSBURY' in black on left side of panel and 'http://www.bloomsbury.com' below panel, in black on purple panel, 7 by 37mm]'. Reading lengthways down right side next to foot of spine 'Cover illustrations based upon original art by Cliff Wright'. All in black on an illustration of a werewolf in swirling mists.

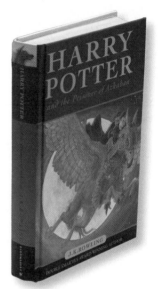

All edges trimmed. Binding measurements: 204 by 128mm (covers), 204 by 37mm (spine). End-papers: wove paper.

Dust-jacket: coated wove paper, 204 by 480mm
Spine, upper and lower covers replicate the binding.
All other details as for A7(a).

Publication: 8 July 1999 (simultaneous with A7(a) and A7(aa)) (confirmed by Bloomsbury)

Price: £10.99

Contents:
Harry Potter and the Prisoner of Azkaban
('Harry Potter was a highly unusual boy in many ways...')

Notes:
The third state of the first edition is identified by the corrected copyright line ('J.K. Rowling'), the omission of a printer, the corrected text-block on page [7] and two publisher's advertisements on additional pages at the end of book. See A7(a) for a comparison. The two publisher's advertisements were black and white reproductions of the upper covers of *Philosopher's Stone* and *Chamber of Secrets*, as follows:

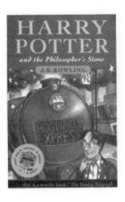

There is anecdotal evidence of a variant version of this state containing only an advertisement for *Chamber of Secrets*. No copies have been examined, however.

Slightly thicker paper was used for this state and the volume is very slightly wider than volumes in the first and second state. The weight changes accordingly. Without dust-jackets, both states one and two weigh 342g. State three weighs 394g (without dust-jacket).

Both the spine and the dust-jacket show a thin column of purple to the left of the werewolf illustration on the spine. In states one and two there is the merest suggestion of a line.

Copies: private collection (PWE)

A7(b)   FIRST AMERICAN EDITION   (1999)
(children's artwork series in hardback)

HARRY POTTER | AND THE PRISONER OF AZKABAN | [black and white illustration of a long-haired man looking at mouse in front of oval window, 58 by 77mm] | BY | J. K. ROWLING | ILLUSTRATIONS BY MARY GRANDPRÉ | [publisher's device of a lantern, 11 by 8mm] | ARTHUR A. LEVINE BOOKS | AN IMPRINT OF SCHOLASTIC PRESS (All width centred on a diamond pattern background)

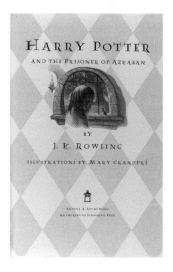

Collation: 224 unsigned leaves bound in fourteen gatherings of sixteen leaves; 226 by 150mm; [I-VI] VII-IX [X-XII] 1-435 [436]

Page contents: [I] half-title: 'HARRY POTTER | AND THE PRISONER OF AZKABAN' (all on a diamond pattern background); [II] 'ALSO BY J. K. ROWLING | [new paragraph] *Harry Potter and the Sorcerer's Stone* | Year One at Hogwarts |

[new paragraph] *Harry Potter and the Chamber of Secrets* | Year Two at Hogwarts'; [III] title-page; [IV] '[device of twelve stars] | Text copyright © 1999 by J. K. Rowling | Illustrations copyright © 1999 by Mary GrandPré | All rights reserved. Published by Scholastic Press, a division of Scholastic Inc., | *Publishers since 1920.* | SCHOLASTIC, SCHOLASTIC PRESS, ARTHUR A. LEVINE BOOKS, and associated logos | are trademarks and/or registered trademarks of Scholastic Inc. | [new paragraph] No part of this publication may be reproduced, or stored in a retrieval system, or transmitted | in any form or by any means, electronic, mechanical, photocopying, recording, or otherwise, | without written permission of the publisher. For information regarding permission, write | to Scholastic Inc., Attention: Permissions Department, 555 Broadway, New York, NY 10012. | [new paragraph] Library of Congress Cataloging-in-Publication Data | [new paragraph] Rowling, J. K. | Harry Potter and the Prisoner of Azkaban / by J. K. Rowling. | p. cm. | Sequel to: Harry Potter and the Chamber of Secrets | Summary: During his third year at Hogwarts School for Witchcraft and Wizardry, | Harry Potter must confront the devious and dangerous wizard responsible for his parents' deaths. | ISBN 0-439-13635-0 | [square bracket]1. Wizards—Fiction. 2. Magic—Fiction. 3. Schools—Fiction. | 4. England—Fiction.[square bracket] I. Title. | PZ7.R79835Ham 1999 | [square bracket]Fic[square bracket] — dc21 99-23982 | [new paragraph] 10 9 8 7 6 5 4 3 2 1   9/9 0/0 1 2 3 4 | Printed in the U.S.A. 37 | First American edition, October 1999'; [V] 'TO JILL PREWETT AND | AINE KIELY, | THE GODMOTHERS OF SWING'; [VI] blank; VII-IX 'CONTENTS' (twenty-two chapters listed with titles and page references); [X] blank; [XI] half-title: 'HARRY POTTER | AND THE PRISONER OF AZKABAN' (all on diamond pattern background); [XII] blank; 1-435 text; [436] colophon: '[publisher's device of a lantern, 17 by 13mm] | *This* | *book was art* | *directed by David Saylor. The* | *art for both the jacket and the interior was* | *created using pastels on toned printmaking paper. The* | *text was set in 12-point Adobe Garamond, a typeface based on the* | *sixteenth-century type designs of Claude Garamond, redrawn by Robert* | *Slimbach in 1989. The book was printed and bound at* | *Berryville Graphics in Berryville, Virginia. The* | *production was supervised by Angela* | *Biola and Mike* | *Derevjanik.*'

Paper: wove paper

Running title: 'CHAPTER' and chapter number on verso, recto title comprises chapter title, pp. 1-435 except for pages on which a new chapter commences. On these pages, the running title comprises 'CHAPTER' and chapter number. Each running title (excluding pages on which new chapters commence) begins and ends with a three star device (in mirror image)

Illustrations: title-page vignette, together with twenty-two vignettes at the beginning of each chapter (after chapter and chapter number but before chapter title). In addition to standard typographical changes (including italics, capitals and small capitals) there are other typographical features, comprising:

p. 8 newspaper headline
p. 10 facsimile of Ron's signature (repeated twice)
p. 11 facsimile of Hermione's signature
p. 14 'handwritten' letter from Hagrid
p. 14 facsimile of Professor M. McGonagall's signature

p. 37 newspaper headline

p. 51 advertisement sign

p. 192 'The Marauder's Map' legend

p. 199 notice

p. 272 'handwritten' letter from Hagrid

p. 287 four different 'handwritten' comments

p. 291 'handwritten' letter from Hagrid

p. 315 'handwritten' exam schedule

p. 325 'handwritten' note from Hagrid

Binding: purple cloth-backed spine with green boards (with diamond pattern in blind).

On spine: 'ROWLING | [rule] | ['YEAR | 3' within concave square]' (horizontally at head) with 'HARRY POTTER | AND THE PRISONER OF AZKABAN' (reading lengthways down spine) and '[publisher's device of a lantern, 19 by 14mm] | ARTHUR A. | LEVINE BOOKS | [rule] | SCHOLASTIC | PRESS' (horizontally at foot). All in green.

Upper and lower covers: blank.

All edges trimmed. Binding measurements: 235 by 150mm (covers), 235 by 47mm (spine). The purple cloth continues onto the covers by 40mm. End-papers: orange wove paper.

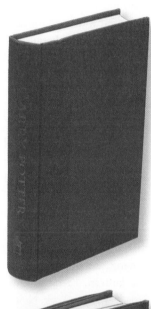

Dust-jacket: uncoated wove paper, 234 by 570mm. A single illustration spans the entire dust-jacket.

On spine: 'ROWLING | [rule] | ['YEAR | 3' within concave square]' (horizontally at head) with 'HARRY POTTER | AND THE PRISONER OF AZKABAN' (reading lengthways down spine) and '[publisher's device of a lantern, 19 by 14mm] | ARTHUR A. | LEVINE BOOKS | [rule] | SCHOLASTIC | PRESS' (horizontally at foot). All embossed in green and all on colour illustration of Buckbeak the Hippogriff's wing and a brick wall with window-frame.

On upper cover: 'Harry Potter [hand-drawn lettering] [embossed in green] | AND [hand-drawn lettering in brown of illustration] | THE Prisoner [hand-drawn lettering in brown of illustration] | of AZKABAN [hand-drawn lettering in brown of illustration] | J. K. ROWLING [embossed in green]' (all width centred). All on colour illustration of Harry Potter and Hermione Granger riding Buckbeak the Hippogriff flying in front of a leaded window.

On lower cover: 'Sequel to the #1 *New York Times* Bestseller | HARRY POTTER | AND THE CHAMBER OF SECRETS | [barcode with smaller barcode to the right (51995) all in black on

orange panel, 20 by 50mm]. All in grey and all on colour illustration of brick wall with a Dementor hiding, together with a tree, moon, etc.

On upper inside flap: '$19.95 | FOR TWELVE | long years, the dread fortress of | Azkaban held an infamous prisoner | named Sirius Black. Convicted of killing | thirteen people with a single curse, he was | said to be the heir apparent to the Dark Lord, | Voldemort. | [new paragraph] Now he has escaped, leaving only two clues as | to where he might be headed: Harry Potter's | defeat of You-Know-Who was Black's downfall as | well. And the Azkaban guards heard Black mut- | tering in his sleep, "He's at Hogwarts … he's at | Hogwarts." | [new paragraph] Harry Potter isn't safe, not even within the | walls of his magical school, surrounded by his | friends. Because on top of it all, there may well | be a traitor in their midst.' All in grey and all on colour illustration of a brick wall with a rat watching the scene.

On lower inside flap: 'ALSO BY J. K. ROWLING | [new paragraph] HARRY POTTER | AND THE CHAMBER OF SECRETS | [new paragraph] [four-sided device, in yellow] #1 *New York Times* Bestseller | [four-sided device, in yellow] #1 *USA Today* Bestseller List | [four-sided device, in yellow] Winner of the National Book Award (UK) | [four-sided device, in yellow] Winner of the Gold Medal Smarties Prize (UK) | [new paragraph] [five-pointed star, in yellow] "Harry Potter's exploits during his second year at | Hogwarts School for Witchcraft and Wizardry completely | live up to the bewitching measure of *Harry Potter and the* | *Sorcerer's Stone*. The mystery, zany humor, student rivalry, | and eccentric faculty… are as expertly crafted here as in | the first book." —*Booklist*, starred review | [new paragraph] HARRY POTTER |AND THE SORCERER'S STONE | [new paragraph] [four-sided device, in yellow] Over six months on the *New York Times* Bestseller List | [four-sided device, in yellow] Winner of the National Book Award (UK) | [four-sided device, in yellow] Cited as one of the best books of 1998 by *Publishers* | *Weekly, School Library Journal*, and *Booklist*. | [new paragraph] "A charming, imaginative, magical confection of a novel." | —*Boston Globe* | [new paragraph] "Funny, moving, and impressive." | —*The New York Times Book Review* | [new paragraph] [publisher's device of a lantern, 15 by 11mm] ARTHUR A. LEVINE BOOKS | *An Imprint of Scholastic Press* | 555 Broadway, New York, New York 10012 | [new paragraph] *Jacket art © 1999 by Mary GrandPré* | *Jacket design by Mary GrandPré and David Saylor*'. All in grey and all on colour illustration of a stag standing by a lake in front of a hut on a hill in front of a forest.

Publication: 8 September 1999

Price: $19.95

Contents:
Harry Potter and the Prisoner of Azkaban
('Harry Potter was a highly unusual boy in many ways. For one thing, he hated…')

Notes:
In an interview with me in March 2012 the publisher Arthur A. Levine stated that it was with publication of the third book in the U.K., prior to American publication, that Amazon's distribution became 'an issue'. Levine noted that Scholastic '… moved the

publication of *Azkaban* to meet demand—it was the only thing we could do. The situation provided an opportunity to clarify laws and the ethical limitations of territorial bookselling. Legally, Scholastic control U.S. rights and Amazon should only have been selling our edition to U.S. customers. The even greater problem was that some British books were showing up in U.S. bookstores… Some bookstores were trying to serve their customers and were importing British editions.'

Although the imprint page notes a publication date of October 1999, the advance reader's edition (see AA4(cc)) cited a publication of September. The date of release, as recorded on an advertising poster issued by the publisher, was 8 September 1999.

Scholastic released a 'dumpbin' display case for this edition at the beginning of October 1999 (Nielsen BookData provides a date of 1 October 1999). The case was filled with 44 copies of this edition.

Each chapter commences with a drop capital.

The American audiobook version, read by Jim Dale, has a duration of approximately eleven and three-quarter hours.

Copies: private collection (PWE)

Reprints include:

20 19	9/9 0/0 1 2 3 4	Printed in the U.S.A. 45
		BL (YA.2000.a.7023) stamped 27 Mar 2000
30 29 28 37 26 25 24 23	0/0 1 2 3 4	Printed in the U.S.A. 45
38 37 36 35 34 33 32 31 30 29 28 27	0/0 1 2 3 4 5	Printed in the U.S.A. 32

ENGLISH DELUXE EDITION **(1999)**
(children's artwork series in deluxe hardback)

HARRY | POTTER | *and the Prisoner of Azkaban* | [illustration of Hogwarts crest with legend 'DRACO DORMIENS NUNQUAM TITILLANDUS' on banner, 70 by 86mm] | J.K.ROWLING | [publisher's device of a dog, 12 by 19mm] | BLOOMSBURY (All width centred)

Collation: 160 unsigned leaves bound in twenty gatherings of eight leaves; 233 by 151mm; [1-7] 8-17 [18] 19-28 [29] 30-41 [42] 43-55 [56] 57-74 [75] 76-93 [94] 95-106 [107] 108-121 [122] 123-36 [137] 138-56 [157] 158-72 [173] 174-86 [187] 188-98 [199] 200-214 [215] 216-30 [231] 232-43 [244] 245-55 [256] 257-62 [263] 264-76 [277] 278-82 [283] 284-303 [304] 305-317 [318-20]

Page contents: [1] half-title: 'HARRY | POTTER | *and the Prisoner of Azkaban* | [illustration of Hogwarts crest with legend 'DRACO DORMIENS NUNQUAM TITILLANDUS' on banner, 49 by 60mm]'; [2] '*Also available:* | Harry Potter and the Philosopher's Stone | Harry Potter and the Chamber of Secrets'; [3] title-page; [4] 'All rights reserved; no part of this publication may be reproduced or | transmitted by any means, electronic, mechanical, photocopying or otherwise, | without the prior permission of the publisher | [new paragraph] This edition first published in Great Britain in 1999 | Bloomsbury Publishing Plc, 38 Soho Square, London, W1V 5DF | [new paragraph] Copyright © Text Joanne Rowling 1999 | Cover illustration based upon original art by Cliff Wright | [new paragraph] The moral right of the author has been asserted | A CIP catalogue record of this book is available from the | British Library | [new paragraph] ISBN 0 7475 4511 1 | [new paragraph] Printed in Great Britain by Clays Ltd, St Ives plc | [new paragraph] 10 9 8 7 6 5 4 3 2 1'; [5] '*To Jill Prewett and Aine Kiely,* | *the Godmothers of Swing*'; [6] blank; [7]-317 text; [318-20] blank

Paper: wove paper

Running title: 'HARRY POTTER' (25mm) on verso, recto title comprises chapter title, pp. 8-317

Binding: light green cloth.
  On spine: 'HARRY POTTER *and the Prisoner of Azkaban* J.K.ROWLING' (reading lengthways down spine) with '[publisher's device of a dog, 12 by 21mm] | BLOOMSBURY' (horizontally at foot of spine). All in gilt.
  On upper cover: 'HARRY | POTTER | *and the Prisoner of Azkaban* | [double ruled border, 107 by 107mm with the outer border thicker than the inner and colour illustration by Cliff Wright laid down] | JKRowling [facsimile signature]' (all width centred). All in gilt.
  Lower cover: blank.

All edges gilt. Yellow sewn bands at head and foot of spine together with yellow marker ribbon. Binding measurements: 241 by 151mm (covers), 241 by 42mm (spine). End-papers: dark green wove paper.

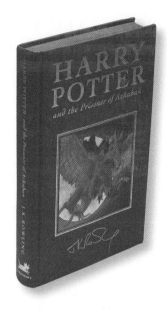

Dust-jacket: none

Publication: 27 September 1999 (see notes)

Price: £18

Contents:

Harry Potter and the Prisoner of Azkaban

('Harry Potter was a highly unusual boy in many ways. For one thing, he hated the…')

Notes:

The publication date for this edition is unclear. Information provided by Bloomsbury gives a date of 28 June 1999. This would pre-date the first trade edition and is evidently incorrect. Bloomsbury's information is replicated by Nielsen BookData. (This source also notes Bloomsbury's publication of an 'Azkaban Mini Hippogriff stand' for the same date which was, obviously, a publicity stand published in advance of the release of the title).

The legal deposit copy in the British Library is dated 13 August 1999. (A comparison with the first trade edition does not help establish a sequence since the British Library copy, stamped 2 August 1999, is a tenth impression.)

The *Bookseller* for 9 July 1999 includes both first English edition and the English deluxe edition as publications for the week. There are no Harry Potter adverts present in the *Bookseller Buyer's Guide* for Spring 1999 or Autumn 1999.

The royalties manager at the Blair Partnership has noted, however, that the files held by the author's agent suggest a publication date of 27 September. This would provide the same publication date for this edition as the English deluxe editions of *Philosopher's Stone* and *Chamber of Secrets* (see A1(d) and A2(e)) and seems the most likely candidate.

Confusion surrounding publication date is also replicated in the Bloomsbury archives with reference to the print-run and no precise figure can be given.

A copy of this edition inscribed by the author to her father and stepmother was offered at auction at Sotheby's New York on 10 December 2003. It was inscribed on the dedication page 'To Dad and Jan, | with lots and lots of love | (and up The Sunday Mail) | Jo x'. On the imprint page the author circled the end of the strike line and wrote, with a pointing arrow, 'Guard it with your lives!!!' Estimated at $20,000/30,000, it sold for $16,000.

Copies: BL (C.194.b.216) stamped 13 Aug 1999; Sotheby's, 17 December 2009, lot 169

A7(d)   TED SMART/'THE BOOK PEOPLE' EDITION   (1999)
(children's artwork series in hardback)

HARRY | POTTER | *and the Prisoner of Azkaban* | [illustration of Hogwarts crest with legend 'DRAGO DORMIENS NUNQUAM TITILLANDUS' on banner, 67 by 82mm] | J.K.ROWLING | [publisher's device of a rule, 39mm | 'TED SMART' | rule, 39mm, all within single ruled border, 7 by 40mm] (Lines 1 and 2 justified on left and right margins, and all width centred)

Collation: 160 unsigned leaves bound in indeterminate gatherings; 197 by 127mm; [1-7] 8-17 [18] 19-28 [29] 30-41 [42] 43-55 [56] 57-74 [75] 76-93 [94] 95-106 [107] 108-121 [122] 123-36 [137] 138-56 [157] 158-72 [173] 174-86 [187] 188-98 [199] 200-214 [215] 216-30 [231] 232-43 [244] 245-55 [256] 257-62 [263] 264-76 [277] 278-82 [283] 284-303 [304] 305-317 [318-20]

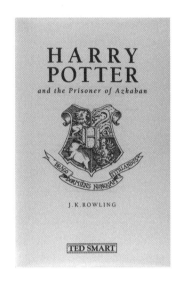

Page contents: [1] half-title: 'HARRY | POTTER | *and the Prisoner of Azkaban* | [illustration of Hogwarts crest with legend 'DRAGO DORMIENS NUNQUAM TITILLANDUS' on banner, 47 by 57mm]'; [2] '*Also available:* | Harry Potter and the Philosopher's Stone | Harry Potter and the Chamber of Secrets'; [3] title-page; [4] 'All rights reserved; no part of this publication may be reproduced or | transmitted by any means, electronic, mechanical, photocopying or otherwise, | without the prior permission of the publisher | [new paragraph] First published in Great Britain in 1999 | Bloomsbury Publishing Plc, 38 Soho Square, London, W1V 5DF | [new paragraph] This edition produced for | The Book People Ltd, | Hall Wood Avenue, | Haydock, St. Helens WA11 9UL | [new paragraph] Copyright © 1999 J.K. Rowling | Cover illustration copyright © Cliff Wright 1999 | Cover illustration from original artwork by Cliff Wright | [new paragraph] The moral right of the author has been asserted | A CIP catalogue record of this book is available from the | British Library | [new paragraph] ISBN 1-85613-617-5 | [new paragraph] Printed in Great Britain by Clays Ltd, St Ives plc | Typeset by Dorchester Typesetting | [new paragraph] 10 9 8 7 6 5 4 3 2 1'; [5] '*To Jill Prewett and Aine Kiely,* | *the Godmothers of Swing*'; [6] blank; [7]-317 text; [318-20] blank

Paper: wove paper

Running title: 'HARRY POTTER' (24mm) on verso, recto title comprises chapter title, pp. 8-317

Binding: pictorial boards.
On spine: '[colour illustration of head of werewolf on coloured panel, 26 by 18mm] HARRY POTTER [in dark yellow on purple panel, 26 by 47mm] *and the Prisoner of Azkaban* J.K.ROWLING [both title conclusion and author in purple on red panel, 26 by 107mm] [publisher's device of a rule, 26mm | 'TED SMART' | rule, 26mm, all within single ruled border, 5 by 27mm] [in dark yellow on black panel, 26 by 33mm]' (reading lengthways down spine).

On upper cover: 'HARRY | POTTER | *and the Prisoner of Azkaban* [lines 1 and 2 in dark yellow, line 3 in green, all on purple panel, 64 by 131mm] | [green rule, 131mm] | [colour illustration of Harry Potter and Hermione Granger riding the back of Buckbeak the Hippogriff, 125 by 131mm] | [green rule, 131mm intersected by orange panel with 'J.K.ROWLING' in purple] | DOUBLE SMARTIES AWARD-WINNING AUTHOR [in orange on black panel, 12 by 131mm]' (all width centred).

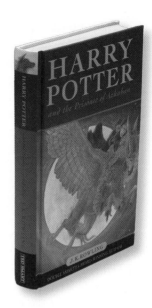

On lower cover: "*Harry Potter and the Philosopher's Stone* started a cult | last year, the emergence of each of the remaining books in | the series of seven deserves to become a major annual | event. Rowling creates a complete and perfect story.' | *The Times* | [new paragraph] 'The Harry Potter books have become a phenomenon … | parents squabble over who gets to read them to the kids, | and teachers say a chapter can silence the most rowdy of | classes.' *The Guardian* | [new paragraph] HARRY POTTER is a | wizard! Along with Ron | and Hermione, his best | friends, Harry is in his | third year at Hogwarts | School of Witchcraft | and Wizardry. Who | knows what will happen | this year? Read on to find | out and immerse yourself | in the magical world of | Hogwarts … | [barcode in black on white panel, 20 by 37mm together with 'http://www.bloomsbury.com' below panel, in black on purple panel, 7 by 37mm]'. Reading lengthways down right side next to foot of spine 'Cover illustrations based upon original art by Cliff Wright'. All in black and all on an illustration of a werewolf in swirling mists.

All edges trimmed. Binding measurements: 204 by 131mm (covers), 204 by 26mm (spine). End-papers: wove paper.

Dust-jacket: coated wove paper, 204 by 487mm

Spine, upper and lower covers replicate the binding.

On upper inside flap: 'HARRY POTTER is a very unusual boy. He | can't wait to get back to school after the | summer holidays! But that's not the only | unusual thing about Harry; Harry's school is | Hogwarts School of Witchcraft and | Wizardry, and Harry is a wizard! | [new paragraph] When Harry, along with his best friends | Ron and Hermione, go back for their third | year at Hogwarts, the atmosphere is tense. | There's an escaped mass murderer on the | loose, and the sinister prison guards of | Azkaban have been called in to guard the | school … | [new paragraph] | A brilliant new story featuring Harry and | his friends, sequel to the award-winning | *Harry Potter and the Philosopher's Stone* and | *Harry Potter and the Chamber of Secrets.* | [new paragraph] HARRY POTTER AND | THE PHILOSOPHER'S STONE | [new paragraph] 'I've yet to meet a 10 year old who hasn't been | entranced by its witty, complex plot and the | character of the eponymous Harry.' | Carolyn

Hart, *The Independent* | [new paragraph] [round point] Gold Award Winner of the 1997 Smarties Nestle | Book Prize | [round point] Winner of the Children's Book Award 1998 | [round point] Winner of the Young Telegraph Book Award 1998 | [round point] Winner of the Sheffield Children's Book Award | 1997 | [round point] Winner of the Birmingham Cable Book Award 1997 | [new paragraph] HARRY POTTER AND | THE CHAMBER OF SECRETS | [new paragraph] 'Such a marriage of good writing, inventiveness, | and sheer child-appeal has not been seen since | Roald Dahl, perhaps even since Tolkien, Lewis, | and Ransome. J. K. Rowling has woken a whole | generation to reading.' *The Times* | £10.99'. All in blue with the exception of the price which is in black and all on orange panel.

On lower inside flap: '[three stars, in yellow] | Dear Joanne Rowling, | [new paragraph] I really, really, really liked "Harry Potter | and the philosopher's stone" and "Harry Potter and | the Chamber of Secrets" was <u>FANTASTIC</u>!!!! I | thought it was <u>very</u> funny when the Memory | Charm backfired and it was driving me mad | when I was trying to think who the bodyless | voice belonged to. | [new paragraph] Please can you write another book, because | I'm dying to read more of Harry's adventures. | [new paragraph] Yours sincerely, | Jamie | Patton | Age eight. | [four stars, in yellow] | ['*TO ORDER FURTHER COPIES &* | *SEE OUR FULL RANGE OF TITLES* | [rule, 38mm] | [telephone symbol] 01942 724444 | Lines are open 7 days a week 8am-8pm | [rule, 38mm] | *CALL US NOW FOR YOUR* | *FREE COLOUR BROCHURE!*' in black on white panel and all within single ruled border, 20 by 40mm]'. All in orange facsimile of child's handwriting, with the exception of panel, and all on blue panel.

Publication: November 1999 (see notes)

Price: no exact price is recorded (see notes)

Contents:

Harry Potter and the Prisoner of Azkaban

('Harry Potter was a highly unusual boy in many ways…')

Notes:

Neither Ted Smart nor Bloomsbury were able to provide any detail about the Ted Smart/'The Book People' editions. Information was provided by the Blair Partnership who noted that this edition was

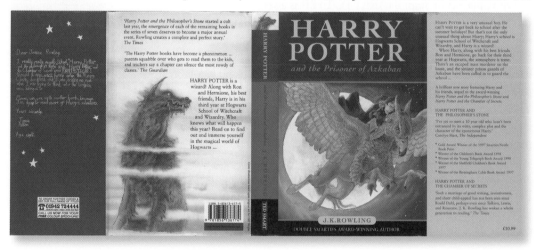

available from November 1999 (presumably at the same time as A2(f)). Production of all the Ted Smart/'The Book People' editions ceased in April 2001.

No exact price has been recorded for this edition. A1(b) was, presumably, sold by itself. A slipcase containing the three volumes A1(b), A2(f) and A7(d) was, probably, available from November 1999 and a slipcase containing the four volumes A1(b), A2(f), A7(d) and A9(c) was, presumably, available from November 2000. In each case the price would have been lower than the single (or combined) prices of the Bloomsbury version.

Copies: private collection (PWE)

Reprints include:
10 9 8 7 6 5 4 3 2
30 29 28 27 26 25 24 23

A7(e) ENGLISH CHILDREN'S EDITION (1999 [2000])
(children's artwork series in paperback)

HARRY | POTTER | *and the Prisoner of Azkaban* | [illustration of Hogwarts crest with legend 'DRAGO DORMIENS NUNQUAM TITILLANDUS' on banner, 67 by 82mm] | J.K.ROWLING | [publisher's device of a dog, 11 by 18mm] | BLOOMSBURY (Lines 1 and 2 justified on left and right margins, and all width centred)

Collation: 160 unsigned leaves bound in indeterminate gatherings; 197 by 128mm; [1-7] 8-17 [18] 19-28 [29] 30-41 [42] 43-55 [56] 57-74 [75] 76-93 [94] 95-106 [107] 108-121 [122] 123-36 [137] 138-56 [157] 158-72 [173] 174-86 [187] 188-98 [199] 200-214 [215] 216-30 [231] 232-43 [244] 245-55 [256] 257-62 [263] 264-76 [277] 278-82 [283] 284-303 [304] 305-317 [318-20]

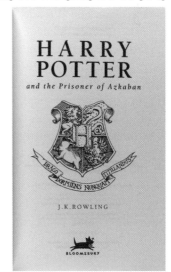

Page contents: [1] half-title: 'HARRY | POTTER | *and the Prisoner of Azkaban* | [illustration of Hogwarts crest with legend 'DRAGO DORMIENS NUNQUAM TITILLANDUS' on banner, 47 by 57mm]'; [2] '*Titles available in the Harry Potter series* | *(in reading order):* | Harry Potter and the Philosopher's Stone | Harry Potter and the Chamber of Secrets | Harry Potter and the Prisoner of Azkaban'; [3] title-page; [4] 'All rights reserved; no part of this publication may be reproduced or | transmitted by any means, electronic, mechanical, photocopying or otherwise, | without the prior permission of the publisher | [new paragraph] First published in Great Britain in 1999 | Bloomsbury Publishing Plc, 38 Soho Square, London, W1V 5DF | [new paragraph] Copyright © 1999

J.K. Rowling | Cover illustration copyright © Cliff Wright 1999 | Cover illustration from original artwork by Cliff Wright | [new paragraph] The moral right of the author has been asserted | A CIP catalogue record of this book is available from the | British Library | [new paragraph] ISBN 0 7475 4629 0 | [new paragraph] Printed in Great Britain by Clays Ltd, St Ives plc | Typeset by Dorchester Typesetting [new paragraph] 10 9 8 7 6 5 4 3 2 1'; [5] 'To Jill Prewett and Aine Kiely, | the Godmothers of Swing'; [6] blank; [7]-317 text; [318-20] blank

Paper: wove paper

Running title: 'HARRY POTTER' (24mm) on verso, recto title comprises chapter title, pp. 8-317

Binding: pictorial wrappers.

On spine: '[colour illustration of head of werewolf on coloured panel, 20 by 16mm] HARRY POTTER [in dark yellow on purple panel, 20 by 45mm] *and the Prisoner of Azkaban* J.K.ROWLING [both title conclusion and author in purple on red panel, 20 by 101mm] BLOOMSBURY [publisher's device of the head of a dog, 3 by 4mm] [both in dark yellow on black panel, 20 by 32mm]' (reading lengthways down spine).

On upper wrapper: 'HARRY | POTTER | *and the Prisoner of Azkaban* [lines 1 and 2 in dark yellow, line 3 in green, all on purple panel, 61 by 128mm] | [green rule, 128mm intersected by dark yellow panel with 'J.K.ROWLING' in purple] | [colour illustration of Harry Potter and Hermione Granger riding the back of Buckbeak the Hippogriff, 124 by 128mm] | [green rule, 128mm] | Winner of the 1999 Whitbread Children's Book of the Year [in dark yellow on black panel, 8 by 128mm]' (all width centred).

On lower wrapper: 'Harry Potter, along with his best friends, Ron and Hermione, is about | to start his third year at Hogwarts School of Witchcraft and Wizardry. | Harry can't wait to get back to school after the summer holidays. | (Who wouldn't if they lived with the horrible Dursleys?) But when | Harry gets to Hogwarts, the atmosphere is tense. There's an escaped | mass murderer on the loose, and the sinister prison guards of | Azkaban have been called in to guard the school … | [new paragraph] A fantastic new story featuring Harry and his friends from the | spellbinding J.K. Rowling. | [new paragraph] 'Children gripped by the funny, quirky and | imaginative storylines of J.K. Rowling's | books will undoubtedly be hooked | again.' *The Daily Mail* | [new paragraph] 'The most eagerly awaited | children's book for years.' | *The Evening Standard* | [new paragraph] 'Spellbinding, enchanting, bewitching | stuff.' *The Mirror* | [new paragraph] 'J.K. Rowling deserves all the plaudits | that are being heaped upon her. For | once, the word phenomenon is an | understatement.' *Scotland on Sunday* | [new paragraph] 'The Harry Potter books are that | rare thing, a series of stories adored | by parents and children alike.' | *The Daily Telegraph* | [barcode in black on white panel, 20 by 38mm together with '[publisher's device of a dog, 6 by 10mm] | BLOOMSBURY | £5.99' in black on left side of panel and 'http://www.bloomsbury.com' below panel, in black on purple panel, 7 by 38mm]'. Reading lengthways down right side next to foot of spine 'Cover illustrations from original artwork by Cliff Wright'. All in black on an illustration of a werewolf in swirling mists.

All edges trimmed. Binding measurements: 197 by 128mm (wrappers), 197 by 20mm (spine).

Publication: 1 April 2000 (simultaneous with A7(ee)) in an edition of 52,636 copies (confirmed by Bloomsbury)

Price: £5.99

Contents:
Harry Potter and the Prisoner of Azkaban
('Harry Potter was a highly unusual boy in many ways…')

Notes:
The publisher's imprint page notes publication in 1999. This paperback edition, however, was first published on 1 April 2000.

Copies: private collection (PWE)

Reprints include:
10 9 8 7 6 5 4
10 9 8 7 6
20 19 18 17 16 15

A7(ee)   ENGLISH ADULT EDITION   (2000)
(original adult artwork series in paperback)

Harry Potter and the | Prisoner of Azkaban | J. K. Rowling | BLOOMSBURY (All width centred)

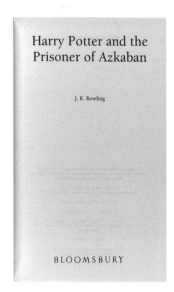

Collation: 160 unsigned leaves bound in indeterminate gatherings; 198 by 128mm; [1-7] 8-17 [18] 19-28 [29] 30-41 [42] 43-55 [56] 57-74 [75] 76-93 [94] 95-106 [107] 108-121 [122] 123-36 [137] 138-56 [157] 158-72 [173] 174-86 [187] 188-98 [199] 200-214 [215] 216-30 [231] 232-43 [244] 245-55 [256] 257-62 [263] 264-76 [277] 278-82 [283] 284-303 [304] 305-317 [318-20]

Page contents: [1] half-title: 'Harry Potter and the | Prisoner of Azkaban'; [2] '*Also available in the Harry Potter series* | (*in reading order*): | Harry Potter and the Philosopher's Stone | Harry Potter and the Chamber of Secrets | Harry Potter and the Prisoner of Azkaban'; [3] title-page; [4] 'All rights reserved; no part of this publication may be reproduced or | transmitted by any means, electronic, mechanical, photocopying or otherwise, | without the prior permission of the publisher | [new paragraph] First published in Great Britain in 1999 | Bloomsbury Publishing Plc, 38 Soho Square, London, W1V 5DF | [new paragraph] This edition first published in 2000 | [new paragraph] Copyright © J.K. Rowling 1999 | [new paragraph] The moral right of the author has been asserted | A CIP catalogue record of this book is available from the | British Library | [new paragraph] ISBN 0 7475 4634 7 | [new paragraph] Printed in Great Britain by Clays Ltd, St Ives plc | Typeset by Dorchester Typesetting | [new paragraph] 10 9 8 7 6 5 4 3 2 1'; [5] 'To Jill Prewett and Aine Kiely, | the Godmothers of Swing'; [6] blank; [7]-317 text; [318-20] blank

Paper: wove paper

Running title: 'HARRY POTTER' (24mm) on verso, recto title comprises chapter title, pp. 8-317

Binding: pictorial wrappers.

On spine: 'HARRY POTTER [in white] | *and the Prisoner of Azkaban* [in red] [black and white photographic illustration of combined horse and eagle in clouds, 20 by 26mm] J. K. ROWLING [in white within red rectangle with rounded ends, 9 by 46mm] [publisher's device of a figure with a bow, 7 by 7mm] [in white]' (reading lengthways down spine). All on black.

On upper wrapper: 'HARRY POTTER | *and the Prisoner of Azkaban* [line 1 in white and line 2 in black, all on red panel, 27 by 128mm] | J. K. ROWLING [in white on black within double red rectangle with rounded ends, 15 by 74mm] | '*A LITERARY EVENT*' – [in white] *THE OBSERVER* [in red] [lines 3 and 4 on black and white photographic illustration of combined horse and eagle in clouds, 171 by 128mm]' (all width centred with the exception of line 2 which is off-set to the right).

On lower wrapper: 'HARRY POTTER [in red] | *and the Prisoner of Azkaban* [in white] | [new paragraph] 'I can honestly say I can't remember the last time I encountered an | author who has had this effect on me. For the first time in years the | book lives up to the hype … perfection' *The Express* | [new paragraph] 'Harry Potter aficionados will revel in the now-familiar narrative and | linguistic landscapes … the weft and warp of this plot is even denser | than its predecessors … JK Rowling's third novel about the world's | favourite wizard hits the ground running' *The Guardian* | [new paragraph] 'The most remarkable publishing success for a generation … | the achievement of JK Rowling is to have created a world in which | anything might happen, yet everything abides by its own tightly | constructed, impossibly wonderful rules. And the story is told with | such momentum, imagination and irrepressible humour that it can | captivate both adults and children' *The Sunday Express* | [new paragraph] 'The pre-publication hype has been justified. This is, simply, | a wizard book' *The Irish Times* | [new paragraph] 'JK Rowling deserves all the plaudits that are being heaped upon her. | For once, the word phenomenon is an understatement' | *Scotland on Sunday* | [new paragraph] 'Wild about Harry? Join the queue' *The Times* [new paragraph] 'Simply marvellous story-telling' *Time Out* | ['BLOOMSBURY [in white on black panel, 6 by 40mm]

| *paperbacks* [in black on red panel, 10 by 40mm]' (all on left side)] [£6.99 [in black] | [barcode in black on white panel, 19 by 39mm] | http://www.bloomsbury.com [in black] (all on red panel, 32 by 40mm and on right side)]'. Reading lengthways down right side next to foot of spine 'Cover image: [in white] Eagle © Michio Hoshino/Robert Harding Horse © Kit Houghton Clouds © John Turner/Tony Stone [in red]'. All in black with the exception of sources which are in red and all on photographic illustration of an opened wing with clouds, 198 by 128mm.

All edges trimmed. Binding measurements: 198 by 128mm (wrappers), 198 by 20mm (spine).

Publication: 1 April 2000 (simultaneous with A7(e)) in an edition of 15,700 copies (confirmed by Bloomsbury)

Price: £6.99

Contents:
Harry Potter and the Prisoner of Azkaban
('Harry Potter was a highly unusual boy in many ways…')

Notes:
Each occurrence of the title on the spine, upper and lower wrappers shows '*and the Prisoner of Azkaban*' off-set to the right of 'HARRY POTTER'.

Copies: private collection (AJH); private collection (SJH); Bloomsbury Archives

Reprints include:
20 19 18 17 16 15 14

A7(f)   AMERICAN CHILDREN'S EDITION   (2001)
(children's artwork series in paperback)

HARRY POTTER | AND THE PRISONER OF AZKABAN | [black and white illustration of a long-haired man looking at mouse in front of oval window, 49 by 68mm] | BY | J. K. ROWLING | ILLUSTRATIONS BY MARY GRANDPRÉ | SCHOLASTIC INC. | NEW YORK [four-sided device] TORONTO [four-sided device] AUCKLAND [four-sided device] SYDNEY | MEXICO CITY [four-sided device] NEW DELHI [four-sided device] HONG KONG [four-sided device] BUENOS AIRES (All width centred on a diamond pattern background)

Collation: 224 unsigned leaves bound in indeterminate gatherings; 193 by 134mm; [I-VI] VII-IX [X-XII] 1-435 [436]

Page contents: [I-II] 'PRAISE FOR J. K. ROWLING'S | HARRY POTTER | AND THE PRISONER OF AZKABAN | [device of nine stars] | [6 reviews and a listing of 7 statements] | [new paragraph] ALSO BY J. K. ROWLING | *Harry Potter and the Sorcerer's Stone* | [new paragraph] *Harry Potter*

and the Chamber of Secrets | Year Two at Hogwarts | *Harry Potter and the Goblet of Fire* | Year Four at Hogwarts'; [III] title-page; [IV] '[device of twelve stars] | Text copyright © 1999 by J. K. Rowling | Illustrations by Mary GrandPré © 1999 by Warner Bros. | [new paragraph] All rights reserved. Published by Scholastic Inc. SCHOLASTIC, the LANTERN DESIGN | and associated logos are trademarks and/or registered trademarks of Scholastic Inc. | [new paragraph] HARRY POTTER and all related characters and elements are trademarks of Warner Bros. | [new paragraph] If you purchased this book without a cover, you should be aware that this book is stolen property. | It was reported as "unsold and destroyed" to the publisher, and neither the author nor | the publisher has received any payment for this "stripped book". | [new paragraph] No part of this publication may be reproduced in whole or in part, | or stored in a retrieval system, or transmitted in any form or

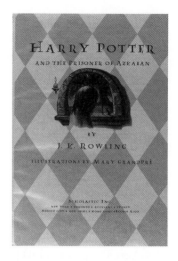

by any means, | electronic, mechanical, photocopying, recording, or otherwise, | without written permission of the publisher. | For information regarding permission, write to Scholastic Inc., | Attention: Permissions Department, 555 Broadway, New York, NY 10012. | [new paragraph] ISBN 0-439-13636-9 | [new paragraph] [publisher's device of a lantern, 7 by 5mm] | [new paragraph] Arthur A. Levine Books hardcover edition | art directed by David Saylor, | published by Arthur A. Levine Books, | an imprint of Scholastic Press, | September 1999 | [new paragraph] 12 11 10 9 8 7 6 5 4 3 2 1   1 2 3 4 5 6/0 | [new paragraph] Printed in the U.S.A. 40 | [new paragraph] First Scholastic trade paperback printing, September 2001'; [V] 'TO JILL PREWETT AND | AINE KIELY, | THE GODMOTHERS OF SWING'; [VI] blank; VII-IX 'CONTENTS' (twenty-two chapters listed with titles and page references); [X] blank; [XI] half-title: 'HARRY POTTER | AND THE PRISONER OF AZKABAN' (all on diamond pattern background); [XII] blank; 1-435 text; [436] '[device of three stars] ABOUT THE AUTHOR [device of three stars] | J. K. ROWLING grew up in England in the Forest of Dean | and is a graduate of Exeter University. She lives in Edinburgh.'

Paper: wove paper

Running title: 'CHAPTER' and chapter number on verso, recto title comprises chapter title, pp. 1-435 except for pages on which a new chapter commences. On these pages, the running title comprises 'CHAPTER' and chapter number. Each running title (excluding pages on which new chapters commence) begins and ends with a three star device (in mirror image).

Illustrations: title-page vignette, together with twenty-two vignettes at the beginning of each chapter (after chapter and chapter number but before chapter title). In addition to standard typographical changes (including italics, capitals and small capitals) there are other typographical features, comprising:

    p. 8 newspaper headline
    p. 10 facsimile of Ron's signature (repeated twice)
    p. 11 facsimile of Hermione's signature
    p. 14 'handwritten' letter from Hagrid

p. 14 facsimile of Professor M. McGonagall's signature

p. 37 newspaper headline

p. 51 advertisement sign

p. 192 'The Marauder's Map' legend

p. 199 notice

p. 272 'handwritten' letter from Hagrid

p. 287 four different 'handwritten' comments

p. 291 'handwritten' letter from Hagrid

p. 315 'handwritten' exam schedule

p. 325 'handwritten' note from Hagrid

Binding: pictorial wrappers.

On spine: 'ROWLING | [rule] | ['YEAR | 3' within concave square]' (horizontally at head) with 'HARRY POTTER | SCHOLASTIC | AND THE PRISONER OF AZKABAN' (reading lengthways down spine). All in green on orange and purple diamond pattern background.

On upper wrapper: 'THE REMARKABLE NATIONAL BESTSELLER [in green] | Harry Potter [hand-drawn lettering] [embossed in green] | AND [hand-drawn lettering in brown of illustration] | THE Prisoner [hand-drawn lettering in brown of illustration] | of AZKABAN [hand-drawn lettering in brown of illustration] | J. K. ROWLING [embossed in green]' (all width centred). All on colour illustration of Harry Potter and Hermione Granger riding Buckbeak the Hippogriff flying in front of a leaded window. In lower left: '[publisher's book device] SCHOLASTIC' in white on red panel, 9 by 47mm.

On lower wrapper: 'For twelve long years, the dread fortress of Azkaban held an | infamous prisoner named Sirius Black. Convicted of killing | thirteen people with a single curse, he was said to be the heir apparent | to the Dark Lord, Voldemort. | [new paragraph] Now he has escaped, leaving only two clues as to where he might be | headed: Harry Potter's defeat of You-Know-Who was Black's downfall as | well. And the Azkaban guards heard Black muttering in his sleep, "He's | at Hogwarts … he's at Hogwarts." | [new paragraph] Harry Potter isn't safe, not even within the walls of his magical school, | surrounded by his friends. Because on top of it all, there may well be a | traitor in their midst. | [new paragraph] [four-sided diamond device] The #1 *New York Times* Bestseller [four-sided diamond device] | [new paragraph] Winner of the Whitbread Award for Children's Literature [four-sided diamond device] *Booklist* 1999 Editor's | Choice [four-sided diamond device] A *Los Angeles Times* Best Book of 1999 [four-sided diamond device] Winner of the 1999 Gold | medal Smarties Prize [four-sided diamond device] An ALA Notable Book [four-sided diamond device] A New York Public Library Title | for Reading and Sharing | Visit Harry Potter on the Web at | www.scholastic.com/harrypotter | COVER ART BY MARY GRANDPRÉ'. All in yellow on colour illustration of brick wall with a

Dementor hiding, together with a tree, moon, etc. In lower right: 'SCHOLASTIC INC. $7.99 US | [rule, 60mm] | [barcode with smaller barcode to the right (13636) together with 'S' within triangle]' all in black on white panel within single black ruled border, 26 by 60mm. The initial 'F' of 'For' is a drop capital.

On inside upper wrapper: barcode with smaller barcode (50799) together with 'S' within triangle below, all in black.

All edges trimmed. Binding measurements: 193 by 134mm (wrappers), 193 by 26mm (spine).

Publication: September 2001 (see notes)

Price: $7.99

Contents:
Harry Potter and the Prisoner of Azkaban
  ('Harry Potter was a highly unusual boy in many ways. For one thing, he hated…')

Notes:
Although no publication date is recorded, 1 September 2000 is assumed. In an email to me from January 2013 Arthur A. Levine noted that 'I'm fairly certain that we didn't have strict "on sale" dates… the publication "day" would simply be the first of the month listed. None of the paperbacks were given a strict "on sale" date either.' Nielsen BookData provides a publication date of 11 September 2001.

Scholastic released a 'dumpbin' display case for this edition at the beginning of September 2001 (Nielsen BookData provides a date of 11 September 2001). The case was filled with 36 copies of this edition. Alternatively, Scholastic made a multiple copy pack available on the same date containing 36 copies of this edition.

This is the first time in the series that the publisher printed the 'stripped book' triangle on the binding. A letter 'S' printed within a triangle denotes that, if the book needs to be returned, the bookseller need only return the stripped wrappers for a refund. The stripped book is then understood by the publisher to have been destroyed. One suspects that, to date, not a single Harry Potter has been stripped due to poor sales.

Each chapter commences with a drop capital.

Copies: private collection (PWE)

Reprints include:

12 11 10 9 8 7 6 5	1 2 3 4 5 6/0	Printed in the U.S.A. 40
48 47	11 12 13/0	Printed in the U.S.A. 40
60 59 58 57 56 55 54 53 52 51	11 12 13/0	Printed in the U.S.A. 40

A7(g) AMERICAN BOOK CLUB EDITION (1999 [2001])
(children's artwork series in hardback)

Publication: between July and December 2001 (see notes)

Notes:

Given that the true American first and the book club editions share a single ISBN, the Blair Partnership noted that book club editions could only be dated to within a half-year period end in their files. This edition was, therefore, published within the period July to December 1999. The Blair Partnership Royalties Manager noted that the American book club editions did not have 'a set price'.

Copies: no copies have been consulted

A7(h) ENGLISH 'CELEBRATORY' EDITION (2004)
(children's artwork series in paperback)

HARRY | POTTER | *and the Prisoner of Azkaban* | [illustration of Hogwarts crest with legend 'DRAGO DORMIENS NUNQUAM TITILLANDUS' on banner, 67 by 82mm] | J.K.ROWLING | [publisher's device of a dog, 11 by 18mm] | BLOOMSBURY (Lines 1 and 2 justified on left and right margins, and all width centred)

Collation: 160 unsigned leaves bound in indeterminate gatherings; 197 by 128mm; [1-7] 8-17 [18] 19-28 [29] 30-41 [42] 43-55 [56] 57-74 [75] 76-93 [94] 95-106 [107] 108-121 [122] 123-36 [137] 138-56 [157] 158-72 [173] 174-86 [187] 188-98 [199] 200-214 [215] 216-30 [231] 232-43 [244] 245-55 [256] 257-62 [263] 264-76 [277] 278-82 [283] 284-303 [304] 305-317 [318-20]

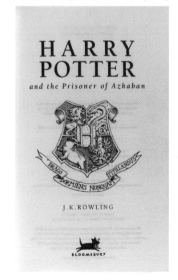

Page contents: [1] half-title: 'HARRY | POTTER | *and the Prisoner of Azkaban* | [illustration of Hogwarts crest with legend 'DRAGO DORMIENS NUNQUAM TITILLANDUS' on banner, 47 by 57mm]'; [2] '*Titles available in the Harry Potter series | (in reading order):* | Harry Potter and the Philosopher's Stone | Harry Potter and the Chamber of Secrets | Harry Potter and the Prisoner of Azkaban | Harry Potter and the Goblet of Fire | Harry Potter and the Order of the Phoenix'; [3] title-page; [4] 'All rights reserved; no part of this publication may be reproduced or | transmitted by any means, electronic, mechanical, photocopying | or otherwise, without the prior permission of the publisher | [new paragraph] First published in Great Britain in 1999 | Bloomsbury Publishing Plc, 38 Soho Square, London, W1D 3HB | [new paragraph] This edition first published in 2004 | [new paragraph] Copyright © J. K. Rowling 1999 | Cover illustration copyright © Cliff Wright 1999 | Cover illustration from original artwork by Cliff Wright | [new paragraph] Harry Potter, names, characters and related indicia | are copyright and trademark Warner Bros., 2000™ | [new paragraph] The moral right of the author has been asserted | A CIP catalogue record of this book is available from the British Library | [new paragraph] ISBN 0 7475 7376 X | [new paragraph] 10 9 8 7 6 5 4 3 2 1 | [new paragraph] Typeset by Dorchester Typesetting | Printed in Great Britain by Clays Ltd, St Ives plc | [new paragraph] All papers used by Bloomsbury are natural, recyclable products made | from wood grown in well-managed forests. The paper used in this book | contains 10% post consumer waste material which was de-inked using | chlorine free methods. The manufacturing processes conform to the | environmental regulations of the country of origin. | [new paragraph] www. bloomsbury.com/harrypotter'; [5] 'To Jill Prewett and Aine Kiely, | the Godmothers of Swing'; [6] blank; [7]-317 text; [318-19] blank; [320] publisher's advertisement: 'Also by | J. K. ROWLING | Get your hands on Harry Potter's very own school books…'

Paper: wove paper

Running title: 'HARRY POTTER' (25mm) on verso, recto title comprises chapter title, pp. 8-317

Binding: pictorial wrappers.

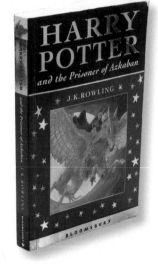

On spine: '[colour illustration of head of werewolf on coloured panel, 17 by 17mm] HARRY POTTER [in purple on gilt panel, 17 by 46mm] *and the Prisoner of Azkaban* [in white] J.K.ROWLING [in gilt, both title conclusion and author on purple panel, 17 by 103mm] BLOOMSBURY [publisher's device of the head of a dog, 3 by 4mm] [both in white on dark blue panel, 16 by 32mm]' (reading lengthways down spine).

On upper wrapper: 'HARRY | POTTER | *and the Prisoner of Azkaban* [lines 1 and 2 in gilt, line 3 in white, all on dark blue panel, 62 by 128mm] | [gilt rule, 128mm] | ['J.K. ROWLING' in gilt] with colour illustration of Harry Potter and Hermione Granger riding the back of Buckbeak the Hippogriff, within single gilt ruled border, 91 by 87mm, all on purple panel with orange, yellow and gilt stars, 123 by 128mm] | [dark blue rule, 128mm] | BLOOMSBURY [in dark blue on gilt panel, 9 by 128mm]' (all width centred).

On lower wrapper: 'Harry Potter, along with his best friends, Ron and Hermione, is about | to start his third year at Hogwarts School of Witchcraft and Wizardry. | Harry can't wait to get back to school after the summer holidays. | (Who wouldn't if they lived with the horrible Dursleys?) But when | Harry gets to Hogwarts, the atmosphere is tense. | There's an escaped | mass murderer on the loose, and the sinister prison guards of | Azkaban have been called in to guard the school … | [new paragraph] A fantastic story featuring Harry and his friends from the | spellbinding J.K. Rowling. | [new paragraph] 'Children gripped by the funny, quirky and | imaginative storylines of J.K. Rowling's | books will undoubtedly be hooked | again.' *The Daily Mail* | [new paragraph] 'Spellbinding, enchanting, | bewitching stuff.' *The Mirror* | [new paragraph] 'J.K. Rowling deserves all the | plaudits that are being heaped upon her. | For once, the word phenomenon is an | understatement.' *Scotland on Sunday* | [new paragraph] 'The Harry Potter books are that rare | thing, a series of stories adored by | parents and children alike.' | *The Daily Telegraph* | [new paragraph] [barcode in black on white panel, 20 by 38mm together with '[publisher's device of a dog, 6 by 10mm] | BLOOMSBURY | £5.99' in black on left side of panel and 'www.bloomsbury.com' below panel, in white on dark purple panel, 7 by 38mm]'. Reading lengthways down right side next to foot of spine 'Cover illustrations from original artwork by Cliff Wright'. All in black on an illustration of a werewolf in swirling mists.

All edges trimmed. Binding measurements: 197 by 128mm (wrappers), 197 by 17mm (spine).

Publication: 3 May 2004 in an edition of 200,080 copies (confirmed by Bloomsbury)

Price: £5.99

Contents:
Harry Potter and the Prisoner of Azkaban
   ('Harry Potter was a highly unusual boy in many ways...')

Notes:
The individual titles in the 'celebratory' edition were each published to celebrate the release of the film version. The UK premiere of *Harry Potter and the Prisoner of Azkaban* took place on 30 May 2004.

Copies: private collection (PWE)

A7(i)   ENGLISH ADULT EDITION   (2004)
(Michael Wildsmith photography adult artwork series in paperback)

Harry Potter and the | Prisoner of Azkaban | J. K. Rowling | BLOOMSBURY (All width centred)

Collation: 240 unsigned leaves bound in indeterminate gatherings; 177 by 110mm; [1-7] 8-22 [23] 24-38 [39] 40-56 [57] 58-78 [79] 80-106 [107] 108-134 [135] 136-53 [154] 155-75 [176] 177-98 [199] 200-228 [229] 230-52 [253] 254-73 [274] 275-91 [292] 293-314 [315] 316-38 [339] 340-57 [358] 359-75 [376] 377-85 [386] 387-406 [407] 408-415 [416] 417-47 [448] 449-68 [469-80]

Page contents: [1] half-title: 'Harry Potter and the | Prisoner of Azkaban'; [2] *'Titles available in the Harry Potter series | (in reading order):* | Harry Potter and the Philosopher's Stone | Harry Potter and the Chamber of Secrets | Harry Potter and the Prisoner of Azkaban | Harry Potter and the Goblet of Fire | Harry Potter and the Order of the Phoenix'; [3] title-page; [4] 'All rights reserved; no part of this publication may be reproduced or | transmitted by any means, electronic, mechanical, photocopying or otherwise, | without the prior permission of the publisher | [new paragraph] First published in Great Britain in 1999 | Bloomsbury Publishing Plc, 38 Soho Square, London, W1D 3HB | [new paragraph] This paperback edition first published in 2004 | [new paragraph] Copyright © J. K. Rowling 1999 | [new paragraph] Harry Potter, names, characters and related indicia are | copyright and trademark Warner Bros., 2000™ | [new paragraph] Thanks to both National Trust Dunstanburgh Castle and to the | building's custodian English Heritage for permission to photograph | the castle for use on the cover image | [new paragraph] The moral right of the author has been asserted | A CIP catalogue record of this book is available from the British Library | [new paragraph] ISBN 0 7475 7449 9 | [new paragraph] 1 3 5 7 9 10 8 6 4 2 | [new paragraph] Typeset by Dorchester Typesetting | Printed in Great Britain by Clays Ltd, St Ives plc | [new paragraph] All papers used by Bloomsbury Publishing are natural, | recyclable products made from wood grown in well-managed forests. | The paper used in this book contains 20% post consumer waste material | which was de-inked using chlorine free methods. The | manufacturing processes conform to the environmental | regulations of the country of origin. | [new paragraph] www.bloomsbury.com/harrypotter'; [5] 'To Jill Prewett and Aine Kiely, | the Godmothers of Swing'; [6] blank; [7]-468 text; [469-80] blank

Paper: wove paper

Running title: 'HARRY POTTER' (24mm) on verso, recto title comprises chapter title, pp. 8-468 (excluding pages on which new chapters commence)

Binding: pictorial wrappers.

On spine: 'HARRY POTTER AND THE [colour photograph of a castle on desolated rocks, surrounded by the sea, 30 by 18mm] | J.K. ROWLING [publisher's device of a figure with a bow, 10 by 10mm] | PRISONER OF AZKABAN' (reading lengthways down spine). All in white with the exception of last line which is in gilt and all on black.

On upper wrapper: 'HARRY POTTER AND THE [in white] | PRISONER OF [embossed in gilt] | AZKABAN [embossed in gilt] | J. K. ROWLING [in white] | BLOOMSBURY [in white]' (all width centred). All on colour photograph of a castle on desolated rocks, surrounded by the sea.

On lower wrapper: '[colour photograph of a castle on desolated rocks, surrounded by the sea, all within single white border, 22 by 22mm] 'I can honestly say I can't remember the last | time I encountered an author who has had | this effect on me. For the first time in years | the book lives up to the hype … perfection' | *Daily Express* | [new paragraph] Harry Potter is lucky to reach the age of thirteen, since he | has already survived the murderous attacks of the feared | Dark Lord on more than one occasion. But his hopes for | a quiet term concentrating on Quidditch are dashed when | a maniacal mass-murderer escapes from Azkaban, pursued | by the soul-sucking Dementors who guard the prison. | It's assumed that Hogwarts is the safest place for Harry to | be. But is it a coincidence that he can feel eyes watching him | in the dark, and should he be taking Professor Trelawney's | ghoulish predictions seriously? | [new paragraph] 'The most remarkable publishing sensation for a generation | … the story is told with such momentum, imagination and | irrepressible humour that it can captivate both adults and | children' *Sunday Express* | [new paragraph] 'Rowling deserves all the plaudits that are being heaped | upon her. For once, the word phenomenon is an | understatement' *Scotland on Sunday* | [new paragraph] 'Extraordinarily vivid and exceptionally well-imagined' | *Independent on Sunday* | [new paragraph] 'Wild about Harry? Join the queue' *The Times* | [new paragraph] [barcode in black on white panel, 24 by 39mm together with 'bloomsbury[in black]pbk[in white]s[in black] | £6.99 [in black] | www.bloomsbury.com [in black]' and all on red panel, 25 by 75mm] | Cover image: Michael Wildsmith Design: William

Webb Author Photograph: © Bill de la HEY'. All in white on black with colour photograph to the left of lines 1-5.

On inside upper wrapper: black and white photograph of J.K. Rowling standing against bookshelves.

On inside lower wrapper: 'Other titles available in the | HARRY POTTER series | [colour illustrations in two columns of four book designs]'. All in white on black.

All edges trimmed. Binding measurements: 177 by 110mm (wrappers), 177 by 30mm (spine).

Publication: 10 July 2004 in an edition of 110,200 copies (confirmed by Bloomsbury)

Price: £6.99

Contents:
Harry Potter and the Prisoner of Azkaban
('Harry Potter was a highly unusual boy in many ways…')

Notes:
See note to A1(f) about this series replacing an existing livery. This volume, A7(i), can be seen as the successor to A7(ee).

Copies: BL (H.2005/1743) stamped 4 May 2004

Reprints include:
11

A7(j)   ENGLISH ADULT EDITION   (2004)
(Michael Wildsmith photography adult artwork series in hardback)

Harry Potter and the | Prisoner of Azkaban | J. K. Rowling | BLOOMSBURY (All width centred)

Collation: 160 unsigned leaves bound in indeterminate gatherings; 197 by 125mm; [1-7] 8-17 [18] 19-28 [29] 30-41 [42] 43-55 [56] 57-74 [75] 76-93 [94] 95-106 [107] 108-121 [122] 123-36 [137] 138-56 [157] 158-72 [173] 174-86 [187] 188-98 [199] 200-214 [215] 216-30 [231] 232-43 [244] 245-55 [256] 257-62 [263] 264-76 [277] 278-82 [283] 284-303 [304] 305-317 [318-20]

Page contents: [1] half-title: 'Harry Potter and the | Prisoner of Azkaban'; [2] *'Titles available in the Harry Potter series | (in reading order):* | Harry Potter and the Philosopher's Stone | Harry Potter and the Chamber of Secrets | Harry Potter and the Prisoner of Azkaban | Harry Potter and the Goblet of Fire | Harry Potter and the Order of the Phoenix | [new paragraph] *Harry Potter and the Philosopher's Stone* | *also available in Latin, Ancient Greek, Welsh and Irish:* | Harrius Potter et Philosophi Lapis (Latin) | Ἄρειος Ποτὴρ καί ἡ τοῦ ψιλοσόψον λίθος (Ancient Greek) | Harri Potter a Maen yr Anthronydd (Welsh) | Harry Potter agus an Órchloch (Irish)'; [3] title-page; [4] 'All rights reserved; no part of this publication may be reproduced or | transmitted by any means, electronic, mechanical, photocopying | or otherwise, without the prior permission of the publisher | [new paragraph] First published in Great Britain in 1999 | Bloomsbury Publishing Plc, 38 Soho Square, London, W1D 3HB | [new paragraph] This edition first published in 2004 | [new paragraph] Copyright © 1999 J. K. Rowling | [new paragraph] Harry Potter, names, characters and related indicia are | copyright and trademark Warner Bros., 2000™ | [new paragraph] Thanks to both National Trust Dunstanburgh Castle and to the building's custodian | English Heritage for permission to photograph the castle for use on the cover image | [new paragraph] The moral right of the author has been asserted | A CIP catalogue record of this book is available from the British Library | [new paragraph] ISBN 0 7475 7362 X | [new paragraph] Typeset by Dorchester Typesetting | [new paragraph] All papers used by Bloomsbury Publishing are natural, recyclable products made | from wood grown in well-managed forests. The manufacturing processes | conform to the environmental regulations of the country of origin. | [new paragraph] Printed in Great Britain by Clays Ltd, St Ives plc | [new paragraph] 1 3 5 7 9 10 8 6 4 2 | [new paragraph] www.bloomsbury.com/harrypotter'; [5] *'To Jill Prewett and Aine Kiely,* | *the Godmothers of Swing';* [6] blank; [7]-317 text; [318-20] blank

Paper: wove paper

Running title: 'HARRY POTTER' (24mm) on verso, recto title comprises chapter title, pp. 8-317 (excluding pages on which new chapters commence)

Binding: black boards.
    On spine: 'HARRY POTTER | J. K. ROWLING | AND THE PRISONER OF AZKABAN [publisher's device of a figure with a bow, 14 by 14mm]' (reading lengthways down spine). All in gilt.
    Upper and lower covers: blank.
    All edges trimmed. Binding measurements: 204 by 128mm (covers), 204 by 40mm (spine). End-papers: wove paper.

Dust-jacket: coated wove paper, 204 by 498mm
    On spine: '[colour photograph of a castle on desolated rocks, surrounded by the sea, all within single white ruled border, 20 by 20mm] HARRY POTTER [in gilt] | J. K. ROWLING [in white] | AND THE PRISONER OF AZKABAN [in white]' (reading lengthways down spine) together with publisher's device of a figure with a bow, 14 by 14mm [in olive beige]' (at foot).
    On upper cover: 'J. K. ROWLING [in white] | HARRY [embossed in gilt] | POTTER [embossed in gilt] | AND THE PRISONER OF AZKABAN [in white] | BLOOMSBURY [in white]' (all width centred). All on colour photograph of a castle on desolated rocks, surrounded by the sea.
    On lower cover: black and white photograph of J.K. Rowling standing against bookshelves with 'www.bloomsbury.com/harrypotter [in black on olive beige panel, 5 by 40mm] | [barcode in black on white panel, 20 by 39mm] | BLOOMSBURY [in black on olive beige panel, 7 by 40mm]' (lower right).
    On upper inside flap: 'Harry Potter is lucky to reach the age of | thirteen, since he has already survived the | murderous attacks of the feared Dark Lord | on more than one occasion. But his hopes | for a quiet term concentrating on | Quidditch are dashed when a maniacal | mass-murderer escapes from Azkaban, | pursued by the soul-sucking Dementors | who guard the prison. It's assumed that | Hogwarts is the safest place for Harry to | be. But is it a coincidence that he can feel | eyes watching him in the

dark, and should | he be taking Professor Trelawney's | ghoulish predictions seriously? | [new paragraph] 'I can honestly say I can't remember the | last time I encountered an author who has | had this effect on me. For the first time in | years the book lives up to the hype … | perfection' *Daily Express* | [new paragraph] 'The most remarkable publishing sensation | for a generation … the story is told with | such momentum, imagination and | irrepressible humour that it can captivate | both adults and children' *Sunday Express* | [new paragraph] 'Rowling deserves all the plaudits that are | being heaped upon her. For once, the word | phenomenon is an understatement' | *Scotland on Sunday* | [new paragraph] 'Extraordinarily vivid and exceptionally | well-imagined' *Independent on Sunday* | [new paragraph] 'Wild about Harry? Join the queue' | *The Times* | [new paragraph] £11.99'. All in white on black.

*On **lower inside flap:*** 'J. K. (JOANNE KATHLEEN) ROWLING | has written fiction since she was a child. | Born in 1965, she grew up in Chepstow | and wrote her first 'book' at the age of six | – a story about a rabbit called Rabbit. | She studied French and Classics at Exeter | University, then moved to London to | work at Amnesty International, and then | to Portugal to teach English as a foreign | language, before settling in Edinburgh. | [new paragraph] The idea for Harry Potter occurred to her | on the train from Manchester to London, | where she says Harry Potter 'just strolled | into my head fully formed', and by the | time she had arrived at King's Cross, | many of the characters had taken shape. | During the next five years she outlined | the plots for each book and began writing | the first in the series, *Harry Potter and* | *the Philosopher's Stone*, which was first | published by Bloomsbury in 1997. The | other Harry Potter titles: *Harry Potter and* | *the Chamber of Secrets, Harry Potter and the* | *Prisoner of Azkaban, Harry Potter and the* | *Goblet of Fire*, and *Harry Potter and the* | *Order of the Phoenix*, followed. | J. K. Rowling has also written two other | companion books, *Quidditch Through the* | *Ages* and *Fantastic Beasts and Where to* | *Find Them*, in aid of Comic Relief. | [new paragraph] Jacket Design: William Webb | Jacket Image: Michael Wildsmith | Author Photograph: © Bill de la HEY'. All in white on black.

Publication: 4 October 2004 in an edition of 12,500 copies (confirmed by Bloomsbury)

Price: £11.99

Contents:
Harry Potter and the Prisoner of Azkaban
  ('Harry Potter was a highly unusual boy in many ways…')

Notes:
Having rebranded the look of the adult artwork edition to feature photography by Michael Wildsmith, it was perhaps inevitable that a hardback version would become available. A1(g), A2(m) and A7(j) were all published on 4 October 2004 with A9(i) following a few days later on 10 October 2004. As the series progressed, later titles published in this livery (see A12(aa), A13(aa) and A14(aa)) would also comprise the simultaneous first edition issues.

Copies: Bloomsbury Archives

Reprints include:
3 5 7 9 10 8 6 4 2
5 7 9 10 8 6 4
10

ENGLISH 'SIGNATURE' EDITION
(Clare Melinsky artwork series in paperback)

Harry Potter ['signature' above 'z' rule with numerous stars] | *and the* | *Prisoner of Azkaban* | [illustration of Hogwarts crest with legend 'DRAGO DORMIENS NUNQUAM TITILLANDUS' on banner, 68 by 84mm] | J.K.ROWLING | [publisher's device of a dog, 8 by 13mm] | BLOOMSBURY | LONDON BERLIN NEW YORK SYDNEY (All width centred)

Collation: 160 unsigned leaves bound in indeterminate gatherings; 197 by 128mm; [1-7] 8-17 [18] 19-28 [29] 30-41 [42] 43-55 [56] 57-74 [75] 76-93 [94] 95-106 [107] 108-121 [122] 123-36 [137] 138-56 [157] 158-72 [173] 174-86 [187] 188-98 [199] 200-214 [215] 216-30 [231] 232-43 [244] 245-55 [256] 257-62 [263] 264-76 [277] 278-82 [283] 284-303 [304] 305-317 [318-20]

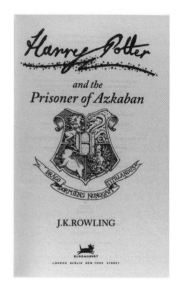

Page contents: [1] half-title: 'Harry Potter ['signature' above 'z' rule with numerous stars] | *and the* | *Prisoner of Azkaban* | [illustration of Hogwarts crest with legend 'DRAGO DORMIENS NUNQUAM TITILLANDUS' on banner, 60 by 75mm]'; [2] *'Titles available in the Harry Potter series* | *(in reading order):* | Harry Potter and the Philosopher's Stone | Harry Potter and the Chamber of Secrets | Harry Potter and the Prisoner of Azkaban | Harry Potter and the Goblet of Fire | Harry Potter and the Order of the Phoenix | Harry Potter and the Half-Blood Prince | Harry Potter and the Deathly Hallows | [new paragraph] *Titles available in the Harry Potter series* | *(in Latin):* | Harry Potter and the Philosopher's Stone | Harry Potter and the Chamber of Secrets | *(in Welsh, Ancient Greek and Irish):* | Harry Potter and the Philosopher's Stone'; [3] title-page; [4] 'All rights reserved; no part of this publication may be reproduced or | transmitted by any means, electronic, mechanical, photocopying | or otherwise, without the prior permission of the publisher | [new paragraph] First published in Great Britain in 1999 by Bloomsbury Publishing Plc | 36 Soho Square, London, W1D 3QY | [new paragraph] Bloomsbury Publishing, London, Berlin, New York and Sydney | [new paragraph] This paperback edition first published in November 2010 | [new paragraph] Copyright © J.K.Rowling 1999 | Cover illustrations by Clare Melinsky copyright © Bloomsbury Publishing Plc 2010 | [new paragraph] Harry Potter, names, characters and related indicia are | copyright and trademark Warner Bros., 2000™ | [new paragraph] The moral right of the author has been asserted | A CIP catalogue record of this book is available from the British Library | [new paragraph] ISBN 978 1 4088 1056 9 | [new paragraph] [Forest Stewardship Council logo, 8 by 9mm together with ® symbol and text: 'FSC | www.fsc.org | MIX | Paper from | responsible sources | FSC® C018072'] | [new paragraph] Typeset by Dorchester Typesetting | Printed in Great Britain by Clays Ltd, St Ives plc | [new paragraph] 1 3 5 7 9 10 8 6 4 2 | [new paragraph]

| www.bloomsbury.com/harrypotter'; [5] *'To Jill Prewett and Aine Kiely,* | *the Godmothers of Swing'*; [6] blank; [7]-317 text; [318-20] blank

Paper: wove paper

Running title: 'HARRY POTTER' (25mm) on verso, recto title comprises chapter title, pp. 8-317

Binding: pictorial wrappers.

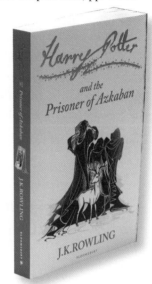

On spine: 'Harry Potter ['signature' above 'z' rule with numerous stars] [in gilt] *and* | *the Prisoner of Azkaban* [black, yellow, orange, white and blue illustration of an hour-glass on a chain, 16 by 21mm] J.K.ROWLING BLOOMSBURY [publisher's device of the head of a dog, 3 by 4mm]' (reading lengthways down spine). All in white on green.

On upper wrapper: 'Harry Potter ['signature' above 'z' rule with numerous stars] [embossed in gilt] | *and the* | *Prisoner of Azkaban* | [light blue, dark blue and green illustration of cloaked and hooded Dementors with a stag, 94 by 116mm] | J.K.ROWLING | BLOOMSBURY' (all width centred). All in green with deckle-edge effect of white leaf on green background at fore-edge.

On lower wrapper: 'Harry Potter, along with his best friends, Ron and | Hermione, is about to start his third year at Hogwarts | School of Witchcraft and Wizardry. Harry can't wait to get | back to school after the summer holidays (who wouldn't if they | lived with the horrible Dursleys?). [*sic*] But when Harry arrives | at Hogwarts, the atmosphere is tense. There's an escaped | mass murderer on the loose, and the sinister prison guards of | Azkaban have been called in to guard the school … | [new paragraph] 'The Harry Potter books are that rare thing, a series of stories | adored by parents and children alike.' | *Daily Telegraph* | [new paragraph] 'Children gripped by the funny, quirky and imaginative storylines | of J.K. Rowling's books will undoubtedly be hooked again.' | *Daily Mail* | [new paragraph] 'Spellbinding, enchanting, | bewitching stuff.' | *Mirror* | [dark blue, light blue and green illustration of Hogwarts castle in front of clouds and rising from swirling waves, 82 by 117mm] | [barcode together with publisher's device of a dog, 6 by 10mm and 'BLOOMSBURY' together with Forest Stewardship Council logo, 7 by 8mm together with © symbol and text: 'FSC | Mixed Sources | Product group from well-managed | forests and other controlled sources | [new paragraph] Cert no. SGS-COC-2061 | www.fsc.org | © 1996 Forest Stewardship Council'] | Designed by Webb & Webb Design | Cover illustrations by Clare Melinsky www.bloomsbury.com/harrypotter £6.99 | Author photograph © J.P.Masclet'. Lines 1-17 in green with all other text in black, together with deckle-edge effect of white leaf on green background at fore-edge. The intial capital 'H' of 'Harry' is a drop capital.

On inside upper wrapper: 'The magical world of … | Harry Potter ['signature' above 'z' rule with numerous stars] | [colour illustrations in three columns of seven book designs] | The internationally bestselling series | [new paragraph] For more from Harry Potter, visit | www.bloomsbury.com/ harrypotter'. All in green with the exception of line 2 which is in gold, together with deckle-edge effect of white leaf on green background at fore-edge.

On inside lower wrapper: colour photograph of J.K. Rowling seated by a window.
All edges trimmed. Binding measurements: 197 by 128mm (wrappers), 197 by 19mm (spine).

Publication: 1 November 2010 in an edition of 63,312 copies(confirmed by Bloomsbury)

Price: £6.99

Contents:
Harry Potter and the Prisoner of Azkaban
   ('Harry Potter was a highly unusual boy in many ways…')

Notes:
Published as a boxed set of seven volumes comprising A1(i), A2(n), A7(k), A9(k), A12(h), A13(g)
and A14(f). Individual volumes were also available separately.

Copies: BL (YK.2011.a.21129) stamped 9 Aug 2010; private collection (PWE)

A7(l)   ENGLISH 'SIGNATURE' EDITION   (2011)
(Clare Melinsky artwork series in hardback)

Harry Potter ['signature' above 'z' rule with numerous stars] | *and the* | *Prisoner of Azkaban* |
[illustration of Hogwarts crest with legend 'DRAGO DORMIENS NUNQUAM TITILLANDUS' on
banner, 68 by 84mm | J.K.ROWLING | [publisher's device of a dog, 8 by 13mm] | BLOOMSBURY
| LONDON BERLIN NEW YORK SYDNEY (All width centred)

Collation: 160 unsigned leaves bound in indeterminate gatherings;
197 by 124mm; [1-7] 8-17 [18] 19-28 [29] 30-41 [42] 43-55 [56]
57-74 [75] 76-93 [94] 95-106 [107] 108-121 [122] 123-36 [137]
138-56 [157] 158-72 [173] 174-86 [187] 188-98 [199] 200-214 [215]
216-30 [231] 232-43 [244] 245-55 [256] 257-62 [263] 264-76 [277]
278-82 [283] 284-303 [304] 305-317 [318-20]

Page contents: [1] half-title: 'Harry Potter ['signature' above 'z' rule
with numerous stars] | *and the* | *Prisoner of Azkaban* | [illustration
of Hogwarts crest with legend 'DRAGO DORMIENS NUNQUAM
TITILLANDUS' on banner, 60 by 75mm]'; [2] *'Titles available in
the Harry Potter series | (in reading order):* | Harry Potter and the
Philosopher's Stone | Harry Potter and the Chamber of Secrets |
Harry Potter and the Prisoner of Azkaban | Harry Potter and the
Goblet of Fire | Harry Potter and the Order of the Phoenix | Harry
Potter and the Half-Blood Prince | Harry Potter and the Deathly
Hallows | [new paragraph] *Titles available in the Harry Potter series* |

(in Latin): | Harry Potter and the Philosopher's Stone | Harry Potter and the Chamber of Secrets | *(in Welsh, Ancient Greek and Irish):* | Harry Potter and the Philosopher's Stone | [new paragraph] *Also available* | *(in aid of Comic Relief):* | Fantastic Beasts and Where to Find Them | Quidditch Through the Ages | *(in aid of Lumos):* | The Tales of Beedle the Bard'; [3] title-page; [4] 'All rights reserved; no part of this publication may be reproduced or | transmitted by any means, electronic, mechanical, photocopying | or otherwise, without the prior permission of the publisher | [new paragraph] First published in Great Britain in 1999 by Bloomsbury Publishing Plc | 49-51 Bedford Square, London, WC1B 3DP | [new paragraph] Bloomsbury Publishing, London, Berlin, New York and Sydney | [new paragraph] This hardback edition first published in November 2011 | [new paragraph] Copyright © J.K.Rowling 1999 | Cover and endpaper illustrations by Clare Melinsky copyright © J.K.Rowling 2010 | [new paragraph] Harry Potter, names, characters and related indicia are | copyright and trademark Warner Bros., 2000™ | [new paragraph] The moral right of the author has been asserted | A CIP catalogue record of this book is available from the British Library | [new paragraph] ISBN 978 1 4088 2585 3 | [new paragraph] [Forest Stewardship Council logo, 8 by 9mm together with ® symbol and text: 'FSC | www.fsc.org | MIX | Paper from | responsible sources | FSC® C018072'] | [new paragraph] Typeset by Dorchester Typesetting | Printed in Great Britain by Clays Ltd, St Ives plc | [new paragraph] 1 3 5 7 9 10 8 6 4 2 | [new paragraph] | www.bloomsbury.com/harrypotter'; [5] 'To Jill Prewett and Aine Kiely, | the Godmothers of Swing'; [6] blank; [7]-317 text; [318-20] blank

Paper: wove paper

Running title: 'HARRY POTTER' (24mm) on verso, recto title comprises chapter title, pp. 8-317

Binding: green boards.

 On spine: 'Harry Potter ['signature' above 'z' rule with numerous stars] *and* | *the Prisoner of Azkaban* [illustration of an hour-glass on a chain, 16 by 21mm] J.K.ROWLING BLOOMSBURY [publisher's device of the head of a dog, 3 by 4mm]' (reading lengthways down spine). All in gilt.

 Upper and lower covers: blank.

 All edges trimmed. Green sewn bands at head and foot of spine together with green marker ribbon. Binding measurements: 205 by 128mm (covers), 205 by 38mm (spine). End-papers: wove paper overprinted in green showing design, in white, of spine motifs from the series (see notes).

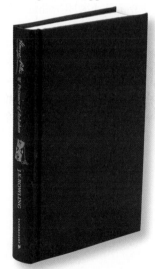

Dust-jacket: coated wove paper, 205 by 490mm

 On spine: 'Harry Potter ['signature' above 'z' rule with numerous stars] [in gilt] *and* | *the Prisoner of Azkaban* [black, yellow, orange, white and blue illustration of an hour-glass on a chain, 16 by 21mm] J.K.ROWLING BLOOMSBURY [publisher's device of the head of a dog, 3 by 4mm]' (reading lengthways down spine). All in white on green.

 On upper cover: 'Harry Potter ['signature' above 'z' rule with numerous stars] [in gilt] | *and the* | *Prisoner of Azkaban* | [light blue, dark blue and green illustration of cloaked and hooded Dementors with a stag, 94 by 116mm] | J.K.ROWLING | BLOOMSBURY' (all width centred). All in green with deckle-edge effect of white leaf on green background at fore-edge.

On lower cover: "Spellbinding, enchanting, | bewitching stuff.' | *Mirror* | [dark blue, light blue and green illustration of Hogwarts castle in front of clouds and rising from swirling waves, 72 by 97mm] | [publisher's device of a dog, 6 by 10mm and 'BLOOMSBURY'] [barcode and 'www.bloomsbury.com/harrypotter' in black on white panel, 24 by 39mm]'. All in green, with deckle-edge effect of white leaf on green background at fore-edge. The initial capital 'S' of 'Spellbinding' is a drop capital.

On upper inside flap: 'Harry Potter, along with his best | friends, Ron and Hermione, is | about to start his third year at Hogwarts | School of Witchcraft and Wizardry. | Harry can't wait to get back to school | after the summer holidays (who wouldn't | if they lived with the horrible Dursleys?). [*sic*] | But when Harry arrives at Hogwarts, the | atmosphere is tense. There's an escaped | mass murderer on the loose, and the | sinister prison guards of Azkaban have | been called in to guard the school … | [new paragraph] 'The Harry Potter books are that rare thing, | a series of stories adored by parents and | children alike.' | *Daily Telegraph* | [new paragraph] 'Children gripped by the funny, quirky and | imaginative storylines of J. K. Rowling's | books will undoubtedly be hooked again.' | *Daily Mail* | [new paragraph] 'Wild about Harry? Join the queue.' | *The Times* | [black, yellow, orange, white and blue illustration of an hour-glass on a chain, 23 by 18mm]'. All in white on green. The initial capital 'H' of 'Harry' is a drop capital.

On lower inside flap: 'J. K. Rowling has written fiction since she was a child, | and she always wanted to be an author. Her parents loved | reading and their house in Chepstow was full of books. | In fact, J. K. Rowling wrote her first 'book' at the age | of six – a story about a rabbit called Rabbit. She studied | French and Classics at Exeter University, then moved to | Edinburgh – via London and Portugal. In 2000 she was | awarded an OBE for services to children's literature. | [new paragraph] The idea for Harry Potter occurred to her on the | train from Manchester to London, where she says | Harry Potter 'just strolled into my head fully formed', | and by the time she had arrived at King's Cross, many | of the characters had taken shape. During the next | five years she outlined the plots

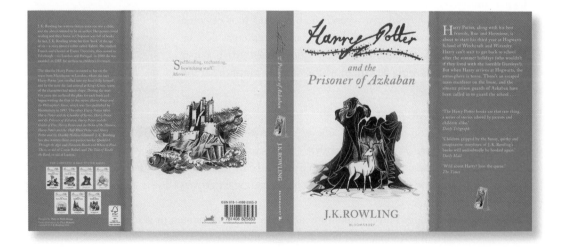

for each book and | began writing the first in the series, *Harry Potter and* | *the Philosopher's Stone*, which was first published by | Bloomsbury in 1997. The other Harry Potter titles: | *Harry Potter and the Chamber of Secrets, Harry Potter* | *and the Prisoner of Azkaban, Harry Potter and the* | *Goblet of Fire, Harry Potter and the Order of the Phoenix,* | *Harry Potter and the Half-Blood Prince* and *Harry* | *Potter and the Deathly Hallows* followed. J. K. Rowling | has also written three companion books: *Quidditch* | *Through the Ages* and *Fantastic Beasts and Where to Find* | *Them*, in aid of Comic Relief, and *The Tales of Beedle* | *the Bard*, in aid of Lumos. | [new paragraph] THE COMPLETE HARRY POTTER SERIES: | [colour illustrations in two rows of seven book designs] | Designed by Webb & Webb Design | Cover illustrations by Clare Melinsky | copyright © J. K. Rowling 2010'. All in white on green with white panel, 19 by 12mm, to right on which in black: '[Forest Stewardship Council logo, 6 by 7mm together with ® symbol] | FSC | www.fsc.org | MIX | Paper from | responsible sources | FSC® C018072'

Publication: 7 November 2011 in an edition of 9,200 copies (confirmed by Bloomsbury)

Price: £115 [together with A1(j), A2(o), A9(l), A12(i), A13(h) and A14(g)]

Contents:
Harry Potter and the Prisoner of Azkaban
　('Harry Potter was a highly unusual boy in many ways…')

Notes:
The end-papers carry a design of eight miniature illustrations. Seven of these reproduce the spine motifs from the series and an eighth comprises a variant of the key-bird from the first book.

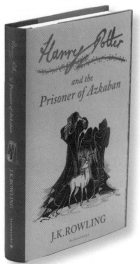

Published as a boxed set of seven volumes comprising A1(j), A2(o), A7(l), A9(l), A12(i), A13(h) and A14(g). Individual volumes were not available separately. The ISBN for the boxed set was ISBN 978 1 4088 2594 5.

Copies: private collection (PWE)

A7(m)　　　ENGLISH ADULT EDITION　　　(2013)
(Andrew Davidson artwork series in paperback)

J.K. [in grey] | ROWLING [in grey] [reading lengthways down title-page] | HARRY | POTTER | &THE [reading lengthways up title-page] PRISONER OF AZKABAN | BLOOMSBURY | LONDON [point] NEW DELHI [point] NEW YORK [point] SYDNEY (Author and final part of title justified on right margin, first part of title justified on left margin, publisher with publisher's offices width centred)

Collation: 160 unsigned leaves bound in indeterminate gatherings; 198 by 128mm; [1-7] 8-17 [18] 19-28 [29] 30-41 [42] 43-55 [56] 57-74 [75] 76-93 [94] 95-106 [107] 108-121 [122] 123-36 [137] 138-56 [157] 158-72 [173] 174-86 [187] 188-98 [199] 200-214 [215] 216-30 [231] 232-43 [244] 245-55 [256] 257-62 [263] 264-76 [277] 278-82 [283] 284-303 [304] 305-317 [318-20]

Page contents: [1] half-title: 'HARRY | POTTER | &THE [reading lengthways up title-page] PRISONER OF AZKABAN'; [2] '*Titles available in the Harry Potter series | (in reading order):* | Harry Potter and the Philosopher's Stone | Harry Potter and the Chamber of Secrets | Harry Potter and the Prisoner of Azkaban | Harry Potter and the Goblet of Fire | Harry Potter and the Order of the Phoenix | Harry Potter and the Half-Blood Prince | Harry Potter and the Deathly Hallows | [new paragraph] *Titles available in the Harry Potter series | (in Latin):* | Harry Potter and the Philosopher's Stone | Harry Potter and the Chamber of Secrets | *(in Welsh, Ancient Greek and Irish):* | Harry Potter and the Philosopher's Stone | [new paragraph] *Also available | (in aid of Comic Relief):* | Fantastic Beasts and Where to Find Them | Quidditch Through the Ages | *(in aid of Lumos):* | The Tales of Beedle the Bard'; [3] title-page; [4] 'All rights reserved; no part of this publication may be reproduced or | transmitted by any means, electronic, mechanical, photocopying | or otherwise, without the prior permission of the publisher | [new paragraph] First published in Great Britain in 1999 by Bloomsbury Publishing Plc | 50 Bedford Square, London WC1B 3DP | [new paragraph] Bloomsbury Publishing, London, New Delhi, New York and Sydney | [new paragraph] This paperback edition first published in 2013 | [new paragraph] Copyright © J.K. Rowling 1999 | Cover illustrations by Andrew Davidson copyright © J.K. Rowling 2013 | [new paragraph] Harry Potter, names, characters and related indicia are | copyright and trademark Warner Bros., 2000™ | [new paragraph] The moral right of the author has been asserted | A CIP catalogue record for this book is available from the British Library | [new paragraph] ISBN 978 1 4088 3498 5 | [new paragraph] [Forest Stewardship Council logo, 6 by 7mm together with ® symbol and text: 'FSC | www.fsc.org' with 'MIX | Paper from | responsible sources | FSC® C020471' to the right and all within single ruled border with rounded corners, 12 by 26mm] | [new paragraph] Typeset by Dorchester Typesetting | Printed and bound in Great Britain by CPI Group (UK) Ltd, Croydon CR0 4YY | [new paragraph] 1 3 5 7 9 10 8 6 4 2 | [new paragraph] | www.bloomsbury. com/harrypotter'; [5] '*To Jill Prewett and Aine Kiely, | the Godmothers of Swing*'; [6] blank; [7]-317 text; [318-20] blank

Paper: wove paper

Running title: 'HARRY POTTER' (24mm) on verso, recto title comprises chapter title, pp. 8-317

Binding: pictorial wrappers.
   On spine: 'J.K. ROWLING [in white] HARRY POTTER [in green] &THE [in white] PRISONER OF AZKABAN [in green] [publisher's device of a figure with a bow, 8 by 6mm] [in white]' (reading

lengthways down spine with the exception of '&THE' and the publisher's device which are horizontal). All on purple.

On upper wrapper: 'J.K. [in white] | ROWLING [in white] [reading lengthways down upper wrapper] | HARRY [in purple] | POTTER [in purple] | &THE [in white] [reading lengthways up upper wrapper] PRISONER OF AZKABAN [in purple] | BLOOMSBURY [in white]' (author and final part of title justified on right margin, first part of title justified on left margin, publisher with publisher's offices width centred). All on light and dark green illustration of Buckbeak the Hippogriff flying over Hogwarts castle.

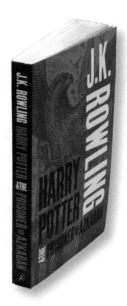

On lower wrapper: 'On the morning of his thirteenth birthday, Harry Potter learns | that mass-murderer Sirius Black has escaped the iron | grasp of Azkaban fortress. Harry has barely survived his first | two years at Hogwarts; now it looks as though Sirius Black | is determined to make sure Harry doesn't finish his third. | [new paragraph] With Ron and Hermione at his side, Harry is forced to confront | this new enemy – while the sinister Dementors of Azkaban | patrol the school grounds threatening to suck the very soul | from those who they encounter with a deadly kiss … | [new paragraph] [section of white illustration of Buckbeak the Hippogriff flying over Hogwarts castle, 69 by 111mm] | BLOOMSBURY www.bloomsbury.com/harrypotter www.pottermore.com £7.99 [in black] | [section of white illustration of Buckbeak the Hippogriff flying over Hogwarts castle, 28 by 111mm upon which: Forest Stewardship Council logo, 5 by 6mm together with ® symbol and text: 'FSC | www.fsc.org | MIX | Paper from | responsible sources | FSC® C020471' all in black on white panel with rounded corners, 19 by 12mm, with barcode in black on white panel, 18 by 38mm, with 'Designed by Webb & Webb Design | Cover illustrations by Andrew Davidson | copyright © J.K. Rowling 2013' in black on purple panel, 9 by 38mm]'. Lines 1-9 in white and all on purple. The initial capital 'O' of 'On' is a drop capital and is printed in green.

On inside upper wrapper: purple and white illustration of Buckbeak the Hippogriff flying over Hogwarts castle.

On inside lower wrapper: purple and white illustration of Hogwarts castle.

All edges trimmed. Binding measurements: 198 by 128mm (wrappers), 198 by 19mm (spine).

Publication: 18 July 2013 in an edition of 57,200 copies (confirmed by Bloomsbury) (see notes)

Price: £7.99

Contents:
Harry Potter and the Prisoner of Azkaban
('Harry Potter was a highly unusual boy in many ways…')

Notes:
The illustrations by Andrew Davidson derive from a single wood engraving. A single illustration is presented on both the upper wrapper and inside upper wrapper. A section is printed on the lower wrapper. A detail from the upper wrapper is shown on the inside lower wrapper.

Although Bloomsbury's 'official' publication date was 18 July 2013, copies were available from amazon.co.uk at the beginning of July.

Copies: private collection (PWE)

A7(n) AMERICAN CHILDREN'S EDITION (2013)
(Kazu Kibuishi artwork in paperback)

HARRY POTTER | AND THE PRISONER OF AZKABAN | [black and white illustration of a long-haired man looking at mouse in front of oval window, 53 by 70mm] | BY | J. K. ROWLING | ILLUSTRATIONS BY MARY GRANDPRÉ | SCHOLASTIC INC. (All width centred on a diamond pattern background)

Collation: 232 unsigned leaves bound in indeterminate gatherings; 204 by 134mm; [I-IV] V-VII [VIII-X] 1-435 [436-54]

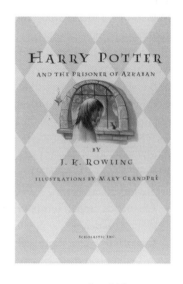

Page contents: [I-II] 'PRAISE FOR J. K. ROWLING'S | HARRY POTTER | AND THE PRISONER OF AZKABAN | [device of nine stars] | [6 reviews and a listing of 7 statements]; [III] title-page; [IV] 'TO JILL PREWETT AND | AINE KIELY, | THE GODMOTHERS OF SWING | [device of twelve stars] | Text © 1999 by J. K. Rowling | Interior illustrations by Mary GrandPré © 1999 by Warner Bros. | Excerpt from *Harry Potter and the Goblet of Fire*, text © 2000 by J. K. Rowling; | illustration by Mary GrandPré © 2000 by Warner Bros. | Cover illustration by Kazu Kibuishi © 2013 by Scholastic Inc. | HARRY POTTER and all related characters and elements are TM of and © WBEI. | Harry Potter Publishing Rights © J. K. Rowling | All rights reserved. Published by Scholastic Inc. SCHOLASTIC, the LANTERN LOGO, and associated | logos are trademarks and/or registered trademarks of Scholastic Inc. | [new paragraph] If you purchased this book without a cover, you should be aware that this book is stolen property. | It was reported as "unsold and destroyed" to the publisher, and neither the author nor the | publisher has received any payment for this "stripped book." | [new paragraph] No part of this publication may be reproduced, stored in a retrieval system, or transmitted in any | form or by any means, electronic, mechanical, photocopying, recording, or otherwise, without | written permission of the publisher. For information regarding permission, write to Scholastic Inc., | Attention: Permissions Department, 557 Broadway, New York, NY 10012. | [new paragraph] [publisher's device of a lantern, 6 by 4mm] | Arthur A. Levine Books hardcover edition art directed by David Saylor, | published by Arthur A. Levine Books, an imprint of Scholastic Inc., October 1999. | [new paragraph] ISBN 978-0-545-58293-3 | [new paragraph] Library of Congress

Control Number: 99-23982 | [new paragraph] 12 11 10 9 8 7 6 5 4 3 2 1   13 14 15 16 17 | [new paragraph] Printed in the U.S.A. 40 | This edition first printing, September 2013 | [new paragraph] We try to produce the most beautiful books possible, and we are extremely concerned about the impact of our | manufacturing process on the forests of the world and the environment as a whole. Accordingly, we made sure | that the text paper contains a minimum of 30% post-consumer waste, and that all the paper has been certified as | coming from forests that are managed to insure the protection of the people and wildlife dependent upon them.'; V-VII 'CONTENTS' (twenty-two chapters listed with titles and page references); [VIII] blank; [IX] half-title: 'HARRY POTTER | AND THE PRISONER OF AZKABAN' (all on diamond pattern background); [X] blank; 1-435 text; [436] blank; [437] 'HARRY POTTER'S | ADVENTURES CONTINUE IN | [new paragraph] HARRY POTTER | AND THE GOBLET OF FIRE | [new paragraph] TURN THE PAGE FOR | A SNEAK PREVIEW!' (all on diamond pattern background); [438] blank; [439-48] text; [449] blank; [450] advertisement for Pottermore; [451] '[black and white photograph of J.K. Rowling seated by curtains, credited 'ANDREW MONTGOMERY' reading lengthways up right margin] | [new paragraph] J. K. ROWLING is the author of the beloved, | bestselling, record-breaking Harry Potter series. She started writing | the series during a delayed Manchester to London King's Cross | train journey, and during the next five years, outlined the plots for | each book and began writing the first novel. *Harry Potter and the* | *Sorcerer's Stone* was published in the United States by Arthur A. | Levine Books in 1998, and the series concluded nearly ten years | later with *Harry Potter and the Deathly Hallows*, published in 2007. | J. K. Rowling is the recipient of numerous awards and honorary | degrees, including an OBE for services to children's literature, | France's Légion d'honneur, and the Hans Christian Andersen | Literature Award. She supports a wide number of causes through | her charitable trust, Volant, and is the founder of Lumos, a charity | working to transform the lives of disadvantaged children. J. K. | Rowling lives in Edinburgh with her husband and three children.'; [452] blank; [453] 'MARY GRANDPRÉ has illustrated more than twenty | beautiful books for children, including the American editions of | the Harry Potter novels. Her work has also appeared in the *New* | *Yorker*, the *Atlantic Monthly*, and the *Wall Street Journal*, and her | paintings and pastels have been shown in galleries across the United | States. Ms. GrandPré lives in Sarasota, Florida, with her family. | [new paragraph] KAZU KIBUISHI is the creator of the *New York Times* | bestselling Amulet series and *Copper*, a collection of his popular | webcomic. He is also the founder and editor of the acclaimed | Flight anthologies. *Daisy Kutter: The Last Train*, his first graphic | novel, was listed as one of the Best Books for Young Adults by | YALSA, and *Amulet, Book One: The Stonekeeper* was an ALA Best | Book for Young Adults and a Children's Choice Book Award | finalist. Kazu lives and works in Alhambra, California, with his | wife and fellow comics artist, Amy Kim Kibuishi, and their two | children. Visit Kazu online at www.boltcity. com.'; [454] blank

Paper: wove paper

Running title: 'CHAPTER' and chapter number on verso, recto title comprises chapter title, pp. 1-435 and pp. [439-48]. Each running title (excluding pages on which new chapters commence) includes a three-star design to left and right of both running-titles on verso and recto. On pages on which a new chapter commences, the three-star design is omitted.

Illustrations: title-page vignette, together with twenty-two vignettes at the beginning of each chapter (after chapter and chapter number but before chapter title). The 'sneak preview' also includes a vignette. In addition to standard typographical changes (including italics, capitals and small capitals) there are other typographical features, comprising:

p. 8 newspaper headline

p. 10 facsimile of Ron's signature (repeated twice)

p. 11 facsimile of Hermione's signature

p. 14 'handwritten' letter from Hagrid

p. 14 facsimile of Professor M. McGonagall's signature

p. 37 newspaper headline

p. 51 advertisement sign

p. 192 'The Marauder's Map' legend

p. 199 notice

p. 272 'handwritten' letter from Hagrid

p. 287 four different 'handwritten' comments

p. 291 'handwritten' letter from Hagrid

p. 315 'handwritten' exam schedule

p. 325 'handwritten' note from Hagrid

Binding: pictorial wrappers.

On spine: 'ROWLING | Harry Potter and the Prisoner of Azkaban [reading lengthways down spine] | 3' and '[publisher's book device] | [rule] | S' in white on red panel, 14 by 6mm. All in white on colour illustration (see notes).

On upper wrapper: 'J. K. ROWLING | Harry Potter [hand-drawn lettering] [embossed in white] | and the | Prisoner of Azkaban' (all width centred). All in white on colour illustration of Harry Potter conjuring a stag Patronus driving away dementors over a lake. In centre at foot: '[publisher's book device] SCHOLASTIC' in white on red panel, 5 by 45mm.

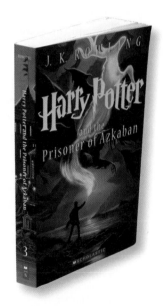

On lower wrapper: '"What you fear most of all is—fear." | — Remus Lupin | [new paragraph] For twelve long years, the dreaded fortress of Azkaban held an infamous | prisoner named Sirius Black. Convicted of killing thirteen people with | a single curse, he was said to be a dedicated follower of the Dark Lord, | Voldemort. Now he's escaped. And the Azkaban guards heard Black | muttering in his sleep, "He's at Hogwarts … he's at Hogwarts." Is he coming | for Harry? | [new paragraph] Harry Potter isn't safe, not even within the walls of his magical school, | surrounded by his friends. Because on top of it all, there may be a traitor in | their midst. | [new paragraph] $12.99 US | [new paragraph] [publisher's book device with 'SCHOLASTIC' in white on red panel, 5 by 45mm] | www.scholastic.com | COVER DESIGN BY KAZU KIBUISHI AND JASON CAFFOE | COVER ART BY KAZU KIBUISHI © 2013 BY SCHOLASTIC INC.' Lines

1-2 in white with other lines in peach and all on colour illustration of pupils and a teacher standing by an ornate closed wardrobe. In lower right: barcode with smaller barcode to the right (51299) together with 'S' within triangle, all in black on white panel, 21 by 53mm.

On inside upper wrapper: barcode with smaller barcode (51299) together with 'S' within triangle below, all in black on white panel, 53 by 21mm. All on purple.

On inside lower wrapper: '[colour illustration of book design] Harry Potter [hand-drawn lettering] [in white] | The Complete Series [in white] | Read All of Harry's [in white] | Magical Adventures! [in white] | [publisher's device of a lantern, 10 by 7mm] [in black] | ARTHUR A. LEVINE BOOKS [in black] | [publisher's book device with 'SCHOLASTIC' in white on red panel, 5 by 45mm] | scholastic.com/harrypotter [in white] | [colour illustrations in three columns of six book designs]'. All on lavender blue.

All edges trimmed. Binding measurements: 204 by 134mm (wrappers), 204 by 22mm (spine).

Publication: 27 August 2013

Price: $12.99

Contents:
Harry Potter and the Prisoner of Azkaban
    ('Harry Potter was a highly unusual boy in many ways. For one thing, he hated...')

Notes:
See notes to A4(h) about this series.

The seven volumes in this edition were available individually or as a set issued in a slipcase. The set, presented in order, reveals a single illustration of Hogwarts castle across the seven spines. Scholastic released images of the new illustrations in a careful marketing campaign: the upper wrapper illustration for *Prisoner of Azkaban* was released on 28 June 2013 at the fourth annual LeakyCon Convention in Portland, Oregon.

The 'sneak preview' of *Goblet of Fire* comprises only the first nine (and approximately three-quarters) (of fifteen) pages of chapter one.

Each chapter commences with a drop capital.

Copies: private collection (PWE)

Reprints include:
12 11 10 9 8 7 6 5 4 3   13 14 15 16 17   Printed in the U.S.A. 40

HARRY | POTTER | AND THE | PRISONER OF | AZKABAN | J.K. ROWLING | [publisher's device of a figure with a bow, 10 by 9mm] | BLOOMSBURY | LONDON NEW DELHI NEW YORK SYDNEY (All width centred and within broken single ruled border, 183 by 114mm)

Collation: 160 unsigned leaves bound in indeterminate gatherings; 198 by 128mm; [1-7] 8-17 [18] 19-28 [29] 30-41 [42] 43-55 [56] 57-74 [75] 76-93 [94] 95-106 [107] 108-121 [122] 123-36 [137] 138-56 [157] 158-72 [173] 174-86 [187] 188-98 [199] 200-214 [215] 216-30 [231] 232-43 [244] 245-55 [256] 257-62 [263] 264-76 [277] 278-82 [283] 284-303 [304] 305-317 [318-20]

Page contents: [1] half-title: 'HARRY | POTTER | AND THE | PRISONER OF | AZKABAN' (all within broken single ruled border, 183 by 114mm); [2] *Titles available in the Harry Potter series | (in reading order):* | Harry Potter and the Philosopher's Stone | Harry Potter and the Chamber of Secrets | Harry Potter and the Prisoner of Azkaban | Harry Potter and the Goblet of Fire | Harry Potter and the Order of the Phoenix | Harry Potter and the Half-Blood Prince | Harry Potter and the Deathly Hallows | [new paragraph] *Titles available in the Harry Potter series | (in Latin):* | Harry Potter and the Philosopher's Stone | Harry Potter and the Chamber of Secrets | *(in Welsh, Ancient Greek and Irish):* | Harry Potter and the Philosopher's Stone | [new paragraph] *Also available | (in aid of Comic Relief):* | Fantastic Beasts and Where to Find Them | Quidditch Through the Ages | *(in aid of Lumos):* | The Tales of Beedle the Bard'; [3] title-page; [4] 'All rights reserved; no part of this publication may be reproduced or | transmitted by any means, electronic, mechanical, photocopying | or otherwise, without the prior permission of the publisher | [new paragraph] First published in Great Britain in 1999 by Bloomsbury Publishing Plc | 50 Bedford Square, London WC1B 3DP | [new paragraph] Bloomsbury Publishing, London, New Delhi, New York and Sydney | [new paragraph] This paperback edition first published in 2013 | [new paragraph] Copyright © J.K. Rowling 1999 | [new paragraph] Harry Potter, names, characters and related indicia are | copyright and trademark Warner Bros., 2000™ | [new paragraph] The moral right of the author has been asserted | A CIP catalogue record for this book is available from the British Library | [new paragraph] ISBN 978 1 4088 4994 1 | [new paragraph] [Forest Stewardship Council logo, 6 by 7mm together with ® symbol and text: 'FSC | www.fsc.org' with 'MIX | Paper from | responsible sources | FSC® C020471' to the right and all within single ruled border with rounded corners, 12 by 26mm] | [new paragraph] Typeset by Dorchester Typesetting | Printed and bound in Great Britain by CPI

Group (UK) Ltd, Croydon CR0 4YY | [new paragraph] 1 3 5 7 9 10 8 6 4 2 | [new paragraph] | www.bloomsbury.com/harrypotter | www.pottermore.com'; [5] 'To Jill Prewett and Aine Kiely, | the Godmothers of Swing'; [6] blank; [7]-317 text; [318-20] blank

Paper: wove paper

Running title: 'HARRY POTTER' (24mm) on verso, recto title comprises chapter title, pp. 8-317

Binding: pictorial wrappers.

On spine: '[triple rule] HARRY POTTER AND THE PRISONER OF AZKABAN J.K. ROWLING [publisher's device of a figure with a bow, 9 by 8mm] [triple rule]' (reading lengthways down spine with rules and publisher's device horizontally at head or foot of spine). All in gilt on green.

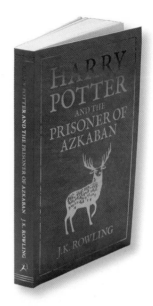

On upper wrapper: 'HARRY | POTTER | AND THE | PRISONER OF | AZKABAN | [illustration of a stag] | J.K. ROWLING | BLOOMSBURY' all width centred and within broken single ruled border, 183 by 114mm. All in gilt on green.

On lower wrapper: '[illustration of a stag] | [new paragraph] On the morning of his thirteenth birthday, Harry Potter | learns that mass-murderer Sirius Black has escaped the | iron grasp of Azkaban fortress. Harry has barely survived | his first two years at Hogwarts; now it looks as though | Sirius Black is determined to make sure Harry | doesn't finish his third. | [new paragraph] With Ron and Hermione at his side, Harry is forced | to confront this new enemy – while the sinister | Dementors of Azkaban patrol the school grounds | threatening to suck the very soul from those who | they encounter with a deadly kiss … | [new paragraph] [barcodes together with '[Forest Stewardship Council logo, 5 by 6mm together with ® symbol] | FSC | www.fsc.org | MIX | Paper from | responsible sources | FSC® C020471' within single ruled border with rounded corners, 18 by 12mm together with '[publisher's device of a figure with a bow, 8 by 7mm] | BLOOMSBURY | www.bloomsbury.com/ harrypotter | www.pottermore.com', all in black on white panel, 23 by 84mm] | [new paragraph] Cover illustration by Joe McLaren' all within broken single ruled border, 183 by 114mm. All in yellow on green.

All edges trimmed. Binding measurements: 198 by 128mm (wrappers), 198 by 19mm (spine).

Slipcase: card slipcase covered in blue paper (see A1(m)).

Publication: 10 October 2013 in an edition of 42,700 copies (confirmed by Bloomsbury)

Price: £21 [together with A1(m) and A2(r)]

Contents:
Harry Potter and the Prisoner of Azkaban
  ('Harry Potter was a highly unusual boy in many ways…')

Notes:
Published as a boxed set of three volumes comprising A1(m), A2(r) and A7(o). Individual volumes were not available separately. Bloomsbury announced the set stating: 'Every great story has a great beginning – and this is where Harry Potter's extraordinary, magical adventure starts... Harry Potter is a milestone in every child's reading life and this gorgeous, collectable boxed set is the perfect introduction for new readers, wizard and Muggle alike.'

Copies: private collection (PWE)

A1(a) spine and upper cover

A1(a) lower cover

A1(aa) spine and upper wrapper

A1(c) spine and upper wrapper

A1(d) spine and upper cover

A1(h) spine and upper wrapper

A1(i) spine and upper wrapper

A1(l) spine and upper wrapper

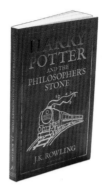

A1(m) spine and upper wrapper

A2(a) spine and upper cover in dust-jacket

A2(c) spine and upper cover in dust-jacket

A2(d) spine and upper wrapper

A2(e) spine and upper cover

A2(i) spine and upper cover

A2(j) spine and upper wrapper

A2(n) spine and upper wrapper

A2(p) spine and upper wrapper

A2(q) spine and upper wrapper

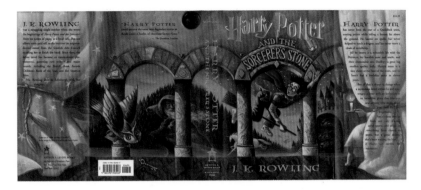

A4(a) dust-jacket

A4(a) spine and upper cover

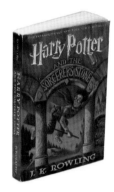

A4(b) spine and upper wrapper

A4(d) spine and upper cover

A4(e) spine and upper wrapper

A4(g) spine and upper cover

A4(h) spine and upper wrapper

A7(a) spine and upper cover in
dust-jacket

A7(b) spine and upper cover in
dust-jacket

A7(c) spine and upper cover

A7(ee) spine and upper wrapper

A7(h) spine and upper wrapper

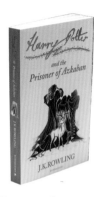

A7(k) spine and upper wrapper

A7(m) spine and upper wrapper

A7(n) spine and upper wrapper

A7(o) spine and upper wrapper

A9(a) spine and upper cover in
dust-jacket

A9(aa) spine and upper cover
in dust-jacket

A9(d) spine and upper wrapper

A9(e) spine and upper wrapper

A9(f) spine and upper wrapper

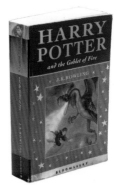

A9(j) spine and upper wrapper

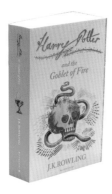

A9(k) spine and upper wrapper

A9(m) spine and upper wrapper

A9(n) spine and upper wrapper

A10(a) spine and upper wrapper

A10(aa) spine and upper wrapper

A10(b) spine and upper cover

A10(d) spine and upper cover

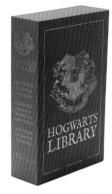

A10(d), A11(d) and A15(b) slipcase

A11(a) spine and upper wrapper

A11(aa) spine and upper wrapper

A11(b) spine and upper cover

A11(d) spine and upper cover

A12(a) spine and upper cover
in dust-jacket

A12(aa) spine and upper cover
in dust-jacket

A12(aaa) spine and upper cover
in dust-jacket

A12(b) dust-jacket

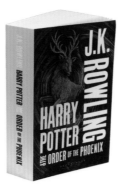

A12(h) spine and upper
wrapper

A12(j) spine and upper wrapper

A12(k) spine and upper
wrapper

A13(a) dust-jacket

A13(aa) dust-jacket

A13(aaaa) dust-jacket

THE DAILY PROPHET – 1 OCTOBER 1999

A8(a)   **FIRST ENGLISH EDITION**   **(1999)**

Banner:
Oct 1ˢᵗ 1999 The Daily Prophet Price: 7 Knuts
(All within single ruled border, 15 by 157mm)

Collation: 4 single leaves with staple upper left corner; 297 by 211mm; [1-4]

Page contents: [1] Headlines section; [2] Quidditch section; [3] Crossword clues; [4] Crossword grid

Paper: wove paper

Running title: none

Publication: 1 October 1999

Price: issued as part of membership of the Harry Potter Fan Club (membership fee: £4.25 per year)

Contents:
[Headlines section, p. 1]
Ministry Imposes Restrictions
    ('Minister for Magic, Cornelius Fudge, has announced Ministry plans to introduce…')
New Potion Gives Hope for Hags
    ('Professor Regulus Moonshine announced at a packed press-conference…')
[Advert]
    ('Poor memory?')

[Quidditch section, p. 2]
Quidditch League Table & Match Information
    ('1. Ballycastle Bats…')
Puddlemere Chaser Vanishes Amid Chaos at Holyhead Match
    ('The Department of Magical Games and Sports was in urgent conference…')
Cannons Blast the Falcons
    ('Chudley Cannons manager Ragmar Dorkins collapsed with shock…')
[Advert]
    ('Buy Your Second-Hand Brooms at…')
[Crossword clues]
    ('Across… 1. She has a backing group of banshees…')

Fiendishly Difficult Crossword
    [grid]

Notes:

After the two stories on page 1 only is there is a large circular point. Compare with A5(a).

There are three sections presented within single ruled borders: the Mnemosyne Clinic for Memory Modification advert (45 by 158mm), 'Quidditch League Table & Match Information' (65 by 158mm) and the Splinter & Kreek's advert (27 by 158mm).

Copyright notes at the foot of pages [1] and [2] ascribe copyright to J.K. Rowling.

Copies: private collection

HARRY POTTER AND THE GOBLET OF FIRE

A9(a) **FIRST ENGLISH EDITION** **(2000)**
(children's artwork series in hardback)

HARRY | POTTER | *and the Goblet of Fire* | [illustration of Hogwarts crest with legend 'DRAGO DORMIENS NUNQUAM TITILLANDUS' on banner, 67 by 82mm] | J.K.ROWLING | [publisher's device of a dog, 11 by 18mm] | BLOOMSBURY (Lines 1 and 2 justified on left and right margins, and all width centred)

Collation: 320 unsigned leaves bound in indeterminate gatherings; 197 by 127mm; [1-7] 8-19 [20] 21-28 [29] 30-38 [39] 40-48 [49] 50-61 [62] 63-69 [70] 71-86 [87] 88-105 [106] 107-129 [130] 131-40 [141] 142-51 [152] 153-70 [171] 172-84 [185] 186-200 [201] 202-218 [219] 220-38 [239] 240-52 [253] 254-74 [275] 276-94 [295] 296-316 [317] 318-35 [336] 337-50 [351] 352-76 [377] 378-97 [398] 399-415 [416] 417-41 [442] 443-64 [465] 466-89 [490] 491-504 [505] 506-525 [526] 527-51 [552] 553-58 [559] 560-71 [572] 573-81 [582] 583-600 [601] 602-620 [621] 622-36 [637-40]

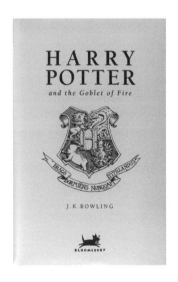

Page contents: [1] half-title: 'HARRY | POTTER | *and the Goblet of Fire* | [illustration of Hogwarts crest with legend 'DRAGO DORMIENS NUNQUAM TITILLANDUS' on banner, 47 by 57mm]'; [2] '*Titles available in the Harry Potter series* | *(in reading order)*: | Harry Potter and the Philosopher's Stone | Harry Potter and the Chamber of Secrets | Harry Potter and the Prisoner of Azkaban | Harry Potter and the Goblet of Fire'; [3] title-page; [4] 'All rights reserved; no part of this publication may be reproduced or | transmitted by any means, electronic, mechanical, photocopying or otherwise, | without the prior permission of the publisher | [new paragraph] First published in Great Britain in 2000 | Bloomsbury Publishing Plc, 38 Soho Square, London, W1V 5DF | [new paragraph] Copyright © 2000 J.K. Rowling | Cover illustrations copyright © by Giles Greenfield 2000 | [new paragraph] The moral right of the author has been asserted | A CIP catalogue record of this book is available from the | British Library | [new paragraph] ISBN 0 7475 4624 X | [new paragraph] Printed in Great Britain by Clays Ltd, St Ives plc | Typeset by Dorchester Typesetting | [new paragraph] First Edition | [new paragraph] www.bloomsbury.com/harrypotter'; [5] '*To Peter Rowling,* | *in memory of Mr Ridley* | *and to Susan Sladden,* | *who helped Harry out of his cupboard*'; [6] blank; [7]-636 text; [637-40] blank

Paper: wove paper

Running title: 'HARRY POTTER' (24mm) on verso, recto title comprises chapter title, pp. 8-636 (excluding pages on which new chapters commence)

Binding: pictorial boards.

On spine: '[colour illustration of an owl on staircase banister on coloured panel, 58 by 18mm] HARRY POTTER [in blue on red panel, 58 by 47mm] *and the Goblet of Fire* [in light blue] J.K.ROWLING [in red, both title conclusion and author on blue panel, 58 by 107mm] BLOOMSBURY [publisher's device of the head of a dog, 3 by 4mm] [both in black on light blue panel, 58 by 34mm]' (reading lengthways down spine).

On upper cover: 'HARRY | POTTER | *and the Goblet of Fire* [lines 1 and 2 in blue, line 3 in black, all on red panel, 64 by 132mm] | [light blue rule, 132mm] | [colour illustration of Harry Potter flying on a broomstick about to seize a golden egg that is protected by a fire-breathing dragon, 124 by 132mm] | [light blue rule, 132mm intersected by blue panel with 'J.K.ROWLING' in red] | BLOOMSBURY [in light blue on black panel, 13 by 132mm]' (all width centred).

On lower cover: 'The summer holidays are dragging on and Harry Potter | can't wait for the start of the school year. It is his fourth | year at Hogwarts School of Witchcraft and Wizardry, | and there are spells to be learnt, potions to be brewed | and Divination lessons (sigh) to be attended. Harry | is expecting these: however, other quite unexpected | events are already on the march… | [new paragraph] A much-awaited new Harry Potter adventure | from an acclaimed story-telling genius. | [new paragraph] 'Like Gameboys, Teletubbies and films by | George Lucas, Harry Potter has permeated | the national child consciousness.' | *The Independent on Sunday* | [new paragraph] 'The world of Hogwarts is complete | in every riotous, headlong detail. The | richness and scale of Rowling's invention | is exhilarating… but the real proof of | quality lies in J.K. Rowling's power to | draw the reader into Harry's world and | make it seem believable.' *The Guardian* | [new paragraph] 'The Harry Potter books are that rare | thing, a series of stories adored by | children and parents alike.' | *The Daily Telegraph* | [barcode in black on white panel, 20 by 37mm together with '[publisher's device of a dog, 6 by 10mm] | BLOOMSBURY' in black on left side of panel and 'http://www.bloomsbury.com' below panel, in light blue on blue panel, 7 by 37mm]'. Reading lengthways down right side next to foot of spine 'Cover illustrations by Giles Greenfield | Cover design by Richard Horne'. All in black on colour illustration of staircase at Hogwarts castle.

All edges trimmed. Binding measurements: 205 by 132mm (covers), 205 by 58mm (spine). End-papers: wove paper.

Dust-jacket: coated wove paper, 205 by 519mm
Spine, upper and lower covers replicate the binding.

On upper inside flap: 'It is the summer holidays, and one night | Harry Potter wakes up with his scar burning. | He has had a strange dream, one that he | can't help worrying about… until a timely | invitation from Ron Weasley arrives: to | nothing less than the Quidditch World Cup! | [new paragraph] Soon Harry is reunited with Ron and | Hermione and gasping at the thrills of an | international Quidditch match. But then | something horrible happens which casts a | shadow over everybody, and Harry in | particular… | [new paragraph] *A fantastic sequel to the existing Harry Potter | adventures:* | [new paragraph] HARRY POTTER AND | THE PHILOSOPHER'S STONE | [new paragraph] 'I've yet to meet a 10 year old who hasn't | been entranced by its witty, complex plot | and the character of the eponymous Harry.' | *The Independent* | [new paragraph] HARRY POTTER AND | THE CHAMBER OF SECRETS | [new paragraph] 'Such a marriage of good writing, inventiveness, | and sheer child-appeal has not been seen since | Roald Dahl, perhaps even since Tolkien, Lewis, | and

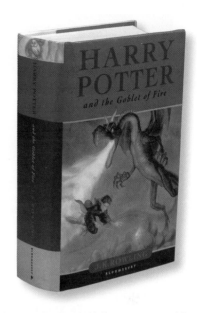

Ransome. J.K. Rowling has woken a whole | generation to reading.' *The Times* | [new paragraph] HARRY POTTER AND | THE PRISONER OF AZKABAN | [new paragraph] 'One warning. If you are going to read this to | your children, make sure you start early in the | evening. There are so many surprising twists that | you will not be allowed to put the book down | even if you wanted to.' *The Sunday Express* | £14.99'. All in black on red panel.

On lower inside flap: '[nine stars, in blue] | Dear Joanne Rowling, | My name's Matthew la Croix, | & I'm 12 years of age. I think your books are | amazing! | [new paragraph] That feeling of looking forward to lunchtimes, so I | could read Harrys world of magic, is great, so | I'd like to thank you for adding that touch | of excitment [*sic*] in my day! [smiley face] | [new paragraph] I've read all three books, | and I think Harry Potter & the Prisoner of Azkaban, | beat all three, and being that it was bigger, it | was twice as much pleaseure [*sic*] reading. | [new paragraph] Please, Please, Please, Please, PLEASE!!!!!!!!!!!! | Bring another one, keeping writing, my Life | depends on it, | [new paragraph] Yours Sincerely, | [new paragraph] Matthew La Croix, Your No°1 fan! | X X X | [twelve stars, in blue] | www.bloomsbury.com/harrypotter'. All in black facsimile of child's handwriting and all on red panel.

Publication: 8 July 2000 (simultaneous with A9(b)) in an edition of 750,000 copies (confirmed by Bloomsbury)

Price: £14.99

Contents:
Harry Potter and the Goblet of Fire
('The villagers of Little Hangleton still called it 'the Riddle House', even though…')

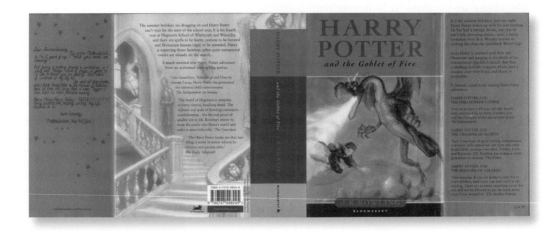

Notes:

Files preserved within the Bloomsbury archives suggest that, in contrast with *Prisoner of Azkaban*, the editorial process continued until close to publication date. A letter from J.K. Rowling to Emma Matthewson is dated 8 March 2000 and included

> … my very preliminary responses to all the points you raised. I thought it would be a good idea to let you have a look at them before we meet…

This letter includes a number of suggestions from the author about the title, comprising: *Harry Potter and the Death Eaters*, *Harry Potter and the Fire Goblet* and *Harry Potter and the Three Champions*. There is also a suggestion that the 'Doomspell Tournament' be renamed the 'Triwizard Tournament', which was evidently accepted. This letter suggests that, in contrast with the first three books in the series, Arthur A. Levine and Scholastic had some editorial input. This was verified in an interview with the American publisher in March 2012.

A set of proofs in the editorial files at Bloomsbury reveal that on 12 April 2000 the book was titled *Harry Potter and*. The file name given to the work was simply 'new book'. This was a deliberate attempt to keep the final title secret until the official press announcement. A set of proofs in the Bloomsbury archives reveal a much earlier state of the text at this stage together with many corrections.

The first English edition of this title is the first book in the series to include details of the typesetter on the publisher's imprint page. It was also the first title in the series to note 'First Edition' rather than print the numerical strike-line.

The advertising campaign for this title included a large banner poster featuring the words 'Harry's Back!' accompanied by an image of the upper cover of the book and the publication date of 8 July 2000. In contrast to the afternoon publication time for *Prisoner of Azkaban*, *Goblet of Fire* was released at midnight. In an interview with me in September 2013, Nigel Newton stated 'I'm not sure where the idea came from. It might have been the movie industry… We came to call this "denial marketing" – what people like most is not being able to get something. It's like life itself: you want most what you can't have. For the month or two months (or six months later on), between when it was announced that Jo had completed and delivered to her publisher the new book and the date it came out, there was just intense press interest in the book and nobody knew what it was because we *were* good at keeping it secret and we had to go to extraordinary lengths to do so.' He also notes that 'we did nothing to promote denial marketing. It just happened.'

A number of book-signing sessions were organized by Bloomsbury. Tickets announced 'Harry's Back!' and noted that the author would 'be signing copies of the new Harry Potter adventure'. Sessions included:

17 July 2000	Harrods, Knightsbridge, London	morning
17 July 2000	Hatchards, 187 Piccadilly, London	3.30 to 5 pm
18 July 2000	Borders Books, Music and Café, Churchill Square, Brighton	6.30 to 8 pm
19 July 2000	Books Etc, 02 Centre, 255 Finchley Road, London	10 to 11.30 am

The editorial files at Bloomsbury include a set of untrimmed and unbound sheets in gatherings for this edition. This is noted as an 'untrimmed set of Harry 4 pages' and comprises collections of folded sheets with the text printed twice (each set starting at opposite ends and reversed by 180 degrees). The first untrimmed gathering therefore presents the first and final signature and the tenth gathering presents the tenth and eleventh signature. Each sheet, as printed, therefore had eight pages on each side and the production of the book created volumes from 20 original gatherings.

The original artwork by Giles Greenfield for this title remained in the possession of Bloomsbury, in contrast to the artwork for earlier titles in the series.

With such large print-runs, I asked Nigel Newton in an interview with me in September 2013 whether a variety of different printers were used to print the first edition. Newton replied in the negative and noted that 'they were all printed by Clays who were absolutely superb'. Two specific requirements were made of the firm. Firstly they were required to 'produce more books in a shorter period of time than anyone had ever done before'. Secondly they had 'to produce those books in conditions of extreme secrecy'. Newton remarked that, later in the series, Clays became the point of distribution given that there was no need to send an edition to Bloomsbury's Macmillan warehouse. Newton noted that 'the other heroes of the logistical side of the story – other than a handful of key people in the office and Clays themselves – were Macmillan Distribution Limited (a third-party warehouse we've used for two decades). Their order processing division was based in Basingstoke and the physical warehouse was in Swansea. So they brought many of their workforce up to Bungay in Suffolk in order to be able to do the distribution… They pre-printed all the invoices down in Basingstoke for 11 million books and then took them up there and then worked with the Clays personel to get all of these books into boxes and despatched.' The arrival of orders on time became significant: early delivery posed a security risk and late delivery would miss the official release date.

Despite Newton's recollection, it appears a variant issue exists with 'Printed in Great Britain by Omnia Books Limited, Glasgow' on the imprint page. Omnia Books printed far fewer copies than Clays. No copies have been consulted.

A copy of this edition inscribed by the author to her father, and therefore a dedication copy, was offered at auction at Sotheby's New York on 10 December 2003. It was inscribed on the dedication page 'Dear Dad – | If I had said 'Ronald (Weasley) | Ridley' they would have | tracked the poor bloke down… | but that's why Ron's called | Ron of course! | Happy Father's Day 2000 | and lots of love | from your first born | JKRowling | xxxxxxxxx'. There is also a sketch of a hand (labelled 'Pesticide') reaching for a running gnome (also labelled). Estimated at $50,000/75,000, it sold for $40,000.

The English audiobook version, read by Stephen Fry, has a duration of approximately twenty-one hours.

Reprints (and subsequent new editions) include a number of corrections to the text. These comprise:

Page 14, line 2	'said the first voice softly' to 'said the second voice softly'
Page 15, line 5	'whispered the first voice' to 'whispered the second voice'
Page 15, line 25	'said the first voice again' to 'said the second voice again'
Page 32, line 1	'Harry would dearly loved to' to 'Harry would have dearly loved to'
Page 34, line 35	'a disgusting swearword' to 'a disgusting swear word'
Page 49, line 21	'dragons in Rumania' to 'dragons in Romania'
Page 82, line 11	'tucking it away into the front of his robes' to 'tucking it away carefully'
Page 93, line 16	'Bertie Botts' Every Flavour Beans' to 'Bertie Bott's Every Flavour Beans'
Page 120, line 3	'Enervate!' to 'Rennervate!'
Page 133, line 10	'Sunday morning' to 'Saturday morning'
Page 136, line 11	'the Gringotts' curse breakers' to 'the Gringotts curse breakers'
Page 144, line 35	'No-Heat, Wet-Start Fireworks' to 'Wet-Start, No-Heat Fireworks'
Page 150, line 18	'Grade Four' to 'Grade 4'
Page 150, line 19	'Malfoy's pale face' to 'Malfoy's pale face.'
Page 155, line 34	'though his half-moon spectacles' to 'through his half-moon spectacles'
Page 171, line 9	'running his finger down the Monday column of his timetable' to 'running his finger down his timetable'
Page 183, line 31	'leaning forwards' to 'leaning forwards.'
Page 185, line 9	'frog guts' to 'toad guts'
Page 203, line 21	'competely' to 'completely'
Page 207, line 18	'Ernie MacMillan' to 'Ernie Macmillan'
Page 215, line 15	'Madam Maxime's' to 'Madame Maxime's'
Page 231, line 29	're-appearance' to 'reappearance'
Page 247, line 23	paragraph break after 'impatience'
Page 248, line 30	'someone else had had considered it' to 'someone else had considered it'
Page 256, line 13	'I don't who put my' to 'I don't know who pit my'
Page 323, line 23	'This is o'ny me second year' to 'This is on'y me second year'
Page 344, line 10	'Eloise Midgeon' to 'Eloise Midgen'
Page 353, line 33	'Conjunctivitus' to 'Conjunctivitis'
Page 357, line 9	'Bertie Botts' Every Flavour Beans' to 'Bertie Bott's Every Flavour Beans'
Page 357, line 10	'Droobles Best Blowing Gum' to 'Drooble's Best Blowing Gum'
Page 362, line 5	'all though dinner' to 'all through dinner'
Page 364, line 5	'Chreetsmas' to 'Chreestmas'
Page 379, line 6	'through the snow' to 'through the snow.'
Page 382, line 11	'reputed to have a developed' to 'reputed to have developed'
Page 434, lines 11-12	'started pointed excitedly' to 'started pointing excitedly'

Page 440, line 18	'Harry stomach leapt' to 'Harry's stomach leapt'
Page 465, line 5	'watched her out of sight' to 'watched her fly out of sight'
Page 466, line 12	'gettting through six bottles' to 'getting through six bottles'
Page 479, line 25	'Don't vont to be overheard' to 'Don't vant to be overheard'
Page 486, line 15	'*Enervate*' to '*Rennervate*'
Page 487, line 8	'he pulled out his wand' to 'he raised his wand'
Page 502, line 25	'Droobles Best Blowing Gum' to 'Drooble's Best Blowing Gum'
Page 502, lines 25-26	'Bertie Botts' Every Flavour Beans' to 'Bertie Bott's Every Flavour Beans'
Page 503, line 28	'said Crouch angrily' to 'said Fudge angrily'
Page 530, lines 2-3	'wrote], 'my priority' to 'wrote], my priority'
Page 548, lines 10-11	'past the the thing' to 'past the thing'
Page 565, line 14	'My Lord, I prostrate' to "My Lord, I prostrate'
Page 579, line 6	'the man appearing' to 'the woman appearing'
Page 579, line 8	'a tall man with untidy hair' to 'a young woman with long hair'
Page 579, line 11	'the ghostly face of his father' to 'the ghostly face of his mother'
Page 579, lines 12-13	"Your mother's coming …' he said quietly. 'She wants to see you …' to "Your father's coming …' she said quietly. 'He wants to see you …'
Page 579, lines 14-15	'And she came … first her head, then her body … a young woman with long hair, the smoky, shadowy form of Lily Potter' to 'And he came … first his head, then his body … tall and untidy-haired like Harry, the smoky, shadowy form of James Potter'
Page 579, line 17	'straightened like her husband' to 'straightened like his wife'
Page 579, line 17	'She walked close' to 'He walked close'
Page 579, line 18	'she spoke' to 'he spoke'
Page 591, lines 15-16	'reopening the trunk each time, and revealing different contents each time' to 'reopening the trunk, and each time revealing different contents'
Page 591, line 25	'thunder-struck' to 'thunderstruck'
Page 593, line 23	'*Enervate*' to '*Rennervate*'
Page 594, line 28	'Moody said' to 'Crouch said'
Page 606, line 35	'given us all we have a right' to 'given us all that we have a right'
Page 613, line 2	'I've heard of a curse scar' to 'I've never heard of a curse scar'
Page 613, line 11	'McNair!' to 'Macnair!'
Page 616, line 22	'staff are playing at Dumbledore' to 'staff are playing at, Dumbledore'
Page 618, line 23	'no hope for any us' to 'no hope for any of us'
Page 629, line 12	'always polite' to 'alvays polite'

Copies: private collection (PWE)

Reprints include:
10 9 8 7 6 5 4 3 2

A report compiled by the printers, Clays Ltd, in October 2013 noted that, to date, they had produced a minimum of 6.1 million paperbacks and 1.5 million hardbacks across 141 printings.

FIRST AMERICAN EDITION
(children's artwork series in hardback)

HARRY POTTER | AND THE GOBLET OF FIRE | [black and white illustration of a flaming goblet on a casket with curtains in background, 54 by 54mm] | BY | J. K. ROWLING | ILLUSTRATIONS BY MARY GRANDPRÉ | [publisher's device of a lantern, 12 by 9mm] | ARTHUR A. LEVINE BOOKS | AN IMPRINT OF SCHOLASTIC PRESS (All width centred on a diamond pattern background)

Collation: 376 unsigned leaves bound in indeterminate gatherings; 228 by 150mm; [I-VI] VII-XI [XII-XIV] 1-734 [735-38]

Page contents: [I] 'HARRY POTTER | AND THE GOBLET OF FIRE' (all on diamond pattern background); [II] 'ALSO BY J. K. ROWLING | [new paragraph] *Harry Potter and the Sorcerer's Stone* | Year One at Hogwarts | [new paragraph] *Harry Potter and the Chamber of Secrets* | Year Two at Hogwarts | [new paragraph] *Harry Potter and the Prisoner of Azkaban* | Year Three at Hogwarts'; [III] title-page; [IV] '[device of twelve stars] | Text copyright © 2000 by J. K. Rowling | Illustrations by Mary GrandPré copyright © 2000 Scholastic Inc. | All rights reserved. Published by Scholastic Press, a division of Scholastic Inc., | *Publishers since 1920.* | SCHOLASTIC, SCHOLASTIC PRESS, and the LANTERN LOGO | are trademarks and/or registered trademarks of Scholastic Inc. | [new paragraph] No part of this publication may be reproduced, or stored in a retrieval system, or transmitted | in any form or by any means, electronic, mechanical, photocopying, recording, or otherwise, | without written permission of the publisher. For information regarding permission, write | to Scholastic Inc., Attention: Permissions Department, 555 Broadway, New York, NY 10012. | [new paragraph] Library of Congress Cataloging-in-Publication Data Available | [new paragraph] Library of Congress catalog card number: 00-131084 | [new paragraph] ISBN 0-439-13959-7 | [new paragraph] 10 9 8 7 6 5 4 3 2 1   0/0 01 02 03 04 | Printed in the U.S.A. 23 | First American edition, July 2000'; [V] 'TO PETER ROWLING, | IN MEMORY OF MR. RIDLEY | AND TO SUSAN SLADDEN, | WHO HELPED HARRY | OUT OF HIS CUPBOARD'; [VI] blank; VII-XI 'CONTENTS' (thirty-seven chapters listed with titles and page references); [XII] blank; [XIII] half-title: 'HARRY POTTER | AND THE GOBLET OF FIRE' (all on diamond pattern background); [XIV] blank; 1-734 text; [735-736] blank; [737] colophon: '[publisher's device of a lantern, 17 by 12mm] | This | book was art | directed by David Saylor. The | art for both the jacket and the interior was | created using pastels on toned printmaking paper. The | text was set in 12-point Adobe Garamond, a typeface based on | the sixteenth-century type designs of Claude Garamond, redrawn by | Robert Slimbach in 1989. The book was typeset by Brad Walrod | and was printed and bound*

at RR Donnelley in | Harrisonberg, Virginia. The Managing | Editor was Manuela Soares and the | Manufacturing Director | was Angela | Biola.'; [738] blank

Paper: wove paper

Running title: 'CHAPTER' and chapter number on verso, recto title comprises chapter title, pp. 1-734. Each running title (excluding pages on which new chapters commence) includes a three-star design to left and right of both running-titles on verso and recto. On pages on which a new chapter commences, the three-star design is omitted.

Illustrations: title-page vignette, together with thirty-seven vignettes at the beginning of each chapter (after chapter and chapter number but before chapter title). In addition to standard typographical changes (including italics, capitals and small capitals) there are other typographical features, comprising:

p. 25 facsimile of Harry's signature

p. 30 facsimile of Molly Weasley's signature

p. 36 facsimiles of Ron and Harry's signatures

pp. 96-97 advertisements written on a gigantic blackboard

p. 102 further advertisements written on a gigantic blackboard, also a Quidditch score

p. 109 lettering displayed on Harry's Omnioculars

p. 113 Quidditch score

p. 202 newspaper headline

p. 226 facsimile of Sirius' signature

p. 228 facsimile of Harry's signature

p. 235 text of announcement sign

p. 240 facsimile of Sirius' signature

p. 292 facsimile of Harry's signature

p. 297 text of badges

p. 298 text of badge

p. 304 facsimile of Rita Skeeter's quill's writing

p. 305 facsimile of Rita Skeeter's quill's writing

p. 306 facsimile of Rita Skeeter's quill's writing

p. 312 facsimile of Sirius' signature

p. 406 facsimile of Sirius' signature

p. 437 newspaper headline

p. 511 magazine headline

p. 541 text of letter in 'poison-pen' style

p. 572 facsimile of Sirius' signature

p. 611 newspaper headline

p. 638 headstone engraved name

Binding: black cloth-backed spine with orange-red boards (with diamond pattern in blind).

On spine: 'ROWLING | [rule] | ['YEAR | 4' within concave square]' (horizontally at head) with 'HARRY POTTER | AND THE GOBLET OF FIRE' (reading lengthways down spine) and '[publisher's device of a lantern, 19 by 14mm] | ARTHUR A. | LEVINE BOOKS | [rule] | SCHOLASTIC' (horizontally at foot). All in gilt.

Upper and lower covers: blank.

All edges trimmed. Binding measurements: 235 by 150mm (covers), 235 by 67mm (spine). The black cloth continues onto the covers by 40mm. End-papers: purple wove paper.

Dust-jacket: uncoated wove paper, 234 by 590mm. A single illustration spans the entire dust-jacket.

On spine: 'ROWLING | [rule] | ['YEAR | 4' within concave square]' (horizontally at head) with 'HARRY POTTER | AND THE GOBLET OF FIRE' (reading lengthways down spine) and '[publisher's device of a lantern, 19 by 14mm] | ARTHUR A. | LEVINE BOOKS | [rule] | SCHOLASTIC' (horizontally at foot). All embossed in gilt on colour illustration of green hedge and back of a Hungarian Horntail dragon.

On upper cover: 'Harry Potter [hand-drawn lettering] [embossed in gilt] | AND THE [hand-drawn lettering in crimson of illustration] | GOBLET OF FIRE [hand-drawn lettering in crimson of illustration] [lines 2-3 in panel of illustration with flame above letter 'E' of 'FIRE'] | J. K. ROWLING [embossed in gilt]' (all width centred). All on colour illustration of Harry Potter clutching wand and golden egg with other characters in background and the back of a Hungarian Horntail dragon in the foreground.

On lower cover: 'Sequel to the #1 *New York Times* Bestseller | HARRY POTTER | AND THE PRISONER OF AZKABAN | [barcode with smaller barcode to the right (52595) all in black on orange panel, 23 by 53mm]. All in black and all on colour illustration of maze hedges, flaming goblet, carriage pulled by winged horses, and a wing and back of a Hungarian Horntail dragon.

On upper inside flap: '$25.95 | YOU HAVE IN YOUR HANDS | the pivotal fourth novel in the seven-part | tale of Harry Potter's training as a wizard and | his coming of age. Harry wants to get away | from the pernicious Dursleys and go to the | International Quidditch Cup with Hermione, | Ron, and the Weasleys. He wants to dream about | Cho Chang, his crush (and maybe do more than | dream). He wants to find out about the mys- | terious event that's supposed to take place at | Hogwarts this year, an event involving two | other rival schools of magic, and a competition | that hasn't happened for a hundred years. He | wants to be a normal, fourteen-year-old wizard. | Unfortunately for Harry Potter, he's not normal— | even by wizarding standards. | [new paragraph] And in this case, different can be deadly.' All in black and all on colour illustration of curling smoke. The initial capital 'Y' of 'YOU' is a drop capital.

On lower inside flap: 'ALSO BY J. K. ROWLING | #1 *New York Times, USA Today,* and international best- | sellers, winners of the National Book Award (UK) and | Gold Medal Smarties prize three years running, and ALA | Notable Books: | [new paragraph] HARRY POTTER | AND THE PRISONER OF AZKABAN | WINNER OF THE WHITBREAD AWARD | "Isn't it reassuring that some things just get better and bet- | ter? This is a fabulously entertaining read that will have | Harry Potter fans cheering for more." | —*School Library Journal* | [new paragraph] HARRY POTTER | AND THE CHAMBER OF SECRETS | [five-pointed star] "Harry Potter's exploits during his second year at | Hogwarts School for Witchcraft and Wizardry completely | live up to the bewitching measure of *Harry Potter and the* | *Sorcerer's Stone.* The mystery, zany humor, student rivalry, | and eccentric faculty… are as expertly crafted here as in | the first book." —*Booklist,* starred review | [new paragraph] HARRY POTTER | AND THE SORCERER'S STONE | "A charming, imaginative, magical confection | of a novel." —*Boston Globe* | "Funny, moving, and impressive." | —*The New York Times Book Review* | [new paragraph] [publisher's device of a lantern, 15 by 10mm] | ARTHUR A. LEVINE BOOKS | *An Imprint of Scholastic Press* | 555 Broadway, New York, New York 10012 | [new paragraph] *Jacket art by Mary GrandPré* | *Jacket design by Mary GrandPré and David Saylor*'. Lines 1-26 in black and lines 27-32 in orange and all on colour illustration of a maze hedge engulfed by tentacles.

Publication: 8 July 2000 (simultaneous with A9(a))

Price: $25.95

Contents:
Harry Potter and the Goblet of Fire
   ('The villagers of Little Hangleton still called it "the Riddle House," even though…')

Notes:

In an interview with me in March 2012 the publisher Arthur A. Levine noted that prior to book four the publishing houses of Bloomsbury and Scholastic had not worked together during the editorial process. However, this situation changed with *Goblet of Fire*. Emma Matthewson from Bloomsbury notes that queries were collated by Bloomsbury who then passed them to Rowling. Scholastic would contact the author directly only for questions resulting from different house-styles or American English.

Goblet of Fire was the first title in the series for which unprecedented demand required printing the first edition at a number of different printers. Copies have been examined with the following printing plant codes on the imprint page:

Printed in the U.S.A.   13
Printed in the U.S.A.   23

An initial print run of 3.8 million copies was reported by PR Newswire on 20 November 2000.

Each chapter commences with a drop capital.

The American audiobook version, read by Jim Dale, has a duration of approximately twenty and a half hours.

Copies: private collection (PWE)

Reprints include:

10 9 8 7 6 5	0/0 01 02 03 04	Printed in the U.S.A. 56
20 19 18 17 16 15 14 13	0/0 01 02 03 04	Printed in the U.S.A. 56
39 38 37 36 35 34 33 32 31 30	02 03 04	Printed in the U.S.A. 23
48 47 46 45 44 43 43 42 41	07 08 09 10 11	Printed in the U.S.A. 12

A9(b)   ENGLISH DELUXE EDITION   (2000)
(children's artwork series in deluxe hardback)

HARRY | POTTER | *and the Goblet of Fire* | [illustration of Hogwarts crest with legend 'DRACO DORMIENS NUNQUAM TITILLANDUS' on banner, 70 by 86mm] | J.K.ROWLING | [publisher's device of a dog, 12 by 19mm] | BLOOMSBURY (All width centred)

Collation: 320 unsigned leaves bound in forty gatherings of eight leaves; 233 by 150mm, [1-7] 8-19 [20] 21-28 [29] 30-38 [39] 40-48 [49] 50-61 [62] 63-69 [70] 71-86 [87] 88-105 [106] 107-129 [130] 131-40 [141] 142-51 [152] 153-70 [171] 172-84 [185] 186-200 [201] 202-218 [219] 220-38 [239] 240-52 [253] 254-74 [275] 276-94 [295] 296-316 [317] 318-35 [336] 337-50 [351] 352-76 [377] 378-97 [398] 399-415 [416] 417-41 [442] 443-64 [465] 466-89 [490] 491-504 [505] 506-525 [526] 527-51 [552] 553-58 [559] 560-71 [572] 573-81 [582] 583-600 [601] 602-620 [621] 622-36 [637-40]

Page contents: [1] half-title: 'HARRY | POTTER | *and the Goblet of Fire* | [illustration of Hogwarts crest with legend 'DRACO DORMIENS NUNQUAM TITILLANDUS' on banner, 49 by 60mm]'; [2] '*Titles available in the Harry Potter series* | *(in reading order):* | Harry Potter and the Philosopher's Stone | Harry Potter and the Chamber of Secrets | Harry Potter and the Prisoner of Azkaban | Harry Potter and the Goblet of Fire'; [3] title-page; [4] 'All rights reserved; no part of this publication may be reproduced or | transmitted by any means, electronic, mechanical, photocopying or otherwise, | without the prior permission of the publisher | [new paragraph] First published in Great Britain in 2000 | Bloomsbury Publishing Plc, 38 Soho Square, London, W1V 5DF | [new paragraph] Copyright © 2000 J.K. Rowling | Cover illustrations copyright © by Giles Greenfield 2000 | [new paragraph] Harry Potter, names, characters and related indicia are | copyright and trademark Warner Bros., 2000™ | [new paragraph] The moral right of the author has been asserted | A CIP catalogue record of this book is available from the | British Library | [new paragraph] ISBN 0 7475 4971 0 | [new paragraph] Printed in Great Britain by Clays Ltd, St Ives plc | Typeset by Dorchester Typesetting | [new paragraph] First Edition | [new paragraph] | www.bloomsbury.com/harrypotter'; [5] '*To Peter Rowling,* | *in memory of Mr Ridley* | *and to Susan Sladden,* | *who helped Harry out of his cupboard*'; [6] blank; [7]-636 text; [637-40] blank

Paper: wove paper

Running title: 'HARRY POTTER' (25mm) on verso, recto title comprises chapter title, pp. 8-636

Binding: light purple cloth.
    On spine: 'HARRY POTTER *and the Goblet of Fire* J.K.ROWLING' (reading lengthways down spine) with '[publisher's device of a dog, 12 by 21mm] | BLOOMSBURY' (horizontally at foot of spine). All in gilt.
    On upper cover: 'HARRY | POTTER | *and the Goblet of Fire* | [double ruled border, 104 by 104mm with the outer border thicker than the inner and colour illustration by Giles Greenfield laid down] | JKRowling [facsimile signature]' (all width centred). All in gilt.
    Lower cover: blank.
    All edges gilt. Red sewn bands at head and foot of spine together with red marker ribbon. Binding measurements: 241 by 151mm (covers), 241 by 62mm (spine). End-papers: navy blue wove paper.

Dust-jacket: none

Publication: 2 October 2000 in an edition of 10,000 copies (confirmed by Bloomsbury)

Price: £25

Contents:
Harry Potter and the Goblet of Fire
    ('The villagers of Little Hangleton still called it 'the Riddle House', even though it had…')

Notes:
This is the first English publication to note Warner Brothers' copyright and trademark of 'Harry Potter, names, characters and related indicia'. Although the film rights for the first two books were

first purchased in October 1998, it took until late 2000 for Warners' rights to be noted in English editions.

Copies: Sotheby's, 17 December 2009, lot 169

A9(c)   TED SMART/'THE BOOK PEOPLE' EDITION   (2000)
(children's artwork series in hardback)

HARRY | POTTER | *and the Goblet of Fire* | [illustration of Hogwarts crest with legend 'DRAGO DORMIENS NUNQUAM TITILLANDUS' on banner, 67 by 82mm] | J.K.ROWLING | [publisher's device of a rule, 31mm | 'TED SMART' | rule, 31mm, all within single ruled border, 6 by 32mm] (Lines 1 and 2 justified on left and right margins, and all width centred)

Collation: 320 unsigned leaves bound in indeterminate gatherings; 197 by 127mm; [1-7] 8-19 [20] 21-28 [29] 30-38 [39] 40-48 [49] 50-61 [62] 63-69 [70] 71-86 [87] 88-105 [106] 107-29 [130] 131-40 [141] 142-51 [152] 153-70 [171] 172-84 [185] 186-200 [201] 202-18 [219] 220-38 [239] 240-52 [253] 254-74 [275] 276-94 [295] 296-316 [317] 318-35 [336] 337-50 [351] 352-76 [377] 378-97 [398] 399-415 [416] 417-41 [442] 443-64 [465] 466-89 [490] 491-504 [505] 506-25 [526] 527-51 [552] 553-58 [559] 560-71 [572] 573-81 [582] 583-600 [601] 602-20 [621] 622-36 [637-40]

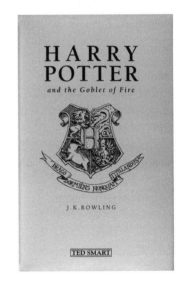

Page contents: [1] half-title: 'HARRY | POTTER | *and the Goblet of Fire* | [illustration of Hogwarts crest with legend 'DRAGO DORMIENS NUNQUAM TITILLANDUS' on banner, 47 by 57mm]'; [2] '*Titles available in the Harry Potter series* | *(in reading order)*: | Harry Potter and the Philosopher's Stone | Harry Potter and the Chamber of Secrets | Harry Potter and the Prisoner of Azkaban | Harry Potter and the Goblet of Fire'; [3] title-page; [4] 'All rights reserved; no part of this publication may be reproduced or | transmitted by any means, electronic, mechanical, photocopying or otherwise, | without the prior permission of the publisher | [new paragraph] First published in Great Britain in 2000 | Bloomsbury Publishing Plc, 38 Soho Square, London, W1V 5DF | [new paragraph] This edition produced for | The Book People Ltd, | Hall Wood Avenue, | Haydock, St. Helens WA11 9UL | [new paragraph] Copyright © 2000 J.K. Rowling | Cover illustrations copyright © by Giles Greenfield 2000 | [new paragraph] Harry Potter, names, characters and related indicia are | copyright and trademark Warner Bros., 2000™ | [new paragraph] The moral right of the author has been asserted | A CIP catalogue record of this book is available from the | British Library | [new paragraph] ISBN 1-85613-769-4 | [new paragraph]

Printed in Great Britain by Clays Ltd, St Ives plc | Typeset by Dorchester Typesetting | [new paragraph] 10 9 8 7 6 5 4 3 2 1 | [new paragraph] www.bloomsbury.com/harrypotter'; [5] 'To Peter Rowling, | in memory of Mr Ridley | and to Susan Sladden, | who helped Harry out of his cupboard'; [6] blank; [7]-636 text; [637-40] blank

Paper: wove paper

Running title: 'HARRY POTTER' (24mm) on verso, recto title comprises chapter title, pp. 8-636 (excluding pages on which new chapters commence)

Binding: pictorial boards.

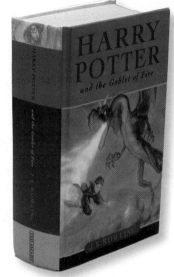

On spine: '[colour illustration of an owl on staircase banister on coloured panel, 58 by 18mm] HARRY POTTER [in blue on red panel, 58 by 47mm] *and the Goblet of Fire* [in light blue] J.K.ROWLING [in red, both title conclusion and author on blue panel, 58 by 107mm] [publisher's device of a rule, 36mm | 'TED SMART' | rule, 36mm, all within single ruled border, 5 by 37mm [in black on light blue panel, 58 by 33mm]' (reading lengthways down spine).

On upper cover: 'HARRY | POTTER | *and the Goblet of Fire* [lines 1 and 2 in blue, line 3 in black, all on red panel, 64 by 132mm] | [light blue rule, 132mm] | [colour illustration of Harry Potter flying on a broomstick about to seize a golden egg that is protected by a fire-breathing dragon, 125 by 132mm] | [light blue rule, 132mm intersected by blue panel with 'J.K.ROWLING' in red] | [black panel, 12 by 132mm]' (all width centred).

On lower cover: 'The summer holidays are dragging on and Harry Potter | can't wait for the start of the school year. It is his fourth | year at Hogwarts School of Witchcraft and Wizardry, | and there are spells to be learnt, potions to be brewed | and Divination lessons (sigh) to be attended. Harry | is expecting these: however, other quite unexpected | events are already on the march... | [new paragraph] A much-awaited new Harry Potter adventure | from an acclaimed story-telling genius. | [new paragraph] 'Like Gameboys, Teletubbies and films by | George Lucas, Harry Potter has permeated | the national child consciousness.' | *The Independent on Sunday* | [new paragraph] 'The world of Hogwarts is complete | in every riotous, headlong detail. The | richness and scale of Rowling's invention | is exhilarating... but the real proof of | quality lies in J.K. Rowling's power to | draw the reader into Harry's world and | make it seem believable.' *The Guardian* | [new paragraph] 'The Harry Potter books are that rare | thing, a series of stories adored by | children and parents alike.' | *The Daily Telegraph* | [barcode in black on white panel, 20 by 37mm] | [blue panel, 7 by 37mm]'. Reading lengthways down right side next to foot of spine 'Cover illustrations by Giles Greenfield | Cover design by Richard Horne'. All in black on colour illustration of staircase at Hogwarts castle.

All edges trimmed. Binding measurements: 205 by 132mm (covers), 205 by 58mm (spine). End-papers: wove paper.

Dust-jacket: coated wove paper, 205 by 524mm

Spine, upper and lower covers replicate the binding.

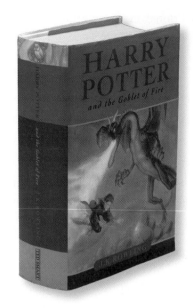

On upper inside flap: 'It is the summer holidays, and one night | Harry Potter wakes up with his scar burning. | He has had a strange dream, one that he | can't help worrying about… until a timely | invitation from Ron Weasley arrives: to | nothing less than the Quidditch World Cup! | [new paragraph] Soon Harry is reunited with Ron and | Hermione and gasping at the thrills of an | international Quidditch match. But then | something horrible happens which casts a | shadow over everybody, and Harry in | particular… | [new paragraph] *A fantastic sequel to the existing Harry Potter* | *adventures:* | [new paragraph] HARRY POTTER AND | THE PHILOSOPHER'S STONE | [new paragraph] 'I've yet to meet a 10 year old who hasn't | been entranced by its witty, complex plot | and the character of the eponymous Harry.' | *The Independent* | [new paragraph] HARRY POTTER AND | THE CHAMBER OF SECRETS | [new paragraph] 'Such a marriage of good writing, inventiveness, | and sheer child-appeal has not been seen since | Roald Dahl, perhaps even since Tolkien, Lewis, | and Ransome. J.K. Rowling has woken a whole | generation to reading.' *The Times* | [new paragraph] HARRY POTTER AND | THE PRISONER OF AZKABAN | [new paragraph] 'One warning. If you are going to read this to | your children, make sure you start early in the | evening. There are so many surprising twists that | you will not be allowed to put the book down | even if you wanted to.' *The Sunday Express* | £14.99'. All in black on red panel.

On lower inside flap: '[nine stars, in blue] | Dear Joanne Rowling, | My name's Matthew la Croix, | & I'm 12 years of age. I think your books are | amazing! | [new paragraph] That feeling of looking forward to lunchtimes, so I | could read Harrys world of magic, is great, so | I'd like to thank you for adding that touch | of excitment [*sic*] in my day! [smiley face] | [new paragraph] I've read all three books, | and I think Harry Potter & the Prisoner of Azkaban, | beat all three, and being that it was bigger, it | was twice as much pleaseure [*sic*] reading. | [new paragraph] Please, Please, Please, Please, PLEASE!!!!!!!!!!!!! | Bring another one, keeping writing, my Life | depends on it, | [new paragraph] Yours Sincerely, | [new paragraph] Matthew La Croix, Your No°1 fan! | X X X | [twelve stars, in blue] | To order further copies & see | our full range of titles phone | [rule, 35mm] 0870 6077740 | LINES ARE OPEN 7 DAYS A WEEK 8AM-8PM | [rule, 35mm] | Please call us today for your | FREE colour catalogue!' (final eight lines within single ruled border, 20 by 37mm). All in black on red panel.

Publication: November 2000 (see notes)

Price: no exact price is recorded (see notes)

Contents:

Harry Potter and the Goblet of Fire

('The villagers of Little Hangleton still called it 'the Riddle House', even though…')

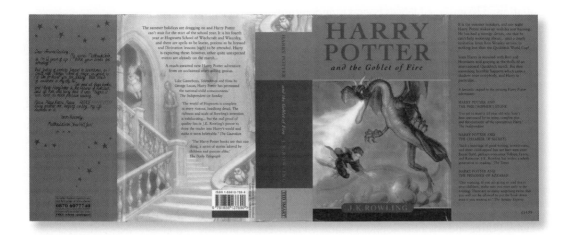

Notes:

The Ted Smart edition includes the Warner Brothers copyright and trademark statement that is not present in A9(a).

Neither Ted Smart nor Bloomsbury were able to provide any detail about the Ted Smart/'The Book People' editions. Information was provided by the Blair Partnership who noted that this edition was available from November 2000. Production of the Ted Smart/'The Book People' editions ceased in April 2001.

   Evidence to support this date is not provided by textual evidence. The correction of text on page 579 in which the ghost of Harry's mother precedes that of Harry's father suggests publication no earlier than January 2001. The *Evening Standard* published details of the error on 18 January 2001 and quoted 'a Bloomsbury spokesman' who stated '… it was a genuine mistake. Lily did come out before James and that was wrong. We decided recently to make the correction, and it has been printed correctly for the last two weeks.'

No exact price has been recorded for this edition. A1(b) was, presumably, sold by itself. A slipcase containing the three volumes A1(b), A2(f) and A7(d) was, probably, available from November 1999 and a slipcase containing the four volumes A1(b), A2(f), A7(d) and A9(c) was, presumably, available from November 2000. In each case the price would have been lower than the single (or combined) prices of the Bloomsbury version.

Copies: private collection (PWE)

A9(d) ENGLISH ADULT EDITION (2001)
(original adult artwork series in paperback)

Harry Potter and the | Goblet of Fire | J. K. Rowling | BLOOMSBURY (All width centred)

Collation: 320 unsigned leaves bound in indeterminate gatherings; 197 by 127mm; [1-7] 8-19 [20] 21-28 [29] 30-38 [39] 40-48 [49] 50-61 [62] 63-69 [70] 71-86 [87] 88-105 [106] 107-129 [130] 131-40 [141] 142-51 [152] 153-70 [171] 172-84 [185] 186-200 [201] 202-218 [219] 220-38 [239] 240-52 [253] 254-74 [275] 276-94 [295] 296-316 [317] 318-35 [336] 337-50 [351] 352-76 [377] 378-97 [398] 399-415 [416] 417-41 [442] 443-64 [465] 466-89 [490] 491-504 [505] 506-525 [526] 527-51 [552] 553-58 [559] 560-71 [572] 573-81 [582] 583-600 [601] 602-620 [621] 622-36 [637-40]

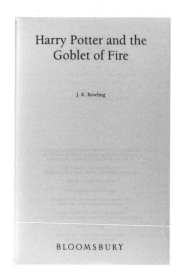

Page contents: [1] half-title: 'Harry Potter and the | Goblet of Fire'; [2] *'Titles available in the Harry Potter series | (in reading order):* | Harry Potter and the Philosopher's Stone | Harry Potter and the Chamber of Secrets | Harry Potter and the Prisoner of Azkaban | Harry Potter and the Goblet of Fire'; [3] title-page; [4] 'All rights reserved; no part of this publication may be reproduced or | transmitted by any means, electronic, mechanical, photocopying | or otherwise, without the prior permission of the publisher | [new paragraph] First published in Great Britain in 2000 | Bloomsbury Publishing Plc, 38 Soho Square, London, W1D 3HB | [new paragraph] Copyright © 2000 J. K. Rowling | [new paragraph] This edition first published in 2001 | [new paragraph] Harry Potter, names, characters and related indicia are | copyright and trademark Warner Bros., 2000™ | [new paragraph] The moral right of the author has been asserted | A CIP catalogue record of this book is available from the British Library | [new paragraph] ISBN 0 7475 5079 4 | [new paragraph] Printed in Great Britain by Clays Ltd, St Ives plc | Typeset by Dorchester Typesetting | [new paragraph] 10 9 8 7 6 5 4 3 2 1'; [5] *'To Peter Rowling, | in memory of Mr Ridley | and to Susan Sladden, | who helped Harry out of his cupboard'*; [6] blank; [7]-636 text; [637] blank; [638-39] publisher's advertisement: *'Wondrous editions available | in the celebrated Harry Potter series:';* [640] blank

Paper: wove paper

Running title: 'HARRY POTTER' (24mm) on verso, recto title comprises chapter title, pp. 8-636

Binding: pictorial wrappers.

On spine: 'HARRY POTTER [in dark red] | *and the Goblet of Fire* [in white] [silver and black photographic illustration of oriental dragon, 39 by 26mm] J. K. ROWLING [in white within dark red rectangle with rounded ends, 9 by 46mm] [publisher's device of a figure with a bow, 7 by 7mm] [in white]' (reading lengthways down spine). All on black.

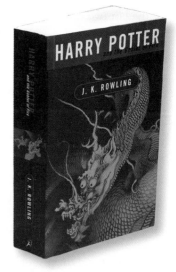

On upper wrapper: 'HARRY POTTER | *and the Goblet of* *Fire* [line 1 in white and line 2 in black, all on dark red panel, 29

by 128mm] | J. K. ROWLING [in white on black within single dark red rectangle with rounded ends, 13 by 73mm] [line 3 on silver and black photographic illustration of oriental dragon, 168 by 128mm]' (all width centred with the exception of line 2 which is off-set to the right).

On lower wrapper: 'HARRY POTTER [in dark red] | *and the Goblet of* Fire [in white] | [new paragraph] "Spectacularly action-packed plot … Rowling's story | exerts a relentless pull' *Heat* | [new paragraph] 'Somewhere in this enchanting mixture is a formula so | brilliant it eludes analysis … Rich and demanding stuff' | *Mail on Sunday* | [new paragraph] '*Harry Potter and the Goblet of Fire* has finally been unleashed. | And is it good? You bet it is. Harry's – and our – fourth year | at Hogwarts is funny, full of delicious parodies of our own | world, and wildly action-packed' *The Times* | [new paragraph] 'There isn't a dull page … The plot fits together like | a wondrous jigsaw' *Sunday Express* | [new paragraph] '*Harry Potter and the Goblet of Fire* is inventive, open- | minded, and carries the hallmark of Rowling's imagination | and scholarship … pure magic' *Mirror* | [new paragraph] 'Every bit as good as Potters 1 through 3' *Stephen King* | [new paragraph] 'A real diamond' *Spectator* | [new paragraph] 'The story is compelling: the humour satisfyingly anarchic, | the moral stance reassuringly strong; JK Rowling has | delivered … her best book yet' *Sunday Telegraph* | [new paragraph] 'JK Rowling's most ambitious and best book so far … full | of good humour and suspense, as well as real and tender | feelings' *Financial Times* | [new paragraph] 'The dazzling plot and pace are more impressive than ever | … there's simply too much to praise. On yer broomstick! | Go get! Go read!' *Irish Times* | [new paragraph] [barcode in black on white panel, 25 by 40mm] ['bloomsbury[in black]pbk[in white]s[in black] | £6.99 [in black] | www.bloomsburymagazine.com [in black]' all on red panel, 25 by 35mm] | [new paragraph] Cover image: © Corbis Images'. All in black with the exception of sources which are in dark red and all on silver with small section of a photographic illustration of a dragon's coils.

All edges trimmed. Binding measurements: 197 by 127mm (wrappers), 197 by 39mm (spine).

Publication: 5 July 2001 in an edition of 20,000 copies (confirmed by Bloomsbury)

Price: £6.99

Contents:
Harry Potter and the Goblet of Fire
   ('The villagers of Little Hangleton still called it 'the Riddle House', even though…')

Notes:
Each occurrence of the title on the spine, upper and lower wrappers shows '*and the Goblet of Fire*' off-set to the right of 'HARRY POTTER'.

Copies: private collection (PWE)

Reprints include:
10

ENGLISH CHILDREN'S EDITION (2000 [2001])
(children's artwork series in paperback)

HARRY | POTTER | *and the Goblet of Fire* | [illustration of Hogwarts crest with legend 'DRAGO DORMIENS NUNQUAM TITILLANDUS' on banner, 67 by 82mm] | J.K.ROWLING | [publisher's device of a dog, 11 by 18mm] | BLOOMSBURY (Lines 1 and 2 justified on left and right margins, and all width centred)

Collation: 320 unsigned leaves bound in indeterminate gatherings; 197 by 127mm; [1-7] 8-19 [20] 21-28 [29] 30-38 [39] 40-48 [49] 50-61 [62] 63-69 [70] 71-86 [87] 88-105 [106] 107-129 [130] 131-40 [141] 142-51 [152] 153-70 [171] 172-84 [185] 186-200 [201] 202-218 [219] 220-38 [239] 240-52 [253] 254-74 [275] 276-94 [295] 296-316 [317] 318-35 [336] 337-50 [351] 352-76 [377] 378-97 [398] 399-415 [416] 417-41 [442] 443-64 [465] 466-89 [490] 491-504 [505] 506-525 [526] 527-51 [552] 553-58 [559] 560-71 [572] 573-81 [582] 583-600 [601] 602-620 [621] 622-36 [637-40]

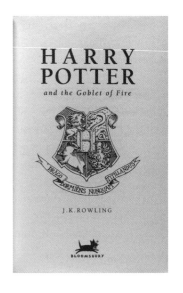

Page contents: [1] half-title: 'HARRY | POTTER | *and the Goblet of Fire* | [illustration of Hogwarts crest with legend 'DRAGO DORMIENS NUNQUAM TITILLANDUS' on banner, 47 by 57mm]'; [2] '*Titles available in the Harry Potter series | (in reading order):* | Harry Potter and the Philosopher's Stone | Harry Potter and the Chamber of Secrets | Harry Potter and the Prisoner of Azkaban | Harry Potter and the Goblet of Fire'; [3] title-page; [4] 'All rights reserved; no part of this publication may be reproduced or | transmitted by any means, electronic, mechanical, photocopying or otherwise, | without the prior permission of the publisher | [new paragraph] First published in Great Britain in 2000 | Bloomsbury Publishing Plc, 38 Soho Square, London, W1D 3HB | [new paragraph] Copyright © 2000 J.K. Rowling | Cover illustrations copyright © by Giles Greenfield 2000 | [new paragraph] Harry Potter, names, characters and related indicia are | copyright and trademark Warner Bros., 2000™ | [new paragraph] The moral right of the author has been asserted | A CIP catalogue record of this book is available from the | British Library | [new paragraph] ISBN 0 7475 5099 9 | [new paragraph] Printed in Great Britain by Clays Ltd, St Ives plc | Typeset by Dorchester Typesetting | [new paragraph] 1 2 3 4 5 6 7 8 9 10 11 12 13 14 15 16 17 18 19 20 | [new paragraph] www.bloomsbury.com/harrypotter'; [5] '*To Peter Rowling,* | *in memory of Mr Ridley* | *and to Susan Sladden,* | *who helped Harry out of his cupboard*'; [6] blank; [7]-636 text; [637] blank; [638-39] publisher's advertisement: '*Wondrous editions available | in the celebrated Harry Potter series:*'; [640] blank

Paper: wove paper

Running title: 'HARRY POTTER' (24mm) on verso, recto title comprises chapter title, pp. 8-636 (excluding pages on which new chapters commence)

Binding: pictorial wrappers.

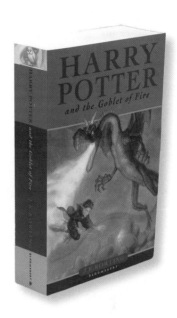

On spine: '[colour illustration of an owl on staircase banister on coloured panel, 39 by 16mm] HARRY POTTER [in blue on red panel, 39 by 45mm] *and the Goblet of Fire* [in light blue] J.K.ROWLING [in red, both title conclusion and author on blue panel, 39 by 103mm] BLOOMSBURY [publisher's device of the head of a dog, 3 by 4mm] [both in black on light blue panel, 39 by 32mm]' (reading lengthways down spine).

On upper wrapper: 'HARRY | POTTER | *and the Goblet of Fire* [lines 1 and 2 in blue, line 3 in black, all on red panel, 61 by 127mm] | [light blue rule, 127mm] | [colour illustration of Harry Potter flying on a broomstick about to seize a golden egg that is protected by a fire-breathing dragon, 135 by 127mm] | [light blue rule, 127mm intersected by blue panel with 'J.K.ROWLING' in red] | BLOOMSBURY [in light blue on black panel, 10 by 127mm]' (all width centred).

On lower wrapper: 'It is the summer holidays and soon Harry Potter will be starting his fourth | year at Hogwarts School of Witchcraft and Wizardry. Harry is counting the | days: there are new spells to be learnt, more Quidditch to be played, and | Hogwarts castle to continue exploring. But Harry needs to be careful – | there are unexpected dangers lurking … | [new paragraph] J.K. Rowling continues to surprise and delight with the power of her | rich, demanding and action-packed storytelling. | [new paragraph] 'From the black heart of Voldemort to the fever pitch excitement | of the Quidditch World Cup, the magical world of Hogwarts and | Harry Potter is more spellbinding than ever. Deep in mystery, | rich in history and sparky in adventure, J.K. Rowling's rare gift | for storytelling enthralls.' *Julia Eccleshare* | [new paragraph] '*Harry Potter and the Goblet of Fire* has finally been | unleashed. And is it good? You bet it is. Harry's – and | our – fourth year at Hogwarts is funny, full of delicious | parodies of our own world, and wildly action-packed.' | *The Times* | [new paragraph] 'There isn't a dull page … The plot fits together | like a wondrous jigsaw.' *The Sunday Express* | [new paragraph] '*Harry Potter and the Goblet of Fire* is inventive, | open-minded, and carries the hallmark of | Rowling's imagination and scholarship … | pure magic.' *The Mirror* | [new paragraph] 'J.K. Rowling has delivered … Her best | book yet.' *The Sunday Telegraph* | [new paragraph] 'Further-reaching than any yet, this is the book | in which Harry and Ron start to notice girls, | with comic consequences, and in which | Voldemort returns, with fatal ones. | It is darker than the previous books, | but just as dazzling.' | *Nicolette Jones* | [barcode in black on white panel, 20 by 38mm together with '[publisher's device of a dog, 6 by 10mm] | BLOOMSBURY' and '£6.99' in black above panel and 'http://www.bloomsbury.com' below panel, in light blue on blue panel, 7 by 38mm]'. Reading lengthways up left side next to fore-edge 'Cover illustrations by Giles Greenfield'. All in black on colour illustration of staircase at Hogwarts castle.

All edges trimmed. Binding measurements: 197 by 127mm (wrappers), 197 by 39mm (spine).

Publication: 6 July 2001 in an edition of 660,000 copies (confirmed by Bloomsbury)

Price: £6.99

Contents:
Harry Potter and the Goblet of Fire
('The villagers of Little Hangleton still called it 'the Riddle House', even though…')

Notes:
The editorial files at Bloomsbury include a letter from an assistant editor to a proof-reader, dated 12 March 2001, noting that 'the typesetters have tried to eliminate the majority of widows and also minimise hypenation, but in doing so have introduced a few new errors'. This was, naturally, a cause for concern and the files include several faxes of selected pages from Dorchester Typesetting, dated 13 March 2001. A complete set of proofs is dated 20 March 2001 which is mostly marked-up to identify widows.

A further set of proofs is dated 17 April 2001 with a revised version dated 23 April 2001. A set with a few final corrections is dated 26 April 2001.

It appears that the wrappers were proofed before the text. The earliest proof of the wrappers preserved in the editorial files at Bloomsbury is dated 16 January 2001.

Editorial files suggest that the collation of the volume should be six gatherings of 24 leaves, followed by two gatherings of 16 leaves and then six final gatherings of 24 leaves.

Copies: private collection (PWE)

A9(f) AMERICAN CHILDREN'S EDITION (2002)
(children's artwork series in paperback)

HARRY POTTER | AND THE GOBLET OF FIRE | [black and white illustration of a flaming goblet on a casket with curtains in background, 47 by 45mm] | BY | J. K. ROWLING | ILLUSTRATIONS BY MARY GRANDPRÉ | SCHOLASTIC INC. | NEW YORK [four-sided device] TORONTO [four-sided device] LONDON [four-sided device] AUCKLAND [four-sided device] SYDNEY | MEXICO CITY [four-sided device] NEW DELHI [four-sided device] HONG KONG [four-sided device] BUENOS AIRES (All width centred on a diamond pattern background)

Collation: 376 unsigned leaves bound in indeterminate gatherings; 192 by 132mm; [I-VI] VII-XI [XII-XIV] 1-734 [735-38]

Page contents: [I-II] 'PRAISE FOR J. K. ROWLING'S | HARRY POTTER | AND THE GOBLET OF FIRE | [device of nine stars] | [9 reviews and a listing of 6 statements] | [new paragraph] ALSO BY J. K. ROWLING | *Harry Potter and the Sorcerer's Stone* | Year One at Hogwarts | [new paragraph] *Harry Potter and the Chamber of Secrets* | Year Two at Hogwarts | [new paragraph] *Harry*

Potter and the Prisoner of Azkaban | Year Three at Hogwarts'; [III] title-page; [IV] '[device of twelve stars] | Text copyright © 2000 by J. K. Rowling. | Illustrations by Mary GrandPré, copyright © 2000 Warner Bros. | All rights reserved. Published by Scholastic Inc. SCHOLASTIC, the LANTERN LOGO, | and associated logos are trademarks and/or registered trademarks of Scholastic Inc. | [new paragraph] HARRY POTTER, characters, names and related indicia are trademarks of Warner Bros. | [new paragraph] If you purchased this book without a cover, you should be aware that this book is stolen property. | It was reported as "unsold and destroyed" to the publisher, and neither the author nor | the publisher has received any payment for this "stripped book." | [new paragraph] No part of this publication may be reproduced in whole or in part, | or stored in a retrieval system, or transmitted in any form or by any means, | electronic, mechanical, photocopying,

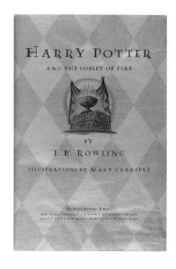

recording, or otherwise, | without written permission of the publisher. | For information regarding permission, write to Scholastic Inc., | Attention: Permissions Department, 557 Broadway, New York, NY 10012. | [new paragraph] ISBN 0-439-13960-0 | [new paragraph] [publisher's device of a lantern, 6 by 4mm] | Arthur A. Levine Books hardcover edition | art directed by David Saylor, | published by Arthur A. Levine Books, | an imprint of Scholastic Press, | July 2000 | [new paragraph] 12 11 10 9 8 7 6 5 4 3 2 1   2 3 4 5 6 7/0 | [new paragraph] Printed in the U.S.A. 40 | [new paragraph] First Scholastic Trade paperback printing, September 2002 | [new paragraph] The art for both the cover and the interior was created using pastels on toned printmaking paper. | The text was set in 12-point Adobe Garamond.'; [V] 'TO PETER ROWLING, | IN MEMORY OF MR. RIDLEY | AND TO SUSAN SLADDEN, | WHO HELPED HARRY | OUT OF HIS CUPBOARD'; [VI] blank; VII-XI 'CONTENTS' (thirty-seven chapters listed with titles and page references); [XII] blank; [XIII] half-title: 'HARRY POTTER | AND THE GOBLET OF FIRE' (all on diamond pattern background); [XIV] blank; 1-734 text; [735] publisher's advertisement: 'Harry Potter | THE MAGICAL BOOKS THAT STARTED IT ALL!'; [736-38] blank

Paper: wove paper

Running title: 'CHAPTER' and chapter number on verso, recto title comprises chapter title, pp. 1-734. Each running title (excluding pages on which new chapters commence) includes a three-star design to left and right of both running-titles on verso and recto. On pages on which a new chapter commences, the three-star design is omitted.

Illustrations: title-page vignette, together with thirty-seven vignettes at the beginning of each chapter (after chapter and chapter number but before chapter title). In addition to standard typographical changes (including italics, capitals and small capitals) there are other typographical features, comprising:

> p. 25 facsimile of Harry's signature
> p. 30 facsimile of Molly Weasley's signature

p. 36 facsimiles of Ron and Harry's signatures

pp. 96-97 advertisements written on a gigantic blackboard

p. 102 further advertisements written on a gigantic blackboard, also a Quidditch score

p. 113 Quidditch score

p. 202 newspaper headline

p. 226 facsimile of Sirius' signature

p. 228 facsimile of Harry's signature

p. 235 text of announcement sign

p. 240 facsimile of Sirius' signature

p. 292 facsimile of Harry's signature

p. 297 text of badges

p. 298 text of badge

p. 304 facsimile of Rita Skeeter's quill's writing

p. 305 facsimile of Rita Skeeter's quill's writing

p. 306 facsimile of Rita Skeeter's quill's writing

p. 312 facsimile of Sirius' signature

p. 406 facsimile of Sirius' signature

p. 437 newspaper headline

p. 511 magazine headline

p. 541 text of letter in 'poison-pen' style

p. 572 facsimile of Sirius' signature

p. 611 newspaper headline

p. 638 headstone engraved name

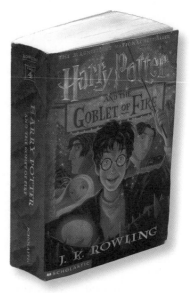

Binding: pictorial wrappers.

On spine: 'ROWLING | [rule] | ['YEAR | 4' within concave square]' (horizontally at head) with 'HARRY POTTER | SCHOLASTIC | AND THE GOBLET OF FIRE' (reading lengthways down spine). All in gilt on green and purple diamond pattern background.

On upper wrapper: 'THE MAGNIFICENT NATIONAL BESTSELLER [in gilt] | Harry Potter [hand-drawn lettering] [embossed in gilt] | AND THE [hand-drawn lettering in crimson of illustration] | GOBLET OF FIRE [hand-drawn lettering in crimson of illustration] [lines 3-4 in panel of illustration with flame above letter 'E' of 'FIRE'] | J. K. ROWLING [embossed in gilt]' (all width centred). All on colour illustration of Harry Potter clutching wand and golden egg with other characters background and the back of a Hungarian Horntail dragon in the foreground. In lower left: '[publisher's book device] SCHOLASTIC' in white on red panel, 9 by 47mm.

On lower wrapper: 'Harry Potter is midway through both his training as a wizard | and his coming of age. Harry wants to get away from the per- | nicious Dursleys and go to the International Quidditch Cup with | Hermione, Ron, and the Weasleys. He wants to dream about Cho | Chang, his crush (and maybe do more than dream). He wants to find out | about the mysterious event that's supposed to take place at Hogwarts | this year, an event involving two other rival schools of magic, and a | competition that hasn't happened for hundreds of years. He wants to be a | normal, fourteen-year-old wizard. But unfortunately for Harry Potter, | he's not normal — even by wizarding standards.

| [new paragraph] And in his case, different can be deadly. | [new paragraph] [four-sided device] The #1 *New York Times* Bestseller [four-sided device] | [new paragraph] Winner of the Hugo Award for Best Novel | A *Publishers Weekly* Best Children's Book of 2000 | A *Booklist* Editors' Choice 2000 | An ALA Notable Book | A New York Public Library Book for the Teen Age | [new paragraph] Visit Harry Potter on the Web at | www.scholastic.com/harrypotter | COVER ART BY MARY GRANDPRÉ'. All in black on colour illustration of a maze hedge engulfed by tentacles. In lower right: 'SCHOLASTIC INC. $8.99 US | [rule, 60mm] | [barcode with smaller barcode to the right (13960) together with 'S' within triangle]' all in black on white panel within single black ruled border, 26 by 60mm. The initial capital 'H' of 'Harry' is a drop capital.

On inside upper wrapper: barcode with smaller barcode (50899) together with 'S' within triangle below, all in black.

All edges trimmed. Binding measurements: 192 by 132mm (wrappers), 192 by 42mm (spine).

Publication: September 2002

Price: $8.99

Contents:
Harry Potter and the Goblet of Fire
  ('The villagers of Little Hangleton still called it "the Riddle House," even though…')

Notes:
Note the slight reworking of the publisher's blurb from the text present in the first American edition (A9(aa)).

Although no publication day is recorded, 1 September 2002 is assumed. In an email to me from January 2013 Arthur A. Levine noted that 'I'm fairly certain that we didn't have strict "on sale" dates… the publication "day" would simply be the first of the month listed. None of the paperbacks were given a strict "on sale" date either.'

Each chapter commences with a drop capital.

Copies: private collection (PWE)

Reprints include:
24 23	7/0	Printed in the U.S.A. 40
45 44 43 42	11 12 13 14 15/0	Printed in the U.S.A. 40

A9(g)   AMERICAN BOOK CLUB EDITION (2000 [2002])
(children's artwork series in hardback)

HARRY POTTER | AND THE GOBLET OF FIRE | [black and white illustration of a flaming goblet on a casket with curtains in background, 51 by 51mm] | BY | J. K. ROWLING | ILLUSTRATIONS

BY MARY GRANDPRÉ | [publisher's device of a lantern, 11 by 8mm] | ARTHUR A. LEVINE BOOKS | AN IMPRINT OF SCHOLASTIC PRESS (All width centred on a diamond pattern background)

Collation: 376 unsigned leaves bound by the 'perfect binding' process; 208 by 135mm; [I-VI] VII-XI [XII-XIV] 1-734 [735-38]

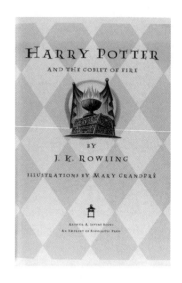

Page contents: [I] 'HARRY POTTER | AND THE GOBLET OF FIRE' (all on diamond pattern background); [II] 'ALSO BY J. K. ROWLING | [new paragraph] *Harry Potter and the Sorcerer's Stone* | Year One at Hogwarts | [new paragraph] *Harry Potter and the Chamber of Secrets* | Year Two at Hogwarts | [new paragraph] *Harry Potter and the Prisoner of Azkaban* | Year Three at Hogwarts'; [III] title-page; [IV] '[device of twelve stars] | Text copyright © 2000 by J. K. Rowling | Illustrations by Mary GrandPré copyright © 2000 Scholastic Inc. | All rights reserved. Published by Scholastic Press, a division of Scholastic Inc., | *Publishers since 1920.* | SCHOLASTIC, SCHOLASTIC PRESS, and the LANTERN LOGO | are trademarks and/or registered trademarks of Scholastic Inc. | [new paragraph] No part of this publication may be reproduced, or stored in a retrieval system, or transmitted | in any form or by any means, electronic, mechanical, photocopying, recording, or otherwise, | without written permission of the publisher. For information regarding permission, write | to Scholastic Inc., Attention: Permissions Department, 555 Broadway, New York, NY 10012. | [new paragraph] ISBN 0-439-13959-7 | [new paragraph] Printed in the U.S.A.'; [V] 'TO PETER ROWLING, | IN MEMORY OF MR. RIDLEY | AND TO SUSAN SLADDEN, | WHO HELPED HARRY | OUT OF HIS CUPBOARD'; [VI] blank; VII-XI 'CONTENTS' (thirty-seven chapters listed with titles and page references); [XII] blank; [XIII] half-title: 'HARRY POTTER | AND THE GOBLET OF FIRE' (all on diamond pattern background); [XIV] blank; 1-734 text; [735-736] blank; [737] colophon: '[publisher's device of a lantern, 16 by 12mm] | *This* | *book was art* | *directed by David Saylor. The* | *art for both the jacket and the interior was* | *created using pastels on toned printmaking paper. The* | *text was set in 12-point Adobe Garamond, a typeface based on* | *the sixteenth-century type designs of Claude Garamond, redrawn by* | *Robert Slimbach in 1989. The book was typeset by Brad Walrod* | *and was printed and bound at Berryville Graphics in* | *Berryville, Virginia. The Managing Editor* | *was Manuela Soares and the* | *Manufacturing Director* | *was Angela* | *Biola.*'; [738] blank

Paper: wove paper

Running title: 'CHAPTER' and chapter number on verso, recto title comprises chapter title, pp. 1-734. Each running title (excluding pages on which new chapters commence) includes a three-star design to left and right of both running-titles on verso and recto. On pages on which a new chapter commences, the three-star design is omitted.

Illustrations: title-page vignette, together with thirty-seven vignettes at the beginning of each chapter (after chapter and chapter number but before chapter title). In addition to standard typographical changes (including italics, capitals and small capitals) there are other typographical features, comprising:

p. 25 facsimile of Harry's signature

p. 30 facsimile of Molly Weasley's signature

p. 36 facsimiles of Ron and Harry's signatures

pp. 96-97 advertisements written on a gigantic blackboard

p. 102 further advertisements written on a gigantic blackboard, also a Quidditch score

p.109 lettering displayed on Harry's Omnioculars

p. 113 Quidditch score

p. 202 newspaper headline

p. 226 facsimile of Sirius' signature

p. 228 facsimile of Harry's signature

p. 235 text of announcement sign

p. 240 facsimile of Sirius' signature

p. 292 facsimile of Harry's signature

p. 297 text of badges

p. 298 text of badge

p. 304 facsimile of Rita Skeeter's quill's writing

p. 305 facsimile of Rita Skeeter's quill's writing

p. 306 facsimile of Rita Skeeter's quill's writing

p. 312 facsimile of Sirius' signature

p. 406 facsimile of Sirius' signature

p. 437 newspaper headline

p. 511 magazine headline

p. 541 text of letter in 'poison-pen' style

p. 572 facsimile of Sirius' signature

p. 611 newspaper headline

p. 638 headstone engraved name

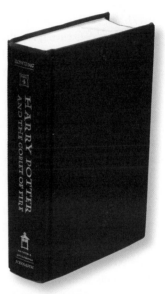

Binding: black boards.

On spine: 'ROWLING | [rule] | ['YEAR | 4' within concave square]' (horizontally at head) with 'HARRY POTTER | AND THE GOBLET OF FIRE' (reading lengthways down spine) and '[publisher's device of a lantern, 16 by 13mm] | ARTHUR A. | LEVINE BOOKS | [rule] | SCHOLASTIC' (horizontally at foot). All in gilt.

Upper and lower covers: blank.

All edges trimmed. Binding measurements: 216 by 139mm (covers), 216 by 57mm (spine). End-papers: white wove paper.

Dust-jacket: uncoated wove paper, 216 by 513mm. A single illustration spans the entire dust-jacket.

On spine: 'ROWLING | [rule] | ['YEAR | 4' within concave square]' (horizontally at head) with 'HARRY POTTER | AND THE GOBLET OF FIRE' (reading lengthways down spine) and '[publisher's device of a lantern, 17 by 13mm] | ARTHUR A. | LEVINE BOOKS | [rule] | SCHOLASTIC' (horizontally at foot). All in orange brown on colour illustration of green hedge and back of a Hungarian Horntail dragon.

On upper cover: 'Harry Potter [hand-drawn lettering] [in orange brown] | AND THE [hand-drawn lettering in crimson of illustration] | GOBLET OF FIRE [hand-drawn lettering in crimson of illustration] [lines 2-3 in panel of illustration with flame above letter 'E' of 'FIRE'] | J. K. ROWLING [in orange brown]' (all width centred). All on colour illustration of Harry Potter clutching wand and golden egg with other characters in background and the back of a Hungarian Horntail dragon in the foreground.

On lower cover: 'Sequel to the #1 *New York Times* Bestseller | HARRY POTTER | AND THE PRISONER OF AZKABAN | [barcode with '03257' to the right, all in black on orange panel, 20 by 47mm]'. All in black and all on colour illustration of maze hedges, flaming goblet, carriage pulled by winged horses, and a wing and back of a Hungarian Horntail dragon.

On upper inside flap: 'YOU HAVE IN YOUR HANDS | the pivotal fourth novel in the seven-part | tale of Harry Potter's training as a wizard and | his coming of age. Harry wants to get away | from the pernicious Dursleys and go to the | International Quidditch Cup with Hermione, | Ron, and the Weasleys. He wants to dream about | Cho Chang, his crush (and maybe do more than | dream). He wants to find out about the mys- | terious event that's supposed to take place at | Hogwarts this year, an event involving two | other rival schools of magic, and a competition | that hasn't happened for a hundred years. He | wants to be a normal, fourteen-year-old wizard. | Unfortunately for Harry Potter, he's not normal—| even by wizarding standards. | [new paragraph] And in this case, different can be deadly.' All in black and all on colour illustration of curling smoke. The initial capital 'Y' of 'YOU' is a drop capital.

On lower inside flap: 'ALSO BY J. K. ROWLING | #1 *New York Times, USA Today,* and international best- | sellers, winners of the National Book Award (UK) and Gold | Medal Smarties prize three years running, and ALA | Notable Books: | [new paragraph] HARRY POTTER | AND THE PRISONER OF AZKABAN | WINNER OF THE WHITBREAD AWARD | "Isn't it reassuring that some things just get better and bet- | ter? This is a fabulously entertaining read that will have | Harry Potter fans cheering for more." |—*School Library Journal* | [new paragraph] HARRY POTTER | AND THE CHAMBER OF SECRETS | [five-pointed star] "Harry Potter's exploits during his second year at | Hogwarts School for Witchcraft and Wizardry completely | live up to the bewitching measure of *Harry Potter and the* | *Sorcerer's Stone.* The mystery, zany humor, student rivalry, | and eccentric faculty… are as expertly crafted here as in the | first book." —*Booklist,* starred review | [new paragraph] HARRY POTTER | AND THE SORCERER'S STONE | "A charming, imaginative, magical confection | of a novel." —*Boston Globe* | "Funny, moving, and impressive." |—*The New York Times Book Review* | [new paragraph] *Jacket art by Mary GrandPré* | *Jacket design by Mary GrandPré and David Saylor* | [new paragraph] Printed in the U.S.A [sic]'. Lines

1-26 in black and lines 27-29 in orange and all on colour illustration of a maze hedge engulfed by tentacles.

Publication: between July and December 2002 (see notes)

Price: see notes

Contents:
Harry Potter and the Goblet of Fire
('The villagers of Little Hangleton still called it "the Riddle House," even though…')

Notes:
Unlike the first book club editions of *Sorcerer's Stone* and *Chamber of Secrets*, the binding of this edition is shorter than the first American edition. Also note that the publisher's imprint page omits mention of the Library of Congress. The strike-line and printer's number is also absent. Also note the change of printer and binder cited in the colophon.

Given that the true American first and the book club editions share a single ISBN, the Blair Partnership noted that book club editions could only be dated to within a half-year period end in their files. This edition was, therefore, published within the period July to December 2002. The Blair Partnership Royalties Manager noted that the American book club editions did not have 'a set price'.

Contrast the barcode panel on the dust-jacket of the First American edition. In A9(aa) there are two barcodes. In this book club edition, the smaller barcode is replaced with the numbers 03257 only. Note also some minor differences in the setting of text on the lower inside panel, including the removal of the publisher's device and name.

Each chapter commences with a drop capital.

Copies: private collection (PWE)

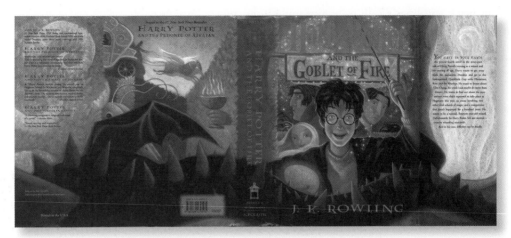

A9(h)   ENGLISH ADULT EDITION   (2004)
(Michael Wildsmith photography adult artwork series in paperback)

Harry Potter and the | Goblet of Fire | J. K. Rowling | BLOOMSBURY (All width centred)

Collation: 400 unsigned leaves bound in indeterminate gatherings; 177 by 111mm; [1-7] 8-22 [23] 24-33 [34] 35-46 [47] 48-59 [60] 61-75 [76] 77-85 [86] 87-107 [108] 109-131 [132] 133-61 [162] 163-75 [176] 177-89 [190] 191-212 [213] 214-29 [230] 231-50 [251] 252-72 [273] 274-98 [299] 300-315 [316] 317-43 [344] 345-69 [370] 371-97 [398] 399-420 [421] 422-39 [440] 441-72 [473] 474-98 [499] 500-521 [522] 523-53 [554] 555-81 [582] 583-612 [613] 614-30 [631] 632-56 [657] 658-88 [689] 690-97 [698] 699-713 [714] 715-25 [726] 727-49 [750] 751-75 [776] 777-96 [797-800]

Page contents: [1] half-title: 'Harry Potter and the | Goblet of Fire'; [2] *'Titles available in the Harry Potter series | (in reading order):* | Harry Potter and the Philosopher's Stone | Harry Potter and the Chamber of Secrets | Harry Potter and the Prisoner of Azkaban | Harry Potter and the Goblet of Fire | Harry Potter and the Order of the Phoenix'; [3] title-page; [4] 'All rights reserved; no part of this publication may be reproduced or | transmitted by any means, electronic, mechanical, photocopying or otherwise, | without the prior permission of the publisher | [new paragraph] First published in Great Britain in 2000 | Bloomsbury Publishing Plc, 38 Soho Square, London, W1D 3HB | [new paragraph] This paperback edition first published in 2004 | [new paragraph] Copyright © J. K. Rowling 2000 | [new paragraph] Harry Potter, names, characters and related indicia are | copyright and trademark Warner Bros., 2000™ | [new paragraph] The moral right of the author has been asserted | A CIP catalogue record of this book is available from the British Library | [new paragraph] ISBN 0 7475 7450 2 | [new paragraph] 1 3 5 7 9 10 8 6 4 2 | [new paragraph] Typeset by Dorchester Typesetting | Printed in Great Britain by Clays Ltd, St Ives plc | [new paragraph] All papers used by Bloomsbury Publishing are natural, | recyclable products made from wood grown in well-managed forests. | The paper used in this book contains 20% post consumer waste material | which was de-inked using chlorine free methods. The | manufacturing processes conform to the environmental

| regulations of the country of origin. | [new paragraph] www.bloomsbury.com/harrypotter'; [5] 'To Peter Rowling, | in memory of Mr Ridley | and to Susan Sladden, | who helped Harry out of his cupboard'; [6] blank; [7]-796 text; [797-800] blank

Paper: wove paper

Running title: 'HARRY POTTER' (24mm) on verso, recto title comprises chapter title, pp. 8-796 (excluding pages on which new chapters commence)

Binding: pictorial wrappers.

On spine: 'HARRY POTTER AND THE [colour photograph of dancing blue flames, 48 by 18mm] | J.K. ROWLING [publisher's device of a figure with a bow, 11 by 11mm] | GOBLET OF FIRE' (reading lengthways down spine). All in white with the exception of last line which is in gilt and all on black.

On upper wrapper: 'HARRY POTTER AND THE [in white] | GOBLET [embossed in gilt] | OF FIRE [embossed in gilt] | J. K. ROWLING [in white] | BLOOMSBURY [in white]' (all width centred). All on colour photograph of a wooden cup with dancing blue flames.

On lower wrapper: '[colour photograph of wooden cup with dancing blue flames, all within single white border, 22 by 22mm] 'Every bit as good as Potters 1 through 3' | Stephen King | [new paragraph] When the Quidditch World Cup is disrupted by Voldemort's | rampaging supporters and the resurrection of the terrifying | Dark Mark, it is obvious to Harry that, far from weakening, | Voldemort is getting stronger. The ultimate signal to the | magic world of the Dark Lord's return would be defeat of | the one and only survivor of his death curse, Harry Potter. | So when Harry is entered for the prestigious yet dangerous | Triwizard Tournament he knows that rather than win it, he | must get through the tasks alive. | [new paragraph] 'Harry's – and our – fourth year at Hogwarts is funny, | full of delicious parodies of our own world, and wildly | action-packed' *The Times* | [new paragraph] 'There isn't a dull page ... The plot fits together like a | wondrous jigsaw' *Sunday Express* | [new paragraph] 'The dazzling plot and pace are more impressive than | ever ... there's simply too much to praise. On yer | broomstick! Go get! Go read!' *Irish Times* | [new paragraph] 'The story is compelling: the humour satisfyingly anarchic, | the moral stance reassuringly strong ... her best book yet' | *Sunday Telegraph* | [new paragraph] [barcode in black on white panel, 24 by 39mm together with 'bloomsbury[in black]pbk[in white]s[in black] | £6.99 [in black] | www.bloomsbury.com [in black]' and all on red panel, 25 by 75mm] | Cover image: Michael Wildsmith Design: William Webb Author Photograph: © Bill de la HEY'. All in white on black with colour photograph to the left of lines 1 and 2.

On inside upper wrapper: black and white photograph of J.K. Rowling standing against bookshelves.

On inside lower wrapper: 'Other titles available in the | HARRY POTTER series | [colour illustrations in two columns of four book designs]'. All in white on black.

All edges trimmed. Binding measurements: 177 by 111mm (wrappers), 177 by 48mm (spine).

Publication: 10 July 2004 in an edition of 110,200 copies (confirmed by Bloomsbury)

Price: £6.99

Contents:
Harry Potter and the Goblet of Fire

('The villagers of Little Hangleton still called it 'the Riddle House', even though…')

Notes:
See note to A1(f) about this series replacing an existing livery. This volume, A9(h), can be seen as the successor to A9(d).

Copies: BL (H.2006/288) stamped 14 May 2004

Reprints include:
3 5 7 9 10 8 6 4
10

A9(i)　　　ENGLISH ADULT EDITION　　　(2004)
(Michael Wildsmith photography adult artwork series in hardback)

Harry Potter and the | Goblet of Fire | J. K. Rowling | BLOOMSBURY (All width centred)

Collation: 320 unsigned leaves bound in indeterminate gatherings; 197 by 125mm; [1-7] 8-19 [20] 21-28 [29] 30-38 [39] 40-48 [49] 50-61 [62] 63-69 [70] 71-86 [87] 88-105 [106] 107-129 [130] 131-40 [141] 142-51 [152] 153-70 [171] 172-84 [185] 186-200 [201] 202-218 [219] 220-38 [239] 240-52 [253] 254-74 [275] 276-94 [295] 296-316 [317] 318-35 [336] 337-50 [351] 352-76 [377] 378-97 [398] 399-415 [416] 417-41 [442] 443-64 [465] 466-89 [490] 491-504 [505] 506-525 [526] 527-51 [552] 553-58 [559] 560-71 [572] 573-81 [582] 583-600 [601] 602-620 [621] 622-36 [637-40]

Page contents: [1] half-title: 'Harry Potter and the | Goblet of Fire'; [2] *Titles available in the Harry Potter series | (in reading order):* | Harry Potter and the Philosopher's Stone | Harry Potter and the Chamber of Secrets | Harry Potter and the Prisoner of Azkaban | Harry Potter and the Goblet of Fire | Harry Potter and the Order of the Phoenix | [new paragraph] *Harry Potter and the Philosopher's Stone | also available in Latin, Ancient Greek, Welsh and Irish:* | Harrius Potter et Philosophi Lapis (Latin) | Ἄρειος Ποτὴρ καί ἡ τοῦ ψιλοσόψον λίθος (Ancient Greek) | Harri Potter a Maen yr Anthronydd (Welsh) | Harry Potter agus an Órchloch (Irish)'; [3] title-page; [4] 'All rights reserved; no part of this publication may be reproduced or | transmitted by any means, electronic, mechanical, photocopying | or otherwise, without the prior permission of the publisher | [new paragraph] First published in Great Britain in 2000 | Bloomsbury Publishing Plc, 38 Soho Square, London, W1D 3HB | [new paragraph] This edition first published in 2004 | [new paragraph] Copyright © 2000 J. K. Rowling | [new paragraph] Harry Potter, names, characters and related indicia are | copyright and trademark Warner Bros., 2000™ | [new paragraph] The moral right of the author has been asserted | A CIP catalogue record of this book is available from the British Library | [new paragraph] ISBN 0 7475 7363 8 | [new paragraph] Typeset by Dorchester Typesetting | [new paragraph] All papers used by Bloomsbury Publishing are natural, recyclable products made | from wood grown in well-managed forests. The manufacturing processes | conform to the environmental regulations of the country of origin. | [new paragraph] Printed in Great Britain by Clays Ltd, St Ives plc | [new paragraph] 1 3 5 7 9 10 8 6 4 2 | [new paragraph] www.bloomsbury.com/harrypotter'; [5] '*To Peter Rowling,* | *in memory of Mr Ridley* | *and to Susan Sladden,* | *who helped Harry out of his cupboard*'; [6] blank; [7]-636 text; [637-40] blank

Paper: wove paper

Running title: 'HARRY POTTER' (24mm) on verso, recto title comprises chapter title, pp. 8-636 (excluding pages on which new chapters commence)

Binding: black boards.

On spine: 'HARRY POTTER | J. K. ROWLING | AND THE GOBLET OF FIRE [publisher's device of a figure with a bow, 14 by 14mm]' (reading lengthways down spine). All in gilt.

Upper and lower covers: blank

All edges trimmed. Binding measurements: 204 by 128mm (covers), 204 by 65mm (spine). End-papers: wove paper.

Dust-jacket: coated wove paper, 204 by 519mm

On spine: '[colour photograph of a wooden cup with dancing blue flames, all within single white ruled border, 20 by 20mm] HARRY POTTER [in gilt] | J. K. ROWLING [in white] | AND THE GOBLET OF FIRE [in white]' (reading lengthways down spine) together with publisher's device of a figure with a bow, 14 by 14mm [in olive beige] (at foot).

On upper cover: 'J. K. ROWLING [in white] | HARRY [embossed in gilt] | POTTER [embossed in gilt] | AND THE GOBLET OF FIRE [in white] | BLOOMSBURY [in white]' (all width centred). All on colour photograph of a wooden cup with dancing blue flames.

On lower cover: black and white photograph of J.K. Rowling standing against bookshelves with 'www.bloomsbury.com/harrypotter [in black on olive beige panel, 5 by 40mm] | [barcode in black on white panel, 20 by 39mm] | BLOOMSBURY [in black on olive beige panel, 7 by 40mm]' (lower right).

On upper inside flap: 'When the Quidditch World Cup is | disrupted by Voldemort's rampaging | supporters and the resurrection of the | terrifying Dark Mark, it is obvious to | Harry that, far from weakening, Voldemort | is getting stronger. The ultimate signal to | the magic world of the Dark Lord's return | would be defeat of the one and only | survivor of his death curse, Harry Potter. | So when Harry is entered for the | prestigious yet dangerous Triwizard | Tournament he knows that rather than win | it, he must get through the tasks alive. | [new paragraph] 'Every bit as good as Potters 1 through 3' | Stephen King | [new paragraph] 'Harry's – and our – fourth year at | Hogwarts is funny, full of delicious | parodies of our own world, and wildly | action-packed' *The Times* | [new paragraph] 'There isn't a dull page ... The plot fits | together like a wondrous jigsaw' | *Sunday Express* | [new paragraph] 'The dazzling plot and pace are more | impressive than ever ... there's simply too | much to praise. On yer broomstick! | Go get! Go read!' *Irish Times* | [new paragraph] 'The story is compelling: the humour | satisfyingly anarchic, the moral stance | reassuringly strong ... her best book yet' | *Sunday Telegraph* | [new paragraph] £14.99'. All in white on black.

On lower inside flap: 'J. K. (JOANNE KATHLEEN) ROWLING | has written fiction since she was a child. | Born in 1965, she grew up in Chepstow | and wrote her first 'book' at the age of six | – a story about a rabbit called Rabbit. | She studied French and Classics at Exeter | University, then moved to London to | work at Amnesty International, and then | to Portugal to teach English as a foreign | language, before settling in Edinburgh. | [new paragraph] The idea for Harry Potter occurred to her | on the train from Manchester to London, | where she says Harry Potter 'just strolled | into my head fully formed', and by the | time she had arrived at King's Cross, | many of the characters had taken shape. | During the next five years she outlined | the plots for each book and began writing | the first in the series, *Harry Potter and* | *the Philosopher's Stone*, which was first | published by Bloomsbury in 1997. The | other Harry Potter titles: *Harry Potter and* | *the Chamber of Secrets, Harry Potter and the* | *Prisoner of Azkaban, Harry Potter and the* | *Goblet of Fire*, and *Harry Potter and the* | *Order of the Phoenix*, followed. | J. K. Rowling has also written two other | companion books, *Quidditch Through the* | *Ages* and *Fantastic Beasts and Where to* | *Find Them*, in aid of Comic Relief. | [new paragraph] Jacket Design: William Webb | Jacket Image: Michael Wildsmith | Author Photograph: © Bill de la HEY'. All in white on black.

Publication: 10 October 2004 in an edition of 12,500 copies (confirmed by Bloomsbury) (see notes)

Price: £14.99

Contents:
Harry Potter and the Goblet of Fire
    ('The villagers of Little Hangleton still called it 'the Riddle House', even though…')

Notes:
Having rebranded the look of the adult artwork edition to feature photography by Michael Wildsmith, it was perhaps inevitable that a hardback version would become available. A1(g), A2(m) and A7(j) were all published on 4 October 2004 with A9(i) following a few days later on 10 October 2004 (although, in contrast to the date provided by Bloomsbury, Nielsen BookData cites a publication date of 4 October 2004 for this title too). As the series progressed, later titles published in this livery (see A12(aa), A13(aa) and A14(aa)) would also comprise the simultaneous first edition issues.

Copies: Bloomsbury Archives

Reprints include:
3 5 7 9 10 8 6 4 2
5 7 9 10 8 6 4
9 10

ENGLISH 'CELEBRATORY' EDITION (2000 [2005])
(children's artwork series in paperback)

HARRY | POTTER | *and the Goblet of Fire* | [illustration of Hogwarts crest with legend 'DRAGO DORMIENS NUNQUAM TITILLANDUS' on banner, 67 by 82mm] | J.K.ROWLING | [publisher's device of a dog, 11 by 18mm] | BLOOMSBURY (Lines 1 and 2 justified on left and right margins, and all width centred)

Collation: 320 unsigned leaves bound in indeterminate gatherings; 197 by 128mm; [1-7] 8-19 [20] 21-28 [29] 30-38 [39] 40-48 [49] 50-61 [62] 63-69 [70] 71-86 [87] 88-105 [106] 107-129 [130] 131-40 [141] 142-51 [152] 153-70 [171] 172-84 [185] 186-200 [201] 202-218 [219] 220-38 [239] 240-52 [253] 254-74 [275] 276-94 [295] 296-316 [317] 318-35 [336] 337-50 [351] 352-76 [377] 378-97 [398] 399-415 [416] 417-41 [442] 443-64 [465] 466-89 [490] 491-504 [505] 506-525 [526] 527-51 [552] 553-58 [559] 560-71 [572] 573-81 [582] 583-600 [601] 602-620 [621] 622-36 [637-40]

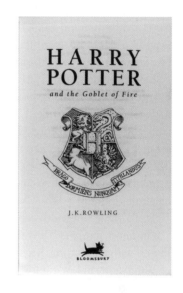

Page contents: [1] half-title: 'HARRY | POTTER | *and the Goblet of Fire* | [illustration of Hogwarts crest with legend 'DRAGO DORMIENS NUNQUAM TITILLANDUS' on banner, 47 by 57mm]'; [2] *'Titles available in the Harry Potter series | (in reading order):* | Harry Potter and the Philosopher's Stone | Harry Potter and the Chamber of Secrets | Harry Potter and the Prisoner of Azkaban | Harry Potter and the Goblet of Fire | Harry Potter and the Order of the Phoenix | Harry Potter and the Half-Blood Prince | [new paragraph] *Harry Potter and the Philosopher's Stone | also available in Latin, Ancient Greek, Welsh and Irish:* | Harrius Potter et Philosophi Lapis (Latin) | Ἄρειος Ποτήρ καί ἡ τοῦ ψιλοσόψον λίθος (Ancient Greek) | Harri Potter a Maen yr Anthronydd (Welsh) | Harry Potter agus an Órchloch (Irish)'; [3] title-page; [4] 'All rights reserved; no part of this publication may be reproduced or | transmitted by any means, electronic, mechanical, photocopying or otherwise, | without the prior permission of the publisher | [new paragraph] First published in Great Britain in 2000 | Bloomsbury Publishing Plc, 36 Soho Square, London, W1D 3QY | [new paragraph] Copyright © 2000 J.K. Rowling | Cover illustrations copyright © by Giles Greenfield 2000 | [new paragraph] Harry Potter, names, characters and related indicia are | copyright and trademark Warner Bros., 2000™ | [new paragraph] The moral right of the author has been asserted | A CIP catalogue record of this book is available from the | British Library | [new paragraph] ISBN 0 7475 8238 6 | ISBN 9780747582380 | [new paragraph] Printed in Great Britain by Clays Ltd, St Ives plc | Typeset by Dorchester Typesetting | [new paragraph] 10 9 8 7 6 5 4 3 2 1 | [new paragraph] www.bloomsbury.com/harrypotter'; [5] *'To Peter Rowling, | in*

memory of Mr Ridley | *and to Susan Sladden,* | *who helped Harry out of his cupboard*'; [6] blank; [7]-636 text; [637-40] blank

Paper: wove paper

Running title: 'HARRY POTTER' (24mm) on verso, recto title comprises chapter title, pp. 8-636 (excluding pages on which new chapters commence)

Binding: pictorial wrappers.

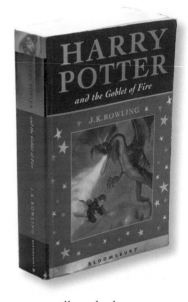

On spine: '[colour illustration of an owl on staircase banister on coloured panel, 38 by 17mm] HARRY POTTER [in red on gilt panel, 38 by 46mm] *and the Goblet of Fire* [in white] J.K.ROWLING [in gilt, both title conclusion and author on red panel, 38 by 103mm] BLOOMSBURY [publisher's device of the head of a dog, 3 by 4mm] [both in white on dark blue panel, 38 by 31mm]' (reading lengthways down spine).

On upper wrapper: 'HARRY | POTTER | *and the Goblet of Fire* [lines 1 and 2 in gilt, line 3 in white, all on dark blue panel, 62 by 127mm] | [gilt rule, 127mm] | ['J.K. ROWLING' [in gilt] with colour illustration of Harry Potter flying on a broomstick about to seize a golden egg that is protected by a fire-breathing dragon, within single gilt ruled border, 91 by 87mm, all on red panel with orange, yellow and gilt stars, 124 by 127mm] | [dark blue rule, 127mm] | BLOOMSBURY [in dark blue on gilt panel, 10 by 127mm]' (all width centred).

On lower wrapper: 'It is the summer holidays and soon Harry Potter will be starting his fourth | year at Hogwarts School of Witchcraft and Wizardry. Harry is counting the | days: there are new spells to be learnt, more Quidditch to be played, and | Hogwarts castle to continue exploring. But Harry needs to be careful – | there are unexpected dangers lurking … | [new paragraph] J.K. Rowling continues to surprise and delight with the power of her | rich, demanding and action-packed storytelling. | [new paragraph] 'From the black heart of Voldemort to the fever pitch excitement | of the Quidditch World Cup, the magical world of Hogwarts and | Harry Potter is more spellbinding than ever. Deep in mystery, | rich in history and sparky in adventure, J.K. Rowling's rare gift | for storytelling enthralls.' *Julia Eccleshare* | [new paragraph] '*Harry Potter and the Goblet of Fire* has finally been | unleashed. And is it good? You bet it is. Harry's – and | our – fourth year at Hogwarts is funny, full of delicious | parodies of our own world, and wildly action-packed.' | *The Times* | [new paragraph] 'There isn't a dull page … The plot fits together | like a wondrous jigsaw.' *The Sunday Express* | [new paragraph] '*Harry Potter and the Goblet of Fire* is inventive, | open-minded, and carries the hallmark of | Rowling's imagination and scholarship … | pure magic.' *The Mirror* | [new paragraph] 'J.K. Rowling has delivered … Her best | book yet.' *The Sunday Telegraph* | [new paragraph] 'Further-reaching than any yet, this is the book | in which Harry and Ron start to notice girls, | with comic consequences, and in which | Voldemort returns, with fatal ones. | It is darker than the previous books, | but just as dazzling.' |

Nicolette Jones | [barcode in black on white panel, 20 by 38mm together with '[publisher's device of a dog, 6 by 10mm] | BLOOMSBURY' and '£6.99' in black above panel and 'http://www.bloomsbury.com' below panel, in white on red panel, 7 by 38mm] | Cover illustrations from original artwork by Cliff Wright'. All in black on colour illustration of staircase at Hogwarts castle.

All edges trimmed. Binding measurements: 197 by 128mm (wrappers), 197 by 38mm (spine).

Publication: 3 October 2005 in an edition of 115,000 copies (confirmed by Bloomsbury)

Price: £6.99

Contents:
Harry Potter and the Goblet of Fire
('The villagers of Little Hangleton still called it 'the Riddle House', even though…')

Notes:
The individual titles in the 'celebratory' edition were each published to celebrate the release of the film version. The UK premiere of *Harry Potter and the Goblet of Fire* took place on 6 November 2005.

Note that no new edition information is provided for this celebratory edition on the publisher's imprint page. The publication year of 2005 is therefore entirely omitted.

Bloomsbury released a 'dumpbin' display case for this edition at the beginning of October 2005 (Nielsen BookData provides a date of 3 October 2005). The case was empty but could be filled with 24 copies of this edition.

Nielsen BookData Online records a *Goblet of Fire* bookmark and also a promotional poster were both issued by Bloomsbury on the same date as this edition was published.

Copies: private collection (PWE); Bloomsbury Archives

Reprints include:
10 9 8 7 6 5 4 3 2

A9(k)   ENGLISH 'SIGNATURE' EDITION   (2010)
(Clare Melinsky artwork series in paperback)

Harry Potter ['signature' above 'z' rule with numerous stars] | *and the* | Goblet of Fire | [illustration of Hogwarts crest with legend 'DRAGO DORMIENS NUNQUAM TITILLANDUS' on banner, 68 by 84mm] | J.K.ROWLING | [publisher's device of a dog, 8 by 13mm] | BLOOMSBURY | LONDON BERLIN NEW YORK SYDNEY (All width centred)

Collation: 320 unsigned leaves bound in indeterminate gatherings; 197 by 128mm; [1-7] 8-19 [20] 21-28 [29] 30-38 [39] 40-48 [49] 50-61 [62] 63-69 [70] 71-86 [87] 88-105 [106] 107-129 [130] 131-40

[141] 142-51 [152] 153-70 [171] 172-84 [185] 186-200 [201] 202-218 [219] 220-38 [239] 240-52 [253] 254-74 [275] 276-94 [295] 296-316 [317] 318-35 [336] 337-50 [351] 352-76 [377] 378-97 [398] 399-415 [416] 417-41 [442] 443-64 [465] 466-89 [490] 491-504 [505] 506-525 [526] 527-51 [552] 553-58 [559] 560-71 [572] 573-81 [582] 583-600 [601] 602-620 [621] 622-36 [637-40]

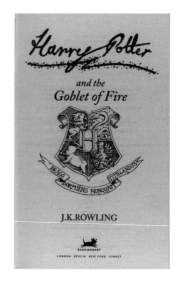

Page contents: [1] half-title: 'Harry Potter ['signature' above 'z' rule with numerous stars] | *and the* | *Goblet of Fire* | [illustration of Hogwarts crest with legend 'DRAGO DORMIENS NUNQUAM TITILLANDUS' on banner, 60 by 75mm']; [2] *'Titles available in the Harry Potter series* | *(in reading order):* | Harry Potter and the Philosopher's Stone | Harry Potter and the Chamber of Secrets | Harry Potter and the Prisoner of Azkaban | Harry Potter and the Goblet of Fire | Harry Potter and the Order of the Phoenix | Harry Potter and the Half-Blood Prince | Harry Potter and the Deathly Hallows | [new paragraph] *Titles available in the Harry Potter series* | *(in Latin):* | Harry Potter and the Philosopher's Stone | Harry Potter and the Chamber of Secrets | *(in Welsh, Ancient Greek and Irish):* | Harry Potter and the Philosopher's Stone'; [3] title-page; [4] 'All rights reserved; no part of this publication may be reproduced or | transmitted by any means, electronic, mechanical, photocopying | or otherwise, without the prior permission of the publisher | [new paragraph] First published in Great Britain in 2000 by Bloomsbury Publishing Plc | 36 Soho Square, London, W1D 3QY | [new paragraph] Bloomsbury Publishing, London, Berlin, New York and Sydney | [new paragraph] This paperback edition first published in November 2010 | [new paragraph] Copyright © J.K.Rowling 2000 | Cover illustrations by Clare Melinsky copyright © Bloomsbury Publishing Plc 2010 | [new paragraph] Harry Potter, names, characters and related indicia are | copyright and trademark Warner Bros., 2000™ | [new paragraph] The moral right of the author has been asserted | A CIP catalogue record of this book is available from the British Library | [new paragraph] ISBN 978 1 4088 1057 6 | [new paragraph] [Forest Stewardship Council logo, 8 by 9mm together with ® symbol and text: 'FSC | www.fsc.org | MIX | Paper from | responsible sources | FSC® C018072'] | [new paragraph] Typeset by Dorchester Typesetting | Printed in Great Britain by Clays Ltd, St Ives plc | [new paragraph] 1 3 5 7 9 10 8 6 4 2 | [new paragraph] | www.bloomsbury.com/harrypotter'; [5] *'To Peter Rowling,* | *in memory of Mr Ridley* | *and to Susan Sladden,* | *who helped Harry out of his cupboard'*; [6] blank; [7]-636 text; [637-40] blank

Paper: wove paper

Running title: 'HARRY POTTER' (25mm) on verso, recto title comprises chapter title, pp. 8-636

Binding: pictorial wrappers.

On spine: 'Harry Potter ['signature' above 'z' rule with numerous stars] [in gilt] *and* | *the Goblet of Fire* [brown, yellow, white and light blue illustration of a flaming goblet, 16 by 28mm] J.K.ROWLING BLOOMSBURY [publisher's device of the head of a dog, 3 by 4mm]' (reading lengthways down spine). All in white on light orange.

On upper wrapper: 'Harry Potter ['signature' above 'z' rule with numerous stars] [embossed in gilt] | *and the* | *Goblet of Fire* | [light green, dark green and red illustration of a snake and skull, 101 by 116mm] | J.K.ROWLING | BLOOMSBURY' (all width centred). All in light orange with deckle-edge effect of white leaf on light orange background at fore-edge.

On lower wrapper: 'The summer holidays seem never-ending and Harry Potter can't | wait for the start of the school term. It is his fourth year at | Hogwarts School of Witchcraft and Wizardry, and there are spells | to learn and (unluckily) Potions and Divination lessons to attend. | But Harry needs to be on his guard at all times – his worst enemy is | preparing a horrifying fate for him … | [new paragraph] *'Harry Potter and the Goblet of Fire* has finally been unleashed. | And is it good? You bet it is. Harry's – and our – fourth year at | Hogwarts is funny, full of delicious parodies of our own world, | and wildly action-packed.' | *The Times* | [new paragraph] 'Inventive, open-minded, and carries the hallmark of Rowling's | imagination and scholarship … pure magic.' | *Mirror* | [new paragraph] 'There isn't a dull page … the plot fits | together like a wondrous jigsaw.' | *Sunday Express* | [dark blue, light blue, dark yellow, light yellow black and green illustration of a giant carriage drawn by two winged horses above clouds, 96 by 112mm] | [barcode together with publisher's device of a dog, 6 by 10mm and 'BLOOMSBURY' together with Forest Stewardship Council logo, 7 by 8mm together with © symbol and text: 'FSC | Mixed Sources | Product group from well-managed | forests and other controlled sources | [new paragraph] Cert no. SGS-COC-2061 | www.fsc.org | © 1996 Forest Stewardship Council'] | Designed by Webb & Webb Design | Cover illustrations by Clare Melinsky www.bloomsbury.com/harrypotter £8.99 | Author photograph © J.P.Masclet'. Lines 1-17 in light orange with all other text in black, together with deckle-edge effect of white leaf on light orange background at fore-edge. The initial capital 'T' of 'The' is a drop capital.

On inside upper wrapper: 'The magical world of … | Harry Potter ['signature' above 'z' rule with numerous stars] | [colour illustrations in three columns of seven book designs] | The internationally bestselling series | [new paragraph] For more from Harry Potter, visit | www.bloomsbury.com/harrypotter'. All in light orange with the exception of line 2 which is in gold, together with deckle-edge effect of white leaf on light orange background at fore-edge.

On inside lower wrapper: colour photograph of J.K. Rowling seated by a window.

All edges trimmed. Binding measurements: 197 by 128mm (wrappers), 197 by 38mm (spine).

Publication: 1 November 2010 in an edition of 65,040 copies (confirmed by Bloomsbury)

Price: £8.99

Contents:
Harry Potter and the Goblet of Fire
   ('The villagers of Little Hangleton still called it 'the Riddle House', even though…')

Notes:
Published as a boxed set of seven volumes comprising A1(i), A2(n), A7(k), A9(k), A12(h), A13(g) and A14(f). Individual volumes were also available separately.

Copies: private collection (PWE)

A9(l)   ENGLISH 'SIGNATURE' EDITION   (2011)
(Clare Melinsky artwork series in hardback)

Harry Potter ['signature' above 'z' rule with numerous stars] | *and the* | *Goblet of Fire* | [illustration of Hogwarts crest with legend 'DRAGO DORMIENS NUNQUAM TITILLANDUS' on banner, 68 by 84mm] | J.K.ROWLING | [publisher's device of a dog, 8 by 13mm] | BLOOMSBURY | LONDON BERLIN NEW YORK SYDNEY (All width centred)

Collation: 320 unsigned leaves bound in indeterminate gatherings; 197 by 124mm; [1-7] 8-19 [20] 21-28 [29] 30-38 [39] 40-48 [49] 50-61 [62] 63-69 [70] 71-86 [87] 88-105 [106] 107-129 [130] 131-40 [141] 142-51 [152] 153-70 [171] 172-84 [185] 186-200 [201] 202-218 [219] 220-38 [239] 240-52 [253] 254-74 [275] 276-94 [295] 296-316 [317] 318-35 [336] 337-50 [351] 352-76 [377] 378-97 [398] 399-415 [416] 417-41 [442] 443-64 [465] 466-89 [490] 491-504 [505] 506-525 [526] 527-51 [552] 553-58 [559] 560-71 [572] 573-81 [582] 583-600 [601] 602-620 [621] 622-36 [637-40]

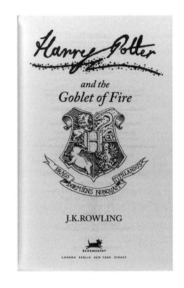

Page contents: [1] half-title: 'Harry Potter ['signature' above 'z' rule with numerous stars] | *and the* | *Goblet of Fire* | [illustration of Hogwarts crest with legend 'DRAGO DORMIENS NUNQUAM TITILLANDUS' on banner, 60 by 75mm]'; [2] '*Titles available in the Harry Potter series* | *(in reading order):* | Harry Potter and the Philosopher's Stone | Harry Potter and the Chamber of Secrets | Harry Potter and the Prisoner of Azkaban | Harry Potter and the Goblet of Fire | Harry Potter and the Order of the Phoenix | Harry Potter and the Half-Blood Prince | Harry Potter and the Deathly Hallows | [new paragraph] *Titles available in the Harry Potter series* | *(in Latin):* | Harry Potter and the Philosopher's Stone | Harry Potter and the Chamber of Secrets | *(in Welsh, Ancient Greek and Irish):* | Harry Potter and the Philosopher's Stone | [new paragraph] *Also available* | *(in aid of Comic Relief):* | Fantastic Beasts and Where to Find Them | Quidditch Through the Ages | *(in aid of Lumos):* | The Tales of Beedle the Bard'; [3] title-page; [4] 'All rights reserved; no part of this publication may be reproduced or | transmitted by any means, electronic, mechanical, photocopying | or otherwise, without the prior permission of the publisher | [new paragraph] First published in Great Britain in 2000 by Bloomsbury Publishing Plc | 49-51 Bedford Square, London, WC1B 3DP | [new paragraph] Bloomsbury Publishing, London, Berlin, New York and Sydney | [new paragraph] This hardback edition first published in November 2011 | [new paragraph] Copyright © J.K.Rowling 2000 | Cover and endpaper illustrations by Clare Melinsky copyright © J.K.Rowling 2010 | [new paragraph] Harry Potter, names, characters and related indicia are | copyright and trademark Warner Bros., 2000™ | [new paragraph] The moral right of the author has been asserted | A CIP catalogue record of this book is available from the British Library | [new paragraph] ISBN 978 1 4088 2583 9 | [new paragraph] [Forest Stewardship Council logo, 8 by 9mm together with ® symbol and text: 'FSC | www.fsc.org | MIX | Paper from | responsible sources | FSC® C018072'] | [new paragraph] Typeset by Dorchester Typesetting | Printed in Great Britain by Clays Ltd, St Ives plc | [new paragraph] 1 3 5 7 9 10 8 6 4 2 | [new paragraph] | www.bloomsbury.com/harrypotter'; [5] 'To Peter Rowling, | in memory of Mr Ridley | and to Susan Sladden, | who helped Harry out of his cupboard'; [6] blank; [7]-636 text; [637-40] blank

Paper: wove paper

Running title: 'HARRY POTTER' (24mm) on verso, recto title comprises chapter title, pp. 8-636

Binding: orange boards.

   On spine: 'Harry Potter ['signature' above 'z' rule with numerous stars] *and* | *the Goblet of Fire* [illustration of a flaming goblet, 16 by 28mm] J.K.ROWLING BLOOMSBURY [publisher's device of the head of a dog, 3 by 4mm]' (reading lengthways down spine). All in gilt.

   Upper and lower covers: blank.

   All edges trimmed. Yellow sewn bands at head and foot of spine together with yellow marker ribbon. Binding measurements: 205 by 128mm (covers), 205 by 59mm (spine). End-papers: wove paper overprinted in orange showing design, in white, of spine motifs from the series (see notes).

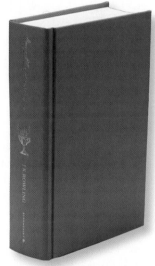

Dust-jacket: coated wove paper, 205 by 511mm

   On spine: 'Harry Potter ['signature' above 'z' rule with numerous stars] [in gilt] *and* | *the Goblet of Fire* [brown, yellow, white and light blue illustration of a flaming goblet, 16 by 28mm] J.K.ROWLING BLOOMSBURY [publisher's device of the head of a dog, 3 by 4mm]' (reading lengthways down spine). All in white on light orange.

   On upper cover: 'Harry Potter ['signature' above 'z' rule with numerous stars] [in gilt] | *and the* | *Goblet of Fire* | [light green, dark green and red illustration of a snake and skull, 101 by 116mm] | J.K.ROWLING | BLOOMSBURY' (all width centred). All in light orange with deckle-edge effect of white leaf on light orange background at fore-edge.

   On lower cover: "Inventive, open-minded, and carries | the hallmark of Rowling's imagination | and scholarship ... pure magic.' | *Mirror* | [dark blue, light blue, dark yellow, light yellow black and green illustration of a giant carriage drawn by two winged horses above clouds, 81 by 94mm] | [publisher's device of a dog, 6 by 10mm and 'BLOOMSBURY'] [barcode and 'www.bloomsbury.

com/harrypotter' in black on white panel, 24 by 39mm]'. All in light orange, with deckle-edge effect of white leaf on light orange background at fore-edge. The initial capital 'I' of 'Inventive' is a drop capital.

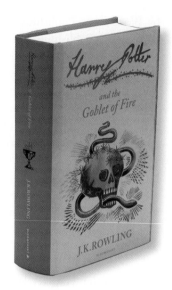

On upper inside flap: 'The summer holidays seem never- | ending and Harry Potter can't wait | for the start of the school term. It is | his fourth year at Hogwarts School of | Witchcraft and Wizardry, and there are | spells to learn and (unluckily) Potions | and Divination lessons to attend. But | Harry needs to be on his guard at all | times – his worst enemy is preparing a | horrifying fate for him … | [new paragraph] '*Harry Potter and the Goblet of Fire* has finally | been unleashed. And is it good? You bet it is. | Harry's – and our – fourth year at Hogwarts | is funny, full of delicious parodies of our own | world, and wildly action-packed.' | *The Times* | [new paragraph] 'The story is compelling: the humour | satisfyingly anarchic, the moral stance | reassuringly strong … her best book yet.' | *Sunday Telegraph* | [new paragraph] 'There isn't a dull page … the plot fits | together like a wondrous jigsaw.' | *Sunday Express* | [brown, yellow, white and light blue illustration of a flaming goblet, 21 by 13mm]'. All in white on light orange. The initial capital 'T' of 'The' is a drop capital.

On lower inside flap: 'J. K. Rowling has written fiction since she was a child, | and she always wanted to be an author. Her parents loved | reading and their house in Chepstow was full of books. | In fact, J. K. Rowling wrote her first 'book' at the age | of six – a story about a rabbit called Rabbit. She studied | French and Classics at Exeter University, then moved to | Edinburgh – via London and Portugal. In 2000 she was | awarded an OBE for services to children's literature. | [new paragraph] The idea for Harry Potter occurred to her on the | train from Manchester to London, where she says | Harry Potter 'just strolled into my head fully formed', | and by the time she had arrived at King's Cross, many | of the characters had taken shape. During the next | five years she outlined the plots for each book and | began writing the first in the series, *Harry Potter and* | *the Philosopher's Stone*, which was first published by | Bloomsbury in 1997. The other Harry Potter titles: | *Harry Potter and the Chamber of Secrets, Harry Potter* | *and the Prisoner of Azkaban, Harry Potter and the* | *Goblet of Fire, Harry Potter and the Order of the Phoenix,* | *Harry Potter and the Half-Blood Prince* and *Harry* | *Potter and the Deathly Hallows* followed. J. K. Rowling | has also written three companion books: *Quidditch* | *Through the Ages* and *Fantastic Beasts and Where to Find* | *Them*, in aid of Comic Relief, and *The Tales of Beedle* | *the Bard*, in aid of Lumos. | [new paragraph] THE COMPLETE HARRY POTTER SERIES: | [colour illustrations in two rows of seven book designs] | Designed by Webb & Webb Design | Cover illustrations by Clare Melinsky | copyright © J. K. Rowling 2010'. All in white on light orange with white panel, 19 by 12mm, to right on which in black: '[Forest Stewardship Council logo, 6 by 7mm together with ® symbol] | FSC | www.fsc.org | MIX | Paper from | responsible sources | FSC® C018072'.

Publication: 7 November 2011 in an edition of 9,200 copies (confirmed by Bloomsbury)

Price: £115 [together with A1(j), A2(o), A7(l), A12(i), A13(h) and A14(g)]

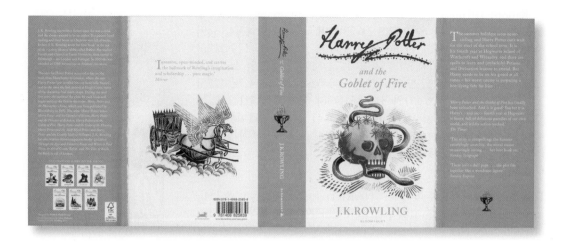

Contents:

Harry Potter and the Goblet of Fire

    ('The villagers of Little Hangleton still called it 'the Riddle House', even though…')

Notes:

The end-papers carry a design of eight miniature illustrations. Seven of these reproduce the spine motifs from the series and an eighth comprises a variant of the key-bird from the first book.

This is the first of the books in the series to carry different press quotes from the equivalent 'signature' paperback edition. For this hardback edition there is an additional quote (from the *Sunday Telegraph*) on the upper inside flap.

Published as a boxed set of seven volumes comprising A1(j), A2(o), A7(l), A9(l), A12(i), A13(h) and A14(g). Individual volumes were not available separately. The ISBN for the boxed set was ISBN 978 1 4088 2594 5.

Copies: private collection (PWE)

A9(m)   ENGLISH ADULT EDITION   (2013)
(Andrew Davidson artwork series in paperback)

J.K. [in grey] | ROWLING [in grey] [reading lengthways down title-page] | HARRY | POTTER | &THE [reading lengthways up title-page] GOBLET OF FIRE | BLOOMSBURY | LONDON [point] NEW DELHI [point] NEW YORK [point] SYDNEY (Author justified on right margin, first part of title justified on left margin, publisher with publisher's offices width centred)

Collation: 320 unsigned leaves bound in indeterminate gatherings; 198 by 128mm; [1-7] 8-19 [20] 21-28 [29] 30-38 [39] 40-48 [49] 50-61 [62] 63-69 [70] 71-86 [87] 88-105 [106] 107-129 [130] 131-40 [141] 142-51 [152] 153-70 [171] 172-84 [185] 186-200 [201] 202-218 [219] 220-38 [239] 240-52 [253] 254-74 [275] 276-94 [295] 296-316 [317] 318-35 [336] 337-50 [351] 352-76 [377] 378-97 [398] 399-415 [416] 417-41 [442] 443-64 [465] 466-89 [490] 491-504 [505] 506-525 [526] 527-51 [552] 553-58 [559] 560-71 [572] 573-81 [582] 583-600 [601] 602-620 [621] 622-36 [637-40]

Page contents: [1] half-title: 'HARRY | POTTER | &THE [reading lengthways up title-page] GOBLET OF FIRE'; [2] *'Titles available in the Harry Potter series | (in reading order):* | Harry Potter and the Philosopher's Stone | Harry Potter and the Chamber of Secrets | Harry Potter and the Prisoner of Azkaban | Harry Potter and the Goblet of Fire | Harry Potter and the Order of the Phoenix | Harry Potter and the Half-Blood Prince | Harry Potter and the Deathly Hallows | [new paragraph] *Titles available in the Harry Potter series* | *(in Latin):* | Harry Potter and the Philosopher's Stone | Harry Potter and the Chamber of Secrets | *(in Welsh, Ancient Greek and Irish):* | Harry Potter and the Philosopher's Stone | [new paragraph] *Also available* | *(in aid of Comic Relief):* | Fantastic Beasts and Where to Find Them | Quidditch Through the Ages | *(in aid of Lumos):* | The Tales of Beedle the Bard'; [3] title-page; [4] 'All rights reserved; no part of this publication may be reproduced or | transmitted by any means, electronic, mechanical, photocopying | or otherwise, without the prior permission of the publisher | [new paragraph] First published in Great Britain in 2000 by Bloomsbury Publishing Plc | 50 Bedford Square, London WC1B 3DP | [new paragraph] Bloomsbury Publishing, London, New Delhi, New York and Sydney | [new paragraph] This paperback edition first published in 2013 | [new paragraph] Copyright © J.K. Rowling 2000 | Cover illustrations by Andrew Davidson copyright © J.K. Rowling 2013 | [new paragraph] Harry Potter, names, characters and related indicia are | copyright and trademark Warner Bros., 2000™ | [new paragraph] The moral right of the author has been asserted | A CIP catalogue record for this book is available from the British Library | [new paragraph] ISBN 978 1 4088 3499 2 | [new paragraph] [Forest Stewardship Council logo, 6 by 7mm together with ® symbol and text: 'FSC | www.fsc.org' with 'MIX | Paper from | responsible sources | FSC® C020471' to the right and all within single ruled border with rounded corners, 12 by 26mm] | [new paragraph] Typeset by Dorchester Typesetting | Printed and bound in Great Britain by CPI Group (UK) Ltd, Croydon CR0 4YY | [new paragraph] 1 3 5 7 9 10 8 6 4 2 | [new paragraph] | www.bloomsbury.com/harrypotter'; [5] *'To Peter Rowling, | in memory of Mr Ridley | and to Susan Sladden, | who helped Harry out of his cupboard'*; [6] blank; [7]-636 text; [637-40] blank

Paper: wove paper

Running title: 'HARRY POTTER' (24mm) on verso, recto title comprises chapter title, pp. 8-636 (excluding pages on which new chapters commence)

Binding: pictorial wrappers.

On spine: 'J.K. ROWLING [in white] HARRY POTTER [in orange] &THE [in white] GOBLET OF FIRE [in orange] [publisher's device of a figure with a bow, 8 by 6mm] [in white]' (reading lengthways down spine with the exception of '&THE' and the publisher's device which are horizontal). All on blue.

On upper wrapper: 'J.K. [in white] | ROWLING [in white] [reading lengthways down upper wrapper] | HARRY [in blue] | POTTER [in blue] | &THE [in white] [reading lengthways up upper wrapper] GOBLET OF FIRE [in blue] | BLOOMSBURY [in white]' (author and final part of title justified on right margin, first part of title justified on left margin, publisher with publisher's offices width centred). All on yellow and orange illustration of dragons flying over Hogwarts castle.

On lower wrapper: 'When Harry Potter wakes one morning with a searing pain | in the lightning-shaped scar on his forehead, he is not sure | what it means. All he knows is that the last time it happened | Lord Voldemort was close by. Three days later, the Quidditch | World Cup ends in carnage at the hands of the Dark Lord's | followers – and Harry steels himself for more trouble ahead. | [new paragraph] Back at Hogwarts for his fourth year, Harry is astonished to be | chosen by the Goblet of Fire to represent the school in the | Triwizard Tournament. The competition is dangerous, the | tasks terrifying, and true courage is no guarantee of survival | – especially when the darkest forces are on the rise … | [new paragraph] [section of white illustration of dragons flying over Hogwarts castle, 57 by 112mm] | BLOOMSBURY www.bloomsbury.com/harrypotter www.pottermore.com £8.99 | [section of white illustration of dragons flying over Hogwarts castle, 27 by 112mm upon which: Forest Stewardship Council logo, 5 by 6mm together with ® symbol and text: 'FSC | www.fsc.org | MIX | Paper from | responsible sources | FSC® C020471' all in black on white panel with rounded corners, 19 by 12mm, with barcode in black on white panel, 18 by 39mm, with 'Designed by Webb & Webb Design | Cover illustrations by Andrew Davidson | copyright © J.K. Rowling 2013' on blue panel, 9 by 39mm]'. All in white on blue. The initial capital 'W' of 'When' is a drop capital and is printed in green.

On inside upper wrapper: blue and white illustration of dragons flying over Hogwarts castle.

On inside lower wrapper: blue and white illustration of dragon's wing, talons and tail.

All edges trimmed. Binding measurements: 198 by 128mm (wrappers), 198 by 38mm (spine).

Publication: 15 August 2013 in an edition of 57,200 copies (confirmed by Bloomsbury) (see notes)

Price: £8.99

Contents:

Harry Potter and the Goblet of Fire

('The villagers of Little Hangleton still called it 'the Riddle House', even though…')

Notes:

The illustrations by Andrew Davidson derive from a single wood engraving. A single illustration is presented on both the upper wrapper and inside upper wrapper. A section is printed on the lower wrapper. A detail from the upper wrapper is shown on the inside lower wrapper.

Although Bloomsbury's 'official' publication date was 15 August 2013, copies were available from amazon.co.uk at the beginning of August.

Copies: private collection (PWE)

A9(n)   AMERICAN CHILDREN'S EDITION   (2013)
(Kazu Kibuishi artwork in paperback)

HARRY POTTER | AND THE GOBLET OF FIRE | [black and white illustration of a flaming goblet on a casket with curtains in background, 49 by 49mm] | BY | J. K. ROWLING | ILLUSTRATIONS BY MARY GRANDPRÉ | SCHOLASTIC INC. (All width centred on a diamond pattern background)

Collation: 384 unsigned leaves bound in indeterminate gatherings; 204 by 134mm; [I-IV] V-IX [X-XII] 1-734 [735-56]

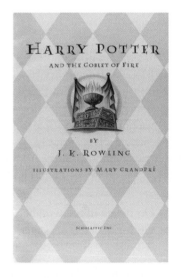

Page contents: [I-II] 'PRAISE FOR J. K. ROWLING'S | HARRY POTTER | AND THE GOBLET OF FIRE | [device of nine stars] | [9 reviews and a listing of 6 statements]'; [III] title-page; [IV] 'TO PETER ROWLING, | IN MEMORY OF MR. RIDLEY | AND TO SUSAN SLADDEN, | WHO HELPED HARRY | OUT OF HIS CUPBOARD | [device of twelve stars] | Text © 2000 by J. K. Rowling | Interior illustrations by Mary GrandPré © 2000 by Warner Bros. | Excerpt from *Harry Potter and the Order of the Phoenix*, text © 2003 by J. K. Rowling; | illustration by Mary GrandPré © 2003 by Warner Bros. | Cover illustration by Kazu Kibuishi © 2013 by Scholastic Inc. | HARRY POTTER and all related characters and elements are TM of and © WBEI. | Harry Potter Publishing Rights © J. K. Rowling | All rights reserved. Published by Scholastic Inc. SCHOLASTIC, the LANTERN LOGO, and associated | logos are trademarks and/or registered trademarks of Scholastic Inc. | [new paragraph] If you purchased this book without a cover, you should be aware that this book is stolen property. | It was reported as "unsold and destroyed" to the publisher, and neither the author nor the | publisher has received any payment for this "stripped book." | [new paragraph] No part of this publication may be reproduced, stored in a retrieval system, or transmitted in any | form or by any means, electronic, mechanical, photocopying, recording, or otherwise, without | written permission of the publisher. For information regarding permission, write to Scholastic Inc., | Attention: Permissions Department, 557 Broadway, New York, NY 10012. | [new paragraph] [publisher's device of a lantern, 6 by 4mm] | Arthur A. Levine Books hardcover edition art directed by David Saylor, | published by Arthur A. Levine Books, an imprint of Scholastic Inc., July 2000. | [new paragraph] ISBN 978-0-545-58295-7 | [new paragraph] Library of Congress Control Number: 00-131084 | [new paragraph] 12 11 10 9 8 7 6 5 4 3 2 1   13 14 15 16 17 | [new paragraph] Printed in the U.S.A. 40 | This edition first printing, September 2013 | [new paragraph] We try to produce the most beautiful books possible, and we are extremely concerned about the impact of our | manufacturing process on the forests of the world and the environment as a whole. Accordingly, we made sure | that the text paper contains a minimum of 30% post-consumer waste, and that all the paper has been certified as | coming from forests that are managed to insure the protection of the people and wildlife dependent upon them.'; V-IX 'CONTENTS' (thirty-seven chapters listed with titles and page references); [X] blank; [XI] half-title: 'HARRY POTTER | AND THE GOBLET OF FIRE' (all on diamond pattern background); [XII] blank; 1-734 text; [735] 'HARRY POTTER'S | ADVENTURES CONTINUE IN | [new paragraph] HARRY POTTER | AND THE ORDER OF THE PHOENIX | [new paragraph] TURN THE PAGE FOR | A SNEAK PREVIEW!' (all on diamond pattern background); [736] blank; [737-52] text; [753] blank; [754] advertisement for Pottermore; [755] '[black and white photograph of J.K. Rowling seated by curtains, credited 'ANDREW MONTGOMERY' reading lengthways up right margin] | [new paragraph] J. K. ROWLING is the author of the beloved, | bestselling, record-breaking Harry Potter series. She started writing | the series during a delayed Manchester to London King's Cross | train journey, and during the next five years, outlined the plots for | each book and began writing the first novel. *Harry Potter and the | Sorcerer's Stone* was published in the United States by Arthur A. | Levine Books in 1998, and the series concluded nearly ten years | later with *Harry Potter and the Deathly Hallows*, published in 2007. | J. K. Rowling is the recipient of numerous awards and honorary | degrees, including an OBE for services to children's literature, | France's Légion d'honneur, and the Hans Christian Andersen | Literature Award. She supports a wide number of causes through | her charitable trust, Volant, and is the founder of Lumos, a charity | working to transform the lives of disadvantaged children. J. K. | Rowling lives in Edinburgh with her husband and three children.'; [756] 'MARY GRANDPRÉ has illustrated more than twenty | beautiful books for children, including the American editions of | the Harry Potter novels. Her work has also appeared in the *New | Yorker*, the *Atlantic Monthly*, and the *Wall Street Journal*, and her | paintings and pastels have been shown in galleries across the Unit- | ed States. Ms. GrandPré lives in Sarasota, Florida, with her family. | [new paragraph] KAZU KIBUISHI is the creator of the *New York Times* | bestselling Amulet series and *Copper*, a collection of his popular | webcomic. He is also the founder and editor of the acclaimed | Flight anthologies. *Daisy Kutter: The Last Train*, his first graphic | novel, was listed as one of the Best Books for Young Adults by | YALSA, and *Amulet, Book One: The Stonekeeper* was an ALA Best | Book for Young Adults and a Children's Choice Book Award | finalist. Kazu lives and works in Alhambra, California, with his | wife and fellow comics artist, Amy Kim Kibuishi, and their two | children. Visit Kazu online at www.boltcity.com.'

Paper: wove paper

Running title: 'CHAPTER' and chapter number on verso, recto title comprises chapter title, pp. 1-734 and pp. [737-52]. Each running title (excluding pages on which new chapters commence) includes a three-star design to left and right of both running-titles on verso and recto. On pages on which a new chapter commences, the three-star design is omitted.

Illustrations: title-page vignette, together with thirty-seven vignettes at the beginning of each chapter (after chapter and chapter number but before chapter title). The 'sneak preview' also includes a vignette. In addition to standard typographical changes (including italics, capitals and small capitals) there are other typographical features, comprising:

p. 25 facsimile of Harry's signature

p. 30 facsimile of Molly Weasley's signature

p. 36 facsimiles of Ron and Harry's signatures

pp. 96-97 advertisements written on a gigantic blackboard

p. 102 further advertisements written on a gigantic blackboard, also a Quidditch score

p. 113 Quidditch score

p. 202 newspaper headline

p. 226 facsimile of Sirius' signature

p. 228 facsimile of Harry's signature

p. 235 text of announcement sign

p. 240 facsimile of Sirius' signature

p. 292 facsimile of Harry's signature

p. 297 text of badges

p. 298 text of badge

p. 304 facsimile of Rita Skeeter's quill's writing

p. 305 facsimile of Rita Skeeter's quill's writing

p. 306 facsimile of Rita Skeeter's quill's writing

p. 312 facsimile of Sirius' signature

p. 406 facsimile of Sirius' signature

p. 437 newspaper headline

p. 511 magazine headline

p. 541 text of letter in 'poison-pen' style

p. 572 facsimile of Sirius' signature

p. 611 newspaper headline

p. 638 headstone engraved name

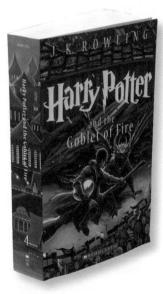

Binding: pictorial wrappers.

On spine: 'ROWLING | Harry Potter and the Goblet of Fire [reading lengthways down spine] | 4' and '[publisher's book device] | [rule] | S' in white on red panel, 14 by 6mm. All in white on colour illustration (see notes).

On upper wrapper: 'J. K. ROWLING | Harry Potter [hand-drawn lettering] [embossed in white] | and the | Goblet of Fire' (all width centred). All in white on colour illustration of Harry Potter clutching a golden egg and challenged, in a spectator's ring, by a Hungarian Horntail dragon. In centre at foot: '[publisher's book device] SCHOLASTIC' in white on red panel, 5 by 45mm.

On lower wrapper: '"It matters not what someone is born, | but what they grow to be!" | — Albus Dumbledore | [new paragraph] Harry Potter wants to get away from the pernicious Dursleys and go to the | Quidditch World Cup with Hermione, Ron, and the Weasleys. He wants to | dream about Cho Chang, his crush (and maybe do more than dream). He | wants to find out about the mysterious event involving two rival schools of | magic, and a competition that hasn't happened for hundreds of years. He | wants to be a normal fourteen-year-old wizard. Unfortunately for Harry | Potter, he's not normal; he's different — even by Wizarding standards. | [new paragraph] And in this case, different can be deadly. | [new paragraph] $14.99 US | [new paragraph] [publisher's book device with 'SCHOLASTIC' in white on red panel, 5 by 45mm] | www.scholastic.com | COVER DESIGN BY KAZU KIBUISHI AND JASON CAFFOE | COVER ART BY KAZU KIBUISHI © 2013 BY SCHOLASTIC INC.' Lines 1-3 in white with other lines in yellow and all on colour illustration of Harry standing before a door opening onto a Hungarian Horntail dragon. In lower right: barcode with smaller barcode to the right (51499) together with 'S' within triangle, all in black on white panel, 21 by 53mm.

On inside upper wrapper: barcode with smaller barcode (51499) together with 'S' within triangle below, all in black on white panel, 53 by 21mm. All on dark green.

On inside lower wrapper: '[colour illustration of book design] Harry Potter [hand-drawn lettering] [in white] | The Complete Series [in white] | Read All of Harry's [in white] | Magical Adventures! [in white] | [publisher's device of a lantern, 10 by 7mm] [in black] | ARTHUR A. LEVINE BOOKS [in black] | [publisher's book device with 'SCHOLASTIC' in white on red panel, 5 by 45mm] | scholastic.com/harrypotter [in white] | [colour illustrations in three columns of six book designs]'. All on lavender blue.

All edges trimmed. Binding measurements: 204 by 134mm (wrappers), 204 by 36mm (spine).

Publication: 27 August 2013

Price: $14.99

Contents:
Harry Potter and the Goblet of Fire
   ('The villagers of Little Hangleton still called it "the Riddle House," even though…')

Notes:
See notes to A4(h) about this series.

The seven volumes in this edition were available individually or as a set issued in a slipcase. The set, presented in order, reveals a single illustration of Hogwarts castle across the seven spines. Scholastic released images of the new illustrations in a careful marketing campaign: the upper wrapper illustration for *Goblet of Fire* was revealed on 29 June 2013 at the American Library Association convention in Chicago.

The 'sneak preview' of *Order of the Phoenix* comprises only the first 16 (of 19) pages of chapter one.

Each chapter commences with a drop capital.

Copies: private collection (PWE)

FANTASTIC BEASTS & WHERE TO FIND THEM

A10(a) **FIRST ENGLISH EDITION** (2001)
(paperback)

FANTASTIC BEASTS | AND WHERE TO FIND THEM | NEWT SCAMANDER | *Special edition with a foreword by* | ALBUS DUMBLEDORE | [publisher's device of a dog, 8 by 14mm] | BLOOMSBURY | *in association with* | [publisher's device of a moon with face within a large black 'O']bscurus Books | 18a Diagon Alley, LONDON (All width centred)

Collation: 32 unsigned leaves bound in indeterminate gatherings; 177 by 111mm; [i-v] vi-vii [viii] ix-xxii 1-42

Page contents: [i] bookplate with picture of a blazing sun and 'THIS BOOK BELONGS TO | Harry Potter [facsimile handwriting]' within double ruled border, 76 by 54mm and below which are nine lines of facsimile handwriting; [ii] 'WITH THANKS | [new paragraph] Bloomsbury and Comic Relief would like to say a big thank you to all | these people for their time, dedication and gorgeous contributions. | [new paragraph] Production: Helena Coryndon and Penny Edwards | Cover design: Richard Horne | Text design, Obscurus logo design and typesetting: Polly Napper | Covers: George Over Limited | Paper supply: Borregaard Hellefos AS, McNaughton Publishing Papers Ltd | Cover board: Iggesund Paperboard Europe | Sales: David Ward, Kathleen Farrar, Barry Horrocks | and the Bloomsbury sales force | Distribution: Macmillan Distribution Limited | Marketing: Minna Fry, Rosamund de la Hey, Colette Whitehouse, and the | Bloomsbury

marketing team | Publicity: Katie Collins and the Bloomsbury publicity team and | Rebecca Salt and Nicky Stonehill at Colman Getty, Edinburgh | Copy-editing and proof-reading: Ingrid von Essen, proof-reading: Dick Clayton | Editor: Emma Matthewson | Christopher Little, Nigel Newton, Sarah Odedina, Colin Adams, | Burt Salvary, Fiddy Henderson, Ele Fountain, Dorchester Typesetting, | and booksellers around the world for their support. | [new paragraph] And of course J. K. Rowling for creating this book and so generously | giving all her royalties from it to Comic Relief. | [new paragraph] *Comic Relief (UK) was set up in 1985 by a group of British comedians to raise | funds for projects promoting social justice and helping to tackle poverty. Every single | penny Comic Relief receives from the public goes to work where it is most needed, | through internationally recognised organisations like Save the Children and Oxfam. | Money from worldwide sales of this book will go to help the very poorest | communities in the very poorest countries in the world; money from sales within the | UK will go to UK projects as well.* | *Comic Relief is a registered charity, number 326568.*' [iii] title-page; [iv] '[facsimile of a game of hangman, graffiti and a noughts and crosses game] | [new paragraph] Text copyright © J. K. Rowling 2001 | Illustrations and hand lettering copyright © J. K. Rowling 2001 | First published in Great Britain in 2001 | Bloomsbury Publishing Plc, 38 Soho Square, London, W1D 3HB | All rights reserved | The moral right of the author has been asserted | A CIP catalogue record of this book is available from the British Library | ISBN 0 7475 5466 8 | Printed in Scotland by Omnia Books Limited | 10 9 8 7 6 5 4 3 2 1'; [v] 'CONTENTS' (ten individual parts listed with titles and page references; also four lines of facsimile handwriting); vi 'ABOUT THE AUTHOR' ('NEWTON ('NEWT') Artemis Fido Scamander was born…'); vii-[viii] 'FOREWORD' ('I was deeply honoured when Newt Scamander asked me…') (signed, 'Albus Dumbledore' [facsimile signature]); ix-xxi 'INTRODUCTION' ('*Fantastic Beasts and Where to Find Them* represents the fruit of many years' travel…') (unsigned); xxii 'MINISTRY OF MAGIC CLASSIFICATIONS' ('The Department for the Regulation and Control of Magical Creatures…'); 1-42 text and illustrations

Paper: wove paper

Running title: none

Illustrations: there are eight illustrations throughout the text of magical creatures:
- p. 4   Billywig
- p. 10   Doxy
- p. 18   Fwooper
- p. 19   Gnome
- p. 23   Kelpie
- p. 33   Plimpy
- p. 35   Quintaped
- p. 37   Runespoor

There are examples of facsimile handwriting comprising marginal notes, graffiti, doodles and games on pp. [i], [iv], [v], vi, x, xiv, xix, xxii, 1, 2, 4, 5, 7, 12, 13, 19, 21, 23, 25, 29, 32, 34, 41 and 42.

Binding: pictorial wrappers, in red with 'stitching' in outline, 'clasps' in yellow at each corner and slashed effect in yellow.

On spine: 'FANTASTIC BEASTS & WHERE TO FIND THEM *Newt Scamander* Obscurus Books' (reading lengthways down spine). All in black on red.

On upper wrapper: 'FANTASTIC BEASTS [in yellow] | & [in yellow] | WHERE TO FIND THEM [in yellow] | *Newt Scamander* [in yellow] | Property of: [in black] | Harry Potter [facsimile signature in black]'). Lines 1-3 within ornate decorative panel, 47 by 92mm in yellow and white (all width centred) with lines 5-6 on white and grey angled panel, 32 by 55mm (off-set to the right).

On lower wrapper: '*A copy of Fantastic Beasts and Where to Find* | *Them resides in almost every wizarding household* | *in the country. Now,*

for a limited period only, Muggles | too have the chance to discover where the Quintaped lives, | what the Puffskein eats and why it is best not to leave | milk out for a Knarl. | [new paragraph] *Proceeds from the sale of this book will go to Comic | Relief, which means that the pounds and Galleons you | exchange for it will do magic beyond the powers of any | wizard. If you feel that this is insufficient reason to part | with your money, I can only hope that passing wizards | feel more charitable if they ever see you being attacked by | a Manticore.* | [new paragraph] Albus Dumbledore [facsimile signature] | [new paragraph] Comic Relief will give the money it gets from the sale of this book to | projects helping some of the poorest and most vulnerable people in | the poorest countries of the world. | [new paragraph] ['COMIC | RELIEF^UK' logo, diameter 20mm at left, with publishers' devices comprising '[publisher's device of a moon with face within a large black 'O']bscurus Books | *in association with* | [publisher's device of a dog, 6 by 10mm] | BLOOMSBURY' at centre, with 'At least £2 from the sale of | this book will go to Comic Relief', barcode in black on white panel, 21 by 37mm and price '£2.50 (14 Sickles 3 Knuts)' in black on light green panel, 7 by 37mm below barcode with both at right] | www.comicrelief. com/harrysbooks | www.bloomsbury.com/harrypotter | World Book Day £1 Book Tokens are not | redeemable against this charity book (UK and Ireland)'. All in black on red. The initial capital 'A' is a drop capital.

All edges trimmed. Binding measurements: 177 by 111mm (wrappers), 177 by 5mm (spine).

Publication: 12 March 2001 (simultaneous with A10(aa)) in an edition of 400,000 copies (confirmed by Bloomsbury)

Price: £2.50

Contents:
About the Author
    ('Newton ('Newt') Artemis Fido Scamander was born in 1897...')
Foreword
    ('I was deeply honoured when Newt Scamander asked me to write the foreword...')
    (signed, 'Albus Dumbledore' [facsimile signature])
Introduction
    ('*Fantastic Beasts and Where to Find Them* represents the fruit of many years' travel...')
Ministry of Magic Classifications
    ('The Department for the Regulation and Control of Magical Creatures...')
An A-Z of Fantastic Beasts
    ('Acromantula | *M.O.M. Classification: XXXXX...*')

Notes:
The Comic Relief books (see also A11) were announced on 16 October 2000. Rowling is reported to have said 'I've always had a secret hankering to write these two books. When Richard Curtis [the screenwriter and Comic Relief co-founder] wrote to me I thought it was a wonderful chance to be involved with a charity I've always supported'. Publication was to be for Red Nose Day on 16 March 2001.

The actual launch date of the books appears to have been 12 March 2001. On that day the author appeared on *Blue Peter* and participated in a question and answer session to launch the two titles.

Printing World reported on 26 March 2001 that the two books had a combined print run of two million copies and that 'the first million were printed free and the second million were printed at a discount'.

Bloomsbury cite a print run of 400,000 copies (in contrast to 2,000,000 copies of A11(a)). This may be explained by the different printers. A10(a) was printed in Scotland by Omnia Books Limited. No printer is given for A11(a) although Clays Ltd may be assumed.

The foreword, sections of the introduction and author note all commence with a drop capital.

Copies: BL (YA.2002.a.6217) stamped 3 Apr 2001; private collection (PWE)

A10(aa)   FIRST AMERICAN EDITION   (2001)
(paperback)

FANTASTIC BEASTS | AND WHERE TO FIND THEM | NEWT SCAMANDER | *Special edition with a foreword by* | ALBUS DUMBLEDORE | [publisher's device of a lantern, 11 by 8mm] | Arthur A. Levine Books | AN IMPRINT OF SCHOLASTIC PRESS | *in association with* | [publisher's device of a moon with face within a large black 'O']bscurus Books | 18a Diagon Alley, LONDON (All width centred)

Collation: 32 unsigned leaves bound in eight gatherings of four leaves; 194 by 133mm; [i-v] vi-vii [viii] ix-xxii 1-42

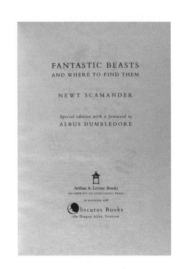

Page contents: [i] bookplate with picture of a blazing sun and 'THIS BOOK BELONGS TO | Harry Potter [facsimile handwriting]' within double ruled border, 75 by 54mm and below which are nine lines of facsimile handwriting; [ii] 'WITH THANKS | J. K. Rowling, Comic Relief U. K., and Scholastic Inc. | would like to thank the following individuals and organizations | for their generous contributions in this endeavor: | [new paragraph] HarperCollins Publishers | Command Web Offset | Quebecor World (USA Corp.) | R. R. Donnelley & Sons | Alliance Forest Product Inc. | Digicon Imaging, Inc. | J. M. Wechter & Associates, Inc. | Rose Printing Company | ICG/Holliston | Lehigh Press, Inc. | The Display Connection Inc. | Universal Printing Company | JY International Inc., Sales Division of LeeFung-Asco Printers | Berryville Graphics | Von Hoffmann | Leo Pacific Pier | Four Lakes Colorgraphics Inc. | Schneider National Inc. | Combined Express, Inc. | Fey Publishing | Delta Corrugated Paper Products Corporation | Webcrafters Inc. | Yellow Corporation | [new paragraph] [four-sided device] And of course, the publisher would especially like to thank | J. K.

Rowling for creating this book and so generously | giving all her royalties from it to Comic Relief.'; [iii] title-page; [iv] '[facsimile of a game of hangman, graffiti and a noughts and crosses game] | [new paragraph] Text and illustrations copyright © 2001 by J. K. Rowling. | All rights reserved. Published by Scholastic Press, a division of Scholastic Inc., *Publishers since 1920*. SCHOLASTIC, | SCHOLASTIC PRESS, and the LANTERN LOGO are trademarks and/or registered trademarks of Scholastic Inc. | HARRY POTTER and all related characters, names, and related indicia are trademarks of Warner Bros. | [new paragraph] No part of this publication may be reproduced, or stored in a retrieval system, or transmitted in any form or by any | means, electronic, mechanical, photocopying, recording, or otherwise, without written permission of the publisher. For | information regarding permissions, write to Scholastic Inc., Attention: Permissions Department, 555 Broadway, New York, | NY 10012. | [new paragraph] Scholastic Inc.'s net proceeds from the sale of this book will go to Comic Relief U.K.'s Harry's Books fund. | J.K. Rowling is donating all royalties to which she would be entitled. The purchase of this book is not tax deductible. Comic | Relief may be contacted at: Comic Relief, 5th Floor, Albert Embankment, London SE1 77P, England | (www.comicrelief.com). Comic Relief in the United Kingdom is not affiliated with the organization of the same name in | the United States. | ISBN 0-439-29501-7 | Library of Congress Cataloging-in-Publication Data Available | 12 11 10 9 8 7 6 5 4 3 2 1 1/0 2/0 3/0 4/0 5/0 | Printed in the U. S. A. 37 | First American edition, February 2001'; [v] 'CONTENTS' (ten individual parts listed with titles and page references; also four lines of facsimile handwriting); vi 'ABOUT THE AUTHOR' ('NEWTON ('NEWT') Artemis Fido Scamander was born…'); vii-[viii] 'FOREWORD' ('I was deeply honoured when Newt Scamander asked me…') (signed, 'Albus Dumbledore' [facsimile signature]); ix-xxi 'INTRODUCTION' ('*Fantastic Beasts and Where to Find Them* represents the fruit of many years' travel…') (unsigned); xxii 'MINISTRY OF MAGIC CLASSIFICATIONS' ('The Department for the Regulation and Control of Magical Creatures…'); 1-42 text and illustrations

Paper: wove paper

Running title: none

Illustrations: there are eight illustrations throughout the text of magical creatures:

- p. 4 Billywig
- p. 10 Doxy
- p. 18 Fwooper
- p. 19 Gnome
- p. 23 Kelpie
- p. 33 Plimpy
- p. 35 Quintaped
- p. 37 Runespoor

There are examples of facsimile handwriting comprising marginal notes, graffiti, doodles and games on pp. [i], [iv], [v], vi, x, xiv, xix, xxii, 1, 2, 4, 5, 7, 12, 13, 19, 21, 23, 25, 29, 32, 34, 40, 41 and 42.

Binding: pictorial wrappers, in red with 'stitching' in outline, 'clasps' in yellow at each corner and slashed effect in yellow.

On spine: 'FANTASTIC BEASTS & WHERE TO FIND THEM *Newt Scamander* Obscurus Books' (reading lengthways down spine) with publisher's book device in black and white on red panel, 5 by 4mm (horizontally at foot of spine). All in black.

On upper wrapper: 'FANTASTIC BEASTS [in yellow] | & [in yellow] | WHERE TO FIND THEM [in yellow] | *Newt Scamander* [in yellow] | Property of: [in black] | Harry Potter [facsimile signature in black]' . Lines 1-3 within ornate decorative panel, 47 by 113mm in yellow and white (all width centred) with lines 5-6 on white and grey angled panel, 35 by 68mm (off-set to the right).

On lower wrapper: '*A copy of Fantastic Beasts & Where to Find | Them resides in almost every wizarding household | in the country. Now, for a limited period only, Muggles | too have the chance to discover where the Quintaped lives, | what the Puffskein eats, and why it is best not to leave | milk out for a Knarl.* | [new paragraph] *Proceeds from the sale of this book will go to improving | and saving the lives of children around the world, which | means that the dollars and Galleons you exchange for it | will do magic beyond the powers of any wizard. If you | feel that this is insufficient reason to part with your | money, I can only hope most sincerely that passing wiz- | ards feel more charitable if they ever see you being | attacked by a Manticore.* | [new paragraph] Albus Dumbledore [facsimile signature] | [new paragraph] J. K. ROWLING and SCHOLASTIC INC.'s net proceeds from the | sale of this book will go to the Harry's Books fund to help needy | children in the poorest countries in the world. | [new paragraph] www.comicrelief.com/harrysbooks | [new paragraph] [device of a moon with face within a large black 'O']bscurus Books | *in association with* | [publisher's device of a lantern, 8 by 6mm] | *Arthur A. Levine Books* | AN IMPRINT OF SCHOLASTIC PRESS | [publisher's book device in white and 'SCHOLASTIC' in white on red panel, 7 by 43mm]'. All in black on red. To left of lines 20-23 is the 'COMIC | RELIEF^UK' logo, diameter 20mm, and to the right of lines 20-25 is a barcode with smaller barcode to the right (29501) all in black on white panel, 22 by 51mm and price '$3.99 US (14 Sickles 3 Knuts)' in black on light green panel, 7 by 51mm below barcode. The initial capital 'A' is a drop capital.

On inside upper wrapper: barcode with smaller barcode below (50399) all in black.

On inside lower wrapper: 'About Comic Relief: A note from J. K. Rowling' ('Comic Relief is one of Britain's most famous and successful charities.') (signed, 'JKRowling' [facsimile signature]) (all within single ruled border, 155 by 95mm). All in black.

All edges trimmed. Binding measurements: 194 by 133mm (wrappers), 194 by 4mm (spine).

Publication: 12 March 2001 (simultaneous with A10(a)) (see notes)

Price: $3.99

Contents:
About the Author
('Newton ('Newt') Artemis Fido Scamander was born in 1897...')
Foreword
('I was deeply honoured when Newt Scamander asked me to write the foreword...')
(signed, 'Albus Dumbledore' [facsimile signature])

Introduction
  ('*Fantastic Beasts and Where to Find Them* represents the fruit of many years' travel…')
Ministry of Magic Classifications
  ('The Department for the Regulation and Control of Magical Creatures…')
An A-Z of Fantastic Beasts
  ('Acromantula | M.O.M. *Classification: XXXXX…*')
About Comic Relief: A note from J.K. Rowling
  ('Comic Relief is one of Britain's most famous and successful charities…')
  (signed, 'JKRowling' [facsimile signature])

Notes:
The Comic Relief books (see also A11) were announced on 16 October 2000. The American *Publishers Weekly* described them as 'a welcome in-joke for Potter fans' (see *Publishers Weekly*, 23 October 2000, p. 20) and noted that 'the titles will be released worldwide (by Scholastic in the U.S., by Bloomsbury everywhere else) on March 16, Comic Relief's Red Nose Day'.

PR Newswire reported on 20 November 2000 the comments of Barbara Marcus, President of Scholastic. She stated 'Scholastic is so fortunate to be J.K.'s publisher and we're delighted to join her in supporting Comic Relief's Fund, which helps children around the world… Millions of children have been touched by J.K. Rowling's magical creation of Harry Potter. This initiative is an opportunity for those fans to express their goodwill and make a difference by helping other children who are less fortunate.' PR Newswire reported that the two books would 'have a worldwire on-sale date of February 13th'.

Despite these dates (and the publication month of February 2001 noted on the imprint page), publication appears to have been on 12 March 2001 (as with the English editions). A report entitled '2 Harry Potter Spinoffs Done for Charity' in the *New York Times* for 12 March noted that '… Scholastic in the United States and Bloomsbury in Britain, are releasing today two new books… to raise money for the British charity Comic Relief…'

In a March 2012 interview with me, the publisher Arthur A. Levine noted that the Comic Relief volumes were not Americanized. He stated '… those are exactly the same – we didn't have time or anything… Did I change the spellings? I might have… I might not have… Because, of course, the conceit is that it's a British school book anyway. It's not narrated…'

The note about Comic Relief is unique to the American edition. The text of the 'Foreword' has also been changed slightly to identify the charity as 'Comic Relief U.K.'

This is the first American publication to note Warner Brothers' trademark of 'Harry Potter and all related characters, names, and related indicia'. Although the film rights for the first two books were first purchased in October 1998, it took until early 2001 for Warners' rights to be noted in English editions. In her paper, 'J.K. Rowling and Harry Potter: Publishing, But Not as We Know It' (see *Journal of the Edinburgh Bibliographical Society*, number 1, Edinburgh: 2006, pp. 11-19), Diana Patterson notes that 'Warner Bros. negotiated something more significant than film rights, and which was clearly linked to controlling the look and visual feel of Potter material'. Significantly, Warner Brothers bought the copyright of the hand-drawn lettering used for 'Harry Potter' and, consequently, the films show a visual kinship with the American books.

The foreword, sections of the introduction and author note all commence with a drop capital.

Information provided by Nielsen BookData suggests that 'Turtleback Books' issued a 'hardback library binding' during March 2001. This edition has the ISBN 0-606-22140-9. No copies have been consulted.

Copies: private collection (PWE)

A10(b)   SECOND AMERICAN EDITION   (2001)
(hardback)

FANTASTIC BEASTS | AND WHERE TO FIND THEM | NEWT SCAMANDER | *Special edition with a foreword by* | ALBUS DUMBLEDORE | [publisher's device of a lantern, 12 by 9mm] | Arthur A. Levine Books | AN IMPRINT OF SCHOLASTIC PRESS | *in association with* | [publisher's device of a moon with face within a large black 'O']bscurus Books | 18a Diagon Alley, LONDON (All width centred)

Collation: 32 unsigned leaves bound in two gatherings of sixteen leaves; 193 by 131mm; [i-v] vi-vii [viii] ix-xxii 1-42

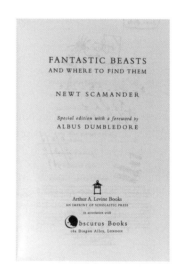

Page contents: [i] bookplate with picture of a blazing sun and 'THIS BOOK BELONGS TO | Harry Potter [facsimile handwriting]' within double ruled border, 83 by 59mm and below which are nine lines of facsimile handwriting; [ii] 'About Comic Relief: A note from J. K. Rowling' ('Comic Relief is one of Britain's most famous and successful charities.') (signed, 'JKRowling' [facsimile signature]) (all within single ruled border, 171 by 105mm); [iii] title-page; [iv] '[facsimile of a game of hangman, graffiti and a noughts and crosses game] | [new paragraph] Text copyright © 2001 by J.K. Rowling. [point] Illustrations and hand lettering copyright © 2001 by J.K. Rowling. | All rights reserved. Published by Scholastic Press, a division of Scholastic Inc., *Publishers since 1920*. SCHOLASTIC, | SCHOLASTIC PRESS, and the LANTERN LOGO are trademarks and/or registered trademarks of Scholastic Inc. | HARRY POTTER and all related characters, names, and related indicia are trademarks of Warner Bros. | [new paragraph] No part of this publication may be reproduced, or stored in a retrieval system, or transmitted in any form or by any | means, electronic, mechanical, photocopying, recording, or otherwise, without written permission of the publisher. For | information regarding permissions, write to Scholastic

Inc., Attention: Permissions Department, 555 Broadway, New York, | NY 10012. | [new paragraph] Scholastic Inc. has arranged for twenty percent of the retail sales price less taxes from the sale of this book to go to Comic | Relief U.K.'s Harry's Books fund. J. K. Rowling is donating all royalties to which she would be entitled. The purchase of this | book is not tax deductible. Comic Relief may be contacted at: Comic Relief, 5th Floor, Albert Embankment, London SE1 | 77P, England (www. comicrelief.com). Comic Relief in the United Kingdom is not affiliated with the organization of the | same name in the United States. | [new paragraph] ISBN 0-439-32160-3 | Library of Congress Cataloging-in-Publication Data Available | 12 11 10 9 8 7 6 5 4 3 2 1 01 02 03 04 05 | Printed in the U. S. A. 37 | First hardback boxset edition, September 2001'; [v] 'CONTENTS' (ten individual parts listed with titles and page references; also four lines of facsimile handwriting); vi 'ABOUT THE AUTHOR' ('NEWTON ('NEWT') Artemis Fido Scamander was born…'); vii-[viii] 'FOREWORD' ('I was deeply honoured when Newt Scamander asked me…') (signed, 'Albus Dumbledore' [facsimile signature]); ix-xxi 'INTRODUCTION' ("*Fantastic Beasts and Where to Find Them* represents the fruit of many years' travel…') (unsigned); xxii 'MINISTRY OF MAGIC CLASSIFICATIONS' ('The Department for the Regulation and Control of Magical Creatures…'); 1-42 text and illustrations

Paper: wove paper

Running title: none

Illustrations: there are eight illustrations throughout the text of magical creatures:
>   p. 4   Billywig
>   p. 10 Doxy
>   p. 18 Fwooper
>   p. 19 Gnome
>   p. 23 Kelpie
>   p. 33 Plimpy
>   p. 35 Quintaped
>   p. 37 Runespoor

There are examples of facsimile handwriting comprising marginal notes, graffiti, doodles and games on pp. [i], [iv], [v], vi, x, xiv, xix, xxii, 1, 2, 4, 5, 7, 12, 13, 19, 21, 23, 25, 29, 32, 34, 40, 41 and 42.

Binding: pictorial boards, in red with 'stitching' in outline, 'clasps' in yellow at each corner and slashed effect in yellow.

  On spine: 'FANTASTIC BEASTS & WHERE TO FIND THEM *Newt Scamander* Obscurus Books' (reading lengthways down spine). All in black.

  On upper cover: 'FANTASTIC BEASTS [in yellow] | & [in yellow] | WHERE TO FIND THEM [in yellow] | *Newt Scamander* [in yellow] | Property of: [in black] | Harry Potter [facsimile signature in black]' Lines 1-3 within ornate decorative panel, 50 by 114mm in yellow and white (all width centred) with lines 5-6 on white and grey angled panel, 35 by 69mm (off-set to the right).

On lower cover: 'A copy of Fantastic Beasts & Where to Find | Them resides in almost every wizarding household | in the country. Now, for a limited period only, Muggles | too have the chance to discover where the Quintaped lives, | what the Puffskein eats, and why it is best not to leave | milk out for a Knarl. | [new paragraph] Proceeds from the sale of this book will go to improving | and saving the lives of children around the world, which | means that the dollars and Galleons you exchange for it | will do magic beyond the powers of any wizard. If you feel | that this is insufficient reason to part with your money, | I can only hope most sincerely that passing wizards feel | more charitable if they ever see you being attacked by a | Manticore. | [new paragraph] Albus Dumbledore [facsimile signature] | [new paragraph] J. K. ROWLING and SCHOLASTIC INC. have arranged for twenty | percent of the retail sales price less taxes of this book to go to the | Harry's Books fund to help needy children in the poorest countries in | the world. | [new paragraph] www.comicrelief.com/harrysbooks | [new paragraph] [three publisher's devices in three columns, in the first column is '[device of a moon with face within a large black 'O']bscurus Books | in association with', in the second column is '[publisher's device of a lantern, 8 by 6mm] | Arthur A. Levine Books | AN IMPRINT OF SCHOLASTIC PRESS' and in the third column is 'COMIC | RELIEF^{UK}' logo, diameter 20mm] | [new paragraph] [publisher's book device in white and 'SCHOLASTIC' in white on red panel, 7 by 43mm] ['ISBN 0-439-32160-3' in black on yellow panel, 7 by 37mm]'. All in black on red. The initial capital 'A' is a drop capital.

All edges trimmed. Binding measurements: 201 by 136mm (covers), 201 by 19mm (spine). End-papers: red wove paper.

Dust-jacket: none

Slipcase: thick card slipcase covered in paper printed in purple.

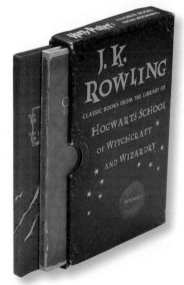

On spine: 'J. K. | Rowling | [star in yellow and orange] | Fantastic | Beasts & | Where to | Find Them | [star in yellow and orange] | Quidditch | Through | the Ages | [publisher's device of a lantern, 16 by 12mm, in yellow and white] | Levine | [rule] | Scholastic'. All in yellow.

On upper side: 'J. K. | ROWLING | CLASSIC BOOKS FROM THE LIBRARY OF | HOGWARTS SCHOOL | OF WITCHCRAFT | AND WIZARDRY' together with device of five stars in yellow and orange to left and device of five stars in yellow and orange to right, 'Property of: [in black] | Harry Potter [facsimile signature in black]' (on white and grey angled panel, 35 by 67mm) and publisher's book device in white and 'SCHOLASTIC' (in white on red panel, 6 by 35mm). All in yellow.

On lower side: 'J. K. | ROWLING | CLASSIC BOOKS FROM THE LIBRARY OF | HOGWARTS SCHOOL | OF WITCHCRAFT | AND WIZARDRY' together with device of five stars in yellow and orange to left and device of five stars in yellow and orange to right and circular red wax stamp stating 'PROPERTY OF | HOGWARTS | LIBRARY'. All in yellow.

On top edge: 'Harry Potter's [hand-drawn lettering] | FAVOURITE BOOKS | FROM HOGWARTS'. All in yellow.

On lower edge: '$12.95 ISBN 0-439-32162-X | Box illustration © 2001 by Scholastic Inc. | Illustration by Peter Bollinger' with barcode with smaller barcode to the right (51295) all in black on yellow panel, 18 by 48mm. All in yellow. The edges of the slipcase feature a metallic effect encasing in brown.

Publication: September 2001 (see notes)

Price: $12.95 [together with A11(b)]

Contents:
About Comic Relief: A note from J.K. Rowling
    ('Comic Relief is one of Britain's most famous and successful charities…')
    (signed, 'JKRowling' [facsimile signature])
About the Author
    ('Newton ('Newt') Artemis Fido Scamander was born in 1897…')
Foreword
    ('I was deeply honoured when Newt Scamander asked me to write the foreword…')
    (signed, 'Albus Dumbledore' [facsimile signature])
Introduction
    ('*Fantastic Beasts and Where to Find Them* represents the fruit of many years' travel…')
Ministry of Magic Classifications
    ('The Department for the Regulation and Control of Magical Creatures…')
An A-Z of Fantastic Beasts
    ('Acromantula | *M.O.M. Classification: XXXXX*…')

Notes:
The note about Comic Relief is unique to the American edition. The text of the 'Foreword' has also been changed slightly to identify the charity as 'Comic Relief U.K.'

Although no publication date is recorded, 1 September 2001 is assumed. In an email to me from January 2013 Arthur A. Levine noted that 'I'm fairly certain that we didn't have strict "on sale" dates… the publication "day" would simply be the first on the month listed.'

The foreword, sections of the introduction and author note all commence with a drop capital.

Copies: private collection (PWE)

FANTASTIC | BEASTS & | WHERE TO | FIND THEM | NEWT SCAMANDER | BY | J.K.ROWLING | [publisher's device of a dog, 9 by 14mm] | BLOOMSBURY | *in association with* | [publisher's device of a moon with face within a large black 'O']bscurus Books | 18a Diagon Alley, LONDON (All width centred)

Collation: 64 unsigned leaves bound in indeterminate gatherings; 196 by 127mm; [i-xii] xiii-xiv [xv-xvi] xvii-xxxiii [xxxiv] xxxv [xxxvi] [1-2] 3-5 [6] 7-9 [10] 11-14 [15-16] 17-25 [26] 27 [28] 29-31 [32] 33-35 [36] 37 [38] 39 [40] 41 [42] 43-44 [45-46] 47-50 [51-52] 53-55 [56] 57 [58] 59 [60] 61-64 [65-66] 67-68 [69-70] 71-73 [74] 75-77 [78] 79 [80] 81 [82] 83 [84] 85 [86] 87-88 [89-92]

Page contents: [i] bookplate with picture of a blazing sun and 'THIS BOOK BELONGS TO | Harry Potter [facsimile handwriting]' within double ruled border, 76 by 54mm and below which are nine lines of facsimile handwriting; [ii] blank; [iii] half-title: 'FANTASTIC | BEASTS & | WHERE TO FIND THEM'; [iv] *'Titles available in the Harry Potter series | (in reading order):* | Harry Potter and the Philosopher's Stone | Harry Potter and the Chamber of Secrets | Harry Potter and the Prisoner of Azkaban | Harry Potter and the Goblet of Fire | Harry Potter and the Order of the Phoenix | Harry Potter and the Half-Blood Prince | Harry Potter and the Deathly Hallows | [new paragraph] *Titles available in the Harry Potter series | (in Latin):* | Harry Potter and the Philosopher's Stone | Harry Potter and the Chamber of Secrets | [new paragraph] *(in Welsh, Ancient Greek and Irish):* | Harry Potter and the Philosopher's Stone | [new paragraph] *Other titles available:* | Quidditch Through the Ages | The Tales of Beedle the Bard'; [v] title-page; [vi] 'Text copyright © J. K. Rowling 2001 | Illustration and hand lettering copyright © J. K. Rowling 2001 | [new paragraph] First published in Great Britain in 2001 | This edition published in 2009 | [new paragraph] Bloomsbury Publishing Plc | 36 Soho Square, London, W1D 3QY | [new paragraph] Bloomsbury Publishing, London, Berlin and New York | [new paragraph] The moral right of the author has been asserted | [new paragraph] All rights reserved | No part of this publication may be reproduced or | transmitted by any means, electronic, mechanical, photocopying | or otherwise, without the prior permission of the publisher | [new paragraph] A CIP catalogue record of this book is available from the British Library | [new paragraph] ISBN 978 1 4088 0301 1 | [new paragraph] The paper this book is printed on is certified by the © 1996 Forest | Stewardship Council A.C. (FSC). It is ancient-forest friendly. The | printer holds FSC chain of custody SGS-COC-2061 | [Forest Stewardship Council logo, 5 by 6mm together with © symbol and text: 'FSC' and, to the right 'Mixed Sources | Product group from well-managed | forests and other controlled sources | [new paragraph] www.fsc.org Cert no. SGS-COC-2061 | © 1996 Forest Stewardship Council'] | [new paragraph] Printed in Great Britain by Clays Ltd, St Ives Plc | [new paragraph] 1 3 5 7 9 10 8 6 4 2 | www.bloomsbury.com | [new paragraph] *Comic Relief (UK) was set up in 1985 by a group of British comedians to raise funds | for projects promoting social justice and helping to tackle poverty. Every single penny | Comic Relief receives from the public goes to work where it is most needed, through | internationally recognised organisations like Save the Children and Oxfam.*

Money | from worldwide sales of this book will go to help the very poorest communities in the | very poorest countries in the world; money from sales within the UK will go to UK | projects as well. | Comic Relief is a registered charity, number 326568.'; [vii] 'With thanks to J. K. Rowling for creating | this book and so generously giving all her | royalties to Comic Relief | [illustration of a Billywig]'; [viii] blank; [ix] illustration of a Plimpy; [x] four lines of facsimile handwriting; [xi] 'Contents' (ten individual parts listed with titles and page references); [xii] blank; xiii-[xv] 'FOREWORD' ('I was deeply honoured when Newt Scamander asked me...') (signed, 'Albus Dumbledore' [facsimile signature]); [xvi] blank; xvii-[xxxiv] 'INTRODUCTION' ('*Fantastic Beasts and Where to Find Them* represents the fruit of many years' travel...') (unsigned); [xxxv] 'MINISTRY OF MAGIC | CLASSIFICATIONS'; [xxxvi] blank; [1] divisional title: 'AN A-Z | OF | FANTASTIC BEASTS' (within decorative border); [2] blank; 3-88 text and illustrations (with blank pages); [89] illustration of a Quintaped; [90] blank; [91] 'COMIC | RELIEF' logo, diameter 23mm and text; [92] facsimile of a game of hangman, graffiti and a noughts and crosses game

Paper: wove paper

Running title: none

Illustrations: there are eight illustrations throughout the text of magical creatures:
    p. 8   Billywig
    p. 18   Doxy
    p. 31   Fwooper
    p. 34   Gnome
    p. 44   Kelpie
    p. 62   Plimpy
    p. 68   Quintaped
    p. 72   Runespoor
Three illustrations are repeated outside the text for additional adornment (Billywig on p. [vii], a part of the Plimpy illustration on p. [ix] and a Quintaped on p. [89]). In addition, letters of the alphabet (lacking letters V, X and Z) are represented in illustrated panels embellished with foliage. A drop capital 'N' is intertwined with an illustration of a newt on p. 87. There are examples of facsimile handwriting comprising marginal notes, graffiti, doodles and games on pp. [i], [x], xviii, xxiv, xxxii, xxxv, 3, 4, 8, 9, 12, 22, 23, 34, [38], 43, 48, 55, 62, 64, 79, 83, 85, 87 and [92].

Binding: pictorial wrappers, in mottled brown.
    On spine: 'FANTASTIC BEASTS & WHERE TO FIND THEM J.K.ROWLING BLOOMSBURY [publisher's device of the head of a dog, 4 by 5mm]' (reading lengthways down spine). All in brown.
    On upper wrapper: 'FANTASTIC | BEASTS & | WHERE TO | FIND THEM | NEWT SCAMANDER | [coloured illustration of Hogwarts crest with legend 'DRAGO DORMIENS NUNQUAM TITILLANDUS' on banner, 54 by 67mm] | BY | J.K.ROWLING | FROM THE WORLD OF | HARRY POTTER' (all within single broken ruled border, 186 by 116mm) (all width centred). All in brown.
    On lower wrapper: 'A copy of *Fantastic Beasts & Where to Find Them* | resides in almost every wizarding household | in the country. Now Muggles too have the chance | to discover where the

Quintaped lives, what the | Puffskein eats and why it is best not to leave milk | out for a Knarl. | [new paragraph] Proceeds from the sale of this book will go to | Comic Relief, which means that the pounds and | Galleons you exchange for it will do magic beyond | the powers of any wizard. If you feel that this is | insufficient reason to part with your money, I can | only hope that passing wizards feel more charitable | if they see you being attacked by a Manticore. | Albus Dumbledore [facsimile signature] | [new paragraph] Comic Relief will give the money | it gets from the sale of this book | to projects helping some of the | poorest and most vulnerable | people in the poorest countries | of the world. | ['COMIC | RELIEF' logo, diameter 17mm, at centre, with publishers' devices comprising '[publisher's device of a moon with face within a large black 'O']bscurus Books | *in association with* | [publisher's device of a dog, 6 by 11mm] | BLOOMSBURY' at right | '[barcode] | £4.99 (1 Galleon 11 Sickles)' at left, '[Forest Stewardship Council logo, 7 by 8mm together with © symbol] | FSC | Mixed Sources | Product group from well-managed | forests and other controlled sources | [new paragraph] Cert no. SGS-COC-2061 | www.fsc.org | © 1996 Forest Stewardship Council' at centre, and '£1.15 from the sale of this book will | go to Comic Relief | [new paragraph] World Book Day £1 Book Tokens | are not redeemable against this | charity book (UK and Ireland) | [new paragraph] www.comicrelief.com | www.bloomsbury.com/harrypotter' at right and all in black on white panel, 27 by 93mm] | Comic Relief, registered charity 326568 (England/Wales); SCO39730 (Scotland)' (all within single broken ruled border, 186 by 115mm). All in brown. The initial capital 'A' is a drop capital.

All edges trimmed. Binding measurements: 196 by 127mm (wrappers), 196 by 11mm (spine).

Publication: 6 July 2009 in an edition of 56,700 copies (confirmed by Bloomsbury)

Price: £4.99

Contents:
Foreword
    ('I was deeply honoured when Newt Scamander asked me to write the foreword…')
    (signed, 'Albus Dumbledore' [facsimile signature])
Introduction
    ('*Fantastic Beasts and Where to Find Them* represents the fruit of many years' travel…')
Ministry of Magic Classifications
    ('The Department for the Regulation and Control of Magical Creatures…')
An A-Z of Fantastic Beasts
    ('A | Acromantula | M.O.M. *Classification: XXXXX*…')
About the Author
    ('Newton ('Newt') Artemis Fido Scamander was born in 1897…')

Notes:
The foreword, sections of the introduction and author note all commence with a drop capital.

Copies: BL (YK.2010.a.21574) stamped 22 Jun 2009

Reprints include:
25

FANTASTIC | BEASTS & | WHERE TO | FIND THEM | [illustration of Hogwarts crest with legend 'DRAGO DORMIENS NUNQUAM TITILLANDUS' on banner, 40 by 49mm] | NEWT | SCAMANDER | [publisher's device of a dog, 5 by 9mm] | BLOOMSBURY | *in association with* | [publisher's device of a moon with face within a large black 'O']bscurus Books | 18a Diagon Alley, LONDON (All width centred)

Collation: 64 unsigned leaves bound in eight gatherings of eight leaves; 198 by 128mm; [i-xii] xiii-xiv [xv-xvi] xvii-xxxiii [xxxiv] xxxv [xxxvi] [1-2] 3-5 [6] 7-9 [10] 11-14 [15-16] 17-25 [26] 27 [28] 29-31 [32] 33-35 [36] 37 [38] 39 [40] 41 [42] 43-44 [45-46] 47-50 [51-52] 53-55 [56] 57 [58] 59 [60] 61-64 [65-66] 67-68 [69-70] 71-73 [74] 75-77 [78] 79 [80] 81 [82] 83 [84] 85 [86] 87-88 [89-92]

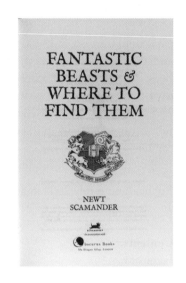

Page contents: [i] bookplate with picture of a blazing sun and 'THIS BOOK BELONGS TO | Harry Potter [facsimile handwriting]' within double ruled border, 76 by 54mm and below which are nine lines of facsimile handwriting; [ii] blank; [iii] half-title: 'FANTASTIC | BEASTS & | WHERE TO | FIND THEM'; [iv] *'Titles available in the Harry Potter series | (in reading order):* | Harry Potter and the Philosopher's Stone | Harry Potter and the Chamber of Secrets | Harry Potter and the Prisoner of Azkaban | Harry Potter and the Goblet of Fire | Harry Potter and the Order of the Phoenix | Harry Potter and the Half-Blood Prince | Harry Potter and the Deathly Hallows | [new paragraph] *Titles available in the Harry Potter series | (in Latin):* | Harry Potter and the Philosopher's Stone | Harry Potter and the Chamber of Secrets | *(in Welsh, Ancient Greek and Irish):* | Harry Potter and the Philosopher's Stone | [new paragraph] *Also available | (in aid of Comic Relief):* | Fantastic Beasts and Where to Find Them | Quidditch Through the Ages | *(in aid of Lumos):* | The Tales of Beedle the Bard'; [v] title-page; [vi] 'Text copyright © J. K. Rowling 2001 | Illustration and hand lettering copyright © J. K. Rowling 2001 | [new paragraph] First published in Great Britain in 2001 | This edition published in 2012 | [new paragraph] Bloomsbury Publishing Plc | 50 Bedford Square, London, WC1B 3DP | [new paragraph] Bloomsbury Publishing, London, New Delhi, New York and Sydney | [new paragraph] The moral right of the author has been asserted | [new paragraph] All rights reserved | No part of this publication may be reproduced or | transmitted by any means, electronic, mechanical, photocopying | or otherwise, without the prior permission of the publisher | [new paragraph] A CIP catalogue record of this book is available from the British Library | [new paragraph] ISBN 978 1 4088 3505 0 [new paragraph] [Forest Stewardship Council logo, 6 by 7mm together with ® symbol and text: 'FSC | www.fsc.org' with 'MIX | Paper from | responsible sources | FSC® C008047' to the right and all within single ruled border with rounded corners, 12 by 26mm] | [new paragraph] Printed in China by C&C Offset Printing Co Ltd, Shenzhen, Guangdong | [new paragraph] 1 3 5 7 9 10 8 6 4 2 | [new paragraph] www.bloomsbury.com | [new paragraph] *Comic Relief (UK) was set up in 1985 by a group of British comedians to raise | funds for projects promoting social justice and helping to tackle poverty. Money from | worldwide sales of this book will go to help the very poorest communities in the very | poorest countries in the world. Money from sales within the UK will go to UK | projects as well. | Comic Relief (UK) is a registered charity number 326568 (England & Wales) and | SCO39730 (Scotland).*'; [vii] 'With thanks to J. K. Rowling for creating | this book and so generously giving all her | royalties to Comic Relief | [illustration of a Billywig]'; [viii] blank; [ix] illustration of a Plimpy; [x] four lines of facsimile handwriting; [xi] 'CONTENTS' (ten individual parts listed with titles and page references); [xii] blank; xiii-[xv] 'FOREWORD' ('I was deeply honoured when Newt Scamander asked me…') (signed, 'Albus Dumbledore' [facsimile signature]); [xvi] blank; xvii-[xxxiv] 'INTRODUCTION' ('*Fantastic Beasts and Where to Find Them* represents the fruit of many years' travel…') (unsigned); [xxxv] 'MINISTRY OF MAGIC | CLASSIFICATIONS'; [xxxvi] blank; [1] divisional title: 'AN A-Z | OF | FANTASTIC BEASTS' (within decorative border); [2] blank; 3-88 text and illustrations (with blank pages); [89] illustration of a Quintaped; [90] blank; [91] 'COMIC | RELIEF^UK' logo and text; [92] facsimile of a game of hangman, graffiti and a noughts and crosses game

Paper: wove paper

Running title: none

Illustrations: there are eight illustrations throughout the text of magical creatures:

- p. 8 Billywig
- p. 18 Doxy
- p. 31 Fwooper
- p. 34 Gnome
- p. 44 Kelpie
- p. 62 Plimpy
- p. 68 Quintaped
- p. 72 Runespoor

Three illustrations are repeated outside the text for additional adornment (Billywig on p. [vii], a part of the Plimpy illustration on p. [ix] and a Quintaped on p. [89]). In addition, letters of the alphabet (lacking letters V, X and Z) are represented in illustrated panels embellished with foliage. A drop capital 'N' is intertwined with an illustration of a newt on p. 87. There are examples of facsimile handwriting comprising marginal notes, graffiti, doodles and games on pp. [i], [x], xviii, xxiv, xxxii, xxxv, 3, 4, 8, 9, 12, 22, 23, 34, [38], 43, 48, 55, 62, 64, 79, 83, 85, 87 and [92].

Binding: decorated boards in 'half-bound' style with spine and corner pieces in green/brown and with covers in light green.

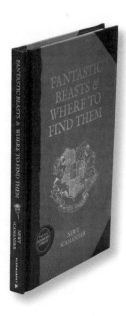

On spine: 'NEWT | FANTASTIC BEASTS & WHERE TO FIND THEM [illustration of a Billywig, 8 by 15mm, in yellow] BLOOMSBURY [publisher's device of the head of a dog, 3 by 4mm] | SCAMANDER' (reading lengthways down spine). All in gilt.

On upper cover: 'FANTASTIC | BEASTS & | WHERE TO | FIND THEM | [illustration of Hogwarts crest with legend 'DRAGO DORMIENS NUNQUAM TITILLANDUS' on banner, 61 by 75mm] | NEWT | SCAMANDER' (all width centred). All in gilt with the exception of the illustration of the crest which is in yellow. To the left of the author is a circular 'wax' stamp in green and black stating '*Property of* | HOGWARTS | LIBRARY' within circular single ruled border, diameter 20mm, with border and lettering in gilt.

On lower cover: '[illustration of Hogwarts crest with legend 'DRAGO DORMIENS NUNQUAM TITILLANDUS' on banner, 25 by 31mm] | A copy of *Fantastic Beasts & Where to Find Them* | resides in almost every wizarding household | in the country. Now Muggles too have | the chance to discover where the Quintaped lives, | what the Puffskein eats and why it is best not | to leave milk out for a Knarl. | [new paragraph] Proceeds from the sale of this book will go to | Comic Relief, which means that the pounds and | Galleons you exchange for it will do magic beyond | the powers of any wizard. If you feel that this | is insufficient reason to part with your money, | I can only hope that passing wizards feel more | charitable if they see you being attacked | by a Manticore. | Albus Dumbledore [facsimile signature] | [new paragraph] [three columns, in the first column is 'Comic Relief will give the money | it gets from the sale of this book | to projects helping some of the | poorest and most vulnerable | people in the UK and some of the | poorest countries of the world.', in the second column is 'COMIC | RELIEF^UK' logo, diameter 15mm and in the third column is '[publisher's device of a moon with face within a large black 'O']bscurus Books | *in association with* | [publisher's device of a dog, 5 by 9mm] | BLOOMSBURY'] | [new paragraph] [three columns, in the first column is the barcode, in the second column is '[Forest Stewardship Council logo, 6 by 7mm] | FSC | MIX | Paper | FSC® C008047' all within single ruled border with rounded corners, 17 by 12mm, and in the third column is 'www.comicrelief.com | www.bloomsbury.com/harrypotter | www.pottermore.com'] | Comic Relief, registered charity 326568 (England/Wales); SCO39730 (Scotland)'. All in yellow with the exception of the Comic Relief logo which is in black and red on white and the final three columns which are in black on a white panel, 23 by 82mm.

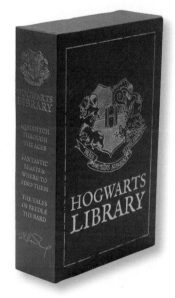

All edges trimmed. Green and yellow sewn bands at head and foot of spine. Binding measurements: 205 by 128mm (covers), 205 by 28mm (spine). End-papers: wove paper. The green/brown spine colour continues onto the covers by approximately 13mm.

Dust-jacket: none

Slipcase: card slipcase covered in red paper.

On spine: '[illustration of Hogwarts crest with legend 'DRAGO DORMIENS NUNQUAM TITILLANDUS' on banner, 30 by 36mm] | [new paragraph] HOGWARTS | LIBRARY | [new paragraph] QUIDDITCH | THROUGH | THE AGES | [new paragraph] FANTASTIC | BEASTS & | WHERE TO | FIND THEM | [new paragraph] THE TALES | OF BEEDLE | THE BARD | [new paragraph] JKRowling [facsimile signature]' (all width centred). All in gilt.

On upper and lower sides: '[illustration of Hogwarts crest with legend 'DRAGO DORMIENS NUNQUAM TITILLANDUS' on banner, 80 by 98mm] | [new paragraph] HOGWARTS | LIBRARY' (all within single broken ruled border, 187 by 117mm) (all width centred). All in gilt.

Top and lower edges: blank.

Publication: 11 October 2012 in an edition of 77,200 copies (confirmed by Bloomsbury)

Price: £25 [together with A11(d) and A15(b)]

Contents:
Foreword
('I was deeply honoured when Newt Scamander asked me to write the foreword...')
(signed, 'Albus Dumbledore' [facsimile signature])
Introduction
(*Fantastic Beasts and Where to Find Them* represents the fruit of many years' travel...')
Ministry of Magic Classifications
('The Department for the Regulation and Control of Magical Creatures...')
An A-Z of Fantastic Beasts
('A | Acromantula | M.O.M. *Classification: XXXXX*...')
About the Author
('Newton ('Newt') Artemis Fido Scamander was born in 1897...')

Notes:
The foreword, sections of the introduction and author note all commence with a drop capital.

Copies: private collection (PWE)

A10(e)   THIRD AMERICAN EDITION   (2013)
(hardback)

FANTASTIC | BEASTS & | WHERE TO | FIND THEM | [illustration of Hogwarts crest with legend 'DRAGO DORMIENS NUNQUAM TITILLANDUS' on banner, 40 by 49mm] | NEWT | SCAMANDER | [publisher's device of a lantern, 9 by 7mm] | ARTHUR A. LEVINE BOOKS | An Imprint of Scholastic Inc. | *in association with* | [publisher's device of a moon with face within a large black 'O']bscurus Books | 18a Diagon Alley, LONDON (All width centred)

Collation: 64 unsigned leaves bound in eight gatherings of eight leaves; 197 by 127mm; [i-xii] xiii-xiv [xv-xvi] xvii-xxxiii [xxxiv] xxxv [xxxvi] [1-2] 3-5 [6] 7-9 [10] 11-14 [15-16] 17-25 [26] 27

[28] 29-31 [32] 33-35 [36] 37 [38] 39 [40] 41 [42] 43-44 [45-46] 47-50 [51-52] 53-55 [56] 57 [58] 59 [60] 61-64 [65-66] 67-68 [69-70] 71-73 [74] 75-77 [78] 79 [80] 81 [82] 83 [84] 85 [86] 87-88 [89-92]

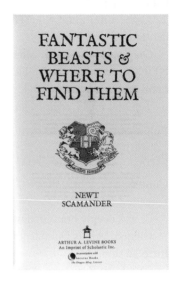

Page contents: [i] bookplate with picture of a blazing sun and 'THIS BOOK BELONGS TO | Harry Potter [facsimile handwriting]' within double ruled border, 76 by 54mm and below which are nine lines of facsimile handwriting; [ii] blank; [iii] half-title: 'FANTASTIC | BEASTS & | WHERE TO | FIND THEM'; [iv] *'Titles available in the Harry Potter series | (in reading order):* | Harry Potter and the Sorcerer's Stone | Harry Potter and the Chamber of Secrets | Harry Potter and the Prisoner of Azkaban | Harry Potter and the Goblet of Fire | Harry Potter and the Order of the Phoenix | Harry Potter and the Half-Blood Prince | Harry Potter and the Deathly Hallows | [new paragraph] *Also available* | *(in aid of Comic Relief):* | Fantastic Beasts and Where to Find Them | Quidditch Through the Ages | *(in aid of Lumos):* | The Tales of Beedle the Bard'; [v] title-page; [vi] 'Text copyright © J. K. Rowling 2001 | Illustration and hand lettering copyright © J. K. Rowling 2001 | HARRY POTTER and all related characters | and elements are TM of and © WBEI. | Harry Potter Publishing Rights © J. K. Rowling | [new paragraph] All rights reserved. Published by Arthur A. Levine Books, an imprint of | Scholastic Inc., *Publishers since 1920.* SCHOLASTIC, the LANTERN | LOGO, and associated logos are trademarks and/or registered trademarks of | Scholastic Inc. | [new paragraph] No part of this publication may be reproduced, stored in a retrieval system, | or transmitted in any form or by any means, electronic, mechanical, | photocopying, recording, or otherwise, without written permission of the | publisher. For information regarding permission, write to Scholastic Inc., | Attention: Permissions Department, 557 Broadway, New York, NY 10012. | [new paragraph] ISBN 978-0-545-61540-2 | [new paragraph] 12 11 10 9 8 7 6 5 4 3 2 1   13 14 15 16 17 | [new paragraph] Printed in China 95 | This edition first printing, November 2013 | [new paragraph] *From every sale of the* Hogwarts Library, *Scholastic will donate twenty percent of* | *the suggested retail sales price less taxes of this boxed set to two charities selected by* | *the author J. K. Rowling: Lumos, a charity founded by J. K. Rowling that works to* | *end the institutionalization of children (wearelumos.org), and Comic Relief,* | *a UK-based charity that strives to create a just world free from poverty* | *(www.comicrelief.com). Purchase of this book is not tax deductible.*'; [vii] 'With thanks to J. K. Rowling for creating | this book and so generously giving all her | royalties to Comic Relief | [illustration of a Billywig]'; [viii] blank; [ix] illustration of a Plimpy; [x] four lines of facsimile handwriting; [xi] 'CONTENTS' (ten individual parts listed with titles and page references); [xii] blank; xiii-[xv] 'FOREWORD' ('I was deeply honoured when Newt Scamander asked me…') (signed, 'Albus Dumbledore' [facsimile signature]); [xvi] blank; xvii-[xxxiv] 'INTRODUCTION' (*'Fantastic Beasts and Where to Find Them* represents the fruit of many years' travel…') (unsigned); [xxxv] 'MINISTRY OF MAGIC | CLASSIFICATIONS'; [xxxvi] blank; [1] divisional title: 'AN A-Z | OF | FANTASTIC BEASTS' (within decorative border); [2] blank; 3-88 text and illustrations (with blank pages); [89] illustration of a Quintaped; [90] blank; [91] 'COMIC | RELIEF^UK' logo and text; [92] facsimile of a game of hangman, graffiti and a noughts and crosses game

Paper: wove paper

Running title: none

Illustrations: there are eight illustrations throughout the text of magical creatures:
- p. 8   Billywig
- p. 18   Doxy
- p. 31   Fwooper
- p. 34   Gnome
- p. 44   Kelpie
- p. 62   Plimpy
- p. 68   Quintaped
- p. 72   Runespoor

Three illustrations are repeated outside the text for additional adornment (Billywig on p. [vii], a part of the Plimpy illustration on p. [ix] and a Quintaped on p. [89]). In addition, letters of the alphabet (lacking letters V, X and Z) are represented in illustrated panels embellished with foliage. A drop capital 'N' is intertwined with an illustration of a newt on p. 87. There are examples of facsimile handwriting comprising marginal notes, graffiti, doodles and games on pp. [i], [x], xviii, xxiv, xxxii, xxxv, 3, 4, 8, 9, 12, 22, 23, 34, [38], 43, 48, 55, 62, 64, 79, 83, 85, 87 and [92].

Binding: decorated boards in 'half-bound' style with spine and corner pieces in green/brown and with covers in light green.
On spine: 'NEWT | FANTASTIC BEASTS & WHERE TO FIND THEM [illustration of a Billywig, 8 by 15mm, in yellow] | SCAMANDER' (reading lengthways down spine) with publisher's device of a lantern, 10 by 7mm and '[publisher's book device] | [rule] | S' within single ruled border, 12 by 6mm (horizontally at foot of spine). All in gilt.
On upper cover: 'FANTASTIC | BEASTS & | WHERE TO | FIND THEM | [illustration of Hogwarts crest with legend 'DRAGO DORMIENS NUNQUAM TITILLANDUS' on banner, 61 by 75mm] | NEWT | SCAMANDER' (all width centred). All in gilt with the exception of the illustration of the crest which is in yellow. To the left of the author is a circular 'wax' stamp in green and black stating '*Property of* | HOGWARTS | LIBRARY' within circular single ruled border, diameter 20mm, with border and lettering in gilt.
On lower cover: '[illustration of Hogwarts crest with legend 'DRAGO DORMIENS NUNQUAM TITILLANDUS' on banner, 25 by 31mm] | A copy of *Fantastic Beasts & Where to Find Them* | resides in almost every wizarding household | in the country. Now Muggles too have | the chance to discover where the Quintaped lives, | what the Puffskein eats and why it is best not | to leave milk out for a Knarl. | [new

paragraph] Proceeds from the sale of this book will go to | Comic Relief, which means that the dollars and | Galleons you exchange for it will do magic beyond | the powers of any wizard. If you feel that this | is insufficient reason to part with your money, | I can only hope that passing wizards feel more | charitable if they see you being attacked | by a Manticore. | Albus Dumbledore [facsimile signature] | [new paragraph] [three columns, in the first column is '[Lumos logo, 9 by 10mm] [in purple] | LUMOS [in purple] | From every sale of the Hogwarts | Library, Scholastic will donate twenty | percent of the suggested retail sales | price less taxes of this boxed set to two | charities selected by the author J. K. | Rowling: Lumos, a charity founded | by J. K. Rowling that works to end | the institutionalization of children | (wearelumos.org), and Comic Relief, | a UK-based charity that strives to | create a just world free from poverty | (www.comicrelief.com).', in the second column is '['COMIC | RELIEF^UK' logo, diameter 15mm] [in red, black and white] | Not to be sold separately.' and in the third column is '[publisher's device of a moon with face within a large black 'O']bscurus Books | *in association with* | [publisher's device of a lantern, 10 by 7mm] | ARTHUR A. LEVINE BOOKS | [publisher's book device with 'SCHOLASTIC' in white on red panel, 5 by 45mm] | scholastic.com']'. All in yellow.

All edges trimmed. Blue and yellow sewn bands at head and foot of spine. Binding measurements: 203 by 128mm (covers), 203 by 24mm (spine). End-papers: wove paper. The green/brown spine colour continues onto the covers by approximately 13mm.

Dust-jacket: none

Slipcase: card slipcase covered in red paper.

On spine: '[illustration of Hogwarts crest with legend 'DRAGO DORMIENS NUNQUAM TITILLANDUS' on banner, 30 by 36mm] | [new paragraph] HOGWARTS | LIBRARY | [new paragraph] QUIDDITCH | THROUGH | THE AGES | [new paragraph] FANTASTIC | BEASTS & | WHERE TO | FIND THEM | [new paragraph] THE TALES | OF BEEDLE | THE BARD | [new paragraph] JKRowling [facsimile signature]' (all width centred). All in gilt.

On upper and lower sides: '[illustration of Hogwarts crest with legend 'DRAGO DORMIENS NUNQUAM TITILLANDUS' on banner, 80 by 98mm] | [new paragraph] HOGWARTS | LIBRARY' (all within single broken ruled border, 187 by 117mm) (all width centred). All in gilt.

Top and lower edges: blank.

Publication: 29 October 2013

Price: $29.99 [together with A11(e) and A15(c)]

Contents:
Foreword
('I was deeply honoured when Newt Scamander asked me to write the foreword…')
(signed, 'Albus Dumbledore' [facsimile signature])

Introduction

('*Fantastic Beasts and Where to Find Them* represents the fruit of many years' travel…')

Ministry of Magic Classifications

('The Department for the Regulation and Control of Magical Creatures…')

An A-Z of Fantastic Beasts

('A | Acromantula | M.O.M. *Classification: XXXXX*…')

About the Author

('Newton ('Newt') Artemis Fido Scamander was born in 1897…')

Notes:

The Scholastic edition is almost exactly the same as the Bloomsbury 'Hogwarts Library' (see A10(d)). Note, however, the different imprint pages and the change of *Philosopher's Stone* to *Sorcerer's Stone* in the list of author's works. The listing of Harry Potter books also omits the Latin, Welsh, Ancient Greek and Irish editions that are unique to Bloomsbury.

The foreword, sections of the introduction and author note all commence with a drop capital.

Copies: private collection (PWE)

QUIDDITCH THROUGH THE AGES

A11(a)   FIRST ENGLISH EDITION   (2001)
(paperback)

QUIDDITCH | THROUGH THE AGES | *Kennilworthy Whisp* | [publisher's device of a dog, 9 by 14mm] | BLOOMSBURY | *in association with* | [publisher's device comprising '*Whizz Hard* | [illustration of a flying Quidditch ball] | *Books*'] | 129B DIAGON ALLEY, LONDON (Lines 1 and 2 justified on left and right margins, and all width centred)

Collation: 32 unsigned leaves bound in indeterminate gatherings; 177 by 111mm; [i-vi] vii [viii] 1-56

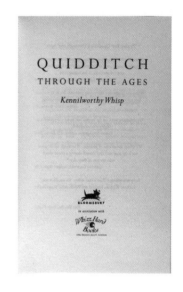

Page contents: [i] four piece panelled table headed 'Property of Hogwarts School Library'; [ii] 'With Thanks | [new paragraph] Bloomsbury and Comic Relief would like to say a big thank you to all these | people for their time, dedication and gorgeous contributions. | [new paragraph] Production: Helena Coryndon and Penny Edwards | Cover design: Richard Horne | Text design, Whizz Hard logo design and typesetting: Polly Napper | Covers: George Over Limited | Paper supply: Borregaard Hellefos AS, McNaughton Publishing Papers Ltd | Cover board: Iggesund Paperboard Europe | Sales: David Ward, Kathleen Farrar, Barry Horrocks | and the Bloomsbury sales force | Distribution: Macmillan Distribution Limited | Marketing: Minna Fry, Rosamund de la Hey, Colette Whitehouse, and the | Bloomsbury marketing team | Publicity: Katie Collins and the Bloomsbury publicity team and | Rebecca Salt and Nicky Stonehill at Colman Getty, Edinburgh | Copy-editing and proof-reading: Ingrid von Essen, proof-reading: Dick Clayton | Editor: Emma Matthewson | Christopher Little, Nigel Newton, Sarah Odedina, Colin Adams, | Burt Salvary, Fiddy Henderson, Ele Fountain, Dorchester Typesetting, | and booksellers around the world for their support. | [new paragraph] And of course J. K. Rowling for creating this book and so generously giving all | her royalties from it to Comic Relief. | [new paragraph] *Comic Relief (UK) was set up in 1985 by a group of British comedians to raise funds for* | *projects promoting social justice and helping to tackle poverty. Every single penny Comic* | *Relief receives from the public goes to work where it is most needed, through internationally* | *recognised organisations like Save the Children and Oxfam. Money from worldwide sales* | *of this book will go to help the very poorest communities in the very poorest countries in* | *the world; money from sales within the UK will go to UK projects as well.* | *Comic Relief is a registered charity, number 326568.* | [new paragraph] Text copyright © J. K. Rowling 2001

| Illustrations and hand lettering copyright © J. K. Rowling 2001 | First published in Great Britain in 2001 | Bloomsbury Publishing Plc, 38 Soho Square, London, W1D 3HB | All rights reserved | The moral right of the author has been asserted | A CIP catalogue record of this book is available from the British Library | ISBN 0 7475 5471 4 | Printed in Great Britain | 10 9 8 7 6 5 4 3 2 1'; [iii] title-page; [iv] 'Praise for *Quidditch through the Ages*' (six quotes with sources); [v] 'About the Author' ('KENNILWORTHY WHISP is a renowned Quidditch expert…'); [vi] 'Contents' (sixteen individual parts listed with titles and page references); vii-[viii] 'Foreword' ('*QUIDDITCH THROUGH THE AGES* is one of the most popular titles…') (signed, 'Albus Dumbledore' [facsimile signature]); 1-56 text and illustrations

Paper: wove paper

Running title: none

Illustrations: there are seven illustrations throughout the text (labelled Fig. A to Fig. G), in addition to an illustration of a flying Quidditch ball at the end of the text (from the 'Whizz Hard Books' device)

Binding: pictorial wrappers, in mottled green with 'stitching' in light green at outer edges and 'ageing' effect in light yellow.

On spine: 'QUIDDITCH THROUGH THE AGES KENNILWORTHY WHISP *Whizz Hard Books*' (reading lengthways down spine). All in black on mottled green.

On upper wrapper: 'QUIDDITCH | THROUGH THE AGES | KENNILWORTHY WHISP | [illustration of a Golden Snitch, 16 by 25mm] | [circular red wax stamp stating 'PROPERTY OF | HOGWARTS | LIBRARY']' (all width centred with the exception of the stamp which is off-set to the right). All in yellow and all on mottled green.

On lower wrapper: '*If you have ever asked yourself where the Golden | Snitch came from, how the Bludgers came into | existence or why the Wigtown Wanderers have pictures | of meat cleavers on their robes, you need Quidditch | Through the Ages. This limited edition is a copy of the | volume in Hogwarts School Library where it is consulted | by young Quidditch fans on an almost daily basis.* | [new paragraph] *Proceeds from the sale of this book will go to Comic | Relief, who will use your money to continue improving | and saving lives – work that is even more important and | astonishing than the three and a half second capture of | the Golden Snitch by Roderick Plumpton in 1921* | Albus Dumbledore [facsimile signature] | [new paragraph] Comic Relief will give the money it gets from the sale of this book to | projects helping some of the poorest and most vulnerable people in | the poorest countries of the world. | [new paragraph] At least £2 from the sale of | this book will go to Comic Relief | ['COMIC | RELIEF^UK' logo, diameter 20mm at left, with publishers' devices comprising '*Whizz Hard* | [illustration of a flying Quidditch ball, 4 by 7mm] | *Books* | *in association with* | [publisher's device of a dog, 6 by 10mm] | BLOOMSBURY' at centre, with 'At least £2 from the sale of | this book will go to Comic Relief', barcode in black on white panel, 21 by 37mm and price '£2.50 (14 Sickles 3 Knuts)' in black on light green panel, 7 by 37mm below barcode with both at right] | www.comicrelief.com/harrysbooks | www.bloomsbury.com/harrypotter | World Book Day £1 Book Tokens are not | redeemable against this charity book (UK and Ireland)'. All in black and all on mottled green. The initial 'I' of 'If' is a drop capital.

All edges trimmed. Binding measurements: 177 by 111mm (wrappers), 177 by 5mm (spine).

Publication: 12 March 2001 (simultaneous with A11(aa)) in an edition of 2,000,000 copies (confirmed by Bloomsbury)

Price: £2.50

Contents:
About the Author
    ('KENNILWORTHY WHISP is a renowned Quidditch expert…')
Foreword
    ('*QUIDDITCH THROUGH THE AGES* is one of the most popular titles…')
    (signed, 'Albus Dumbledore' [facsimile signature])
Quidditch Through the Ages
    ('No spell yet devised enables wizards to fly unaided in human form…')

Notes:
See A10(a) for notes on publication date.

Bloomsbury cite a print run of 2,000,000 copies (in contrast to 400,000 copies of A10(a)). This may be explained by the different printers. A10(a) was printed in Scotland by Omnia Books Limited. No printer is given for A11(a) although Clays Ltd may be assumed.

Immediatley before the release of *Harry Potter and the Order of the Phoenix*, Bloomsbury noted that customers who bought the new book directly from their website would also receive a free copy of *Quidditch Through the Ages*. This would suggest that by 2003 the different printruns of A10(a) and A11(a) had left the publishers with a significant stock of *Quidditch Through the Ages*.

Each section (foreword, chapter or author note) commences with a drop capital.

Copies: BL (YA.2002.a.20724) stamped 3 Apr 2001; private collection (PWE)

A11(aa)   FIRST AMERICAN EDITION   (2001)
(paperback)

QUIDDITCH | THROUGH THE AGES | *Kennilworthy Whisp* | [publisher's device of a lantern, 11 by 8mm] | Arthur A. Levine Books | AN IMPRINT OF SCHOLASTIC PRESS | *in association with* | [publisher's device comprising '*Whizz Hard* | [illustration of a flying Quidditch ball] | *Books*'] | 129B DIAGON ALLEY, LONDON (Lines 1 and 2 justified on left and right margins, and all width centred)

Collation: 32 unsigned leaves bound in eight gatherings of four leaves; 192 by 133mm; [i-v] vi [viii] 1-56

Page contents: [i] four piece panelled table headed 'Property of Hogwarts School Library'; [ii] 'With Thanks | [new paragraph] J. K. Rowling, Comic Relief U. K., and Scholastic Inc. | would like to thank the following individuals and organizations | for their generous contributions in this endeavor: | [new paragraph] HarperCollins Publishers | Command Web Offset | Quebecor World (USA Corp.) | R. R. Donnelley & Sons | Alliance Forest Product Inc. | Digicon Imaging, Inc. | J. M. Wechter & Associates, Inc. | Rose Printing Company | ICG/Holliston | Lehigh Press, Inc. | The Display Connection Inc. | Universal Printing Company | JY International Inc., Sales Division of LeeFung-Asco Printers | Berryville Graphics | Von Hoffmann | Leo Pacific Pier | Four

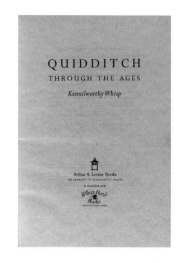

Lakes Colorgraphics Inc. | Schneider National Inc. | Combined Express, Inc. | Fey Publishing | Delta Corrugated Paper Products Corporation | Webcrafters Inc. | Yellow Corporation | [new paragraph] [four-sided device] And of course, the publisher would especially like to thank | J. K. Rowling for creating this book and so generously | giving all her royalties from it to Comic Relief.'; [iii] title-page; [iv] 'Praise for *Quidditch Through the Ages* | [six quotes with sources] | [new paragraph] Text and illustrations copyright © 2001 by J. K. Rowling. | All rights reserved. Published by Scholastic Press, a division of Scholastic Inc., *Publishers since 1920*. SCHOLASTIC, | SCHOLASTIC PRESS, and the LANTERN LOGO are trademarks and/or registered trademarks of Scholastic Inc. HARRY | POTTER and all related characters, names, and related indicia are trademarks of Warner Bros. | [new paragraph] No part of this publication may be reproduced, or stored in a retrieval system, or transmitted in any form or by any means, | electronic, mechanical, photocopying, recording, or otherwise, without written permission of the publisher. For information | regarding permissions, write to Scholastic Inc., Attention: Permissions Department, 555 Broadway, New York, NY 10012. | [new paragraph] Scholastic Inc.'s net proceeds from the sale of this book will go to The Harry Potter Fund established by Comic Relief U. K. | J. K. Rowling is donating all royalties to which she would be entitled. The purchase of this book is not tax deductible. Comic | Relief may be contacted at: Comic Relief, 5th Floor, Albert Embankment, London SE1 77P, England (www.comicrelief.com). | Comic Relief in the United Kingdom is not affiliated with the organization of the same name in the United States. | ISBN 0-439-29502-5 | Library of Congress Cataloging-in-Publication Data Available | 12 11 10 9 8 7 6 5 4 3 2 1   1/0 2/0 3/0 4/0 5/0 | Printed in the U. S. A. | First American edition, February 2001'; [v] 'About the Author' ('KENNILWORTHY WHISP is a renowned Quidditch expert...'); vi 'Contents' (sixteen individual parts listed with titles and page references); vii-[viii] 'Foreword' ('*QUIDDITCH THROUGH THE AGES* is one of the most popular titles...') (signed, 'Albus Dumbledore' [facsimile signature]); 1-56 text and illustrations

Paper: wove paper

Running title: none

Illustrations: there are seven illustrations throughout the text (labelled Fig. A to Fig. G), in addition to an illustration of a flying Quidditch ball at the end of the text (from the 'Whizz Hard Books' device)

Binding: pictorial wrappers, in mottled green with 'stitching' in light green at outer edges and 'ageing' effect in light yellow.

On spine: 'QUIDDITCH THROUGH THE AGES KENNILWORTHY WHISP *Whizz Hard* Books' (reading lengthways down spine) with publisher's book device in black and white on red panel, 5 by 4mm (horizontally at foot of spine). All in black.

On upper wrapper: 'QUIDDITCH | THROUGH THE AGES | KENNILWORTHY WHISP | [illustration of a Golden Snitch, 17 by 30mm] | [circular red wax stamp stating 'PROPERTY OF | HOGWARTS | LIBRARY']' (all width centred with the exception of the stamp which is off-set to the right). All in yellow and all on mottled green.

On lower wrapper: '*If you have ever asked yourself where the Golden | Snitch came from, how the Bludgers came into | existence, or why the Wigtown Wanderers have pictures | of meat cleavers on their robes, you need Quidditch | Through the Ages. This limited edition is a copy of the | volume in Hogwarts School Library, where it is | consulted by young Quidditch fans on an almost daily basis.* | [new paragraph] *Proceeds from the sale of this book will go to improving | and saving the lives of children around the world – work | that is even more important and astonishing than the | three-and-a-half-second capture of the Golden Snitch by | Roderick Plumpton in 1921* | Albus Dumbledore [facsimile signature] | [new paragraph] J. K. ROWLING and SCHOLASTIC INC.'s net proceeds from the | sale of this book will go to the Harry's Books fund to help needy | children in the poorest countries in the world. | [new paragraph] www.comicrelief.com/harrysbooks | [new paragraph] [publisher's device comprising '*Whizz Hard* | [illustration of a flying Quidditch ball] | Books'] | *in association with* | [publisher's device of a lantern, 8 by 6mm] | *Arthur A. Levine Books* | AN IMPRINT OF SCHOLASTIC PRESS | [publisher's book device in white and 'SCHOLASTIC' in white on red panel, 7 by 43mm]'. All in black and all on mottled green. To right of lines 20-24 is the 'COMIC | RELIEF^UK' logo, diameter 20mm, and to the extreme right of lines 22-27 is a barcode with smaller barcode to the right (29502) all in black on white panel, 22 by 51mm and price '$3.99 US (*14 Sickles 3 Knuts*)' in black on light green panel, 7 by 51mm below barcode. The initial '*I*' of '*If*' is a drop capital.

On inside upper wrapper: barcodes.

On inside lower wrapper: 'About Comic Relief: A note from J. K. Rowling' ('Comic Relief is one of Britain's most famous and successful charities.') (signed, 'JKRowling' [facsimile signature]) (all within single ruled border, 155 by 95mm). All in black.

All edges trimmed. Binding measurements: 192 by 133mm (wrappers), 192 by 4mm (spine).

Publication: 12 March 2001 (simultaneous with A11(a)) (see notes)

Price: $3.99

Contents:

About the Author

('KENNILWORTHY WHISP is a renowned Quidditch expert…')

Foreword

('*QUIDDITCH THROUGH THE AGES* is one of the most popular titles…')

(signed, 'Albus Dumbledore' [facsimile signature])

Quidditch Through the Ages

('No spell yet devised enables wizards to fly unaided in human form…')

About Comic Relief: A note from J.K. Rowling

('Comic Relief is one of Britain's most famous and successful charities…')

(signed, 'JKRowling' [facsimile signature])

Notes:

The note about Comic Relief is unique to the American edition. The text of the 'Foreword' has also been changed slightly to identify the charity as 'Comic Relief U.K.'

See A10(aa) for notes on publication date.

Each section (foreword, chapter or author note) commences with a drop capital.

Information provided by Nielsen BookData suggests that 'Turtleback Books' issued a 'hardback library binding' during March 2001. This edition has the ISBN 0-613-32974-0. No copies have been consulted.

Copies: private collection (PWE)

A11(b)   SECOND AMERICAN EDITION   (2001)
(hardback)

QUIDDITCH | THROUGH THE AGES | *Kennilworthy Whisp* | [publisher's device of a lantern, 12 by 9mm] | Arthur A. Levine Books | AN IMPRINT OF SCHOLASTIC PRESS | *in association with* | [publisher's device comprising '*Whizz Hard* | [illustration of a flying Quidditch ball] | *Books*'] | 129B DIAGON ALLEY, LONDON (Lines 1 and 2 justified on left and right margins, and all width centred)

Collation: 32 unsigned leaves bound in two gatherings of sixteen leaves; 193 by 131mm; [i-v] vi [viii] 1-56

Page contents: [i] four piece panelled table headed 'Property of Hogwarts School Library'; [ii] 'About Comic Relief: A note from J. K. Rowling' ('Comic Relief is one of Britain's most famous and successful charities.') (signed, 'JKRowling' [facsimile signature]) (all within single ruled border, 171 by 105mm); [iii] title-page; [iv] 'Praise for *Quidditch Through the Ages* | [six quotes with sources] | [new paragraph] Text copyright © 2001 by J.K. Rowling. [point] Illustrations and hand lettering copyright © 2001 by

J.K. Rowling. | All rights reserved. Published by Scholastic Press, a division of Scholastic Inc., *Publishers since 1920.* SCHOLASTIC, | SCHOLASTIC PRESS, and the LANTERN LOGO are trademarks and/or registered trademarks of Scholastic Inc. HARRY | POTTER and all related characters, names, and related indicia are trademarks of Warner Bros. | [new paragraph] No part of this publication may be reproduced, or stored in a retrieval system, or transmitted in any form or by any means, | electronic, mechanical, photocopying, recording, or otherwise, without written permission of the publisher. For information | regarding permissions, write to Scholastic Inc., Attention: Permissions Department, 555 Broadway, New York, NY 10012. | [new paragraph] Scholastic Inc. has arranged for twenty percent of the retail sales price less taxes from the sale of this book to go to Comic | Relief U.K.'s Harry's Books fund. J. K. Rowling is donating all royalties to which she would be

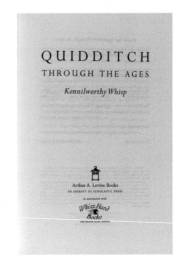

entitled. The purchase of this | book is not tax deductible. Comic Relief may be contacted at: Comic Relief, 5th Floor, Albert Embankment, London SE1 77P, | England (www.comicrelief.com). Comic Relief in the United Kingdom is not affiliated with the organization of the same name | in the United States. | [new paragraph] ISBN 0-439-32161-1 | Library of Congress Cataloging-in-Publication Data Available | 12 11 10 9 8 7 6 5 4 3 2 1   01 02 03 04 05 | Printed in the U. S. A. 37 | First hardback boxset edition, September 2001'; [v] 'About the Author' ('KENNILWORTHY WHISP is a renowned Quidditch expert...'); vi 'Contents' (sixteen individual parts listed with titles and page references); vii-[viii] 'Foreword' ('*QUIDDITCH THROUGH THE AGES* is one of the most popular titles...') (signed, 'Albus Dumbledore' [facsimile signature]); 1-56 text and illustrations

Paper: wove paper

Running title: none

Illustrations: there are seven illustrations throughout the text (labelled Fig. A to Fig. G), in addition to an illustration of a flying Quidditch ball at the end of the text (from the 'Whizz Hard Books' device)

Binding: pictorial boards, in mottled green with 'stitching' in light green at outer edges and 'ageing' effect in light yellow.

On spine: 'QUIDDITCH THROUGH THE AGES KENNILWORTHY WHISP *Whizz Hard* Books' (reading lengthways down spine). All in black.

On upper cover: 'QUIDDITCH | THROUGH THE AGES | KENNILWORTHY WHISP | [illustration of a Golden Snitch, 17 by 21mm] | [circular red wax stamp stating 'PROPERTY OF | HOGWARTS | LIBRARY']' (all width centred with the exception of the stamp which is off-set to the right). All in yellow and all on mottled green.

On lower cover: '*If you have ever asked yourself where the Golden* | *Snitch came from, how the Bludgers came into* | *existence, or why the Wigtown*

Wanderers have pictures | of meat cleavers on their robes, you need Quidditch | Through the Ages. This limited edition is a copy of the | volume in Hogwarts School Library, where it is consulted | by young Quidditch fans on an almost daily basis. | [new paragraph] Proceeds from the sale of this book will go to improving | and saving the lives of children around the world – work | that is even more important and astonishing than the | three-and-a-half-second capture of the Golden Snitch by | Roderick Plumpton in 1921 | Albus Dumbledore [facsimile signature] [new paragraph] J. K. ROWLING and SCHOLASTIC INC. have arranged for twenty | percent of the retail sales price less taxes of this book to go to the | Harry's Books fund to help needy children in the poorest countries in | the world. | [new paragraph] www.comicrelief.com/harrysbooks | [new paragraph] [three publisher's devices in three columns, in the first column is publisher's device comprising '*Whizz Hard* | [illustration of a flying Quidditch ball] | *Books* | *in association with*, in the second column is '[publisher's device of a lantern, 8 by 6mm] | *Arthur A. Levine Books* | *AN IMPRINT OF SCHOLASTIC PRESS*' and in the third column is 'COMIC | RELIEF^UK' logo, diameter 20mm] | [new paragraph] [publisher's book device in white and 'SCHOLASTIC' in white on red panel, 7 by 43mm] ['ISBN 0-439-32161-1' in black on yellow panel, 7 by 37mm]'. All in black and all on mottled green. The initial '*I*' of '*If*' is a drop capital.

All edges trimmed. Binding measurements: 201 by 136mm (covers), 201 by 19mm (spine). End-papers: green wove paper.

Dust-jacket: none

Slipcase: see A10(b)

Publication: September 2001 (see notes)

Price: $12.95 [together with A10(b)]

Contents:
About Comic Relief: A note from J.K. Rowling
   ('Comic Relief is one of Britain's most famous and successful charities…')
   (signed, 'JKRowling' [facsimile signature])
About the Author
   ('KENNILWORTHY WHISP is a renowned Quidditch expert…')
Foreword
   ('*QUIDDITCH THROUGH THE AGES* is one of the most popular titles…')
   (signed, 'Albus Dumbledore' [facsimile signature])
Quidditch Through the Ages
   ('No spell yet devised enables wizards to fly unaided in human form…')

Notes:
Although no publication date is recorded, 1 September 2001 is assumed. In an email to me from January 2013 Arthur A. Levine noted that 'I'm fairly certain that we didn't have strict "on sale" dates… the publication "day" would simply be the first on the month listed.'

Each section (foreword, chapter or author note) commences with a drop capital.

Copies: private collection (PWE)

A11(c)   SECOND ENGLISH EDITION   (2009)
(paperback)

QUIDDITCH | THROUGH | THE AGES | KENNILWORTHY | WHISP | BY | J.K.ROWLING | [publisher's device of a dog, 9 by 14mm] | BLOOMSBURY | *in association with* | [publisher's device comprising *'Whizz Hard* | [illustration of a flying Quidditch ball] | *Books'*] | 129B DIAGON ALLEY, LONDON (All width centred)

Collation: 64 unsigned leaves bound in indeterminate gatherings; 196 by 127mm; [i-xiv] xv-xvii [xviii] [1-2] 3-5 [6-8] 9-12 [13-16] 17-20 [21-24] 25-30 [31-34] 35-36 [37-40] 41-58 [59-62] 63-71 [72-74] 75-85 [86-88] 89-93 [94-96] 97-100 [101-102] 103 [104] 105 [106-110]

Page contents: [i] twenty-four piece panelled table headed 'HOGWARTS | LIBRARY' below which is an illustration of Hogwarts crest with legend 'DRAGO DORMIENS NUNQUAM TITILLANDUS' on banner, 28 by 34mm and, to the right, a noughts and crosses game; [ii] blank; [iii-iv] 'Praise for *Quidditch through the Ages*' (six quotes with sources); [v] half-title: 'QUIDDITCH | THROUGH | THE AGES'; [vi] *'Titles available in the Harry Potter series* | *(in reading order):* | Harry Potter and the Philosopher's Stone | Harry Potter and the Chamber of Secrets | Harry Potter and the Prisoner of Azkaban | Harry Potter and the Goblet of Fire | Harry Potter and the Order of the Phoenix | Harry Potter and the Half-Blood Prince | Harry Potter and the Deathly Hallows | [new paragraph] *Titles available in the Harry Potter series* | *(in Latin):* | Harry Potter and the Philosopher's Stone | Harry Potter and the Chamber of Secrets | [new paragraph] *(in Welsh, Ancient Greek and Irish):* | Harry Potter and the Philosopher's Stone | [new paragraph] *Other titles available:* | Fantastic Beasts and Where to Find Them | The Tales of Beedle the Bard'; [vii] title-page; [viii] 'Text copyright © J. K. Rowling 2001 | Illustration and hand lettering copyright © J. K. Rowling 2001 | [new paragraph] First published in Great Britain in 2001 | This edition published in 2009 | [new paragraph] Bloomsbury Publishing Plc | 36 Soho Square, London, W1D 3QY | [new paragraph] Bloomsbury Publishing, London, Berlin and New York | [new paragraph] The moral right of the author has been asserted | [new paragraph] All rights reserved | No part of this publication may be reproduced or | transmitted by any means, electronic, mechanical, photocopying | or otherwise, without the prior permission of the publisher | [new paragraph] A CIP catalogue record of this book is available from the British Library | [new paragraph] ISBN 978 1 4088 0302 8 | [new paragraph] The paper this book is printed on is certified by the © 1996 Forest | Stewardship Council A.C. (FSC). It is ancient-forest friendly. The | printer holds FSC chain of custody SGS-COC-2061 | [Forest Stewardship Council logo, 5 by 6mm together with © symbol and text: 'FSC' and, to the right 'Mixed Sources | Product group from well-managed | forests and other controlled sources | [new paragraph] www.fsc.org Cert no. SGS-COC-2061 | © 1996 Forest Stewardship Council'] | [new paragraph] Printed in Great Britain by Clays Ltd, St Ives Plc | [new paragraph] 1 3 5 7 9 10 8 6 4 2 | www.bloomsbury.com | [new paragraph] *Comic Relief (UK) was set up in 1985 by a group of British comedians to raise funds* | *for projects promoting social justice and helping to tackle poverty. Every single penny* | *Comic Relief receives* *from the public goes to work where it is most needed, through* | *internationally recognised organisations like*

Save the Children and Oxfam. Money | from worldwide sales of this book will go to help the very poorest communities in the | very poorest countries in the world; money from sales within the UK will go to UK | projects as well. | Comic Relief is a registered charity, number 326568.'; [ix] 'With thanks to J. K. Rowling for creating | this book and so generously giving all her | royalties to Comic Relief | [illustration of a Golden Snidget]'; [x] blank; [xi] illustration of a flying Quidditch ball; [xii] blank; [xiii] 'Contents' (seventeen individual parts listed with titles and page references); [xiv] blank; xv-[xviii] 'Foreword' ('*QUIDDITCH THROUGH THE AGES* is one of the most popular titles…') (signed, 'Albus Dumbledore' [facsimile signature]); [1]-103 text and illustrations (with blank pages); [104] blank; 105 'About the Author' ('KENNILWORTHY WHISP is a renowned Quidditch expert…'); [106] blank; [107] illustration of a flying Quidditch ball; [108] blank; [109] 'COMIC | RELIEF' logo, diameter 23mm and text; [110] blank

Paper: wove paper

Running title: '*Foreword*' (14mm) on both verso and recto, pp. xvi-[xviii]; '*Quidditch Through the Ages*' (45mm) on both verso and recto, pp. 4-[101]

Illustrations: there are seven illustrations throughout the text (labelled Fig. A to Fig. G), in addition to the repetition of figure B, an illustration of a flying Quidditch ball at the beginning and end of the text (from the 'Whizz Hard Books' device) and a Golden Snitch before each section. Page numbers are each centred within a further illustration of a Golden Snitch.

Binding: pictorial wrappers, in mottled blue.

On spine: 'QUIDDITCH THROUGH THE AGES J.K.ROWLING BLOOMSBURY [publisher's device of the head of a dog, 4 by 5mm]' (reading lengthways down spine). All in yellow.

On upper wrapper: 'QUIDDITCH | THROUGH | THE AGES | KENNILWORTHY | WHISP | [illustration of a Golden Snitch, 43 by 77mm] | BY | J.K.ROWLING | FROM THE WORLD OF | HARRY POTTER' (all within single broken ruled border, 186 by 116mm) (all width centred). All in yellow.

On lower wrapper: 'If you have ever asked yourself where the | Golden Snitch came from, how the Bludgers | came into existence or why the Wigtown Wanderers | have pictures of meat cleavers on their robes, you | need *Quidditch Through the Ages*. This edition is a copy | of the volume in Hogwarts School Library, where it | is consulted by young Quidditch fans on an almost | daily basis. | [new paragraph] Proceeds from the sale of this book will go to | Comic Relief, who will use your money to continue | improving and changing lives – work that is even | more important and astonishing than the three | and a half second capture of the Golden Snitch by | Roderick Plumpton in 1921. | Albus Dumbledore [facsimile signature] | [new paragraph] Comic Relief will give the money | it gets from the sale of this book | to projects helping some of the | poorest and most vulnerable | people in the poorest countries | of the world. | ['COMIC | RELIEF' logo, diameter 17mm, at centre, with publishers' devices comprising '*Whizz Hard* | [illustration of a flying Quidditch ball] | *Books* | *in association with* | [publisher's device of a dog, 6 by 11mm] | BLOOMSBURY' at right | '[barcode] | £4.99 (1 Galleon 11 Sickles)' at left, '[Forest Stewardship Council logo, 7 by 8mm together with © symbol] | FSC | Mixed Sources | Product group from well-managed | forests and other controlled sources | [new paragraph] Cert no. SGS-COC-2061 | www.fsc.org | © 1996 Forest Stewardship Council' at centre, and '£1.15

from the sale of this book will | go to Comic Relief | [new paragraph] World Book Day £1 Book Tokens | are not redeemable against this | charity book (UK and Ireland) | [new paragraph] www. comicrelief.com | www.bloomsbury.com/harrypotter' at right and all in black on white panel, 27 by 94mm] | Comic Relief, registered charity 326568 (England/Wales); SCO39730 (Scotland)' (all within single broken ruled border, 186 by 116mm). All in yellow. The initial 'I' of 'If' is a drop capital.

All edges trimmed. Binding measurements: 196 by 127mm (wrappers), 196 by 9mm (spine).

Publication: 6 July 2009 in an edition of 56,700 copies (confirmed by Bloomsbury)

Price: £4.99

Contents:
Foreword
('*Quidditch Through the Ages* is one of the most popular titles...')
(signed, 'Albus Dumbledore' [facsimile signature])
Quidditch Through the Ages
('No spell yet devised enables wizards to fly unaided in human form...')
About the Author
('Kennilworthy Whisp is a renowned Quidditch expert...')

Notes:
Each section (foreword, chapter or author note) commences with a drop capital.

Copies: BL (YK.2010.a.21575) stamped 22 Jun 2009

Reprints include:
21

A11(d)　　　THIRD ENGLISH EDITION　　　(2012)
(hardback)

QUIDDITCH | THROUGH | THE AGES | [illustration of a Golden Snitch, 26 by 47mm] | KENNILWORTHY | WHISP | [publisher's device of a dog, 5 by 9mm] | BLOOMSBURY | *in association with* | [publisher's device comprising '*Whizz Hard* | [illustration of a flying Quidditch ball] | *Books*'] | 129B Diagon Alley, LONDON (All width centred)

Collation: 64 unsigned leaves bound in eight gatherings of eight leaves; 199 by 128mm; [i-xiv] xv-xvii [xviii] [1-2] 3-5 [6-8] 9-12 [13-16] 17-20 [21-24] 25-30 [31-34] 35-36 [37-40] 41-58 [59-62] 63-71 [72-74] 75-85 [86-88] 89-93 [94-96] 97-100 [101-102] 103 [104] 105 [106-110]

Page contents: [i] twenty-four piece panelled table headed 'HOGWARTS | LIBRARY' below which is an illustration of Hogwarts crest with legend 'DRAGO DORMIENS NUNQUAM TITILLANDUS' on banner, 28 by 34mm and, to the right, a noughts and crosses game, an arrow and heart appear upper left; [ii] blank; [iii-iv] 'Praise for *Quidditch through the Ages*' (six quotes with sources); [v] half-title: 'QUIDDITCH | THROUGH | THE AGES'; [vi] *'Titles available in the Harry Potter series | (in reading order):* | Harry Potter and the Philosopher's Stone | Harry Potter and the Chamber of Secrets | Harry Potter and the Prisoner of Azkaban | Harry Potter and the Goblet of Fire | Harry Potter and the Order of the Phoenix | Harry Potter and the Half-Blood Prince | Harry Potter and the Deathly Hallows | [new paragraph] *Titles available in the Harry Potter series | (in Latin):* | Harry Potter and the Philosopher's Stone | Harry Potter and the Chamber of Secrets | *(in Welsh, Ancient Greek and Irish):* | Harry Potter and the Philosopher's Stone | [new paragraph] *Also available | (in aid of Comic Relief):* | Fantastic Beasts and Where to Find Them | Quidditch Through the Ages | *(in aid of Lumos):* | The Tales of Beedle the Bard'; [vii] title-page; [viii] 'Text

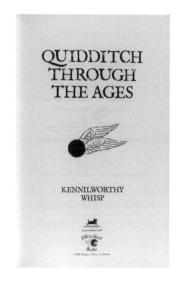

copyright © J. K. Rowling 2001 | Illustration and hand lettering copyright © J. K. Rowling 2001 | [new paragraph] First published in Great Britain in 2001 | This edition published in 2012 | [new paragraph] Bloomsbury Publishing Plc | 50 Bedford Square, London, WC1B 3DP | [new paragraph] Bloomsbury Publishing, London, New Delhi, New York and Sydney | [new paragraph] The moral right of the author has been asserted | [new paragraph] All rights reserved | No part of this publication may be reproduced or | transmitted by any means, electronic, mechanical, photocopying | or otherwise, without the prior permission of the publisher | [new paragraph] A CIP catalogue record of this book is available from the British Library | [new paragraph] ISBN 978 1 4088 3503 6 | [new paragraph] [Forest Stewardship Council logo, 6 by 7mm together with ® symbol and text: 'FSC | www.fsc.org' with 'MIX | Paper from | responsible sources | FSC® C008047' to the right and all within single ruled border with rounded corners, 12 by 26mm] | [new paragraph] Printed in China by C&C Offset Printing Co Ltd, Shenzhen, Guangdong | [new paragraph] 1 3 5 7 9 10 8 6 4 2 | [new paragraph] www.bloomsbury.com | [new paragraph] *Comic Relief (UK) was set up in 1985 by a group of British comedians to raise | funds for projects promoting social justice and helping to tackle poverty. Money from | worldwide sales of this book will go to help the very poorest communities in the very | poorest countries in the world. Money from sales within the UK will go to UK | projects as well. | Comic Relief (UK) is a registered charity number 326568 (England & Wales) and | SCO39730 (Scotland)*.'; [ix] 'With thanks to J. K. Rowling for creating | this book and so generously giving all her | royalties to Comic Relief | [illustration of a Golden Snidget]'; [x] blank; [xi] illustration of a flying Quidditch ball; [xii] blank; [xiii] 'Contents' (seventeen individual parts listed with titles and page references); [xiv] blank; xv-[xviii] 'Foreword' ('*QUIDDITCH THROUGH THE AGES* is one of the most popular titles…') (signed, 'Albus Dumbledore' [facsimile signature]); [1]-103 text and illustrations (with blank pages); [104] blank; 105 'About the Author' ('KENNILWORTHY WHISP is a renowned Quidditch expert…'); [106] blank; [107] illustration of a flying Quidditch ball; [108] blank; [109] 'COMIC | RELIEF^UK' logo and text; [110] blank

Paper: wove paper

Running title: '*Foreword*' (14mm) on both verso and recto, pp. xvi-[xviii]; '*Quidditch Through the Ages*' (45mm) on both verso and recto, pp. 4-[101]

Illustrations: there are seven illustrations throughout the text (labelled Fig. A to Fig. G), in addition to the repetition of figure B, an illustration of a flying Quidditch ball at the beginning and end of the text (from the 'Whizz Hard Books' device) and a Golden Snitch before each section. Page numbers are each centred within a further illustration of a Golden Snitch.

Binding: decorated boards in 'half-bound' style with spine and corner pieces in brown and with covers in red.

On spine: 'KENNILWORTHY | QUIDDITCH THROUGH THE AGES [illustration of a flying Quidditch ball, 7 by 14mm, in yellow] BLOOMSBURY [publisher's device of the head of a dog, 3 by 4mm] | WHISP' (reading lengthways down spine). All in gilt.

On upper cover: 'QUIDDITCH | THROUGH | THE AGES | [illustration of a Golden Snitch, 38 by 69mm, in yellow] | KENNILWORTHY | WHISP' (all width centred). All in gilt. To the left of the author is a circular 'wax' stamp in crimson and black stating '*Property of* | HOGWARTS | LIBRARY' within circular single ruled border, diameter 20mm, with border and lettering in gilt.

On lower cover: '[illustration of a Golden Snitch, 24 by 42mm] | If you have ever asked yourself where the | Golden Snitch came from, how the Bludgers | came into existence or why the Wigtown Wanderers | have pictures of meat cleavers on their robes, | you need *Quidditch Through the Ages*. | This invaluable volume is consulted by young | Quidditch fans on an almost daily basis. | [new paragraph] Proceeds from the sale of this book will go to | Comic Relief, who will use your money to | continue improving and changing lives – work that | is even more important and astonishing than | the three and a half second capture of the Golden | Snitch by Roderick Plumpton in 1921. | Albus Dumbledore [facsimile signature] | [new paragraph] [three columns, in the first column is 'Comic Relief will give the money | it gets from the sale of this book | to projects helping some of the | poorest and most vulnerable | people in the UK and some of the | poorest countries of the world.', in the second column is 'COMIC | RELIEF[UK]' logo, diameter 15mm and in the third column is '*Whizz Hard* | [illustration of a flying Quidditch ball] | *Books* | *in association with* | [publisher's device of a dog, 5 by 9mm] | BLOOMSBURY'] | [new paragraph] [three columns, in the first column is the barcode, in the second column is '[Forest Stewardship Council logo, 6 by 7mm] | FSC | MIX | Paper | FSC® C008047' all within single ruled border with rounded corners, 17 by 12mm, and in the third column is 'www.comicrelief.com | www.bloomsbury.com/harrypotter | www.pottermore.com'] | Comic Relief, registered charity 326568 (England/Wales); SCO39730 (Scotland)'. All in yellow with the exception of the Comic Relief logo which is in black and red on white and the final three columns which are in black on a white panel, 23 by 82mm.

All edges trimmed. Red and yellow sewn bands at head and foot of spine. Binding measurements: 205 by 128mm (covers), 205 by 28mm (spine). End-papers: wove paper. The brown spine colour continues onto the covers by approximately 13mm.

Dust-jacket: none

Slipcase: card slipcase covered in red paper (see description for A10(d))

Publication: 11 October 2012 in an edition of 77,200 copies (confirmed by Bloomsbury)

Price: £25 [together with A10(d) and A15(b)]

Contents:
Foreword
    ('*Quidditch Through the Ages* is one of the most popular titles…')
    (signed, 'Albus Dumbledore' [facsimile signature])
Quidditch Through the Ages
    ('No spell yet devised enables wizards to fly unaided in human form…')
About the Author
    ('Kennilworthy Whisp is a renowned Quidditch expert…')

Notes:
Note the appearance of the arrow and heart drawing on page [i]. This is not present in previous editions.

Each section (foreword, chapter or author note) commences with a drop capital.

Copies: private collection (PWE)

A11(e) THIRD AMERICAN EDITION (2013)
(hardback)

QUIDDITCH | THROUGH | THE AGES | [illustration of a Golden Snitch, 28 by 53mm] | KENNILWORTHY | WHISP | [publisher's device of a lantern, 9 by 7mm] | ARTHUR A. LEVINE BOOKS | An Imprint of Scholastic Inc. | *in association with* | [publisher's device comprising '*Whizz Hard* | [illustration of a flying Quidditch ball] | *Books*'] | 129B Diagon Alley, LONDON (All width centred)

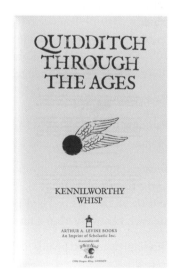

Collation: 64 unsigned leaves bound in eight gatherings of eight leaves; 197 by 127mm; [i-xiv] xv-xvii [xviii] [1-2] 3-5 [6-8] 9-12 [13-16] 17-20 [21-24] 25-30 [31-34] 35-36 [37-40] 41-58 [59-62] 63-71 [72-74] 75-85 [86-88] 89-93 [94-96] 97-100 [101-102] 103 [104] 105 [106-110]

Page contents: [i] twenty-four piece panelled table headed 'HOGWARTS | LIBRARY' below which is an illustration of

Hogwarts crest with legend 'DRAGO DORMIENS NUNQUAM TITILLANDUS' on banner, 28 by 34mm and, to the right, a noughts and crosses game, an arrow and heart appear upper left; [ii] blank; [iii-iv] 'Praise for *Quidditch through the Ages*' (six quotes with sources); [v] half-title: 'QUIDDITCH | THROUGH | THE AGES'; [vi] *'Titles available in the Harry Potter series | (in reading order):* | Harry Potter and the Sorcerer's Stone | Harry Potter and the Chamber of Secrets | Harry Potter and the Prisoner of Azkaban | Harry Potter and the Goblet of Fire | Harry Potter and the Order of the Phoenix | Harry Potter and the Half-Blood Prince | Harry Potter and the Deathly Hallows | [new paragraph] *Also available | (in aid of Comic Relief):* | Fantastic Beasts and Where to Find Them | Quidditch Through the Ages | *(in aid of Lumos):* | The Tales of Beedle the Bard'; [vii] title-page; [viii] 'Text copyright © J. K. Rowling 2001 | Illustration and hand lettering copyright © J. K. Rowling 2001 | HARRY POTTER and all related characters | and elements are TM of and © WBEI. | Harry Potter Publishing Rights © J. K. Rowling | [new paragraph] All rights reserved. Published by Arthur A. Levine Books, an imprint of | Scholastic Inc., *Publishers since 1920.* SCHOLASTIC, the LANTERN | LOGO, and associated logos are trademarks and/or registered trademarks of | Scholastic Inc. | [new paragraph] No part of this publication may be reproduced, stored in a retrieval system, | or transmitted in any form or by any means, electronic, mechanical, | photocopying, recording, or otherwise, without written permission of the | publisher. For information regarding permission, write to Scholastic Inc., | Attention: Permissions Department, 557 Broadway, New York, NY 10012. | [new paragraph] ISBN 978-0-545-61540-2 | [new paragraph] 12 11 10 9 8 7 6 5 4 3 2 1   13 14 15 16 17 | [new paragraph] Printed in China 95 | This edition first printing, November 2013 | [new paragraph] *From every sale of the Hogwarts Library, Scholastic will donate twenty percent of | the suggested retail sales price less taxes of this boxed set to two charities selected by | the author J. K. Rowling: Lumos, a charity founded by J. K. Rowling that works to | end the institutionalization of children (wearelumos.org), and Comic Relief, | a UK-based charity that strives to create a just world free from poverty | (www.comicrelief.com). Purchase of this book is not tax deductible.';* [ix] 'With thanks to J. K. Rowling for creating | this book and so generously giving all her | royalties to Comic Relief | [illustration of a Golden Snidget]'; [x] blank; [xi] illustration of a flying Quidditch ball; [xii] blank; [xiii] 'Contents' (seventeen individual parts listed with titles and page references); [xiv] blank; xv-[xviii] 'Foreword' (*'Quidditch through the Ages* is one of the most popular titles...') (signed, 'Albus Dumbledore' [facsimile signature]); [1]-103 text and illustrations (with blank pages); [104] blank; 105 'About the Author' ('Kennilworthy Whisp is a renowned Quidditch expert...'); [106] blank; [107] illustration of a flying Quidditch ball; [108] blank; [109] 'COMIC | RELIEF^UK' logo and text; [110] blank

Paper: wove paper

Running title: '*Foreword*' (14mm) on both verso and recto, pp. xvi-[xviii]; '*Quidditch Through the Ages*' (45mm) on both verso and recto, pp. 4-[101]

Illustrations: there are seven illustrations throughout the text (labelled Fig. A to Fig. G), in addition to the repetition of figure B, an illustration of a flying Quidditch ball at the beginning and end of the text (from the 'Whizz Hard Books' device) and a Golden Snitch before each section. Page numbers are each centred within a further illustration of a Golden Snitch.

Binding: decorated boards in 'half-bound' style with spine and corner pieces in brown and with covers in red.

On spine: 'KENNILWORTHY | QUIDDITCH THROUGH THE AGES [illustration of a flying Quidditch ball, 7 by 14mm, in yellow] | WHISP' (reading lengthways down spine) with publisher's device of a lantern, 10 by 7mm and '[publisher's book device] | [rule] | S' within single ruled border, 12 by 6mm (horizontally at foot of spine). All in gilt.

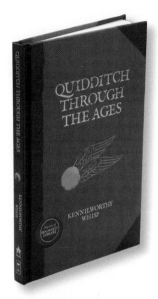

On upper cover: 'QUIDDITCH | THROUGH | THE AGES | [illustration of a Golden Snitch, 38 by 69mm, in yellow] | KENNILWORTHY | WHISP' (all width centred). All in gilt. To the left of the author is a circular 'wax' stamp in crimson and black stating '*Property of* | HOGWARTS | LIBRARY' within circular single ruled border, diameter 20mm, with border and lettering in gilt.

On lower cover: '[illustration of a Golden Snitch, 24 by 42mm] | If you have ever asked yourself where the | Golden Snitch came from, how the Bludgers | came into existence or why the Wigtown Wanderers | have pictures of meat cleavers on their robes, | you need *Quidditch Through the Ages*. | This invaluable volume is consulted by young | Quidditch fans on an almost daily basis. | [new paragraph] Proceeds from the sale of this book will go to | Comic Relief, who will use your money to | continue improving and changing lives – work that | is even more important and astonishing than | the three and a half second capture of the Golden | Snitch by Roderick Plumpton in 1921. | Albus Dumbledore [facsimile signature] | [new paragraph] [three columns, in the first column is '[Lumos logo, 9 by 10mm] [in purple] | LUMOS [in purple] | From every sale of the Hogwarts | Library, Scholastic will donate twenty | percent of the suggested retail sales | price less taxes of this boxed set to two | charities selected by the author J. K. | Rowling: Lumos, a charity founded | by J. K. Rowling that works to end | the institutionalization of children | (wearelumos.org), and Comic Relief, | a UK-based charity that strives to | create a just world free from poverty | (www.comicrelief. com).', in the second column is '['COMIC | RELIEF[UK]' logo, diameter 15mm] [in red, black and white] | Not to be sold separately.' and in the third column is '*Whizz Hard* | [illustration of a flying Quidditch ball] | *Books* | *in association with* | [publisher's device of a lantern, 10 by 7mm] | ARTHUR A. LEVINE BOOKS | [publisher's book device with 'SCHOLASTIC' in white on red panel enclosed by white single ruled border in white, 5 by 45mm] | scholastic.com']'. All in yellow.

All edges trimmed. Red and yellow sewn bands at head and foot of spine. Binding measurements: 203 by 128mm (covers), 203 by 24mm (spine). End-papers: wove paper. The green/brown spine colour continues onto the covers by approximately 13mm.

Dust-jacket: none

Slipcase: card slipcase covered in red paper (see description for A10(e)).

Publication: 29 October 2013

Price: $29.99 [together with A10(e) and A15(c)]

Contents:

Foreword

    ('*Quidditch through the Ages* is one of the most popular titles…')

    (signed, 'Albus Dumbledore' [facsimile signature])

Quidditch Through the Ages

    ('No spell yet devised enables wizards to fly unaided in human form…')

About the Author

    ('Kennilworthy Whisp is a renowned Quidditch expert…')

Notes:

The Scholastic edition is almost exactly the same as the Bloomsbury 'Hogwarts Library' (see A11(d)). Note, however, the different imprint pages and the change of *Philosopher's Stone* to *Sorcerer's Stone* in the list of author's works. The listing of Harry Potter books also omits the Latin, Welsh, Ancient Greek and Irish editions that are unique to Bloomsbury.

Note that the lower cover includes two minor features specific to this volume in the Scholastic 'Hogwarts Library' set. The note 'Not to be sold separately.' is slightly off-set to the left and the publisher's 'SCHOLASTIC' banner is enclosed by a single ruled border in white.

Each section (foreword, chapter or author note) commences with a drop capital.

Copies: private collection (PWE)

HARRY POTTER AND THE
ORDER OF THE PHOENIX

A12(a)   **FIRST ENGLISH EDITION**   (2003)
(children's artwork series in hardback)

HARRY | POTTER | *and the Order of the Phoenix* | [illustration of Hogwarts crest with legend 'DRAGO DORMIENS NUNQUAM TITILLANDUS' on banner, 66 by 81mm] | J. K. ROWLING | [publisher's device of a dog, 11 by 18mm] | BLOOMSBURY (Lines 1 and 2 justified on left and right margins, and all width centred)

Collation: 384 unsigned leaves bound in indeterminate gatherings; 197 by 127mm; [1-7] 8-23 [24] 25-42 [43] 44-57 [58] 59-75 [76] 77-91 [92] 93-111 [112] 113-25 [126] 127-38 [139] 140-62 [163] 164-80 [181] 182-99 [200] 201-225 [226] 227-50 [251] 252-73 [274] 275-94 [295] 296-311 [312] 313-31 [332] 333-51 [352] 353-71 [372] 373-89 [390] 391-411 [412] 413-34 [435] 436-55 [456] 457-79 [480] 481-502 [503] 504-527 [528] 529-49 [550] 551-73 [574] 575-95 [596] 597-619 [620] 621-42 [643] 644-61 [662] 663-73 [674] 675-88 [689] 690-711 [712] 713-22 [723] 724-44 [745] 746-66 [767-68]

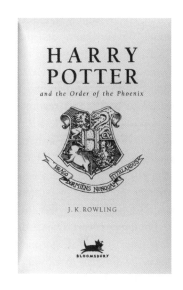

Page contents: [1] half-title: 'HARRY | POTTER | *and the Order of the Phoenix* | [illustration of Hogwarts crest with legend 'DRAGO DORMIENS NUNQUAM TITILLANDUS' on banner, 46 by 57mm]'; [2] '*Titles available in the Harry Potter series | (in reading order):* | Harry Potter and the Philosopher's Stone | Harry Potter and the Chamber of Secrets | Harry Potter and the Prisoner of Azkaban | Harry Potter and the Goblet of Fire | Harry Potter and the Order of the Phoenix | [new paragraph] Harry Potter and the Philosopher's Stone | *also available in Latin and Welsh:* | Harrius Potter et Philosophi Lapis (Latin) | Harri Potter a Maen yr Athronydd (Welsh)'; [3] title-page; [4] 'All rights reserved; no part of this publication may be reproduced or | transmitted by any means, electronic, mechanical, photocopying or otherwise, | without the prior permission of the publisher | [new paragraph] First published in Great Britain in 2003 | Bloomsbury Publishing Plc, 38 Soho Square, London W1D 3HB | [new paragraph] Copyright © 2003 J.K. Rowling | Cover illustrations by Jason Cockcroft © 2003 Bloomsbury Publishing Plc | [new paragraph] Harry Potter, names, characters and related indicia are | copyright and trademark Warner Bros., 2000™ | [new paragraph] The moral right of the author has been asserted | A CIP catalogue record for this book is available | from the British Library | [new paragraph] ISBN 0 7475 5100 6 | [new paragraph] Typeset by Palimpsest Book Production Limited, | Polmont, Stirlingshire | [new paragraph] All paper used by Bloomsbury Publishing, including that in this book, | is a natural, recyclable product made from wood grown in sustainable, | well-managed forests. The manufacturing processes conform to the | environmental regulations of the country of origin. | [new paragraph] Printed in Great Britain by Clays Ltd, St Ives plc | [new paragraph] First edition | [new paragraph] www.bloomsbury.com/harrypotter'; [5] 'To Neil, Jessica and David, | who make my world magical'; [6] blank; [7]-766 text; [767-68] blank

Paper: wove paper

Running title: 'HARRY POTTER' (24mm) on verso, recto title comprises chapter title, pp. 8-766 (excluding pages on which new chapters commence)

Binding: pictorial boards.

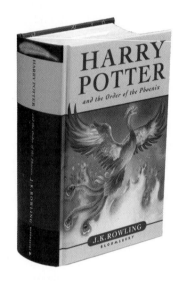

On spine: '[colour illustration of a golden feather on blue panel, 65 by 15mm] HARRY POTTER [in burgundy on yellow panel, 65 by 47mm] *and the Order of the Phoenix* [in yellow] J.K.ROWLING [in white, both title conclusion and author on burgundy panel, 65 by 109mm] BLOOMSBURY [publisher's device of the head of a dog, 4 by 3mm] [both in yellow on blue panel, 65 by 35mm]' (reading lengthways down spine).

On upper cover: 'HARRY | POTTER | *and the Order of the Phoenix* [lines 1 and 2 in burgundy, line 3 in blue, all on yellow panel, 62 by 131mm] | [blue rule, 131mm] | [colour illustration of a phoenix rising from flames, 125 by 131mm] | [blue rule, 131mm intersected by burgundy panel with 'J.K.ROWLING' in white] | BLOOMSBURY [in burgundy on yellow panel, 15 by 131mm]' (all width centred).

On lower cover: '*Dumbledore lowered | his hands and surveyed Harry | through his half-moon glasses.* '*It is time,*' | *he said,* '*for me to tell you what I should have | told you five years ago, Harry. Please sit down.* | *I am going to tell you everything.*' | [new paragraph] Harry Potter is due to start his fifth year at Hogwarts School | of Witchcraft and Wizardry. He is desperate to get back to | school and find out why his friends Ron and Hermione | have been so secretive all summer. However, | what Harry is about to discover in his | new year at Hogwarts will turn | his world upside down ... | [new paragraph] This is a gripping and | electrifying new novel, | full of suspense, secrets, | and – of course – magic, | from the incomparable | J.K. Rowling. | [barcode in black on white panel, 21 by 40mm together with '[publisher's device of a dog, 5 by 9mm] | BLOOMSBURY' in black on right side of panel and 'http:// www.bloomsbury.com' below panel, in burgundy on yellow panel, 5 by 40mm]'. Reading lengthways down right side next to foot of spine 'Cover illustrations by Jason Cockcroft'. All in black and all on colour illustration of an arch, with runic characters above, a candle-lit vaulted ceiling passage and a wizard, witch, centaur, goblin and house-elf comprising characters in the fountain of magical brethren with pouring water.

All edges trimmed. Binding measurements: 205 by 131mm (covers), 205 by 65mm (spine). End-papers: wove paper.

Dust-jacket: coated wove paper, 206 by 527mm

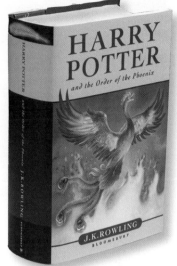

Spine, upper and lower covers replicate the binding, with the exception of the illustration note which is omitted.

On upper inside flap: '*Dumbledore lowered his hands and surveyed Harry | through his half-moon glasses. 'It is time,' he said, | 'for me to tell you what I should have told you five | years ago, Harry. Please sit down. I am | going to tell you everything.'* | [new paragraph] Harry Potter is about to start his fifth year at | Hogwarts School of Witchcraft and Wizardry. | Unlike most schoolboys, Harry never enjoys his | summer holidays, but this summer is even worse | than usual. The Dursleys, of course, are making | his life a misery, but even his best friends, Ron | and Hermione, seem to be neglecting him. | Harry has had enough. He is beginning to think | he must do something, *anything*, to change his | situation, when the summer holidays come to an | end in a very dramatic fashion. What Harry is | about to discover in his new year at Hogwarts | will turn his world upside down ... | [new paragraph] This is a gripping and electrifying new novel, | full of suspense, secrets, and – of course – magic, | from the incomparable J.K. Rowling. | £16.99'. All in white on burgundy panel with the exception of the price which is in black, and all on an illustration of flames.

On lower inside flap: 'J.K. (Joanne Kathleen) Rowling has written | fiction since she was a child, and always wanted | to be an author. Her parents loved reading, and | their house in Chepstow was full of books. In | fact, J.K. Rowling wrote her first 'book' at the | age of six – a story about a rabbit called Rabbit! | [new paragraph] The idea for Harry Potter occurred to | J.K. Rowling on the train from Manchester to | London, where she says Harry Potter 'just strolled | into my head fully formed', and by the time she | had arrived at King's Cross, many of the characters | had taken shape. During the next five years she | outlined the plots for each book and began | writing the first in the series, *Harry Potter and* | *the Philosopher's Stone*, which was first published | by Bloomsbury in 1997. The other Harry Potter | titles: *Harry Potter and the Chamber of Secrets,* | *Harry Potter and the Prisoner of Azkaban,* and | *Harry Potter and the Goblet of Fire,* followed. | J.K. Rowling has also written two other | companion books, *Quidditch Through the Ages* | and *Fantastic Beasts and Where to Find Them,* in | aid of Comic Relief. | Cover illustrations by Jason Cockcroft'. All in white on burgundy panel with the exception of the illustration note, which is in burgundy on an illustration of flames.

Publication: 21 June 2003 (simultaneous with A12(aa) and A12(aaa)) in an edition of 4 million copies (confirmed by Bloomsbury)

Price: £16.99

Contents:
Harry Potter and the Order of the Phoenix
('The hottest day of the summer so far was drawing to a close and a drowsy silence lay...')

Notes:

In an interview with me in September 2013, Nigel Newton recalled receiving the manuscript of this title. He noted 'Christopher Little phoned me out of the blue and said, "Nigel, drink at the Pelican tonight?" and I said, "Drink at the Pelican? Yes, Chris, 6 pm." That was where he had delivered the previous book to me. So I drove to the Pelican, a pub off the Fulham Road not far from Stamford Bridge, in a state of high alert. And I went in and there was a massive Sainsbury's plastic carrier bag at his feet... he said nothing about that and I said nothing and he just said "Drink?" and I said, "a pint, please". So we stood at the bar and drank our pints and said nothing about Harry Potter. But when we left I walked out with the carrier bag. It was a classic dead letter drop. So I put this bag into the back of my car and drove it home. By this stage the series was so enormous that I was almost frightened to be in physical possession of it. My three children and wife were all enormous fans themselves so I couldn't say anything to them. I shoved it under the bed. I had another typescript sitting there (publisher's lives are about reading typescripts, not books)... so I stuck [the] top four pages of David Guterson's *East of the Mountains* on the top and then stayed up all night reading it, which my wife did find a bit odd. I think I did tell her (because you tell your wife everything don't you?) There was no question of showing any of it to her. Even then I was putting bits of it in the safe. The next morning at about 10 am I rung up Emma Matthewson, Jo's editor at Bloomsbury, and, having finished it, drove it over to her... I was so relieved to hand it over. By this stage we had done quite a lot to secure her house and we had various common-sense systems. People seem to love editing online (I don't know why) and so the first thing we did was to make sure she had a computer that wasn't attached to the internet. No hacking in the world could get at something that wasn't plugged-in.'

The editorial files preserved at Bloomsbury include an early proposed schedule for the book:

December 2002	—	delivery of manuscript and briefing of artists
January 2003	—	editing of manuscript and finalisation of visuals
February 2003	—	copy-editing and proofs of artwork
March 2003	—	text sent for proofing

March/April 2003	—	'rest period' scheduled
		(the author's son was born at the end of March)
May 2003	—	revised proofs due
June 2003	—	book ready to print
July 2003	—	12 July proposed publication date

There is a letter from Emma Matthewson to J.K. Rowling dated 4 February 2003 thanking the author 'for going through everything so fast …'. On 11 March 2003 Bloomsbury sent the author a 'long fax with copy-edit questions'. Matthewson explained that '… it looks more daunting than it is. These are combined from the UK and US copy-editors'. The earliest preserved set of proofs is dated 16 March 2003. This is a proof-reader's marked-up set. The text, in this state, lacks the dedication. Certainly by March the text was available to Scholastic since 'two copyediting queries' from Scholastic were communicated to the Christopher Little Agency on 20 March. These were sent to the editorial team at Bloomsbury. Another proof of the text was printed on 18 April 2003. Two global search and replace requests were communicated to the typesetters on 24 April. These were the change of 'unforgiveable' to 'unforgivable' and the name 'Prewitt' changed to 'Prewett'.

While working on the commission for the English children's edition, the artist Giles Greenfield suffered a devastating loss when his six-month-old daughter was diagnosed with a terminal genetic illness. Greenfield's original designs were, consequently, developed by Jason Cockcroft. Proof sheets for dust-jackets for both the children's edition and the adult edition are preserved in the Bloomsbury archives dated 25 April 2003.

Publication was slightly later than originally scheduled.

This title enjoyed a publicity campaign hitherto unknown in the series. As early as February 2003 posters were available. On 2 June posters were released to retailers together with a two-week countdown card. Then, on 16 June, Bloomsbury released additional publicity material. This included a 'dumpbin' display case (empty), a 'cut-out' and posters. A 'window-piece' was also available for the publication date.

To cope with demand for duplicate copies, Bloomsbury released:

- A 'triple pack' comprising three copies of this edition, three door signs and three bookmarks (priced at £50.97).
- A 'family triple pack' comprising two copies of this edition, one copy of the adult edition (see A12(aa)), three door signs and three bookmarks (priced at £50.97).
- A 'family four pack' comprising two copies of this edition, two copies of the adult edition (see A12(aa)), four door signs and four bookmarks (priced at £67.96).

This title was the first new Harry Potter novel to be published after the release of the first Harry Potter film (in November 2001). Nigel Newton, in an interview with me in September 2013, noted that the movie opened up the audience from 'people who shopped in Waterstone's and read the *Daily Telegraph*' to 'a wider group of people'. He also recalled that the movies caused the supermarkets to 'swing into action'. They had only recently begun to sell books due to the repeal of the net book agreement and were still working out that books were items that would respond to the supermarket model of sales. As Newton recalls '… they hadn't been selling the new Harry Potters originally, but whenever the movie of number one came along they all said, "right we'll try this". So then what we witnessed was that *Philosopher's Stone* went back to number one on the bestseller list even though it was some years old by then, and then two weeks later, the *Chamber of Secrets* went to number one. And you could watch this cascade as new readers became completely hooked – just like everyone else – and read right the way through to being up-to-date to whatever book we were at by then.' With the release, therefore, of *Order of the Phoenix*, demand had grown to an unprecedented extent.

With such a significant print-run there are occasional anomalies in the printing. One anomaly occurs on page [7], where 'boy' on the ninth line of text is printed as 'bo ' only. Such oddities cannot, I suggest, be regarded as issue points but rather as minor errors in book production on an unprecedented scale.

The English audiobook version, read by Stephen Fry, has a duration of approximately twenty-nine and a quarter hours.

Reprints (and subsequent new editions) include a number of corrections to the text. These comprise:

Page 18, line 25	'beat up a ten year old' to 'beat up a ten-year-old'
Page 20, line 19	'Harry stood stock still' to 'Harry stood stock-still'
Page 23, line 9	'he span on his heel' to 'he spun on his heel'
Page 33, line 24	'Harry supplied dully' to 'Harry supplied tonelessly'
Page 36, line 5	'what ARE Dementoids?' to 'what ARE Dementoids?'
Page 38, line 31	'Harry said dully' to 'Harry said'
Page 40, line 23	'don't know, Marge was right' to 'don't know. Marge was right'
Page 56, line 11	'yelled Moody' to 'yelled Moody.'
Page 66, line 18	'Apparation tests' to 'Apparition tests'
Page 70, line 70	'said Ron dully' to 'said Ron'
Page 79, line 34	'closely examining' to 'minutely examining'
Page 96, line 6	'a shifty at it' to a 'shufti at it'
Page 99, line 26	'closely' to 'intently'
Page 103, lines 24-25	'the bottom of the tree closely' to 'the bottom of the tree'
Page 105, line 19	'examining the tapestry closely' to 'examining the tapestry carefully'
Page 119, line 32	'Apparation Test Centre' to 'Apparition Test Centre'
Page 128, line 17	'surveyed Fudge' to 'looked at Fudge'
Page 131, line 33	'eyeing her closely' to 'eying her suspiciously'
Page 138, line 4	'clearing the witness' to 'clearing the accused'
Page 145, line 23	'SPEW' to 'S.P.E.W.'
Page 145, line 27	'SPEW' to 'S.P.E.W.'
Page 145, line 29	'*SPEW*' to '*S.P.E.W.*'
Page 151, lines 20-21	'Harry hurried across the room, closed the door, then returned slowly to his bed and sank on to it' to 'Harry returned slowly to his bed and sank on to it'
Page 153, line 13	'lying it on his folded robes' to 'laying it on his folded robes'
Page 161, line 16	'The Order are better prepared' to 'The Order is better prepared'

Page 167, lines 35-36   'He wondered dully' to 'He wondered bleakly'
Page 171, lines 7-8   'bit off the frog's head' to 'bit off the Frog's head'
Page 172, line 17   '...*like*' to '... *like*'
Page 176, lines 32-33   "We'd better change,' said Hermione at last, and all of them opened their trunks with difficulty and pulled on their school robes.' to "We'd better change,' said Hermione at last.'
Page 178, line 2   'Hogsmeade Station' to 'Hogsmeade station'
Page 178, line 15   'the gathering gloom' to 'the gloom'
Page 193, line 36   'said Hermione through gritted teeth' to 'said Hermione ominously'
Page 194, line 20   'he said dully' to 'he said'
Page 206, line 29   'SPEW' to 'S.P.E.W.'
Page 207, line 3   'an hour and a half's' to 'three quarters of an hour's'
Page 207, lines 7-8   'remaining hour and twenty minutes' to 'remaining thirty-five minutes'
Page 207, line 24   'around the edges of the yard' to 'around the yard'
Page 208, line 36   'said Harry dully' to 'said Harry listlessly'
Page 209, lines 17-18   'where he sat down between Ron and Hermione and ignored' to 'ignoring'
Page 212, line 22   " ... now he's in' to "... now he's in'
Page 217, line 6   'observing them all closely' to 'observing them all'
Page 222, lines 9-10   'without saying a word, turned on his heel and left' to 'without saying a word and left'
Page 223, lines 21-22   'watching Harry closely' to 'frowning at Harry'
Page 225, line 1   'eyed him closely' to 'eyed him'
Page 226, line 14   'through clenched teeth' to 'in a shaking voice'
Page 231, line 2   'She turned on her heel and left' to 'She left'
Page 235, lines 26-27   'said Harry through gritted teeth' to 'snarled Harry'
Page 237, line 24   'up to the castle an hour and a half later' to 'up to the castle'
Page 238, line 12   'She turned on her heel and stormed away' to 'She stormed away'
Page 239, line 11   'a large technicolour kitten' to 'a large technicoloured kitten'
Page 247, line 16   'shining with blood' to 'dotted with blood'
Page 247, line 27   'dotted with drops of blood' to 'shining with drops of blood'
Page 256, lines 7-8   'the caretaker turned on his heel and shuffled back' to 'the caretaker turned and shuffled back'
Page 259, line 25   'for a week' to 'all week'
Page 276, lines 12-13   '*This is a further, disgusting attempt*' to '*This is a further disgusting attempt*'
Page 277, lines 6-7   'turned on his heel to face then' to 'turned to face them'
Page 282, lines 8-9   'Professor Umbridge surveyed Professor Trelawney' to 'Professor Umbridge's eyebrows were still raised'
Page 283, line 30   "You disagree?' she repeated.' to "You disagree?'
Page 288, lines 23-24   'Harry saw Malfoy look up eagerly and watch Umbridge and Grubbly-Plank closely.' to 'Harry saw Malfoy look up eagerly.'
Page 290, line 17   'said Harry dully' to 'said Harry'
Page 293, line 19   'The whole time you're sure you know' to 'The whole time you know'

Page 302, line 1	'and Terry Boot, Ginny, followed by' to 'and Terry Boot; then Ginny, followed by'
Page 303, lines 26-27	'said Michael Corner, who was watching her closely' to 'said Michael Corner'
Page 304, line 16	'he repeated' to 'he asked'
Page 313, line 1	'noticeboard;' to 'noticeboard,'
Page 319, line 15	'screwed it into her eye, to examine' to 'screwed it into her eye to examine'
Page 323, line 23	'Harry, watching him closely, added' to 'His eyes on Snape, Harry added'
Page 326, line 23	'they chanted dully' to 'they chanted drearily'
Page 333, line 23	'said Ron through clenched teeth' to 'said Ron testily'
Page 337, line 19	'said George, through clenched teeth' to 'said George, wincing'
Page 341, line 33	'Surveying Dobby more closely' to 'Looking back at Dobby'
Page 343, lines 36-37	'It was, after all, very late, he was exhausted, and had Snape's essay to finish' to 'It was, after all, very late, and he was exhausted'
Page 359, line 20	'into the dazzling sunlight' to 'into the dazzling sky'
Page 359, line 27	'blinking stupidly in the sunlight' to 'blinking stupidly'
Page 361, line 12	'he wheeled around to watch Ron' to 'he turned his Firebolt towards Ron'
Page 366, line 29	'turned on their heels and marched off' to 'turned and marched off'
Page 367, line 22	'wheeled round' to 'spun round'
Page 374, line 22	'surveying her sternly' to 'fixing her sternly'
Page 376, line 8	'Harry repeated' to 'Harry asked'
Page 376, lines 20-21	'he surveyed Ron' to 'he squinted at Ron'
Page 387, line 13	'repeated Professor Umbridge' to 'said Professor Umbridge'
Page 387, line 37	'Hagrid repeated blankly' to 'Hagrid echoed blankly'
Page 393, line 16	'It surveyed the class' to 'It looked around at the class'
Page 400, line 9	'bearing the legend: 'HAVE A VERY HARRY CHRISTMAS!"' to 'bearing the legend: HAVE A VERY HARRY CHRISTMAS!'
Page 400, line 20	'Nargles are' to 'Nargles were'
Page 404, line 15	'Harry gave a half-hearted shrug. In truth, he didn't know whether he was all right or not. 'What's up?' said Ron' to '"What's up?' said Ron'
Page 418, line 25	'repeated Phineas' to 'recited Phineas'
Page 423, line 24	'the kitchen door' to 'the door'
Page 428, line 30	'eyeing the Weasley party closely as though counting' to 'eyeing the Weasley party as though counting'
Page 437, line 37	'Harry span round' to 'Harry spun round'
Page 441, line 6	'first thing this morning' to 'yesterday morning'
Page 442, line 2	'he wheeled round' to 'he turned on the spot to face her'
Page 446, line 23	'two years' to 'three years'
Page 453, line 7	'Harry's head span round' to 'Harry's head spun round'
Page 453, line 28	'looking closely at Harry' to 'peering at Harry'
Page 453, line 32	'surveyed his own feet' to 'stared at his own feet'
Page 460, lines 34-35	'Snape pocketed his wand, turned on his heel and swept back' to 'Snape pocketed his wand and swept back'

Page 468, line 16	'Snape continued to survey him through narrowed eyes for a moment, then said, 'Now, Occlumency.' to "Now, Occlumency.'
Page 472, line 22	'said Snape, watching him closely' to 'said Snape contemptuously'
Page 474, line 37	'watching Snape's face closely' to 'watching Snape closely for a reaction'
Page 477, line 19	'watching Fred and George closely' to 'watching Fred and George'
Page 480, line 18	'*Algernon Rookwood*' to '*Augustus Rookwood*'
Page 487, line 16	'she predicted students' answers' to 'she predict students' answers'
Page 492, lines 6-7	"Remember the first time we played against each other, in the third year?' she asked' to "Remember the first time we played against each other?' she asked'
Page 519, lines 27-33	delete paragraph ('Harry was so angry with her he did not talk to her for the rest of the day, which proved to be another bad one. When people were not discussing the escaped Death Eaters in the corridors, they were laughing at Gryffindor's abysmal performance in their match against Hufflepuff; the Slytherins were singing 'Weasley is our King' so loudly and frequently that by sundown Filch had banned it from the corridors out of sheer irritation.')
Page 526, line 24	'*Locomotor trunks!*' to '*Locomotor trunks!*'
Page 526, line 27	'standing stock still' to 'standing stock-still'
Page 533, line 9	'Firenze surveyed Harry' to 'Firenze looked at Harry'
Page 533, line 24	'he'd repeated Firenze's words' to 'he'd passed on Firenze's message'
Page 536, line 9	'the elf tried to kick himself and fell to the floor' to 'Dobby tried to kick himself and sank to his knees'
Page 536, lines 11-12	'Dobby let out a howl, and began beating his bare feet hard on the floor to 'Dobby let out a howl'
Page 551, lines 13-14	'Draco Malfoy had slid out from behind the door, closely followed' to 'Draco Malfoy had slid out from behind the door, followed'
Page 551, line 18	'It's only teachers who can dock points from houses, Malfoy' to 'You can't take points from fellow prefects, Malfoy'
Page 551, line 20	delete line ("Yeah, we're prefects, too, remember?' snarled Ron.')
Page 551, line 21	'I know *prefects* can't dock points, Weasel King' to 'I know *prefects* can't dock points from each other'
Page 554, lines 35-36	'surveying him complacently, like a toad' to 'looking like a toad'
Page 555, lines 24-25	'watching him closely' to 'watching him'
Page 555, line 36	"I don't know where he is,' Harry repeated.' to "I don't know where he is.'
Page 555, line 37	'He pretended to drink again. She was watching him very closely' to 'Harry pretended to drink again.'
Page 556, line 1	"Very well,' she said, though she looked displeased' to "Very well,' said Umbridge, looking displeased'
Page 572, line 32	'You will not repeat what you saw to anybody!' to 'You will not tell anybody what you saw!'
Page 575, line 2	'he said dully' to 'he said'
Page 575, line 31	'*wasn't he?*' to '*wasn't he?*'

Page 577, line 20	'asked Ginny, watching him closely' to 'asked Ginny'
Page 577, line 26	delete first sentence ('Ginny continued to watch him thoughtfully.')
Page 577, line 33	'said Harry dully' to 'said Harry hopelessly'
Page 582, line 29	'Snape was surveying him' to 'Snape was watching him'
Page 595, line 3	'Wizarding Wheezes' to 'Wizard Wheezes'
Page 602, line 33	'the topmost row' to 'the second topmost row'
Page 607, line 37	'need yeh two ter help me' to 'need you two ter help me'
Page 608, line 26	'*What* is it?' to 'What is it?'
Page 625, line 32	'he thought dully' to 'he thought'
Page 644, line 20	'He wheeled around and strode blindly' to 'He strode blindly'
Page 647, line 6	'said Harry through gritted teeth' to 'said Harry in a trembling voice'
Page 648, line 11	'closely followed by Luna' to 'followed by Luna'
Page 656, lines 1-2	'Draco Malfoy entered the room, closely followed by Snape' to 'Draco Malfoy came back into the room, holding open the door for Snape'
Page 656, lines 9-10	'surveying her coolly' to 'observing her coolly'
Page 656, line 27	'repeated Umbridge angrily' to 'shouted Umbridge angrily'
Page 668, lines 34-35	'Devoid of a wand' to 'Wandless'
Page 670, lines 5-6	'Ron came into sight, closely followed by Ginny, Neville and Luna' to 'Ron came into sight with Ginny, Neville and Luna hurrying along behind him'
Page 670, line 18	'Bat Bogey' to 'Bat-Bogey'
Page 671, line 24	'said Harry through gritted teeth' to 'said Harry frustratedly'
Page 678, line 17	'closely followed by' to 'closely followed'
Page 679, lines 17-18	'he marched over the threshold, the others at his heels' to 'he marched forwards, leading the others over the threshold'
Page 683, lines 20-21	'angrier than the occasion warranted, 'there isn't any' to 'angrier than the occasion warranted. 'There isn't any'
Page 684, line 7	'the wall span' to 'the wall spun'
Page 702, line 32	'Harry span around' to 'Harry spun round'
Page 705, line 10	'He climbed backwards onto it' to 'He climbed backwards on to it'
Page 709, line 10	'Neville span himself' to 'Neville spun himself'
Page 709, line 25	'Neville sank to the ground' to 'Neville sank on to the bench above'
Page 710, lines 17-20	'Dumbledore sped down the steps past Neville and Harry, who had no more thoughts of leaving. Dumbledore was already at the foot of the steps when the Death Eaters nearest realised he was there and yelled' to 'Dumbledore had already sped past Neville and Harry, who had no more thoughts of leaving, when the Death Eaters nearest realised Dumbledore was there and yelled'
Page 710, lines 32-33	'He was jumping down the steps again' to 'He jumped to the ground'
Page 711, line 10	'He had reached the floor, his breath coming in searing gasps' to 'Harry's breath was coming in searing gasps'
Page 711, line 13	'But as he reached the ground and sprinted towards the dais' to 'But as he sprinted towards the dais'

Page 715, line 17	'span off' to 'spun off'
Page 721, line 8	'Anti-Disapparation Jinx' to 'Anti-Disapparition Jinx'
Page 721, line 31	'Fudge wheeled around' to 'Fudge spun round'
Page 721, line 34	"He - here?' said Fudge, goggling at Harry' to "He - here?' said Fudge'
Page 722, line 15	'and surveyed it' to 'and glanced at it'
Page 724, line 4	'surveyed Harry out of' to 'watched Harry with'
Page 724, line 19	'The wizard was surveying him' to 'The wizard was eyeing him'
Page 725, line 20	'listening closely' to 'listening eagerly'
Page 727, lines 6-7	'He turned on his heel and ran to the door' to 'He ran to the door'
Page 742, line 4	'Dumbledore surveyed him for a moment through his glasses' to 'Dumbledore took a deep breath'
Page 746, line 17	'boy who lived' to 'Boy Who Lived'
Page 753, line 12	delete sentence ('He was watching Harry closely')
Page 755, lines 15-16	'end-of-term leaving feast' to 'end-of-term Leaving Feast'
Page 766, line 18	'He turned away from Uncle Vernon to survey Harry' to 'He turned from Uncle Vernon to Harry'

In addition to these there are four global corrections throughout the text: 'OWL to 'O.W.L.', 'OWLs' to 'O.W.L.s', 'NEWT' to 'N.E.W.T.' and 'NEWTs' to 'N.E.W.T.s'.

Copies: private collection (PWE)

Reprints include:
3 5 7 9 10 8 6 4 2

A report compiled by the printers, Clays Ltd, in October 2013 noted that, after the first edition 1.2 million copies were reprinted within the following month across four different impressions. Clays also noted that, to date, they had produced a minimum of 2.9 million paperbacks and 5.5 million hardbacks across 63 printings. This is therefore the first book in the series in which the sales of hardbacks has, to date, been greater than paperbacks and reflects the surge in sales of the first edition.

A12(aa)   FIRST ENGLISH EDITION   (2003)
(Michael Wildsmith photography adult artwork series in hardback)

Harry Potter and the | Order of the Phoenix | J. K. Rowling | BLOOMSBURY (All width centred)

Collation: 384 unsigned leaves bound in indeterminate gatherings; 197 by 127mm; [1-7] 8-23 [24] 25-42 [43] 44-57 [58] 59-75 [76] 77-91 [92] 93-111 [112] 113-25 [126] 127-38 [139] 140-62 [163] 164-80 [181] 182-99 [200] 201-225 [226] 227-50 [251] 252-73 [274] 275-94 [295] 296-311 [312] 313-31 [332] 333-51 [352] 353-71 [372] 373-89 [390] 391-411 [412] 413-34 [435] 436-55 [456] 457-79 [480] 481-502 [503] 504-527 [528] 529-49 [550] 551-73 [574] 575-95 [596] 597-619 [620] 621-42 [643]

644-61 [662] 663-73 [674] 675-88 [689] 690-711 [712] 713-22 [723] 724-44 [745] 746-66 [767-68]

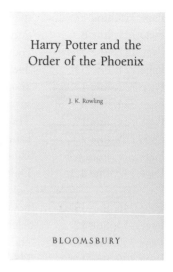

Page contents: [1] half-title: 'Harry Potter and the | Order of the Phoenix'; [2] '*Titles available in the Harry Potter series* | *(in reading order):* | Harry Potter and the Philosopher's Stone | Harry Potter and the Chamber of Secrets | Harry Potter and the Prisoner of Azkaban | Harry Potter and the Goblet of Fire | Harry Potter and the Order of the Phoenix | [new paragraph] *Harry Potter and the Philosopher's Stone* | *also available in Latin and Welsh:* | Harrius Potter et Philosophi Lapis (Latin) | Harri Potter a Maen yr Athronydd (Welsh)'; [3] title-page; [4] 'All rights reserved; no part of this publication may be reproduced or | transmitted by any means, electronic, mechanical, photocopying or otherwise, | without the prior permission of the publisher | [new paragraph] First published in Great Britain in 2003 | Bloomsbury Publishing Plc, 38 Soho Square, London W1D 3HB | [new paragraph] Copyright © 2003 J.K. Rowling | [new paragraph] Harry Potter, names, characters and related indicia are | copyright and trademark Warner Bros., 2000™ | [new paragraph] The moral right of the author has been asserted | A CIP catalogue record for this book is available | from the British Library | [new paragraph] ISBN 0 7475 6940 1 | [new paragraph] Typeset by Palimpsest Book Production Limited, | Polmont, Stirlingshire | [new paragraph] All paper used by Bloomsbury Publishing, including that in this book, | is a natural, recyclable product made from wood grown in sustainable, | well-managed forests. The manufacturing processes conform to the | environmental regulations of the country of origin. | [new paragraph] Printed in Great Britain by Clays Ltd, St Ives plc | [new paragraph] First edition | [new paragraph] www. bloomsbury.com/harrypotter'; [5] '*To Neil, Jessica and David,* | *who make my world magical*'; [6] blank; [7]-766 text; [767-68] blank

Paper: wove paper

Running title: 'HARRY POTTER' (24mm) on verso, recto title comprises chapter title, pp. 8-766 (excluding pages on which new chapters commence)

Binding: black boards.
   On spine: 'J.K. ROWLING | HARRY | POTTER | AND THE ORDER OF THE PHOENIX | [publisher's device of a figure with a bow, 13 by 12mm]'. All in gilt.
   Upper and lower covers: blank.
   All edges trimmed. Binding measurements: 205 by 128mm (covers), 205 by 73mm (spine). End-papers: wove paper.

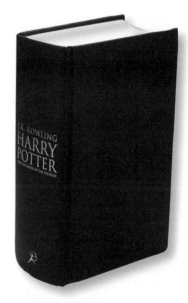

Dust-jacket: coated wove paper, 205 by 526mm

On spine: '[colour photograph of a metallic phoenix rising through flame, all within single white ruled border, 58 by 54mm] | J.K. ROWLING [in white] | HARRY [in gilt] | POTTER [in gilt] | AND THE ORDER OF THE PHOENIX [in white] | [publisher's device of a figure with a bow, 13 by 12mm] [in olive beige]'. All on black.

On upper cover: 'J. K. ROWLING [in white] | HARRY [embossed in gilt] | POTTER [embossed in gilt] | AND THE ORDER OF THE PHOENIX [in white] | BLOOMSBURY [in white]' (all width centred). All on colour photograph of a metallic phoenix rising through flame.

On lower cover: black and white photograph of J.K. Rowling standing against bookshelves with 'www.bloomsbury.com/harrypotter [in black on olive beige panel, 5 by 40mm] | [barcode in black on white panel, 20 by 39mm] | BLOOMSBURY [in black on olive beige panel, 7 by 40mm]' (lower right).

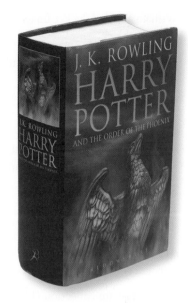

On upper inside flap: '*Dumbledore lowered his hands and surveyed* | *Harry through his half-moon glasses.* | *'It is time,' he said, 'for me to tell you what* | *I should have told you five years ago,* | *Harry. Please sit down. I am going to tell* | *you everything.'* | [new paragraph] Harry Potter is due to start his fifth year | at Hogwarts School of Witchcraft and | Wizardry. Unusually for a schoolboy, | however, Harry is not enjoying his | summer holidays. He is feeling neglected | by his friends, and, as ever, the Dursleys | are making his life a misery. But Harry | has had enough. He is beginning to think | he must do something, *anything*, to change | his situation. Then the summer holidays | come to an unexpectedly dramatic end, | and Harry is thrown back into life at | Hogwarts School. What Harry is about to | discover at Hogwarts will turn his world | upside down … | [new paragraph] This is a stunning tour de force, in which | J.K. Rowling weaves together with | consummate skill the magical ingredients | of humour, suspense and drama which | have become her trademark. | [new paragraph] £16.99'. All in white on black.

On lower inside flap: 'J. K. (JOANNE KATHLEEN) ROWLING | has written fiction since she was a child. | Born in 1965, she grew up in Chepstow | and wrote her first 'book' at the age of six | – a story about a rabbit called Rabbit. | She studied French and Classics at Exeter | University, then moved to London to | work at Amnesty International, and then | to Portugal to teach English as a foreign | language, before settling in Edinburgh. | [new paragraph] The idea for Harry Potter occurred to her | on the train from Manchester to London, | where she says Harry Potter 'just strolled | into my head fully formed', and by the | time she had arrived at King's Cross, | many of the characters had taken shape. | During the next five years she outlined | the plots for each book and began writing | the first in the series, *Harry Potter and* | *the Philosopher's Stone*, which was first | published by Bloomsbury in 1997. The | other Harry Potter titles: *Harry Potter and* | *the Chamber of Secrets, Harry Potter and the* | *Prisoner of Azkaban*, and *Harry Potter and* | *the Goblet of Fire*, followed. J. K. Rowling | has also written two other companion | books, *Quidditch Through the Ages* and | *Fantastic Beasts and Where to Find Them*, in | aid of Comic Relief. | [new paragraph] Jacket Design:

William Webb | Jacket Image: Michael Wildsmith | Author Photograph: © Bill de la HEY'. All in white on black.

Publication: 21 June 2003 (simultaneous with A12(a) and A12(aaa)) in an edition of 500,000 copies (confirmed by Bloomsbury)

Price: £16.99

Contents:
Harry Potter and the Order of the Phoenix
('The hottest day of the summer so far was drawing to a close and a drowsy silence lay...')

Notes:
This was the first title in the series for which the children's and adult editions were published simultaneously.

At least one reprint of this edition (sixth impression) included the Hogwarts crest on both the half-title and title-page (from the children's edition).

Copies: private collection (PWE)

Reprints include:
7 9 10 8 6
9 10 8

A12(aaa)   FIRST AMERICAN EDITION   (2003)
(children's artwork series in hardback)

HARRY POTTER | AND THE ORDER OF THE PHOENIX | [black and white illustration of a black dog passing through a doorway, with knarled tree on right, 70 by 52mm] | BY | J. K.

ROWLING | ILLUSTRATIONS BY MARY GRANDPRÉ | [publisher's device of a lantern, 12 by 9mm] | ARTHUR A. LEVINE BOOKS | AN IMPRINT OF SCHOLASTIC PRESS (All width centred on a diamond pattern background)

Collation: 448 unsigned leaves bound in indeterminate gatherings; 228 by 150mm; [I-VI] VII-XI [XII-XIV] 1-870 [871-82]

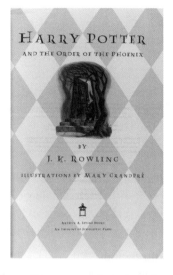

Page contents: [I] half-title: 'HARRY POTTER | AND THE ORDER OF THE PHOENIX' (all on diamond pattern background); [II] 'ALSO BY J. K. ROWLING | [new paragraph] *Harry Potter and the Sorcerer's Stone* | Year One at Hogwarts | [new paragraph] *Harry Potter and the Chamber of Secrets* | Year Two at Hogwarts | [new paragraph] *Harry Potter and the Prisoner of Azkaban* | Year Three at Hogwarts | [new paragraph] *Harry Potter and the Goblet of Fire* | Year Four at Hogwarts'; [III] title-page; [IV] '[device of twelve stars] | Text copyright © 2003 by J. K. Rowling | Illustrations by Mary GrandPré copyright © 2003 by Warner Bros. | HARRY POTTER, characters, names and related indicia are trademarks of | and © Warner Bros. Harry Potter Publishing Rights © J. K. Rowling. | All rights reserved. Published by Scholastic Press, a division of Scholastic Inc., | *Publishers since 1920.* | SCHOLASTIC, SCHOLASTIC PRESS, and the LANTERN LOGO | are trademarks and/or registered trademarks of Scholastic Inc. | [new paragraph] No part of this publication may be reproduced, or stored in a retrieval system, or transmitted | in any form or by any means, electronic, mechanical, photocopying, recording, or otherwise, | without written permission of the publisher. For information regarding permission, write | to Scholastic Inc., Attention: Permissions Department, 557 Broadway, New York, NY 10012. | [new paragraph] Library of Congress Cataloging-in-Publication Data Available | [new paragraph] Library of Congress Control Number: 2003102525 | [new paragraph] ISBN 0-439-35806-X [new paragraph] 10 9 8 7 6 5 4 3 2 1   03 04 05 06 07 | Printed in the U.S.A. 23 | First American edition, July 2003'; [V] 'TO NEIL, JESSICA, AND DAVID, | WHO MAKE MY WORLD MAGICAL.'; [VI] blank; VII-XI 'CONTENTS' (thirty-eight chapters listed with titles and page references); [XII] blank; [XIII] half-title: 'HARRY POTTER | AND THE ORDER OF THE PHOENIX' (all on diamond pattern background); [XIV] blank; 1-870 text; [871-72] blank; [873] 'ABOUT THE AUTHOR | [new paragraph] J. K. Rowling is the author of five magnificent novels in the | Harry Potter series. Her books have been honored with the | Hugo Award, the Bram Stoker Award, the Whitbread | Children's Book Award, the Nestlé Smarties Book Prize, | the British Book Awards Children's Book of the Year, and | numerous state, magazine, and children's choice citations. | Ms. Rowling herself has received a special certificate for be- | ing a three-year winner of the Nestlé Smarties Book Prize | as well as a special commendation from the Anne Spencer | Lindbergh Prize for her outstanding contribution to chil- | dren's fantasy literature. She has also been named an Offi- | cer of the Order of the British Empire. | [new paragraph] Ms. Rowling lives in Scotland with her husband and | two children.'; [874] blank; [875] 'ABOUT THE ILLUSTRATOR | [new paragraph]

Mary GrandPré works in a style she calls "soft geometry," | combining her concerns for color, light, drawing, and de- | sign with her signature chalk pastels. She has illustrated | more than fifteen beautiful books, including *Plum*, a col- | lection of poetry by Tony Mitton, and the American edi- | tions of all five Harry Potter novels. Her work has also | appeared in *The New Yorker, The Atlantic Monthly*, and | *Communication Arts*, and on the cover of *Time*. | [new paragraph] Ms. GrandPré lives in St. Paul, Minnesota, with her | family.'; [876] blank; [877] colophon: '[publisher's device of a lantern, 17 by 12mm] | *This* | *book was art* | *directed by David Saylor.* | *The art for both the jacket and the* | *interior was created using pastels on toned* | *printmaking paper. The text was set in 11.5-point Adobe* | *Garamond, a typeface based on the sixteenth-century type designs of* | *Claude Garamond, redrawn by Robert Slimbach in 1989. The book was typeset* | *by Brad Walrod and was printed and bound at RR Donnelley in* | *Crawsfordsville, Indiana. No old-growth forests were used to* | *create the paper for this book. The Managing* | *Editor was Manuela Soares and the* | *Manufacturing Director* | *was Angela* | *Biola.*'; [878-82] blank

Paper: wove paper

Running title: 'CHAPTER' and chapter number on verso, recto title comprises chapter title, pp. 1-870. Each running title (excluding pages on which new chapters commence) includes a three-star design to left and right of both running-titles on verso and recto. On pages on which a new chapter commences, the three-star design is omitted.

Illustrations: title-page vignette, together with thirty-eight vignettes at the beginning of each chapter (after chapter and chapter number but before chapter title). In addition to standard typographical changes (including italics, capitals and small capitals) there are other typographical features, comprising:

p. 27 facsimile of Mafalda Hopkirk's signature

p. 28 facsimile of Arthur Weasley's signature

p. 33 facsimile of Mafalda Hopkirk's signature

p. 35 note from Sirius Black

p. 58 facsimile of handwriting

p. 111 embroidered tapestry title

p. 127 text of sign

p. 190 magazine headlines

p. 191 magazine headline

pp. 191-93 texts of magazine articles

p. 222 text of sign

p. 239 blackboard text

p. 240 blackboard text

p. 280 facsimile of Harry's signature

p. 287 newspaper headline

p. 298 facsimile of Percy's signature

p. 306 newspaper headline

p. 351-52 text (together with facsimile signature and seal) of sign

p. 359 note from Sirius Black

p. 404 text and outline of badge

p. 485 text of portrait label

pp. 485-86 text of floor guide

p. 544 newspaper headline

p. 546 newspaper headline

p. 551 text (together with facsimile signature and seal) of sign

p. 578 facsimile of envelope address

p. 579 magazine headline

p. 581 text (together with facsimile signature and seal) of sign

p. 624 text (together with facsimile signature and seal) of sign

p. 656 text of notice

p. 768 text of badge

p. 780 text appearing on glass sphere's label

p. 841 text of prophecy

p. 845 newspaper headline

p. 858 note from Sirius Black

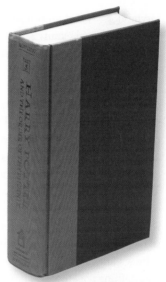

Binding: grey cloth-backed spine with light blue boards (with diamond pattern in blind).

On spine: 'ROWLING | [rule] | ['YEAR | 5' within concave square]' (horizontally at head) with 'HARRY POTTER | AND THE ORDER OF THE PHOENIX' (reading lengthways down spine) and '[publisher's device of a lantern, 19 by 14mm] | ARTHUR A. | LEVINE BOOKS | [rule] | SCHOLASTIC' (horizontally at foot). All in blue.

Upper and lower covers: blank.

All edges trimmed. Binding measurements: 235 by 150mm (covers), 235 by 65mm (spine). The grey cloth continues onto the covers by 40mm. End-papers: navy blue wove paper.

Dust-jacket: uncoated wove paper, 235 by 589mm. A single illustration in two parts spans the entire dust-jacket.

On spine: 'ROWLING | [rule] | ['YEAR | 5' within concave square]' (horizontally at head) with 'HARRY POTTER | AND THE ORDER OF THE PHOENIX' (reading lengthways down spine) and '[publisher's device of a lantern, 19 by 14mm] | ARTHUR A. | LEVINE BOOKS | [rule] | SCHOLASTIC' (horizontally at foot). All embossed in blue on colour illustration of candles.

On upper cover: 'Harry Potter [hand-drawn lettering] [embossed in blue] | and the [hand-drawn lettering in grey of illustration] | Order of the Phoenix [hand-drawn lettering in grey of illustration]

| J. K. ROWLING [embossed in blue]' (all width centred). All on colour illustration of Harry Potter clutching wand surrounded by doors and candles.

On *lower cover*: 'Sequel to the #1 *New York Times* Bestseller | HARRY POTTER | AND THE GOBLET OF FIRE | [barcode with smaller barcode to the right (52999) all in black on red panel, 23 by 53mm]. All in light blue and all on colour illustration of three figures behind a door.

On *upper inside flap*: '$29.99 | THERE IS A DOOR at the end | of a silent corridor. And it's haunting Harry | Potter's dreams. Why else would he be waking in | the middle of the night, screaming in terror? | [new paragraph] Here are just a few things on Harry's mind: | [new paragraph] [six-pointed star] A Defense Against the Dark Arts teacher | with a personality like poisoned honey | [six-pointed star] A venomous, disgruntled house-elf | [six-pointed star] Ron as keeper of the Gryffindor | Quidditch team | [six-pointed star] The looming terror of the end-of-term | Ordinary Wizarding Level exams | [new paragraph] ... and of course, the growing threat of | He-Who-Must-Not-Be-Named. In the richest | installment yet of J. K. Rowling's seven-part | story, Harry Potter is faced with the unreliability | of the very government of the magical world and | the impotence of the authorities at Hogwarts. | [new paragraph] Despite this (or perhaps because of it), he | finds depth and strength in his friends, beyond | what even he knew; boundless loyalty; and | unbearable sacrifice. | [new paragraph] Though thick runs the plot (as well as the | spine), readers will race through these pages and | leave Hogwarts, wishing only for the | next train back.' All in light blue and all on colour illustration of swirling misty wind and candles.

On *lower inside flap*: 'ALSO BY J. K. ROWLING: | [new paragraph] HARRY POTTER | AND THE GOBLET OF FIRE | [new paragraph] "Another grand tale of magic and mystery, of wheels | within wheels oiled in equal measure by terror and comedy, | featuring an engaging young hero-in-training who's not | above the occasional snit, and clicking along so smoothly | that it seems shorter than it is." — *Kirkus Reviews* | [new paragraph] HARRY POTTER | AND THE PRISONER OF AZKABAN | [new paragraph] "Isn't it reassuring that some things just get better and | better? This is a fabulously entertaining read that will have | Harry Potter fans cheering for more." | —*School Library Journal* | [new paragraph] HARRY POTTER | AND THE CHAMBER OF SECRETS | [new paragraph] "Rowling might be a Hogwarts graduate herself, for her | ability to create such an engaging, imaginative, funny, and, above all, heart-poundingly suspenseful yarn is nothing | short of magical." — *Publishers Weekly* | [new paragraph] HARRY POTTER | AND THE SORCERER'S STONE | [new paragraph] "You don't have to be a wizard or a kid to appreciate the | spell cast by Harry Potter." — *USA Today* | [new paragraph] *Jacket art by Mary GrandPré © 2003 Warner Bros.* | *Jacket design by Mary GrandPré and David Saylor* | [new paragraph] [publisher's device of a lantern, 19 by 14mm] ARTHUR A. LEVINE BOOKS | *An Imprint of Scholastic Press* | 557 Broadway, New York, New York 10012 | WWW.SCHOLASTIC.COM'. All in light blue and all on colour illustration of swirling misty wind.

Publication: 21 July 2003 (simultaneous with A12(a) and A12(aa))

Price: $29.99

Contents:
Harry Potter and the Order of the Phoenix
  ('The hottest day of the summer so far was drawing to a close and a drowsy silence...')

Notes:

Copies have been examined with the following printing plant codes on the imprint page:

Printed in the U.S.A.   12

Printed in the U.S.A.   23

Printed in the U.S.A.   58

The editorial files at Bloomsbury provide one suggested alteration from the English text. Page 860, line 28 reads '… only wizards.' The files state that '…Jo does not want this changed in English language editions, but if you feel the need to make it clear that it is not just the male form, you may add 'and witches' …'. The alteration was not made.

Each chapter commences with a drop capital.

The American audiobook version, read by Jim Dale, has a duration of approximately twenty-four hours.

Copies: private collection (PWE)

Reprints include:

10 9 8 7 6 5 4 3   03 04 05 06 07   Printed in the U.S.A. 55

10 9 8 7 6 5 4   03 04 05 06 07   Printed in the U.S.A. 55

A12(b)   AMERICAN DELUXE EDITION   (2003)
(children's artwork series in deluxe hardback)

HARRY POTTER | AND THE ORDER OF THE PHOENIX | [black and white illustration of a black dog passing through a doorway, with knarled tree on right, 70 by 52mm] | BY | J. K.

ROWLING | ILLUSTRATIONS BY MARY GRANDPRÉ | [publisher's device of a lantern, 12 by 9mm] | ARTHUR A. LEVINE BOOKS | AN IMPRINT OF SCHOLASTIC PRESS (All width centred on a diamond pattern background)

Collation: 448 unsigned leaves bound in indeterminate gatherings; 229 by 146mm; [I-VI] VII-XI [XII-XIV] 1-870 [871-82]

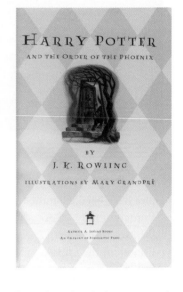

Page contents: [I] half-title: 'HARRY POTTER | AND THE ORDER OF THE PHOENIX' (all on diamond pattern background); [II] 'ALSO BY J. K. ROWLING | [new paragraph] *Harry Potter and the Sorcerer's Stone* | Year One at Hogwarts | [new paragraph] *Harry Potter and the Chamber of Secrets* | Year Two at Hogwarts | [new paragraph] *Harry Potter and the Prisoner of Azkaban* | Year Three at Hogwarts | [new paragraph] *Harry Potter and the Goblet of Fire* | Year Four at Hogwarts'; [III] title-page; [IV] '[device of twelve stars] | Text copyright © 2003 by J. K. Rowling | Illustrations by Mary GrandPré copyright © 2003 by Warner Bros. | HARRY POTTER, characters, names and related indicia are trademarks of | and © Warner Bros. Harry Potter Publishing Rights © J. K. Rowling. | All rights reserved. Published by Scholastic Press, a division of Scholastic Inc., | *Publishers since 1920.* | SCHOLASTIC, SCHOLASTIC PRESS, and the LANTERN LOGO | are trademarks and/or registered trademarks of Scholastic Inc. | [new paragraph] No part of this publication may be reproduced, or stored in a retrieval system, or transmitted | in any form or by any means, electronic, mechanical, photocopying, recording, or otherwise, | without written permission of the publisher. For information regarding permission, write | to Scholastic Inc., Attention: Permissions Department, 557 Broadway, New York, NY 10012. | [new paragraph] Library of Congress Cataloging-in-Publication Data Available | [new paragraph] Library of Congress Control Number: 2003102525 | [new paragraph] ISBN 0-439-56762-9 [new paragraph] 10 9 8 7 6 5 4 3 2 1   03 04 05 06 07 | Printed in the U.S.A. 23 | This deluxe edition, July 2003'; [V] 'TO NEIL, JESSICA, AND DAVID, | WHO MAKE MY WORLD MAGICAL.'; [VI] blank; VII-XI 'CONTENTS' (thirty-eight chapters listed with titles and page references); [XII] blank; [XIII] half-title: 'HARRY POTTER | AND THE ORDER OF THE PHOENIX' (all on diamond pattern background); [XIV] blank; 1-870 text; [871-72] blank; [873] 'ABOUT THE AUTHOR | [new paragraph] J. K. Rowling is the author of five magnificent novels in the | Harry Potter series. Her books have been honored with the | Hugo Award, the Bram Stoker Award, the Whitbread | Children's Book Award, the Nestlé Smarties Book Prize, | the British Book Awards Children's Book of the Year, and | numerous state, magazine, and children's choice citations. | Ms. Rowling herself has received a special certificate for be- | ing a three-year winner of the Nestlé Smarties Book Prize | as well as a special commendation from the Anne Spencer | Lindbergh Prize for her outstanding contribution to chil- | dren's fantasy literature. She has also been named an Offi- | cer of the Order of the British Empire. | [new paragraph] Ms.

Rowling lives in Scotland with her husband and | two children.'; [874] blank; [875] 'ABOUT THE ILLUSTRATOR | [new paragraph] Mary GrandPré works in a style she calls "soft geometry," | combining her concerns for color, light, drawing, and de- | sign with her signature chalk pastels. She has illustrated | more than fifteen beautiful books, including *Plum*, a col- | lection of poetry by Tony Mitton, and the American edi- | tions of all five Harry Potter novels. Her work has also | appeared in *The New Yorker, The Atlantic Monthly*, and | *Communication Arts*, and on the cover of *Time*. | [new paragraph] Ms. GrandPré lives in St. Paul, Minnesota, with her | family.'; [876] blank; [877] colophon: '[publisher's device of a lantern, 17 by 12mm] | *This Deluxe | Edition was art | directed and designed by | David Saylor. Mary GrandPré's | artwork for the slipcase, the endpapers, the | interior, and the special jacket illustration was | created using pastels on toned printmaking paper. The | text was set in 11.5-point Adobe Garamond, a typeface based | on the sixteenth-century type designs of Claude Garamond, redrawn | by Robert Slimbach in 1989. The book was typeset by Brad Walrod and | printed on acid-free 55-pound offset paper manufactured for Scholastic by Fraser | Papers in Berlin, New Hampshire. No old-growth forests were used to | create the paper in this book. The case is wrapped in Sierra cloth, | an acid-free rayon-based material manufactured in Europe | exclusively for Ecological Fibers. This edition was | printed, bound, and packaged by RR Donnelley | in Crawfordsville, Indiana. The Managing | Editor was Manuela Soares and | the Manufacturing Director | was Angela Biola.* | [device of six stars]'; [878-82] blank

Paper: wove paper

Running title: 'CHAPTER' and chapter number on verso, recto title comprises chapter title, pp. 1-870. Each running title (excluding pages on which new chapters commence) includes a three-star design to left and right of both running-titles on verso and recto. On pages on which a new chapter commences, the three-star design is omitted.

Illustrations: title-page vignette, together with thirty-eight vignettes at the beginning of each chapter (after chapter and chapter number but before chapter title). In addition to standard typographical changes (including italics, capitals and small capitals) there are other typographical features, comprising:

p. 27 facsimile of Mafalda Hopkirk's signature

p. 28 facsimile of Arthur Weasley's signature

p. 33 facsimile of Mafalda Hopkirk's signature

p. 35 note from Sirius Black

p. 58 facsimile of handwriting

p. 111 embroidered tapestry title

p. 127 text of sign

p. 190 magazine headlines

p. 191 magazine headline

pp. 191-93 texts of magazine articles

p. 222 text of sign

p. 239 blackboard text

p. 240 blackboard text

p. 280 facsimile of Harry's signature

p. 287 newspaper headline

p. 298 facsimile of Percy's signature

p. 306 newspaper headline

p. 351-52 text (together with facsimile signature and seal) of sign

p. 359 note from Sirius Black

p. 404 text and outline of badge

p. 485 text of portrait label

pp. 485-86 text of floor guide

p. 544 newspaper headline

p. 546 newspaper headline

p. 551 text (together with facsimile signature and seal) of sign

p. 578 facsimile of envelope address

p. 579 magazine headline

p. 581 text (together with facsimile signature and seal) of sign

p. 624 text (together with facsimile signature and seal) of sign

p. 656 text of notice

p. 768 text of badge

p. 780 text appearing on glass sphere's label

p. 841 text of prophecy

p. 845 newspaper headline

p. 858 note from Sirius Black

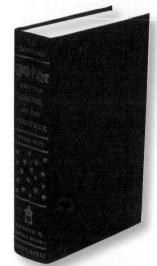

Binding: black cloth with diamond pattern in blind on upper and lower covers.

On spine: 'J. K. | ROWLING | [double rule, 48mm] | Harry Potter [hand-drawn lettering] | AND THE | ORDER | OF THE | PHOENIX | [double rule, 48mm] | YEAR FIVE | [double rule, 48mm] | [eighteen stars] | [double rule, 48mm] | [publisher's device of a lantern, 19 by 14mm] | ARTHUR A. | LEVINE BOOKS | [double rule, 48mm] | SCHOLASTIC'. All in metallic blue.

Upper and lower covers: blank with diamond pattern in blind.

All edges trimmed. Black and white sewn bands at head and foot of spine. Binding measurements: 235 by 150mm (covers), 235 by 65mm (spine). End-papers: wove paper with colour illustration of Harry Potter clutching wand surrounded by doors and candles on front endpapers, and colour illustration of three figures behind a door on rear endpapers.

Dust-jacket: uncoated wove paper, 235 by 589mm. A single illustration spans the entire dust-jacket comprising a colour illustration of number twelve Grimmauld Place together with an owl carrying parchment.

On upper inside flap: '*Illustration by Mary GrandPré © 2003 Warner Bros.*' All in grey.

Slipcase: card slipcase covered in navy blue paper.

On spine: 'J. K. | ROWLING | [double rule, 48mm] | Harry Potter [hand-drawn lettering] | AND THE | ORDER | OF THE | PHOENIX | [double rule, 48mm] | YEAR FIVE | [double rule, 48mm] | [eighteen stars] | [double rule, 48mm] | [publisher's device of a lantern, 19 by 14mm] | ARTHUR A. | LEVINE BOOKS | [double rule, 48mm] | SCHOLASTIC'. All in metallic blue.

On upper side: colour illustration of three figures behind a door, all within single rule in metallic blue, 221 by 136mm.

On lower side: 'Harry Potter [hand-drawn lettering] [in metallic blue] | and the [hand-drawn lettering in grey of illustration] | Order of the Phoenix [hand-drawn lettering in grey of illustration]' (all width centred). All on colour illustration of Harry Potter clutching wand surrounded by doors and candles and all within single rule in metallic blue, 221 by 135mm.

On top edge: author's signature 'JK Rowling' in metallic blue.

On lower edge: *'Illustrations by Mary GrandPré © 2003 Warner Bros.'* All in grey.

Publication: July 2003 (see notes)

Price: $60

Contents:
Harry Potter and the Order of the Phoenix
  ('The hottest day of the summer so far was drawing to a close and a drowsy silence…')

Notes:
The dust-jacket for the first American edition (see A12(aaa)) and slipcase design for this edition, both show Harry with wand in left hand on one cover and three figures facing left behind a door on the other cover. These single panel illustrations appear

to have originated from the full double-page versions reproduced in this edition on the endpapers. Both are reversed so that Harry's wand is in his right hand and the three figures face right. These full double-page versions and entirely new dust-jacket design are unique to this deluxe edition.

Note the change from a 'collector's edition' for *Sorcerer's Stone* and *Chamber of Secrets* to 'deluxe edition' for this edition of *Order of the Phoenix*. There were no Scholastic collector's or deluxe editions for *Prisoner of Azkaban* or *Goblet of Fire*.

Although no publication day is recorded, 1 July 2003 is assumed. In an email to me from January 2013 Arthur A. Levine noted that 'I'm fairly certain that we didn't have strict "on sale" dates… the publication "day" would simply be the first of the month listed.'

Each chapter commences with a drop capital.

Copies: private collection (PWE)

Reprints include:
10 9 8 7 6 5 4 3 2   03 04 05 06 07

A12(c)   ENGLISH DELUXE EDITION   (2003)
(children's artwork series in deluxe hardback)

HARRY | POTTER | *and the Order of the Phoenix* | [illustration of Hogwarts crest with legend 'DRACO DORMIENS NUNQUAM TITILLANDUS' on banner, 70 by 85mm] | J.K.ROWLING | [publisher's device of a dog, 12 by 19mm] | BLOOMSBURY (All width centred)

Collation: 384 unsigned leaves bound in forty-eight gatherings of eight leaves; 233 by 150mm, [1-7] 8-23 [24] 25-42 [43] 44-57 [58] 59-75 [76] 77-91 [92] 93-111 [112] 113-25 [126] 127-38 [139] 140-62 [163] 164-80 [181] 182-99 [200] 201-225 [226] 227-50 [251] 252-73 [274] 275-94 [295] 296-311 [312] 313-31 [332] 333-51 [352] 353-71 [372] 373-89 [390] 391-411 [412] 413-34 [435] 436-55 [456] 457-79 [480] 481-502 [503] 504-527 [528] 529-49 [550] 551-73 [574] 575-95 [596] 597-619 [620] 621-42 [643] 644-61 [662] 663-73 [674] 675-88 [689] 690-711 [712] 713-22 [723] 724-44 [745] 746-66 [767-68]

Page contents: [1] half-title: 'HARRY | POTTER | *and the Order of the Pheonix* | [illustration of Hogwarts crest with legend 'DRACO DORMIENS NUNQUAM TITILLANDUS' on banner, 49 by 60mm]'; [2] '*Titles available in the Harry Potter series* | *(in reading order):* | Harry Potter and the Philosopher's Stone | Harry Potter and the Chamber of Secrets | Harry Potter and the Prisoner of Azkaban | Harry Potter and the Goblet of Fire | Harry Potter and the Order of the Phoenix | [new paragraph] *Harry Potter and the Philosopher's Stone* | *also available in Latin and Welsh:* | Harrius Potter et Philosophi Lapis (Latin) | Harri Potter a Maen yr Athronydd (Welsh)'; [3] title-page; [4] 'All rights reserved; no part of this publication may be reproduced or | transmitted by any means, electronic, mechanical, photocopying or otherwise, | without the prior permission of the publisher | [new paragraph] First published in Great Britain in 2003 | Bloomsbury Publishing Plc, 38 Soho Square, London W1D 3HB | [new paragraph] Copyright © 2003 J.K. Rowling | Cover illustration by Jason Cockcroft © 2003 Bloomsbury Publishing Plc | [new paragraph] Harry Potter, names, characters and related indicia are | copyright and trademark Warner Bros., 2000™ | [new paragraph] The moral right of the author has been asserted | A CIP catalogue record of this book is available | from the British Library | [new paragraph] ISBN 0 7475 6961 4 | [new paragraph] Typeset by Palimpsest Book Production Limited, | Polmont, Stirlingshire | [new paragraph] All paper used by Bloomsbury Publishing, including that in this book, | is a natural, recyclable product made from wood grown in sustainable, | well-managed forests. The manufacturing processes conform to the | environmental regulations of the country of origin. | [new paragraph] Printed in Great Britain by Clays Ltd, St Ives plc | [new paragraph] First Edition | [new paragraph] | www.bloomsbury.com/harrypotter'; [5] 'To Neil, Jessica and David, | who make my world magical'; [6] blank; [7]-766 text; [767-68] blank

Paper: wove paper

Running title: 'HARRY POTTER' (25mm) on verso, recto title comprises chapter title, pp. 8-766

Binding: burgundy cloth.

On spine: 'HARRY POTTER *and the Order of the Phoenix* J.K.ROWLING' (reading lengthways down spine) with '[publisher's device of a dog, 12 by 21mm] | BLOOMSBURY' (horizontally at foot). All in gilt.

On upper cover: 'HARRY | POTTER | *and the Order of the Phoenix* | [double ruled border, 103 by 103mm with the outer border thicker than the inner and colour illustration by Jason Cockcroft laid down] | JKRowling [facsimile signature]' (all width centred). All in gilt.

Lower cover: blank.

All edges gilt. Yellow sewn bands at head and foot of spine together with yellow marker ribbon. Binding measurements: 241 by 151mm (covers), 241 by 70mm (spine). End-papers: burgundy wove paper.

Dust-jacket: none

Publication: 6 October 2003 in an edition of 26,700 copies (confirmed by Bloomsbury)

Price: £30

Contents:
Harry Potter and the Order of the Phoenix
  ('The hottest day of the summer so far was drawing to a close and a drowsy silence lay…')

Copies: Sotheby's, 17 December 2009, lot 169

ENGLISH CHILDREN'S EDITION
(children's artwork series in paperback)

HARRY | POTTER | *and the Order of the Phoenix* | [illustration of Hogwarts crest with legend 'DRAGO DORMIENS NUNQUAM TITILLANDUS' on banner, 66 by 81mm] | J. K. ROWLING | [publisher's device of a dog, 11 by 18mm] | BLOOMSBURY (Lines 1 and 2 justified on left and right margins, and all width centred)

Collation: 384 unsigned leaves bound in indeterminate gatherings; 197 by 128mm; [1-7] 8-23 [24] 25-42 [43] 44-57 [58] 59-75 [76] 77-91 [92] 93-111 [112] 113-25 [126] 127-38 [139] 140-62 [163] 164-80 [181] 182-99 [200] 201-225 [226] 227-50 [251] 252-73 [274] 275-94 [295] 296-311 [312] 313-31 [332] 333-51 [352] 353-71 [372] 373-89 [390] 391-411 [412] 413-34 [435] 436-55 [456] 457-79 [480] 481-502 [503] 504-527 [528] 529-49 [550] 551-73 [574] 575-95 [596] 597-619 [620] 621-42 [643] 644-61 [662] 663-73 [674] 675-88 [689] 690-711 [712] 713-22 [723] 724-44 [745] 746-66 [767-68]

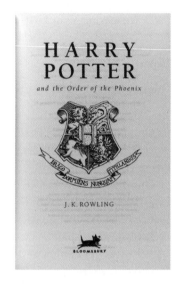

Page contents: [1] half-title: 'HARRY | POTTER | *and the Order of the Phoenix* | [illustration of Hogwarts crest with legend 'DRAGO DORMIENS NUNQUAM TITILLANDUS' on banner, 46 by 57mm]'; [2] '*Titles available in the Harry Potter series* | *(in reading order):* | Harry Potter and the Philosopher's Stone | Harry Potter and the Chamber of Secrets | Harry Potter and the Prisoner of Azkaban | Harry Potter and the Goblet of Fire | Harry Potter and the Order of the Phoenix | [new paragraph] *Harry Potter and the Philosopher's Stone* | *also available in Latin and Welsh:* | Harrius Potter et Philosophi Lapis (Latin) | Harri Potter a Maen yr Athronydd (Welsh)'; [3] title-page; [4] 'All rights reserved; no part of this publication may be reproduced or | transmitted by any means, electronic, mechanical, photocopying or otherwise, | without the prior permission of the publisher | [new paragraph] First published in Great Britain in 2003 | Bloomsbury Publishing Plc, 38 Soho Square, London W1D 3HB | [new paragraph] This paperback edition first published in 2004 | [new paragraph] Copyright © J.K. Rowling 2003 | Cover illustration by Jason Cockcroft © 2003 Bloomsbury Publishing Plc | [new paragraph] Harry Potter, names, characters and related indicia are | copyright and trademark Warner Bros., 2000™ | [new paragraph] The moral right of the author has been asserted | A CIP catalogue record for this book is available | from the British Library | [new paragraph] ISBN 0 7475 6107 9 | [new paragraph] 1 3 5 9 10 8 6 4 2 | [new paragraph] Typeset by Palimpsest Book Production Limited, | Polmont, Stirlingshire | Printed in Great Britain by Clays Ltd, St Ives plc | [new paragraph] All papers used by Bloomsbury Publishing are natural, | recyclable products made from wood grown in well-managed forests. | The paper used in this book contains 10% post consumer waste | material which was de-inked using chlorine free methods. The | manufacturing processes conform to the environmental | regulations of the country of origin. | www.bloomsbury.com/harrypotter'; [5] '*To Neil, Jessica and David,* | *who make my world magical*'; [6] blank; [7]-766 text; [767-68] blank

Paper: wove paper

Running title: 'HARRY POTTER' (24mm) on verso, recto title comprises chapter title, pp. 8-766 (excluding pages on which new chapters commence)

Binding: pictorial wrappers.

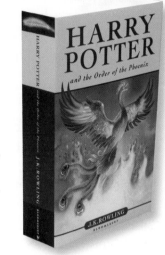

On spine: '[colour illustration of a golden feather on blue panel, 41 by 16mm] HARRY POTTER [in burgundy on yellow panel, 41 by 45mm] *and the Order of the Phoenix* [in yellow] J.K.ROWLING' [in white, both title conclusion and author on burgundy panel, 41 by 103mm] BLOOMSBURY [publisher's device of the head of a dog, 4 by 3mm] [both in yellow on blue panel, 41 by 32mm]' (reading lengthways down spine).

On upper wrapper: 'HARRY | POTTER | *and the Order of the Phoenix* [lines 1 and 2 in burgundy, line 3 in blue, all on yellow panel, 62 by 128mm] | [blue rule, 128mm] | [colour illustration of a phoenix rising from flames, 132 by 128mm] | [blue rule, 128mm intersected by burgundy panel with 'J.K.ROWLING' in white] | BLOOMSBURY [in burgundy on yellow panel, 10 by 128mm]' (all width centred).

On lower wrapper: 'Harry Potter is due to start | his fifth year at Hogwarts School of | Witchcraft and Wizardry. His best friends Ron | and Hermione have been very secretive all summer | and he is desperate to get back to school and find out | what has been going on. However, what Harry discovers | is far more devastating than he could ever have expected … | [new paragraph] Suspense, secrets and thrilling action from the pen of J.K. Rowling | ensure an electrifying adventure that is impossible to put down. | [new paragraph] 'Rowling's imagination and daring put | her in a class of her own.' *The Times* | [new paragraph] 'Every seven-year-old I know is desperate | to read that great paving slab of a book, | *The Order of the Phoenix.' Daily Mail* | 'For Christmas I would like | *The Order of the Phoenix,* as it's | wonderfully written and is a story | the whole family is following.' | Anne Diamond, *Sunday Express* | [publisher's device of a dog, 6 by 10mm] | BLOOMSBURY | [barcode in black on white panel, 21 by 38mm together with 'http://www.bloomsbury.com' below panel, in burgundy on yellow panel, 6 by 38mm and '£7.99' to the right]'. Reading lengthways up left side next to fore-edge 'Cover illustrations by Jason Cockcroft'. All in white with the exception of the illustration credit which is in black, and all on an illustration of an arch, with runic characters above, a candle-lit vaulted ceiling passage and a wizard, witch, centaur, goblin and house-elf comprising characters in the fountain of magical brethren with pouring water.

All edges trimmed. Binding measurements: 197 by 128mm (wrappers), 197 by 41mm (spine).

Publication: 10 July 2004 (simultaneous with A12(dd)) in an edition of 1,635,828 copies (confirmed by Bloomsbury)

Price: £7.99

Contents:

Harry Potter and the Order of the Phoenix

('The hottest day of the summer so far was drawing to a close and a drowsy silence lay...')

Notes:

Bloomsbury released a 'dumpbin' display case for this edition at the beginning of July (Nielsen BookData provides a date of 10 July 2004). The case was available empty or filled with 48 copies of this edition. A promotional poster was apparently released on the same date.

Copies: private collection (PWE)

A12(dd)   ENGLISH ADULT EDITION   (2004)
(Michael Wildsmith photography adult artwork series in paperback)

Harry Potter and the | Order of the Phoenix | J. K. Rowling | BLOOMSBURY (All width centred)

Collation: 480 unsigned leaves bound in forty gatherings of twelve leaves; 177 by 111mm; [1-7] 8-27 [28] 29-51 [52] 53-70 [71] 72-92 [93] 94-112 [113] 114-37 [138] 139-54 [155] 156-70 [171] 172-200 [201] 202-222 [223] 224-45 [246] 247-77 [278] 279-309 [310] 311-39 [340] 341-65 [366] 367-87 [388] 389-412 [413] 414-38 [439] 440-63 [464] 465-85 [486] 487-512 [513] 514-41 [542] 543-68 [569] 570-98 [599] 600-627 [628] 629-58 [659] 660-86 [687] 688-715 [716] 717-43 [744] 745-73 [774] 775-801 [802] 803-824 [825] 826-39 [840] 841-58 [859] 860-86 [887] 888-900 [901] 902-928 [929] 930-56 [957-60]

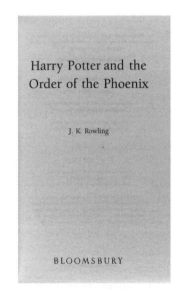

Page contents: [1] half-title: 'Harry Potter and the | Order of the Phoenix'; [2] *'Titles available in the Harry Potter series | (in reading order):* | Harry Potter and the Philosopher's Stone | Harry Potter and the Chamber of Secrets | Harry Potter and the Prisoner of Azkaban | Harry Potter and the Goblet of Fire | Harry Potter and the Order of the Phoenix'; [3] title-page; [4] 'All rights reserved; no part of this publication may be reproduced or | transmitted by any means, electronic, mechanical, photocopying or otherwise, | without the prior permission of the publisher | [new paragraph] First published in Great Britain in 2003 | Bloomsbury Publishing Plc, 38 Soho Square, London W1D 3HB | [new paragraph] This edition first published in 2004 | [new paragraph] Copyright © 2003 J.K. Rowling | [new paragraph] Harry Potter, names, characters and related indicia are | copyright and trademark Warner Bros., 2000™ | [new paragraph] The moral right of the author has been asserted | A CIP catalogue record of this book is available | from the British Library | [new paragraph] ISBN 0 7475 7073 6 | [new paragraph] 1 3 5 7 9 10 8 6 4 2 | [new paragraph] Typeset by Palimpsest Book Production Limited, | Polmont, Stirlingshire | Printed in Great Britain by Clays Ltd, St Ives plc | [new paragraph] All papers used by Bloomsbury Publishing are natural, | recyclable products made from wood grown in well-managed forests. | The paper used in this book contains 20% post consumer waste | material which was de-inked using chlorine free methods. The | manufacturing processes conform to the environmental | regulations of the country of origin. | [new paragraph] www.bloomsbury.com/harrypotter'; [5] '*To Neil, Jessica and David,* | *who make my world magical*'; [6] blank; [7]-956 text; [957-60] blank

Paper: wove paper

Running title: 'HARRY POTTER' (24mm) on verso, recto title comprises chapter title, pp. 8-956 (excluding pages on which new chapters commence)

Binding: pictorial wrappers.

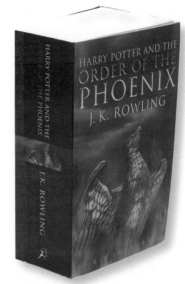

On spine: 'HARRY POTTER AND THE [colour photograph of a metallic phoenix rising through flame, 58 by 18mm] | J.K. ROWLING [publisher's device of a figure with a bow, 11 by 11mm] | ORDER OF THE PHOENIX' (reading lengthways down spine). All in white with the exception of last line which is in gilt and all on black.

On upper wrapper: 'HARRY POTTER AND THE [in white] | ORDER OF THE [embossed in gilt] | PHOENIX [embossed in gilt] | J. K. ROWLING [in white] | BLOOMSBURY [in white]' (all width centred). All on colour photograph of a metallic phoenix rising through flame.

On lower wrapper: '[colour photograph of a metallic phoenix rising through flame, all within single white border, 22 by 22mm] 'What more could one want? ... Rowling's | take on 15-year-old boyhood is masterfully | done and places humanity, not magic, at | the centre of the book' *Time Out* | [new paragraph] Harry is furious that he has been abandoned at the | Dursleys' house for the summer, for he suspects that | Voldemort is gathering an army, that he himself could | be attacked, and that his so-called friends are keeping him | in the dark. Finally rescued by wizard bodyguards, he | discovers that Dumbledore is regrouping the Order of the | Phoenix – a secret society first formed years ago to fight | Voldemort. But the Ministry of Magic is against the Order, | lies are being spread by the wizards' tabloid the *Daily* | *Prophet*, and Harry fears that he may have to take on | this epic battle against evil alone. | [new paragraph] 'Don't be alienated by the hype, Rowling's imagination | and daring put her in a class of her own' *The Times* | [new paragraph] 'In discovering the magical world of Hogwarts and Harry | himself, I found more than just great characters and stories | ... *Harry Potter and the Order of the Phoenix* is even | better than its predecessors' *Ireland's Sunday Independent* | [new paragraph] 'Read it yet? Five is bigger and better than ever' *Heat* | [new paragraph] [barcode in black on white panel,

24 by 39mm together with 'bloomsbury[in black]pbk[in white]s[in black] | £7.99 [in black] | www.bloomsbury.com [in black]' and all on red panel, 25 by 75mm] | Cover image: Michael Wildsmith Design: William Webb Author Photograph: © Bill de la HEY'. All in white on black with colour photograph to the left of lines 1-4.

On inside upper wrapper: black and white photograph of J.K. Rowling standing against bookshelves.

On inside lower wrapper: 'Other titles available in the | HARRY POTTER series | [colour illustrations in two columns of four book designs]'. All in white on black.

All edges trimmed. Binding measurements: 177 by 111mm (wrappers), 177 by 58mm (spine).

Publication: 10 July 2004 (simultaneous with A12(d)) in an edition of 325,200 copies (confirmed by Bloomsbury)

Price: £7.99

Contents:
Harry Potter and the Order of the Phoenix
('The hottest day of the summer so far was drawing to a close and a drowsy silence lay…')

Notes:
Previous titles in the Michael Wildsmith photography adult artwork series in paperback had replaced existing 'adult' livery editions. However, this was the first title in this guise which did not replace a previous edition. See note to A1(f) about earlier titles in this series.

Copies: private collection (PWE)

Reprints include:
3 5 7 9 10 8 6 4 2

A12(e)   AMERICAN CHILDREN'S EDITION   (2004)
(children's artwork series in paperback)

HARRY POTTER | AND THE ORDER OF THE PHOENIX | [black and white illustration of a black dog passing through a doorway, with knarled tree on right, 61 by 46mm] | BY | J. K. ROWLING | ILLUSTRATIONS BY MARY GRANDPRÉ | SCHOLASTIC INC. | NEW YORK [four-sided device] TORONTO [four-sided device] LONDON [four-sided device] AUCKLAND [four-sided device] SYDNEY | MEXICO CITY [four-sided device] NEW DELHI [four-sided device] HONG KONG [four-sided device] BUENOS AIRES (All width centred on a diamond pattern background)

Collation: 448 unsigned leaves bound in indeterminate gatherings; 192 by 132mm; [I-X] XI-XV [XVI-XVIII] 1-870 [871-78]

Page contents: [I-II] 'PRAISE FOR J. K. ROWLING'S | HARRY POTTER | AND THE ORDER OF THE PHOENIX | [device of nine stars] | [6 reviews and a listing of 5 statements]'; [III] 'ALSO BY J. K. ROWLING | *Harry Potter and the Sorcerer's Stone* | Year One at Hogwarts | [new paragraph] *Harry Potter and the Chamber of Secrets* | Year Two at Hogwarts | [new paragraph] *Harry Potter and the Prisoner of Azkaban* | Year Three at Hogwarts | [new paragraph] | *Harry Potter and the Goblet of Fire* | Year Four at Hogwarts'; [IV] blank; [V] half-title: 'HARRY POTTER | AND THE ORDER OF THE PHOENIX' (all on diamond pattern background); [VI] blank; [VII] title-page; [VIII] '[device of twelve stars] | Text copyright © 2003 by J. K. Rowling. | Illustrations by Mary GrandPré copyright © 2003 by Warner Bros. | HARRY POTTER, characters, names and related indicia are trademarks of | and © Warner Bros. Harry Potter Publishing Rights © J. K.

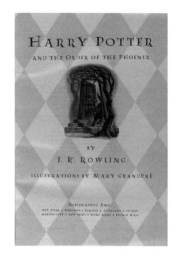

Rowling. | All rights reserved. Published by Scholastic Inc. | SCHOLASTIC, the LANTERN LOGO, and associated logos | are trademarks and/or registered trademarks of Scholastic Inc. | [new paragraph] If you purchased this book without a cover, you should be aware that this book is stolen property. | It was reported as "unsold and destroyed" to the publisher, and neither the author nor | the publisher has received any payment for this "stripped book." | [new paragraph] No part of this publication may be reproduced in whole or in part, | or stored in a retrieval system, or transmitted in any form or by any means, | electronic, mechanical, photocopying, recording, or otherwise, | without written permission of the publisher. | For information regarding permission, write to Scholastic Inc., | Attention: Permissions Department, 557 Broadway, New York, NY 10012. | [new paragraph] [publisher's device of a lantern, 6 by 4mm] | Arthur A. Levine Books hardcover edition | art directed by David Saylor, | published by Arthur A. Levine Books, | an imprint of Scholastic Inc. | July 2003 | [new paragraph] ISBN 0-439-35807-8 | [new paragraph] Library of Congress Control Number: 2003102525 | [new paragraph] 12 11 10 9 8 7 6 5 4 3 2 1   4 5 6 7 8 9/0 | [new paragraph] Printed in the U.S.A. 40 | [new paragraph] First Scholastic trade paperback printing, September 2004 | [new paragraph] This book is printed on paper containing a minimum of 20% post-consumer recycled fiber.'; [IX] 'TO NEIL, JESSICA, AND DAVID, | WHO MAKE MY WORLD MAGICAL.'; [X] blank; XI-XV 'CONTENTS' (thirty-eight chapters listed with titles and page references); [XVI] blank; [XVII] half-title: 'HARRY POTTER | AND THE ORDER OF THE PHOENIX' (all on diamond pattern background); [XVIII] blank; 1-870 text; [871-72] blank; [873] 'ABOUT THE AUTHOR | [new paragraph] J. K. Rowling is the author of five magnificent novels in the Harry | Potter series. Her books have been honored with the Hugo Award, the | Bram Stoker Award, the Whitbread Children's Book Award, the Nestlé | Smarties Book Prize, the British Book Awards Children's Book of the | Year, and numerous state, magazine, and children's choice citations. | Ms. Rowling herself has received a special certificate for being a three- | year winner of the Nestlé Smarties Book Prize as well as a special | commendation from the Anne Spencer Lindbergh Prize for her out- | standing contribution to children's fantasy literature. She has also been | named an Officer of the Order of the British Empire. | [new paragraph] Ms. Rowling lives in

Scotland with her husband and two children.'; [874] blank; [875] 'ABOUT THE ILLUSTRATOR | [new paragraph] Mary GrandPré works in a style she calls "soft geometry," combining | her concerns for color, light, drawing, and design with her signature | chalk pastels. She has illustrated more than fifteen beautiful books, | including *Plum*, a collection of poetry by Tony Mitton, and the | American editions of all five Harry Potter novels. Her work has also | appeared in *The New Yorker*, *The Atlantic Monthly*, and | *Communication Arts*, and on the cover of *Time*. | [new paragraph] Ms. GrandPré lives in Sarasota, Florida, with her family.'; [876] blank; [877] publisher's advertisement: 'Harry Potter [hand-drawn lettering] | THE MAGICAL BOOKS THAT STARTED IT ALL!'; [878] blank

Paper: wove paper

Running title: 'CHAPTER' and chapter number on verso, recto title comprises chapter title, pp. 1-870. Each running title (excluding pages on which new chapters commence) includes a three-star design to left and right of both running-titles on verso and recto. On pages on which a new chapter commences, the three-star design is omitted.

Illustrations: title-page vignette, together with thirty-eight vignettes at the beginning of each chapter (after chapter and chapter number but before chapter title). In addition to standard typographical changes (including italics, capitals and small capitals) there are other typographical features, comprising:

    p. 27 facsimile of Mafalda Hopkirk's signature
    p. 28 facsimile of Arthur Weasley's signature
    p. 33 facsimile of Mafalda Hopkirk's signature
    p. 35 note from Sirius Black
    p. 58 facsimile of handwriting
    p. 111 embroidered tapestry title
    p. 127 text of sign
    p. 190 magazine headlines
    p. 191 magazine headline
    pp. 191-93 texts of magazine articles
    p. 222 text of sign
    p. 239 blackboard text
    p. 240 blackboard text
    p. 280 facsimile of Harry's signature
    p. 287 newspaper headline
    p. 298 facsimile of Percy's signature
    p. 306 newspaper headline
    p. 351-52 text (together with facsimile signature and seal) of sign
    p. 359 note from Sirius Black
    p. 404 text and outline of badge
    p. 485 text of portrait label
    pp. 485-86 text of floor guide

Binding: pictorial wrappers.

On spine: 'ROWLING | [rule] | ['YEAR | 5' within concave square]' (horizontally at head) with 'HARRY POTTER | SCHOLASTIC | AND THE ORDER OF THE PHOENIX' (reading lengthways down spine). All in silver on blue and purple diamond pattern background.

On upper wrapper: 'THE SPELLBINDING NATIONAL BESTSELLER [in silver] | Harry Potter [hand-drawn lettering] [embossed in silver] | and the [hand-drawn lettering in grey of illustration] | Order of the Phoenix [hand-drawn lettering in grey of illustration] | J. K. ROWLING [embossed in silver]' (all width centred). All on colour illustration of Harry Potter clutching wand surrounded by doors and candles. In centre at foot: '[publisher's book device] SCHOLASTIC' in white on red panel, 5 by 45mm.

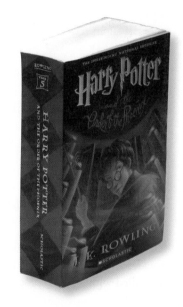

On lower wrapper: 'There is a door at the end of a silent corridor. And it's haunting | Harry Potter's dreams. Why else would he be waking in the middle | of the night, screaming in terror? | [new paragraph] Harry has a lot on his mind for this, his fifth year at Hogwarts: a | Defense Against the Dark Arts teacher with a personality like poisoned | honey; a big surprise on the Gryffindor Quidditch team; and the | looming | terror of the Ordinary Wizarding Level exams. But all these things pale | next to the growing threat of He-Who-Must-Not-Be-Named — a threat that | neither the magical government nor the authorities at Hogwarts can stop. | [new paragraph] As the grasp of darkness tightens, Harry must discover the true depth | and strength of his friends, the importance of boundless loyalty, and the | shocking price of unbearable sacrifice. | [new paragraph] His fate depends on them all. | [new paragraph] [four-sided device] The #1 *New York Times* Bestseller [four-sided device] | [new paragraph] A *Booklist* Editors' Choice [four-sided device] An ALA Notable Book | An ALA Best Book for Young Adults | Shortlisted for the WH Smith Books Award | [publisher's book device with

'SCHOLASTIC' in white on red panel, 5 by 45mm] | www.scholastic.com/harrypotter | COVER ART BY MARY GRANDPRÉ'. All in white on colour illustration of three figures behind a door, with barcode with smaller barcode (35807) together with 'S' within triangle and '$9.99 US', all in black on white panel with black border, 28 by 60mm, to the left of final three lines. The initial 'T' of 'There' is a drop capital.

On inside upper wrapper: barcode with smaller barcode (50999) together with 'S' within triangle below, all in black.

All edges trimmed. Binding measurements: 192 by 132mm (wrappers), 192 by 46mm (spine).

Publication: September 2004 (see notes)

Price: $9.99

Contents:
Harry Potter and the Order of the Phoenix
('The hottest day of the summer so far was drawing to a close and a drowsy silence...')

Notes:
Note the slight reworking of the publisher's blurb from the text present in the first American edition – see A12(aaa).

The two half-titles from the first American edition are retained for this paperback edition. Previous titles in the paperback series saw the deletion of the first half-title (and deletion of all half-titles in A4(b)). Subsequent titles in the original paperback series would see the second half-title retained for A13(b) and both half-titles, as here, retained for A14(c).

Although no publication day is recorded, 1 September 2004 is assumed. In an email to me from January 2013 Arthur L. Levine noted that 'I'm fairly certain that we didn't have strict "on sale" dates… the publication "day" would simply be the first of the month listed. None of the paperbacks were given a strict "on sale" date either.' Nielsen BookData provides a publication date of 10 August 2004.

Scholastic released a 'dumpbin' display case for this edition prior to publication (Nielsen BookData provides a date of 1 August 2004). The case was filled with 12 copies of this edition. Alternatively, cases filled with 18 or 24 copies are provided with a publication date of 10 August 2004 by Nielsen BookData.

Each chapter commences with a drop capital.

Copies: private collection (PWE)

Reprints include:

26	11 12 13/0	Printed in the U.S.A. 40
39 38 37 36 35 34 33 32 31 30 29	11 12 13 14 15 16/0	Printed in the U.S.A. 40

A12(f) AMERICAN BOOK CLUB EDITION (2003 [2004])
(children's artwork series in hardback)

HARRY POTTER | AND THE ORDER OF THE PHOENIX | [black and white illustration of a black dog passing through a doorway, with knarled tree on right, 65 by 49mm] | BY | J. K. ROWLING | ILLUSTRATIONS BY MARY GRANDPRÉ | [publisher's device of a lantern, 11 by 8mm] | ARTHUR A. LEVINE BOOKS | AN IMPRINT OF SCHOLASTIC PRESS (All width centred on a diamond pattern background)

Collation: 448 unsigned leaves bound in twenty-eight gatherings of sixteen leaves; 209 by 136mm; [I-VI] VII-XI [XII-XIV] 1-870 [871-82]

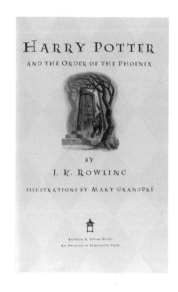

Page contents: [I] half-title: 'HARRY POTTER | AND THE ORDER OF THE PHOENIX' (all on diamond pattern background); [II] 'ALSO BY J. K. ROWLING | [new paragraph] *Harry Potter and the Sorcerer's Stone* | Year One at Hogwarts | [new paragraph] *Harry Potter and the Chamber of Secrets* | Year Two at Hogwarts | [new paragraph] *Harry Potter and the Prisoner of Azkaban* | Year Three at Hogwarts | [new paragraph] *Harry Potter and the Goblet of Fire* | Year Four at Hogwarts'; [III] title-page; [IV] '[device of twelve stars] | Text copyright © 2003 by J. K. Rowling | Illustrations by Mary GrandPré copyright © 2003 by Warner Bros. | HARRY POTTER, characters, names and related indicia are trademarks of | and © Warner Bros. Harry Potter Publishing Rights © J. K. Rowling. | All rights reserved. Published by Scholastic Press, a division of Scholastic Inc., | *Publishers since 1920.* | SCHOLASTIC, SCHOLASTIC PRESS, and the LANTERN LOGO | are trademarks and/or registered trademarks of Scholastic Inc. | [new paragraph] No part of this publication may be reproduced, or stored in a retrieval system, or transmitted | in any form or by any means, electronic, mechanical, photocopying, recording, or otherwise, | without written permission of the publisher. For information regarding permission, write | to Scholastic Inc., Attention: Permissions Department, 557 Broadway, New York, NY 10012. | [new paragraph] ISBN 0-439-35806-X [new paragraph] Printed in the U.S.A.'; [V] 'TO NEIL, JESSICA, AND DAVID, | WHO MAKE MY WORLD MAGICAL.'; [VI] blank; VII-XI 'CONTENTS' (thirty-eight chapters listed with titles and page references); [XII] blank; [XIII] half-title: 'HARRY POTTER | AND THE ORDER OF THE PHOENIX' (all on diamond pattern background); [XIV] blank; 1-870 text; [871-72] blank; [873] 'ABOUT THE AUTHOR | [new paragraph] J. K. Rowling is the author of five magnificent novels in the | Harry Potter series. Her books have been honored with the | Hugo Award, the Bram Stoker Award, the Whitbread | Children's Book Award, the Nestlé Smarties Book Prize, | the British Book Awards Children's Book of the Year, and | numerous state, magazine, and children's choice citations. | Ms. Rowling herself has received a special certificate for be- | ing a three-year winner of the Nestlé Smarties Book Prize | as well as a special commendation from the Anne Spencer | Lindbergh Prize for her outstanding contribution to chil- | dren's fantasy literature. She has also been named an Offi- | cer of the Order of the British Empire. | [new paragraph] Ms. Rowling lives in Scotland with her husband and | two children.'; [874] blank; [875] 'ABOUT THE ILLUSTRATOR | [new paragraph] Mary GrandPré works in a style she calls "soft geometry," | combining her concerns for color, light, drawing, and de- | sign with her signature chalk pastels. She has illustrated | more than fifteen beautiful books, including *Plum*, a col- | lection of poetry by Tony Mitton, and the American edi- | tions of all five Harry Potter novels. Her work has also | appeared in *The New Yorker, The Atlantic Monthly*, and | *Communication Arts*, and on the cover of *Time*. | [new paragraph] Ms. GrandPré lives in St. Paul, Minnesota, with her | family.'; [876] blank; [877] colophon: '[publisher's device of a lantern, 15 by 12mm] | *This* | *book was art* | *directed by David Saylor.* | *The art for both the jacket and the* | *interior was created using pastels on toned* | *printmaking paper. The text was set in 11.5-point Adobe* | *Garamond, a typeface based on the sixteenth-century type designs of* | *Claude Garamond, redrawn by Robert Slimbach in 1989. The book was typeset* | *by Brad Walrod and was printed and bound at Berryville Graphics in* | *Beryville, Virginia. No old-growth forests were used to* | *create the paper for this book. The Managing* | *Editor was Manuela Soares and the* | *Manufacturing Director* | *was Angela* | *Biola.*'; [878-82] blank

Paper: wove paper

Running title: 'CHAPTER' and chapter number on verso, recto title comprises chapter title, pp. 1-870. Each running title (excluding pages on which new chapters commence) includes a three-star design to left and right of both running-titles on verso and recto. On pages on which a new chapter commences, the three-star design is omitted.

Illustrations: title-page vignette, together with thirty-eight vignettes at the beginning of each chapter (after chapter and chapter number but before chapter title). In addition to standard typographical changes (including italics, capitals and small capitals) there are other typographical features, comprising:

p. 27 facsimile of Mafalda Hopkirk's signature

p. 28 facsimile of Arthur Weasley's signature

p. 33 facsimile of Mafalda Hopkirk's signature

p. 35 note from Sirius Black

p. 58 facsimile of handwriting

p. 111 embroidered tapestry title

p. 127 text of sign

p. 190 magazine headlines

p. 191 magazine headline

pp. 191-93 texts of magazine articles

p. 222 text of sign

p. 239 blackboard text

p. 240 blackboard text

p. 280 facsimile of Harry's signature

p. 287 newspaper headline

p. 298 facsimile of Percy's signature

p. 306 newspaper headline

p. 351-52 text (together with facsimile signature and seal) of sign

p. 359 note from Sirius Black

p. 404 text and outline of badge

p. 485 text of portrait label

pp. 485-86 text of floor guide

p. 544 newspaper headline

p. 546 newspaper headline

p. 551 text (together with facsimile signature and seal) of sign

p. 578 facsimile of envelope address

p. 579 magazine headline

p. 581 text (together with facsimile signature and seal) of sign

p. 624 text (together with facsimile signature and seal) of sign

p. 656 text of notice

p. 768 text of badge

p. 780 text appearing on glass sphere's label

p. 841 text of prophecy

p. 845 newspaper headline

p. 858 note from Sirius Black

Binding: black boards.

On spine: 'ROWLING | [rule] | ['YEAR | 5' within concave square]' (horizontally at head) with 'HARRY POTTER | AND THE ORDER OF THE PHOENIX' (reading lengthways down spine) and '[publisher's device of a lantern, 16 by 12mm] | ARTHUR A. | LEVINE BOOKS | [rule] | SCHOLASTIC' (horizontally at foot). All in gilt.

Upper and lower covers: blank.

All edges trimmed. Binding measurements: 216 by 139mm (covers), 216 by 62mm (spine). End-papers: wove paper.

Dust-jacket: uncoated wove paper, 216 by 533mm. A single illustration in two parts spans the entire dust-jacket.

On spine: 'ROWLING | [rule] | ['YEAR | 5' within concave square]' (horizontally at head) with 'HARRY POTTER | AND THE ORDER OF THE PHOENIX' (reading lengthways down spine) and '[publisher's device of a lantern, 18 by 14mm] | ARTHUR A. | LEVINE BOOKS | [rule] | SCHOLASTIC' (horizontally at foot). All in blue with the exception of the publisher's information which is in light blue and all on colour illustration of candles.

On upper cover: 'Harry Potter [hand-drawn lettering] [in blue] | and the [hand-drawn lettering in grey of illustration] | Order of the Phoenix [hand-drawn lettering in grey of illustration] | J. K. ROWLING [in light blue]' (all width centred). All on colour illustration of Harry Potter clutching wand surrounded by doors and candles.

On lower cover: 'Sequel to the #1 *New York Times* Bestseller | HARRY POTTER | AND THE GOBLET OF FIRE | [barcode in black on red panel, 23 by 49mm] ['116133' in black on white panel, 6 by 17mm] ['64951' in black on white panel, 6 by 13mm]'. All in white and all on colour illustration of three figures behind a door.

On upper inside flap: 'THERE IS A DOOR at the end | of a silent corridor. And it's haunting Harry | Potter's dreams. Why else would he be waking in | the middle of the night, screaming in terror? | [new paragraph] Here are just a few things on Harry's mind: | [new paragraph] [six-pointed star] A Defense Against the Dark Arts teacher | with a personality like poisoned honey | [six-pointed star] A venomous, disgruntled house-elf | [six-pointed star] Ron as keeper of the Gryffindor | Quidditch team | [six-pointed star] The looming terror of the end-of-term | Ordinary Wizarding Level exams | [new paragraph] … and of course, the growing threat of | He-Who-Must-Not-Be-Named. In the richest | installment yet of J. K. Rowling's seven-part | story, Harry Potter is faced with the unreliability | of the very government of the magical world and | the impotence of the authorities at Hogwarts. | [new paragraph] Despite this (or perhaps because of it), he | finds depth and strength in his friends, beyond | what even he knew; boundless loyalty; and | unbearable sacrifice. | [new paragraph] Though thick runs the plot (as well as the | spine), readers will race through these pages and | leave Hogwarts, wishing only for the | next train back.' All in light blue and all on colour illustration of swirling misty wind and candles.

On lower inside flap: 'ALSO BY J. K. ROWLING: | [new paragraph] HARRY POTTER | AND THE GOBLET OF FIRE | [new paragraph] "Another grand tale of magic and mystery, of wheels | within wheels oiled in equal measure by terror and comedy, | featuring an engaging young hero-in-training who's not | above the occasional snit, and clicking along so smoothly | that it seems shorter than it is." — *Kirkus Reviews* | [new paragraph] HARRY POTTER | AND THE PRISONER OF AZKABAN | [new paragraph] "Isn't it reassuring that some things just get better and | better? This is a fabulously entertaining read that will have | Harry Potter fans cheering for more." | —*School Library Journal* | [new paragraph] HARRY POTTER | AND THE CHAMBER OF SECRETS | [new paragraph] "Rowling might be a Hogwarts graduate herself, for her | ability to create such an engaging, imaginative, funny, and, above all, heart-poundingly suspenseful yarn is nothing | short of magical." — *Publishers Weekly* | [new paragraph] HARRY POTTER | AND THE SORCERER'S STONE | [new paragraph] "You don't have to be a wizard or a kid to appreciate the | spell cast by Harry Potter." — *USA Today* | [new paragraph] *Jacket art by Mary GrandPré* © *2003 Warner Bros.* | *Jacket design by Mary GrandPré and David Saylor* | [new paragraph] Printed in the U.S.A.' All in light blue and all on colour illustration of swirling misty wind.

Publication: between July and December 2004 (see notes)

Price: see notes

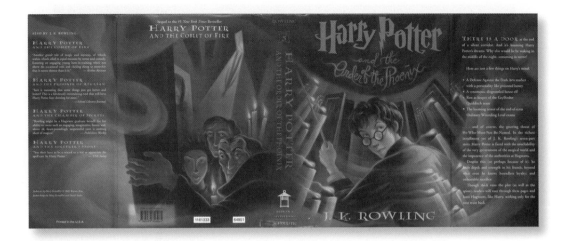

Contents:

Harry Potter and the Order of the Phoenix

('The hottest day of the summer so far was drawing to a close and a drowsy silence…')

Notes:

As with the first book club edition of *Goblet of Fire* (see A9(g)), the binding of this edition is smaller than that for the first American edition. Also note that the publisher's imprint page omits mention of the Library of Congress. The strike-line and printer's number is also absent. Also note the change of printer and binder noted in the colophon.

Given that the true American first and the book club editions share a single ISBN, the Blair Partnership noted that book club editions could only be dated to within a half-year period end in their files. This edition was, therefore, published within the period July to December 2004. The Blair Partnership Royalties Manager noted that the American book club editions did not have 'a set price'.

Contrast the barcode panel on the dust-jacket of the First American edition. In A12(aaa) there are two barcodes. In this book club edition, the smaller barcode is omitted and two white panels appear to the right of the barcode. Note also the removal of the publisher's device and name from the lower inside flap.

Each chapter commences with a drop capital.

Copies: private collection (PWE)

A12(g) ENGLISH 'CELEBRATORY' EDITION (2007)
(children's artwork series in paperback)

HARRY | POTTER | *and the Order of the Phoenix* | [illustration of Hogwarts crest with legend 'DRAGO DORMIENS NUNQUAM TITILLANDUS' on banner, 66 by 81mm] | J. K. ROWLING | [publisher's device of a dog, 11 by 18mm] | BLOOMSBURY (Lines 1 and 2 justified on left and right margins, and all width centred)

Collation: 384 unsigned leaves bound by the 'perfect binding' process; 197 by 128mm; [1-7] 8-23 [24] 25-42 [43] 44-57 [58] 59-75 [76] 77-91 [92] 93-111 [112] 113-25 [126] 127-38 [139] 140-62 [163] 164-80 [181] 182-99 [200] 201-225 [226] 227-50 [251] 252-73 [274] 275-94 [295] 296-311 [312] 313-31 [332] 333-51 [352] 353-71 [372] 373-89 [390] 391-411 [412] 413-34 [435] 436-55 [456] 457-79 [480] 481-502 [503] 504-27 [528] 529-49 [550] 551-73 [574] 575-95 [596] 597-619 [620] 621-42 [643] 644-61 [662] 663-73 [674] 675-88 [689] 690-711 [712] 713-22 [723] 724-44 [745] 746-66 [767-68]

Page contents: [1] half-title: 'HARRY | POTTER | *and the Order of the Phoenix* | [illustration of Hogwarts crest with legend 'DRAGO DORMIENS NUNQUAM TITILLANDUS' on banner, 46 by 57mm]'; [2] *'Titles available in the Harry Potter series | (in reading order):* | Harry Potter and the Philosopher's Stone | Harry Potter and the Chamber of Secrets | Harry Potter and the Prisoner of Azkaban | Harry Potter and the Goblet of Fire | Harry Potter and the Order of the Phoenix | Harry Potter and the Half-Blood Prince| [new paragraph] *Titles available in the Harry Potter series | (in Latin):* | Harry Potter and the Philosopher's Stone | Harry Potter and the Chamber of Secrets | *(in Welsh, Ancient Greek and Irish):* | Harry Potter and the Philosopher's Stone'; [3] title-page; [4] 'All rights reserved; no part of this publication may be reproduced or | transmitted by any means, electronic, mechanical, photocopying or otherwise, | without the prior permission of the publisher | [new paragraph] First published in Great Britain in 2003 | Bloomsbury Publishing Plc, 36 Soho Square, London W1D 3QY | [new paragraph] This edition first published in 2007 |

[new paragraph] Copyright © J.K. Rowling 2003 | Cover illustration by Jason Cockcroft © 2003 Bloomsbury Publishing Plc | [new paragraph] Harry Potter, names, characters and related indicia are | copyright and trademark Warner Bros., 2000™ | [new paragraph] The moral right of the author has been asserted | A CIP catalogue record for this book is available | from the British Library | [new paragraph] ISBN 978 0 7475 9126 9 | [new paragraph] 1 3 5 7 9 10 8 6 4 2 | [new paragraph] Typeset by Palimpsest Book Production Limited, | Grangemouth, Stirlingshire | Printed in Great Britain by Clays Ltd, St Ives plc | [new paragraph] The paper this book is printed on is 100% post-consumer waste recycled | [new paragraph] www.bloomsbury.com/harrypotter'; [5] 'To Neil, Jessica and David, | who make my world magical'; [6] blank; [7]-766 text; [767-68] blank

Paper: wove paper

Running title: 'HARRY POTTER' (24mm) on verso, recto title comprises chapter title, pp. 8-766 (excluding pages on which new chapters commence)

Binding: pictorial wrappers.

On spine: '[colour illustration of a golden feather on blue panel, 25 by 17mm] HARRY POTTER [in yellowish red on metallic brown panel, 25 by 45mm] *and the Order of the Phoenix* [in blue] J.K.ROWLING [in metallic brown, both title conclusion and author on yellow panel, 25 by 102mm] BLOOMSBURY [publisher's device of the head of a dog, 3 by 4mm] [both in white on blue panel, 25 by 31mm]' (reading lengthways down spine).

On upper wrapper: 'HARRY | POTTER | *and the Order of the Phoenix* [lines 1 and 2 in metallic brown, line 3 in white, all on blue panel, 62 by 128mm] | [metallic brown rule, 128mm] | ['J.K. ROWLING' [in metallic brown] with colour illustration of a phoenix rising from flames, within single metallic brown ruled border, 91 by 86mm, all on yellow panel with orange, yellow and metallic brown stars, 123 by 128mm] | [blue rule, 128mm] | BLOOMSBURY [in dark blue on metallic brown panel, 10 by 128mm]' (all width centred).

On lower wrapper: 'Harry Potter is due to start | his fifth year at Hogwarts School of | Witchcraft and Wizardry. His best friends Ron | and Hermione have been very secretive all summer | and he is desperate to get back to school and find out | what has been going on. However, what Harry discovers | is far more devastating than he could ever have expected … | [new paragraph] Suspense, secrets and thrilling action from the pen of J.K. Rowling | ensure an electrifying adventure that is impossible to put down. | [new paragraph] 'Rowling's imagination and daring put | her in a class of her own.' *The Times* | [new paragraph] 'I can't put it down. It is THE BEST.' | Sarah Poynton, aged 10, *Observer* | [new paragraph] 'Wonderfully written … a story | the whole family is following.' | Anne Diamond, *Sunday Express* | [new paragraph] [publisher's device of a dog, 6 by 10mm] | BLOOMSBURY | [new paragraph] [barcode in black on white panel, 21 by 38mm] [recycling device of three arrows] [in green] | The paper that this [in green] | book is printed on is [in green] | 100% post-consumer [in green] | waste recycled [in green] [these five lines to the right of the barcode panel] | ['www.bloomsbury.com/harrypotter' below barcode panel, in burgundy on yellow panel, 6 by 38mm] £7.99 [to the right of the web address panel]'. Reading lengthways up left side from foot of spine 'Cover illustrations by Jason Cockcroft' (in white). All in black on colour illustration of an arch, with runic characters above, a candle-lit vaulted ceiling passage and a wizard, witch, centaur, goblin and house-elf comprising characters in the fountain of magical brethren with pouring water.

All edges trimmed. Binding measurements: 197 by 128mm (wrappers), 197 by 25mm (spine).

Publication: 4 June 2007 in an edition of 47,660 copies (confirmed by Bloomsbury)

Price: £7.99

Contents:
Harry Potter and the Order of the Phoenix
('The hottest day of the summer so far was drawing to a close and a drowsy silence lay…')

Notes:
The individual titles in the 'celebratory' edition were each published to celebrate the release of the film version. The UK premiere of *Harry Potter and the Order of the Phoenix* took place on 3 July 2007.

The first edition of this 'celebratory' edition featured thin paper (with a spine width of only 25mm). Reprints would use thicker paper (with a spine width of 46mm).

Copies: Bloomsbury Archives

Reprints include:
5 7 9 10 8 6
7 9 10 8

A12(h)   ENGLISH 'SIGNATURE' EDITION   (2010)
(Clare Melinsky artwork series in paperback)

Harry Potter ['signature' above 'z' rule with numerous stars] | *and the* | *Order of the Phoenix* | [illustration of Hogwarts crest with legend 'DRAGO DORMIENS NUNQUAM TITILLANDUS' on banner, 68 by 84mm] | J.K.ROWLING | [publisher's device of a dog, 8 by 13mm] | BLOOMSBURY | LONDON BERLIN NEW YORK SYDNEY (All width centred)

Collation: 384 unsigned leaves bound in indeterminate gatherings; 197 by 128mm; [1-7] 8-23 [24] 25-42 [43] 44-57 [58] 59-75 [76] 77-91 [92] 93-111 [112] 113-25 [126] 127-38 [139] 140-62 [163] 164-80 [181] 182-99 [200] 201-225 [226] 227-50 [251] 252-73 [274] 275-94 [295] 296-311 [312] 313-31 [332] 333-51 [352] 353-71 [372] 373-89 [390] 391-411 [412] 413-34 [435] 436-55 [456] 457-79 [480] 481-502 [503] 504-527 [528] 529-49 [550] 551-73 [574] 575-95 [596] 597-619 [620] 621-42 [643] 644-61 [662] 663-73 [674] 675-88 [689] 690-711 [712] 713-22 [723] 724-44 [745] 746-66 [767-68]

Page contents: [1] half-title: 'Harry Potter ['signature' above 'z' rule with numerous stars] | *and the* | *Order of the Phoenix* | [illustration of Hogwarts crest with legend 'DRAGO DORMIENS

NUNQUAM TITILLANDUS' on banner, 60 by 75mm]'; [2] *'Titles available in the Harry Potter series | (in reading order): |* Harry Potter and the Philosopher's Stone | Harry Potter and the Chamber of Secrets | Harry Potter and the Prisoner of Azkaban | Harry Potter and the Goblet of Fire | Harry Potter and the Order of the Phoenix | Harry Potter and the Half-Blood Prince | Harry Potter and the Deathly Hallows | [new paragraph] *Titles available in the Harry Potter series | (in Latin):* | Harry Potter and the Philosopher's Stone | Harry Potter and the Chamber of Secrets | *(in Welsh, Ancient Greek and Irish):* | Harry Potter and the Philosopher's Stone'; [3] title-page; [4] 'All rights reserved; no part of this publication may be reproduced or | transmitted by any means, electronic, mechanical, photocopying | or otherwise, without the prior permission of the publisher | [new paragraph] First published in Great Britain in 2003 by Bloomsbury Publishing Plc | 36 Soho Square, London, W1D 3QY | [new paragraph]

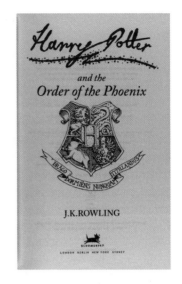

Bloomsbury Publishing, London, Berlin, New York and Sydney | [new paragraph] This paperback edition first published in November 2010 | [new paragraph] Copyright © J. K. Rowling 2003 | Cover illustrations by Clare Melinsky copyright © Bloomsbury Publishing Plc 2010 | [new paragraph] Harry Potter, names, characters and related indicia are | copyright and trademark Warner Bros., 2000™ | [new paragraph] The moral right of the author has been asserted | A CIP catalogue record of this book is available from the British Library | [new paragraph] ISBN 978 1 4088 1059 0 | [new paragraph] [Forest Stewardship Council logo, 8 by 9mm together with ® symbol and text: 'FSC | www.fsc.org | MIX | Paper from | responsible sources | FSC® C018072'] | [new paragraph] Typeset by Palimpset Book Production Limited, Grangemouth, Stirlingshire | Printed in Great Britain by Clays Ltd, St Ives plc | [new paragraph] 1 3 5 7 9 10 8 6 4 2 | [new paragraph] | www.bloomsbury. com/harrypotter'; [5] *'To Neil, Jessica and David, | who make my world magical'*; [6] blank; [7]-766 text; [767-68] blank

Paper: wove paper

Running title: 'HARRY POTTER' (24mm) on verso, recto title comprises chapter title, pp. 8-766 (excluding pages on which new chapters commence)

Binding: pictorial wrappers.

    On spine: 'Harry Potter ['signature' above 'z' rule with numerous stars] [in gilt] *and* | *the Order of the Phoenix* [red, orange, yellow and green illustration of a phoenix with flames at feet, 23 by 18mm] J.K.ROWLING BLOOMSBURY [publisher's device of the head of a dog, 3 by 4mm]' (reading lengthways down spine). All in white on purple.

    On upper wrapper: 'Harry Potter ['signature' above 'z' rule with numerous stars] [embossed in gilt] | *and the* | *Order of the Phoenix* | [light green, dark green, brown, light blue, dark blue and yellow illustration of a small glass sphere on a shelf with a label, 89 by 104mm] | J.K.ROWLING | BLOOMSBURY' (all width centred). All in purple with deckle-edge effect of white leaf on purple background at fore-edge.

On lower wrapper: 'Harry Potter is due to start his fifth year at Hogwarts School | of Witchcraft and Wizardry. He is desperate to return to | Hogwarts and find out why his friends, Ron and Hermione, have | been so secretive all summer. But before he even gets to school, | Harry survives a terrifying encounter with two Dementors, attends | a court hearing at the Ministry of Magic and is escorted on a night- | time broomstick ride to | the secret headquarters | of a mysterious group | called the Order of the | Phoenix … | [new paragraph] 'Hooray for Harry | Potter … as funny as | Roald Dahl's stories and | as vivid as the Narnia | books.' | *Daily Mail* | [new paragraph] 'The Harry Potter books | are that rare thing, a | series of stories adored | by parents and children | alike.' | *Daily Telegraph* | [dark blue and olive green illustration of stairs, railing and door in cracked doorway, 132 by 86mm to the left of lines 7-23] | [barcode together with publisher's device of a dog, 6 by 10mm and 'BLOOMSBURY' together with Forest 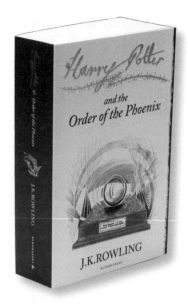 Stewardship Council logo, 7 by 8mm together with © symbol and text: 'FSC | Mixed Sources | Product group from well-managed | forests and other controlled sources | [new paragraph] Cert no. SGS-COC-2061 | www.fsc.org | © 1996 Forest Stewardship Council'] | Designed by Webb & Webb Design | Cover illustrations by Clare Melinsky www.bloomsbury.com/harrypotter £8.99 | Author photograph © J.P.Masclet'. Lines 1-23 in purple with all other text in black, together with deckle-edge effect of white leaf on purple background at fore-edge. The initial 'H' of 'Harry' is a drop capital.

On inside upper wrapper: 'The magical world of … | Harry Potter ['signature' above 'z' rule with numerous stars] | [colour illustrations in three columns of seven book designs] | The internationally bestselling series | [new paragraph] For more from Harry Potter, visit | www.bloomsbury.com/ harrypotter'. All in purple with the exception of line 2 which is in gold, together with deckle-edge effect of white leaf on purple background at fore-edge.

On inside lower wrapper: colour photograph of J.K. Rowling seated by a window.

All edges trimmed. Binding measurements: 197 by 128mm (wrappers), 197 by 47mm (spine).

Publication: 1 November 2010 in an edition of 63,435 copies (confirmed by Bloomsbury)

Price: £8.99

Contents:
Harry Potter and the Order of the Phoenix
   ('The hottest day of the summer so far was drawing to a close and a drowsy silence lay…')

Notes:
The ISBN numbers within the signature paperback edition are not sequential for *Order of the Phoenix* and *Half-Blood Prince*. The earlier book, *Order of the Phoenix*, has the ISBN number 978-1-4088-1059-0 while the later book, *Half-Blood Prince*, has the ISBN number 978-1-4088-1058-3.

Published as a boxed set of seven volumes comprising A1(i), A2(n), A7(k), A9(k), A12(h), A13(g) and A14(f). Individual volumes were also available separately.

Copies: private collection (PWE)

A12(i)   ENGLISH 'SIGNATURE' EDITION   (2011)
(Clare Melinsky artwork series in hardback)

Harry Potter ['signature' above 'z' rule with numerous stars] | *and the* | *Order of the Phoenix* | [illustration of Hogwarts crest with legend 'DRAGO DORMIENS NUNQUAM TITILLANDUS' on banner, 68 by 84mm] | J.K.ROWLING | [publisher's device of a dog, 8 by 13mm] | BLOOMSBURY | LONDON BERLIN NEW YORK SYDNEY (All width centred)

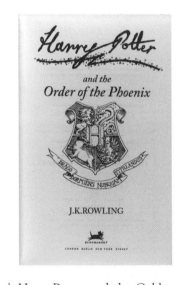

Collation: 384 unsigned leaves bound in indeterminate gatherings; 197 by 124mm; [1-7] 8-23 [24] 25-42 [43] 44-57 [58] 59-75 [76] 77-91 [92] 93-111 [112] 113-25 [126] 127-38 [139] 140-62 [163] 164-80 [181] 182-99 [200] 201-225 [226] 227-50 [251] 252-73 [274] 275-94 [295] 296-311 [312] 313-31 [332] 333-51 [352] 353-71 [372] 373-89 [390] 391-411 [412] 413-34 [435] 436-55 [456] 457-79 [480] 481-502 [503] 504-527 [528] 529-49 [550] 551-73 [574] 575-95 [596] 597-619 [620] 621-42 [643] 644-61 [662] 663-73 [674] 675-88 [689] 690-711 [712] 713-22 [723] 724-44 [745] 746-66 [767-68]

Page contents: [1] half-title: 'Harry Potter ['signature' above 'z' rule with numerous stars] | *and the* | *Order of the Phoenix* | [illustration of Hogwarts crest with legend 'DRAGO DORMIENS NUNQUAM TITILLANDUS' on banner, 60 by 75mm]'; [2] '*Titles available in the Harry Potter series* | *(in reading order):* | Harry Potter and the Philosopher's Stone | Harry Potter and the Chamber of Secrets | Harry Potter and the Prisoner of Azkaban | Harry Potter and the Goblet of Fire | Harry Potter and the Order of the Phoenix | Harry Potter and the Half-Blood Prince | Harry Potter and the Deathly Hallows | [new paragraph] *Titles available in the Harry Potter series* | *(in Latin):* | Harry Potter and the Philosopher's Stone | Harry Potter and the Chamber of Secrets | *(in Welsh, Ancient Greek and Irish):* | Harry Potter and the Philosopher's Stone | [new paragraph] *Also available* | *(in aid of Comic Relief):* | Fantastic Beasts and Where to Find Them | Quidditch Through the Ages | *(in aid of Lumos):* | The Tales of Beedle the Bard'; [3] title-page; [4] 'All rights reserved; no part of this publication may be reproduced or | transmitted by any means, electronic, mechanical, photocopying | or otherwise, without the prior permission of the publisher | [new paragraph] First published in Great Britain in 2003 by Bloomsbury Publishing Plc | 49-51

Bedford Square, London, WC1B 3DP | [new paragraph] Bloomsbury Publishing, London, Berlin, New York and Sydney | [new paragraph] This hardback edition first published in November 2011 | [new paragraph] Copyright © J. K. Rowling 2003 | Cover and endpaper illustrations by Clare Melinsky copyright © J. K. Rowling 2010 | [new paragraph] Harry Potter, names, characters and related indicia are | copyright and trademark Warner Bros., 2000™ | [new paragraph] The moral right of the author has been asserted | A CIP catalogue record of this book is available from the British Library | [new paragraph] ISBN 978 1 4088 2587 7 | [new paragraph] [Forest Stewardship Council logo, 8 by 9mm together with ® symbol and text: 'FSC | www.fsc.org | MIX | Paper from | responsible sources | FSC® C018072'] | [new paragraph] Typeset by Palimpsest Book Production Limited, Falkirk, Stirlingshire | Printed in Great Britain by Clays Ltd, St Ives plc | [new paragraph] 1 3 5 7 9 10 8 6 4 2 | [new paragraph] | www.bloomsbury.com/harrypotter'; [5] 'To Neil, Jessica and David, | who make my world magical'; [6] blank; [7]-766 text; [767-68] blank

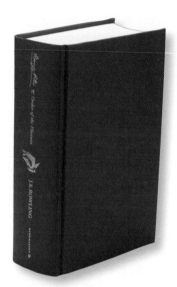

Paper: wove paper

Running title: 'HARRY POTTER' (24mm) on verso, recto title comprises chapter title, pp. 8-766

Binding: purple boards.
　　On spine: 'Harry Potter ['signature' above 'z' rule with numerous stars] *and* | *the Order of the Phoenix* [illustration of a phoenix with flames at feet, 23 by 18mm] J.K.ROWLING BLOOMSBURY [publisher's device of the head of a dog, 3 by 4mm]' (reading lengthways down spine). All in gilt.
　　Upper and lower covers: blank.
　　All edges trimmed. Purple sewn bands at head and foot of spine together with purple marker ribbon. Binding measurements: 205 by 128mm (covers), 205 by 66mm (spine). End-papers: wove paper overprinted in purple showing design, in white, of spine motifs from the series (see notes).

Dust-jacket: coated wove paper, 205 by 521mm
　　On spine: 'Harry Potter ['signature' above 'z' rule with numerous stars] [in gilt] *and* | *the Order of the Phoenix* [red, orange, yellow and green illustration of a phoenix with flames at feet, 23 by 18mm] J.K.ROWLING BLOOMSBURY [publisher's device of the head of a dog, 3 by 4mm]' (reading lengthways down spine). All in white on purple.
　　On upper cover: 'Harry Potter ['signature' above 'z' rule with numerous stars] [in gilt] | *and the* | *Order of the Phoenix* | [light green, dark green, brown, light blue, dark blue and yellow illustration of a small glass sphere on a shelf with a label, 89 by

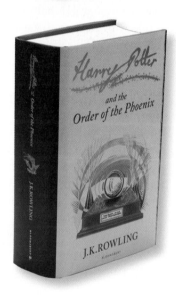

104mm] | J.K.ROWLING | BLOOMSBURY' (all width centred). All in purple with deckle-edge effect of white leaf on purple background at fore-edge.

On lower cover: "The Harry Potter books | are that rare thing, | a series of stories adored by | parents and children alike.' | *Daily Telegraph* [dark blue and olive green illustration of stairs, railing and door in cracked doorway, 91 by 59mm to the left of lines 1-5] | [publisher's device of a dog, 6 by 10mm and 'BLOOMSBURY'] [barcode and 'www.bloomsbury.com/harrypotter' in black on white panel, 24 by 39mm]'. All in purple, with deckle-edge effect of white leaf on purple background at fore-edge. The initial 'T' of 'The' is a drop capital.

On upper inside flap: 'Harry Potter is due to start his | fifth year at Hogwarts School | of Witchcraft and Wizardry. He is | desperate to return to Hogwarts and | find out why his friends, Ron and | Hermione, have been so secretive all | summer. But before he even gets to | school, Harry survives a terrifying | encounter with two Dementors, attends | a court hearing at the Ministry of | Magic and is escorted on a night-time | broomstick ride to the secret | headquarters of a mysterious group | called the Order of the Phoenix … | [new paragraph] 'Hooray for Harry Potter … as funny as | Roald Dahl's stories and as vivid as the | Narnia books.' | *Daily Mail* | [new paragraph] 'Rowling's imagination and daring put her | in a class of her own.' | *The Times* | [red, orange, yellow and green illustration of a phoenix with flames at feet, 20 by 25mm]'. All in white on purple. The initial 'H' of 'Harry' is a drop capital.

On lower inside flap: 'J. K. Rowling has written fiction since she was a child, | and she always wanted to be an author. Her parents loved | reading and their house in Chepstow was full of books. | In fact, J. K. Rowling wrote her first 'book' at the age | of six – a story about a rabbit called Rabbit. She studied | French and Classics at Exeter University, then moved to | Edinburgh – via London and Portugal. In 2000 she was | awarded an OBE for services to children's literature. | [new paragraph] The idea for Harry Potter occurred to her on the | train from Manchester to London, where she says | Harry Potter 'just strolled into my head fully formed', | and by the time she had arrived at King's Cross, many | of the characters had taken shape. During the next | five years she outlined the plots for each book and | began writing the first in the series, *Harry Potter and* | *the Philosopher's Stone*, which was first published by | Bloomsbury in 1997. The other Harry Potter titles: | *Harry Potter and the Chamber of Secrets, Harry Potter* | *and the Prisoner of Azkaban, Harry Potter and the* | *Goblet of Fire, Harry Potter and the Order of the Phoenix,* | *Harry Potter and the Half-Blood Prince* and *Harry* | *Potter and the Deathly Hallows* followed. J. K. Rowling | has also written three companion books: *Quidditch* | *Through the Ages* and *Fantastic Beasts and Where to Find* | *Them*, in aid of Comic Relief, and *The Tales of Beedle* | *the Bard*, in aid of Lumos. | [new paragraph] THE COMPLETE HARRY POTTER SERIES: | [colour illustrations in two rows of seven book designs] | Designed by Webb & Webb Design | Cover illustrations by Clare Melinsky | copyright © J. K. Rowling 2010'. All in white on purple with white panel, 19 by 12mm, to right on which in black: '[Forest Stewardship Council logo, 6 by 7mm together with ® symbol] | FSC | www.fsc.org | MIX | Paper from | responsible sources | FSC® C018072'.

Publication: 7 November 2011 in an edition of 9,200 copies (confirmed by Bloomsbury)

Price: £115 [together with A1(j), A2(o), A7(l), A9(l), A13(h) and A14(g)]

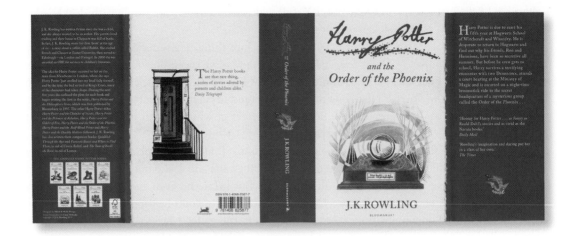

Contents:

Harry Potter and the Order of the Phoenix

('The hottest day of the summer so far was drawing to a close and a drowsy silence lay…')

Notes:

The end-papers carry a design of eight miniature illustrations. Seven of these reproduce the spine motifs from the series and an eighth comprises a variant of the key-bird from the first book.

This is the second of the books in the series to carry different press quotes from the equivalent 'signature' paperback edition – see A12(h). For this hardback edition there is an additional quote (from *The Times*) on the upper inside flap.

Published as a boxed set of seven volumes comprising A1(j), A2(o), A7(l), A9(l), A12(i), A13(h) and A14(g). Individual volumes were not available separately. The ISBN for the boxed set was ISBN 978 1 4088 2594 5.

Copies: private collection (PWE)

A12(j)   ENGLISH ADULT EDITION   (2013)
(Andrew Davidson artwork series in paperback)

J.K. [in grey] | ROWLING [in grey] [reading lengthways down title-page] | HARRY | POTTER | &THE [reading lengthways up title-page] ORDER OF THE PHOENIX | BLOOMSBURY | LONDON [point] NEW DELHI [point] NEW YORK [point] SYDNEY (Author and final part of title justified on right margin, first part of title justified on left margin, publisher with publisher's offices width centred)

Collation: 384 unsigned leaves bound in indeterminate gatherings; 198 by 128mm; [1-7] 8-23 [24] 25-42 [43] 44-57 [58] 59-75 [76] 77-91 [92] 93-111 [112] 113-25 [126] 127-38 [139] 140-62 [163] 164-80 [181] 182-99 [200] 201-225 [226] 227-50 [251] 252-73 [274] 275-94 [295] 296-311 [312] 313-31 [332] 333-51 [352] 353-71 [372] 373-89 [390] 391-411 [412] 413-34 [435] 436-55 [456] 457-79 [480] 481-502 [503] 504-527 [528] 529-49 [550] 551-73 [574] 575-95 [596] 597-619 [620] 621-42 [643] 644-61 [662] 663-73 [674] 675-88 [689] 690-711 [712] 713-22 [723] 724-44 [745] 746-66 [767-68]

Page contents: [1] half-title: 'HARRY | POTTER | &THE [reading lengthways up title-page] ORDER OF THE PHOENIX'; [2] '*Titles available in the Harry Potter series | (in reading order):* | Harry Potter and the Philosopher's Stone | Harry Potter and the Chamber of Secrets | Harry Potter and the Prisoner of Azkaban | Harry Potter and the Goblet of Fire | Harry Potter and the Order of the Phoenix | Harry Potter and the Half-Blood Prince | Harry Potter and the Deathly Hallows | [new paragraph] *Titles available in the Harry Potter series | (in Latin):* | Harry Potter and the Philosopher's Stone | Harry Potter and the Chamber of Secrets | *(in Welsh, Ancient Greek and Irish):* | Harry Potter and the Philosopher's Stone | [new paragraph] *Also available | (in aid of Comic Relief):* | Fantastic Beasts and Where to Find Them | Quidditch Through the Ages | *(in aid of Lumos):* | The Tales of Beedle the Bard'; [3] title-page; [4] 'All rights reserved; no part of this publication may be reproduced or | transmitted by any means, electronic, mechanical, photocopying | or otherwise, without the prior permission of the publisher | [new paragraph] First published in Great Britain in 2003 by Bloomsbury Publishing Plc | 50 Bedford Square, London WC1B 3DP | [new paragraph] Bloomsbury Publishing, London, New Delhi, New York and Sydney | [new paragraph] This paperback edition first published in 2013 | [new paragraph] Copyright © J.K. Rowling 2003 | Cover illustrations by Andrew Davidson copyright © J.K. Rowling 2013 | [new paragraph] Harry Potter, names, characters and related indicia are | copyright and trademark Warner Bros., 2000™ | [new paragraph] The moral right of the author has been asserted | A CIP catalogue record for this book is available from the British Library | [new paragraph] ISBN 978 1 4088 3500 5 | [new paragraph] [Forest Stewardship Council logo, 6 by 7mm together with ® symbol and text: 'FSC | www.fsc.org' with 'MIX | Paper from | responsible sources | FSC® C020471' to the right and all within single ruled border with rounded corners, 12 by 26mm] | [new paragraph] Typeset by Palimpsest Book Production Limited, Polmont, Stirlingshire | Printed and bound in Great Britain by CPI Group (UK) Ltd, Croydon CR0 4YY | [new paragraph] 1 3 5 7 9 10 8 6 4 2 | [new paragraph] | www.bloomsbury.com/harrypotter'; [5] '*To Neil, Jessica and David, | who make my world magical*'; [6] blank; [7]-766 text; [767-68] blank

Paper: wove paper

Running title: 'HARRY POTTER' (24mm) on verso, recto title comprises chapter title, pp. 8-766

Binding: pictorial wrappers.

On spine: 'J.K. ROWLING [in white] HARRY POTTER [in purple] &THE [in white] ORDER OF THE PHOENIX [in purple] [publisher's device of a figure with a bow, 8 by 6mm] [in white]' (reading lengthways down spine with the exception of '&THE' and the publisher's device which are horizontal). All on yellow.

On upper wrapper: 'J.K. [in white] | ROWLING [in white] [reading lengthways down upper wrapper] | HARRY [in yellow] | POTTER [in yellow] | &THE [in white] [reading lengthways up upper wrapper] ORDER OF THE PHOENIX [in yellow] | BLOOMSBURY [in white]' (author and final part of title justified on right margin, first part of title justified on left margin, publisher with publisher's offices width centred). All on light and dark purple illustration of an enormous silver stag emerging from a swirl of mist to confront two Dementors.

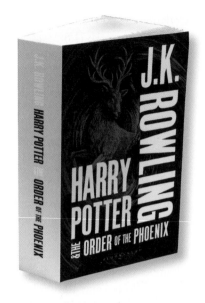

On lower wrapper: 'Harry Potter is stuck with the Dursleys in Privet Drive for a | long, hot summer. Sirius Black has told him to lie low – but | how can he, when the Darkest wizard in history is gathering | strength, and the wizarding authorities seem unwilling to do | anything about it? Harry knows that Voldemort's Dark Forces | will find him, wherever he is. | [new paragraph] Two Dementors soon bring their death-cold breath to Little | Whinging, and Harry uses magic to save his cousin Dudley's | life. Expelled from Hogwarts and accused of illegal magical | activity, Harry discovers the secret domain of the Order of the | Phoenix – and that maybe he's not alone in his battle after all … | [new paragraph] [section of white illustration of an enormous silver stag, 57 by 111mm] | BLOOMSBURY www.bloomsbury. com/harrypotter www.pottermore.com £8.99 [in black] | [section of white illustration of an enormous silver stag, 26 by 111mm upon which: Forest Stewardship Council logo, 5 by 6mm together with ® symbol and text: 'FSC | www.fsc.org | MIX | Paper from | responsible sources | FSC® C020471' all in black on white panel with rounded corners, 18 by 12mm, with barcode in black on white panel, 18 by 38mm, with 'Designed by Webb & Webb Design | Cover illustrations by Andrew Davidson | copyright © J.K. Rowling 2013' in black on yellow panel, 9 by 38mm]'. Lines 1-11 in white and all on yellow. The initial 'H' of 'Harry' is a drop capital and is printed in green.

On inside upper wrapper: yellow and white illustration of an enormous silver stag emerging from a swirl of mist to confront two Dementors.

On inside lower wrapper: yellow and white illustration of swirl of mist.

All edges trimmed. Binding measurements: 198 by 128mm (wrappers), 198 by 45mm (spine).

Publication: 15 August 2013 in an edition of 57,200 copies (confirmed by Bloomsbury) (see notes)

Price: £8.99

Contents:
Harry Potter and the Order of the Phoenix
   ('The hottest day of the summer so far was drawing to a close and a drowsy silence lay…')

Notes:

The illustrations by Andrew Davidson derive from a single wood engraving. A single illustration is presented on both the upper wrapper and inside upper wrapper. A section is printed on the lower wrapper. A detail from the upper wrapper is shown on the inside lower wrapper.

Although Bloomsbury's 'official' publication date was 15 August 2013, copies were available from amazon.co.uk at the beginning of August.

Copies: private collection (PWE)

A12(k) AMERICAN CHILDREN'S EDITION (2013)
(Kazu Kibuishi artwork in paperback)

HARRY POTTER | AND THE ORDER OF THE PHOENIX | [black and white illustration of a black dog passing through a doorway, with knarled tree on right, 63 by 48mm] | BY | J. K. ROWLING | ILLUSTRATIONS BY MARY GRANDPRÉ | SCHOLASTIC INC. (All width centred on a diamond pattern background)

Collation: 456 unsigned leaves bound in indeterminate gatherings; 204 by 134mm; [I-VI] VII-XI [XII-XIV] 1-870 [871-98]

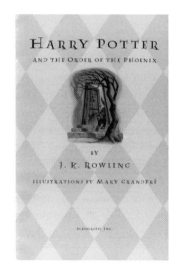

Page contents: [I-II] 'PRAISE FOR J. K. ROWLING'S | HARRY POTTER | AND THE ORDER OF THE PHOENIX | [device of nine stars] | [6 reviews and a listing of 5 statements]'; [III] 'ALSO BY J. K. ROWLING | [new paragraph] *Harry Potter and the Sorcerer's Stone* | Year One at Hogwarts | [new paragraph] *Harry Potter and the Chamber of Secrets* | Year Two at Hogwarts | [new paragraph] *Harry Potter and the Prisoner of Azkaban* | Year Three at Hogwarts | [new paragraph] | *Harry Potter and the Goblet of Fire* | Year Four at Hogwarts | [new paragraph] *Harry Potter and the Half-Blood Prince* | Year Six at Hogwarts | [new paragraph] *Harry Potter and the Deathly Hallows* | Year Seven'; [IV] blank; [V] title-page; [VI] 'TO NEIL, JESSICA, AND DAVID, | WHO MAKE MY WORLD MAGICAL. | [device of twelve stars] | Text © 2003 by J. K. Rowling | Interior illustrations by Mary GrandPré © 2003 by Warner Bros. | Excerpt from *Harry Potter and the Half-Blood Prince*, text © 2005 by J. K. Rowling; | illustration by Mary GrandPré © 2005 by Warner Bros. | Cover illustration by Kazu Kibuishi © 2013 by Scholastic Inc. | HARRY POTTER and all related characters and elements are TM of and © WBEI. | Harry Potter Publishing Rights © J. K. Rowling | All rights reserved. Published by Scholastic Inc. SCHOLASTIC, the LANTERN LOGO, and associated | logos are trademarks and/or registered trademarks of Scholastic Inc. | [new paragraph] If you purchased this book without a cover, you should be aware that this book is stolen property. | It was reported as "unsold and destroyed" to the publisher, and neither the author nor the | publisher has received any payment for this "stripped book." | [new paragraph] No part of this publication may be reproduced, stored in a retrieval system, or transmitted in any | form or by any means, electronic, mechanical, photocopying, recording, or otherwise, without | written permission of the publisher. For information regarding permission, write to Scholastic Inc., | Attention: Permissions Department, 557 Broadway, New York, NY 10012. | [new paragraph] [publisher's device of a lantern, 6 by 4mm] | Arthur A. Levine Books hardcover edition art directed by David Saylor, | published by Arthur A. Levine Books, an imprint of Scholastic Inc., July 2003. | [new paragraph] ISBN 978-0-545-58297-1 | [new paragraph] Library of Congress Control Number: 2003102525 | [new paragraph] 12 11 10 9 8 7 6 5 4 3 2 1   13 14 15 16 17 | [new paragraph] Printed in the U.S.A. 40 | This edition first printing, September 2013 | [new paragraph] We try to produce the most beautiful books possible, and we are extremely concerned about the impact of our | manufacturing process on the forests of the world and the environment as a whole. Accordingly, we made sure | that the text paper contains a minimum of 30% post-consumer waste, and that all the paper has been certified as | coming from forests that are managed to insure the protection of the people and wildlife dependent upon them.'; VII-XI 'CONTENTS' (thirty-eight chapters listed with titles and page references); [XII] blank; [XIII] half-title: 'HARRY POTTER | AND THE ORDER OF THE PHOENIX' (all on diamond pattern background); [XIV] blank; 1-870 text; [871-72] blank; [873] 'HARRY POTTER'S | ADVENTURES CONTINUE IN | [new paragraph] HARRY POTTER | AND THE HALF-BLOOD PRINCE | [new paragraph] TURN THE PAGE FOR | A SNEAK PREVIEW!' (all on diamond pattern background); [874] blank; [875-92] text; [893] blank; [894] advertisement for Pottermore; [895] '[black and white photograph of J.K. Rowling seated by curtains, credited 'ANDREW MONTGOMERY' reading lengthways up right margin] | [new paragraph] J. K. ROWLING is the author of the beloved, | bestselling, record-breaking Harry Potter series. She started writing | the series during a delayed Manchester to London King's Cross | train journey, and during the next five years, outlined the plots for | each book and began writing the first novel. *Harry Potter and the* | *Sorcerer's Stone* was published in the United States by Arthur A. | Levine Books in 1998, and the series concluded nearly ten years | later with *Harry Potter and the Deathly Hallows*, published in 2007. | J. K. Rowling is the recipient of numerous awards and honorary | degrees, including an OBE for services to children's literature, | France's Légion d'honneur, and the Hans Christian Andersen | Literature Award. She supports a wide number of causes through | her charitable trust, Volant, and is the founder of Lumos, a charity | working to transform the lives of disadvantaged children. J. K. | Rowling lives in Edinburgh with her husband and three children.'; [896] blank; [897] 'MARY GRANDPRÉ has illustrated more than twenty | beautiful books for children, including the American editions of | the Harry Potter novels. Her work has also appeared in the *New* | *Yorker*, the *Atlantic Monthly*, and the *Wall Street Journal*, and her | paintings and pastels have been shown in galleries across the United | States. Ms. GrandPré lives in Sarasota, Florida, with her family. | [new paragraph] KAZU KIBUISHI is the creator of the *New York Times* | bestselling Amulet series and *Copper*, a collection of his popular | webcomic. He is also the founder and editor of the acclaimed | Flight anthologies. *Daisy Kutter: The Last Train*, his first graphic | novel, was listed as one of the Best Books for Young Adults by | YALSA, and *Amulet,*

Book One: The Stonekeeper was an ALA Best | Book for Young Adults and a Children's Choice Book Award | finalist. Kazu lives and works in Alhambra, California, with his | wife and fellow comics artist, Amy Kim Kibuishi, and their two | children. Visit Kazu online at www.boltcity.com.'; [898] blank

Paper: wove paper

Running title: 'CHAPTER' and chapter number on verso, recto title comprises chapter title, pp. 1-870 and pp. [875-92]. Each running title (excluding pages on which new chapters commence) includes a three-star design to left and right of both running-titles on verso and recto. On pages on which a new chapter commences, the three-star design is omitted.

Illustrations: title-page vignette, together with thirty-eight vignettes at the beginning of each chapter (after chapter and chapter number but before chapter title). The 'sneak preview' also includes a vignette. In addition to standard typographical changes (including italics, capitals and small capitals) there are other typographical features, comprising:

p. 27 facsimile of Mafalda Hopkirk's signature
p. 28 facsimile of Arthur Weasley's signature
p. 33 facsimile of Mafalda Hopkirk's signature
p. 35 note from Sirius Black
p. 58 facsimile of handwriting
p. 111 embroidered tapestry title
p. 127 text of sign
p. 190 magazine headlines
p. 191 magazine headline
pp. 191-93 texts of magazine articles
p. 222 text of sign
p. 239 blackboard text
p. 240 blackboard text
p. 280 facsimile of Harry's signature
p. 287 newspaper headline
p. 298 facsimile of Percy's signature
p. 306 newspaper headline
p. 351-52 text (together with facsimile signature and seal) of sign
p. 359 note from Sirius Black
p. 404 text and outline of badge
p. 485 text of portrait label
pp. 485-86 text of floor guide
p. 544 newspaper headline
p. 546 newspaper headline
p. 551 text (together with facsimile signature and seal) of sign
p. 578 facsimile of envelope address
p. 579 magazine headline

p. 581 text (together with facsimile signature and seal) of sign

p. 624 text (together with facsimile signature and seal) of sign

p. 656 text of notice

p. 768 text of badge

p. 780 text appearing on glass sphere's label

p. 841 text of prophecy

p. 845 newspaper headline

p. 858 note from Sirius Black

Binding: pictorial wrappers.

On spine: 'ROWLING | Harry Potter and the Order of the Phoenix [reading lengthways down spine] | 5' and '[publisher's book device] | [rule] | S' in white on red panel, 14 by 6mm. All in white on colour illustration (see notes).

On upper wrapper: 'J. K. ROWLING | Harry Potter [hand-drawn lettering] [embossed in white] | and the | Order of the Phoenix' (all width centred). All in white on colour illustration of three figures, including Harry Potter, each riding a flying thestral. In centre at foot: '[publisher's book device] SCHOLASTIC' in white on red panel, 5 by 45mm.

On lower wrapper: '"We're coming with you, Harry." | — Neville Longbottom | [new paragraph] There is a door at the end of a silent corridor. And it's haunting Harry Potter's | dreams. Why else would he be waking in the middle of the night, screaming | in terror? | [new paragraph] It's not just the upcoming O.W.L. exams; a new teacher with a personality | like poisoned honey; a venomous, disgruntled house-elf; or even the | growing threat of He-Who-Must-Not-Be-Named. Now Harry Potter is | faced with the unreliability of the very government of the magical world | and the impotence of the authorities at Hogwarts. | [new paragraph] Despite this (or perhaps because of it), he finds depth and strength in his | friends, beyond what even he knew; boundless loyalty; and unbearable | sacrifice. | [new paragraph] $14.99 US | [new paragraph] [publisher's book device with 'SCHOLASTIC' in white on red panel, 5 by 45mm] | www.scholastic.com | COVER DESIGN BY KAZU KIBUISHI AND JASON CAFFOE | COVER ART BY KAZU KIBUISHI © 2013 BY SCHOLASTIC INC.' Lines 1-2 in white with other lines in light blue and all on colour illustration of six students standing in the centre of a large circular room with unmarked doors. In lower right: barcode with smaller barcode to the right (51499) together with 'S' within triangle, all in black on white panel, 21 by 53mm.

On inside upper wrapper: barcode with smaller barcode (51499) together with 'S' within triangle below, all in black on white panel, 53 by 21mm. All on salmon pink.

On inside lower wrapper: '[colour illustration of book design] Harry Potter [hand-drawn lettering] [in white] | The Complete Series [in white] | Read All of Harry's [in white] | Magical Adventures! [in white] | [publisher's device of a lantern, 10 by 7mm] [in black] | ARTHUR A. LEVINE BOOKS [in black] | [publisher's book device with 'SCHOLASTIC' in white on red panel, 5 by 45mm] | scholastic.com/harrypotter [in white] | [colour illustrations in three columns of six book designs]'. All on lavender blue.

All edges trimmed. Binding measurements: 204 by 134mm (wrappers), 204 by 42mm (spine).

Publication: 27 August 2013

Price: $14.99

Contents:
Harry Potter and the Order of the Phoenix
('The hottest day of the summer so far was drawing to a close and a drowsy silence...')

Notes:
See notes to A4(h) about this series.

The seven volumes in this edition were available individually or as a set issued in a slipcase. The set, presented in order, reveals a single illustration of Hogwarts castle across the seven spines. Scholastic released images of the new illustrations in a careful marketing campaign: the upper wrapper illustration for *Order of the Phoenix* was released on 1 July on the publisher's website.

In contrast with A12(e), this edition only includes the second half-title.

The 'sneak preview' of *Half-Blood Prince* comprises the entire first chapter.

Each chapter commences with a drop capital.

Copies: private collection (PWE)

Reprints include:
12 11 10 9 8 7 6 5 4 3 2   13 14 15 16 17   Printed in the U.S.A. 40

HARRY POTTER AND THE HALF-BLOOD PRINCE

A13(a) **FIRST ENGLISH EDITION** **(2005)**
(children's artwork series in hardback)

HARRY | POTTER | *and the Half-Blood Prince* | [illustration of Hogwarts crest with legend 'DRAGO DORMIENS NUNQUAM TITILLANDUS' on banner, 66 by 81mm] | J. K. ROWLING | [publisher's device of a dog, 11 by 18mm] | BLOOMSBURY (Lines 1 and 2 justified on left and right margins, and all width centred)

Collation: 304 unsigned leaves bound in indeterminate gatherings; 197 by 127mm; [1-7] 8-24 [25] 26-41 [42] 43-58 [59] 60-80 [81] 82-102 [103] 104-123 [124] 125-47 [148] 149-62 [163] 164-83 [184] 185-204 [205] 206-222 [223] 224-41 [242] 243-60 [261] 262-83 [284] 285-304 [305] 306-326 [327] 328-49 [350] 351-73 [374] 375-395 [396] 397-418 [419] 420-38 [439] 440-59 [460] 461-79 [480] 481-499 [500] 501-518 [519] 520-40 [541] 542-56 [557] 558-69 [570] 571-89 [590] 591-607 [608]

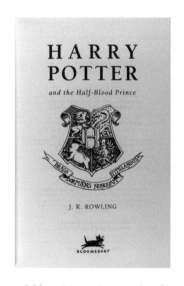

Page contents: [1] half-title: 'HARRY | POTTER | *and the Half-Blood Prince* | [illustration of Hogwarts crest with legend 'DRAGO DORMIENS NUNQUAM TITILLANDUS' on banner, 46 by 57mm]'; [2] '*Titles available in the Harry Potter series* | *(in reading order):* | Harry Potter and the Philosopher's Stone | Harry Potter and the Chamber of Secrets | Harry Potter and the Prisoner of Azkaban | Harry Potter and the Goblet of Fire | Harry Potter and the Order of the Phoenix | Harry Potter and the Half-Blood Prince | [new paragraph] *Harry Potter and the Philosopher's Stone* | *also available in Latin, Ancient Greek, Welsh and Irish:* | Harrius Potter et Philosophi Lapis (Latin) | Ἄρειος Ποτήρ καί ἡ τοῦ φιλοσόφου λίθος (Ancient Greek) | Harri Potter a Maen yr Anthronydd (Welsh) | Harry Potter agus an Órchloch (Irish)'; [3] title-page; [4] 'All rights reserved; no part of this publication may be reproduced or | transmitted by any means, electronic, mechanical, photocopying | or otherwise, without the prior permission of the publisher | [new paragraph] First published in Great Britain in 2005 | Bloomsbury Publishing Plc, 38 Soho Square, London, W1D 3HB | [new paragraph] Copyright © 2005 J. K. Rowling | Cover illustrations by Jason Cockcroft copyright © 2005 Bloomsbury Publishing Plc | Harry Potter, names, characters and related indicia are | copyright and trademark Warner Bros., 2000™ | [new paragraph] J. K. Rowling has asserted her moral rights | A CIP catalogue record of this book is available from the British Library | [new paragraph] ISBN 0 7475 8108 8 | [new paragraph] The paper this book is printed on is certified by the Forest Stewardship | Council (FSC). It is made up of 30% FSC certified pulp and 70% pulp from | controlled sources. FSC products with percentage claims meet environmental | requirements to be ancient-forest friendly. The printer holds FSC chain of | custody SGS-COC-2061. | [new paragraph] Typeset by RefineCatch Limited, Bungay, Suffolk | Printed in Great Britain by Clays Ltd, St Ives plc | [new paragraph] First Edition | [new paragraph] www.bloomsbury.com/harrypotter'; [5] 'To Mackenzie, | my beautiful daughter, | I dedicate | her ink and paper twin'; [6] blank; [7]-607 text; [608] blank

Paper: wove paper

Running title: 'HARRY POTTER' (24mm) on verso, recto title comprises chapter title, pp. 10-607 (excluding pages on which new chapters commence)

Binding: pictorial boards.

   On spine: '[colour illustration of a ring on burgundy panel, 53 by 16mm] HARRY POTTER [in green on blue panel, 53 by 47mm] *and the Half-Blood Prince* [in white] J.K.ROWLING [in blue, both title conclusion and author on green panel, 53 by 109mm] BLOOMSBURY [publisher's device of the head of a dog, 4 by 3mm] [both in white on blue panel, 53 by 34mm]' (reading lengthways down spine).

   On upper cover: 'HARRY | POTTER | *and the Half-Blood Prince* [lines 1 and 2 in green, line 3 in white, all on blue panel, 62 by 132mm] | [green rule, 132mm] | [colour illustration of Dumbledore and Harry Potter clutching wands and engulfed by swirls of fire, 125 by 132mm] | [green rule, 132mm intersected by green panel with 'J.K.ROWLING' in blue] | BLOOMSBURY [in white on blue panel, 15 by 132mm]' (all width centred).

   On lower cover: 'It is the middle of the summer, but there is an unseasonal mist | pressing against the windowpanes. Harry is waiting | nervously in his bedroom at the Dursleys' house in Privet Drive | for a visit from Professor Dumbledore himself. One of the last | times he saw the Headmaster was in a fierce one-to-one duel with | Lord Voldemort, and Harry can't quite believe that Professor | Dumbledore will actually appear at the Dursleys' of all places. | Why is the Professor coming to visit him now? What is it that | cannot wait until Harry returns to Hogwarts in a few weeks' | times? Harry's sixth year at Hogwarts has already got off to | an unusual start, as the worlds of Muggle and magic | start to intertwine ... | [new paragraph] J.K. Rowling charts Harry Potter's latest adventures | in his sixth year at Hogwarts with | consummate skill and in | breathtaking fashion. | [barcode in black on white panel, 21 by 40mm together with '[publisher's device of a dog, 5 by 9mm] | BLOOMSBURY' in white on right side of panel and 'http://www.bloomsbury.com' below panel, in white on green panel, 5 by 40mm]'. Reading lengthways down right side next to foot of spine 'Cover illustrations by Jason Cockcroft'. All in white with the exception of the illustrations credit which is in black, and all on an illustration of a stone basin on top of a pedestal, emitting a phosphorescent glow, situated in the middle of a small island of smooth rock by a great black lake with a tiny boat to the left.

All edges trimmed. Binding measurements: 205 by 132mm (covers), 205 by 53mm (spine). End-papers: wove paper.

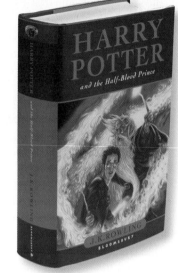

Dust-jacket: coated wove paper, 204 by 516mm

Spine, upper and lower covers replicate the binding, with the exception of the illustrations credit which is omitted.

On upper inside flap: '£16.99 | Harry has yet again spent the summer holidays | at the Dursleys'. He has had plenty to think | about, though – from the death of his beloved | godfather Sirius Black, to the terrifying chase | through the Ministry of Magic by the Death | Eaters, to the fierce duel he witnessed between | Professor Dumbledore and Lord Voldemort. | Now he is waiting nervously in his bedroom | at the Dursleys' for a visit from his headmaster. | Harry can't think why Dumbledore would | want to visit him now. What is it that cannot | possibly wait until the beginning of term? He | is also not quite sure how the Dursleys will | react to the Headmaster's sudden appearance | in their own home … | [new paragraph] J.K. Rowling charts Harry Potter's adventure | in his sixth year at Hogwarts with a mix of detail | and humour that is unsurpassed, pace that is | breathless and above all a flair that is magical | [colour illustration of an old lower arm and hand locked in a clench with a young lower arm and hand, 45 by 90mm]'. All in white on green panel with the exception of the price which is in black.

On lower inside flap: 'J.K. (Joanne Kathleen) Rowling has written | fiction since she was a child, and always wanted | to be an author. Her parents loved reading, and | their house in Chepstow was full of books. In | fact, J.K. Rowling wrote her first 'book' at the | age of six – a story about a rabbit called Rabbit! | [new paragraph] The idea for Harry Potter occurred to | J.K. Rowling on the train from Manchester to | London, where she says Harry Potter 'just | strolled into my head fully formed', and by | the time she had arrived at King's Cross, many | of the characters had taken shape. During the | next five years she outlined the plots for each | book and began writing the first in the series, | *Harry Potter and the Philosopher's Stone*, which | was first published by Bloomsbury in 1997. | The other Harry Potter titles: *Harry Potter | and the Chamber of Secrets, Harry Potter and | the Prisoner of Azkaban, Harry Potter and the | Goblet of Fire*, and *Harry Potter and the Order | of the Phoenix* followed. | [new paragraph] J.K. Rowling has also written two other | companion books, *Quidditch Through the Ages | and Fantastic Beasts and Where to Find Them,* | in aid of Comic Relief. | Cover illustrations by Jason Cockcroft | [colour illustration of an old lower arm and hand locked in a clench with a young lower arm and hand, 45 by 90mm]'. All in white on green panel with the exception of the illustrations credit which is in black on an illustration of flames.

Publication: 16 July 2005 (simultaneous with A13(aa), A13(aaa) and A13(aaaa)) in an edition of 6.3 million copies (confirmed by Bloomsbury)

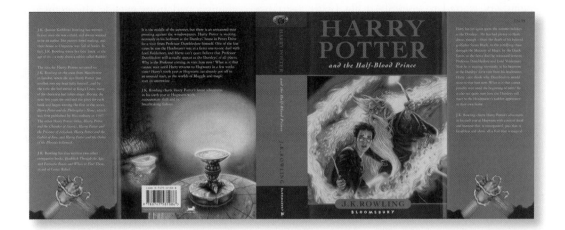

Price: £16.99

Contents:

Harry Potter and the Half-Blood Prince

('It was nearing midnight and the Prime Minister was sitting alone in his office…')

Notes:

The manuscript was delivered to Bloomsbury at the end of 2004. The editorial files at the publisher include an email from Emma Matthewson to J.K. Rowling dated 3 December 2004. Matthewson wrote:

> … what a marvellous book (book seems too small a word) you have created. I do think that revised opening is a masterstroke… what I think is wonderful about this book is that for the first time readers will really and truly begin to appreciate the breadth of the vision you have. They will really begin to appreciate all those carefully and painstakingly laid plots and clues and important objects and scenes. This is the marvel of your writing…

There was then a period of copy-editing throughout December. An email from Rowling to Matthewson, dated 16 December 2004, provided 'responses to your queries'. A few days later, on Christmas Eve, Rowling emailed Matthewson detailing 'the further edits we have agreed are needed…'

Within Bloomsbury itself, Nigel Newton communicated with an internal email noting that 'Emma Matthewson is working on the percentage of editorial changes made to the… typescripts, which she guesses might be about 1%.'

A publication announcement poster was released at the beginning of February 2005. Promotional countdown posters were then issued at the beginning of July 2005. Furthermore, Bloomsbury released packs of 20 *Half-Blood Prince* bags for retailers as part of the their marketing campaign. Other promotional material included double-sided banners and window displays.

A set of proofs is preserved within the editorial files at Bloomsbury. They are dated 27 February 2005 and reveal some small copy-editing changes.

Bloomsbury started to compile a file (with assistance commissioned from outside the company) known as the 'HP Bible' around September 2004. This was to assist with consistency across the series.

The English audiobook version, read by Stephen Fry, has a duration of approximately twenty and a half hours.

Reprints (and subsequent new editions) include a number of corrections to the text. These comprise:

Page 99, line 9	'eleven' to 'ten'
Page 101, line 27	'ten' to 'nine'
Page 139, line 31	'Bat Bogey Hex' to 'Bat-Bogey Hex'
Page 212, lines 16-17	'They now joined Katie, Demelza and Ginny' to 'They now joined the spectators'
Page 252, line 7	'an old wardrobe and an iron bedstead' to 'an old wardrobe, a wooden chair and an iron bedstead'
Page 272, line 12	'Bat Bogey Hex' to 'Bat-Bogey Hex'

Copies: private collection (PWE)

Reprints include:
5 7 9 10 8 6

A report compiled by the printers, Clays Ltd, in October 2013 noted that, to date, they had produced a minimum of 2.3 million paperbacks and 7.6 million hardbacks across 75 printings.

A13(aa) FIRST ENGLISH EDITION (2005)
(Michael Wildsmith photography adult artwork series in hardback)

Harry Potter and the | Half-Blood Prince | J. K. Rowling | BLOOMSBURY (All width centred)

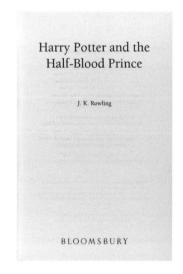

Collation: 304 unsigned leaves bound in indeterminate gatherings; 197 by 127mm; [1-7] 8-24 [25] 26-41 [42] 43-58 [59] 60-80 [81] 82-102 [103] 104-123 [124] 125-47 [148] 149-62 [163] 164-83 [184] 185-204 [205] 206-222 [223] 224-41 [242] 243-60 [261] 262-83 [284] 285-304 [305] 306-326 [327] 328-49 [350] 351-73 [374] 375-395 [396] 397-418 [419] 420-38 [439] 440-59 [460] 461-79 [480] 481-499 [500] 501-518 [519] 520-40 [541] 542-56 [557] 558-69 [570] 571-89 [590] 591-607 [608]

Page contents: [1] half-title: 'Harry Potter and the | Half-Blood Prince'; [2] *'Titles available in the Harry Potter series | (in reading order):* | Harry Potter and the Philosopher's Stone | Harry Potter and the Chamber of Secrets | Harry Potter and the Prisoner of Azkaban | Harry Potter and the Goblet of Fire | Harry Potter and the Order of the Phoenix | Harry Potter and the Half-Blood Prince | [new paragraph] *Harry Potter and the Philosopher's Stone* | *also available in Latin, Ancient Greek, Welsh and Irish:* | Harrius Potter et Philosophi Lapis (Latin) | Ἄρειος Ποτήρ καί ἡ τοῦ ψιλοσόψον λίθος (Ancient Greek) | Harri Potter a Maen yr Anthronydd (Welsh) | Harry Potter agus an Órchloch (Irish)'; [3] title-page; [4] 'All rights reserved; no part of this publication may be reproduced or | transmitted by any means, electronic, mechanical, photocopying | or otherwise, without the prior permission of the publisher | [new paragraph] First published in Great Britain in 2005 | Bloomsbury Publishing Plc, 38 Soho Square, London, W1D 3HB | [new paragraph] Copyright © 2005 J. K. Rowling | Harry Potter, names, characters and related indicia are | copyright and trademark Warner Bros., 2000™ | [new paragraph] J. K. Rowling has asserted her moral rights | A CIP catalogue record of this book is available from the British Library | [new paragraph] ISBN 0 7475 8110 X | [new paragraph] The paper this book is printed on is certified by the Forest Stewardship | Council (FSC). It is made up of 30% FSC certified pulp and 70% pulp from | controlled sources. FSC products with percentage claims meet environmental | requirements to be ancient-forest friendly. The printer holds FSC chain of | custody SGS-COC-2061. | [new paragraph] Typeset by RefineCatch Limited, Bungay, Suffolk | Printed in Great Britain by Clays Ltd, St Ives plc | [new paragraph] First Edition | [new paragraph] www.bloomsbury.com/harrypotter'; [5] '*To Mackenzie,* | *my beautiful daughter,* | *I dedicate* | *her ink and paper twin*'; [6] blank; [7]-607 text; [608] blank

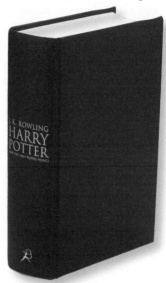

Paper: wove paper

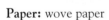

Running title: 'HARRY POTTER' (24mm) on verso, recto title comprises chapter title, pp. 8-607 (excluding pages on which new chapters commence)

Binding: black boards.

    On spine: 'J. K. ROWLING | HARRY | POTTER | AND THE HALF-BLOOD PRINCE | [publisher's device of a figure with a bow, 13 by 12mm]'. All in gilt.

    Upper and lower covers: blank.

    All edges trimmed. Binding measurements: 205 by 128mm (covers), 205 by 60mm (spine). End-papers: wove paper.

Dust-jacket: coated wove paper, 205 by 517mm

    On spine: '[colour photograph of a battered-looking copy of *Advanced Potion-Making* by Libatius Borage lying on desk, all within single white ruled border, 58 by 42mm] | J. K. ROWLING

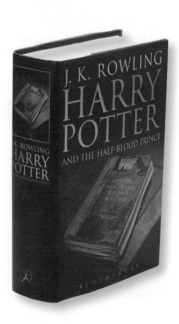

[in white] | HARRY [in gilt] | POTTER [in gilt] | AND THE HALF-BLOOD PRINCE [in white] | [publisher's device of a figure with a bow, 13 by 12mm] [in olive beige]'. All on black.

On upper cover: 'J. K. ROWLING [in white] | HARRY [embossed in gilt] | POTTER [embossed in gilt] | AND THE HALF-BLOOD PRINCE [in white] | BLOOMSBURY [in white]' (all width centred). All on colour photograph of a battered-looking copy of *Advanced Potion-Making* by Libatius Borage lying on desk.

On lower cover: black and white photograph of J.K. Rowling standing against bookshelves with 'www.bloomsbury.com/harrypotter [in black on olive beige panel, 5 by 40mm] | [barcode in black on white panel, 20 by 39mm] | BLOOMSBURY [in black on olive beige panel, 7 by 40mm]' (lower right).

On upper inside flap: 'Harry's sixth year at Hogwarts begins, | and it feels like a reassuring place to | return to after the strange events of the | summer. Disappearances, murder and an | ominous chilling mist which swirls | through both the Muggle and wizarding | worlds are harbingers of more sinister | purpose. Voldemort's army is swelling, | and with it the Death Eaters are growing | bolder and more deadly. Suspicions are | rife, and allegiances questioned as even | the safest havens cease to feel secure from | the Dark wizards. As the storm gathers | strength, Harry must face the terrifying | truth of his destiny. | [new paragraph] With her irresistibly deft mix of suspense | and humour, J.K. Rowling reveals the | sheer intricacy and brilliance of the world | she has created, as the pieces of the jigsaw | start to fall into place. | [new paragraph] £16.99'. All in white on black.

On lower inside flap: 'J. K. (JOANNE KATHLEEN) ROWLING | has written fiction since she was a child. | Born in 1965, she grew up in Chepstow | and wrote her first 'book' at the age of six | – a story about a rabbit called Rabbit. | She studied French and Classics at Exeter | University, then moved to London to | work at Amnesty International, and then | to Portugal to teach English as a foreign | language, before settling in Edinburgh. | [new paragraph] The idea for Harry Potter occurred to her | on the train from Manchester to London, | where she says Harry Potter 'just strolled | into my head fully formed', and by the | time she had arrived at King's Cross, | many of the characters had taken shape. | During the next five years she outlined | the plots for each book and began writing | the first in the series, *Harry Potter and* | *the Philosopher's Stone*, which was first | published by Bloomsbury in 1997. The | other Harry Potter titles: *Harry Potter and* | *the Chamber*

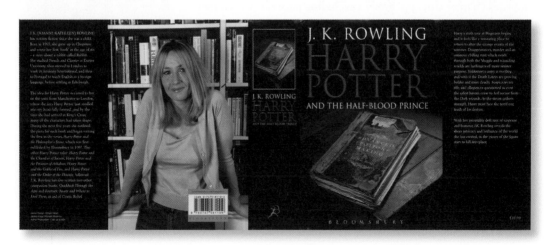

of Secrets, Harry Potter and | the Prisoner of Azkaban, Harry Potter | and the Goblet of Fire, and Harry Potter | and the Order of the Phoenix, followed. | J. K. Rowling has also written two other | companion books, *Quidditch Through the* | *Ages* and *Fantastic Beasts and Where to* | *Find Them*, in aid of Comic Relief. | [new paragraph] Jacket Design: William Webb | Jacket Image: Michael Wildsmith | Author Photograph: © Bill de la HEY'. All in white on black.

Publication: 16 July 2005 (simultaneous with A13(a), A13(aaa) and A13(aaaa)) in an edition of 1 million copies (confirmed by Bloomsbury)

Price: £16.99

Contents:
Harry Potter and the Half-Blood Prince
('It was nearing midnight and the Prime Minister was sitting alone in his office...')

Copies: private collection (PWE)

A13(aaa) FIRST AMERICAN EDITION (2005)
(children's artwork series in hardback)

HARRY POTTER | AND THE HALF-BLOOD PRINCE | [black and white illustration of a battered book, with swirl of bubbling potion and a lit candle in holder, 68 by 57mm] | BY | J. K. ROWLING | ILLUSTRATIONS BY MARY GRANDPRÉ | [publisher's device of a lantern, 12 by 9mm] | ARTHUR A. LEVINE BOOKS | AN IMPRINT OF SCHOLASTIC INC. (All width centred on a diamond pattern background)

Collation: 336 unsigned leaves bound in twenty-one gatherings of sixteen leaves; 228 by 150mm; [I-VI] VII-X [XI-XII] 1-652 [653-60]

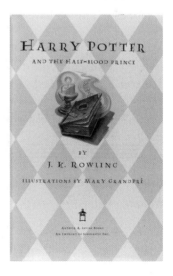

Page contents: [I] 'HARRY POTTER | AND THE HALF-BLOOD PRINCE' (all on diamond pattern background); [II] 'ALSO BY J. K. ROWLING | [new paragraph] *Harry Potter and the Sorcerer's Stone* | Year One at Hogwarts | [new paragraph] *Harry Potter and the Chamber of Secrets* | Year Two at Hogwarts | [new paragraph] *Harry Potter and the Prisoner of Azkaban* | Year Three at Hogwarts | [new paragraph] *Harry Potter and the Goblet of Fire* | Year Four at Hogwarts | [new paragraph] *Harry Potter and the Order of the Phoenix* | Year Five at Hogwarts'; [III] title-page; [IV] '[device of twelve stars] | Text copyright © 2005 by J. K. Rowling | Illustrations by Mary GrandPré copyright © 2005 by Warner Bros. | HARRY POTTER, characters, names and related indicia are trademarks of | and © Warner Bros. Harry Potter Publishing Rights © J. K. Rowling. | All rights reserved. Published by Arthur A. Levine Books, | an imprint of Scholastic Inc., *Publishers since 1920.* | SCHOLASTIC, the LANTERN LOGO, and associated logos are | trademarks and/or registered trademarks of Scholastic Inc. | [new paragraph] No part of this publication may be reproduced, or stored in a retrieval system, or transmitted | in any form or by any means, electronic, mechanical, photocopying, recording, or otherwise, | without written permission of the publisher. For information regarding permission, write | to Scholastic Inc., Attention: Permissions Department, 557 Broadway, New York, NY 10012. | [new paragraph] Library of Congress Control Number: 2005921149 | [new paragraph] ISBN 0-439-78454-9 | [new paragraph] 10 9 8 7 6 5 4 3 2 1   05 06 07 08 09 | Printed in the U.S.A. 37 | First American edition, July 2005'; [V] 'TO MACKENZIE, | MY BEAUTIFUL DAUGHTER, | I DEDICATE | HER INK-AND-PAPER TWIN.'; [VI] blank; VII-X 'CONTENTS' (thirty chapters listed with titles and page references); [XI] half-title: 'HARRY POTTER | AND THE HALF-BLOOD PRINCE' (all on diamond pattern background); [XII] blank; 1-652 text; [653-54] blank; [655] 'ABOUT THE AUTHOR | [new paragraph] J. K. Rowling is the author of six celebrated novels in the | Harry Potter sequence. Her most recent book, *Harry Potter* | *and the Order of the Phoenix,* was named an ALA Notable | Book and recognized with prizes as diverse as an Anthony | Award for Best Young Adult Mystery and a Best Science- | Fiction/Fantasy Novel award from *Disney Adventures* mag- | azine. Ms. Rowling's first four books have been honored | with the Hugo Award, the Bram Stoker Award, the Whit- | bread Children's Book Award, the Nestlé Smarties Book | Prize, the British Book Awards Children's Book of the Year, | and numerous state, magazine, and children's choice cita- | tions. She has also been named an Officer of the Order of | the British Empire. | [new paragraph] Ms. Rowling lives in Scotland with her family.'; [656] blank; [657] 'ABOUT THE ILLUSTRATOR | [new paragraph] Mary GrandPré has illustrated nineteen beautiful books, | including *Henry and Pawl and the Round Yellow Ball,* co- | written with her husband Tom Casmer; *Plum,* a collection | of poetry by Tony Mitton; *The Sea Chest,* by Toni Buzzeo; | *Sweep Dreams,* by Nancy Willard; and the American edi- | tions of all six Harry Potter novels. Her work has also | appeared in *The New Yorker, The Atlantic Monthly,* and | *The Wall Street Journal,* and her paintings and pastels have | been shown in galleries across the United States. | [new paragraph] Ms. GrandPré lives in Sarasota, Florida, with her family.'; [658] blank; [659] colophon: '[publisher's device of a lantern, 17 by 12mm] | *This* | *book was art* | *directed by David Saylor.* | *The art for both the jacket and the* | *interior was created using pastels on toned* | *printmaking paper. The text was set in 12-point Adobe* | *Garamond, a typeface based on the sixteenth-century type designs of* | *Claude Garamond, redrawn by Robert Slimbach in 1989. The book was typeset* | *by Brad Walrod and was printed and bound at Berryville Graphics in* | *Berryville, Virginia, on paper that is free of fiber from ancient* | *forests. The Managing Editor was Karyn Browne;* | *the Continuity Editor was Cheryl* | *Klein; and the Manufacturing* | *Director was Angela* | *Biola.'*; [660] blank

Paper: wove paper

Running title: 'CHAPTER' and chapter number on verso, recto title comprises chapter title, pp. 1-652. Each running title (excluding pages on which new chapters commence) includes a three-star design to left and right of both running-titles on verso and recto. On pages on which a new chapter commences, the three-star design is omitted.

Illustrations: title-page vignette, together with thirty vignettes at the beginning of each chapter (after chapter and chapter number but before chapter title). In addition to standard typographical changes (including italics, capitals and small capitals) there are other typographical features, comprising:

p. 39 newspaper headline

p. 40 newspaper headline

p. 42 leaflet title

p. 43 facsimile of Albus Dumbledore's signature

p. 102 O.W.L. results

p. 110 cardboard sign

p. 116 window display lettering

p. 141 facsimile of Professor H.E.F. Slughorn's signature

p. 181 facsimile of Albus Dumbledore's signature

p. 189 textbook scribble

p. 193 textbook ownership inscription

p. 238 textbook scribble

p. 338 gold chain lettering

p. 354 text of sign

p. 377 textbook scribble

p. 470 note from Hagrid

p. 609 note from R.A.B.

Binding: black cloth-backed spine with purple boards (with diamond pattern in blind).

On spine: 'ROWLING | [rule] | ['YEAR | 6' within concave square]' (horizontally at head) with 'HARRY POTTER | AND THE HALF-BLOOD PRINCE' (reading lengthways down spine) and '[publisher's device of a lantern, 19 by 14mm] | ARTHUR A. | LEVINE BOOKS | [rule] | SCHOLASTIC' (horizontally at foot). All in purple.

Upper and lower covers: blank.

All edges trimmed. Binding measurements: 235 by 150mm (covers), 235 by 60mm (spine). The black cloth continues onto the covers by 40mm. End-papers: green wove paper.

Dust-jacket: uncoated wove paper, 235 by 583mm. A single illustration in two parts spans the entire dust-jacket.

On spine: 'ROWLING | [rule] | ['YEAR | 6' within concave square]' (horizontally at head) with 'HARRY POTTER | AND THE HALF-BLOOD PRINCE' (reading lengthways down spine) and '[publisher's device of a lantern, 19 by 14mm] | ARTHUR A. | LEVINE BOOKS | [rule] | SCHOLASTIC' (horizontally at foot). All embossed in purple and all on colour illustration of swirling mists.

On upper cover: 'Harry Potter [hand-drawn lettering] [embossed in purple] | and the Half-Blood Prince [hand-drawn lettering in brown of illustration] | J. K. ROWLING [embossed in purple]' (all width centred). All on colour illustration of Harry Potter and Dumbledore gazing into a stone basin surrounded by swirling mists.

On lower cover: colour illustration of children gazing at green glowing Dark Mark in the sky with outline of Hogwarts in background together with barcode with smaller barcode to the right (52999) all in black on orange panel, 23 by 50mm.

On upper inside flap: '$29.99 | [new paragraph] THE WAR AGAINST VOLDEMORT | is not going well; even Muggle governments are | noticing. Ron scans the obituary pages of the *Daily* | *Prophet*, looking for familiar names. Dumbledore | is absent from Hogwarts for long stretches of time, | and the Order of the Phoenix has already suffered | losses. | [new paragraph] And yet … | [new paragraph] As in all wars, life goes on. Sixth-year students | learn to Apparate — and lose a few eyebrows in the | process. The Weasley twins expand their business. | Teenagers flirt and fight and fall in love. Classes are | never straightforward, though Harry receives some | extraordinary help from the mysterious Half- | Blood Prince. | [new paragraph] So it's the home front that takes center stage in | the multilayered sixth installment of the story of | Harry Potter. Here at Hogwarts, Harry will search | for the full and complex story of the boy who | became Lord Voldemort — and thereby find what | may be his only vulnerability. | [new paragraph] *Jacket art by Mary GrandPré © 2005 Warner Bros. | Jacket design by Mary GrandPré and David Saylor*'. All in yellow and all on colour illustration of swirling mists.

On lower inside flap: 'PRAISE FOR | HARRY POTTER | AND THE ORDER OF THE PHOENIX | [new paragraph] | — The #1 *New York Times* Bestseller — | [new paragraph] "As Harry gets older, Rowling gets better…. She has looted the | shelves of literature and mythology, fairy tales and folklore, anthro- | pology and comparative religion, firing up a pop-culture crockpot | and adding pratfalls, wordplay and dread…. *Harry Potter and the* | *Order of the Phoenix* is rich and satisfying." | — John Leonard, *The New York Times Book Review* | [new paragraph] "Rowling has not lost her flair as a storyteller or her ability to keep | coming up with new gimcracks to astound her readers. But her true | skills lie in the way she ages Harry, successfully evolving him from | the once downtrodden yet hopeful young boy to this new, gangly | teenager showing all the symptoms of adolescence." — *Booklist* | [new paragraph] "By the time we finish *The Order of the Phoenix*, with its extraordi- | nary passages of fear and despair, the distinction between 'children's | literature' and plain old 'literature' has ceased to exist…. This is | one series not just for the decade, but for the ages." | — Stephen King, *Entertainment Weekly* | [new paragraph] [publisher's device of a lantern, 14 by 10mm] | ARTHUR A. LEVINE BOOKS | WWW.ARTHURALEVINEBOOKS.COM | An Imprint of | [publisher's book device with 'SCHOLASTIC' in white on red panel, 5 by 44mm] | WWW.SCHOLASTIC.COM | 557 Broadway, New York, NY 10012'. All in yellow and all on colour illustration of outline of Hogwarts in background.

Publication: 16 July 2005 (simultaneous with A13(a), A13(aa) and A13(aaaa))

Price: $29.99

Contents:
Harry Potter and the Half-Blood Prince
('It was nearing midnight and the Prime Minister was sitting alone in his office…')

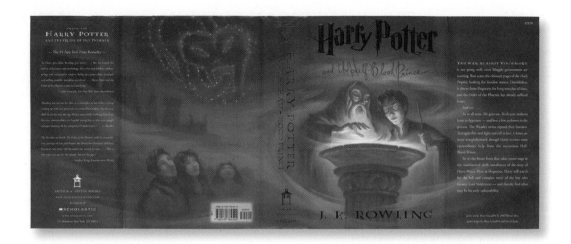

Notes:

Copies have been examined with the following printing plant codes on the imprint page:

Printed in the U.S.A.   23
Printed in the U.S.A.   37
Printed in the U.S.A.   55
Printed in the U.S.A.   58

The print run was announced as 10.8 million copies (see PRNewswire, 11 May 2005).

Information provided by Nielsen BookData suggests that the publishers also issued a 'sewn' edition on the same date as the first American edition (described, in contrast, as 'unsewn / adhesive bound'). The 'sewn' edition has a different ISBN (ISBN 0-439-78677-0) and was probably a more durable version intended for libraries. No copies have been consulted.

Each chapter commences with a drop capital.

The American audiobook version, read by Jim Dale, has a duration of approximately eighteen and a half hours.

Copies: private collection (PWE)

Reprints include:

10 9 8 7 6 5 4 3 2   05 06 07 08 09   Printed in the U.S.A. 58

FIRST AMERICAN EDITION (2005)
(children's artwork series in deluxe hardback)

HARRY POTTER | AND THE HALF-BLOOD PRINCE | [black and white illustration of a battered book, with swirl of bubbling potion and a lit candle in holder, 68 by 57mm] | BY | J. K. ROWLING | ILLUSTRATIONS BY MARY GRANDPRÉ | [publisher's device of a lantern, 11 by 8mm] | ARTHUR A. LEVINE BOOKS | AN IMPRINT OF SCHOLASTIC INC. (All width centred on a diamond pattern background)

Collation: 352 unsigned leaves bound in twenty-two gatherings of sixteen leaves with an additional plate leaf inserted between leaves one and two; 228 by 150mm; [I-II] [additional illustration leaf] [III-VI] VII-X [XI-XII] 1-652 [653-92]

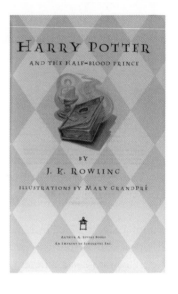

Page contents: [I] 'HARRY POTTER | AND THE HALF-BLOOD PRINCE' (all on diamond pattern background); [II] 'ALSO BY J. K. ROWLING | [new paragraph] *Harry Potter and the Sorcerer's Stone* | Year One at Hogwarts | [new paragraph] *Harry Potter and the Chamber of Secrets* | Year Two at Hogwarts | [new paragraph] *Harry Potter and the Prisoner of Azkaban* | Year Three at Hogwarts | [new paragraph] *Harry Potter and the Goblet of Fire* | Year Four at Hogwarts | [new paragraph] *Harry Potter and the Order of the Phoenix* | Year Five at Hogwarts' (with additional leaf inserted on the verso of which is the frontispiece, 177 by 114mm); [III] title-page; [IV] '[device of twelve stars] | Text copyright © 2005 by J. K. Rowling | Illustrations by Mary GrandPré copyright © 2005 by Warner Bros. | HARRY POTTER, characters, names and related indicia are trademarks of | and © Warner Bros. Harry Potter Publishing Rights © J. K. Rowling. | All rights reserved. Published by Arthur A. Levine Books, | an imprint of Scholastic Inc., *Publishers since 1920.* | SCHOLASTIC, the LANTERN LOGO, and associated logos are | trademarks and/ or registered trademarks of Scholastic Inc. | [new paragraph] No part of this publication may be reproduced, or stored in a retrieval system, or transmitted | in any form or by any means, electronic, mechanical, photocopying, recording, or otherwise, | without written permission of the publisher. For information regarding permission, write | to Scholastic Inc., Attention: Permissions Department, 557 Broadway, New York, NY 10012. | [new paragraph] Library of Congress Control Number: 2005921149 | [new paragraph] ISBN 0-439-79132-4 | [new paragraph] 10 9 8 7 6 5 4 3 2 1   05 06 07 08 09 | Printed in the U.S.A. 23 | This deluxe edition, July 2005'; [V] 'TO MACKENZIE, | MY BEAUTIFUL DAUGHTER, | I DEDICATE | HER INK-AND-PAPER TWIN.'; [VI] blank; VII-X 'CONTENTS' (thirty chapters and illustration showcase listed with titles and page references); [XI] half-title: 'HARRY POTTER | AND THE HALF-BLOOD PRINCE' (all on diamond pattern background); [XII] blank; 1-652 text; [653] 'ILLUSTRATION SHOWCASE' (all on diamond pattern background); [654-84] chapter numbers, illustrations and captions; [685-86] blank; [687] 'ABOUT THE AUTHOR | [new paragraph] J. K. Rowling is the author of six celebrated novels in the | Harry Potter sequence. Her most recent book, *Harry Potter* | *and the Order of the Phoenix*, was named an ALA Notable | Book and recognized with prizes as diverse as an Anthony | Award for Best Young Adult Mystery and a Best Science- | Fiction/Fantasy Novel award from *Disney Adventures* mag- | azine. Ms. Rowling's first four books have been honored | with the Hugo Award, the Bram Stoker Award, the Whit- | bread Children's Book Award, the Nestlé Smarties Book | Prize, the British Book Awards Children's Book of the Year, | and numerous state, magazine, and children's choice cita- | tions. She has also been named an Officer of the Order of | the British Empire. | [new paragraph] Ms. Rowling lives in Scotland with her family.'; [688] blank; [689] 'ABOUT THE ILLUSTRATOR | [new paragraph] Mary GrandPré has illustrated nineteen beautiful books, | including *Henry and Pawl and the Round Yellow Ball*, co- | written with her husband Tom Casmer; *Plum*, a collection | of poetry by Tony Mitton; *The Sea Chest*, by Toni Buzzeo; | *Sweep Dreams*, by Nancy Willard; and the American edi- | tions of all six Harry Potter novels. Her work has also | appeared in *The New Yorker*, *The Atlantic Monthly*, and | *The Wall Street Journal*, and her paintings and pastels have | been shown in galleries across the United States. | [new paragraph] Ms. GrandPré lives in Sarasota, Florida, with her family.'; [690] blank; [691] colophon: '[publisher's device of a lantern, 17 by 12mm] | *This Deluxe* | *Edition was art* | *directed and designed by* | *David Saylor. Mary GrandPré's* | *artwork for the slipcase,* | *the endpapers, the* | *frontispiece, the interior, and the special cover illustration* | *was created using pastels on* | *toned printmaking paper. The text was* | *set in 12-point Adobe Garamond, a typeface based on the sixteenth-* | *century* | *type designs of Claude Garamond, redrawn by Robert Slimbach in 1989. The book* | *was typeset* | *by Brad Walrod and printed on acid-free paper manufactured for Scholastic by* | *Glatfelter Paper in Neenah,* | *Wisconsin. This paper does not include any fiber from ancient* | *forests. The case is wrapped in Sierra cloth,* | *an acid-free rayon-based material* | *manufactured in Europe exclusively for Ecological Fibers. This edition* | *was printed, bound, and packaged by RR Donnelley in* | *Crawfordsville, Indiana. The Managing Editor was* | *Karyn Browne; the Continuity Editor was* | *Cheryl Klein; and the Manufacturing* | *Director was Angela* | *Biola.* | [device of six stars]'; [692] blank

Paper: wove paper

Running title: 'CHAPTER' and chapter number on verso, recto title comprises chapter title, pp. 1-652. Each running title (excluding pages on which new chapters commence) includes a three-star design to left and right of both running-titles on verso and recto. On pages on which a new chapter commences, the three-star design is omitted.

Illustrations: colour frontispiece, title-page vignette, together with thirty vignettes at the beginning of each chapter (after chapter and chapter number but before chapter title). These vignettes are repeated as larger illustrations within the 'Illustration Showcase'. In addition to standard typographical changes (including italics, capitals and small capitals) there are other typographical features, comprising:

p. 39 newspaper headline
p. 40 newspaper headline
p. 42 leaflet title
p. 43 facsimile of Albus Dumbledore's signature

p. 102 O.W.L. results

p. 110 cardboard sign

p. 116 window display lettering

p. 141 facsimile of Professor H.E.F. Slughorn's signature

p. 181 facsimile of Albus Dumbledore's signature

p. 189 textbook scribble

p. 193 textbook ownership inscription

p. 238 textbook scribble

p. 338 gold chain lettering

p. 354 text of sign

p. 377 textbook scribble

p. 470 note from Hagrid

p. 609 note from R.A.B.

Binding: black cloth with diamond pattern in blind on upper and lower covers.

On spine: 'J. K. | ROWLING | [double rule, 48mm] | Harry Potter [hand-drawn lettering] | AND THE | HALF- | BLOOD | PRINCE | [double rule, 48mm] | YEAR SIX | [double rule, 48mm] | [eighteen stars] | [double rule, 48mm] | [publisher's device of a lantern, 19 by 14mm] | ARTHUR A. | LEVINE BOOKS | [double rule, 48mm] | SCHOLASTIC'. All in purple.

Upper and lower covers: blank.

All edges trimmed. Green and white sewn bands at head and foot of spine. Binding measurements: 235 by 150mm (covers), 235 by 68mm (spine). End-papers: wove paper with colour illustration of Harry Potter and Dumbledore gazing into a stone basin surrounded by swirling mists on front endpapers, and colour illustration of children gazing at green glowing Dark Mark in the sky with outline of Hogwarts in background on rear endpapers.

Dust-jacket: uncoated wove paper, 235 by 587mm

A single illustration spans the entire dust-jacket comprising a colour illustration of Harry Potter and Dumbledore watching from within a clump of trees a hatted figure (with a wooden staff) approaching a building half-hidden amongst a tangle of tree trunks.

On lower inside flap: '*Illustration by Mary GrandPré © 2005 Warner Bros.*' All in light green.

Slipcase: card slipcase covered in green paper.

On spine: 'J. K. | ROWLING | [double rule, 48mm] | Harry Potter [hand-drawn lettering] | AND THE | HALF- | BLOOD | PRINCE | [double rule, 48mm] | YEAR SIX | [double rule, 48mm]

| [eighteen stars] | [double rule, 48mm] | [publisher's device of a lantern, 19 by 14mm] | ARTHUR A. | LEVINE BOOKS | [double rule, 48mm] | SCHOLASTIC'. All in gilt.

On upper side: 'Harry Potter [hand-drawn lettering] | AND THE | HALF-BLOOD PRINCE' on colour illustration of a hatted figure with wooden staff approaching a building half-hidden amongst a tangle of tree trunks and all within single rule in gilt, 221 by 137mm. All in gilt.

On lower side: 'Harry Potter [hand-drawn lettering] | AND THE | HALF-BLOOD PRINCE' on colour illustration of Harry Potter and Dumbledore watching from within a clump of trees and all within single rule in gilt, 221 by 137mm. All in gilt.

On top edge: author's signature 'JK Rowling' in gilt.

On lower edge: *Illustration by Mary GrandPré © 2005 Warner Bros.'* All in light green.

The slipcase was shrink-wrapped with two labels attached. The first, 51 by 51mm with rounded corners, with text in black on gilt, 'EXCLUSIVE | [rule] | FULL-COLOR | [rule] | ARTWORK AND | [rule] | ILLUSTRATION | [rule] | SHOWCASE' together with 30 stars. The second, 37 by 56mm with rounded corners, with price, barcode with smaller barcode to the right (56000) all in black on white.

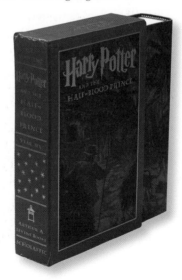

Publication: 16 July 2005 (simultaneous with A13(a), A13(aa) and A13(aaa)

Price: $60

Contents:
Harry Potter and the Half-Blood Prince
   ('It was nearing midnight and the Prime Minister was sitting alone in his office…')

Notes:

The dust-jacket for the first American edition (see A13(aaa)) shows Dumbledore on the left and Harry on the right of the upper panel. The lower panel shows children gazing towards the right at a green glowing Dark Mark in the sky. These single panel illustrations appear to have originated from the full double-page versions reproduced in this edition on the endpapers. Both are reversed so that Harry is on the left and Dumbledore on the right of the front endpapers. The children gaze towards the left of the lower endpapers. These full double-page versions are unique to this deluxe edition. The colour frontispiece is also unique to this edition.

Scholastic released the exclusive artwork for this edition on 11 May 2005. A news announcement noted that the deluxe edition would be published simultaneously with the trade edition. David Saylor from Scholastic stated '… in this spectacular artwork for the deluxe edition, layers of mystery unfold in a forested glen, where we find Harry Potter and Dumbledore peering through dense branches… once again, Mary GrandPré's mysterious artwork beautifully features an eerie scene that tantalizes the reader with hints from the soon-to-be-released, *Harry Potter and the Half-Blood Prince*'. The print run was announced as 100,000 copies (see PRNewswire, 11 May 2005).

Each chapter commences with a drop capital.

Copies: private collection (PWE)

A13(b)   ENGLISH DELUXE EDITION   (2005)
(children's artwork series in deluxe hardback)

HARRY | POTTER | *and the Half-Blood Prince* | [illustration of Hogwarts crest with legend 'DRACO DORMIENS NUNQUAM TITILLANDUS' on banner, 70 by 85mm] | J. K. ROWLING | [publisher's device of a dog, 12 by 19mm] | BLOOMSBURY (All width centred)

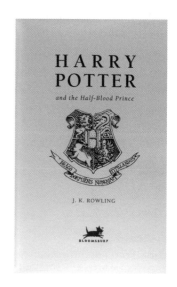

Collation: 304 unsigned leaves bound in thirty-eight gatherings of eight leaves; 233 by 150mm, [1-7] 8-24 [25] 26-41 [42] 43-58 [59] 60-80 [81] 82-102 [103] 104-123 [124] 125-47 [148] 149-62 [163] 164-83 [184] 185-204 [205] 206-222 [223] 224-41 [242] 243-60 [261] 262-83 [284] 285-304 [305] 306-326 [327] 328-49 [350] 351-73 [374] 375-395 [396] 397-418 [419] 420-38 [439] 440-59 [460] 461-79 [480] 481-499 [500] 501-518 [519] 520-40 [541] 542-56 [557] 558-69 [570] 571-89 [590] 591-607 [608]

Page contents: [1] half-title: 'HARRY | POTTER | *and the Half-Blood Prince* | [illustration of Hogwarts crest with legend

'DRACO DORMIENS NUNQUAM TITILLANDUS' on banner, 50 by 61mm]'; [2] *'Titles available in the Harry Potter series* | *(in reading order):* | Harry Potter and the Philosopher's Stone | Harry Potter and the Chamber of Secrets | Harry Potter and the Prisoner of Azkaban | Harry Potter and the Goblet of Fire | Harry Potter and the Order of the Phoenix | Harry Potter and the Half-Blood Prince | [new paragraph] *Harry Potter and the Philosopher's Stone* | *also available in Latin, Ancient Greek, Welsh and Irish:* | Harrius Potter et Philosophi Lapis (Latin) | Ἄρειος Ποτήρ καί ἡ τοῦ ψιλοσόψον λίθος (Ancient Greek) | Harri Potter a Maen yr Athronydd (Welsh) | Harry Potter agus an Órchloch (Irish)'; [3] title-page; [4] 'All rights reserved; no part of this publication may be reproduced or | transmitted by any means, electronic, mechanical, photocopying | or otherwise, without the prior permission of the publisher | [new paragraph] First published in Great Britain in 2005 | Bloomsbury Publishing Plc, 36 Soho Square, London, W1D 3QY | [new paragraph] Copyright © 2005 J. K. Rowling | Cover illustrations by Jason Cockcroft copyright © 2005 Bloomsbury Publishing Plc | Harry Potter, names, characters and related indicia are | copyright and trademark Warner Bros., 2000™ | [new paragraph] J. K. Rowling has asserted her moral rights | A CIP catalogue record of this book is available from the British Library | [new paragraph] ISBN 0 7475 8142 8 | [new paragraph] The paper this book is printed on is certified by the © Forest Stewardship Council | 1996 A.C. (FSC). It is ancient-forest friendly. The printer holds FSC chain of | custody SGS-COC-2061. | [Forest Stewardship Council logo, 7 by 9mm together with © symbol and text: 'FSC | Mixed Sources | Product group from well-managed | forests and other controlled sources | [new paragraph] Cert no. SGS-COC-2061 | www fsc org | © 1996 Forest Stewardship Council'] | [new paragraph] Typeset by RefineCatch Limited, Bungay, Suffolk | Printed in Great Britain by Clays Ltd, St Ives plc | [new paragraph] | First Edition | [new paragraph] | www.bloomsbury.com/harrypotter'; [5] *'To Mackenzie,* | *my beautiful daughter,* | *I dedicate* | *her ink and paper twin'*; [6] blank; [7]-607 text; [608] blank

Paper: wove paper

Running title: 'HARRY POTTER' (25mm) on verso, recto title comprises chapter title, pp. 8-607

Binding: dark blue cloth.

On spine: 'HARRY POTTER *and the Half-Blood Prince* J.K.ROWLING' (reading lengthways down spine) with '[publisher's device of a dog, 12 by 21mm] | BLOOMSBURY' (horizontally at foot of spine). All in gilt.

On upper cover: 'HARRY | POTTER | *and the Half-Blood Prince* | [double ruled border, 104 by 104mm with the outer border thicker than the inner and colour illustration by Jason Cockcroft laid down] | [facsimile of author's signature]' (all width centred). All in gilt.

Lower cover: blank.

All edges gilt. Green sewn bands at head and foot of spine together with green marker ribbon. Binding measurements: 241 by 151mm (covers), 241 by 61mm (spine). End-papers: dark blue wove paper.

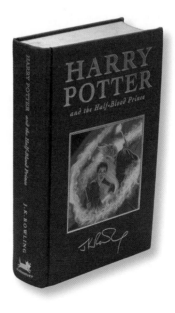

Dust-jacket: none

Publication: 3 October 2005 in an edition of 26,310 copies (confirmed by Bloomsbury)

Price: £30

Contents:
Harry Potter and the Half-Blood Prince
  ('It was nearing midnight and the Prime Minister was sitting alone in his office…')

Copies: Sotheby's, 17 December 2009, lot 169; private collection (PWE)

A13(c)   ENGLISH CHILDREN'S EDITION   (2006)
(children's artwork series in paperback)

HARRY | POTTER | *and the Half-Blood Prince* | [illustration of Hogwarts crest with legend 'DRAGO DORMIENS NUNQUAM TITILLANDUS' on banner, 66 by 81mm] | J. K. ROWLING | [publisher's device of a dog, 11 by 18mm] | BLOOMSBURY (Lines 1 and 2 justified on left and right margins, and all width centred)

Collation: 304 unsigned leaves bound in indeterminate gatherings; 197 by 128mm; [1-7] 8-24 [25] 26-41 [42] 43-58 [59] 60-80 [81] 82-102 [103] 104-123 [124] 125-47 [148] 149-62 [163] 164-83 [184] 185-204 [205] 206-222 [223] 224-41 [242] 243-60 [261] 262-83 [284] 285-304 [305] 306-326 [327] 328-49 [350] 351-73 [374] 375-395 [396] 397-418 [419] 420-38 [439] 440-59 [460] 461-79 [480] 481-499 [500] 501-518 [519] 520-40 [541] 542-56 [557] 558-69 [570] 571-89 [590] 591-607 [608]

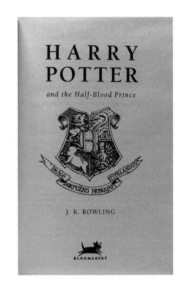

Page contents: [1] half-title: 'HARRY | POTTER | *and the Half-Blood Prince* | [illustration of Hogwarts crest with legend 'DRAGO DORMIENS NUNQUAM TITILLANDUS' on banner, 46 by 57mm]'; [2] *'Titles available in the Harry Potter series | (in reading order):* | Harry Potter and the Philosopher's Stone | Harry Potter and the Chamber of Secrets | Harry Potter and the Prisoner of Azkaban | Harry Potter and the Goblet of Fire | Harry Potter and the Order of the Phoenix | Harry Potter and the Half-Blood Prince | [new paragraph] *Harry Potter and the Philosopher's Stone* | *also available in Latin, Ancient Greek, Welsh and Irish:* | Harrius Potter et Philosophi Lapis (Latin) | Ἄρειος Ποτήρ καί ἡ τοῦ ψιλοσόψου λίθος (Ancient Greek) | Harri Potter a Maen yr Anthronydd (Welsh) | Harry Potter agus an Órchloch (Irish)'; [3] title-page;

[4] 'All rights reserved; no part of this publication may be reproduced or | transmitted by any means, electronic, mechanical, photocopying | or otherwise, without the prior permission of the publisher | [new paragraph] First published in Great Britain in 2005 | Bloomsbury Publishing Plc, 36 Soho Square, London, W1D 3QY | [new paragraph] This paperback edition first published in 2006 | [new paragraph] Copyright © 2005 J. K. Rowling | Cover illustrations by Jason Cockcroft copyright © 2005 Bloomsbury Publishing Plc | [new paragraph] Harry Potter, names, characters and related indicia are | copyright and trademark Warner Bros., 2000™ | [new paragraph] J. K. Rowling has asserted her moral rights | A CIP catalogue record of this book is available from the British Library | [new paragraph] ISBN 0 7475 8468 0 | 978 0 7475 8468 1 | [new paragraph] All papers used by Bloomsbury Publishing are made from wood grown in | well-managed forests. The paper used in this book contains 50% post | consumer waste recycled material which was de-inked using chlorine-free | methods. The manufacturing processes conform to the | environmental regulations of the country of origin. | [new paragraph] Typeset by RefineCatch Limited, Bungay, Suffolk | Printed in Great Britain by Clays Ltd, St Ives plc | [new paragraph] First Edition | [new paragraph] www.bloomsbury.com/harrypotter'; [5] 'To Mackenzie, | my beautiful daughter, | I dedicate | her ink and paper twin'; [6] blank; [7]-607 text; [608] blank

Paper: wove paper

Running title: 'HARRY POTTER' (24mm) on verso, recto title comprises chapter title, pp. 10-607 (excluding pages on which new chapters commence)

Binding: pictorial wrappers.

    On spine: '[colour illustration of a ring on burgundy panel, 34 by 16mm] HARRY POTTER [in green on blue panel, 34 by 45mm] *and the Half-Blood Prince* [in white] J.K.ROWLING [in blue, both title conclusion and author on green panel, 34 by 103mm] BLOOMSBURY [publisher's device of the head of a dog, 4 by 3mm] [both in white on blue panel, 34 by 32mm]' (reading lengthways down spine).

    On upper wrapper: 'HARRY | POTTER | *and the Half-Blood Prince* [lines 1 and 2 in green, line 3 in white, all on blue panel, 61 by 128mm] | [green rule, 128mm] | [colour illustration of Dumbledore and Harry Potter clutching wands and engulfed by swirls of fire, phoenix rising from flames, 123 by 128mm] | [green rule, 128mm intersected by green panel with 'J.K.ROWLING' in blue] | BLOOMSBURY [in white on blue panel, 10 by 128mm]' (all width centred).

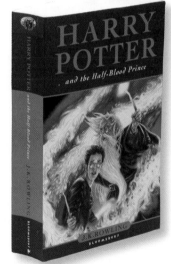

    On lower wrapper: 'It is Harry Potter's sixth year at Hogwarts School of Witchcraft | and Wizardry. As Voldemort's sinister forces amass and a spirit of | gloom and fear sweeps the land, it becomes more and more clear | to Harry that he will soon have to confront his destiny. But is he | up to the challenges ahead of him? | [new paragraph] In her darkest and most breathtaking adventure yet, J.K. Rowling | skilfully begins to unravel the complex web she has woven, as we | discover more of the truth about Harry, Dumbledore, Snape and, | of course, He Who Must Not Be Named … | [new paragraph] 'Fast, dark, exciting and tightly plotted.' *Daily Mail* | [new paragraph] 'A gripping story with its clues trailed through the text, chills, spills and | some excellent, new comic characters. There is a measure of sadness too … | one of the elements of Rowling's writing that I think entitles her to a | seat in the pantheon.' Julian Fellowes, *Sunday Telegraph* | [new paragraph] 'Everything in the series starts to come to fruition … | This ingenious setting up is intriguing for aficionados | who have been hungry to discover what | happens next.' Nicolette Jones, | *Sunday Times* | [new paragraph] 'Taut, witty, effortlessly engaging, | and very, very nasty. How we | yearn for more.' *TLS* | [new paragraph] [barcode in black on white panel, 21 by 40mm together with '[publisher's device of a dog, 5 by 9mm] | BLOOMSBURY | £7.99' in black on right side of panel and 'http://www.bloomsbury.com/harrypotter' below panel, in white on green panel, 5 by 40mm]'. Reading lengthways down right side next to foot of spine, in black: 'Cover illustrations by Jason Cockcroft | Author photograph © Bill de la HEY'. All in white with the exception of the illustration and photography credit which are in black, and all on an illustration of a stone basin on top of a pedestal, emitting a phosphorescent glow, situated in the middle of a small island of smooth rock by a great black lake with a tiny boat to the left.

   On inside upper wrapper: black and white photograph of J.K. Rowling standing against bookshelves.

   On inside lower wrapper: 'Other titles available | in the HARRY POTTER series | [colour illustrations in three columns of six book designs] | Audio editions read by Stephen Fry | and co-published by HNP | also available'. All in black on white.

   All edges trimmed. Binding measurements: 197 by 128mm (wrappers), 197 by 34mm (spine).

Publication: 23 June 2006 (simultaneous with A13(cc)) in an edition of 501,700 copies (confirmed by Bloomsbury)

Price: £7.99

Contents:
Harry Potter and the Half-Blood Prince
   ('It was nearing midnight and the Prime Minister was sitting alone in his office…')

Notes:
Bloomsbury released a 'dumpbin' display case for this edition. The case was available filled with 48 copies. A poster advertising this edition was also released.

The artwork on the lower wrapper has (in contrast to A13(a)) been moved very slightly to the right edge and also positioned lower. This shows less of the smooth rock island but more of the black lake.

Copies: private collection (PWE)

ENGLISH ADULT EDITION
(Michael Wildsmith photography adult artwork series in paperback)

HARRY | POTTER | *and the Half-Blood Prince* | [illustration of Hogwarts crest with legend 'DRAGO DORMIENS NUNQUAM TITILLANDUS' on banner, 66 by 81mm] | J. K. ROWLING | [publisher's device of a dog, 11 by 18mm] | BLOOMSBURY (Lines 1 and 2 justified on left and right margins, and all width centred)

Collation: 384 unsigned leaves bound in indeterminate gatherings; 177 by 110mm; [1-7] 8-28 [29] 30-50 [51] 52-72 [73] 74-100 [101] 102-127 [128] 129-54 [155] 156-84 [185] 186-203 [204] 205-230 [231] 232-57 [258] 259-80 [281] 282-305 [306] 307-329 [330] 331-58 [359] 360-85 [386] 387-413 [414] 415-42 [443] 444-72 [473] 474-500 [501] 502-529 [530] 531-54 [555] 556-80 [581] 582-605 [606] 607-631 [632] 633-55 [656] 657-83 [684] 685-703 [704] 705-719 [720] 721-44 [745] 746-68

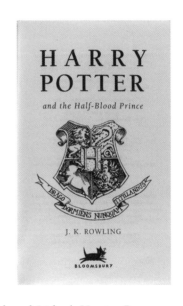

Page contents: [1] half-title: 'HARRY | POTTER | *and the Half-Blood Prince* | [illustration of Hogwarts crest with legend 'DRAGO DORMIENS NUNQUAM TITILLANDUS' on banner, 47 by 58mm]'; [2] *'Titles available in the Harry Potter series | (in reading order):* | Harry Potter and the Philosopher's Stone | Harry Potter and the Chamber of Secrets | Harry Potter and the Prisoner of Azkaban | Harry Potter and the Goblet of Fire | Harry Potter and the Order of the Phoenix | Harry Potter and the Half-Blood Prince | [new paragraph] *Harry Potter and the Philosopher's Stone | also available in Latin, Ancient Greek, | Welsh and Irish:* | Harrius Potter et Philosophi Lapis (Latin) | Ἄρειος Ποτὴρ καί ἡ τοῦ ψιλοσόψον λίθος | (Ancient Greek) | Harri Potter a Maen yr Anthronydd (Welsh) | Harry Potter agus an Órchloch (Irish)'; [3] title-page; [4] 'All rights reserved; no part of this publication may be reproduced or | transmitted by any means, electronic, mechanical, photocopying | or otherwise, without the prior permission of the publisher | [new paragraph] First published in Great Britain in 2005 | Bloomsbury Publishing Plc, 36 Soho Square, London, W1D 3QY | [new paragraph] This paperback edition first published in 2006 | [new paragraph] Copyright © 2005 J. K. Rowling | Cover illustrations by Jason Cockcroft copyright © 2005 | Bloomsbury Publishing Plc | [new paragraph] Harry Potter, names, characters and related indicia are | copyright and trademark Warner Bros., 2000™ | [new paragraph] J. K. Rowling has asserted her moral rights | A CIP catalogue record of this book is available from the British Library | [new paragraph] ISBN 0 7475 8467 2 | 978 0 7475 8467 4 | [new paragraph] All papers used by Bloomsbury Publishing are made from wood grown in | well-managed forests. The paper used in this book contains 50% post | consumer waste recycled material which was de-inked using chlorine-free | methods. The manufacturing processes conform to the | environmental regulations of the country of origin. | [new paragraph] Typeset by RefineCatch Limited, Bungay, Suffolk | Printed in Great Britain by Clays Ltd, St Ives plc | [new paragraph] First Edition | [new paragraph] www.bloomsbury. com/harrypotter'; [5] '*To Mackenzie,* | *my beautiful daughter,* | *I dedicate* | *her ink and paper twin*'; [6] blank; [7]-768 text

Paper: wove paper

Running title: 'HARRY POTTER' (25mm) on verso, recto title comprises chapter title, pp. 8-768 (excluding pages on which new chapters commence)

Binding: pictorial wrappers.

On spine: 'HARRY POTTER AND THE [top portion of colour photograph of a battered-looking copy of *Advanced Potion-Making* by Libatius Borage lying on desk, 45 by 18mm] | J.K. ROWLING [publisher's device of a figure with a bow, 11 by 11mm] | HALF-BLOOD PRINCE' (reading lengthways down spine). All in white with the exception of last line which is in gilt and all on black.

On upper wrapper: 'HARRY POTTER AND THE [in white] | HALF-BLOOD [embossed in gilt] | PRINCE [embossed in gilt] | J. K. ROWLING [in white] | BLOOMSBURY [in white]' (all width centred). All on colour photograph of a battered-looking copy of *Advanced Potion-Making* by Libatius Borage lying on desk.

On lower wrapper: '[colour photograph of a battered-looking copy of *Advanced Potion-Making* by Libatius Borage lying on desk, all within single white border, 21 by 21mm] 'Everything in the series starts to come | to fruition ... This ingenious setting up is | intriguing for aficionados who have been | hungry to discover what happens next' | Nicolette Jones, *Sunday Times* | [new paragraph] It is Harry Potter's sixth year at Hogwarts School of | Witchcraft and Wizardry. As Voldemort's sinister forces | amass and a spirit of gloom and fear sweeps the land, it | becomes more and more clear to Harry that he will soon | have to confront his destiny. But is he up to the challenges | ahead of him? | [new paragraph] In her darkest and most breathtaking adventure yet, | J.K. Rowling skilfully begins to unravel the complex web | she has woven, as we discover more of the truth about | Harry, Dumbledore, Snape and, of course, He Who Must | Not Be Named ... | [new paragraph] 'Fast, dark, exciting and tightly plotted' *Daily Mail* | [new paragraph] 'A gripping story with its clues trailed through the text, chills, | spills and some excellent, new comic characters. There is a | measure of sadness too ... one of the elements of Rowling's | writing that I think entitles her to a seat in the pantheon' | Julian Fellowes, *Sunday Telegraph* | [new paragraph] 'Taut, witty, effortlessly engaging, and very, very nasty. | How we yearn for more' *TLS* | [new paragraph] [barcode in white on black panel, 24 by 39mm together with 'bloomsbury[in black]pbk[in white]s[in black] | £7.99 [in black] | www.bloomsbury.com [in black]' and all on red panel, 25 by 75mm] | Cover image: Michael Wildsmith Design: William Webb Author photograph: © Bill de la HEY'. All in white on black with colour photograph to the left of lines 1-5.

On inside upper wrapper: black and white photograph of J.K. Rowling standing against bookshelves.

On inside lower wrapper: 'Other titles available | in the HARRY POTTER series | [colour illustrations in three columns of six book designs] | Audio editions read by Stephen Fry | and co-published by HNP | also available'. All in white on black.

All edges trimmed. Binding measurements: 177 by 110mm (wrappers), 177 by 45mm (spine).

Publication: 23 June 2006 (simultaneous with A13(c)) in an edition of 200,000 copies (confirmed by Bloomsbury)

Price: £7.99

Contents:
Harry Potter and the Half-Blood Prince
('It was nearing midnight and the Prime Minister was sitting alone in his office…')

Notes:
Note that the publisher's imprint page refers to the 'cover illustrations by Jason Cockcroft'. These illustrations do not feature on this 'adult' edition of the book. However, the Hogwarts crest is present on the half-title and title-page. For all other titles in the series, the crest was omitted from the adult editions. Reprints (as seen in a copy of the fourteenth reprint) would dispense with the Hogwarts crest on the title-page and credit the cover image to Michael Wildsmith.

Copies: private collection (SJH); Bloomsbury Archives

Reprints include:
14

A13(d)   AMERICAN CHILDREN'S EDITION   (2006)
(children's artwork series in paperback)

HARRY POTTER | AND THE HALF-BLOOD PRINCE | [black and white illustration of a battered book, with swirl of bubbling potion and a lit candle in holder, 61 by 50mm] | BY | J. K. ROWLING | ILLUSTRATIONS BY MARY GRANDPRÉ | SCHOLASTIC INC. | NEW YORK [four-sided device] TORONTO [four-sided device] LONDON [four-sided device] AUCKLAND [four-sided device] SYDNEY | MEXICO CITY [four-sided device] NEW DELHI [four-sided device] HONG KONG [four-sided device] BUENOS AIRES (All width centred on a diamond pattern background)

Collation: 336 unsigned leaves bound in indeterminate gatherings; 192 by 133mm; [I-VI] VII-X [XI-XII] 1-652 [653-60]

Page contents: [I-II] 'PRAISE FOR J. K. ROWLING'S | HARRY POTTER | AND THE HALF-BLOOD PRINCE | [device of nine stars] | [5 reviews and a listing of 4 statements] | [device of nine stars] | ALSO BY J. K. ROWLING | *Harry Potter and the Sorcerer's Stone* | Year One at Hogwarts | *Harry Potter and the Chamber of Secrets* | Year Two at Hogwarts | *Harry Potter and the Prisoner of Azkaban* | Year Three at Hogwarts | *Harry Potter and the Goblet of Fire* | Year Four at Hogwarts | *Harry Potter and the Order of the Phoenix* | Year Five at Hogwarts'; [III] title-page; [IV] '[device of twelve stars] | Text copyright © 2005 by J. K. Rowling. | Illustrations by Mary GrandPré copyright © 2005 by Warner Bros. | HARRY POTTER, characters, names and related indicia are trademarks of | and © Warner Bros. Harry Potter Publishing Rights © J. K. Rowling. | All rights reserved. Published by Scholastic Inc. | SCHOLASTIC, the LANTERN LOGO, and associated logos | are trademarks and/or registered trademarks of Scholastic Inc. | [new paragraph] If you purchased this book without a cover, you should be aware that this book

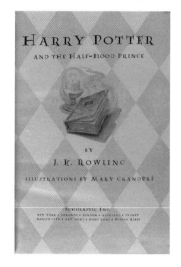

is stolen property. | It was reported as "unsold and destroyed" to the publisher, and neither the author nor | the publisher has received any payment for this "stripped book." | [new paragraph] No part of this publication may be reproduced, | stored in a retrieval system, or transmitted in any form or by any means, | electronic, mechanical, photocopying, recording, or otherwise, | without written permission of the publisher. | For information regarding permission, write to Scholastic Inc., | Attention: Permissions Department, 557 Broadway, New York, NY 10012. | [new paragraph] [publisher's device of a lantern, 6 by 4mm] | Arthur A. Levine Books hardcover edition | art directed by David Saylor, | published by Arthur A. Levine Books, | an imprint of Scholastic Inc. | July 2005. | [new paragraph] ISBN 0-439-78596-0 | [new paragraph] Library of Congress Control Number: 2005921149 | [new paragraph] 12 11 10 9 8 7 6 5 4 3 2 1   6 7 8 9 10 11/0 | [new paragraph] | Printed in the U.S.A. 40 | [new paragraph] First Scholastic trade paperback printing, September 2006 | [new paragraph] This book is printed on paper containing a minimum of 20% post-consumer recycled fiber.'; [V] 'TO MACKENZIE, | MY BEAUTIFUL DAUGHTER, | I DEDICATE | HER INK-AND-PAPER TWIN.'; [VI] blank; VII-X 'CONTENTS' (thirty chapters listed with titles and page references); [XI] half-title: 'HARRY POTTER | AND THE HALF-BLOOD PRINCE' (all on diamond pattern background); [XII] blank; 1-652 text; [653-54] blank; [655] 'ABOUT THE AUTHOR | [new paragraph] J. K. Rowling is the author of six celebrated novels in the | Harry Potter sequence. Her most recent book, *Harry Potter | and the Order of the Phoenix*, was named an ALA Notable | Book and recognized with prizes as diverse as an Anthony | Award for Best Young Adult Mystery and a Best Science- | Fiction/Fantasy Novel award from *Disney Adventures* mag- | azine. Ms. Rowling's first four books have been honored | with the Hugo Award, the Bram Stoker Award, the Whit- | bread Children's Book Award, the Nestlé Smarties Book | Prize, the British Book Awards Children's Book of the Year, | and numerous state, magazine, and children's choice cita- | tions. She has also been named an Officer of the Order of | the British Empire. | [new paragraph] Ms. Rowling lives in Scotland with her family.'; [656] blank; [657] 'ABOUT THE ILLUSTRATOR | [new paragraph] Mary GrandPré has illustrated nineteen beautiful books, | including *Henry and Pawl and the Round Yellow Ball*, co- | written with her husband Tom Casmer; *Plum*, a collection |

of poetry by Tony Mitton; *The Sea Chest*, by Toni Buzzeo; | *Sweep Dreams*, by Nancy Willard; and the American edi- | tions of all six Harry Potter novels. Her work has also | appeared in *The New Yorker*, *The Atlantic Monthly*, and | *The Wall Street Journal*, and her paintings and pastels have | been shown in galleries across the United States. | [new paragraph] Ms. GrandPré lives in Sarasota, Florida, with her family.'; [658] blank; [659] publisher's advertisement: 'Harry Potter [hand-drawn lettering] | READ ALL OF HARRY'S ADVENTURES!'; [660] blank

Paper: wove paper

Running title: 'CHAPTER' and chapter number on verso, recto title comprises chapter title, pp. 1-652. Each running title (excluding pages on which new chapters commence) includes a three-star design to left and right of both running-titles on verso and recto. On pages on which a new chapter commences, the three-star design is omitted.

Illustrations: title-page vignette, together with thirty vignettes at the beginning of each chapter (after chapter and chapter number but before chapter title). In addition to standard typographical changes (including italics, capitals and small capitals) there are other typographical features, comprising:

    p. 39 newspaper headline
    p. 40 newspaper headline
    p. 42 leaflet title
    p. 43 facsimile of Albus Dumbledore's signature
    p. 102 O.W.L. results
    p. 110 cardboard sign
    p. 116 window display lettering
    p. 141 facsimile of Professor H.E.F. Slughorn's signature
    p. 181 facsimile of Albus Dumbledore's signature
    p. 189 textbook scribble
    p. 193 textbook ownership inscription
    p. 238 textbook scribble
    p. 338 gold chain lettering
    p. 354 text of sign
    p. 377 textbook scribble
    p. 470 note from Hagrid
    p. 609 note from R.A.B.

Binding: pictorial wrappers.

On spine: 'ROWLING | [rule] | ['YEAR | 6' logo within concave square]' (horizontally at head) with 'HARRY POTTER | SCHOLASTIC | AND THE HALF-BLOOD PRINCE' (reading lengthways down spine). All in gilt on light and dark green diamond pattern background.

On upper wrapper: 'THE ENTHRALLING NATIONAL BESTSELLER [in gilt] | Harry Potter [hand-drawn lettering] [embossed in gilt] | and the Half-Blood Prince [hand-drawn lettering

in brown of illustration] | J. K. ROWLING [embossed in gilt]' (all width centred). All on colour illustration of Harry Potter and Dumbledore gazing into a stone basin surrounded by swirling mists. In centre at foot: '[publisher's book device] SCHOLASTIC' in white on red panel, 5 by 45mm.

On lower wrapper: 'The war against Voldemort is not going well; even Muggle | governments are noticing. Ron scans the obituary pages of | the *Daily Prophet*, looking for familiar names. Dumbledore is absent from | Hogwarts for long stretches of time, and the Order of the Phoenix has | already suffered losses. | [new paragraph] And yet … | [new paragraph] As in all wars, life goes on. The Weasley twins expand their busi- | ness. Sixth-year students learn to Apparate — and lose a few eyebrows | in the process. Teenagers flirt and fight and fall in love. Classes are never | straightforward, though Harry receives some extraordinary help from the | mysterious Half-Blood Prince. | [new paragraph] So it's the home front that takes center stage in the multilayered | sixth installment of the story of Harry Potter. Here at Hogwarts, Harry | will search for the full and complex story of the boy who became Lord | Voldemort — and thereby find what may be his only vulnerability. | [new paragraph] [four-sided device in light green] The #1 *New York Times* Bestseller [four-sided device in light green] | [new paragraph] The 2005 Quill Book of the Year | A *New York Times* Notable Book | An ALA Best Book for Young Adults | [publisher's book device with 'SCHOLASTIC' in white on red panel, 5 by 45mm] | www.scholastic.com/harrypotter | COVER ART BY MARY GRANDPRÉ'. All in white on colour illustration of children gazing at green glowing Dark Mark in the sky with outline of Hogwarts in background, with barcode with smaller barcode (50999) together with 'S' within triangle and '$9.99 US', all in black on white panel, 28 by 61mm, to the left of final three lines. The initial capital 'T' of 'The' is a drop capital.

On inside upper wrapper: barcode with smaller barcode (50999) together with 'S' within triangle below, all in black.

All edges trimmed. Binding measurements: 192 by 133mm (wrappers), 192 by 36mm (spine).

Publication: September 2006

Price: $9.99

Contents:
Harry Potter and the Half-Blood Prince
('It was nearing midnight and the Prime Minister was sitting alone in his office…')

Notes:
In contrast with the first American edition (see A13(aaa)), the listing of Rowling's works is not presented with paragraph breaks between titles.

Each chapter commences with a drop capital.

Copies: private collection (PWE)

Reprints include:
20 19   11 12 13/0   Printed in the U.S.A. 40
20   11 12 13/0   Printed in the U.S.A. 40

A13(e)   AMERICAN BOOK CLUB EDITION   [2006]
(children's artwork series in hardback)

Publication: between July and December 2006 (see notes)

Notes:
Given that the true American first and the book club editions share a single ISBN, the Blair Partnership noted that book club editions could only be dated to within a half-year period end in their files. This edition was, therefore, published within the period July to December 2006. The Blair Partnership Royalties Manager noted that the American book club editions did not have 'a set price'.

Copies: no copies have been consulted

A13(f)   ENGLISH 'CELEBRATORY' EDITION   (2009)
(children's artwork series in paperback)

HARRY | POTTER | *and the Half-Blood Prince* | [illustration of Hogwarts crest with legend 'DRAGO DORMIENS NUNQUAM TITILLANDUS' on banner, 66 by 81mm] | J.K.ROWLING | [publisher's device of a dog, 9 by 15mm] | BLOOMSBURY | LONDON BERLIN NEW YORK (Lines 1 and 2 justified on left and right margins, and all width centred)

Collation: 304 unsigned leaves bound in indeterminate gatherings; 197 by 128mm; [1-7] 8-24 [25] 26-41 [42] 43-58 [59] 60-80 [81] 82-102 [103] 104-123 [124] 125-47 [148] 149-62 [163] 164-83 [184] 185-204 [205] 206-222 [223] 224-41 [242] 243-60 [261] 262-83 [284] 285-304 [305] 306-326 [327] 328-49 [350] 351-73 [374] 375-95 [396] 397-418 [419] 420-38 [439] 440-59 [460] 461-79 [480] 481-99 [500] 501-518 [519] 520-40 [541] 542-56 [557] 558-69 [570] 571-89 [590] 591-607 [608]

Page contents: [1] half-title: 'HARRY | POTTER | *and the Half-Blood Prince* | [illustration of Hogwarts crest with legend 'DRAGO DORMIENS NUNQUAM TITILLANDUS' on banner, 47 by 58mm]'; [2] '*Titles available in the Harry Potter series* | *(in reading order):* | Harry Potter and the Philosopher's Stone | Harry Potter and the Chamber of Secrets | Harry Potter and the Prisoner of Azkaban | Harry Potter and the Goblet of Fire | Harry Potter and the Order of the Phoenix | Harry Potter and the Half-Blood Prince | Harry Potter and the Deathly Hallows | [new paragraph] *Titles available in the Harry Potter series* | *(in Latin):* | Harry Potter and the Philosopher's Stone | Harry Potter and the Chamber of Secrets | *(in Welsh, Ancient Greek and Irish):* | Harry Potter and the Philosopher's Stone'; [3] title-page; [4] 'All rights reserved; no part of this publication may be reproduced or | transmitted by any means, electronic, mechanical, photocopying | or otherwise, without the prior permission of the publisher | [new paragraph] First published in Great Britain in 2005 | Bloomsbury Publishing Plc, 36 Soho Square, London, W1D 3QY | [new paragraph] This edition first published in 2009 | [new paragraph] Copyright © J.K.Rowling 2005 | Cover illustrations by Jason Cockcroft copyright © Bloomsbury Publishing Plc 2005 | [new paragraph] Harry Potter, names, characters and related indicia are | copyright and trademark Warner Bros., 2000™ | [new paragraph] J.K.Rowling has asserted her moral rights | A CIP catalogue record of this book is available from the British Library | [new paragraph] ISBN 978 0 7475 9846 6 | [new paragraph] [FSC symbol, 7 by 8mm together with © symbol and text: 'FSC | Mixed Sources | Product group from well-managed | forests and other controlled sources | [new paragraph] Cert no. SGS-COC-2061 | www fsc org | © 1996 Forest Stewardship Council'] | [new paragraph] Typeset by RefineCatch Limited, Bungay, Suffolk | Printed in Great Britain by Clays Ltd, St Ives plc | [new paragraph] 1 3 5 7 9 10 8 6 4 2 | [new paragraph] www.bloomsbury.com/harrypotter'; [5] 'To Mackenzie, | *my beautiful daughter,* | *I dedicate* | *her ink and paper twin*'; [6] blank; [7]-607 text; [608] blank

Paper: wove paper

Running title: 'HARRY POTTER' (24mm) on verso, recto title comprises chapter title, pp. 8-607

Binding: pictorial wrappers.

On spine: '[colour illustration of a ring on burgundy panel, 36 by 17mm] HARRY POTTER [in green on gilt panel, 36 by 46mm] *and the Half-Blood Prince* [in white] J.K.ROWLING [in gilt, both title conclusion and author on green panel, 36 by 102mm] BLOOMSBURY [publisher's device of the head of a dog, 3 by 4mm] [both in white on dark blue panel, 36 by 31mm]' (reading lengthways down spine).

On upper wrapper: 'HARRY | POTTER | *and the Half-Blood Prince* [lines 1 and 2 in gilt, line 3 in white, all on dark blue panel, 62 by 128mm] | [gilt rule, 128mm] | ['J.K. ROWLING' [in gilt] with colour illustration of Dumbledore and Harry Potter clutching wands and engulfed by swirls of fire, within single gilt ruled border, 91 by 86mm, all on green panel with orange, yellow and gilt stars, 123 by 128mm] | [blue rule, 128mm] | BLOOMSBURY [in dark blue on gilt panel, 10 by 128mm]' (all width centred).

On lower wrapper: 'It is Harry Potter's sixth year at Hogwarts School of Witchcraft | and Wizardry. As Voldemort's sinister forces amass and a spirit of | gloom and fear sweeps the land, it becomes more and more clear | to Harry that he will soon have to confront his destiny. But is he | up to the challenges ahead of him? | [new paragraph] In this dark and breathtaking adventure, J.K. Rowling skilfully | begins to unravel the complex web she has woven, as we discover | more of the truth about Harry, Dumbledore, Snape and, of course, | He Who Must Not Be Named ... | [new paragraph] 'Fast, dark, exciting and tightly plotted.' *Daily Mail* | [new paragraph] 'A gripping story with its clues trailed through the text, chills, spills and | some excellent, new comic characters. There is a measure of sadness too ... | one of the elements of Rowling's writing that I think entitles her to | a seat in the pantheon.' Julian Fellowes, *Sunday Telegraph* | [new paragraph] 'Everything in the series starts to come to fruition ... | This ingenious setting up is intriguing for aficionados | who have been hungry to discover what | happens next.' Nicolette Jones, | *Sunday Times* | [new paragraph] 'Taut, witty, effortlessly engaging, | and very, very nasty. How we | yearn for more.' *TLS* | [new paragraph] [publisher's device of a dog, 6 by 10mm] | BLOOMSBURY | [new paragraph] [barcode in black on white panel, 21 by 38mm] [FSC symbol, 7 by 8mm together with © symbol and text: 'FSC | Mixed Sources | Product group from well-managed | forests and other controlled sources | [new paragraph]

Cert no. SGS-COC-2061 | www.fsc.org | © 1996 Forest Stewardship Council'] [these eight lines to the right of the barcode panel] | ['www.bloomsbury.com/harrypotter' below barcode panel, in white on green panel, 6 by 38mm]'. Reading lengthways down right side towards foot of spine 'Cover illustration by Jason Cockcroft'. All in white with the exception of the illustration credit which is in black, and all on an illustration of a stone basin on top of a pedestal, emitting a phosphorescent glow, situated in the middle of a small island of smooth rock by a great lake with a tiny boat to the left.

All edges trimmed. Binding measurements: 197 by 128mm (wrappers), 197 by 36mm (spine).

Publication: 6 July 2009 in an edition of 14,040 copies (confirmed by Bloomsbury)

Price: £8.99

Contents:
Harry Potter and the Half-Blood Prince
('It was nearing midnight and the Prime Minister was sitting alone in his office...')

Notes:
The individual titles in the 'celebratory' edition were each published to celebrate the release of the film version. The UK premiere of *Harry Potter and the Half-Blood Prince* took place on 7 July 2009.

The first issue omits a publication price on the lower wrapper.

As with A13(c), the artwork on the lower wrapper has been moved very slightly (in contrast to A13(a)). The position of the publisher's device suggests that the dog is in the tiny boat.

Copies: Bloomsbury Archives

A13(g)   ENGLISH 'SIGNATURE' EDITION   (2010)
(Clare Melinsky artwork series in paperback)

Harry Potter ['signature' above 'z' rule with numerous stars] | *and the* | *Half-Blood Prince* | [illustration of Hogwarts crest with legend 'DRAGO DORMIENS NUNQUAM TITILLANDUS' on banner, 68 by 84mm] | J.K.ROWLING | [publisher's device of a dog, 8 by 13mm] | BLOOMSBURY | LONDON BERLIN NEW YORK SYDNEY (All width centred)

Collation: 304 unsigned leaves bound in indeterminate gatherings; 197 by 128mm; [1-7] 8-24 [25] 26-41 [42] 43-58 [59] 60-80 [81] 82-102 [103] 104-123 [124] 125-47 [148] 149-62 [163] 164-83 [184] 185-204 [205] 206-222 [223] 224-41 [242] 243-60 [261] 262-83 [284] 285-304 [305] 306-326 [327] 328-49 [350] 351-73 [374] 375-395 [396] 397-418 [419] 420-38 [439] 440-59 [460] 461-79 [480] 481-499 [500] 501-518 [519] 520-40 [541] 542-56 [557] 558-69 [570] 571-89 [590] 591-607 [608]

Page contents: [1] half-title: 'Harry Potter ['signature' above 'z' rule with numerous stars] | *and the* | *Half-Blood Prince* | [illustration of Hogwarts crest with legend 'DRAGO DORMIENS NUNQUAM

TITILLANDUS' on banner, 60 by 75mm]'; [2] *'Titles available in the Harry Potter series | (in reading order):* | Harry Potter and the Philosopher's Stone | Harry Potter and the Chamber of Secrets | Harry Potter and the Prisoner of Azkaban | Harry Potter and the Goblet of Fire | Harry Potter and the Order of the Phoenix | Harry Potter and the Half-Blood Prince | Harry Potter and the Deathly Hallows | [new paragraph] *Titles available in the Harry Potter series | (in Latin):* | Harry Potter and the Philosopher's Stone | Harry Potter and the Chamber of Secrets | *(in Welsh, Ancient Greek and Irish):* | Harry Potter and the Philosopher's Stone'; [3] title-page; [4] 'All rights reserved; no part of this publication may be reproduced or | transmitted by any means, electronic, mechanical, photocopying | or otherwise, without the prior permission of the publisher | [new paragraph] First published in Great Britain in 2005 by Bloomsbury Publishing Plc | 36 Soho Square, London, W1D 3QY | [new paragraph] Bloomsbury Publishing, London,

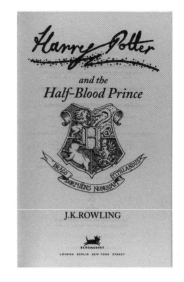

Berlin, New York and Sydney | [new paragraph] This paperback edition first published in November 2010 | [new paragraph] Copyright © J.K.Rowling 2005 | Cover illustrations by Clare Melinsky copyright © Bloomsbury Publishing Plc 2010 | [new paragraph] Harry Potter, names, characters and related indicia are | copyright and trademark Warner Bros., 2000™ | [new paragraph] J.K. Rowling has asserted her moral rights | A CIP catalogue record of this book is available from the British Library | [new paragraph] ISBN 978 1 4088 1058 3 | [new paragraph] [Forest Stewardship Council logo, 8 by 9mm together with ® symbol and text: 'FSC | www.fsc. org | MIX | Paper from | responsible sources | FSC® C018072'] | [new paragraph] Typeset by RefineCatch Limited, Bungay, Suffolk | Printed in Great Britain by Clays Ltd, St Ives plc | [new paragraph] 1 3 5 7 9 10 8 6 4 2 | [new paragraph] | www.bloomsbury.com/ harrypotter'; [5] *'To Mackenzie, | my beautiful daughter, | I dedicate | her ink and paper twin'*; [6] blank; [7]-607 text; [608] blank

Paper: wove paper

Running title: 'HARRY POTTER' (24mm) on verso, recto title comprises chapter title, pp. 10-607 (excluding pages on which new chapters commence)

Binding: pictorial wrappers.

On spine: 'Harry Potter ['signature' above 'z' rule with numerous stars] [in gilt] *and* | *the Half-Blood Prince* [red, orange, yellow and white illustration of a stoppered bottle of potion, 7 by 21mm] J.K.ROWLING BLOOMSBURY [publisher's device of the head of a dog, 3 by 4mm]' (reading lengthways down spine). All in white on red.

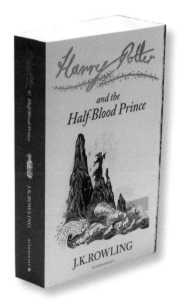

A13(aa) spine and upper cover

A13(aaa) spine and upper cover in dust-jacket

A13(aaaa) spine and upper cover

A13(b) spine and upper cover

A13(cc) spine and upper wrapper

A13(d) spine and upper wrapper

A13(h) spine and upper cover in dust-jacket

A13(i) spine and upper wrapper

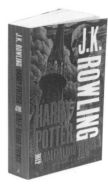

A13(j) spine and upper wrapper

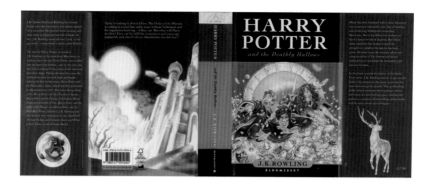

A14(*a*) dust-jacket

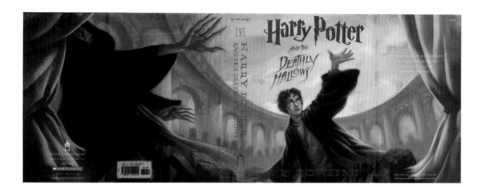

A14(*aaaa*) dust-jacket

A14(*aaaaa*) dust-jacket

A14(aa) spine and upper cover in dust-jacket

A14(aaa) spine and upper cover

A14(aaaaa) slipcase

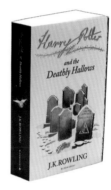

A14(b) spine and upper wrapper

A14(c) spine and upper wrapper

A14(f) spine and upper wrapper

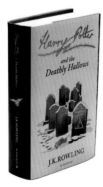

A14(g) spine and upper wrapper in dust-jacket

A14(h) spine and upper wrapper

A14(i) spine and upper wrapper

A15(a) spine and upper cover

A15(aa) spine and upper cover

A15(c) spine and upper cover

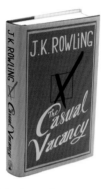

*A16(a) spine and upper cover
in dust-jacket*

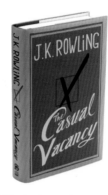

*A16(aa) spine and upper cover
in dust-jacket*

*A16(b) spine and upper
wrapper*

*A16(c) spine and upper
wrapper*

*A17(a) spine and upper cover
in dust-jacket*

A17(a) spine and upper cover

AA1(a) spine and upper wrapper

AA2(a) spine and upper wrapper

AA2(b) spine and upper wrapper

AA3(a) spine and upper wrapper

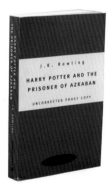

AA4(a) spine and upper wrapper

AA4(b) spine and upper wrapper

AA4(c) spine and upper wrapper

B1(a) spine and upper wrapper

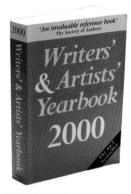

B3(a) spine and upper wrapper

B4(b) spine and upper wrapper

B4(c) spine and upper wrapper

B5(a) spine and upper wrapper

B6(a) spine and upper wrapper

B7(a) spine and upper wrapper

B8(a) spine and upper wrapper

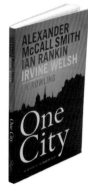

B9(a) spine and upper wrapper

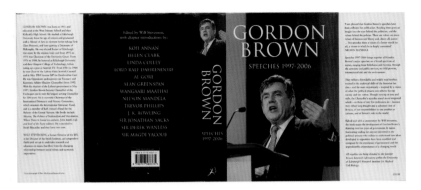

B10(a) dust-jacket

B11(a) spine and upper wrapper

B12(a) spine and upper cover

B12(a) spine and upper cover in dust-jacket

B12(b) spine and upper wrapper

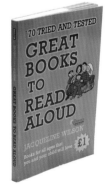

B13(a) spine and upper wrapper

B14(a) spine and upper wrapper

B15(a) spine and upper
wrapper

B16(a) spine and upper
wrapper

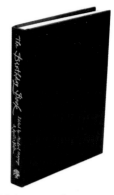

B17(a) spine and upper cover

B17(a) dust-jacket

B18(a) spine and upper
wrapper

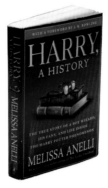

B19(a) spine and upper
wrapper

B20(a) spine and upper cover in
dust-jacket

On upper wrapper: 'Harry Potter ['signature' above 'z' rule with numerous stars] [embossed in gilt] | *and the* | *Half-Blood Prince* | [light green, light blue, dark blue and yellow illustration of two figures standing on rocks above a raging sea, 96 by 107mm] | J.K.ROWLING | BLOOMSBURY' (all width centred). All in red with deckle-edge effect of white leaf on red background at fore-edge.

On lower wrapper: 'It is Harry Potter's sixth year at Hogwarts School of Witchcraft | and Wizardry. As Voldemort's sinister forces amass and a spirit | of gloom and fear sweeps the land, it becomes clear to Harry that | he will soon have no choice but to confront his destiny. | Can Harry succeed in the death-defying tasks ahead? | [new paragraph] 'Fast, dark, exciting and tightly plotted.' | *Daily Mail* | [new paragraph] 'A gripping story with its clues trailed through the | text, chills, spills and some excellent, new comic | characters. There is a measure of sadness too ... | one of the elements of Rowling's writing that | I think entitles her to a seat in the pantheon.' | *Sunday Telegraph* | [dark blue, yellow and olive green illustration of Hogwarts castle, 172 by 122mm to the left of lines 4-13 and with white panel overlaid at foot] | [barcode together with 'www. bloomsbury.com/harrypotter', publisher's device of a dog, 6 by 10mm, 'BLOOMSBURY', '£8.99' together with Forest Stewardship Council logo, 7 by 8mm together with © symbol and text: 'FSC | Mixed Sources | Product group from well-managed | forests and other controlled sources | [new paragraph] Cert no. SGS-COC-2061 | www.fsc.org | © 1996 Forest Stewardship Council' (all on white panel, 24 by 73mm)] | Designed by Webb & Webb Design | Cover illustrations by Clare Melinsky | Author photograph © J.P.Masclet'. Lines 1-13 in red with all other text in black, together with deckle-edge effect of white leaf on red background at fore-edge. The initial 'I' of 'It' is a drop capital.

On inside upper wrapper: 'The magical world of ... | Harry Potter ['signature' above 'z' rule with numerous stars] | [colour illustrations in three columns of seven book designs] | The internationally bestselling series | [new paragraph] For more from Harry Potter, visit | www.bloomsbury.com/harrypotter'. All in red with the exception of line 2 which is in gold, together with deckle-edge effect of white leaf on red background at fore-edge.

On inside lower wrapper: colour photograph of J.K. Rowling seated by a window.

All edges trimmed. Binding measurements: 197 by 128mm (wrappers), 197 by 36mm (spine).

Publication: 1 November 2010 in an edition of 64,252 copies (confirmed by Bloomsbury)

Price: £8.99

Contents:

Harry Potter and the Half-Blood Prince

('It was nearing midnight and the Prime Minister was sitting alone in his office...')

Notes:

This is the only volume in the paperback 'signature' edition to include a white panel on the lower wrapper that overlays the illustration.

The ISBN numbers within the signature paperback edition are not sequential for *Order of the Phoenix* and *Half-Blood Prince*. The earlier book, *Order of the Phoenix*, has the ISBN number 978-1-4088-1059-0 while the later book, *Half-Blood Prince*, has the ISBN number 978-1-4088-1058-3.

Published as a boxed set of seven volumes comprising A1(i), A2(n), A7(k), A9(k), A12(h), A13(g) and A14(f). Individual volumes were also available separately.

Copies: private collection (PWE)

A13(h) ENGLISH 'SIGNATURE' EDITION (2011)
(Clare Melinsky artwork series in hardback)

Harry Potter ['signature' above 'z' rule with numerous stars] | *and the* | *Half-Blood Prince* | [illustration of Hogwarts crest with legend 'DRAGO DORMIENS NUNQUAM TITILLANDUS' on banner, 68 by 84mm] | J.K.ROWLING | [publisher's device of a dog, 8 by 13mm] | BLOOMSBURY | LONDON BERLIN NEW YORK SYDNEY (All width centred)

Collation: 304 unsigned leaves bound in indeterminate gatherings; 197 by 124mm; [1-7] 8-24 [25] 26-41 [42] 43-58 [59] 60-80 [81] 82-102 [103] 104-123 [124] 125-47 [148] 149-62 [163] 164-83 [184] 185-204 [205] 206-222 [223] 224-41 [242] 243-60 [261] 262-83 [284] 285-304 [305] 306-326 [327] 328-49 [350] 351-73 [374] 375-395 [396] 397-418 [419] 420-38 [439] 440-59 [460] 461-79 [480] 481-499 [500] 501-518 [519] 520-40 [541] 542-56 [557] 558-69 [570] 571-89 [590] 591-607 [608]

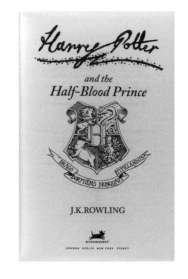

Page contents: [1] half-title: 'Harry Potter ['signature' above 'z' rule with numerous stars] | *and the* | *Half-Blood Prince* | [illustration of Hogwarts crest with legend 'DRAGO DORMIENS NUNQUAM TITILLANDUS' on banner, 60 by 75mm]'; [2] *'Titles available in the Harry Potter series* | *(in reading order):* | Harry Potter and the Philosopher's Stone | Harry Potter and the Chamber of Secrets | Harry Potter and the Prisoner of Azkaban | Harry Potter and the Goblet of Fire | Harry Potter and the Order of the Phoenix | Harry Potter and the Half-Blood Prince | Harry Potter and the Deathly Hallows | [new paragraph] *Titles available in the Harry Potter series* | *(in Latin):* | Harry Potter and the Philosopher's Stone | Harry Potter and the Chamber of Secrets | *(in Welsh, Ancient Greek and Irish):* | Harry Potter and the Philosopher's Stone | [new paragraph] *Also available* | *(in aid of Comic Relief):* | Fantastic Beasts and Where to Find Them | Quidditch Through the Ages | *(in aid of Lumos):* | The Tales of Beedle the Bard'; [3] title-page; [4] 'All rights reserved; no part of this publication may be reproduced or | transmitted by any means, electronic, mechanical, photocopying | or otherwise, without the prior permission of the publisher | [new paragraph] First published in Great Britain in 2005 by Bloomsbury Publishing Plc | 49-51 Bedford Square, London, WC1B 3DP | [new paragraph] Bloomsbury Publishing, London, Berlin, New York and Sydney | [new paragraph] This hardback edition first published in November 2011 | [new paragraph] Copyright © J.K.Rowling 2005 | Cover and endpaper illustrations by Clare Melinsky copyright © J.K.Rowling 2010 | [new paragraph] Harry Potter, names, characters and related indicia are | copyright and trademark Warner Bros., 2000™ | [new paragraph] J.K.Rowling has asserted her moral rights | A CIP catalogue record of this book is available from the British Library | [new paragraph] ISBN 978 1 4088 2582 2 | [new paragraph] [Forest Stewardship Council logo, 8 by 9mm together with ® symbol and text: 'FSC | www.fsc. org | MIX | Paper from | responsible sources | FSC® C018072'] | [new paragraph] Typeset by RefineCatch Limited, Bungay, Suffolk | Printed in Great Britain by Clays Ltd, St Ives plc | [new paragraph] 1 3 5 7 9 10 8 6 4 2 | [new paragraph] | www.bloomsbury.com/harrypotter'; [5] *'To Mackenzie,* | *my beautiful daughter,* | *I dedicate* | *her ink and paper twin'*; [6] blank; [7]-607 text; [608] blank

Paper: wove paper

Running title: 'HARRY POTTER' (24mm) on verso, recto title comprises chapter title, pp. 8-607

Binding: red boards.

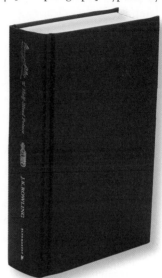

    On spine: 'Harry Potter ['signature' above 'z' rule with numerous stars] *and* | *the Half-Blood Prince* [illustration of a stoppered bottle of potion, 7 by 21mm] J.K.ROWLING BLOOMSBURY [publisher's device of the head of a dog, 3 by 4mm]' (reading lengthways down spine). All in gilt.

    Upper and lower covers: blank.

    All edges trimmed. Red sewn bands at head and foot of spine together with red marker ribbon. Binding measurements: 205 by 128mm (covers), 205 by 59mm (spine). End-papers: wove paper overprinted in pink showing design, in white, of spine motifs from the series (see notes).

Dust-jacket: coated wove paper, 205 by 512mm

    On spine: 'Harry Potter ['signature' above 'z' rule with numerous stars] [in gilt] *and* | *the Half-Blood Prince* [red, orange, yellow and white illustration of a stoppered bottle of potion, 7 by 21mm] J.K.ROWLING BLOOMSBURY [publisher's device of the head of a dog, 3 by 4mm]' (reading lengthways down spine). All in white on red.

    On upper cover: 'Harry Potter ['signature' above 'z' rule with numerous stars] [in gilt] | *and the* | *Half-Blood Prince* | [light green, light blue, dark blue and yellow illustration of two figures standing on rocks above a raging sea, 96 by 107mm] | J.K.ROWLING | BLOOMSBURY' (all width centred). All in red with deckle-edge effect of white leaf on red background at fore-edge.

On lower cover: "Fast, dark, exciting and | tightly plotted.' | *Daily Mail* [dark blue, yellow and olive green illustration of Hogwarts castle, 127 by 98mm to the left of lines 1-3] | [publisher's device of a dog, 6 by 10mm and 'BLOOMSBURY'] [barcode and 'www.bloomsbury.com/harrypotter' in black on white panel, 24 by 39mm]'. All in red, with deckle-edge effect of white leaf on red background at fore-edge. The initial 'F' of 'Fast' is a drop capital.

On upper inside flap: 'It is Harry Potter's sixth year at | Hogwarts School of Witchcraft | and Wizardry. As Voldemort's sinister | forces amass and a spirit of gloom and | fear sweeps the land, it becomes clear to | Harry that he will soon have no choice | but to confront his destiny. Can Harry | succeed in the death-defying tasks ahead? | [new paragraph] 'Taut, witty, effortlessly engaging ... how | we yearn for more.' | *Times Literary Supplement* | [new paragraph] 'A gripping story with its clues trailed | through the text, chills, spills and some | excellent, new comic characters. There is | a measure of sadness too ... one of the | elements of Rowling's writing that I think | entitles her to a seat in the pantheon.' | *Sunday Telegraph* | [red, orange, yellow and white illustration of a stoppered bottle of potion, 23 by 8mm]'. All in white on red. The initial 'I' of 'It' is a drop capital.

On lower inside flap: 'J. K. Rowling has written fiction since she was a child, | and she always wanted to be an author. Her parents loved | reading and their house in Chepstow was full of books. | In fact, J. K. Rowling wrote her first 'book' at the age | of six – a story about a rabbit called Rabbit. She studied | French and Classics at Exeter University, then moved to | Edinburgh – via London and Portugal. In 2000 she was | awarded an OBE for services to children's literature. | [new paragraph] The idea for Harry Potter occurred to her on the | train from Manchester to London, where she says | Harry Potter 'just strolled into my head fully formed', | and by the time she had arrived at King's Cross, many | of the characters had taken shape. During the next | five years she outlined the plots for each book and | began writing the first in the series, *Harry Potter and* | *the Philosopher's Stone*, which was first published by | Bloomsbury in 1997. The other Harry Potter titles: | *Harry Potter and the Chamber of Secrets, Harry Potter* | *and the Prisoner of Azkaban, Harry Potter and the* | *Goblet of Fire, Harry Potter and the Order of the Phoenix,* | *Harry Potter and the Half-Blood Prince* and *Harry* | *Potter and the Deathly Hallows* followed. J. K. Rowling | has also written three companion books: *Quidditch* | *Through the Ages* and *Fantastic Beasts and Where to Find* | *Them*, in aid of Comic Relief, and *The Tales of Beedle* | *the Bard*, in aid of Lumos. | [new paragraph] THE COMPLETE HARRY POTTER SERIES: | [colour illustrations in two rows of seven book designs] | Designed by Webb & Webb Design | Cover illustrations by Clare Melinsky | copyright © J. K. Rowling 2010'. All in white on red with white panel, 19 by 12mm, to right on which in black: '[Forest Stewardship Council logo, 6 by 7mm together with ® symbol] | FSC | www.fsc.org | MIX | Paper from | responsible sources | FSC® C018072'.

Publication: 7 November 2011 in an edition of 9,200 copies (confirmed by Bloomsbury)

Price: £115 [together with A1(j), A2(o), A7(l), A9(l), A12(i) and A14(g)]

Contents:
Harry Potter and the Half-Blood Prince
('It was nearing midnight and the Prime Minister was sitting alone in his office...')

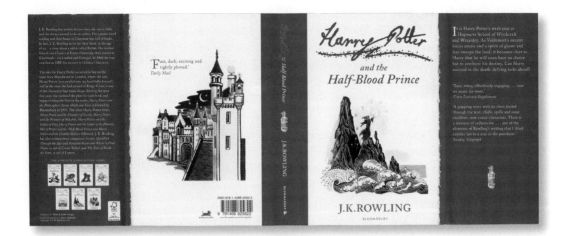

Notes:

The end-papers carry a design of eight miniature illustrations. Seven of these reproduce the spine motifs from the series and an eighth comprises a variant of the key-bird from the first book.

This is the third of the books in the series to carry different press quotes from the equivalent 'signature' paperback edition. For this hardback edition there is an additional quote (from *The Times Literary Supplement*) on the upper inside flap.

Published as a boxed set of seven volumes comprising A1(j), A2(o), A7(l), A9(l), A12(i), A13(h) and A14(g). Individual volumes were not available separately. The ISBN for the boxed set was ISBN 978 1 4088 2594 5.

Copies: private collection (PWE)

A13(i)   AMERICAN CHILDREN'S EDITION   (2013)
(Kazu Kibuishi artwork in paperback)

HARRY POTTER | AND THE HALF-BLOOD PRINCE | [black and white illustration of a battered book, with swirl of bubbling potion and a lit candle in holder, 61 by 52mm] | BY | J. K. ROWLING | ILLUSTRATIONS BY MARY GRANDPRÉ | SCHOLASTIC INC. (All width centred on a diamond pattern background)

Collation: 344 unsigned leaves bound in indeterminate gatherings; 204 by 133mm; [I-VI] VII-X [XI-XII] 1-652 [653-76]

Page contents: [I-II] 'PRAISE FOR J. K. ROWLING'S | HARRY POTTER | AND THE HALF-BLOOD PRINCE | [device of seven stars] | [5 reviews and a listing of 4 statements] | [device of nine stars]'; [III] title-page; [IV] '[device of twelve stars] | Text © 2005 by J. K. Rowling | Interior illustrations by Mary GrandPré © 2005 by Warner Bros. | Excerpt from *Harry Potter and the Deathly Hallows*, text © 2007 by J. K. Rowling; | illustration by Mary GrandPré © 2007 by Warner Bros. | Cover illustration by Kazu Kibuishi © 2013 by Scholastic Inc. | HARRY POTTER and all related characters and elements are TM of and © WBEI. | Harry Potter Publishing Rights © J. K. Rowling | All rights reserved. Published by Scholastic Inc. SCHOLASTIC, the LANTERN LOGO, and associated | logos are trademarks and/or registered trademarks of Scholastic Inc. | [new paragraph] If you purchased this book without a cover, you should be aware that this book is stolen property. | It was reported as "unsold and destroyed" to the

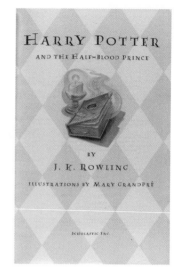

publisher, and neither the author nor the | publisher has received any payment for this "stripped book." | [new paragraph] No part of this publication may be reproduced, stored in a retrieval system, or transmitted in any | form or by any means, electronic, mechanical, photocopying, recording, or otherwise, without | written permission of the publisher. For information regarding permission, write to Scholastic Inc., | Attention: Permissions Department, 557 Broadway, New York, NY 10012. | [new paragraph] [publisher's device of a lantern, 6 by 4mm] | Arthur A. Levine Books hardcover edition art directed by David Saylor, | published by Arthur A. Levine Books, an imprint of Scholastic Inc., July 2005. | [new paragraph] ISBN 978-0-545-58299-5 | [new paragraph] Library of Congress Control Number: 2005921149 | [new paragraph] 12 11 10 9 8 7 6 5 4 3 2 1   13 14 15 16 17 | [new paragraph] Printed in the U.S.A. 40 | This edition first printing, September 2013 | [new paragraph] We try to produce the most beautiful books possible, and we are extremely concerned about the impact of our | manufacturing process on the forests of the world and the environment as a whole. Accordingly, we made sure | that the text paper contains a minimum of 30% post-consumer waste, and that all the paper has been certified as | coming from forests that are managed to insure the protection of the people and wildlife dependent upon them.'; [V] 'TO MACKENZIE, | MY BEAUTIFUL DAUGHTER, | I DEDICATE | HER INK-AND-PAPER TWIN.'; [VI] blank; VII-X 'CONTENTS' (thirty chapters listed with titles and page references); [XI] half-title: 'HARRY POTTER | AND THE HALF-BLOOD PRINCE' (all on diamond pattern background); [VIII] blank; 1-652 text; [653-54] blank; [655] 'HARRY POTTER'S | ADVENTURES CONTINUE IN | [new paragraph] HARRY POTTER | AND THE DEATHLY HALLOWS | [new paragraph] TURN THE PAGE FOR | A SNEAK PREVIEW!' (all on diamond pattern background); [656] blank; [657-68] text; [669] blank; [670] advertisement for Pottermore; [671] '[black and white photograph of J.K. Rowling seated by curtains, credited 'ANDREW MONTGOMERY' reading lengthways up right margin] | [new paragraph] J. K. ROWLING is the author of the beloved, | bestselling, record-breaking Harry Potter series. She started writing | the series during a delayed Manchester to London King's Cross | train journey, and during the next five years, outlined the plots for | each book and began writing the first novel. *Harry Potter and the* | *Sorcerer's Stone* was published in the United States by Arthur A. | Levine Books in 1998, and the series concluded nearly ten years | later with *Harry Potter and the Deathly Hallows*, published in 2007. | J. K. Rowling is the recipient of numerous awards and honorary | degrees, including an OBE for services to children's literature, | France's Légion d'honneur, and the Hans Christian Andersen | Literature Award. She supports a wide number of causes through | her charitable trust, Volant, and is the founder of Lumos, a charity | working to transform the lives of disadvantaged children. J. K. | Rowling lives in Edinburgh with her husband and three children.'; [672] blank; [673] 'MARY GRANDPRÉ has illustrated more than twenty | beautiful books for children, including the American editions of | the Harry Potter novels. Her work has also appeared in the *New* | *Yorker*, the *Atlantic Monthly*, and the *Wall Street Journal*, and her | paintings and pastels have been shown in galleries across the United | States. Ms. GrandPré lives in Sarasota, Florida, with her family. | [new paragraph] KAZU KIBUISHI is the creator of the *New York Times* | bestselling Amulet series and *Copper*, a collection of his popular | webcomic. He is also the founder and editor of the acclaimed | Flight anthologies. *Daisy Kutter: The Last Train*, his first graphic | novel, was listed as one of the Best Books for Young Adults by | YALSA, and *Amulet, Book One: The Stonekeeper* was an ALA Best | Book for Young Adults and a Children's Choice Book Award | finalist. Kazu lives and works in Alhambra, California, with his | wife and fellow comics artist, Amy Kim Kibuishi, and their two | children. Visit Kazu online at www.boltcity.com.'; [674-76] blank

Paper: wove paper

Running title: 'CHAPTER' and chapter number on verso, recto title comprises chapter title, pp. 1-652 and pp. [657-68]. Each running title (excluding pages on which new chapters commence) includes a three-star design to left and right of both running-titles on verso and recto. On pages on which a new chapter commences, the three-star design is omitted.

Illustrations: title-page vignette, together with thirty vignettes at the beginning of each chapter (after chapter and chapter number but before chapter title). The 'sneak preview' also includes a vignette. In addition to standard typographical changes (including italics, capitals and small capitals) there are other typographical features, comprising:

    p. 39 newspaper headline
    p. 40 newspaper headline
    p. 42 leaflet title
    p. 43 facsimile of Albus Dumbledore's signature
    p. 102 O.W.L. results
    p. 110 cardboard sign
    p. 116 window display lettering
    p. 141 facsimile of Professor H.E.F. Slughorn's signature
    p. 181 facsimile of Albus Dumbledore's signature
    p. 189 textbook scribble
    p. 193 textbook ownership inscription
    p. 238 textbook scribble

p. 338 gold chain lettering

p. 354 text of sign

p. 377 textbook scribble

p. 470 note from Hagrid

p. 609 note from R.A.B.

Binding: pictorial wrappers.

On spine: 'ROWLING | Harry Potter and the Half-Blood Prince [reading lengthways down spine] | 6' and '[publisher's book device] | [rule] | S' in white on red panel, 14 by 6mm. All in white on colour illustration (see notes).

On upper wrapper: 'J. K. ROWLING | Harry Potter [hand-drawn lettering] [embossed in white] | and the | Half-Blood Prince' (all width centred). All in white on colour illustration of Harry Potter with Professor Dumbledore standing on a rock, with a cliff behind, looking out to sea. In centre at foot: '[publisher's book device] SCHOLASTIC' in white on red panel, 5 by 45mm.

On lower wrapper: '"When you have that last piece of the jigsaw, | everything will, I hope, be clear …" | — Albus Dumbledore | [new paragraph] The war against Voldemort is not going well. Hermione scans the pages of | the *Daily Prophet*, reading out terrible news. Dumbledore is absent from | Hogwarts for long stretches of time, and yet … | [new paragraph] As in all wars, life goes on. Sixth-year students learn to Apparate — and | lose a few eyebrows in the process. Teenagers flirt and fight and fall in love. | Classes are tough, though Harry receives some extraordinary help from | the mysterious Half-Blood Prince. | [new paragraph] And all the while Harry searches for the full and complex story of the | boy who became Lord Voldemort — hoping to find what may be his only | vulnerability. | [new paragraph] $14.99 US | [new paragraph] [publisher's book device with 'SCHOLASTIC' in white on red panel, 5 by 45mm] | www.scholastic.com | COVER DESIGN BY KAZU KIBUISHI AND JASON CAFFOE | COVER ART BY KAZU KIBUISHI © 2013 BY SCHOLASTIC INC.' Lines 1-3 in white with other lines in light yellow and all on colour illustration of Harry standing before Professor Dumbledore in his office with a stone basin between them. In lower right: barcode with smaller barcode to the right (51499) together with 'S' within triangle, all in black on white panel, 21 by 53mm.

On inside upper wrapper: barcode with smaller barcode (51499) together with 'S' within triangle below, all in black on white panel, 53 by 21mm. All on green.

On inside lower wrapper: '[colour illustration of book design] Harry Potter [hand-drawn lettering] [in white] | The Complete Series [in white] | Read All of Harry's [in white] | Magical Adventures! [in white] | [publisher's device of a lantern, 10 by 7mm] [in black] | ARTHUR A. LEVINE BOOKS [in black] | [publisher's book device with 'SCHOLASTIC' in white on red panel, 5 by 45mm] |

scholastic.com/harrypotter [in white] | [colour illustrations in three columns of six book designs]'. All on lavender blue.

All edges trimmed. Binding measurements: 204 by 134mm (wrappers), 204 by 33mm (spine).

Publication: 27 August 2013

Price: $14.99

Contents:
Harry Potter and the Half-Blood Prince
('It was nearing midnight and the Prime Minister was sitting alone in his office…')

Notes:
See notes to A4(h) about this series.

The seven volumes in this edition were available individually or as a set issued in a slipcase. The set, presented in order, reveals a single illustration of Hogwarts castle across the seven spines. Scholastic released images of the new illustrations in a careful marketing campaign: the upper wrapper illustration for *Harry Potter and the Half-Blood Prince* was shown at the annual Comic-Con Convention in San Diego on 19 July 2013.

The 'sneak preview' of *Deathly Hallows* comprises the complete text of chapter one.

Each chapter commences with a drop capital.

Copies: private collection (PWE)

A13(j)   ENGLISH ADULT EDITION   (2013)
(Andrew Davidson artwork series in paperback)

J.K. [in grey] | ROWLING [in grey] [reading lengthways down title-page] | HARRY | POTTER | &THE [reading lengthways up title-page] HALF-BLOOD PRINCE | BLOOMSBURY | LONDON [point] NEW DELHI [point] NEW YORK [point] SYDNEY (Author and final part of title justified on right margin, first part of title justified on left margin, publisher with publisher's offices width centred)

Collation: 304 unsigned leaves bound in indeterminate gatherings; 198 by 128mm; [1-7] 8-24 [25] 26-41 [42] 43-58 [59] 60-80 [81] 82-102 [103] 104-123 [124] 125-47 [148] 149-62 [163] 164-83 [184] 185-204 [205] 206-222 [223] 224-41 [242] 243-60 [261] 262-83 [284] 285-304 [305] 306-326 [327] 328-49 [350] 351-73 [374] 375-395 [396] 397-418 [419] 420-38 [439] 440-59 [460] 461-79 [480] 481-499 [500] 501-518 [519] 520-40 [541] 542-56 [557] 558-69 [570] 571-89 [590] 591-607 [608]

Page contents: [1] half-title: 'HARRY | POTTER | &THE [reading lengthways up title-page] HALF-BLOOD PRINCE'; [2] '*Titles available in the Harry Potter series* | *(in reading order)*: | Harry Potter and the Philosopher's Stone | Harry Potter and the Chamber of Secrets | Harry Potter and the Prisoner of Azkaban | Harry Potter and the Goblet of Fire | Harry Potter and the Order of the Phoenix | Harry Potter and the Half-Blood Prince | Harry Potter and the Deathly Hallows | [new paragraph] *Titles available in the Harry Potter series | (in Latin):* | Harry Potter and the Philosopher's Stone | Harry Potter and the Chamber of Secrets | *(in Welsh, Ancient Greek and Irish):* | Harry Potter and the Philosopher's Stone | [new paragraph] *Also available | (in aid of Comic Relief):* | Fantastic Beasts and Where to Find Them | Quidditch Through the Ages | *(in aid of Lumos):* | The Tales of Beedle the Bard'; [3] title-page; [4] 'All rights reserved; no part of this publication may be reproduced or | transmitted by any means, electronic, mechanical, photocopying | or otherwise, without the prior permission of the publisher | [new paragraph] First published in Great Britain in 2005 by Bloomsbury Publishing Plc | 50 Bedford Square, London WC1B 3DP | [new

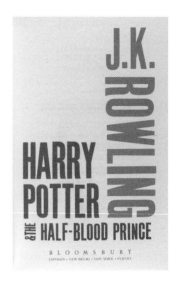

paragraph] Bloomsbury Publishing, London, New Delhi, New York and Sydney | [new paragraph] This paperback edition first published in 2013 | [new paragraph] Copyright © J.K. Rowling 2005 | Cover illustrations by Andrew Davidson copyright © J.K. Rowling 2013 | [new paragraph] Harry Potter, names, characters and related indicia are | copyright and trademark Warner Bros., 2000™ | [new paragraph] J.K. Rowling has asserted her moral rights | A CIP catalogue record for this book is available from the British Library | [new paragraph] ISBN 978 1 4088 3501 2 | [new paragraph] [Forest Stewardship Council logo, 6 by 7mm together with ® symbol and text: 'FSC | www.fsc.org' with 'MIX | Paper from | responsible sources | FSC® C020471' to the right and all within single ruled border with rounded corners, 12 by 26mm] | [new paragraph] Typeset by RefineCatch Limited, Bungay, Suffolk | Printed and bound in Great Britain by CPI Group (UK) Ltd, Croydon CR0 4YY | [new paragraph] 1 3 5 7 9 10 8 6 4 2 | [new paragraph] | www.bloomsbury.com/ harrypotter'; [5] 'To Mackenzie, | my beautiful daughter, | I dedicate | her ink and paper twin'; [6] blank; [7]-607 text; [608] blank

Paper: wove paper

Running title: 'HARRY POTTER' (24mm) on verso, recto title comprises chapter title, pp. 8-607

Binding: pictorial wrappers.

On spine: 'J.K. ROWLING [in white] HARRY POTTER [in red] &THE [in white] HALF-BLOOD PRINCE [in red] [publisher's device of a figure with a bow, 8 by 6mm] [in white]' (reading lengthways down spine with the exception of '&THE' and the publisher's device which are horizontal). All on blue.

On upper wrapper: 'J.K. [in white] | ROWLING [in white] [reading lengthways down upper wrapper] | HARRY [in blue] |

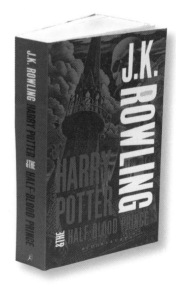

POTTER [in blue] | &THE [in white] [reading lengthways up upper wrapper] HALF-BLOOD PRINCE [in blue] | BLOOMSBURY [in white]' (author and final part of title justified on right margin, first part of title justified on left margin, publisher with publisher's offices width centred). All on orange and red illustration of Hogwarts castle with a blazing skull hanging in the sky.

On lower wrapper: 'Suspicion and fear blow through the wizarding world as news | of the Dark Lord's attack on the Ministry of Magic spreads. | Harry has not told anyone about the future predicted by the | prophecy in the Department of Mysteries, nor how deeply what | happened to Sirius Black has affected him. He's desperate | for Professor Dumbledore to arrive and take him away from | the Dursleys – but Hogwarts may not be the safe haven from | Voldemort's Dark Forces that it once was. | [new paragraph] In his sixth year, the names Black, Malfoy, Lestrange and Snape | will haunt Harry with shades of trust and treachery as he discovers | the secret behind the mysterious Half-Blood Prince – and | Dumbledore prepares him to face his own terrifying destiny … | [new paragraph] [section of white illustration of Hogwarts castle with a blazing skull hanging in the sky, 50 by 111mm] | BLOOMSBURY www.bloomsbury.com/harrypotter www.pottermore.com £8.99 [in black] | [section of white illustration of Hogwarts castle with a blazing skull hanging in the sky, 27 by 111mm upon which: Forest Stewardship Council logo, 5 by 6mm together with ® symbol and text: 'FSC | www.fsc.org | MIX | Paper from | responsible sources | FSC® C020471' all in black on white panel with rounded corners, 19 by 12mm, with barcode in black on white panel, 18 by 38mm, with 'Designed by Webb & Webb Design | Cover illustrations by Andrew Davidson | copyright © J.K. Rowling 2013' in black on blue panel, 9 by 38mm]'. Lines 1-12 in white and all on blue. The initial 'S' of 'Suspicion' is a drop capital and is printed in blue.

On inside upper wrapper: blue and white illustration of Hogwarts castle with a blazing skull hanging in the sky.

On inside lower wrapper: blue and white illustration of roof of Hogwarts castle.

All edges trimmed. Binding measurements: 198 by 128mm (wrappers), 198 by 36mm (spine).

Publication: 26 September 2013 in an edition of 57,200 copies (confirmed by Bloomsbury) (see notes)

Price: £8.99

Contents:
Harry Potter and the Half-Blood Prince
  ('It was nearing midnight and the Prime Minister was sitting alone in his office…')

Notes:
The illustrations by Andrew Davidson derive from a single wood engraving. A single illustration is presented on both the upper wrapper and inside upper wrapper. A section is printed on the lower wrapper. A detail from the upper wrapper is shown on the inside lower wrapper.

Although Bloomsbury's 'official' publication date was 26 September 2013, copies were available from amazon.co.uk two or three days beforehand.

Copies: private collection (PWE)

HARRY POTTER AND THE DEATHLY HALLOWS

A14(a)   **FIRST ENGLISH EDITION**   **(2007)**
(children's artwork series in hardback)

HARRY | POTTER | *and the Deathly Hallows* | [illustration of Hogwarts crest with legend 'DRAGO DORMIENS NUNQUAM TITILLANDUS' on banner, 66 by 81mm] | J. K. ROWLING | [publisher's device of a dog, 11 by 18mm] | BLOOMSBURY (Lines 1 and 2 justified on left and right margins, and all width centred)

Collation: 304 unsigned leaves bound in indeterminate gatherings; 198 by 127mm; [1-9] 10-18 [19] 20-30 [31] 32-41 [42] 43-57 [58] 59-75 [76] 77-94 [95] 96-114 [115] 116-33 [134] 135-45 [146] 147-65 [166] 167-83 [184] 185-202 [203] 204-220 [221] 222-33 [234] 235-54 [255] 256-69 [270] 271-85 [286] 287-95 [296] 297-314 [315] 316-28 [329] 330-43 [344] 345-61 [362] 363-85 [386] 387-405 [406] 407-418 [419] 420-38 [439] 440-46 [447] 448-59 [460] 461-73 [474] 475-88 [489] 490-512 [513] 514-28 [529] 530-53 [554] 555-64 [565] 566-79 [580] 581-600 [601-603] 604-607 [608]

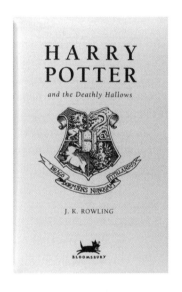

Page contents: [1] half-title: 'HARRY | POTTER | *and the Deathly Hallows* | [illustration of Hogwarts crest with legend 'DRAGO DORMIENS NUNQUAM TITILLANDUS' on banner, 47 by 58mm]'; [2] '*Titles available in the Harry Potter series* | *(in reading order):* | Harry Potter and the Philosopher's Stone | Harry Potter and the Chamber of Secrets | Harry Potter and the Prisoner of Azkaban | Harry Potter and the Goblet of Fire | Harry Potter and the Order of the Phoenix | Harry Potter and the Half-Blood Prince | Harry Potter and the Deathly Hallows | [new paragraph] *Titles available in the Harry Potter series* | *(in Latin):* | Harry Potter and the Philosopher's Stone | Harry Potter and the Chamber of Secrets | *(in Welsh, Ancient Greek and Irish):* | Harry Potter and the Philosopher's Stone'; [3] title-page; [4] 'All rights reserved; no part of this publication may be reproduced or | transmitted by any means, electronic, mechanical, photocopying | or otherwise, without the prior permission of the publisher | [new paragraph] First published in Great Britain in 2007 by Bloomsbury Publishing Plc | 36 Soho Square, London, W1D 3QY | [new paragraph] Copyright © J. K. Rowling 2007 | Cover illustrations by Jason Cockcroft copyright © Bloomsbury Publishing Plc 2007 | Harry Potter, names, characters and related indicia are | copyright and trademark Warner Bros., 2000™ | [new paragraph] J. K.

Rowling has asserted her moral rights | [new paragraph] The extract from *The Libation Bearers* is taken from the Penguin Classics edition | of *The Oresteia*, translated by Robert Fagles, copyright © Robert Fagles, 1966, | 1967, 1975, 1977 | [new paragraph] The extract from *More Fruits of Solitude* is taken from *More Fruits of Solitude* | by William Penn, first included in Everyman's Library, 1915 | [new paragraph] A CIP catalogue record of this book is available from the British Library | [new paragraph] ISBN 978 0 7475 9105 4 | [new paragraph] The pages of this book are printed on 100% Ancient-Forest Friendly paper | [Forest Stewardship Council logo, 7 by 8mm together with © symbol and text: 'FSC | Mixed Sources | Product group from well-managed | forests and other controlled sources | [new paragraph] Cert no. SGS-COC-2061 |www fsc org | © 1996 Forest Stewardship Council'] | The papers on which this book is printed are manufactured from a composition | of © 1996 Forest Stewardship Council A.C. (FSC) approved and post-consumer | waste recycled materials. The FSC promotes environmentally appropriate, socially | beneficial and economically viable management of the world's forests. | [new paragraph] Typeset by RefineCatch Limited, Bungay, Suffolk | Printed in Great Britain by Clays Ltd, St Ives plc | [new paragraph] First Edition | [new paragraph] www. bloomsbury.com/harrypotter'; [5] '*The | dedication | of this book | is split | seven ways: | to Neil, | to Jessica, | to David, | to Kenzie, | to Di, | to Anne, | and to you, | if you have | stuck | with Harry | until the | very | end.*'; [6] blank; [7] three stanzas from 'Aeschylus, *The Libation Bearers*' and one paragraph from 'William Penn, *More Fruits of Solitude*'; [8] blank; [9]-600 text; [601] '*Nineteen Years Later*'; [602] blank; [603]-607 text; [608] blank

Paper: wove paper

Running title: 'HARRY POTTER' (24mm) on verso, recto title comprises chapter title, pp. 10-607 (excluding pages on which new chapters commence)

Binding: pictorial boards.

On spine: '[light blue / grey illustration of a triangular eye symbol on light blue / grey panel, 47 by 16mm] HARRY POTTER [in white on purple panel, 47 by 47mm] *and the Deathly Hallows* [in black] J.K.ROWLING [in white, both title conclusion and author on red panel, 47 by 109mm] BLOOMSBURY [publisher's device of the head of a dog, 4 by 3mm] [both in white on black panel, 47 by 33mm]' (reading lengthways down spine).

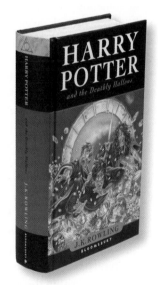

On upper cover: 'HARRY | POTTER | *and the Deathly Hallows* [lines 1 and 2 in white, line 3 in grey, all on black panel, 62 by 131mm] | [red rule, 131mm] | [colour illustration of Harry Potter, Ron Weasley and Hermione Granger within a cave-like opening on top of a sea of golden coins and other treasures with Griphook the goblin clutching Harry's back and a sword, 125 by 131mm] | [red rule, 131mm intersected by grey panel with 'J.K.ROWLING' in black] | BLOOMSBURY [in white on black panel, 14 by 132mm]' (all width centred).

On lower cover: 'Harry is waiting in Privet Drive. The Order of the Phoenix | is coming to escort him safely away without Voldemort and | his supporters knowing – if they can. But what will

Harry | do then? How can he fulfil the momentous and seemingly | impossible task that Professor Dumbledore has left him? | [barcode in black on white panel (with red border), 21 by 40mm together with '[Forest Stewardship Council logo, 6 by 7mm together with © symbol and text: 'FSC | Mixed Sources | Product group from well-managed | forests and other controlled sources | [new paragraph] Cert no. SGS-COC-2061 | www.fsc.org | © 1996 Forest Stewardship Council'] | [publisher's device of a dog, 5 by 9mm] | BLOOMSBURY' in black on right side of panel and 'http://www.bloomsbury.com' below panel, in black on red panel, 6 by 40mm] | Cover illustrations by Jason Cockcroft [in black]'. All in white on colour illustration of Hogwarts castle, a full moon, clouds and a tree.

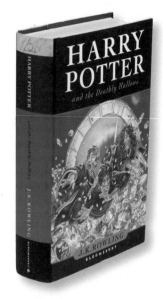

All edges trimmed. Binding measurements: 205 by 131mm (covers), 205 by 47mm (spine). End-papers: wove paper.

Dust-jacket: coated wove paper, 205 by 507mm

Spine, upper and lower covers replicate the binding, with the exception of the illustration note which is omitted.

On upper inside flap: 'Harry has been burdened with a dark, dangerous | and seemingly impossible task: that of locating | and destroying Voldemort's remaining | Horcruxes. Never has Harry felt so alone, or | faced a future so full of shadows. But Harry | must somehow find within himself the | strength to complete the task he has been | given. He must leave the warmth, safety and | companionship of The Burrow and follow | without fear or hesitation the inexorable path | laid out for him … | [new paragraph] In this final, seventh instalment of the *Harry* | *Potter* series, J.K. Rowling unveils in spectacular | fashion the answers to the many questions that | have been so eagerly awaited. The spellbinding, | richly woven narrative, which plunges, twists | and turns at a breathtaking pace, confirms the | author as a mistress of storytelling, whose books | will be read, reread and read again. | [colour illustration of a stag, 85 by 43mm] | £17.99'. All in white on purple panel.

On lower inside flap: 'J.K. (Joanne Kathleen) Rowling has written | fiction since she was a child, and always wanted | to be an author. Her parents loved reading, and | their house in Chepstow was full of books. In | fact, J.K. Rowling wrote her first 'book' at the | age of six – a story about a rabbit called Rabbit! | [new paragraph] The idea for Harry Potter occurred to | J.K. Rowling on the train from Manchester to | London, where she says Harry Potter 'just strolled | into my head fully formed', and by the time she | had arrived at King's Cross, many of the characters | had taken shape. During the next five years she | outlined the plots for each book and began | writing the first in the series, *Harry Potter and* | *the Philosopher's Stone*, which was first published | by Bloomsbury in 1997. The other *Harry Potter* | titles: *Harry Potter and the Chamber of Secrets,* | *Harry Potter and the Prisoner of Azkaban, Harry* | *Potter and the Goblet of Fire, Harry Potter* *and the* | *Order of the Phoenix* and *Harry Potter and the* | *Half-Blood Prince*, followed. J.K. Rowling has | also written two companion books, *Quidditch* | *Through the Ages* and *Fantastic Beasts and* *Where* | *to Find Them*, in aid of Comic Relief. | [colour illustration of a snake contained within a globe reflecting a window, 46 by 46mm] | Cover illustrations by Jason Cockcroft'. All in white on purple panel.

Publication: 21 July 2007 (simultaneous with A14(aa), A14(aaa), A14(aaaa) and A14(aaaaa)) in an edition of 8 million copies (confirmed by Bloomsbury)

Price: £17.99

Contents:
Harry Potter and the Deathly Hallows
('The two men appeared out of nowhere, a few yards apart in the narrow, moonlit lane.')

Notes:
It appears that editing was done by Emma Matthewson at Bloomsbury in conversation (by phone) with Arthur A. Levine at Scholastic. A notebook preserved in the editorial files of Bloomsbury suggests that copy-editing commenced on 12 March 2007 with email queries sent to Rowling the following day. A response was received on 21 March and the manuscript was sent to production on 23 March.

An early set of proofs (given the file title *Edinburgh Potmakers*) is dated 25 March. This was not the only spurious title given to the novel. Another print-out of the text in the editorial files at Bloomsbury is entitled *The Life and Times of Clara Rose Lovett* with the thrilling sub-title, 'An epic novel covering many generations'.

Collated proofs from copy-editors were produced by 20 April. A further email was sent to the author on 23 April with a response received on 27 April. Marked proofs finalised on 4 May 2007.

The email dated 23 April from Matthewson to Rowling presented proof queries and was headed 'Final Final Edits'. It included detailed plot queries and a few notes about consistency throughout the entire series. It noted, for example, that within paragraph four of page 11 Rowling had written 'He

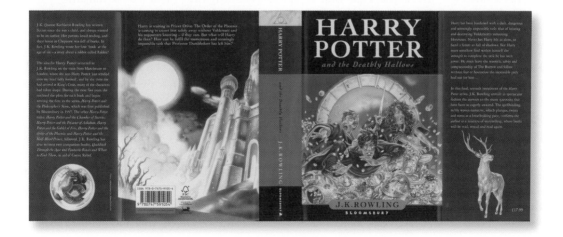

had never learned how to repair wounds' and pointed out that Harry had used 'Episkey' on Demelza's lip on page 267 of *Half-Blood Prince*. The question was therefore asked 'But this is ok as it is not really learning *properly* to repair wounds?'

The launch event for the final title in the series was called 'J.K. Rowling and the Moonlight Signing'. This event, as noted on an admission ticket, was held at the Natural History Museum in London 'to celebrate the publication' of the book. Admission time was 10 pm on Friday 20 July. Copies signed by the author on that night carry the author's hologram sticker.

In a promotional statement on the launch of A14(b), Bloomsbury noted that the title 'sold 2,652,656 copies in the UK on the first day of its release, making it the fastest-selling book of all time'. Nigel Newton recalled, in an interview with me in September 2013, that the impact of the supermarkets was huge (see note to A12(a)) and noted that 'with the last book Tesco's initial order was three quarters of a million hardcovers'. Distribution was also an issue. By the end of the series, distribution was direct from the printers (see notes to A9(a)). Nigel Newton proudly stated that 'by the end of the series we were drop-shipping 11 million hardcovers into 83 countries around the world all to arrive within 48 to 24 hours of the on-sale time'.

Note that the Forest Stewardship Council text on page [4] excludes dots in the web address. These are present on the lower cover and dust-jacket.

The English audiobook version, read by Stephen Fry, has a duration of approximately twenty-four hours.

Reprints (and subsequent new editions) include a number of corrections to the text. These comprise:

Page 27, line 15	*'hear the word 'no' and a nice sharp'* to *'hear the word "no" and a nice sharp'*
Page 98, line 16	'first floor' to 'first-floor'
Page 116, line 19	'*permettez-moi*' to '*permettez-moi*' (final i to be italic)
Page 167, line 32	'dust-figure' to 'dust figure'
Page 237, line 21	'Voldemort had lived or visited' to 'Voldemort had lived in or visited'
Page 246, line 27	'the *Prophet's* ignoring' to 'the *Prophet*'s ignoring' (final 's to be roman)
Page 249, line 11	"*Muggle-borns*,' he said' to "*Muggle-borns*,' he said' (comma in italic)
Page 287, line 34	""*Dear Batty*' to ""*Dear Batty*' (opening single quote to be roman)
Page 323, line 18	'hawk-like head, peered down' to 'hawk-head head peered down'
Page 336, line 31	'Ron said, 'the wand', and Harry said' to 'Ron said, 'the wand,' and Harry said'
Page 344, line 9	'*Cave inimicum*' to '*Cave inimicum*' (first word entirely in italic)
Page 358, line 21	'said Lupin' to 'said Lupin.'
Page 364, line 29	"*Dean?*" to "*Dean?*" (opening quote to be italic)
Page 383, line 34	"*Stupefy!*" to "*Stupefy!*" (closing quote to be italic)
Page 385, line 10	'needed too' to 'needed to'
Page 427, line 10	'murmured, '*Confundo*,' twice' to 'murmured, '*Confundo*,' twice' (opening quote to be italic)
Page 434, line 11	'said Harry,' to 'said Harry.'
Page 447, line 21	"*Accio Cloak!*' roared one' to "*Accio Cloak!*' roared one' (opening quote to be italic)

Page 504, line 23	"*Accio diadem*,' cried Hermione' to "*Accio diadem*,' cried Hermione' (punctuation to be italic)
Page 506, line 6	"*Descendo!*" to "*Descendo!*" (opening quote to be italic)
Page 506, line 12	'cried, '*Finite!*' and it steadied' to 'cried, '*Finite!*' and it steadied' (opening quote to be italic)
Page 507, line 36	"*Aguamenti!*' Harry bawled' to "*Aguamenti!*' Harry bawled' (opening quote to be italic)

Copies: private collection (PWE)

Reprints include:
5 7 9 10 8 6

A report compiled by the printers, Clays Ltd, in October 2013 noted that, to date, they had produced a minimum of 1.1 million paperbacks and 9.2 million hardbacks across 55 printings.

A14(aa)   FIRST ENGLISH EDITION   (2007)
(Michael Wildsmith photography adult artwork series in hardback)

Harry Potter and the | Deathly Hallows | J. K. Rowling | BLOOMSBURY (All width centred)

Collation: 304 unsigned leaves bound in indeterminate gatherings; 197 by 127mm; [1-9] 10-18 [19] 20-30 [31] 32-41 [42] 43-57 [58] 59-75 [76] 77-94 [95] 96-114 [115] 116-33 [134] 135-45 [146] 147-65 [166] 167-83 [184] 185-202 [203] 204-220 [221] 222-33 [234] 235-54 [255] 256-69 [270] 271-85 [286] 287-95 [296] 297-314 [315] 316-28 [329] 330-43 [344] 345-61 [362] 363-85 [386] 387-405 [406] 407-418 [419] 420-38 [439] 440-46 [447] 448-59 [460] 461-73 [474] 475-88 [489] 490-512 [513] 514-28 [529] 530-53 [554] 555-64 [565] 566-79 [580] 581-600 [601-603] 604-607 [608]

Harry Potter and the
Deathly Hallows

J. K. Rowling

BLOOMSBURY

Page contents: [1] half-title: 'Harry Potter and the | Deathly Hallows'; [2] '*Titles available in the Harry Potter series* | *(in reading order):* | Harry Potter and the Philosopher's Stone | Harry Potter and the Chamber of Secrets | Harry Potter and the Prisoner of Azkaban | Harry Potter and the Goblet of Fire | Harry Potter and the Order of the Phoenix | Harry Potter and the Half-Blood Prince | Harry Potter and the Deathly Hallows | [new paragraph]
Titles available in the Harry Potter series | *(in Latin):* | Harry Potter and the Philosopher's Stone | Harry Potter and the Chamber of Secrets | *(in Welsh, Ancient Greek and Irish):* | Harry Potter and the Philosopher's Stone'; [3] title-page; [4] 'All rights reserved; no part of this publication may be

reproduced or | transmitted by any means, electronic, mechanical, photocopying | or otherwise, without the prior permission of the publisher | [new paragraph] First published in Great Britain in 2007 by Bloomsbury Publishing Plc | 36 Soho Square, London, W1D 3QY | [new paragraph] Copyright © J. K. Rowling 2007 | Front cover and spine photographs copyright © Michael Wildsmith, 2007 | Harry Potter, names, characters and related indicia are | copyright and trademark Warner Bros., 2000™ | [new paragraph] J. K. Rowling has asserted her moral rights | [new paragraph] The extract from *The Libation Bearers* is taken from the Penguin Classics edition | of *The Oresteia*, translated by Robert Fagles, copyright © Robert Fagles, 1966, | 1967, 1975, 1977 | [new paragraph] The extract from *More Fruits of Solitude* is taken from *More Fruits of Solitude* | by William Penn, first included in Everyman's Library, 1915 | [new paragraph] A CIP catalogue record of this book is available from the British Library | [new paragraph] ISBN 978 0 7475 9106 1 | [new paragraph] The pages of this book are printed on 100% Ancient-Forest Friendly paper | [Forest Stewardship Council logo, 7 by 8mm together with © symbol and text: 'FSC | Mixed Sources | Product group from well-managed | forests and other controlled sources | [new paragraph] Cert no. SGS-COC-2061 | www fsc org | © 1996 Forest Stewardship Council'] | The papers on which this book is printed are manufactured from a composition | of © 1996 Forest Stewardship Council A.C. (FSC) approved and post-consumer | waste recycled materials. The FSC promotes environmentally appropriate, socially | beneficial and economically viable management of the world's forests. | [new paragraph] Typeset by RefineCatch Limited, Bungay, Suffolk | Printed in Great Britain by Clays Ltd, St Ives plc | [new paragraph] First Edition | [new paragraph] www.bloomsbury.com/harrypotter'; [5] 'The | dedication | of this book | is split | seven ways: | to Neil, | to Jessica, | to David, | to Kenzie, | to Di, | to Anne, | and to you, | if you have | stuck | with Harry | until the | very | end.'; [6] blank; [7] three stanzas from 'Aeschylus, *The Libation Bearers*' and one paragraph from 'William Penn, *More Fruits of Solitude*'; [8] blank; [9]-600 text; [601] '*Nineteen Years Later*'; [602] blank; [603]-607 text; [608] blank

Paper: wove paper

Running title: 'HARRY POTTER' (24mm) on verso, recto title comprises chapter title, pp. 10-607 (excluding pages on which new chapters commence)

Binding: black boards.
On spine: 'J. K. ROWLING | HARRY | POTTER | AND THE DEATHLY HALLOWS | [publisher's device of a figure with a bow, 13 by 12mm]'. All in gilt.
Upper and lower covers: blank.
All edges trimmed. Binding measurements: 204 by 128mm (covers), 204 by 55mm (spine). End-papers: wove paper.

Dust-jacket: coated wove paper, 204 by 507mm
On spine: '[colour photograph of a golden medallion encrusted with green gems, on a slate, all within single white ruled border, 58 by 33mm] | J. K. ROWLING [in white] | HARRY [in gilt] | POTTER [in gilt] | AND THE DEATHLY HALLOWS [in white]

| [publisher's device of a figure with a bow, 13 by 12mm] [in olive beige]' (all width centred). All on black.

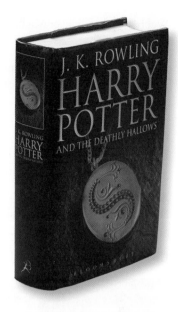

On upper cover: 'J. K. ROWLING [in white] | HARRY [embossed in gilt] | POTTER [embossed in gilt] | AND THE DEATHLY HALLOWS [in white] | BLOOMSBURY [in white]' (all width centred). All on colour photograph of a golden medallion encrusted with green gems, on a slate.

On lower cover: black and white photograph of J.K. Rowling standing against bookshelves with 'www.bloomsbury. com/harrypotter [in black on olive beige panel, 5 by 41mm] | [barcode in black on white panel, 20 by 40mm] | BLOOMSBURY [in black on olive beige panel, 6 by 41mm]' (lower right) and Forest Stewardship Council logo, 6 by 7mm together with © symbol and text: 'FSC | Mixed Sources | Product group from well-managed | forests and other controlled sources | [new paragraph] Cert no. SGS-COC-2061 | www.fsc.org | © 1996 Forest Stewardship Council' in black (lower right).

On upper inside flap: 'Harry has been burdened with a dark, | dangerous and seemingly impossible task: | that of locating and destroying Voldemort's | remaining Horcruxes. Never has Harry | felt so alone, or faced a future so full of | shadows. But Harry must somehow find | within himself the strength to complete | the task he has been given. He must leave | the warmth, safety and companionship | of The Burrow and follow without fear | or hesitation the inexorable path laid | out for him. | [new paragraph] In this final, seventh instalment of the | *Harry Potter* series, J. K. Rowling unveils | in spectacular fashion the answers to the | many questions that have been so eagerly | awaited. The spellbinding, richly woven | narrative, which plunges, twists and turns | at a breathtaking pace, confirms the author | as a mistress of storytelling, whose books | will be read, reread and read again. | [new paragraph] £17.99'. All in white on black.

On lower inside flap: 'J. K. (JOANNE KATHLEEN) ROWLING | has written fiction since she was a child. | Born in 1965, she grew up in Chepstow | and wrote her first 'book' at the age of six | – a story about a rabbit called Rabbit. | She studied French and Classics at Exeter | University, then moved to London to work | at Amnesty International, and then to | Portugal to teach English as a foreign | language, before settling in Edinburgh. | [new paragraph] The idea for Harry Potter occurred to her | on the train from Manchester to London, | where she says Harry Potter 'just strolled | into my head fully formed', and by the time | she had arrived at King's Cross, many of the | characters had taken shape. During the | next five years she outlined the plots for | each book and began writing the first in the | series, *Harry Potter and the Philosopher's* | *Stone*, which was first published by | Bloomsbury in 1997. The other *Harry* | *Potter* titles: *Harry Potter and the Chamber* | *of Secrets*, *Harry Potter and the Prisoner of* | *Azkaban*, *Harry Potter and the Goblet of* | *Fire*, *Harry Potter and the Order of the* | *Phoenix* and *Harry Potter and the Half-Blood* | *Prince*, followed. J. K. Rowling has also | written two companion books, *Quidditch* | *Through the Ages* and *Fantastic Beasts and* | *Where to Find Them*, in aid of Comic Relief. | [new paragraph] Jacket Design: William

Webb | Jacket Image: Michael Wildsmith | Author Photograph: © Bill de la HEY'. All in white on black.

Publication: 21 July 2007 (simultaneous with A14(a), A14(aaa), A14(aaaa) and A14(aaaaa)) in an edition of 2,080,718 copies (confirmed by Bloomsbury)

Price: £17.99

Contents:
Harry Potter and the Deathly Hallows
    ('The two men appeared out of nowhere, a few yards apart in the narrow, moonlit lane.')

Notes:
Note that the Forest Stewardship Council text on page [4] excludes dots in the web address. These are present on the dust-jacket.

Copies: private collection (AJH)

A14(aaa)   FIRST ENGLISH EDITION   (2007)
(children's artwork series in deluxe hardback)

HARRY | POTTER | *and the Deathly Hallows* | [illustration of Hogwarts crest with legend 'DRACO DORMIENS NUNQUAM TITILLANDUS' on banner, 70 by 85mm] | J. K. ROWLING | [publisher's device of a dog, 12 by 20mm] | BLOOMSBURY (All width centred)

Collation: 304 unsigned leaves bound in thirty-eight gatherings of eight leaves; 233 by 152mm, [1-9] 10-18 [19] 20-30 [31] 32-41 [42] 43-57 [58] 59-75 [76] 77-94 [95] 96-114 [115] 116-33 [134] 135-45 [146] 147-65 [166] 167-83 [184] 185-202 [203] 204-220 [221] 222-33 [234] 235-54 [255] 256-69 [270]

271-85 [286] 287-95 [296] 297-314 [315] 316-28 [329] 330-43 [344] 345-61 [362] 363-85 [386] 387-405 [406] 407-418 [419] 420-38 [439] 440-46 [447] 448-59 [460] 461-73 [474] 475-88 [489] 490-512 [513] 514-28 [529] 530-53 [554] 555-64 [565] 566-79 [580] 581-600 [601-603] 604-607 [608]

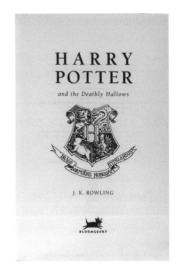

Page contents: [1] half-title: 'HARRY | POTTER | *and the Deathly Hallows* | [illustration of Hogwarts crest with legend 'DRACO DORMIENS NUNQUAM TITILLANDUS' on banner, 50 by 61mm]'; [2] *Titles available in the Harry Potter series* | *(in reading order):* | Harry Potter and the Philosopher's Stone | Harry Potter and the Chamber of Secrets | Harry Potter and the Prisoner of Azkaban | Harry Potter and the Goblet of Fire | Harry Potter and the Order of the Phoenix | Harry Potter and the Half-Blood Prince | Harry Potter and the Deathly Hallows | [new paragraph] *Titles available in the Harry Potter series* | *(in Latin):* | Harry Potter and the Philosopher's Stone | Harry Potter and the Chamber of Secrets | *(in Welsh, Ancient Greek and Irish):* | Harry Potter and the Philosopher's Stone'; [3] title-page; [4] 'All rights reserved; no part of this publication may be reproduced or | transmitted by any means, electronic, mechanical, photocopying | or otherwise, without the prior permission of the publisher | [new paragraph] First published in Great Britain in 2007 by Bloomsbury Publishing Plc | 36 Soho Square, London, W1D 3QY | [new paragraph] Copyright © J. K. Rowling 2007 | Cover illustration by Jason Cockcroft copyright © Bloomsbury Publishing Plc 2007 | Harry Potter, names, characters and related indicia are | copyright and trademark Warner Bros., 2000™ | [new paragraph] J. K. Rowling has asserted her moral rights | [new paragraph] The extract from *The Libation Bearers* is taken from the Penguin Classics edition | of *The Oresteia*, translated by Robert Fagles, copyright © Robert Fagles, 1966, | 1967, 1975, 1977 | [new paragraph] The extract from *More Fruits of Solitude* is taken from *More Fruits of Solitude* | by William Penn, first included in Everyman's Library, 1915 | [new paragraph] A CIP catalogue record of this book is available from the British Library | [new paragraph] ISBN 978 0 7475 9107 8 | [new paragraph] [Forest Stewardship Council logo, 7 by 9mm together with © symbol and text: 'FSC | Mixed Sources | Product group from well-managed | forests and other controlled sources | [new paragraph] Cert no. SGS-COC-2061 |www fsc org | © 1996 Forest Stewardship Council'] | [new paragraph] Typeset by RefineCatch Limited, Bungay, Suffolk | Printed in Great Britain by Clays Ltd, St Ives plc | [new paragraph] First Edition | [new paragraph] | www.bloomsbury.com/harrypotter'; [5] '*The* | *dedication* | *of this book* | *is split* | *seven ways:* | *to Neil,* | *to Jessica,* | *to David,* | *to Kenzie,* | *to Di,* | *to Anne,* | *and to you,* | *if you have* | *stuck* | *with Harry* | *until the* | *very* | *end.*'; [6] blank; [7] three stanzas from 'Aeschylus, *The Libation Bearers*' and one paragraph from 'William Penn, *More Fruits of Solitude*'; [8] blank; [9]-600 text; [601] *'Nineteen Years Later'*; [602] blank; [603]-607 text; [608] blank

Paper: wove paper

Running title: 'HARRY POTTER' (25mm) on verso, recto title comprises chapter title, pp. 10-607

Binding: black cloth.

On spine: 'HARRY POTTER *and the Deathly Hallows* J.K.ROWLING' (reading lengthways down spine) with '[publisher's device of a dog, 12 by 21mm] | BLOOMSBURY' (horizontally at foot). All in gilt.

On upper cover: 'HARRY | POTTER | *and the Deathly Hallows* | [double ruled border, 103 by 103mm with the outer border thicker than the inner and colour illustration by Jason Cockcroft laid down] | JKRowling [facsimile signature]' (all width centred). All in gilt.

Lower cover: blank.

All edges gilt. Purple sewn bands at head and foot of spine together with green marker ribbon. Binding measurements: 240 by 151mm (covers), 240 by 60mm (spine). End-papers: purple wove paper.

Dust-jacket: none

Publication: 21 July 2007 (simultaneous with A14(a), A14(aa), A14(aaaa) and A14(aaaaa)) in an edition of 46,500 copies (confirmed by Bloomsbury)

Price: £35

Contents:
Harry Potter and the Deathly Hallows
   ('The two men appeared out of nowhere, a few yards apart in the narrow, moonlit lane.')

Notes:
It was only with the final title in the series that the English deluxe edition was published simultaneously with the children's and adult editions (A14(a) and A14(aa)).

Copies: Sotheby's, 17 December 2009, lot 169; private collection (PWE)

Reprints include:
5 7 9 10 8 6 4

A14(aaaa)   FIRST AMERICAN EDITION   (2007)
(children's artwork series in hardback)

HARRY POTTER | AND THE DEATHLY HALLOWS | [black and white illustration of an owl in cage with books and wand all by a window, 66 by 52mm] | BY | J. K. ROWLING | ILLUSTRATIONS BY MARY GRANDPRÉ | [publisher's device of a lantern, 12 by 9mm] | ARTHUR A. LEVINE BOOKS | AN IMPRINT OF SCHOLASTIC INC. (All width centred on a diamond pattern background)

Collation: 392 unsigned leaves bound in twenty-four gatherings of sixteen leaves and one gathering of eight leaves; 228 by 150mm; [I-VI] VII-X [XI-XIV] 1-749 [750-52] 753-59 [760-70]

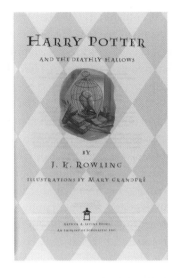

Page contents: [I] 'HARRY POTTER | AND THE DEATHLY HALLOWS' (all on diamond pattern background); [II] 'ALSO BY J. K. ROWLING | [new paragraph] *Harry Potter and the Sorcerer's Stone* | Year One at Hogwarts | [new paragraph] *Harry Potter and the Chamber of Secrets* | Year Two at Hogwarts | [new paragraph] *Harry Potter and the Prisoner of Azkaban* | Year Three at Hogwarts | [new paragraph] *Harry Potter and the Goblet of Fire* | Year Four at Hogwarts | [new paragraph] *Harry Potter and the Order of the Phoenix* | Year Five at Hogwarts | [new paragraph] *Harry Potter and the Half-Blood Prince* | Year Six at Hogwarts'; [III] title-page; [IV] '[device of twelve stars] | Text copyright © 2007 by J. K. Rowling | Illustrations by Mary GrandPré copyright © 2007 by Warner Bros. | HARRY POTTER & all related characters and elements are TM of and © WBEI. | Harry Potter Publishing Rights © J. K. Rowling. | All rights reserved. Published by Arthur A. Levine Books, | an imprint of Scholastic Inc., *Publishers since 1920.* | SCHOLASTIC, the LANTERN LOGO, and associated logos are | trademarks and/or registered trademarks of Scholastic Inc. | [new paragraph] "The Libation Bearers" by Aeschylus, from THE ORESTEIA by Aeschylus, | translated by Robert Fagles, copyright © 1966, 1967, 1975, 1977 by Robert Fagles. | Used by permission of Viking Penguin, a division of Penguin Group (USA) Inc. | "More Fruits of Solitude," reprinted from William Penn, *Fruits of Solitude*, Vol I., | Part 3, the Harvard Classics (New York: P.F. Collier & Son, 1909-14). | [new paragraph] No part of this publication may be reproduced, or stored in a retrieval system, or transmitted | in any form or by any means, electronic, mechanical, photocopying, recording, or otherwise, | without written permission of the publisher. For information regarding permission, write to | Scholastic Inc., Attention: Permissions Department, 557 Broadway, New York, NY 10012. | [new paragraph] Library of Congress Control Number: 2007925449 | [new paragraph] ISBN-13: 978-0-545-01022-1 | ISBN-10: 0-545-01022-5 | [new paragraph] 10 9 8 7 6 5 4 3 2 1   07 08 09 10 11 | Printed in the U.S.A. 12 | First edition, July 2007 | [new paragraph] We try to produce the most beautiful books possible, and we are also extremely concerned | about the impact of our manufacturing process on the forests of the world and the | environment as a whole. Accordingly, we make sure that all of the paper we used contains 30% | post-consumer recycled fiber, and that over 65% has been certified as coming from forests | that are managed to insure the protection of the people and wildlife dependent upon them.'; [V] 'THE | DEDICATION | OF THIS BOOK | IS SPLIT | SEVEN WAYS: | TO NEIL, | TO JESSICA, | TO DAVID, | TO KENZIE, | TO DI, | TO ANNE, | AND TO YOU, | IF YOU HAVE | STUCK | WITH HARRY | UNTIL THE | VERY | END.'; [VI] blank; VII-X 'CONTENTS' (thirty-six chapters and one epilogue listed with titles and page references); [XI] three stanzas from 'Aeschylus, *The Libation Bearers*' and one paragraph from 'William Penn, *More Fruits of Solitude*'; [XII] blank; [XIII] half-title: 'HARRY POTTER | AND THE DEATHLY HALLOWS' (all on diamond pattern background);

[XIV] blank; 1-749 text; [750] blank; [751] divisional title: 'NINETEEN YEARS LATER' (all on diamond pattern background); [752] blank; 753-759 text; [760-66] blank; [767] 'ABOUT THE AUTHOR | [new paragraph] J. K. Rowling began writing stories when she was six | years old. She started working on the Harry Potter se- | quence in 1990, when, she says, "the idea ... simply | fell into my head." The first book, *Harry Potter and the* | *Sorcerer's Stone*, was published in the United Kingdom | in 1997 and the United States in 1998. Since then, books | in the Harry Potter series have been honored with many | prizes, including the Anthony Award, the Hugo Award, | the Bram Stoker Award, the Whitbread Children's Book | Award, the Nestlé Smarties Book Prize, and the Brit- | ish Book Awards Children's Book of the Year, as well as | *New York Times* Notable Book, ALA Notable Children's | Book, and ALA Best Book for Young Adults citations. | Ms. Rowling has also been named an Officer of the Order | of the British Empire. | [new paragraph] She lives in Scotland with her family.'; [768] blank; [769] 'ABOUT THE ILLUSTRATOR | [new paragraph] Mary GrandPré has illustrated more than twenty beau- | tiful books, including *Henry and Pawl and the Round* | *Yellow Ball*, cowritten with her husband Tom Casmer; | *Plum*, a collection of poetry by Tony Mitton; *Lucia and* | *the Light*, by Phyllis Root; and the American editions of | all seven Harry Potter novels. Her work has also appeared | in *The New Yorker*, *The Atlantic Monthly*, and *The Wall* | *Street Journal*, and her paintings and pastels have been | shown in galleries across the United States. | [new paragraph] Ms. GrandPré lives in Sarasota, Florida, with her | family.'; [770] '[publisher's device of a lantern, 17 by 12mm] | *This* | *book was art* | *directed by David Saylor.* | *The art for both the jacket and the* | *interior was created using pastels on toned* | *printmaking paper. The text was set in 12-point Adobe* | *Garamond, a typeface based on the sixteenth-century type designs* | *of Claude Garamond, redrawn by Robert Slimbach in 1989. The book was* | *typeset by Brad Walrod and was printed and bound at Quebecor* | *World Fairfield in Fairfield, Pennsylvania. The Managing* | *Editor was Karyn Browne; the Continuity* | *Editor was Cheryl Klein; and the* | *Manufacturing Director* | *was Angela* | *Biola.*'

Paper: wove paper

Running title: 'CHAPTER' and chapter number on verso, recto title comprises chapter title, pp. 1-749 also 'EPILOGUE' on verso, recto title comprises 'NINETEEN YEARS LATER', pp. 753-59. Each running title (excluding pages on which new chapters commence) includes a three-star design to left and right of both running-titles on verso and recto. On pages on which a new chapter commences, the three-star design is omitted.

Illustrations: title-page vignette, together with thirty-seven vignettes at the beginning of each chapter (after chapter and chapter number but before chapter title) and epilogue. In addition to standard typographical changes (including italics, capitals and small capitals) there are other typographical features, comprising:

    p. 16 newspaper headline and illustration

    p. 22 newspaper headline

    p. 134 facsimile of Dumbledore's handwriting

    p. 186 facsimile of Regulus Arcturus Black's handwriting

    p. 207 newspaper headline

Binding: yellow cloth-backed spine with light green boards (with diamond pattern in blind).

On spine: 'ROWLING | [rule] | ['YEAR | 7' within concave square]' (horizontally at head) with 'HARRY POTTER | AND THE DEATHLY HALLOWS' (reading lengthways down spine) and '[publisher's device of a lantern, 19 by 14mm] | ARTHUR A. | LEVINE BOOKS | [rule] | SCHOLASTIC' (horizontally at foot). All in purple.

Upper and lower covers: blank.

All edges trimmed. Binding measurements: 235 by 150mm (covers), 235 by 65mm (spine). The yellow cloth continues onto the covers by 40mm. End-papers: red wove paper.

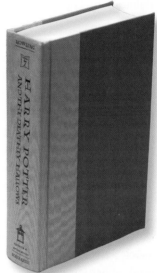

Dust-jacket: uncoated wove paper, 235 by 626mm. A single illustration spans the entire dust-jacket.

On spine: 'ROWLING | [rule] | ['YEAR | 7' within concave square]' (horizontally at head) with 'HARRY POTTER | AND THE DEATHLY HALLOWS' (reading lengthways down spine) and '[publisher's device of a lantern, 19 by 14mm] | ARTHUR A. | LEVINE BOOKS | [rule] | SCHOLASTIC' (horizontally at foot). All embossed in red and all on colour illustration of orange sky and circular bridge-like wall.

On upper cover: 'Harry Potter [hand-drawn lettering] [embossed in red] | AND THE [hand-drawn lettering in brown of illustration] | DEATHLY [hand-drawn lettering in brown of illustration] | HALLOWS [hand-drawn lettering in brown of illustration] | J. K. ROWLING [embossed in red]' (title and author width centred with other lines off-set to the left). All on colour illustration of Harry Potter against an orange sky and circular bridge-like wall.

On lower cover: colour illustration of hands reaching out from cloak sleeves together with barcode with smaller barcode to the right (53499) all in black on orange panel, 24 by 50mm.

On upper inside flap: '$34.99 | [new paragraph] WE NOW PRESENT THE SEVENTH | AND FINAL INSTALLMENT | IN THE EPIC TALE OF | HARRY POTTER. | [new paragraph] *Jacket art by Mary GrandPré © 2007 Warner Bros. | Jacket design by Mary GrandPré and David Saylor*'. All in white on colour illustration of orange sky and curtain.

On lower inside flap: '[publisher's device of a lantern, 14 by 10mm] | ARTHUR A. LEVINE BOOKS | WWW.ARTHURALEVINEBOOKS.COM | An Imprint of | [publisher's book device with 'SCHOLASTIC' in white on red panel, 5 by 44mm] | WWW.SCHOLASTIC.COM | 557 Broadway, New York, NY 10012'. All in cream and all on colour illustration of outline of red eyes peering from hood of a dark robe together with a curtain.

Publication: 21 July 2007 (simultaneous with A14(a), A14(aa), A14(aaa) and A14(aaaaa))

Price: $34.99

Contents:

Harry Potter and the Deathly Hallows

('The two men appeared out of nowhere, a few yards apart in the narrow, moonlit lane.')

Notes:

An email from Arthur A. Levine to Emma Matthewson, dated 23 March 2007, provided some follow-up queries from America and noted 'We will attempt to finish the rest by tomorrow. If that's not possible we'll certainly have it done by Saturday because we MUST have our electronic file ready for our typesetter on Monday'.

During the copy-editing of the text Levine sent 71 questions by email to Matthewson on 18 April 2007 as a result of reading through 'first and second pass galleys'. Levine wrote 'I truly hope it won't feel stressful for Jo. I wish we could convey adequately our feeling that all of these detail questions are merely a result of the absolutely PHENOMENAL level of detail in Harry's saga, and the extraordinary depth of her imagination.' (The author later wrote 'correct' on a copy of the email.)

American and English diction was, once again, an issue of editorial discussion. Correspondence emails in the Bloomsbury files include the note 'if you mean underpants and not trousers here, can we

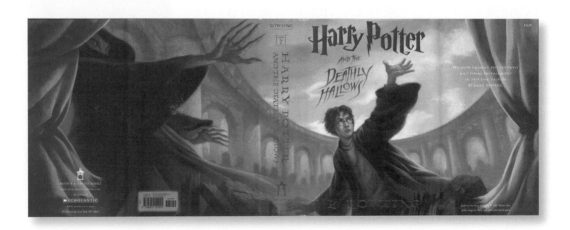

spell out 'underpants' for the U.S., so readers understand fully how embarrassing this is for Ron?' This request was annotated 'OK (U.S. only)'.

Copies have been examined with the following printing plant codes on the imprint page:

Printed in the U.S.A.   12
Printed in the U.S.A.   23
Printed in the U.S.A.   55
Printed in the U.S.A.   58

Each chapter together with the epilogue commences with a drop capital.

Information provided by Nielsen BookData suggests that the publisher also issued a 'library edition' on 1 August 2007. This edition has a different ISBN (ISBN 0-545-02936-8). No copies have been consulted.

The American audiobook version, read by Jim Dale, has a duration of approximately twenty-one and a half hours.

Copies: private collection (PWE)

A14(aaaaa) FIRST AMERICAN EDITION (2007)
(children's artwork series in deluxe hardback)

HARRY POTTER | AND THE DEATHLY HALLOWS | [black and white illustration of an owl in cage with books and wand all by a window, 66 by 52mm] | BY | J. K. ROWLING | ILLUSTRATIONS BY MARY GRANDPRÉ | [publisher's device of a lantern, 12 by 9mm] | ARTHUR A. LEVINE BOOKS | AN IMPRINT OF SCHOLASTIC INC. (All width centred on a diamond pattern background)

Collation: 392 unsigned leaves bound in twenty-five gatherings of sixteen leaves and one gathering of eight leaves with an additional plate leaf inserted between leaves one and two; 227 by 150mm; [I-II] [additional illustration leaf] [III-VI] VII-X [XI-XIV] 1-749 [750-52] 753-59 [760-802]

Page contents: [I] 'HARRY POTTER | AND THE DEATHLY HALLOWS' (all on diamond pattern background); [II] 'ALSO BY J. K. ROWLING | [new paragraph] *Harry Potter and the Sorcerer's Stone* | Year One at Hogwarts | [new paragraph] *Harry Potter and the Chamber of Secrets* | Year Two at Hogwarts | [new paragraph] *Harry Potter and the Prisoner of Azkaban* | Year Three at Hogwarts | [new paragraph] *Harry Potter and the Goblet of Fire* | Year Four at Hogwarts | [new paragraph] *Harry Potter and the Order of the Phoenix* | Year Five at Hogwarts | [new paragraph] *Harry Potter and the Half-Blood Prince* | Year Six at Hogwarts' (with additional leaf inserted on the verso of which is the frontispiece, 188 by 125mm within single ruled border, 190 by 127mm); [III] title-page; [IV] '[device of twelve stars] | Text copyright © 2007 by J. K. Rowling | Illustrations by Mary GrandPré copyright © 2007 by Warner Bros. | HARRY POTTER & all related characters and elements are TM of and © WBEI. | Harry Potter Publishing Rights © J. K. Rowling. | All rights reserved. Published by Arthur A. Levine Books, | an imprint of Scholastic Inc., *Publishers since 1920.* | SCHOLASTIC, the LANTERN LOGO, and associated logos are | trademarks and/or registered trademarks of Scholastic Inc. | [new paragraph] "The Libation Bearers" by Aeschylus, from THE ORESTEIA by Aeschylus, | translated by Robert Fagles, copyright © 1966, 1967, 1975, 1977 by Robert Fagles. | Used by permission of Viking Penguin, a division of Penguin Group (USA) Inc. | "More Fruits of Solitude," reprinted from William Penn, *Fruits of Solitude*, Vol I., | Part 3, the Harvard Classics (New York: P.F. Collier & Son, 1909-14). | [new paragraph] No part of this publication may be reproduced, or stored in a retrieval system, or transmitted | in any form or by any means, electronic, mechanical, photocopying, recording, or otherwise, | without written permission of the publisher. For information regarding permission, write to | Scholastic Inc., Attention: Permissions Department, 557 Broadway, New York, NY 10012. | [new paragraph] Library of Congress Control Number: 2007925449 | [new paragraph] ISBN-13: 978-0-545-02937-7 | ISBN-10: 0-545-02937-6 | [new paragraph] 10 9 8 7 6 5 4 3 2 1   07 08 09 10 11 | Printed in the U.S.A. 23 | Deluxe edition, July 2007 | [new paragraph] [Forest Stewardship Council logo, 4 by 5mm together with © symbol and text 'FSC', together with text 'Recycled | Cert no. SCS-COC-00648 | © 1996 FSC' to the right] | [new paragraph] We try to produce the most beautiful books possible, and we are also extremely concerned | about the impact of our manufacturing process on the forests of the world and the | environment as a whole. Therefore we are pleased that all of the paper in your hands is | certified to the standards of the Forest Stewardship Council (FSC). The text is made | from 100% post-consumer waste fiber. The jacket contains 30% post-consumer waste | fiber and was manufactured using Green-e certified wind-generated electricity.'; [V] 'THE | DEDICATION | OF THIS BOOK | IS SPLIT | SEVEN WAYS: | TO NEIL, | TO JESSICA, | TO DAVID, | TO KENZIE, | TO DI, | TO ANNE, | AND TO YOU, | IF YOU HAVE | STUCK | WITH HARRY | UNTIL THE | VERY | END.'; [VI] blank; VII-X 'CONTENTS' (thirty-six chapters, one epilogue and illustration showcase listed with titles and page references); [XI] three stanzas from 'Aeschylus, *The Libation Bearers*' and one paragraph from 'William Penn, *More Fruits of Solitude*'; [XII] blank; [XIII] half-title: 'HARRY POTTER | AND THE DEATHLY HALLOWS' (all on diamond pattern background); [XIV] blank; 1-749 text; [750] blank; [751] divisional title: 'NINETEEN YEARS LATER' (all on diamond pattern background); [752] blank; 753-759 text; [760] blank; [761] 'ILLUSTRATION SHOWCASE' (all on diamond pattern background); [762-800] chapter numbers, illustrations and captions; [801] 'ABOUT THE AUTHOR | [new paragraph] J. K. Rowling began writing stories when she was six years old. | She started working on the Harry Potter sequence in 1990, | when, she says, "the idea … simply fell into my head." The | first book, *Harry Potter and the Sorcerer's Stone*, was published | in the United Kingdom in 1997 and the United States in 1998. | Since then, books in the Harry Potter series have been honored | with many prizes, including the Anthony Award, the Hugo | Award, the Bram Stoker Award, the Whitbread Children's | Book

Award, the Nestlé Smarties Book Prize, and the British | Book Awards Children's Book of the Year, as well as *New York* | *Times* Notable Book, ALA Notable Children's Book, and ALA | Best Book for Young Adults citations. Ms. Rowling has also | been named an Officer of the Order of the British Empire. | [new paragraph] She lives in Scotland with her family. | [new paragraph] ABOUT THE ILLUSTRATOR | [new paragraph] Mary GrandPré has illustrated more than twenty beauty- | ful books, including *Henry and Pawl and the Round Yellow* | *Ball*, cowritten with her husband Tom Casmer; *Plum*, a col- | lection of poetry by Tony Mitton; *Lucia and the Light*, by | Phyllis Root; and the American editions of all seven Harry | Potter novels. Her work has also appeared in *The New Yorker*, | *The Atlantic Monthly*, and *The Wall Street Journal*, and her | paintings and pastels have been shown in galleries across the | United States. | [new paragraph] Ms. GrandPré lives in Sarasota, Florida, with her family.'; [802] '[publisher's device of a lantern, 17 by 12mm] | *This Deluxe* | *Edition was art* | *directed and designed by* | *David Saylor. Mary Grandpré's* | *artwork for the slipcase, the jacket, the* | *endpapers, the frontispiece, and the interior was created* | *using pastels on toned printmaking paper. The text was set in* | *12-point Adobe Garamond, a typeface based on the sixteenth-century* | *type designs of Claude Garamond, redrawn by Robert Slimbach in 1989. The book* | *was typeset by Brad Walrod and was printed and bound at RR Donnelley in* | *Crawfordsville, Indiana. The case is wrapped in Sierra cloth, an acid-* | *free rayon-based material manufactured in Europe exclusively* | *for Ecological Fibers. The Managing Editor was Karyn* | *Browne; the Continuity Editor was Cheryl* | *Klein; and the Manufacturing* | *Director was Angela Biola.* | [device of six stars]'

Paper: wove paper

Running title: 'CHAPTER' and chapter number on verso, recto title comprises chapter title, pp. 1-749 also 'EPILOGUE' on verso, recto title comprises 'NINETEEN YEARS LATER', pp. 753-59. Each running title (excluding pages on which new chapters commence) includes a three-star design to left and right of both running-titles on verso and recto. On pages on which a new chapter commences, the three-star design is omitted.

Illustrations: colour frontispiece, title-page vignette, together with thirty-seven vignettes at the beginning of each chapter (after chapter and chapter number but before chapter title) and epilogue. These vignettes are repeated as larger illustrations within the 'Illustration Showcase'. In addition to standard typographical changes (including italics, capitals and small capitals) there are other typographical features, comprising:

   p. 16 newspaper headline and illustration
   p. 22 newspaper headline
   p. 134 facsimile of Dumbledore's handwriting
   p. 186 facsimile of Regulus Arcturus Black's handwriting
   p. 207 newspaper headline
   p. 217 newspaper headline
   p. 225 newspaper headline
   p. 249 title of pamphlet
   p. 325 tombstone engraving
   p. 328 tombstone engraving

p. 333 text of magical graffiti

p. 353 photograph caption

p. 398 text of hand-painted signs

p. 481 stone engraving

p. 689 facsimile of Lily Potter's Christian name signature

Binding: black cloth with diamond pattern in blind on upper and lower covers.

On spine: 'J. K. | ROWLING | [double rule, 48mm] | Harry Potter [hand-drawn lettering] | AND THE | DEATHLY | HALLOWS | [double rule, 48mm] | YEAR SEVEN | [double rule, 48mm] | [eighteen stars] | [double rule, 48mm] | [publisher's device of a lantern, 19 by 14mm] | ARTHUR A. | LEVINE BOOKS | [double rule, 48mm] | SCHOLASTIC' (all width centred). All in red.

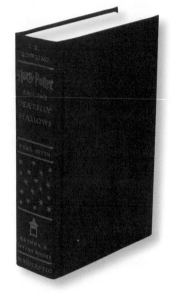

Upper and lower covers: blank.

All edges trimmed. Red and yellow sewn bands at head and foot of spine. Binding measurements: 235 by 150mm (covers), 235 by 66mm (spine). End-papers: wove paper with colour illustration of Harry Potter against an orange sky with curtain to the right on front endpapers, and colour illustration of hands reaching out from cloak sleeves with curtain to the left on rear endpapers.

Dust-jacket: uncoated wove paper, 234 by 627mm. A single illustration spans the entire dust-jacket comprising a colour illustration of Harry Potter, Hermione Granger and Ron Weasley riding on the back of an airborne dragon.

On lower inside flap: '*Illustration by Mary GrandPré © 2007 Warner Bros.*' All in white.

Slipcase: card slipcase covered in gold paper.

On spine: 'J. K. | ROWLING | [double rule, 48mm] | Harry Potter [hand-drawn lettering] | AND THE | DEATHLY | HALLOWS | [double rule, 48mm] | YEAR SEVEN | [double rule, 48mm] | [eighteen stars] | [double rule, 48mm] | [publisher's device of a lantern, 19 by 14mm] | ARTHUR A. | LEVINE BOOKS | [double rule, 48mm] | SCHOLASTIC' (all width centred). All in metallic red.

On upper side: colour illustration of hooded figure with curtain to the left, all within single rule in metallic red, 222 by 137mm.

On lower side: 'Harry Potter [hand-drawn lettering] [in metallic red] | AND THE [hand-drawn lettering in brown of illustration] | DEATHLY [hand-drawn lettering in brown of illustration] | HALLOWS [hand-drawn lettering in brown of illustration]'. All on illustration of Harry Potter against an orange sky and all within single rule in metallic red, 222 by 137mm.

On top edge: author's signature 'JK Rowling' in metallic red.

On lower edge: '*Illustration by Mary GrandPré © 2007 Warner Bros.*' All in white.

Publication: 21 July 2007 (simultaneous with A14(a), A14(aa), A14(aaa) and A14(aaaa))

Price: $65

Contents:
Harry Potter and the Deathly Hallows
('The two men appeared out of nowhere, a few yards apart in the narrow, moonlit lane.')

Notes:
The press widely reported that the edition comprised 100,000 copies.

Each chapter together with the epilogue commences with a drop capital.

Copies: private collection (PWE)

A14(b) ENGLISH CHILDREN'S EDITION (2008)
(children's artwork series in paperback)

HARRY | POTTER | *and the Deathly Hallows* | [illustration of Hogwarts crest with legend 'DRAGO DORMIENS NUNQUAM TITILLANDUS' on banner, 66 by 81mm] | J. K. ROWLING |

[publisher's device of a dog, 11 by 19mm] | BLOOMSBURY (Lines 1 and 2 justified on left and right margins, and all width centred)

Collation: 304 unsigned leaves bound in indeterminate gatherings; 198 by 127mm; [1-9] 10-18 [19] 20-30 [31] 32-41 [42] 43-57 [58] 59-75 [76] 77-94 [95] 96-114 [115] 116-33 [134] 135-45 [146] 147-65 [166] 167-83 [184] 185-202 [203] 204-220 [221] 222-33 [234] 235-54 [255] 256-69 [270] 271-85 [286] 287-95 [296] 297-314 [315] 316-28 [329] 330-43 [344] 345-61 [362] 363-85 [386] 387-405 [406] 407-418 [419] 420-38 [439] 440-46 [447] 448-59 [460] 461-73 [474] 475-88 [489] 490-512 [513] 514-28 [529] 530-53 [554] 555-64 [565] 566-79 [580] 581-600 [601-603] 604-607 [608]

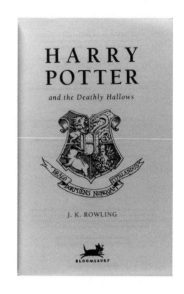

Page contents: [1] half-title: 'HARRY | POTTER | *and the Deathly Hallows* | [illustration of Hogwarts crest with legend 'DRAGO DORMIENS NUNQUAM TITILLANDUS' on banner, 47 by 58mm]'; [2] *'Titles available in the Harry Potter series | (in reading order):* | Harry Potter and the Philosopher's Stone | Harry Potter and the Chamber of Secrets | Harry Potter and the Prisoner of Azkaban | Harry Potter and the Goblet of Fire | Harry Potter and the Order of the Phoenix | Harry Potter and the Half-Blood Prince | Harry Potter and the Deathly Hallows | [new paragraph] *Titles available in the Harry Potter series | (in Latin):* | Harry Potter and the Philosopher's Stone | Harry Potter and the Chamber of Secrets | *(in Welsh, Ancient Greek and Irish):* | Harry Potter and the Philosopher's Stone'; [3] title-page; [4] 'All rights reserved; no part of this publication may be reproduced or | transmitted by any means, electronic, mechanical, photocopying | or otherwise, without the prior permission of the publisher | [new paragraph] First published in Great Britain in 2007 by Bloomsbury Publishing Plc | 36 Soho Square, London, W1D 3QY | [new paragraph] This paperback edition first published in 2008 | [new paragraph] Copyright © J. K. Rowling 2007 | Cover illustrations by Jason Cockcroft copyright © Bloomsbury Publishing Plc 2007 | Harry Potter, names, characters and related indicia are | copyright and trademark Warner Bros., 2000™ | [new paragraph] J. K. Rowling has asserted her moral rights | [new paragraph] The extract from *The Libation Bearers* is taken from the Penguin Classics edition | of *The Oresteia*, translated by Robert Fagles, copyright © Robert Fagles, 1966, | 1967, 1975, 1977 | [new paragraph] The extract from *More Fruits of Solitude* is taken from *More Fruits of Solitude* | by William Penn, first included in Everyman's Library, 1915 | [new paragraph] A CIP catalogue record of this book is available from the British Library | [new paragraph] ISBN 978 0 7475 9583 0 | [new paragraph] The pages of this book are printed on 100% Ancient-Forest Friendly paper | [Forest Stewardship Council logo, 7 by 9mm together with © symbol and text: 'FSC | Mixed Sources | Product group from well-managed | forests and other controlled sources | [new paragraph] Cert no. SGS-COC-2061 | www fsc org | © 1996 Forest Stewardship Council'] | The papers on which this book is printed are manufactured from a composition | of © 1996 Forest

Stewardship Council A.C. (FSC) approved and post-consumer | waste recycled materials. The FSC promotes environmentally appropriate, socially | beneficial and economically viable management of the world's forests. | [new paragraph] Typeset by RefineCatch Limited, Bungay, Suffolk | Printed in Great Britain by Clays Ltd, St Ives plc | [new paragraph] 1 3 5 7 9 10 8 6 4 2 | [new paragraph] www.bloomsbury.com/harrypotter'; [5] 'The | dedication | of this book | is split | seven ways: | to Neil, | to Jessica, | to David, | to Kenzie, | to Di, | to Anne, | and to you, | if you have | stuck | with Harry | until the | very | end.'; [6] blank; [7] three stanzas from 'Aeschylus, *The Libation Bearers*' and one paragraph from 'William Penn, *More Fruits of Solitude*'; [8] blank; [9]-600 text; [601] '*Nineteen Years Later*'; [602] blank; [603]-607 text; [608] blank

Paper: wove paper

Running title: 'HARRY POTTER' (24mm) on verso, recto title comprises chapter title, pp. 10-607 (excluding pages on which new chapters commence)

Binding: pictorial wrappers.

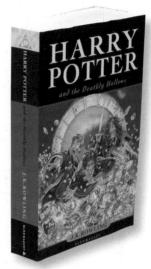

On spine: '[light blue / grey illustration of a triangular eye symbol on light blue / grey panel, 31 by 17mm] HARRY POTTER [in white on purple panel, 31 by 45mm] *and the Deathly Hallows* [in black] J.K.ROWLING' [in white, both title conclusion and author on red panel, 31 by 103mm] BLOOMSBURY [publisher's device of the head of a dog, 4 by 3mm] [both in white on black panel, 31 by 31mm]' (reading lengthways down spine).

On upper wrapper: 'HARRY | POTTER | *and the Deathly Hallows* [lines 1 and 2 in white, line 3 in grey, all on black panel, 62 by 128mm] | [red rule, 128mm] | [colour illustration of Harry Potter, Ron Weasley and Hermione Granger within a cave-like opening on top of a sea of golden coins and other treasures with Griphook the goblin clutching Harry's back and a sword, 123 by 128mm] | [red rule, 128mm intersected by grey panel with 'J.K.ROWLING' in black] | BLOOMSBURY [in grey on black panel, 10 by 128mm]' (all width centred).

On lower wrapper: 'Harry Potter is preparing to leave the Dursleys and Privet Drive for | the last time. But the future that awaits him is full of danger, not | only for him, but for anyone close to him – and Harry has already lost | so much. Only by destroying Voldemort's remaining Horcruxes can | Harry free himself and overcome the Dark Lord's forces of evil. | [new paragraph] In this dramatic conclusion to the Harry Potter series, Harry must | leave his most loyal friends behind, and in a final perilous journey | find the strength and the will to face his terrifying destiny: a deadly | confrontation that is his alone to fight. | [new paragraph] 'A nail-biting rollercoaster. A finale that ticks every box. If Harry's journey | had to come to an end, *Deathly Hallows* is the best possible way.' *Heat* | [new paragraph] 'The best thing about this book is that it finally answers the | questions we have been longing to know.' *Daily Mirror* | [new paragraph] 'The final chapter in the final book of one of the greatest | literary adventures of modern times.' *Sunday Telegraph* | [new paragraph] 'Rowling has woven together clues, hints and characters | from previous books into a prodigiously rewarding, | suspenseful conclusion.' | *Guardian* | [new paragraph] [barcode in black on white panel, 21 by 40mm together with '[Forest Stewardship Council logo, 6 by 7mm together with © symbol and text: 'FSC | Mixed Sources | Product group from well-managed | forests and other controlled sources | [new paragraph] Cert no. SGS-COC-2061 | www.fsc.org | © 1996 Forest Stewardship Council'] | [publisher's device of a dog, 5 by 9mm] | BLOOMSBURY' in black on right side of panel and '£8.99' further to right and 'http://www.bloomsbury.com/harrypotter' below panel, in black on red panel, 5 by 40mm]'. Reading lengthways down right side next to spine 'Cover illustrations by Jason Cockcroft | Author photograph © Bill de la HEY'. All in white with the exception of the illustration and photography credit which are in black, and all on colour illustration of Hogwarts castle and clouds.

On inside upper wrapper: black and white photograph of J.K. Rowling standing against bookshelves.

On inside lower wrapper: 'Titles available in the | HARRY POTTER series | [colour illustrations in three columns of seven book designs] | Audio editions read by Stephen Fry | and co-published by HNP also available'. All in black.

All edges trimmed. Binding measurements: 198 by 127mm (wrappers), 198 by 31mm (spine).

Publication: 10 July 2008 (simultaneous with A14(bb)) in an edition of 314,605 copies (confirmed by Bloomsbury)

Price: £8.99

Contents:

Harry Potter and the Deathly Hallows

('The two men appeared out of nowhere, a few yards apart in the narrow, moonlit lane.')

Notes:

Note that the Forest Stewardship Council text on page [4] excludes dots in the web address. These are present on the lower cover.

Copies: private collection (KTh)

A14(bb)   ENGLISH ADULT EDITION   (2008)
(Michael Wildsmith photography adult artwork series in paperback)

Harry Potter and the | Deathly Hallows | J. K. Rowling | BLOOMSBURY (All width centred)

Collation: 416 unsigned leaves bound by the 'perfect binding' process; 177 by 111mm; [1-9] 10-22 [23] 24-38 [39] 40-52 [53] 54-74 [75] 76-99 [100] 101-126 [127] 128-54 [155] 156-80 [181] 182-97 [198] 199-224 [225] 226-47 [248] 249-73 [274] 275-98 [299] 300-315 [316] 317-44 [345] 346-65 [366] 367-87 [388] 389-401 [402] 403-428 [429] 430-47 [448] 449-67 [468] 469-91 [492] 493-524 [525] 526-52 [553]

554-70 [571] 572-97 [598] 599-608 [609] 610-26 [627] 628-45 [646] 647-66 [667] 668-99 [700] 701-721 [722] 723-56 [757] 758-72 [773] 774-92 [793] 794-821 [822-25] 826-31 [832]

Page contents: [1] half-title: 'Harry Potter and the | Deathly Hallows'; [2] *Titles available in the Harry Potter series | (in reading order):* | Harry Potter and the Philosopher's Stone | Harry Potter and the Chamber of Secrets | Harry Potter and the Prisoner of Azkaban | Harry Potter and the Goblet of Fire | Harry Potter and the Order of the Phoenix | Harry Potter and the Half-Blood Prince | Harry Potter and the Deathly Hallows | [new paragraph] *Titles available in the Harry Potter series | (in Latin):* | Harry Potter and the Philosopher's Stone | Harry Potter and the Chamber of Secrets | *(in Welsh, Ancient Greek and Irish):* | Harry Potter and the Philosopher's Stone'; [3] title-page; [4] 'All rights reserved; no part of this publication may be reproduced or | transmitted by any means, electronic, mechanical, photocopying | or otherwise, without the prior permission of the publisher | [new paragraph] First published in Great Britain in 2007 by Bloomsbury Publishing Plc | 36 Soho Square, London, W1D 3QY | [new paragraph] This paperback edition first published in 2008 | [new paragraph] Copyright © J. K. Rowling 2007 | Front cover and spine photographs copyright © Michael Wildsmith, 2007 | Harry Potter, names, characters and related indicia are | copyright and trademark Warner Bros., 2000™ | [new paragraph] J. K. Rowling has asserted her moral rights | [new paragraph] The extract from *The Libation Bearers* is taken from the Penguin Classics | edition of *The Oresteia*, translated by Robert Fagles, copyright | © Robert Fagles, 1966, 1967, 1975, 1977 | [new paragraph] The extract from *More Fruits of Solitude* is taken from *More Fruits of | Solitude* by William Penn, first included in Everyman's Library, 1915 | [new paragraph] A CIP catalogue record of this book is available from the British Library | [new paragraph] ISBN 978 0 7475 9582 3 | [new paragraph] The pages of this book are printed on 100% Ancient-Forest Friendly paper | [Forest Stewardship Council logo, 7 by 8mm together with © symbol and text: 'FSC | Mixed Sources | Product group from well-managed | forests and other controlled sources | [new paragraph] Cert no. SGS-COC-2061 | www fsc org | © 1996 Forest Stewardship Council'] | The papers on which this book is printed are manufactured from a | composition of © 1996 Forest Stewardship Council A.C. (FSC) approved | and post-consumer waste recycled materials. The FSC promotes | environmentally appropriate, socially beneficial and economically viable | management of the world's forests. | [new paragraph] Typeset by RefineCatch Limited, Bungay, Suffolk | Printed in Great Britain by Clays Ltd, St Ives plc | [new paragraph] 1 3 5 7 9 10 8 6 4 2 | [new paragraph] www.bloomsbury.com/harrypotter'; [5] 'The | dedication | of this book | is split | seven ways: | to Neil, | to Jessica, | to David, | to Kenzie, | to Di, | to Anne, | and to you, | if you have | stuck | with Harry | until the | very | end.'; [6] blank; [7] three stanzas from 'Aeschylus, *The Libation Bearers*' and one paragraph from 'William Penn, *More Fruits of Solitude*'; [8] blank; [9]-821 text; [822] blank; [823] '*Nineteen Years Later*'; [824] blank; [825]-31 text; [832] blank

Paper: wove paper

Running title: 'HARRY POTTER' (24mm) on verso, recto title comprises chapter title, pp. 10-821 and pp. 826-31 (excluding pages on which new chapters commence)

Binding: pictorial wrappers.
   On spine: 'HARRY POTTER AND THE [top portion of colour photograph of a golden medallion encrusted with green gems, on a slate, 42 by 18mm] | J.K. ROWLING [publisher's device of a figure

with a bow, 11 by 11mm] | DEATHLY HALLOWS' (reading lengthways down spine). All in white with the exception of last line which is in gilt, and all on black.

On upper wrapper: 'HARRY POTTER AND THE [in white] | DEATHLY [embossed in gilt] | HALLOWS [embossed in gilt] | J. K. ROWLING [in white] | BLOOMSBURY [in white]' (all width centred). All on colour photograph of a golden medallion encrusted with green gems, on a slate.

On lower wrapper: '[portion of colour photograph of a golden medallion encrusted with green gems, on a slate, all within single white border, 22 by 22mm] 'A nail-biting rollercoaster. A finale that | ticks every box. If Harry's journey had to | come to an end, *Deathly Hallows* is the best | possible way' | *Heat* | [new paragraph] Harry Potter is preparing to leave the Dursleys and Privet | Drive for the last time. But the future that awaits him is full | of danger, not only for him, but for anyone close to him | – and Harry has already lost so much. Only by destroying | Voldemort's remaining Horcruxes can Harry free himself | and overcome the Dark Lord's forces of evil. | [new paragraph] In this dramatic conclusion to the Harry Potter series, | Harry must leave his most loyal friends behind and in a | final perilous journey finds the strength and the will to face | his terrifying destiny: a deadly confrontation that is his | alone to fight. | [new paragraph] 'The best thing about this book is that it finally | answers the questions we have been longing to know' | *Daily Mirror* | [new paragraph] 'The final chapter in the final book of one of the | greatest literary adventures of modern times' | *Sunday Telegraph* | [new paragraph] 'Rowling has woven together clues, hints and characters | from previous books into a prodigiously rewarding, | suspenseful conclusion' *Guardian* | [new paragraph] 'You engage better for reading it' *Observer* | [new paragraph] [barcode in black on white panel, 24 by 39mm together with 'bloomsbury[in black]pbk[in white]s[in black] | £8.99 [in black] | www.bloomsbury.com [in black]' and all on red panel, 25 by 75mm] [Forest Stewardship Council logo, 7 by 8mm together with © symbol and text: 'FSC | Mixed Sources | Product group from well-managed | forests and other controlled sources | [new paragraph] Cert no. SGS-COC-2061 | www.fsc.org | © 1996 Forest Stewardship Council'] | [new paragraph] Cover image: Michael Wildsmith Design: William Webb Author photograph: © Bill de la HEY'. All in white on black with colour photograph to the left of lines 1-5.

On inside upper wrapper: black and white photograph of J.K. Rowling standing against bookshelves.

On inside lower wrapper: 'Titles available in the | HARRY POTTER series | [colour illustrations in three columns of seven book designs] | Audio editions read by Stephen Fry | and co-published by HNP | also available'. All in white on black.

All edges trimmed. Binding measurements: 177 by 111mm (wrappers), 177 by 42mm (spine).

Publication: 10 July 2008 (simultaneous with A14(b)) in an edition of 180,200 copies (confirmed by Bloomsbury)

Price: £8.99

Contents:
Harry Potter and the Deathly Hallows
('The two men appeared out of nowhere, a few yards apart in the narrow, moonlit lane.')

Notes:
Note that the Forest Stewardship Council text on page [4] excludes dots in the web address. These are present on the lower wrapper.

Reprints include:
3 5 7 9 10 8 6 4

A14(c)   AMERICAN CHILDREN'S EDITION   (2009)
(children's artwork series in paperback)

HARRY POTTER | AND THE DEATHLY HALLOWS | [black and white illustration of an owl in cage with books and wand all by a window, 66 by 52mm] | BY | J. K. ROWLING | ILLUSTRATIONS BY MARY GRANDPRÉ | [publisher's device of a lantern, 12 by 9mm] | ARTHUR A. LEVINE BOOKS | AN IMPRINT OF SCHOLASTIC INC. (All width centred on a diamond pattern background)

Collation: 392 unsigned leaves bound in indeterminate gatherings; 194 by 132mm; [I-XII] XIII-XVI [XVII-XX] 1-749 [750-52] 753-59 [760-64]

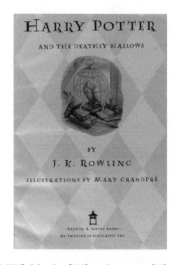

Page contents: [I-III] 'PRAISE FOR J. K. ROWLING'S | HARRY POTTER | AND THE DEATHLY HALLOWS | [device of nine stars] | [10 reviews and a listing of 9 statements]'; [IV] blank; [V] half-title: 'HARRY POTTER | AND THE DEATHLY HALLOWS' (all on diamond pattern background); [VI] blank; [VII] 'ALSO BY J. K. ROWLING | [new paragraph] *Harry Potter and the Sorcerer's Stone* | Year One at Hogwarts | [new paragraph] *Harry Potter and the Chamber of Secrets* | Year Two at Hogwarts | [new paragraph] *Harry Potter and the Prisoner of Azkaban* | Year Three at Hogwarts | [new paragraph] | *Harry Potter and the Goblet of Fire* | Year Four at Hogwarts | [new paragraph] *Harry Potter and the Order of the Phoenix* | Year Five at Hogwarts | [new paragraph] *Harry Potter and the Half-Blood Prince* | Year Six at Hogwarts'; [VIII] blank; [IX] title-page; [X] '[device of twelve stars] | Text © 2007 by J. K. Rowling | Illustrations by Mary GrandPré © 2007 by Warner Bros. | HARRY POTTER & all related characters and elements are TM of and © WBEI. | Harry Potter Publishing Rights © J. K. Rowling. | All rights reserved. Published by Scholastic Inc. | SCHOLASTIC, the LANTERN LOGO, and associated logos are | trademarks and/or registered trademarks of Scholastic Inc. | [new paragraph] "The Libation Bearers" by Aeschylus, from THE ORESTEIA by Aeschylus, | translated by Robert Fagles, copyright © 1966, 1967, 1975, 1977 by Robert Fagles. | Used by permission of Viking Penguin, a division of Penguin Group (USA) Inc. | "More Fruits of Solitude," reprinted from William Penn, *Fruits of Solitude*, | Vol I., the Harvard Classics (New York: P.F. Collier & Son, 1909). | [new paragraph] If you purchased this book without a cover, you should be aware that this book is stolen property. | It was reported as "unsold and destroyed" to the publisher, and neither the author nor | the publisher has received any payment for this "stripped book." | [new paragraph] No part of this publication may be reproduced, stored in a retrieval system, or transmitted | in any form or by any means, electronic, mechanical, photocopying, recording, or otherwise, | without written permission of the publisher. | For information regarding permission, write | to Scholastic Inc., Attention: Permissions Department, 557 Broadway, New York, NY 10012. | [new paragraph] [publisher's device of a lantern, 6 by 4mm] | Arthur A. Levine Books hardcover edition | art directed by David Saylor, | published by Arthur A. Levine Books, | an imprint of Scholastic Inc., | July 2007 | [new paragraph] ISBN-13: 978-0-545-13970-0 | ISBN-10: 0-545-13970-8 | [new paragraph] Library of Congress Control Number: 2007925449 | [new paragraph] 10 9 8 7 6 5 4 3 2 1   09 10 11 12 13/0 | [new paragraph] Printed in the U.S.A. 40 | [new paragraph] First Scholastic trade paperback printing, July 2009'; [XI] 'THE | DEDICATION | OF THIS BOOK | IS SPLIT | SEVEN WAYS: | TO NEIL, | TO JESSICA, | TO DAVID, | TO KENZIE, | TO DI, | TO ANNE, | AND TO YOU, | IF YOU HAVE | STUCK | WITH HARRY | UNTIL THE | VERY | END.'; [XII] blank; XIII-XVI 'CONTENTS' (thirty-six chapters and one epilogue listed with titles and page references); [XVII] three stanzas from 'Aeschylus, *The Libation Bearers*' and one paragraph from 'William Penn, *More Fruits of Solitude*'; [XVIII] blank; [XIX] half-title: 'HARRY POTTER | AND THE DEATHLY HALLOWS' (all on diamond pattern background); [XX] blank; 1-749 text; [750] blank; [751] divisional title: 'NINETEEN YEARS LATER' (all on diamond pattern background); [752] blank; 753-759 text; [760] blank; [761] '[black and white photograph of J.K. Rowling seated by a window, all within single black ruled border, 87 by 62mm, and credited 'JP MASCLET' lower right] | J. K. ROWLING began writing stories when she was | six years old. She started working on the Harry Potter sequence | in 1990, when, she says, "the idea … simply fell into my | head." The first book, *Harry Potter and the Sorcerer's Stone*, was | published in the United Kingdom in 1997 and the United | States in 1998. Since then, books in the Harry Potter series | have been honored with many prizes, including the Anthony | Award, the Hugo Award, the Bram Stoker Award, the | Whitbread Children's Book Award, the Nestlé Smarties Book | Prize, and the British Book Awards Children's Book of the | Year, as well as *New York Times* Notable Book, ALA Notable | Children's Book, and ALA Best Book for Young Adults | citations. Ms. Rowling has also been named an Officer of the | Order of the British Empire. | [new paragraph] She lives in Scotland with her family.'; [762] blank; [763] 'MARY GRANDPRÉ has illustrated more than | twenty beautiful books, including *Henry and Pawl and the* | *Round Yellow Ball*, cowritten with her husband Tom Casmer; | *Plum*, a collection of poetry by Tony Mitton; *Lucia and | the Light*, by Phyllis Root; and the American editions of all | seven Harry Potter novels. Her work has also appeared in | *The New Yorker, The Atlantic Monthly*, and *The Wall Street* | *Journal*, and her paintings and pastels have been shown in | galleries across the United States. | [new paragraph] Ms. GrandPré lives in Sarasota, Florida, with her family.'; [764] publisher's advertisement: 'Harry Potter [hand-drawn lettering] | READ ALL OF HARRY'S | MAGICAL ADVENTURES!'

Paper: wove paper

Running title: 'CHAPTER' and chapter number on verso, recto title comprises chapter title, pp. 1-749 also 'EPILOGUE' on verso, recto title comprises 'NINETEEN YEARS LATER', pp. 753-59.

Each running title (excluding pages on which new chapters commence) includes a three-star design to left and right of both running-titles on verso and recto. On pages on which a new chapter commences, the three-star design is omitted.

Illustrations: title-page vignette, together with thirty-seven vignettes at the beginning of each chapter (after chapter and chapter number but before chapter title) and epilogue. In addition to standard typographical changes (including italics, capitals and small capitals) there are other typographical features, comprising:

    p. 16 newspaper headline and illustration

    p. 22 newspaper headline

    p. 134 facsimile of Dumbledore's handwriting

    p. 186 facsimile of Regulus Arcturus Black's handwriting

    p. 207 newspaper headline

    p. 217 newspaper headline

    p. 225 newspaper headline

    p. 249 title of pamphlet

    p. 325 tombstone engraving

    p. 328 tombstone engraving

    p. 333 text of magical graffiti

    p. 353 photograph caption

    p. 398 text of hand-painted signs

    p. 481 stone engraving

    p. 689 facsimile of Lily Potter's Christian name signature

Binding: pictorial wrappers.

    On spine: 'ROWLING | [rule] | ['YEAR | 7' within concave square] [in white]' (horizontally at head) with 'HARRY POTTER | AND THE DEATHLY HALLOWS' (reading lengthways down spine) and '[publisher's book device] | [rule] | S' in white on red panel, 14 by 6mm (horizontally at foot). All in grey and dark yellow on a dark and light orange diamond pattern background.

    On upper wrapper: 'THE BREATHTAKING SERIES FINALE [in white] | Harry Potter [hand-drawn lettering] [embossed in gilt] | AND THE [hand-drawn lettering in brown of illustration] | DEATHLY [hand-drawn lettering in brown of illustration] | HALLOWS [hand-drawn lettering in brown of illustration] | J. K. ROWLING [embossed in gilt]' (all width centred). All on colour illustration of Harry Potter against an orange sky and circular bridge-like wall. In centre at foot: '[publisher's book device] SCHOLASTIC' in white on red panel, 5 by 45mm.

    On lower wrapper: 'WE NOW PRESENT THE SEVENTH AND FINAL | INSTALLMENT IN THE EPIC TALE OF

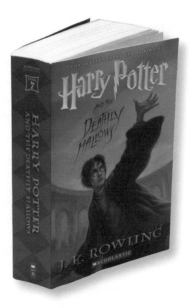

HARRY POTTER. | [rule of four-sided devices, 106mm] | [new paragraph] "Writing a decent sequel to a good novel is hard.... Writing six of them is | almost unheard of. Each of the 'Harry Potters' deserves to stand on the shelf | with its mates, and the last one more than fulfils the promise of the first six." | — Malcolm Jones, *Newsweek* | [new paragraph] "It's pure pleasure to watch Rowling showing off her chops, managing the | tension and throttling the pace up and down, and it's also a precious gift to | the reader ... As a farewell to the series, *Deathly Hallows* is everything fans | of Harry Potter could hope for." — Lev Grossman, *Time* | [new paragraph] "Author J. K. Rowling gives her readers, and her characters, precisely what they | crave — excitement, insight, closure and catharsis galore. Weddings, births, | dragons, bank robberies, stolen kisses, stolen swords, broken tombs, exploding | horns, long-lost siblings and of course all the magic, loyalty, treachery and wizard | battles 759 pages can hold...." — Mary McNamara, *The Los Angeles Times* | [new paragraph] "There's a lot of meat on the bones of these books — good writing, honest | feeling, a sweet but uncompromising view of human nature ... and hard | reality.... The fact that Harry attracted adults as well as children has | never surprised me. J. K. Rowling has set the standard: It's a high one, and | God bless her for it." — Stephen King, *Entertainment Weekly* | [new paragraph] "Exhilarating ... Worth the wait? It is indeed." — Sue Corbett, *People* | [new paragraph] [publisher's book device with 'SCHOLASTIC' in white on red panel, 5 by 45mm] | www.scholastic.com/harrypotter | COVER ART BY MARY GRANDPRÉ'. All in white on dark orange, with barcode with smaller barcode (51499) together with 'S' within triangle and '$14.99 US', all in black on white panel, 22 by 61mm, to the left of final three lines.

On inside upper wrapper: barcode with smaller barcode (51499) together with 'S' within triangle below, all in black.

On inside lower wrapper: publisher's advertisement: "'Fans can't get a copy fast enough! | *Beedle* has a direct connection to... | *Harry Potter and the Deathly Hallows*." | — New York *Daily News...*' (advert for *The Tales of Beedle the Bard*).

All edges trimmed. Binding measurements: 194 by 132mm (wrappers), 194 by 39mm (spine).

Publication: 7 July 2009

Price: $14.99

Contents:
Harry Potter and the Deathly Hallows
('The two men appeared out of nowhere, a few yards apart in the narrow, moonlit lane.')

Notes:
As with A12(e), the two half-titles from the first American edition are retained for this paperback edition.

This is the only book in the American children's edition (children's artwork series in paperback) to replace the publisher's name on the spine with the publisher's device.

On 7 July 2009, from 10 am to 6 pm, Scholastic's flagship store at 557 Broadway hosted a paperback release party.

Each chapter together with the epilogue commences with a drop capital.

Copies: private collection (PWE)

Reprints include:
20 19 18 17 16 15 14 13 12   11 12 13 0   Printed in the U.S.A. 40

A14(d)   AMERICAN BOOK CLUB EDITION   [2009]
(children's artwork series in hardback)

Publication: between July and December 2009 (see notes)

Notes:
Given that the true American first and the book club editions share a single ISBN, the Blair Partnership noted that book club editions could only be dated to within a half-year period end in their files. This edition was, therefore, published within the period July to December 2006. The Blair Partnership Royalties Manager noted that the American book club editions did not have 'a set price'.

Copies: no copies have been consulted

A14(e)   ENGLISH 'CELEBRATORY' EDITION   (2010)
(children's artwork series in paperback)

HARRY | POTTER | *and the Deathly Hallows* | [illustration of Hogwarts crest with legend 'DRAGO DORMIENS NUNQUAM TITILLANDUS' on banner, 66 by 81mm] | J. K. ROWLING | [publisher's device of a dog, 9 by 15mm] | BLOOMSBURY | LONDON BERLIN NEW YORK SYDNEY (Lines 1 and 2 justified on left and right margins, and all width centred)

Collation: 304 unsigned leaves bound in indeterminate gatherings; 197 by 128mm; [1-9] 10-18 [19] 20-30 [31] 32-41 [42] 43-57 [58] 59-75 [76] 77-94 [95] 96-114 [115] 116-33 [134] 135-45 [146] 147-65 [166] 167-83 [184] 185-202 [203] 204-220 [221] 222-33 [234] 235-54 [255] 256-69 [270] 271-85 [286] 287-95 [296] 297-314 [315] 316-28 [329] 330-43 [344] 345-61 [362] 363-85 [386] 387-405 [406] 407-418 [419] 420-38 [439] 440-46 [447] 448-59 [460] 461-73 [474] 475-88 [489] 490-512 [513] 514-28 [529] 530-53 [554] 555-64 [565] 566-79 [580] 581-600 [601-603] 604-607 [608]

Page contents: [1] half-title: 'HARRY | POTTER | *and the Deathly Hallows* | [illustration of Hogwarts crest with legend 'DRAGO DORMIENS NUNQUAM TITILLANDUS' on banner, 47 by 58mm]'; [2] *'Titles available in the Harry Potter series | (in reading order):* | Harry Potter and the Philosopher's Stone | Harry Potter and the Chamber of Secrets | Harry Potter and the Prisoner of Azkaban | Harry Potter and the Goblet of Fire | Harry Potter and the Order of the Phoenix | Harry Potter and the Half-Blood Prince | Harry Potter and the Deathly Hallows | [new paragraph] *Titles available in the Harry Potter series*

| *(in Latin)*: | Harry Potter and the Philosopher's Stone | Harry Potter and the Chamber of Secrets | *(in Welsh, Ancient Greek and Irish)*: | Harry Potter and the Philosopher's Stone'; [3] title-page; [4] 'All rights reserved; no part of this publication may be reproduced or | transmitted by any means, electronic, mechanical, photocopying | or otherwise, without the prior permission of the publisher | [new paragraph] First published in Great Britain in 2007 by Bloomsbury Publishing Plc | 36 Soho Square, London, W1D 3QY | [new paragraph] Bloomsbury Publishing, London, Berlin, New York and Sydney | [new paragraph] This paperback edition first published in October 2010 | [new paragraph] Copyright © J. K. Rowling 2007 | Cover illustrations by Jason Cockcroft copyright © Bloomsbury Publishing Plc 2007 | Harry Potter, names, characters and related indicia are | copyright and trademark Warner Bros., 2000™ | [new paragraph] J. K. Rowling has asserted her moral rights | [new paragraph] The extract from *The Libation Bearers* is taken from the Penguin Classics edition | of *The Oresteia*, translated by Robert Fagles, copyright © Robert Fagles, 1966, | 1967, 1975, 1977 | [new paragraph] The extract from *More Fruits of Solitude* is taken from *More Fruits of Solitude* | by William Penn, first included in Everyman's Library, 1915 | [new paragraph] A CIP catalogue record of this book is available from the British Library | [new paragraph] ISBN 978 1 4088 1029 3 | [new paragraph] [Forest Stewardship Council logo, 6 by 7mm together with ® symbol and text: 'FSC | www.fsc.org | [new paragraph] MIX | [new paragraph] Paper from | responsible sources | [new paragraph] FSC® C018072'] | [new paragraph] Typeset by RefineCatch Limited, Bungay, Suffolk | Printed in Great Britain by Clays Ltd, St Ives plc | [new paragraph] 1 3 5 7 9 10 8 6 4 2 | [new paragraph] www.bloomsbury.com/harrypotter'; [5] 'The | dedication | of this book | is split | seven ways: | to Neil, | to Jessica, | to David, | to Kenzie, | to Di, | to Anne, | and to you, | if you have | stuck | with Harry | until the | very | end.'; [6] blank; [7] three stanzas from 'Aeschylus, *The Libation Bearers*' and one paragraph from 'William Penn, *More Fruits of Solitude*'; [8] blank; [9]-600 text; [601] '*Nineteen Years Later*'; [602] blank; [603]-607 text; [608] blank

Paper: wove paper

Running title: 'HARRY POTTER' (24mm) on verso, recto title comprises chapter title, pp. 10-600 and pp. [604]-607 (excluding pages on which new chapters commence)

Binding: pictorial wrappers.

    On spine: '[light blue / grey illustration of a triangular eye symbol on light blue / grey panel, 36 by 15mm] HARRY POTTER [in black on gilt panel, 36 by 46mm] *and the Deathly Hallows* [in white] J.K.ROWLING' [in gilt, both title conclusion and author on black panel, 36 by 102mm] BLOOMSBURY [publisher's device of the head of a dog, 3 by 4mm] [both in white on purple panel, 36 by 33mm]' (reading lengthways down spine).

    On upper wrapper: 'HARRY | POTTER | *and the Deathly Hallows* [lines 1 and 2 in gilt, line 3 in white, all on purple panel, 61 by 128mm] | [gilt rule, 128mm] | ['J.K. ROWLING' [in gilt] with colour illustration of Harry Potter, Ron Weasley and Hermione Granger within a cave-like opening on top of a sea of golden coins and other treasures with Griphook the goblin clutching Harry's back and a sword, within single gilt ruled border, 91 by 86mm, all on black panel with orange, yellow and gilt stars, 123 by 128mm] | [purple rule, 128mm] | BLOOMSBURY [in black on gilt panel, 11 by 128mm]' (all width centred).

    On lower wrapper: 'Harry Potter is preparing to leave the Dursleys and Privet Drive for | the last time. But the future that awaits him is full of danger, not | only for him, but for anyone close to him – and Harry has already lost | so much. Only by destroying Voldemort's remaining Horcruxes can | Harry free himself and overcome the Dark Lord's forces of evil. | [new paragraph] In this dramatic conclusion to the Harry Potter series, Harry must | leave his most loyal friends behind, and in a final perilous journey | find the strength and the will to face his terrifying destiny: a deadly | confrontation that is his alone to fight. | [new paragraph] 'A nail-biting rollercoaster. A finale that ticks every box. If Harry's journey | had to come to an end, *Deathly Hallows* is the best possible way.' *Heat* | [new paragraph] 'The best thing about this book is that it finally answers the | questions we have been longing to know.' *Daily Mirror* | [new paragraph] 'The final chapter in the final book of one of the greatest | literary adventures of modern times.' *Sunday Telegraph* | [new paragraph] 'Rowling has woven together clues, hints and characters | from previous books into a prodigiously rewarding, | suspenseful conclusion.' | *Guardian* | [new paragraph] [barcode in black on white panel, 21 by 40mm] [FSC symbol, 7 by 8mm together with © symbol and text: 'FSC | Mixed Sources | Product group from well-managed | forests and other controlled sources | [new paragraph] Cert no. SGS-COC-2061 | www.fsc.org | © 1996 Forest Stewardship Council'] [these eight lines to the right of the barcode panel] | ['www.bloomsbury.com/harrypotter' below barcode panel, in black on red panel, 5 by 40mm] [publisher's device of a dog, 5 by 9mm] | BLOOMSBURY £8.99' [these two lines to the right of the web address panel]'. Note that the barcode panel and the web address panel are enclosed by a single red ruled border, 27 by 40mm. Reading lengthways down right side towards foot of spine 'Cover illustration by Jason Cockcroft'. All in white on colour illustration of Hogwarts castle and clouds.

All edges trimmed. Binding measurements: 197 by 128mm (wrappers), 197 by 36mm (spine).

Publication: 4 October 2010 in an edition of 36,200 copies (confirmed by Bloomsbury)

Price: £8.99

Contents:
Harry Potter and the Deathly Hallows
('The two men appeared out of nowhere, a few yards apart in the narrow, moonlit lane.')

Notes:
The individual titles in the 'celebratory' edition were each published to celebrate the release of the film version. The UK premiere of *Harry Potter and the Deathly Hallows, part 1* took place on 11 November 2010. *Harry Potter and the Deathly Hallows, part 2* premiered in the UK on 7 July 2011.

Copies: Bloomsbury Archives

A14(f)   ENGLISH 'SIGNATURE' EDITION   (2010)
(Clare Melinsky artwork series in paperback)

Harry Potter ['signature' above 'z' rule with numerous stars] | *and the* | *Deathly Hallows* | [illustration of Hogwarts crest with legend 'DRAGO DORMIENS NUNQUAM TITILLANDUS' on banner,

68 by 84mm] | J.K.ROWLING | [publisher's device of a dog, 8 by 13mm] | BLOOMSBURY | LONDON BERLIN NEW YORK SYDNEY (All width centred)

Collation: 304 unsigned leaves bound in indeterminate gatherings; 198 by 127mm; [1-9] 10-18 [19] 20-30 [31] 32-41 [42] 43-57 [58] 59-75 [76] 77-94 [95] 96-114 [115] 116-33 [134] 135-45 [146] 147-65 [166] 167-83 [184] 185-202 [203] 204-220 [221] 222-33 [234] 235-54 [255] 256-69 [270] 271-85 [286] 287-95 [296] 297-314 [315] 316-28 [329] 330-43 [344] 345-61 [362] 363-85 [386] 387-405 [406] 407-418 [419] 420-38 [439] 440-46 [447] 448-59 [460] 461-73 [474] 475-88 [489] 490-512 [513] 514-28 [529] 530-53 [554] 555-64 [565] 566-79 [580] 581-600 [601-603] 604-607 [608]

Page contents: [1] half-title: 'Harry Potter ['signature' above 'z' rule with numerous stars] | *and the* | *Deathly Hallows* | [illustration of Hogwarts crest with legend 'DRAGO DORMIENS NUNQUAM TITILLANDUS' on banner, 60 by 75mm]'; [2] '*Titles available in the Harry Potter series* | *(in reading order):* | Harry Potter and the Philosopher's Stone | Harry Potter and the Chamber of Secrets | Harry Potter and the Prisoner of Azkaban | Harry Potter and the Goblet of Fire | Harry Potter and the Order of the Phoenix | Harry Potter and the Half-Blood Prince | Harry Potter and the Deathly Hallows | [new paragraph] *Titles available in the Harry Potter series* | *(in Latin):* | Harry Potter and the Philosopher's Stone | Harry Potter and the Chamber of Secrets | *(in Welsh, Ancient Greek and Irish):* | Harry Potter and the Philosopher's Stone'; [3] title-page; [4] 'All rights reserved; no part of this publication may be reproduced or | transmitted by any means, electronic, mechanical, photocopying | or otherwise, without the prior permission of the publisher | [new paragraph] First published in Great Britain in 2007 by Bloomsbury Publishing Plc | 36 Soho Square, London, W1D 3QY | [new paragraph] Bloomsbury Publishing, London, Berlin, New York and Sydney | [new paragraph] This paperback edition first published in November 2010 | [new paragraph] Copyright © J.K.Rowling 2007 | Cover illustrations by Clare Melinsky copyright © Bloomsbury Publishing Plc 2010 | Harry Potter, names, characters and related indicia are | copyright and trademark Warner Bros., 2000™ | [new paragraph] J.K.Rowling has asserted her moral rights | [new paragraph] The extract from *The Libation Bearers* is taken from the Penguin Classics edition | of *The Oresteia*, translated by Robert Fagles, copyright © Robert Fagles, 1966, | 1967, 1975, 1977 | [new paragraph] The extract from *More Fruits of Solitude* is taken from *More Fruits of Solitude* | by William Penn, first included in Everyman's Library, 1915 | [new paragraph] A CIP catalogue record of this book is available from the British Library | [new paragraph] ISBN 978 1 4088 1060 6 | [new paragraph] [Forest Stewardship Council logo, 8 by 9mm together with ® symbol and text: 'FSC | www.fsc.org | MIX | Paper from | responsible sources | FSC® C018072'] | [new paragraph] Typeset by RefineCatch Limited, Bungay, Suffolk | Printed in Great Britain by Clays Ltd, St Ives plc | [new paragraph] 1 3 5 7 9 10 8 6 4 2 | [new paragraph] | www.bloomsbury.

com/harrypotter'; [5] 'The | dedication | of this book | is split | seven ways: | to Neil, | to Jessica, | to David, | to Kenzie, | to Di, | to Anne, | and to you, | if you have | stuck | with Harry | until the | very | end.'; [6] blank; [7] three stanzas from 'Aeschylus, *The Libation Bearers*' and one paragraph from 'William Penn, *More Fruits of Solitude*'; [8] blank; [9]-600 text; [601] '*Nineteen Years Later*'; [602] blank; [603]-607 text; [608] blank

Paper: wove paper

Running title: 'HARRY POTTER' (24mm) on verso, recto title comprises chapter title, pp. 10-607 (excluding pages on which new chapters commence)

Binding: pictorial wrappers.

On spine: 'Harry Potter ['signature' above 'z' rule with numerous stars] [in gilt] *and* | *the Deathly Hallows* [red, orange, light blue and white illustration of a Golden Snitch, 28 by 15mm] J.K.ROWLING BLOOMSBURY [publisher's device of the head of a dog, 3 by 4mm]' (reading lengthways down spine). All in white on dark green.

On upper wrapper: 'Harry Potter ['signature' above 'z' rule with numerous stars] [embossed in gilt] | *and the* | *Deathly Hallows* | [olive green, dark blue, light blue, brown, grey and black illustration of eleven snowy tombstones, 87 by 115mm] | J.K.ROWLING | BLOOMSBURY' (all width centred). All in dark green with deckle-edge effect of white leaf on dark green background at fore-edge.

On lower wrapper: 'Harry Potter is preparing to leave the Durlseys and Privet Drive | for the last time. The future that awaits him is full of danger, not | only for him, but for anyone close to him – and Harry has already lost | so much. Only by destroying Voldemort's remaining Horcruxes can | Harry free himself and overcome the Dark Lord's forces of evil. In a | final and perilous journey, Harry must find the strength and the will | to face a deadly confrontation that is his alone to fight. | [new paragraph] 'The best thing about this book is that it finally answers the questions | we have been longing to know.' | *Daily Mirror* | [new paragraph] 'The final chapter in the final book of one of the greatest literary | adventures of modern times.' | *Sunday Telegraph* | [new paragraph] 'Rowling has woven together clues, hints and characters from previous | books into a prodigiously rewarding, suspenseful conclusion.' | *Guardian* | [olive green, light blue, dark blue and red illustration of a sword with glittering rubies in its hilt lying at the bottom of a forest pool, 84 by 121mm] | [barcode together with publisher's device of a dog, 6 by 10mm and 'BLOOMSBURY' together with Forest Stewardship Council logo, 7 by 8mm together with © symbol and text: 'FSC | Mixed Sources | Product group from well-managed | forests and other controlled sources | [new paragraph] Cert no. SGS-COC-2061 | www.fsc.org | © 1996 Forest Stewardship Council'] | Designed by Webb & Webb Design | Cover illustrations by Clare Melinsky www. bloomsbury.com/harrypotter £8.99 | Author photograph © J.P.Masclet'. Lines 1-16 in dark green with all other text in black, together with deckle-edge effect of white leaf on dark green background at fore-edge. The initial 'H' of 'Harry' is a drop capital.

On inside upper wrapper: 'The magical world of … | Harry Potter ['signature' above 'z' rule with numerous stars] | [colour illustrations in three columns of seven book designs] | The internationally bestselling series | [new paragraph] For more from Harry Potter, visit | www.bloomsbury.com/ harrypotter'. All in dark green with the exception of line 2 which is in gold, together with deckle-edge effect of white leaf on dark green background at fore-edge.

On inside lower wrapper: colour photograph of J.K. Rowling seated by a window.

All edges trimmed. Binding measurements: 197 by 128mm (wrappers), 197 by 36mm (spine).

Publication: 1 November 2010 in an edition of 65,200 copies (confirmed by Bloomsbury)

Price: £8.99

Contents:

Harry Potter and the Deathly Hallows

('The two men appeared out of nowhere, a few yards apart in the narrow, moonlit lane.')

Notes:

Published as a boxed set of seven volumes comprising A1(i), A2(n), A7(k), A9(k), A12(h), A13(g) and A14(f). Individual volumes were also available separately.

Copies: private collection (PWE)

A14(g) ENGLISH 'SIGNATURE' EDITION (2011)
(Clare Melinsky artwork series in hardback)

Harry Potter ['signature' above 'z' rule with numerous stars] | *and the* | *Deathly Hallows* | [illustration of Hogwarts crest with legend 'DRAGO DORMIENS NUNQUAM TITILLANDUS' on banner, 68 by 84mm] | J.K.ROWLING | [publisher's device of a dog, 8 by 13mm] | BLOOMSBURY | LONDON BERLIN NEW YORK SYDNEY (All width centred)

Collation: 304 unsigned leaves bound in indeterminate gatherings; 197 by 124mm; [1-9] 10-18 [19] 20-30 [31] 32-41 [42] 43-57 [58] 59-75 [76] 77-94 [95] 96-114 [115] 116-33 [134] 135-45 [146] 147-65 [166] 167-83 [184] 185-202 [203] 204-220 [221] 222-33 [234] 235-54 [255] 256-69 [270] 271-85 [286] 287-95 [296] 297-314 [315] 316-28 [329] 330-43 [344] 345-61 [362] 363-85 [386] 387-405 [406] 407-418 [419] 420-38 [439] 440-46 [447] 448-59 [460] 461-73 [474] 475-88 [489] 490-512 [513] 514-28 [529] 530-53 [554] 555-64 [565] 566-79 [580] 581-600 [601-603] 604-607 [608]

Page contents: [1] half-title: 'Harry Potter ['signature' above 'z' rule with numerous stars] | *and the* | *Deathly Hallows* | [illustration of Hogwarts crest with legend 'DRAGO DORMIENS NUNQUAM TITILLANDUS' on banner, 60 by 75mm]'; [2] '*Titles available in the Harry Potter series | (in reading* *order*): | Harry Potter and the Philosopher's Stone | Harry Potter and the Chamber of Secrets | Harry Potter and the Prisoner of Azkaban | Harry Potter and the Goblet of Fire | Harry Potter and the Order of the Phoenix | Harry Potter and the Half-Blood Prince | Harry Potter and the Deathly Hallows | [new paragraph] *Titles available in the Harry Potter series* | *(in Latin):* | Harry Potter and the Philosopher's Stone | Harry Potter and the Chamber of Secrets | *(in Welsh, Ancient Greek and Irish):* | Harry Potter and the Philosopher's Stone | [new paragraph] *Also available* | *(in aid of Comic Relief):* | Fantastic Beasts and Where to Find Them | Quidditch Through the Ages | *(in aid of Lumos):* | The Tales of Beedle the Bard'; [3] title-page; [4] 'All rights reserved; no part of this publication may be reproduced or | transmitted by any means, electronic, mechanical, photocopying | or otherwise, without the prior permission of the publisher | [new paragraph] First published in Great Britain in 2007 by Bloomsbury Publishing Plc | 49-51

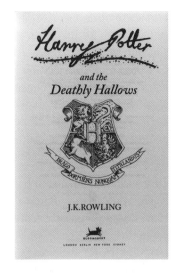

Bedford Square, London, WC1B 3DP | [new paragraph] Bloomsbury Publishing, London, Berlin, New York and Sydney | [new paragraph] This hardback edition first published in November 2011 | [new paragraph] Copyright © J.K.Rowling 2007 | Cover and endpaper illustrations by Clare Melinsky copyright © J.K.Rowling 2010 | Harry Potter, names, characters and related indicia are | copyright and trademark Warner Bros., 2000™ | [new paragraph] J.K.Rowling has asserted her moral rights | [new paragraph] The extract from *The Libation Bearers* is taken from the Penguin Classics edition | of *The Oresteia*, translated by Robert Fagles, copyright © Robert Fagles, 1966, | 1967, 1975, 1977 | [new paragraph] The extract from *More Fruits of Solitude* is taken from *More Fruits of Solitude* | by William Penn, first included in Everyman's Library, 1915 | [new paragraph] A CIP catalogue record of this book is available from the British Library | [new paragraph] ISBN 978 1 4088 2584 6 | [new paragraph] [Forest Stewardship Council logo, 8 by 9mm together with ® symbol and text: 'FSC | www.fsc.org | MIX | Paper from | responsible sources | FSC® C018072'] | [new paragraph] Typeset by RefineCatch Limited, Bungay, Suffolk | Printed in Great Britain by Clays Ltd, St Ives plc | [new paragraph] 1 3 5 7 9 10 8 6 4 2 | [new paragraph] | www.bloomsbury. com/harrypotter'; [5] 'The | dedication | of this book | is split | seven ways: | to Neil, | to Jessica, | to David, | to Kenzie, | to Di, | to Anne, | and to you, | if you have | stuck | with Harry | until the | very | end.'; [6] blank; [7] three stanzas from 'Aeschylus, *The Libation Bearers*' and one paragraph from 'William Penn, *More Fruits of Solitude*'; [8] blank; [9]-600 text; [601] *'Nineteen Years Later'*; [602] blank; [603]-607 text; [608] blank

Paper: wove paper

Running title: 'HARRY POTTER' (24mm) on verso, recto title comprises chapter title, pp. 10-607 (excluding pages on which new chapters commence)

Binding: green boards.
    On spine: 'Harry Potter ['signature' above 'z' rule with numerous stars] *and* | *the Deathly*

Hallows [illustration of a Golden Snitch, 28 by 15mm] J.K.ROWLING BLOOMSBURY [publisher's device of the head of a dog, 3 by 4mm]' (reading lengthways down spine). All in gilt.

Upper and lower covers: blank.

All edges trimmed. Green sewn bands at head and foot of spine together with green marker ribbon. Binding measurements: 205 by 128mm (covers), 205 by 56mm (spine). End-papers: wove paper overprinted in green showing design, in white, of spine motifs from the series (see notes).

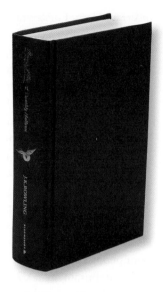

Dust-jacket: coated wove paper, 205 by 510mm

On spine: 'Harry Potter ['signature' above 'z' rule with numerous stars] [in gilt] *and* | *the Deathly Hallows* [red, orange, light blue and white illustration of a Golden Snitch, 28 by 15mm] J.K.ROWLING BLOOMSBURY [publisher's device of the head of a dog, 3 by 4mm]' (reading lengthways down spine). All in white on dark green.

On upper cover: 'Harry Potter ['signature' above 'z' rule with numerous stars] [in gilt] | *and the* | *Deathly Hallows* | [olive green, dark blue, light blue, brown, grey and black illustration of eleven snowy tombstones, 87 by 115mm] | J.K.ROWLING | BLOOMSBURY' (all width centred). All in dark green with deckle-edge effect of white leaf on dark green background at fore-edge.

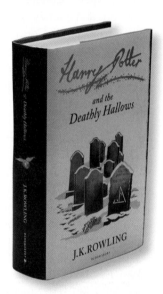

On lower cover: "The final chapter in the final book | of one of the greatest literary | adventures of modern times.' | *Sunday Telegraph* | [olive green, light blue, dark blue and red illustration of a sword with glittering rubies in its hilt lying at the bottom of a forest pool, 75 by 107mm] | [publisher's device of a dog, 6 by 10mm and 'BLOOMSBURY'] [barcode and 'www.bloomsbury.com/harrypotter' in black on white panel, 24 by 39mm]'. All in dark green, with deckle-edge effect of white leaf on dark green background at fore-edge. The initial 'T' of 'The' is a drop capital.

On upper inside flap: 'Harry Potter is preparing to leave | the Durlseys and Privet Drive | for the last time. The future that awaits | him is full of danger, not only for him, | but for anyone close to him – and | Harry has already lost so much. Only | by destroying Voldemort's remaining | Horcruxes can Harry free himself and | overcome the Dark Lord's forces of evil. | In a final and perilous journey, Harry | must find the strength and the will to | face a deadly confrontation that is his | alone to fight. | [new paragraph] 'The best thing about this book is that it | finally answers the questions we have been | longing to know.' | *Daily Mirror* | [new paragraph] 'You emerge better for reading it.' | *Observer* | [new paragraph] 'Rowling has woven together clues, hints | and characters from previous books into | a prodigiously rewarding, suspenseful | conclusion.' | *Guardian* | [red, orange, light blue and white illustration of a Golden Snitch, 13 by 25mm]'. All in white on dark green. The initial 'H' of 'Harry' is a drop capital.

On lower inside flap: 'J. K. Rowling has written fiction since she was a child, | and she always wanted to be an author. Her parents loved | reading and their house in Chepstow was full of books. | In fact, J. K. Rowling wrote her first 'book' at the age | of six – a story about a rabbit called Rabbit. She studied | French and Classics at Exeter University, then moved to | Edinburgh – via London and Portugal. In 2000 she was | awarded an OBE for services to children's literature. | [new paragraph] The idea for Harry Potter occurred to her on the | train from Manchester to London, where she says | Harry Potter 'just strolled into my head fully formed', | and by the time she had arrived at King's Cross, many | of the characters had taken shape. During the next | five years she outlined the plots for each book and | began writing the first in the series, *Harry Potter and* | *the Philosopher's Stone,* which was first published by | Bloomsbury in 1997. The other Harry Potter titles: | *Harry Potter and the Chamber of Secrets, Harry Potter* | *and the Prisoner of Azkaban, Harry Potter and the* | *Goblet of Fire, Harry Potter and the Order of the Phoenix,* | *Harry Potter and the Half-Blood Prince* and *Harry* | *Potter and the Deathly Hallows* followed. J. K. Rowling | has also written three companion books: *Quidditch* | *Through the Ages* and *Fantastic Beasts and Where to Find* | *Them,* in aid of Comic Relief, and *The Tales of Beedle* | *the Bard,* in aid of Lumos. | [new paragraph] THE COMPLETE HARRY POTTER SERIES: | [colour illustrations in two rows of seven book designs] | Designed by Webb & Webb Design | Cover illustrations by Clare Melinsky | copyright © J. K. Rowling 2010'. All in white on dark green with white panel, 19 by 12mm, to right on which in black: '[Forest Stewardship Council logo, 6 by 7mm together with ® symbol] | FSC | www.fsc.org | MIX | Paper from | responsible sources | FSC® C018072'.

Publication: 7 November 2011 in an edition of 9,200 copies (confirmed by Bloomsbury)

Price: £115 [together with A1(j), A2(o), A7(l), A9(l), A12(i) and A13(h)]

Contents:

Harry Potter and the Deathly Hallows

    ('The two men appeared out of nowhere, a few yards apart in the narrow, moonlit lane.')

Notes:

The end-papers carry a design of eight miniature illustrations. Seven of these reproduce the spine motifs from the series and an eighth comprises a variant of the key-bird from the first book.

This is the fourth of the books in the series to carry different press quotes from the equivalent 'signature' paperback edition. For this hardback edition there is an additional quote (from the *Observer*) on the upper inside flap.

Published as a boxed set of seven volumes comprising A1(j), A2(o), A7(l), A9(l), A12(i), A13(h) and A14(g). Individual volumes were not available separately. The ISBN for the boxed set was ISBN 978 1 4088 2594 5.

Copies: private collection (PWE)

A14(h)   AMERICAN CHILDREN'S EDITION   (2013)
(Kazu Kibuishi artwork in paperback)

HARRY POTTER | AND THE DEATHLY HALLOWS | [black and white illustration of an owl in cage with books and wand all by a window, 60 by 48mm] | BY | J. K. ROWLING | ILLUSTRATIONS BY MARY GRANDPRÉ | SCHOLASTIC INC. (All width centred on a diamond pattern background)

Collation: 392 unsigned leaves bound in indeterminate gatherings; 204 by 133mm; [I-XII] XIII-XVI [XVII-XX] 1-749 [750-52] 753-59 [760-64]

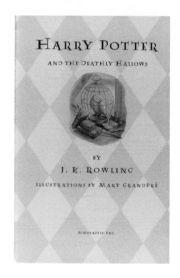

Page contents: [I-III] 'PRAISE FOR J. K. ROWLING'S | HARRY POTTER | AND THE DEATHLY HALLOWS | [device of nine stars] | [10 reviews and a listing of 9 statements]'; [IV] blank; [V] half-title: 'HARRY POTTER | AND THE DEATHLY HALLOWS' (all on diamond pattern background); [VI] blank; [VII] 'ALSO BY J. K. ROWLING | [new paragraph] *Harry Potter and the Sorcerer's Stone* | Year One at Hogwarts | [new paragraph] *Harry Potter and the Chamber of Secrets* | Year Two at Hogwarts | [new paragraph] *Harry Potter and the Prisoner of Azkaban* | Year Three at Hogwarts | [new paragraph] | *Harry Potter and the Goblet of Fire* | Year Four at Hogwarts | [new paragraph] *Harry Potter and the Order of the*

Phoenix | Year Five at Hogwarts | [new paragraph] *Harry Potter and the Half-Blood Prince* | Year Six at Hogwarts'; [VIII] blank; [IX] title-page; [X] '[device of twelve stars] | Text © 2007 by J. K. Rowling | Interior illustrations by Mary GrandPré © 2007 by Warner Bros. | Cover illustration by Kazu Kibuishi © 2013 by Scholastic Inc. | HARRY POTTER & all related characters and elements are TM of and © WBEI. | Harry Potter Publishing Rights © J. K. Rowling | All rights reserved. Published by Scholastic Inc. SCHOLASTIC, the LANTERN LOGO, and associated | logos are trademarks and/ or registered trademarks of Scholastic Inc. | [new paragraph] "The Libation Bearers" by Aeschylus, from THE ORESTEIA by Aeschylus, translated by Robert | Fagles, copyright © 1966, 1967, 1975, 1977 by Robert Fagles. Used by permission of Viking | Penguin, a division of Penguin Group (USA) Inc. | "More Fruits of Solitude," reprinted from William Penn, *Fruits of Solitude*, Vol I., the Harvard | Classics (New York: P.F. Collier & Son, 1909). | [new paragraph] If you purchased this book without a cover, you should be aware that this book is stolen property. | It was reported as "unsold and destroyed" to the publisher, and neither the author nor the | publisher has received any payment for this "stripped book." | [new paragraph] No part of this publication may be reproduced, stored in a retrieval system, or transmitted in any | form or by any means, electronic, mechanical, photocopying, recording, or otherwise, without | written permission of the publisher. For information regarding permission, write to Scholastic Inc., | Attention: Permissions Department, 557 Broadway, New York, NY 10012. | [new paragraph] [publisher's device of a lantern, 6 by 4mm] | Arthur A. Levine Books hardcover edition art directed by David Saylor, | published by Arthur A. Levine Books, an imprint of Scholastic Inc., July 2007. | [new paragraph] ISBN 978-0-545-58300-8 | [new paragraph] Library of Congress Control Number: 2007925449 | [new paragraph] 10 9 8 7 6 5 4 3 2 1   13 14 15 16 17 | [new paragraph] Printed in the U.S.A. 40 | This edition first printing, September 2013 | [new paragraph] We try to produce the most beautiful books possible, and we are extremely concerned about the impact of our | manufacturing process on the forests of the world and the environment as a whole. Accordingly, we made sure | that the text paper contains a minimum of 30% post-consumer waste, and that all the paper has been certified as | coming from forests that are managed to insure the protection of the people and wildlife dependent upon them.'; [XI] 'THE | DEDICATION | OF THIS BOOK | IS SPLIT | SEVEN WAYS: | TO NEIL, | TO JESSICA, | TO DAVID, | TO KENZIE, | TO DI, | TO ANNE, | AND TO YOU, | IF YOU HAVE | STUCK | WITH HARRY | UNTIL THE | VERY | END.'; [XII] blank; XIII-XVI 'CONTENTS' (thirty-six chapters and one epilogue listed with titles and page references); [XVII] three stanzas from 'Aeschylus, *The Libation Bearers*' and one paragraph from 'William Penn, *More Fruits of Solitude*'; [XVIII] blank; [XIX] half-title: 'HARRY POTTER | AND THE DEATHLY HALLOWS' (all on diamond pattern background); [XX] blank; 1-749 text; [750] blank; [751] divisional title: 'NINETEEN YEARS LATER' (all on diamond pattern background); [752] blank; 753-759 text; [760] advertisement for Pottermore; [761] '[black and white photograph of J.K. Rowling seated by curtains, credited 'ANDREW MONTGOMERY' reading lengthways up right margin] | [new paragraph] J. K. ROWLING is the author of the beloved, | bestselling, record-breaking Harry Potter series. She started writing | the series during a delayed Manchester to London King's Cross | train journey, and during the next five years, outlined the plots for | each book and began writing the first novel. *Harry Potter and the* | *Sorcerer's Stone* was published in the United States by Arthur A. | Levine Books in 1998, and the series concluded nearly ten years | later with *Harry Potter and the Deathly Hallows*, published in 2007. | J. K. Rowling is the recipient of numerous awards and honorary | degrees, including an OBE for services to children's literature, | France's Légion d'honneur, and the Hans Christian Andersen | Literature Award. She supports a wide number of causes through | her charitable trust, Volant, and is the founder of Lumos, a charity | working to transform the lives of disadvantaged children. J. K. | Rowling lives in Edinburgh with her husband and three children.'; [762] blank; [763] 'MARY GRANDPRÉ has illustrated more than twenty | beautiful books for children, including the American editions of | the Harry Potter novels. Her work has also appeared in the *New* | *Yorker*, the *Atlantic Monthly*, and the *Wall Street Journal*, and her | paintings and pastels have been shown in galleries across the United | States. Ms. GrandPré lives in Sarasota, Florida, with her family. | [new paragraph] KAZU KIBUISHI is the creator of the *New York Times* | bestselling Amulet series and *Copper*, a collection of his popular | webcomic. He is also the founder and editor of the acclaimed | Flight anthologies. *Daisy Kutter: The Last Train*, his first graphic | novel, was listed as one of the Best Books for Young Adults by | YALSA, and *Amulet, Book One: The Stonekeeper* was an ALA Best | Book for Young Adults and a Children's Choice Book Award | finalist. Kazu lives and works in Alhambra, California, with his | wife and fellow comics artist, Amy Kim Kibuishi, and their two | children. Visit Kazu online at www.boltcity.com.'; [764] blank

Paper: wove paper

Running title: 'CHAPTER' and chapter number on verso, recto title comprises chapter title, pp. 1-749 also 'EPILOGUE' on verso, recto title comprises 'NINETEEN YEARS LATER', pp. 753-59. Each running title (excluding pages on which new chapters commence) includes a three-star design to left and right of both running-titles on verso and recto. On pages on which a new chapter commences, the three-star design is omitted.

Illustrations: title-page vignette, together with thirty-seven vignettes at the beginning of each chapter (after chapter and chapter number but before chapter title) and epilogue. In addition to standard typographical changes (including italics, capitals and small capitals) there are other typographical features, comprising:
  p. 16 newspaper headline and illustration
  p. 22 newspaper headline
  p. 134 facsimile of Dumbledore's handwriting
  p. 186 facsimile of Regulus Arcturus Black's handwriting
  p. 207 newspaper headline
  p. 217 newspaper headline
  p. 225 newspaper headline
  p. 249 title of pamphlet
  p. 325 tombstone engraving
  p. 328 tombstone engraving
  p. 333 text of magical graffiti
  p. 353 photograph caption
  p. 398 text of hand-painted signs
  p. 481 stone engraving
  p. 689 facsimile of Lily Potter's Christian name signature

Binding: pictorial wrappers.

On spine: 'ROWLING | Harry Potter and the Deathly Hallows [reading lengthways down spine] | 7' and '[publisher's book device] | [rule] | S' in white on red panel, 14 by 6mm. All in white on colour illustration (see notes).

On upper wrapper: 'J. K. ROWLING | Harry Potter [hand-drawn lettering] [embossed in white] | and the | Deathly Hallows' (all width centred). All in white on colour illustration of Harry Potter, Hermione Granger and Ron Weasley riding on the back of a gigantic dragon. In centre at foot: '[publisher's book device] SCHOLASTIC' in white on red panel, 5 by 45mm.

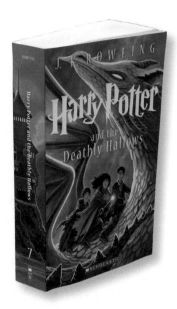

On lower wrapper: '"Neither can live while the other survives, and one | of us is about to leave for good ...." | — Harry Potter | [new paragraph] We now present the seventh and final installment | in the epic tale of Harry Potter. | [new paragraph] $16.99 US | [new paragraph] [publisher's book device with 'SCHOLASTIC' in white on red panel, 5 by 45mm] | www.scholastic.com | COVER DESIGN BY KAZU KIBUISHI AND JASON CAFFOE | COVER ART BY KAZU KIBUISHI © 2013 BY SCHOLASTIC INC.' Lines 1-3 in white with other lines in light purple and all on colour illustration of Harry facing Lord Voldemort. In lower right: barcode with smaller barcode to the right (51699) together with 'S' within triangle, all in black on white panel, 21 by 53mm.

On inside upper wrapper: barcode with smaller barcode (51699) together with 'S' within triangle below, all in black on white panel, 53 by 21mm. All on orange.

On inside lower wrapper: '[colour illustration of book design] Harry Potter [hand-drawn lettering] [in white] | The Complete Series [in white] | Read All of Harry's [in white] | Magical Adventures! [in white] | [publisher's device of a lantern, 10 by 7mm] [in black] | ARTHUR A. LEVINE BOOKS [in black] | [publisher's book device with 'SCHOLASTIC' in white on red panel, 5 by 45mm] | scholastic.com/harrypotter [in white] | [colour illustrations in three columns of six book designs]'. All on lavender blue.

All edges trimmed. Binding measurements: 204 by 134mm (wrappers), 204 by 36mm (spine).

Publication: 27 August 2013

Price: $16.99

Contents:
Harry Potter and the Deathly Hallows
   ('The two men appeared out of nowhere, a few yards apart in the narrow, moonlit lane.')

Notes:
See notes to A4(h) about this series.

The seven volumes in this edition were available individually or as a set issued in a slipcase. The set, presented in order, reveals a single illustration of Hogwarts castle across the seven spines. Scholastic released images of the new illustrations in a careful marketing campaign: the upper wrapper illustration for *Deathly Hallows* was revealed on 31 July 2013 at the Scholastic Store in New York.

Each chapter together with the epilogue commences with a drop capital.

Copies: private collection (PWE)

Reprints include:
10 9 8 7 6 5 4 3 2   13 14 15 16 17   Printed in the U.S.A. 40

A14(i)   ENGLISH ADULT EDITION   (2013)
(Andrew Davidson artwork series in paperback)

J.K. [in grey] | ROWLING [in grey] [reading lengthways down title-page] | HARRY | POTTER | &THE [reading lengthways up title-page] DEATHLY HALLOWS | BLOOMSBURY | LONDON [point] NEW DELHI [point] NEW YORK [point] SYDNEY (Author and final part of title justified on right margin, first part of title justified on left margin, publisher with publisher's offices width centred)

Collation: 304 unsigned leaves bound in indeterminate gatherings; 198 by 128mm; [1-9] 10-18 [19] 20-30 [31] 32-41 [42] 43-57 [58] 59-75 [76] 77-94 [95] 96-114 [115] 116-33 [134] 135-45 [146] 147-65 [166] 167-83 [184] 185-202 [203] 204-220 [221] 222-33 [234] 235-54 [255] 256-69 [270] 271-85 [286] 287-95 [296] 297-314 [315] 316-28 [329] 330-43 [344] 345-61 [362] 363-85 [386] 387-405 [406] 407-418 [419] 420-38 [439] 440-46 [447] 448-59 [460] 461-73 [474] 475-88 [489] 490-512 [513] 514-28 [529] 530-53 [554] 555-64 [565] 566-79 [580] 581-600 [601-603] 604-607 [608]

Page contents: [1] half-title: 'HARRY | POTTER | &THE [reading lengthways up title-page] DEATHLY HALLOWS'; [2] '*Titles available in the Harry Potter series* | (*in reading order*): | Harry Potter and the Philosopher's Stone | Harry Potter and the Chamber of Secrets | Harry Potter and the Prisoner of Azkaban | Harry Potter and the Goblet of Fire | Harry Potter and the Order of the Phoenix | Harry Potter and the Half-Blood Prince | Harry Potter and the Deathly Hallows | [new paragraph] *Titles available in the Harry Potter series* | (*in Latin*): | Harry Potter and the Philosopher's Stone | Harry Potter and the Chamber of Secrets | (*in Welsh, Ancient Greek and Irish*): | Harry Potter and the Philosopher's Stone | [new paragraph] *Also available* | (*in aid of Comic Relief*): | Fantastic Beasts and Where to Find Them | Quidditch Through the Ages | (*in aid of Lumos*): | The Tales of Beedle the Bard'; [3] title-page; [4] 'All rights reserved; no part of this publication may be reproduced or | transmitted by any means, electronic, mechanical, photocopying | or otherwise, without the prior permission of the publisher | [new paragraph] First published in Great Britain in 2007 by Bloomsbury Publishing Plc | 50 Bedford Square, London WC1B 3DP | [new paragraph] Bloomsbury Publishing, London, New Delhi, New York and Sydney | [new paragraph] This paperback edition first published 2013 | [new paragraph] Copyright © J.K. Rowling 2007 | Cover illustrations by Andrew Davidson copyright © J.K. Rowling 2013 | Harry Potter, names, characters and related indicia are | copyright and trademark Warner Bros., 2000™ | [new paragraph] J.K. Rowling has asserted her moral rights | [new paragraph] The extract from *The Libation Bearers* is taken from the Penguin Classics edition | of *The Oresteia*, translated by Robert Fagles, copyright © Robert Fagles, 1966, | 1967, 1975, 1977 | [new paragraph] The extract from *More Fruits of Solitude* is taken from *More Fruits of Solitude* | by William Penn, first included in Everyman's Library, 1915 | [new paragraph] A CIP catalogue record for this book is available from the British Library | [new paragraph] ISBN 978 1 4088 3502 9 | [new paragraph] [Forest Stewardship Council logo, 6 by 7mm together with ® symbol and text: 'FSC | www.fsc.org' with 'MIX | Paper from | responsible sources | FSC® C020471' to the right and all within single ruled border with rounded corners, 12 by 26mm] | [new paragraph] Typeset by RefineCatch Limited, Bungay, Suffolk | Printed and bound in Great Britain by CPI Group (UK) Ltd, Croydon CR0 4YY | [new paragraph] 1 3 5 7 9 10 8 6 4 2 | [new paragraph] | www.bloomsbury.com/harrypotter'; [5] '*The | dedication | of this book | is split | seven ways: | to Neil, | to Jessica, | to David, | to Kenzie, | to Di, | to Anne, | and to you, | if you have | stuck | with Harry | until the | very | end.*'; [6] blank; [7] three stanzas from 'Aeschylus, *The Libation Bearers*' and one paragraph from 'William Penn, *More Fruits of Solitude*'; [8] blank; [9]-600 text; [601] '*Nineteen Years Later*'; [602] blank; [603]-607 text; [608] blank

Paper: wove paper

Running title: 'HARRY POTTER' (24mm) on verso, recto title comprises chapter title, pp. 8-607

Binding: pictorial wrappers.

On spine: 'J.K. ROWLING [in white] HARRY POTTER [in dark green] &THE [in white] DEATHLY HALLOWS [in dark green] [publisher's device of a figure with a bow, 8 by 6mm] [in white]' (reading lengthways down spine with the exception of '&THE' and the publisher's device which are horizontal). All on orange.

On upper wrapper: 'J.K. [in white] | ROWLING [in white] [reading lengthways down upper wrapper] | HARRY [in orange] | POTTER [in orange] | &THE [in white] [reading lengthways up upper wrapper] DEATHLY HALLOWS [in orange] | BLOOMSBURY [in white]' (author and final part of title justified on right margin, first part of title justified on left margin, publisher with publisher's offices width centred). All on light and dark green illustration of a giant snake revealing its fangs within the courtyard of Hogwarts castle.

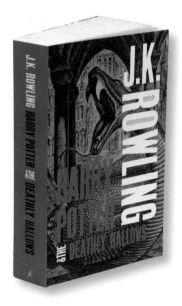

On lower wrapper: 'Harry Potter faces a seemingly impossible task. He will | not return to Hogwarts for his seventh year; instead, he | will finish the quest started by Albus Dumbledore. He must | hunt down and destroy Voldmort's remaining Horcruxes. | Only then will he be able to rid the world of the Dark Lord's | shadow once and for all. | [new paragraph] This final battle is Harry's destiny, and destiny demands that | he rise to meet his true fate without fear … | [new paragraph] [section of white illustration of a giant snake revealing its fangs within the courtyard of Hogwarts castle, 78 by 111mm] | BLOOMSBURY www.bloomsbury.com/harrypotter www.pottermore.com £8.99 [in black] | [section of white illustration of a giant snake revealing its fangs within the courtyard of Hogwarts castle, 27 by 111mm upon which: Forest Stewardship Council logo, 5 by 6mm together with ® symbol and text: 'FSC | www.fsc.org | MIX | Paper from | responsible sources | FSC® C020471' all in black on white panel with rounded corners, 19 by 12mm, with barcode in black on white panel, 18 by 38mm, with 'Designed by Webb & Webb Design | Cover illustrations by Andrew Davidson | copyright © J.K. Rowling 2013' in black on orange panel, 9 by 38mm]'. Lines 1-8 in white and all on orange. The initial 'H' of 'Harry' is a drop capital and is printed in dark green.

On inside upper wrapper: orange and white illustration of a giant snake revealing its fangs within the courtyard of Hogwarts castle.

On inside lower wrapper: orange and white illustration of snakes's scales.

All edges trimmed. Binding measurements: 198 by 128mm (wrappers), 198 by 37mm (spine).

Publication: 26 September 2013 in an edition of 57,200 copies (confirmed by Bloomsbury) (see notes)

Price: £8.99

Contents:

Harry Potter and the Deathly Hallows

('The two men appeared out of nowhere, a few yards apart in the narrow, moonlit lane.')

Notes:

All other volumes in this Andrew Davidson artwork series read 'This paperback edition first published in' on the imprint page. This volume omits 'in'.

The illustrations by Andrew Davidson derive from a single wood engraving. A single illustration is presented on both the upper wrapper and inside upper wrapper. A section is printed on the lower wrapper. A detail from the upper wrapper is shown on the inside lower wrapper.

Although Bloomsbury's 'official' publication date was 26 September 2013, copies were available from amazon.co.uk two or three days beforehand.

Copies: private collection (PWE)

A15(a)   **FIRST ENGLISH EDITION**   **(2008)**
(hardback)

THE | TALES OF | BEEDLE | THE | BARD | Translated from the original | runes by Hermione Granger | BY | J.K.ROWLING [all within decorated border including skull, heart and tree stump, 150 by 114mm with 'children's | HIGH LEVEL GROUP | health. education. welfare.' at left foot and '[publisher's device of a dog, 7 by 11mm] | BLOOMSBURY' at right foot] (All width centred except charity and publisher's devices which are slightly inset from outer margins)

Collation: 64 unsigned leaves bound in indeterminate gatherings (see notes); 178 by 123mm; [i-x] xi-xvii [xviii] [1-2] 3-17 [18-20] 21-25 [26] 27-31 [32] 33-40 [41-44] 45-59 [60-62] 63-70 [71] 72-83 [84-86] 87 [88] 89-104 [105-106] 107-108 [109-110]

Page contents: [i] half-title: 'THE | TALES OF | BEEDLE | THE | BARD | [leaf and flower motif]'; [ii] *Titles available in the Harry Potter series | (in reading order):* | Harry Potter and the Philosopher's Stone | Harry Potter and the Chamber of Secrets | Harry Potter and the Prisoner of Azkaban | Harry Potter and the Goblet of Fire | Harry Potter and the Order of the Phoenix | Harry Potter and the Half-Blood Prince | Harry Potter and the Deathly Hallows | [new paragraph] *Titles available in the Harry Potter series | (in Latin):* | Harry Potter and the Philosopher's Stone | Harry Potter and the Chamber of Secrets | *(in Welsh, Ancient Greek and Irish):* | Harry Potter and the Philosopher's

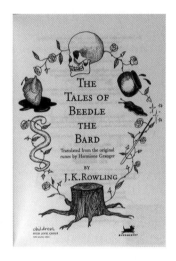

Stone | [new paragraph] *Other titles available:* | Quidditch Through the Ages | Fantastic Beasts and Where to Find Them'; [iii] title-page; [iv] 'First published in Great Britain in 2008 by the Children's High Level Group, | 45 Great Peter Street, London, SW1P 3LT, | in association with Bloomsbury Publishing Plc, | 36 Soho Square, London, W1D 3QY | [new paragraph] Text and illustrations copyright © J. K. Rowling 2007/2008 | [new paragraph] The Children's High Level Group and the Children's High | Level Group logo and associated logos are trademarks of | the Children's High Level Group | [new paragraph] The Children's High Level Group (CHLG) is a charity established | under English law. Registered charity number 1112575 | [new paragraph] J. K. Rowling has asserted her moral rights | [new paragraph] All rights reserved | No part of this publication may be reproduced or | transmitted by any means, electronic, mechanical, photocopying | or otherwise, without the prior permission of the publisher | [new paragraph] A CIP catalogue record of this book is available from the British Library | [new paragraph] ISBN 978 0 7475 9987 6 | [new paragraph]

[Forest Stewardship Council logo, 7 by 9mm together with © symbol and 'FSC' to the right is the text: 'Mixed Sources | Product group from well-managed | forests and other controlled sources | [new paragraph] www.fsc.org Cert no. SGS-COC-2061 | © 1996 Forest Stewardship Council'] | [new paragraph] The paper on which this book is printed has © 1996 Forest | Stewardship Council A.C. (FSC) accreditation. The FSC promotes | environmentally appropriate, socially beneficial and economically | viable management of the world's forests. | [new paragraph] Typeset by RefineCatch Limited, Bungay, Suffolk | Printed in Great Britain by Clays Ltd, St Ives Plc | [new paragraph] 1 3 5 7 9 10 8 6 4 2 | [new paragraph] www.chlg.org | www.bloomsbury.com/beedlebard'; [v] illustration of skull, wand, stone, cloak and ten stars, 34 by 56mm; [vi] blank; [vii] 'CONTENTS' (seven individual parts listed with titles and page references); [viii] blank; [ix] illustration of wand lying over rose with ten stars, 22 by 47mm; [x] blank; xi-xvi 'Introduction' ('*The Tales of Beedle the Bard* is a collection of stories written for young wizards…') (signed, 'J K Rowling | 2008'); xvii 'A Note on the Footnotes' ('Professor Dumbledore appears to have been writing for a wizarding audience…') (signed, 'JKR'); [xviii] blank; [1] illustration of puddle, three slugs, a thick slipper and eleven stars, 16 by 35mm; [2] blank; 3-11 text and illustrations; 12-[18] text of commentary; [19] illustration of sword, shield and foliage, 16 by 38mm; [20] blank; 21-35 text and illustrations; 36-[41] text of commentary; [42] blank; [43] illustration of book, lute, key, goblet and dagger, 21 by 36mm; [44] blank; 45-54 text and illustrations; 55-[60] text of commentary; [61] illustration of branch, axe, crown, dog's collar and pair of hound footprints, 20 by 38mm; [62] blank; 63-77 text and illustrations; 78-[84] text of commentary; [85] illustration of skull, wand, stone, cloak and ten stars, 31 by 50mm; [86] blank; 87-93 text and illustrations; 94-[105] text of commentary; [106] blank; 107-[109] [A personal message from Baroness Nicholson of Winterbourne] ('children's | HIGH LEVEL GROUP | health. education. welfare. | [new paragraph] Dear Reader, | [new paragraph] Thank you very much for buying this unique…') (signed, 'Baroness Nicholson of Winterbourne MEP | Co-Chair of CHLG'); [110] blank

Paper: wove paper

Running title: '*The Tales of Beedle the Bard*' (37mm) on verso, recto title comprises story or section title, pp. xii-[105] (excluding blank pages, pages on which a new story or section commences, or pages with a full-page illustration). Running titles are enclosed within two vignettes of foliage (in mirror image)

Illustrations: In addition to an illustrated title-page, (p. [iii]) and embellishments to 'Contents' (p. [vii]), there are a large number of illustrations through the volume. There are seven vignettes (all printed on an otherwise blank page) that separate the volume into component parts (pp. [v], [ix], [1], [19], [43], [61] and [85]). Within the pages noted above as 'text and illustrations', there are two small drawings with text (less than ¼ page) (pp. 51 and [105]), six ¼ page drawings with text (pp. 3, 21, 45, 54, 63 and 87) which, with the exception of that on page 54 repeat the previous divisional vignette, two ⅓ page drawings with text (pp. 9 and 11), two ½ page drawings with text (pp. 75 and 93) and four full-page drawings without text (pp. [26], [32], [71] and [88]). In addition, an illustration of a wand and ten stars is present at the start of each section of commentary text (on pp. 12, 36, 55, 78 and 94). Page numbers are enclosed within two vignettes of foliage (in mirror image).

Binding: pictorial boards.

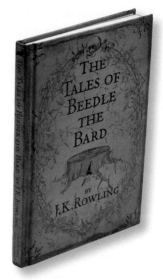

On spine: publisher's device of a dog, 10 by 7mm (horizontally at head) with 'children's [in red] | THE TALES OF BEEDLE THE BARD BY J.K. ROWLING | HIGH LEVEL GROUP' [in black]' (reading lengthways down spine). All in blue.

On upper cover: 'THE | TALES OF | BEEDLE | THE | BARD | [illustration of a tree stump] | BY | J.K.ROWLING' (all width centred). All in blue and all within decorated border of foliage with skull at top.

On lower cover: '*The Tales of Beedle the Bard* | contains five richly diverse fairy tales, | each with its own magical character, | that will variously bring delight, laughter | and the thrill of mortal peril. | [new paragraph] Additional notes for each story penned | by Professor Albus Dumbledore | will be enjoyed by Muggles and wizards alike, | as the Professor muses on the morals illuminated | by the tales, and reveals snippets of information | about life at Hogwarts. | [new paragraph] A uniquely magical volume, with illustrations | by the author, J.K.Rowling, that will be treasured for years to come. | [new paragraph] £1.61 from the sale of this book will be donated to the | Children's High Level Group | [new paragraph (with 'children's [in red] | HIGH LEVEL GROUP [in black] | health. education. welfare. [in black]' on left)] The Children's High Level | Group (CHLG) campaigns to | protect and promote children's | rights and make life better for | vulnerable young people. [all within decorated border of foliage with skull at top] | [barcode in black on white panel, 27 by 39mm (on left)] ['[publisher's device of a dog, 7 by 12mm] | BLOOMSBURY | £6.99' on left and '[Forest Stewardship Council logo, 6 by 7mm together with © symbol] | FSC | Mixed Sources | Product group from well-managed | forests and other controlled sources | [new paragraph] Cert no. SGS-COC-2061 | www.fsc.org | © 1996 Forest Stewardship Council' on right with 'www.chlg.org | www.bloomsbury.com/beedlebard' at centre, all in dark blue (with the exception of the price which is in black) on light blue panel, 27 by 41mm (on right)]'. All in blue and, with the exception of the two panels, all within decorated border of foliage with skull at top.

All edges trimmed. Binding measurements: 184 by 125mm (covers), 184 by 23mm (spine). End-papers: wove paper.

Dust-jacket: none

Publication: 4 December 2008 (simultaneous with A15(aa) and A15(aaa)) in an edition of 1.67 million copies (confirmed by Bloomsbury)

Price: £6.99

Contents:
Introduction
('*The Tales of Beedle the Bard* is a collection of stories written for young wizards…')
(signed, 'J K Rowling | 2008')

A Note on the Footnotes
('Professor Dumbledore appears to have been writing for a wizarding audience…')
(signed, 'JKR')
The Wizard and the Hopping Pot
('There was once a kindly old wizard who used his magic generously…')
Albus Dumbledore on 'The Wizard and the Hopping Pot'
('A kind old wizard decides to teach his hard-hearted son a lesson…')
The Fountain of Fair Fortune
('High on a hill in an enchanted garden, enclosed by tall walls and protected…')
Albus Dumbledore on 'The Fountain of Fair Fortune'
("'The Fountain of Fair Fortune' is a perennial favourite…')
The Warlock's Hairy Heart
('There was once a handsome, rich and talented young warlock…')
Albus Dumbledore on 'The Warlock's Hairy Heart'
('As we have already seen, Beedle's first two tales attracted criticism…')
Babbitty Rabbitty and her Cackling Stump
('A long time ago, in a far-off land, there lived a foolish king…')
Albus Dumbledore on 'Babbitty Rabbitty and her Cackling Stump'
('The story of 'Babbitty Rabbitty and her Cackling Stump' is, in many ways…')
The Tale of the Three Brothers
('There were once three brothers who were travelling along a lonely, winding road…')
Albus Dumbledore on 'The Tale of the Three Brothers'
('This story made a profound impression on me as a boy.')

Notes:

On 13 December 2007 Sotheby's sold one of seven handwritten copies of *The Tales of Beedle the Bard* (see D5). Recipients of the other copies were important people in the history of Harry Potter and the gift was intended as a thank you present by the author. The purchaser, however, was amazon.com who received some significant publicity. Although the author's work was protected by copyright laws, the online merchant posted reviews of the individual tales and numerous photographs. It was announced that the volume would tour libraries and schools. Amazon also ran a competition with a prize allowing the winner access to read the book.

On 31 July 2008 it was announced on the author's website that the text was to be published with additional notes.

The earliest dated proofs in the editorial files at Bloomsbury reveal a date of 10 July 2008. An email dated 24 June 2008 provides an early draft of pre-publication publicity. Production files suggest that 11 August 2008 was intended as the date for final approval of text. This timetable was later abandoned.

Editorial files reveal that the text was edited and revised during the production process. There were minor changes throughout the book and discussion with the author. A note, for example, on 'The Wizard and the Hopping Pot' queries 'garbage pail' and notes that this 'may sound a little American to a British ear but – and this is probably precisely why you selected this word – it does have Middle

English derivations! Did you want to look though at using a word that *appears* at least less American? Or leave?' The published text includes a 'rubbish pail' (in both English and American editions).

An early set of proofs (dated 10 July 2008) included number headings to each story. These were later deleted.

At least three proof states were produced by Bloomsbury before publication.

During July 2008 it was discovered that 'The Children's Voice' (the original name of the charity) was trademarked in the United States. The name, therefore, reverted to the original 'The Children's High Level Group'. On 12 August 2008 Colman Getty, then the author's PR agency, noted the need for the charity's registered charity number to be included in the publication. It had been omitted from early proofs.

Editorial files suggest that the collation of the volume should comprise one gathering of 24 leaves, one gathering of 16 leaves and then a final gathering of 24 leaves. This has not been possible to verify from copies of the book without causing damage.

The official launch of *The Tales of Beedle the Bard* was at a tea party held at 4 pm at the National Library of Scotland on the day of publication. Attending were local children and those who had won a competition organized by the publisher.

The 'Personal Message from Baroness Nicholson of Winterbourne' starts below a letterhead ('children's | HIGH LEVEL GROUP | health. education.welfare.') including 'children's' in a handwritten script. This was the logo of the charity.

Copies: private collection (PWE)

Reprints include:
7 9 10 8 6

A15(aa)   FIRST AMERICAN EDITION   (2008)
(hardback)

THE | TALES | OF | BEEDLE | THE | BARD | JKRowling [facsimile signature] (All width centred within decorated border including skull, heart and tree stump, 172 by 128mm)

Collation: 64 unsigned leaves bound in indeterminate gatherings; 210 by 136mm; [I-VI] VII-XIV [XV-XVI] 1-107 [108] 109-111 [112]

Page contents: [I] 'THE | TALES | OF | BEEDLE | THE | BARD'; [II] *'Translated from the Ancient Runes by* | HERMIONE GRANGER | *Commentary by* | ALBUS DUMBLEDORE | *Introduction, Notes, and Illustrations by* | J.K. ROWLING | [three stars] | children's | HIGH LEVEL GROUP | [rule, 63mm] | *In association with* | ARTHUR A. LEVINE BOOKS | An Imprint of Scholastic

Inc.'; [III] title-page; [IV] 'Text and interior illustrations copyright © 2007, 2008 by J. K. Rowling | Cover illustration by Mary GrandPré copyright © 2008 by J. K. Rowling | [new paragraph] All rights reserved. | J. K. Rowling has asserted her moral rights. | Published by the Children's High Level Group, | in association with ARTHUR A. LEVINE BOOKS, an imprint of Scholastic Inc., | *Publishers since 1920.* SCHOLASTIC, the LANTERN LOGO, and associated logos | are trademarks and/or registered trademarks of Scholastic Inc. | The Children's High Level Group and the Children's High Level Group logo and | associated logos are trademarks of the Children's High Level Group. | [new paragraph] No part of this publication may be reproduced, stored in a retrieval system, | or transmitted in any form or by any means, electronic, mechanical, photocopying, | recording, or otherwise, without written permission of the publisher. | For information regarding permission, write to Scholastic Inc., Attention: | Permissions

Department, 557 Broadway, New York, NY 10012. | [new paragraph] Scholastic's net proceeds from every sale of this book will go to the | Children's High Level Group. The purchase of this book is not tax deductible. | The Children's High Level Group may be contacted at: CHLG, Hope House, | 45 Great Peter Street, London, SW1P 3LT, United Kingdom. www.chlg.org | [new paragraph] Library of Congress Control Number: 2008934360 | ISBN-13: 978-0-545-12828-5 [point] ISBN-10: 0-545-12828-5 | [new paragraph] 10 9 8 7 6 5 4 3 2 1   08 09 10 11 12 | [new paragraph] Printed in the U.S.A. 58 | First edition, December 2008 | [new paragraph] [Forest Stewardship Council logo, 6 by 8mm together with © symbol and 'FSC' to the right is the text: 'Mixed Sources | Product group from well-managed | forests, controlled sources and | recycled wood or fiber | [new paragraph] www.fsc.org Cert no. SW-COC-002550 | © 1996 Forest Stewardship Council'] | [new paragraph] We try to produce the most beautiful books possible, and we are also extremely | concerned about the impact of our manufacturing process on the forests of the | world and the environment as a whole. Accordingly, we made sure that all of the | paper we used contains 30% post-consumer recycled fiber, and has been | certified as coming from forests that are managed to insure the protection | of the people and wildlife dependent upon them.'; [V] 'CONTENTS' (twelve individual parts listed with titles and page references); [VI] blank; VII-XIV 'INTRODUCTION' ('THE TALES OF BEEDLE THE BARD is a collection of stories written for young wizards...') (signed, 'J. K. Rowling | 2008') together with panel in grey on p. XIV, 40 by 82mm, containing 'A NOTE ON THE FOOTNOTES | Professor Dumbledore appears to have been writing | for a Wizarding audience, so I have occasionally | inserted an explanation of a term or fact that | might need clarification for Muggle readers. |—JKR—'; [XV] half-title: 'THE | TALES | OF | BEEDLE | THE BARD'; [XVI] blank; 1-10 text and illustrations; 11-19 text of commentary; 20-34 text and illustrations; 35-42 text of commentary; 43-53 text and illustrations; 54-60 text of commentary; 61-77 text and illustrations; 78-86 text of commentary; 87-93 text and illustrations; 94-107 text of commentary; [108] illustration of wand lying over rose with ten stars, 32 by 65mm; 109-111 [A personal message from Baroness Nicholson of Winterbourne] ('ABOUT THE CHILDREN'S | HIGH LEVEL GROUP | [new paragraph] *Dear*

Reader, | [new paragraph] *Thank you very much for buying this unique…'*) (signed, *'Baroness Nicholson of Winterbourne MEP* | *Co-Chair of CHLG'*); [112] colophon: '[publisher's device of a lantern, 17 by 13mm] | *This book was edited by Arthur A. Levine and* | *art directed by David Saylor. The art for the cover was* | *created using pastels on toned printmaking paper.* | *The art for the interiors was created using pen and ink* | *on paper. The book was designed by Elizabeth B. Parisi* | *and typeset by Brad Walrod. The text was set in Adobe* | *Garamond Pro. The book was printed and bound at* | *Quebecor World in Taunton, Massachusetts. The Managing* | *Editor was Karyn Browne; the Continuity Editor was* | *Cheryl Klein; and the Manufacturing* | *Director was Meryl Wolfe.'*

Paper: wove paper

Running title: 'THE TALES OF | BEEDLE THE BARD' on verso, recto title comprises story title, pp. 2-10, pp. 21-34, pp. 44-53, pp. 62-77 and pp. 88-93 only. Each running title includes a three-star design to left and right of both running-titles on verso and recto.

Illustrations: In addition to an illustrated title-page, (p. [III]), there are a large number of illustrations through the volume. Within the pages noted above as 'text and illustrations', there are seven small drawings with text (less than ⅓ page) (pp. 1, 20, 43, 53, 61, 77 and 87), five ½ page drawings with text (pp. 8, 10, 25, 50 and 90), two ¾ page drawings with text (pp. 34 and 93) and one full-page drawing without text (p. 70). Page numbers are enclosed within single six-pointed stars,

Binding: pictorial boards.

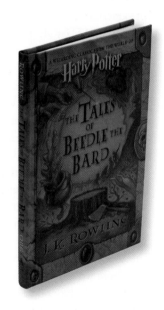

 On spine: 'ROWLING [in dark yellow] THE TALES OF BEEDLE THE BARD [in purple] CHLG [in dark yellow]' (reading lengthways down spine) with publisher's device of a lantern,12 by 9mm [in brown] (horizontally at foot of spine).

 On upper cover: 'A WIZARDING CLASSIC FROM THE WORLD OF [in black] | Harry Potter [hand-drawn lettering] [in dark yellow and grey] | THE TALES [in purple] | OF [in purple] | BEEDLE THE [in purple] | BARD [in purple] | J. K. ROWLING [in purple]' (all width centred). All on colour illustration of vignettes from all stories. The outer border imitates an old binding with a green gem in each corner, a purple gem at the centre foot and half a skull for a clasp.

 On lower cover: 'WITH EXTENSIVE COMMENTARY BY [in black] | ALBUS DUMBLEDORE | [illustration of a pair of half-moon spectacles] | THE TALE OF BEEDLE THE BARD, a Wizarding classic, first | came to Muggle readers' attention in the book known as HARRY | POTTER AND THE DEATHLY HALLOWS. Now, thanks to | Hermione Granger's new translation from the ancient runes, we | present this stunning edition with an introduction, notes, and | illustrations by J. K. Rowling, and extensive commentary by Albus | Dumbledore. Never before have Muggles been privy to these richly | imaginative tales: "The Wizard and the Hopping Pot," "The | Fountain of Fair Fortune," "The Warlock's Hairy Heart," "Babbitty | Rabbitty and Her Cackling Stump," and of course, "The

Tale | of the Three Brothers." But not only are they the equal of fairy | tales we now know and love, reading them gives new insight into | the world of Harry Potter. | [new paragraph] This purchase also represents another very important form of giving: | From every sale of this book, Scholastic will give its net proceeds to the | CHILDREN'S HIGH LEVEL GROUP, a charity cofounded in 2005 by J. K. Rowling | and Baroness Nicholson of Winterbourne, MEP. | [new paragraph] CHLG campaigns to protect and promote children's rights and make | life better for vulnerable young people. www.chlg. org | [barcode with smaller barcode to the right (51299) to the right all in black on yellow panel, 22 by 50mm] children's [in red] | HIGH LEVEL GROUP [in white] | health. education. welfare. [in white] | $12.99 US | Cover art by Mary GrandPré © 2008 by J. K. Rowling [in black]' (lines 1 and 2 centred, lines 3-15 justified on left and right margins, lines 16-21 centred, line 26 centred). All in yellow and all on dark brown panel. The outer border imitates an old binding with a blue gem in each corner and half a skull for a clasp.

All edges trimmed. Binding measurements: 217 by 139mm (covers), 217 by 21mm (spine). End-papers: purple wove paper. Red and yellow sewn bands at head and foot of spine.

Dust-jacket: none

Publication: 4 December 2008 (simultaneous with A15(a) and A15(aaa))

Price: $12.99

Contents:
Introduction
    ('THE TALES OF BEEDLE THE BARD is a collection of stories written for young wizards…')
    (signed, 'J. K. Rowling | 2008')
A Note on the Footnotes
    ('Professor Dumbledore appears to have been writing for a Wizarding audience…')
    (signed, 'JKR')
The Wizard and the Hopping Pot
    ('There was once a kindly old wizard who used his magic generously…')
Albus Dumbledore on "The Wizard and the Hopping Pot"
    ('A kind old wizard decides to teach his hard-hearted son a lesson…')
The Fountain of Fair Fortune
    ('High on a hill in an enchanted garden, enclosed by tall walls and protected…')
Albus Dumbledore on "The Fountain of Fair Fortune"
    ('"The Fountain of Fair Fortune" is a perennial favorite…')
The Warlock's Hairy Heart
    ('There was once a handsome, rich, and talented young warlock…')
Albus Dumbledore on "The Warlock's Hairy Heart"
    ('As we have already seen, Beedle's first two tales attracted criticism…')
Babbitty Rabbitty and her Cackling Stump
    ('A long time ago, in a far-off land, there lived a foolish King…')
Albus Dumbledore on "Babbitty Rabbitty and Her Cackling Stump"
    ('The story of "Babbitty Rabbitty and Her Cackling Stump" is, in many ways…')

The Tale of the Three Brothers

('There were once three brothers who were traveling along a lonely, winding road…')

Albus Dumbledore on "The Tale of the Three Brothers"

('This story made a profound impression on me as a boy.')

Notes:

The commentary notes 'by Albus Dumbledore' (together with Rowling's elucidations) are printed on grey panels. There are three six-pointed stars at each corner.

Editorial files at Bloomsbury suggest that they provided Scholastic with editorial changes of text. A set of proofs labelled 'Complete Mark-Up' and 'includes amends from JKR email' notes, for example, 'we didn't tell U.S. this 'of' deletion' for the fifth paragraph of Dumbledore's commentary on 'The Warlock's Hairy Heart'. The original final sentence read 'He wants to remain forever uninfected by what he regards as a kind of sickness, and therefore performs a piece of Dark magic that would not be possible outside of a story book: he locks away his own heart.' The final 'of' is not present in A15(a) but is included here.

Files at Bloomsbury note 'one of the global questions that came up for us while copy-editing this manuscript was whether to Americanize the spellings. In the previous charity books, we opted to leave the British spellings alone… In this case, however, we've decided that this book seems more like the U.S. edition of a wizarding classic, and therefore we're using American spellings …'

At least one slang connotation was highlighted: in Dumbledore's commentary on 'The Wizard and the Hopping Pot' the phrase 'such fruity seventeenth-century insults…' prompted the comment that 'in American slang, "fruity" means insane with connotations of being gay, though it's not the most common insult used against gay people anymore. Does it bother you to possibly have this distracting association here?' In both the U.K. and U.S. editions the phrase appears as 'such fruity epithets'. It was also felt that Dumbledore's commentary on 'The Fountain of Fair Fortune' needed a footnote to explain 'Christmas pantomine' to American readers. In the U.S. edition a note by Rowling is included, which is absent from the U.K. edition.

Each tale commences with a drop capital.

Copies: private collection (PWE)

A15(aaa)　　　AMAZON EDITION　　　(2008)
(hardback)

The Tales | of | Beedle the Bard | Translated from the original | runes by | Hermione Granger | JKRowling [facsimile signature] [all within decorated border including skull, heart and tree stump, 129 by 95mm] | With Commentary by Professor | Albus Dumbledore (All width centred)

Collation: 90 unsigned leaves bound in nine gatherings of eight leaves, one gathering of ten leaves and one gathering of eight leaves; 165 by 110mm; [1-8] 9-20 [21-24] 25-31 [32] 33-36 [37] 38-48

[49-52] 53-57 [58] 59-68 [69] 70 [71-72] 73-81 [82-84] 85-89 [90] 91-96 [97-98] 99-106 [107-110] 111-14 [115] 116-18 [119-20] 121-22 [123] 124-31 [132] 133-42 [143-46] 147 [148] 149-52 [153] 154 [155] 156 [157-58] 159-73 [174-75] 176-79 [180]

Page contents: [1] half-title: 'The Tales | of | Beedle the Bard'; [2] blank; [3] title-page; [4] 'Text and illustrations copyright © 2007/2008 by J. K. Rowling | [new paragraph] All rights reserved. | J.K. Rowling has asserted her moral rights. | Published by the Children's High Level Group. | [new paragraph] Produced by Amazon in association with | Andrews McMeel Publishing, LLC, and LionheartBooks,Ltd. | Designed by Michael Reagan. | [new paragraph] The Children's High Level Group and the Children's High Level Group logo | and associated logos are trademarks of the Children's High Level Group. | The Children's High Level Group (CHLG) is a charity established | under English law. Registered charity number 1112575. | [new paragraph] No part of this publication may be reproduced, stored in a retrieval system, or | transmitted in any form or by any means, electronic, mechanical, photocopying, | recording, or otherwise, without written permission of the publisher. For | information regarding permission, write to: The Children's High Level Group | c/o Christopher Little Literary Agency, Eel Brook Studios | 125 Moore Park Road, London, SW6 4PS | [new paragraph] Amazon's net proceeds from every sale of this book will go to the Children's | High Level Group (CHLG). Net proceeds for sales of the book from www. | amazon.co.uk in the United Kingdom are estimated to be £20 GBP per | unit. The purchase of this book is not tax deductible. Children's High | Level Group (CHLG) can be contacted at: CHLG, Hope House, 45 Great | Peter Street, London SW1P 3LT, United Kingdom, www.chlg.org. | [new paragraph] Library of Congress Control Number: 2008935436 | A CIP catalogue record of this book is available from the British Library | [new paragraph] ISBN-13: 978-0-956-01090-2 [point] ISBN-10: 0-956-01090-3 | 10 9 8 7 6 5 4 3 2 1   08 09 10 11 12 | [new paragraph] Printed in China | Through Asia Pacific Offset | [new paragraph] First edition, December 2008'; [5] 'The Tales of Beedle the Bard | Translated from the original runes by | Hermione Granger | Commentary by | Albus Dumbledore | Introduction, Notes, and Illustrations by | J.K. Rowling | [device of ten stars] | children's | HIGH LEVEL GROUP | health. education.welfare.'; [6-7] 'Contents' (twelve individual parts listed with titles and page references); [8] illustration of wand lying over rose with ten stars, 25 by 52mm; 9-20 'Introduction' ('"The Tales of Beedle the Bard" is a collection of stories written for young witches...') (signed, 'JKRowling | 2008'); [21] illustration of wand with ten stars, 50 by 35mm; [22] illustration of ten stars, 15 by 12mm; [23] divisional title: 'The Wizard and the | Hopping Pot'; [24] blank; 25-[37] text and illustrations; [38] 'A Note on the Footnotes | Professor Dumbledore appears to have been writing | for a wizarding audience, so I have occasionally | inserted an explanation of a term or fact that | might need explaining for Muggle readers. | JKR'; [39]-[49] text of commentary; [50] illustration of ten stars, 15 by 12mm; [51] divisional title: 'The Fountain of | Fair Fortune'; [52] blank; 53-[71] text and illustrations; [72] illustration of worm entwined with rose, 38 by 19mm; 73-81 text of commentary; [82] illustration of ten stars, 15 by 12mm; [83] divisional title: 'The Warlock's Hairy Heart'; [84] blank; 85-[98] text and illustrations; 99-106 text of commentary; [107] illustration of wand with ten stars, 45 by 31mm; [108] illustration of ten stars, 15 by 12mm; [109] divisional title: 'Babbitty Rabbitty and her | Cackling Stump'; [110] blank; 111-[132] text and illustrations; 133-142 text of commentary; [143] illustration of wand with ten stars, 45 by 31mm; [144] illustration of ten stars, 15 by 12mm; [145] divisional title: 'The Tale of the Three Brothers'; [146] blank; 147-[157] text and illustrations; [158] illustration of skull and roses, 24 by 60mm; 159-[175] text of commentary; 176-179 [A personal message from Baroness Nicholson of Winterbourne] ('children's | HIGH LEVEL GROUP | health. education. welfare. | [new paragraph] Dear Reader, | [new paragraph] Thank you very much for buying this unique…') (signed, '*Baroness Nicholson of Winterbourne MEP* | *Co-Chair of CHLG*'); [180] 'Amazon's net proceeds from every sale of | this book will go to the Children's High | Level Group (CHLG). Net proceeds for | sales of the book from www.amazon.co.uk | in the United Kingdom are estimated to be | £20 GBP per unit. The purchase of this | book is not tax deductible. Children's High | Level Group (CHLG) can be contacted at: | CHLG, Hope House, 45 Great Peter Street, | London SW1P 3LT, United Kindgom, | www.chlg.org.'

Paper: wove paper

Running title: none

Illustrations: In addition to an illustrated title-page, (p. [3]) and embellishments to 'Contents' (on both pp. [6] and [7]), there are a large number of illustrations through the volume. There are thirteen vignettes (often printed on a full-page) that separate the volume into component parts (pp. [5], [8], [21], [22], [50], [72], [82], [107], [108], [132], [143], [144] and [158]). Within the pages noted above as 'text and illustrations', there are two small drawings (less than ¼ page) (pp. 93 and 94), ten ¼ page drawings with text (pp. 25, 27, 35, 53, 64, 67, 85, 111, 129 and 147), ten full-page drawings without text (pp. [32], [37], [69], [71], [90], [98], [115], [120], [123] and [157]) and five drawings with text which span two pages (pp. [58]-59, 96-[97], [148]-149, 152-[153] and 154-[155]).

Binding: imitation brown morocco with metal embellishments.
    Spine: blank with four raised bands.
    On upper cover: five embellished metal panels. Centre: panel with skull and two beads, 98 by 83mm. Top left corner: panel with leaf and one bead, 45 by 45mm. Top right corner: panel with heart and one bead, 45 by 45mm. Lower left corner: panel with foot and one bead, 45 by 45mm. Lower right corner: panel with fountain, 45 by 45mm.
    On lower cover: metal clasp which clips on to upper cover.
    All edges trimmed. Binding measurements: 172 by 114mm (covers), 172 by 32mm (spine). End-papers: wove paper with printed marbled paper effect. Brown sewn bands at head and foot of spine together with green marker ribbon.

Dust-jacket: none

Publication: 4 December 2008 (simultaneous with A15(a) and A15(aa))

Price: £50 / $100

Contents:
Introduction
    ('"The Tales of Beedle the Bard" is a collection of stories written for young witches…')
    (signed, 'JKRowling | 2008')

The Wizard and the Hopping Pot

('There was once a kindly old wizard who used his magic generously...')

A Note on the Footnotes

('Professor Dumbledore appears to have been writing for a wizarding audience...')

(signed, 'JKR')

Albus Dumbledore on 'The Wizard and the Hopping Pot'

('A kind old wizard decides to teach his hard-hearted son a lesson...')

The Fountain of Fair Fortune

('High on a hill in an enchanted garden, enclosed by tall walls and protected...')

Albus Dumbledore on 'The Fountain of Fair Fortune'

("'The Fountain of Fair Fortune' is a perennial favourite...')

The Warlock's Hairy Heart

('There was once a handsome, rich and talented young warlock...')

Albus Dumbledore on 'The Warlock's Hairy Heart'

('As we have already seen, Beedle's first two tales attracted criticism...')

Babbitty Rabbitty and her Cackling Stump

('A long time ago, in a far-off land, there lived a foolish king...')

Albus Dumbledore on 'Babbitty Rabbitty and her Cackling Stump'

('The story of 'Babbitty Rabbitty and her Cackling Stump' is, in many ways...')

The Tale of the Three Brothers

('There were once three brothers who were travelling along a lonely, winding road...')

Albus Dumbledore on 'The Tale of the Three Brothers'

('This story made a profound impression on me as a boy.')

Notes:

The commentary notes 'by Albus Dumbledore' (together with Rowling's elucidations) are printed within single ruled borders. The first page of each section has additional embellishments at each corner.

Each tale commences with an embellished drop capital.

Note that the number on page 36 is in a different style.

The volume was presented in a large folding box measuring 316 by 250mm (covers), 316 by 83mm (spine). The box mimics a half-bound book with the dark brown colour of the spine encroaching onto the covers. There are also brown corner pieces. The edges are in gilt and imitate paper. On spine: '[imitation raised band] | The | Tales of | Beedle the | Bard | [imitation raised band] | [illustration of wand entwined with rose, 63 by 51mm] | [imitation raised band] | J. K. | Rowling | [imitation raised band]' (all width centred). On upper cover: 'The Tales | of | Beedle the Bard | by | JKRowling [facsimile signature]' (all width centred and within decorated border including skull, heart and tree stump, 205 by 157mm). On lower cover: illustration of skull and roses, 44 by 107mm. Internally the box is lined with black cloth. There is a pocket on the inside of the upper cover and a padded recess for the volume, 203 by 137mm (with a depth of 41mm).

The volume was contained in a deep purple velvet bag with a gold draw string, 226 by 163mm. On one side 'JKRowling', as a facsimile signature, is present in gold thread. The bag is stitched with purple thread.

The pocket contained an envelope of ten prints. The wove paper envelope, measuring 267 by 190mm, was printed with a background to imitate a textured paper with pink, white and orange hues. On upper panel: 'Collector's | Edition | Prints | JKRowling [facsimile signature]' (all width centred and within decorated border including skull, heart, and tree stump, 147 by 113mm). On flap, 45 by 190mm (with tapered left and right edges and rounded corners): 'children's | HIGH LEVEL GROUP | health. education. welfare.' (lines 1 and 2 width centred and line 3 of left margin). The ten prints, each on wove paper, are printed in blue black and replicate Rowling's illustrations as follows:

1 Cooking pot, slipper and parchment (from p. 27)
2 Young woman with baby appealing for help at wizard's door (from p. [32])
3 Three witches, followed by a knight, venturing into the enchanted garden (from pp. [58]-59)
4 Stream bearing the words 'Pay Me The Treasure of Your Past' (from p. 64)
5 The fountain of fair fortune (from p. [69])
6 Warlock looking upon a beautiful witch (from p. [90])
7 Ornate key (from p. 93)
8 Two men, 'the charlatan and the foolish King' waving wands (from p. [115])
9 Babbitty Rabbitty, an old crone (from p. [120])
10 Man lying dead with head on a pillow, together with bottle of poison and apparition (from pp. [154]-155)

Published as the 'collector's edition' and offered exclusively by Amazon, the volume was intended to reproduce the binding of the author's original offered for sale at auction (see D5). Amazon stated that their edition was 'available in limited quantities'. It was reported at the time of publication that 100,000 copies were printed. This is unverified.

A comparison with the text of Rowling's introduction (as set in type for A15(a) and A15(aa)), suggests that there would be some minor revisions and that this handwritten version is in an earlier state than that set in type. Page 12, line 8 includes 'fate' (set in type as 'fates') and page 18 line 10 includes 'they' (set in type as 'the notes'). Note, also, the 'wizards' or 'witches' in the opening sentence.

Editorial files at Bloomsbury suggest that the Amazon edition was separately proof-read from the standard trade edition but that the Bloomsbury team were part of the project.

Copies: private collection

THE | TALES OF | BEEDLE | THE | BARD | Translated from the original | runes by Hermione Granger | *With additional notes by* | Professor Albus Dumbledore [all within decorated border including skull, heart and tree stump, 155 by 118mm with '[Lumos logo, 6 by 8mm] | LUMOS | Working to transform the lives | of disadvantaged children' at left foot and '[publisher's device of a dog, 7 by 13mm] | BLOOMSBURY' at right foot] (All width centred except charity and publisher's devices which are slightly inset from outer margins)

Collation: 64 unsigned leaves bound in eight gatherings of eight leaves; 198 by 128mm; [i-x] xi-xvii [xviii] [1-2] 3-17 [18-20] 21-25 [26] 27-31 [32] 33-40 [41-44] 45-59 [60-62] 63-70 [71] 72-83 [84-86] 87 [88] 89-104 [105-106] 107-108 [109-110]

Page contents: [i] half-title: 'THE | TALES OF | BEEDLE | THE | BARD' with floral motif; [ii] *'Titles available in the Harry Potter series | (in reading order):* | Harry Potter and the Philosopher's Stone | Harry Potter and the Chamber of Secrets | Harry Potter and the Prisoner of Azkaban | Harry Potter and the Goblet of Fire | Harry Potter and the Order of the Phoenix | Harry Potter and the Half-Blood Prince | Harry Potter and the Deathly Hallows | [new paragraph] *Titles available in the Harry Potter series | (in Latin):* | Harry Potter and the Philosopher's Stone | Harry Potter and the Chamber of Secrets | *(in Welsh, Ancient Greek and Irish):* | Harry Potter and the Philosopher's Stone | [new paragraph] *Also available | (in aid of Comic Relief):* | Fantastic Beasts and Where to Find Them | Quidditch Through the Ages | *(in aid of Lumos):* | The Tales of Beedle the Bard'; [iii] title-page; [iv] 'First published in Great Britain in 2008 by Lumos (formerly the Children's | High Level Group), 12-14 Berry Street, London, EC1V 0AU, | in association with Bloomsbury Publishing Plc, | 50 Bedford Square, London, WC1B 3DP | [new paragraph] This edition published in 2012 | [new paragraph] Text and illustrations copyright © J. K. Rowling 2007/2008 | [new paragraph] Lumos and the Lumos logo and associated logos | are trademarks of the Lumos Foundation | [new paragraph] Lumos is the operating name of Lumos Foundation (formerly the | Children's High Level Group), a company limited by guarantee | registered in England and Wales, number: 5611912. | Registered charity number 1112575 | [new paragraph] J. K. Rowling has asserted her moral rights | [new paragraph] All rights reserved | No part of this publication may be reproduced or | transmitted by any means, electronic, mechanical, photocopying | or otherwise, without the prior permission of the publisher. | [new paragraph] A CIP catalogue record of this book is available from the British Library | [new paragraph] ISBN 978 1 4088 3504 3 | [new paragraph] [Forest Stewardship Council logo, 6 by 7mm together with ® symbol and text: 'FSC | www.fsc.org' with 'MIX | Paper from | responsible sources | FSC® C008047' to the right and all within single ruled border with rounded corners, 12 by 26mm] | [new paragraph] Typeset by RefineCatch Limited, Bungay, Suffolk | Printed in China by C&C Offset Printing Co Ltd, Shenzhen, Guangdong | [new paragraph] 1 3 5 7 9 10 8 6 4 2 | [new paragraph] www.lumos.org.uk | www.bloomsbury.com'; [v] illustration of skull, wand, stone, cloak and ten stars, 34 by 57mm; [vi] blank; [vii] 'CONTENTS' (seven individual parts listed with titles and page references); [viii] blank; [ix] illustration of wand lying over rose with ten stars, 22 by 47mm; [x] blank; xi-xvi 'Introduction' ('*The Tales of Beedle the Bard* is a collection of stories written for young wizards…') (signed, 'J K Rowling | 2008'); xvii 'A Note on the Footnotes' ('Professor Dumbledore appears to have been writing for a wizarding audience…') (signed, 'JKR'); [xviii] blank; [1] illustration of puddle, three slugs, a thick slipper and eleven stars, 16 by 35mm; [2] blank; 3-11 text and illustrations; 12-[18] text of commentary; [19] illustration of sword, shield and foliage, 16 by 38mm; [20] blank; 21-35 text and illustrations; 36-[41] text of commentary; [42] blank; [43] illustration of book, lute, key, goblet and dagger, 21 by 36mm; [44] blank; 45-54 text and illustrations; 55-[60] text of commentary; [61] illustration of branch, axe, crown, dog's collar and pair of hound footprints, 20 by 38mm; [62] blank; 63-77 text and illustrations; 78-[84] text of commentary; [85] illustration of skull, wand, stone, cloak and ten stars, 31 by 50mm; [86] blank; 87-93 text and illustrations; 94-[105] text of commentary; [106] blank; 107-[109] [A personal message from Georgette Mulheir, Chief Executive of Lumos] ('[Lumos logo, 8 by 9mm] | LUMOS | Working to transform the lives | of disadvantaged children | [new paragraph] Dear Reader, | [new paragraph] Thank you very much for buying this unique…') (signed, 'Georgette Mulheir | Chief Executive, Lumos'); [110] blank

Paper: wove paper

Running title: '*The Tales of Beedle the Bard*' (37mm) on verso, recto title comprises story or section title, pp. xii-[105] (excluding blank pages, pages on which a new story or section commences, or pages with a full-page illustration). Running titles are enclosed within two vignettes of foliage (in mirror image)

Illustrations: as for A15(a)

Binding: decorated boards in 'half-bound' style with spine and corner pieces in black and with covers in blue.

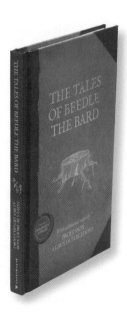

On spine: 'NOTES BY PROFESSOR | THE TALES OF BEEDLE THE BARD [illustration of foliage, 12 by 13mm, in yellow] BLOOMSBURY [publisher's device of the head of a dog, 3 by 4mm] | ALBUS DUMBLEDORE' (reading down spine). All in gilt.

On upper cover: 'THE TALES | OF BEEDLE | THE BARD | [illustration of a tree stump, 40 by 71mm] | *With additional notes by* | PROFESSOR | ALBUS DUMBLEDORE' (all width centred). All in gilt with the exception of the illustration of the tree stump which is in yellow. To the left of the author is a circular 'wax' stamp in dark blue and black stating '*Property of* | HOGWARTS | LIBRARY' within circular single ruled border, diameter 20mm, with border and lettering in gilt.

On lower cover: '[illustration of a tree stump, 27 by 48mm] | *The Tales of Beedle the Bard* contains | five richly diverse fairy tales, each with its own | magical character, that will variously bring delight, | laughter and the thrill of mortal peril. | [new paragraph] Essential and enjoyable reading for Muggles | and wizards alike, *The Tales of Beedle the Bard* | is a uniquely magical volume. | With illuminating notes by | Albus Dumbledore [facsimile signature] | [new paragraph] Proceeds from the sale of this book will be | donated to Lumos, a charity working to transform | the lives of disadvantaged children. | [new paragraph] [two columns, in the first column is '[Lumos logo, 9 by 10mm] | LUMOS', in the second column is '[publisher's device of a dog, 5 by 9mm] | BLOOMSBURY'] | [new paragraph] [three columns, in the first column is the barcode, in the second column is '[Forest Stewardship Council logo, 6 by 7mm] | FSC | MIX | Paper | FSC® C008047' all within single ruled border with rounded corners, 17 by 12mm, and in the third column is 'www.lumos.org.uk | www.bloomsbury.com/harrypotter | www.pottermore.com']'. All in yellow with the exception of the Lumos logo and name which is in light and dark purple and the final three columns which are in black on a white panel, 23 by 81mm.

All edges trimmed. Blue and grey sewn bands at head and foot of spine. Binding measurements: 205 by 128mm (covers), 205 by 28mm (spine). End-papers: wove paper. The black spine colour continues onto the covers by approximately 13mm.

Dust-jacket: none

Slipcase: card slipcase covered in red paper (see description for A10(d)).

Publication: 11 October 2012 in an edition of 77,200 copies (confirmed by Bloomsbury)

Price: £25 [together with A10(d) and A11(d)]

Contents:
Introduction
    ('*The Tales of Beedle the Bard* is a collection of stories written for young wizards…')
    (signed, 'J K Rowling | 2008')
A Note on the Footnotes
    ('Professor Dumbledore appears to have been writing for a wizarding audience…')
    (signed, 'JKR')
The Wizard and the Hopping Pot
    ('There was once a kindly old wizard who used his magic generously…')
Albus Dumbledore on 'The Wizard and the Hopping Pot'
    ('A kind old wizard decides to teach his hard-hearted son a lesson…')
The Fountain of Fair Fortune
    ('High on a hill in an enchanted garden, enclosed by tall walls and protected…')
Albus Dumbledore on 'The Fountain of Fair Fortune'
    ("The Fountain of Fair Fortune' is a perennial favourite…')

The Warlock's Hairy Heart

('There was once a handsome, rich and talented young warlock…')

Albus Dumbledore on 'The Warlock's Hairy Heart'

('As we have already seen, Beedle's first two tales attracted criticism…')

Babbitty Rabbitty and her Cackling Stump

('A long time ago, in a far-off land, there lived a foolish king…')

Albus Dumbledore on 'Babbitty Rabbitty and her Cackling Stump'

('The story of 'Babbitty Rabbitty and her Cackling Stump' is, in many ways…')

The Tale of the Three Brothers

('There were once three brothers who were travelling along a lonely, winding road…')

Albus Dumbledore on 'The Tale of the Three Brothers'

('This story made a profound impression on me as a boy.')

Notes:

The core text of this edition appears to use the same setting as A15(a).

Note the change of the charity's name from the Children's High Level Group to Lumos.

The 'Personal Message from Georgette Mulheir' uses much of the text of the 'Personal Message from Baroness Nicholson of Winterbourne' from A15(a).

Copies: private collection (PWE)

A15(c)   SECOND AMERICAN EDITION   (2013)
(hardback)

THE | TALES | OF | BEEDLE | THE | BARD | JKRowling [facsimile signature] (All width centred within decorated border including skull, heart and tree stump, 148 by 114mm)

Collation: 64 unsigned leaves bound in eight gatherings of eight leaves; 197 by 127mm; [i-x] xi-xvii [xviii] [1-2] 3-17 [18-20] 21-25 [26] 27-31 [32] 33-40 [41-44] 45-59 [60-62] 63-70 [71] 72-83 [84-86] 87 [88] 89-104 [105-106] 107-108 [109-110]

Page contents: [i] 'THE | TALES OF | BEEDLE | THE | BARD'; [ii] 'Translated from the Ancient Runes by | HERMIONE GRANGER | Commentary by | ALBUS DUMBLEDORE | Introduction, Notes, and Illustrations by | J. K. ROWLING | [three stars] | [Lumos logo, 10 by 11mm] | LUMOS | Working to transform the lives | of disadvantaged children | [rule, 63mm] | In *association with* | ARTHUR A. LEVINE BOOKS | An Imprint of Scholastic Inc.'; [iii] title-page; [iv] 'Text and illustrations copyright © 2007, 2008 by J. K. Rowling | HARRY POTTER and all related characters | and elements are TM of and © WBEI. | Harry Potter Publishing Rights © J. K. Rowling | [new paragraph] All rights reserved. J. K. Rowling has asserted her moral rights. | Published by Lumos (formerly the Children's High Level Group), in | association with Arthur A. Levine Books, an imprint of Scholastic Inc., | *Publishers since 1920.* SCHOLASTIC, the LANTERN LOGO, | and associated logos are trademarks and/or registered trademarks of | Scholastic Inc. LUMOS, the LUMOS LOGO, and associated logos | are trademarks of the Lumos Foundation. | [new paragraph] No part of this publication may be reproduced, stored in a retrieval system, | or transmitted in any form or by any means, electronic, mechanical, | photocopying, recording, or otherwise, without written permission of the | publisher. For information regarding permission, write to Scholastic Inc., | Attention: Permissions Department, 557 Broadway, New York, NY 10012. | [new paragraph] ISBN 978-0-545-61540-2 | [new paragraph] 12 11 10 9 8 7 6 5 4 3 2 1   13 14 15 16 17 | [new paragraph] Printed in China 95 | This edition first printing, November 2013 | [new paragraph] *From every sale of the* Hogwarts Library, *Scholastic will donate twenty percent of* | *the suggested retail sales price less taxes of this boxed set to two charities selected by* | *the author J. K. Rowling: Lumos, a charity founded by J. K. Rowling that works* | *to end the institutionalization of children (wearelumos.org), and Comic Relief, a* | *UK-based charity that strives to create a just world free from poverty* | *(www.comicrelief.com). Purchase of this book is not tax deductible.*'; [v] illustration of skull, wand, stone, cloak and ten stars, 34 by 57mm; [vi] blank; [vii] 'CONTENTS' (seven individual parts listed with titles and page references); [viii] blank; [ix] illustration of wand lying over rose with ten stars, 22 by 47mm; [x] blank; xi-xvi 'Introduction' ('*The Tales of Beedle the Bard* is a collection of stories written for young wizards...') (signed, 'J K Rowling | 2008'); xvii 'A Note on the Footnotes' ('Professor Dumbledore appears to have been writing for a wizarding audience...') (signed, 'JKR'); [xviii] blank; [1] illustration of puddle, three slugs, a thick slipper and eleven stars, 16 by 35mm; [2] blank; 3-11 text and illustrations; 12-[18] text of commentary; [19] illustration of sword, shield and foliage, 16 by 38mm; [20] blank; 21-35 text and illustrations; 36-[41] text of commentary; [42] blank; [43] illustration of book, lute, key, goblet and dagger, 21 by 36mm; [44] blank; 45-54 text and illustrations; 55-[60] text of commentary; [61] illustration of branch, axe, crown, dog's collar and pair of hound footprints, 20 by 38mm; [62] blank; 63-77 text and illustrations; 78-[84] text of commentary; [85] illustration of skull, wand, stone, cloak and ten stars, 31 by 50mm; [86] blank; 87-93 text and illustrations; 94-[105] text of commentary; [106] blank; 107-[109] [A personal message from Georgette Mulheir, Chief Executive of Lumos] ('[Lumos logo, 8 by 9mm] | LUMOS | Working to transform the lives | of disadvantaged children | [new paragraph] Dear Reader, | [new paragraph] Thank you very much for buying this unique...') (signed, 'Georgette Mulheir | Chief Executive, Lumos'); [110] blank

Paper: wove paper

Running title: '*The Tales of Beedle the Bard*' (37mm) on verso, recto title comprises story or section title, pp. xii-[105] (excluding blank pages, pages on which a new story or section commences, or pages with a full-page illustration). Running titles are enclosed within two vignettes of foliage (in mirror image)

Illustrations: as for A15(a)

Binding: decorated boards in 'half-bound' style with spine and corner pieces in black and with covers in blue.

On spine: 'NOTES BY PROFESSOR | THE TALES OF BEEDLE THE BARD [illustration of foliage, 12 by 13mm, in yellow] | ALBUS DUMBLEDORE' (reading lengthways down spine) with publisher's device of a lantern, 10 by 7mm and '[publisher's book device] | [rule] | S' within single ruled border, 12 by 6mm (horizontally at foot of spine). All in gilt.

On upper cover: 'THE TALES | OF BEEDLE | THE BARD | [illustration of a tree stump, 40 by 71mm] | *With additional notes by* | PROFESSOR | ALBUS DUMBLEDORE' (all width centred). All in gilt with the exception of the illustration of the tree stump which is in yellow. To the left of the author is a circular 'wax' stamp in dark blue and black stating '*Property of* | HOGWARTS | LIBRARY' within circular single ruled border, diameter 20mm, with border and lettering in gilt.

On lower cover: '[illustration of a tree stump, 27 by 48mm] | *The Tales of Beedle the Bard* contains | five richly diverse fairy tales, each with its own | magical character, that will variously bring delight, | laughter and the thrill of mortal peril. | [new paragraph] Essential and enjoyable reading for Muggles | and wizards alike, *The Tales of Beedle the Bard* | is a uniquely magical volume. | With illuminating notes by | Albus Dumbledore [facsimile signature] | [new paragraph] Proceeds from the sale of this book will be | donated to Lumos, a charity working to transform | the lives of disadvantaged children. | [new paragraph] [three columns, in the first column is '[Lumos logo, 9 by 10mm] [in purple] | LUMOS [in purple] | From every sale of the Hogwarts | Library, Scholastic will donate twenty | percent of the suggested retail sales | price less taxes of this boxed set to two | charities selected by the author J. K. | Rowling: Lumos, a charity founded | by J. K. Rowling that works to end | the institutionalization of children | (wearelumos.org), and Comic Relief, | a UK-based charity that strives to | create a just world free from poverty | (www.comicrelief.com).', in the second column is '[COMIC | RELIEF^UK' logo, diameter 15mm] [in red, black and white] | Not to be sold separately.' and in the third column is '[publisher's device of a lantern, 10 by 7mm] | ARTHUR A. LEVINE BOOKS | [publisher's book device with 'SCHOLASTIC' in white on red panel, 5 by 45mm] | scholastic.com']'. All in yellow.

All edges trimmed. Blue and grey sewn bands at head and foot of spine. Binding measurements: 203 by 128mm (covers), 203 by 24mm (spine). End-papers: wove paper. The green/brown spine colour continues onto the covers by approximately 13mm.

Dust-jacket: none

Slipcase: card slipcase covered in red paper (see description for A10(e)).

Publication: 29 October 2013

Price: $29.99 [together with A10(e) and A11(e)]

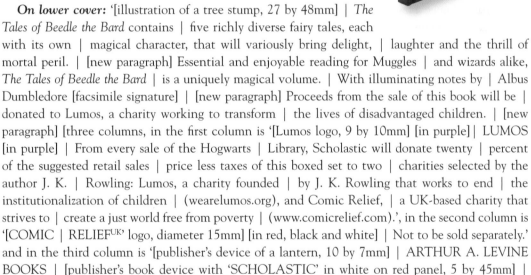

Contents:

Introduction

('*The Tales of Beedle the Bard* is a collection of stories written for young wizards...')

(signed, 'J K Rowling | 2008')

A Note on the Footnotes

('Professor Dumbledore appears to have been writing for a wizarding audience...')

(signed, 'JKR')

The Wizard and the Hopping Pot

('There was once a kindly old wizard who used his magic generously...')

Albus Dumbledore on 'The Wizard and the Hopping Pot'

('A kind old wizard decides to teach his hard-hearted son a lesson...')

The Fountain of Fair Fortune

('High on a hill in an enchanted garden, enclosed by tall walls and protected...')

Albus Dumbledore on 'The Fountain of Fair Fortune'

("The Fountain of Fair Fortune' is a perennial favourite...')

The Warlock's Hairy Heart

('There was once a handsome, rich and talented young warlock...')

Albus Dumbledore on 'The Warlock's Hairy Heart'

('As we have already seen, Beedle's first two tales attracted criticism...')

Babbitty Rabbitty and her Cackling Stump

('A long time ago, in a far-off land, there lived a foolish king...')

Albus Dumbledore on 'Babbitty Rabbitty and her Cackling Stump'

('The story of 'Babbitty Rabbitty and her Cackling Stump' is, in many ways...')

The Tale of the Three Brothers

('There were once three brothers who were travelling along a lonely, winding road...')

Albus Dumbledore on 'The Tale of the Three Brothers'

('This story made a profound impression on me as a boy.')

Notes:

The core text of this edition appears to use the same setting as A15(b), and therefore A15(a). Note, however, that the 'double title-page' of A15(aa) is retained although the distinctive type used there has been abandoned.

Copies: private collection (PWE)

THE CASUAL VACANCY

A16(a)　　　　　**FIRST ENGLISH EDITION**　　　　　**(2012)**
　　　　　　　　　　　　　　(hardback)

J.K.ROWLiNG | [rule, 36mm] | The | Casual | Vacancy | [publisher's device of 'L', 'B' and column within single oval border, 17 by 12mm] | Little, Brown (Lines 1-5 in hand-drawn lettering and all width centred)

Collation: 256 unsigned leaves bound in indeterminate gatherings; 234 by 151mm; [i-vi] [1-2] 3-5 [6] 7-50 [51-52] 53-175 [176-78] 179-255 [256-58] 259-328 [329-30] 331-401 [402-404] 405-465 [466-68] 469-81 [482-84] 485-503 [504-506]

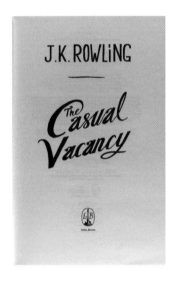

Page contents: [i] half-title: 'The | Casual | Vacancy' (hand-drawn lettering); [ii] '*Also by J.K. Rowling* | [new paragraph] Harry Potter and the Philosopher's Stone | Harry Potter and the Chamber of Secrets | Harry Potter and the Prisoner of Azkaban | Harry Potter and the Goblet of Fire | Harry Potter and the Order of the Phoenix | Harry Potter and the Half-Blood Prince | Harry Potter and the Deathly Hallows | [new paragraph] (in Latin) | Harry Potter and the Philosopher's Stone | Harry Potter and the Chamber of Secrets | [new paragraph] (in Welsh, Ancient Greek and Irish) | Harry Potter and the Philosopher's Stone | [new paragraph] Fantastic Beasts and Where to Find Them | Quidditch Through the Ages | The Tales of Beedle the Bard'; [iii] title-page; [iv] 'LITTLE, BROWN | [new paragraph] First published in Great Britain in 2012 by Little, Brown | [new paragraph] Copyright © J.K. Rowling 2012 | [new paragraph] The moral right of the author has been asserted. | [new paragraph] *All characters and events in this publication, other than those* | *clearly in the public domain, are fictitious and any resemblance* | *to real persons, living or dead, is purely* | *coincidental.* | [new paragraph] All rights reserved. | No part of this publication may be reproduced, stored in a | retrieval system, or transmitted, in any form or by any means, without | the prior permission in writing of the publisher, nor be otherwise circulated | in any form of binding or cover other than that in which it is published | and without a similar condition including this condition being | imposed on the subsequent purchaser. | [new paragraph] 'Umbrella': Written by Terius Nash, Christopher 'Tricky' Stewart, Shawn Carter and Thaddis | Harrell © 2007 by 2082 Music Publishing (ASCAP)/Songs of Peer, Ltd. (ASCAP)/March | Ninth Music Publishing (ASCAP)/ Carter Boys Music (ASCAP)/EMI Music Publishing Ltd | (PRS)/Sony/ATV Music Publishing (PRS). All rights on behalf of WB Music Corp. and | 2082 Music Publishing Administered by

[v] *'To Neil'*; [vi] blank; [1] 'Part One' together with quotation from Arnold-Baker; [2] blank; 3-5 text; [6] blank; 7-50 text; [51] '(Olden Days)' together with quotation from Arnold-Baker; [52] blank; 53-175 text [176] blank; [177] 'Part Two' together with quotation from Arnold-Baker; [178] blank; 179-255 text; [256] blank; [257] 'Part Three' together with quotation from Arnold-Baker; [258] blank; 259-328 text; [329] 'Part Four' together with quotation from Arnold-Baker; [330] blank; 331-401 text; [402] blank; [403] 'Part Five' together with quotation from Arnold-Baker; [404] blank; 405-465 text; [466] blank; [467] 'Part Six' together with quotation from Arnold-Baker; [468] blank; 469-81 text; [482] blank; [483] 'Part Seven' together with quotation from Arnold-Baker; [484] blank; 485-503 text; [504-506] blank

Paper: wove paper

Running title: none

Binding: black boards.

On spine: 'The | J.K.ROWLiNG [square with large cross] Casual Vacancy' (reading lengthways down spine) with publisher's device of 'L', 'B', and column within single oval border, 17 by 12mm (horizontally at foot). All in gilt.

Upper and lower covers: blank.

All edges trimmed. Yellow and red sewn bands at head and foot of spine. Binding measurements: 241 by 151mm (covers), 241 by 50mm (spine). End-papers: orange wove paper.

Dust-jacket: coated wove paper, 241 by 565mm

On spine: 'The | J.K.ROWLiNG [square with large cross] [in red] Casual Vacancy' (reading lengthways down spine) with publisher's device of 'L', 'B', and column within single oval border, 17 by 12mm (horizontally at foot). All in black on yellow.

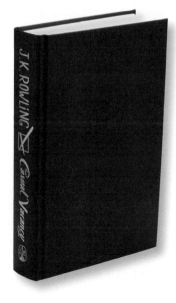

On upper cover: 'J.K.ROWLiNG [in white] | [square with large cross] [in black] | The [in white] | Casual [in white] | Vacancy [in white]' (all width centred with the exception of the title which is at an angle and slightly off-set to the right). All on red panel, 215 by 133mm, enclosed by single border in red, 226 by 141mm, and all on yellow.

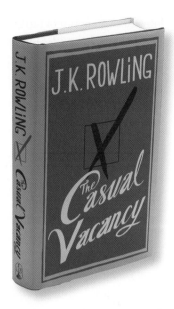

On lower cover: '[black silhouette of town skyline dominated by steeple with trees in blind in foreground, 50 by 103mm] | [Forest Stewardship Council logo, 8 by 9mm together with ® symbol and text: 'FSC' (all in black) and '[rule, 7mm] | Natural | Renewable | & Recyclable' (all in grey) on white panel, 25 by 12mm] ['visit littlebrown.co.uk' in black on yellow panel, 7 by 30mm] | [barcode in black together with 'GENERAL FICTION' in grey on white panel, 17 by 30mm]' with e-book logo in black (with text 'ebook+audio | also available'), 9 by 18mm, to the right of the three panels. All on red panel, 215 by 133mm, enclosed by single border in red, 226 by 141mm, and all on yellow.

On upper inside flap: 'A BIG NOVEL ABOUT | A SMALL TOWN … | [new paragraph] When Barry Fairbrother dies in his early forties, | the town of Pagford is left in shock. Pagford | is, seemingly, an English idyll, with a cobbled market | square and an ancient abbey, but what lies behind the | pretty façade is a town at war. | [new paragraph] Rich at war with poor, teenagers at war with their | parents, wives at war with their husbands, teachers at | war with their pupils … Pagford is not what it | first seems. | [new paragraph] And the empty seat left by Barry on the Parish | Council soon becomes the catalyst for the biggest | war the town has yet seen. Who will triumph in | an election fraught with passion, duplicity and | unexpected revelations? | [new paragraph] A big novel about a small town, | *The Casual Vacancy* is | J.K. Rowling's first novel for | adults. It is the work of a | storyteller like no other. | [new paragraph] UK £20.00'. Lines 1 and 2 in red, lines 3-16 in black, lines 17-21 in red and line 22 in black all on light yellow. The initial capital 'W' of 'When' is a drop capital.

On lower inside flap: '[colour photograph of J.K. Rowling, 80 by 71mm] | J.K. ROWLING [in red] is the author of the bestselling | Harry Potter series of seven books, published | between 1997 and 2007, which have sold over | 450 million copies worldwide, are distributed in | more than 200 territories, have been translated | into 73 languages and have been turned into eight | blockbuster films. | [new paragraph] As well as an OBE for services to children's literature, | J.K. Rowling is the recipient of numerous awards and | honorary degrees, including the Prince of Asturias | Award for Concord, France's Légion d'honneur, | and the Hans Christian Andersen Award, and she | has been a Commencement Speaker at Harvard | University. She supports a wide range of charitable | causes and is the founder of Lumos, which works to | transform the lives of disadvantaged children. | [new paragraph] www.jkrowling.com | www.littlebrown.co.uk | [new paragraph] JACKET DESIGN BY MARIO J. PULICE | JACKET ILLUSTRATION AND HAND-LETTERING BY JOEL HOLLAND | AUTHOR PHOTOGRAPH © WALL TO WALL MEDIA LTD. | PHOTOGRAPHER: ANDREW MONTGOMERY | JACKET © 2012 HACHETTE BOOK GROUP, INC. | [new paragraph] little, brown | An imprint of Little, Brown Book Group | www.littlebrown.co.uk'. Lines 1-16 in black, lines 17-18 in red, lines 19-23 in grey and lines 24-26 in black all on light yellow.

Publication: 27 September 2012 (simultaneous with A16(aa))

Price: £20

Contents:
The Casual Vacancy
  ('Barry Fairbrother did not want to go out to dinner...')

Notes:
The hand-drawn lettering of the title includes 'The' nestled in the top part of the capital 'C' of 'Casual'. This hand-drawn lettering is used on the half-title, title-page, spine, dust-jacket spine and dust-jacket upper cover.

The divisional titles throughout the book quote from the seventh edition of Charles Arnold-Baker's *Local Council Administration*. This work was first published in 1975 and is fully titled *Local Council Administration in English parishes and Welsh communities*.

The Little, Brown book group issued a press announcement on 4 July 2012. This released the cover design, provided updated information about the story (including the correction from previous publicity of the name 'Barry Fairweather' to 'Barry Fairbrother'), noted details of the reader for the audiobooks version and supplied a confirmed page count.

As with the Harry Potter series, online retailers were quick to announce a pre-publication discount price. On the day of publication, the price listed on Amazon.co.uk was £9.86.

Copies: private collection (PWE)

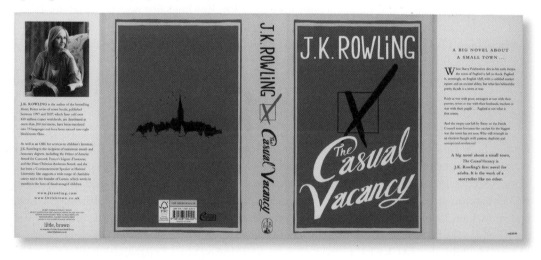

J.K.ROWLiNG | [rule, 36mm] | The | Casual | Vacancy | [publisher's device of '175 | YEARS' with 'L' and 'B' in white on black points with circular single ruled borders at centre, 13 by 14mm] | LITTLE, BROWN AND COMPANY | NEW YORK BOSTON LONDON (Lines 1-5 in hand-drawn lettering and all width centred)

Collation: 256 unsigned leaves bound in indeterminate gatherings; 234 by 151mm; [i-vi] [1-2] 3-5 [6] 7-50 [51-52] 53-175 [176-78] 179-255 [256-58] 259-328 [329-30] 331-401 [402-404] 405-465 [466-68] 469-81 [482-84] 485-503 [504-506]

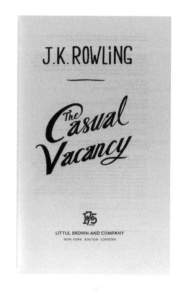

Page contents: [i] half-title: 'The | Casual | Vacancy' (hand-drawn lettering); [ii] '*Also by J.K. Rowling* | [new paragraph] Harry Potter and the Philosopher's Stone | (published in the U.S. as *The Sorcerer's Stone*) | Harry Potter and the Chamber of Secrets | Harry Potter and the Prisoner of Azkaban | Harry Potter and the Goblet of Fire | Harry Potter and the Order of the Phoenix | Harry Potter and the Half-Blood Prince | Harry Potter and the Deathly Hallows | [new paragraph] (in Latin) | Harry Potter and the Philosopher's Stone | Harry Potter and the Chamber of Secrets | [new paragraph] (in Welsh, Ancient Greek and Irish) | Harry Potter and the Philosopher's Stone | [new paragraph] Fantastic Beasts and Where to Find Them | Quidditch Through the Ages | The Tales of Beedle the Bard'; [iii] title-page; [iv] 'The characters and events in this book are fictitious. Any similarity to real persons, | living or dead, is coincidental and not intended by the author. | [new paragraph] Copyright © 2012 by J.K. Rowling | [new paragraph] All rights reserved. In accordance with the U.S. Copyright Act of 1976, the scanning, | uploading, and electronic sharing of any part of this book without the permission of the | publisher constitute unlawful piracy and theft of the author's intellectual property. If you | would like to use material from the book (other than for review purposes), prior written | permission must be obtained by contacting the publisher at permissions@hbgusa.com. | Thank you for your support of the author's rights | [new paragraph] Little, Brown and Company | Hachette Book Group | 237 Park Avenue, New York, NY 10017 | littlebrown.com | [new paragraph] First Edition: September 2012 | Published simultaneously in Great Britain by Little, Brown Book Group, | September 2012 | [new paragraph] Little, Brown and Company is a division of Hachette Book Group, Inc., and is | celebrating its 175th anniversary in 2012. The Little, Brown name and logo are | trademarks of Hachette Book Group, Inc. | [new paragraph] The publisher is not responsible for websites (or their content) that are not | owned by the publisher. | [new paragraph] The Hachette Speakers Bureau provides a wide range of authors for | speaking events. To find out more, go to hachettespeakersbureau.com or |

call (866) 376-6591 | [new paragraph] "Umbrella": Written by Terius Nash, Christopher "Tricky" Stewart, Shawn Carter, | and Thaddis Harrell © 2007 by 2082 Music Publishing (ASCAP)/Songs of Peer Ltd. | (ASCAP)/March Ninth Music Publishing (ASCAP)/Carter Boys Music (ASCAP)/ EMI | Music Publishing Ltd. (PRS)/Sony/ATV Music Publishing (PRS). All rights on behalf | of WB Music Corp. and 2082 Music Publishing Administered by Warner/Chappell | North America Ltd. All rights on behalf of March Ninth Music Publishing Controlled | and Administered by Songs of Peer Ltd. (ASCAP). All rights on behalf of Carter Boys | Music Controlled and Administered by EMI Music Publishing Ltd. All rights on behalf | of Thaddis Harrell Controlled and Administered by Sony/ATV Music Publishing. | "Green, Green Grass of Home": ©1965 Sony/ATV Music Publishing LLC. All rights | administered by Sony/ATV Music Publishing LLC, 8 Music Square West, Nashville, | TN 37203. All rights reserved. Used by permission. | [new paragraph] ISBN 978-0-316-22853-4 (hc) / 978-0-316-22854-1 (large print) | Library of Congress Control Number 2012943788 | [new paragraph] 10 9 8 7 6 5 4 3 2 1 | [new paragraph] RRD-C | [new paragraph] Printed in the United States of America'; [v] 'To Neil'; [vi] blank; [1] 'Part One' together with quotation from Arnold-Baker; [2] blank; 3-5 text; [6] blank; 7-50 text; [51] '(Olden Days)' together with quotation from Arnold-Baker; [52] blank; 53-175 text [176] blank; [177] 'Part Two' together with quotation from Arnold-Baker; [178] blank; 179-255 text; [256] blank; [257] 'Part Three' together with quotation from Arnold-Baker; [258] blank; 259-328 text; [329] 'Part Four' together with quotation from Arnold-Baker; [330] blank; 331-401 text; [402] blank; [403] 'Part Five' together with quotation from Arnold-Baker; [404] blank; 405-465 text; [466] blank; [467] 'Part Six' together with quotation from Arnold-Baker; [468] blank; 469-81 text; [482] blank; [483] 'Part Seven' together with quotation from Arnold-Baker; [484] blank; 485-503 text; [504] blank; [505] 'J.K. ROWLING is the author of the bestselling Harry Potter series | of seven books, published between 1997 and 2007, which have sold |over 450 million copies worldwide, are distributed in more than 200 | territories, have been translated into 73 languages, and have been | turned into 8 blockbuster films. | [new paragraph] As well as an Order of the British Empire for services to children's | literature, J.K. Rowling is the recipient of numerous awards and hon- | orary degrees, including the Prince of Asturias Award for Concord, | France's Légion d'honneur, and the Hans Christian Andersen Award, | and she has been a commencement speaker at Harvard University. | She supports a wide number of causes and is the founder of Lumos, | which works to transform the lives of disadvantaged children.'; [506] blank

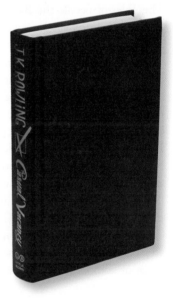

Paper: wove paper

Running title: none

Binding: black boards.
  On spine: 'The | J.K.ROWLiNG [square with large cross] Casual Vacancy' (reading lengthways down spine) with publisher's device of 'L' and 'B' within circular single ruled borders and 'LITTLE, | BROWN', 16 by 15mm, (horizontally at foot). All in gilt.

On upper cover: publisher's device of 'L' and 'B' within circular single ruled borders, 13 by 26mm (all width centred). All in blind.

Lower cover: blank.

All edges trimmed. Grey sewn bands at head and foot of spine. Binding measurements: 241 by 151mm (covers), 241 by 50mm (spine). End-papers: orange wove paper.

Dust-jacket: coated wove paper, 241 by 569mm

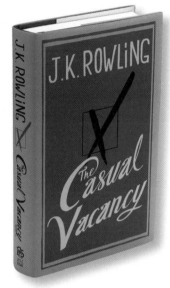

On spine: 'The | J.K.ROWLiNG [square with large cross] [in red] Casual Vacancy' (reading lengthways down spine) with publisher's device of '175 | YEARS' with 'L' and 'B' in white on black points with circular single dark yellow ruled borders at centre, 11 by 12mm and 'LiTTLE, | BROWN' (horizontally at foot). All in black on yellow.

On upper cover: 'J.K.ROWLiNG [in white] | [square with large cross] [in black] | The [in white] | Casual [in white] | Vacancy [in white]' (all width centred with the exception of the title which is at an angle and slightly off-set to the right). All on red panel, 215 by 133mm, enclosed by single border in red, 226 by 141mm, and all on yellow.

On lower cover: '[black silhouette of town skyline dominated by steeple with trees in blind in foreground, 50 by 103mm] | [barcode with smaller barcode to the right (53500) all in black on white panel, 17 by 51mm]'. All on red panel, 215 by 133mm, enclosed by single border in red, 226 by 141mm, and all on yellow.

On upper inside flap: '$35.00 | $36.99 in Canada | [new paragraph] A BIG NOVEL ABOUT | A SMALL TOWN … | [new paragraph] WHEN BARRY FAIRBROTHER DIES | in his early forties, the town of Pagford is left in shock. | [new paragraph] Pagford is, seemingly, an English idyll, with a | cobbled market square and an ancient abbey, but | what lies behind the pretty facade is a town at war. | [new paragraph] Rich at war with poor, teenagers at war with | their parents, wives at war with their husbands, | teachers at war with their pupils…Pagford is not | what it first seems. | [new paragraph] And the empty seat left by Barry on the parish | council soon becomes the catalyst for the biggest | war the town has yet seen. Who will triumph in | an election fraught with passion, duplicity, and | unexpected revelations? | [new paragraph] A big novel about a small town, | *The Casual Vacancy* is J.K. Rowling's | first novel for adults. It is the work of | a storyteller like no other.' Lines 1 and 2 in black, lines 3-4 in red, lines 5-18 in black and lines 19-22 in red all on light yellow.

On lower inside flap: '[colour photograph of J.K. Rowling, 80 by 70mm] | J.K. ROWLING [in red] is the author of the bestselling | Harry Potter series of seven books, published | between 1997 and 2007, which have sold over 450 | million copies worldwide, are distributed in more | than 200 territories, have been translated into | 73 languages, and have been turned into eight | blockbuster films. | [new paragraph] As well as an Order of the British Empire for | services to children's literature, J.K. Rowling | is the recipient of numerous awards and honorary | degrees, including the Prince of Asturias Award for | Concord, France's Légion d'honneur, and the Hans | Christian Andersen

Award, and she has been a | commencement speaker at Harvard University. | She supports a wide range of causes and is the | founder of Lumos, which works to transform the | lives of disadvantaged children. | [new paragraph] www.jkrowling.com | www.littlebrown.co.uk | [new paragraph] ALSO AVAILABLE FROM [publisher's 'H' logo] hachette | AUDIO | JACKET DESIGN BY MARIO J. PULICE | JACKET ILLUSTRATION AND HAND-LETTERING BY JOEL HOLLAND | AUTHOR PHOTOGRAPH © WALL TO WALL MEDIA LTD. | PHOTOGRAPHER: ANDREW MONTGOMERY | JACKET © 2012 HACHETTE BOOK GROUP, INC. | PRINTED IN THE U.S.A.' Lines 1-17 in black, lines 18-19 in red, lines 20-27 in black all on light yellow.

Publication: 27 September 2012 (simultaneous with A16(a))

Price: $35

Contents:
The Casual Vacancy
('Barry Fairbrother did not want to go out to dinner...')

Notes:
The hand-drawn lettering of the title includes 'The' nestled in the top part of the capital 'C' of 'Casual'. This hand-drawn lettering is used on the half-title, title-page, spine, dust-jacket spine and dust-jacket upper cover.

The setting of text is not the same as the First English edition (A16(a)). Single quotation marks in the English edition appear here as double quotation marks. Other features include hypenation of words (the English 'goodbye' appears as 'good-bye') and American spellings of words.

As with the Harry Potter series, online retailers were quick to announce a pre-publication discount price. On the day of publication, the price listed on Amazon.com was $20.90. Copies from Amazon Fulfillment Services in Lexington, KT, were sent out on the day of publication.

Copies: private collection (PWE)

SECOND ENGLISH EDITION
(paperback)

J. K. | ROWLING | THE | CASUAL | VACANCY | [curved line] | sphere (All width centred with curved line and publisher on black silhouette of town skyline dominated by steeple, 57 by 126mm)

Collation: 288 unsigned leaves bound in indeterminate gatherings; 197 by 126mm; [i-viii] [1-2] 3-5 [6] 7-56 [57-58] 59-197 [198-200] 201-288 [289-90] 291-371 [372-74] 375-455 [456-58] 459-527 [528-30] 531-44 [545-46] 547-68

Page contents: [i-ii] extracts from 11 reviews; [iii] 'J.K. Rowling is the author of the bestselling Harry Potter series | of seven books, published between 1997 and 2007, which have | sold over 450 million copies worldwide, are distributed in more | than 200 territories, translated into 73 languages, and have been | turned into eight blockbuster films. She has also written two small | volumes, which appear as the titles of Harry's schoolbooks within | the novels. *Fantastic Beasts and Where to Find Them* and *Quidditch* | *Through the Ages* were published by Bloomsbury Children's Books | in March 2001 in aid of Comic Relief. In December 2008, *The* | *Tales of Beedle the Bard* was published in aid of the Children's High | Level Group, and quickly became the fastest selling book of the | year. *The Casual Vacancy* is her first novel for adults. | [new paragraph] As well as an OBE for services to children's literature, J.K. | Rowling is the recipient of numerous awards and honorary | degrees including the Prince of Asturias Award for Concord, | France's Légion d'Honneur, and the Hans Christian Andersen | Award, and she has been a Commencement Speaker at Harvard | University. She supports a wide number of charitable causes | through her charitable trust Volant, and is the founder of Lumos, | a charity working to transform the lives of disadvantaged children.'; [iv] '*By J.K. Rowling* | [new paragraph] Harry Potter and the Philosopher's Stone | Harry Potter and the Chamber of Secrets | Harry Potter and the Prisoner of Azkaban | Harry Potter and the Goblet of Fire | Harry Potter and the Order of the Phoenix | Harry Potter and the Half-Blood Prince | Harry Potter and the Deathly Hallows | [new paragraph] (in Latin) | Harry Potter and the Philosopher's Stone | Harry Potter and the Chamber of Secrets | [new paragraph] (in Welsh, Ancient Greek and Irish) | Harry Potter and the Philosopher's Stone | [new paragraph] Fantastic Beasts and Where to Find Them | Quidditch Through the Ages | The Tales of Beedle the Bard | [new paragraph] The Casual Vacancy'; [v] title-page; [vi] 'SPHERE | [new paragraph] First published in Great Britain in 2012 by Sphere | This paperback edition published in 2013 by Sphere | [new paragraph] Copyright © J.K. Rowling 2012 | [new paragraph] The moral right of the author has been asserted. | [new paragraph] *All characters and events in this publication, other than those* | *clearly in*

the public domain, are fictitious and any resemblance | *to real persons, living or dead, is purely coincidental.* | [new paragraph] | [new paragraph] 'Umbrella': Written by Terius Nash, Christopher 'Tricky' Stewart, | Shawn Carter and Thaddis Harrell © 2007 by 2082 Music Publishing (ASCAP)/Songs of Peer, Ltd. | (ASCAP)/March Ninth Music Publishing (ASCAP)/Carter Boys Music (ASCAP)/ EMI Music Publishing Ltd | (PRS)/Sony/ATV Music Publishing (PRS). All rights on behalf of WB Music Corp. and 2082 Music | Publishing Administered by Warner/Chappell North America Ltd. All Rights on behalf of March | Ninth Music Publishing Controlled and Administered by Songs of Peer Ltd. (ASCAP). All Rights on | behalf of Carter Boys Music Controlled and Administered by EMI Music Publishing Ltd. All rights on | behalf of Thaddis Harrell Controlled and Administered by Sony/ATV Music Publishing. | [new paragraph] 'Green, Green Grass of Home': ©1965 Sony/ ATV Music Publishing LLC. All rights | administered by Sony/ATV Music Publishing LLC, 8 Music Square West, Nashville, | TN 37203. All rights reserved. Used by permission. | [new paragraph] A CIP catalogue record for this book | is available from the British Library. | [new paragraph] ISBN 978-0-7515-5286-7 | [new paragraph] Typeset in Bembo by M Rules | Printed and bound in Great Britain by | Clays Ltd, St Ives plc | [new paragraph] Papers used by Sphere are from well-managed forests | and other responsible sources. | [new paragraph] [Forest Stewardship Council logo, 7 by 9mm together with ® symbol and text: 'FSC | www.fsc.org' with 'MIX | Paper from | responsible sources | FSC® C104740' to right] | [new paragraph] Sphere | An imprint of | Little, Brown Book Group | 100 Victoria Embankment | London EC4Y 0DY | [new paragraph] An Hachette UK Company | www. hachette.co.uk | [new paragraph] www.littlebrown.co.uk'; [vii] *'To Neil'*; [viii] blank; [1] 'PART ONE' together with quotation from Arnold-Baker; [2] blank; 3-5 text; [6] blank; 7-56 text; [57] '(OLDEN DAYS)' together with quotation from Arnold-Baker; [58] blank; 59-197 text [198] blank; [199] 'PART TWO' together with quotation from Arnold-Baker; [200] blank; 201-288 text; [289] 'PART THREE' together with quotation from Arnold-Baker; [290] blank; 291-371 text; [372] blank; [373] 'PART FOUR' together with quotation from Arnold-Baker; [374] blank; 375-455 text; [456] blank; [457] 'PART FIVE' together with quotation from Arnold-Baker; [458] blank; 459-527 text; [528] blank; [529] 'PART SIX' together with quotation from Arnold-Baker; [530] blank; 531-44 text; [545] 'PART SEVEN' together with quotation from Arnold-Baker; [546] blank; 547-68 text

Paper: wove paper

Running title: none

Binding: pictorial wrappers.

On spine: 'J.K. [in metallic blue silver] | THE | CASUAL VACANCY | ROWLING [in metallic blue silver] (reading lengthways down spine) with '[curved line] | sphere' (horizontally at foot). All in white on illustration of sky, horizon, silhouette of town skyline and hill.

On upper wrapper: "This is a wonderful novel' [in black] | Melvyn Bragg, THE OBSERVER [in grey] | J.K. [in metallic blue silver] | ROWLING [in metallic blue silver] | THE [in white]

| CASUAL [in white] | VACANCY [in white] | 'A big, ambitious, brilliant, profance, funny, deeply unsetting and [in blue] | magnificently eloquent novel of contemporary England' [in blue] | TIME MAGAZINE [in grey]' (all width centred). All on illustration of sky, horizon, silhouette of town skyline dominated by steeple, and hill with a bench.

On lower wrapper: 'In the idyllic small town of Pagford, | a councillor dies and leaves a 'casual vacancy' – | an empty seat on the Parish Council. | [new paragraph] In the election for his successor that follows, it is clear | that behind the pretty surface this is a town at war. Rich at | war with poor, wives at war with husbands, teachers at war | with pupils … Pagford is not what it first seems. | [new paragraph] From the smallest of elections in a | sleepy British town, J.K. Rowling conjures an epic, | emotional and compulsively readable tale that | has had millions of readers hooked. | [new paragraph] 'I had come under the spell of a great novel … a deeply moving | book by somebody who understands both human | beings and novels very, very well' | TIME MAGAZINE | [new paragraph] 'This is a wonderful novel. J.K. Rowling's skills as a storyteller are | on a par with R.L. Stevenson, Conan Doyle and P.D. James. | Here, they are combined with her ability to create memorable and | moving characters to produce a state-of-England novel | driven by tenderness and fury' | THE OBSERVER | [new paragraph] '*The Casual Vacancy* is a brilliant novel, entertaining, intelligent, moving, | passionate and hard-hitting … Moreover, it's unputdownable … | The novel is a triumph' | IRISH TIMES | [new paragraph] 'A stunning, brilliant, outrageously gripping and entertaining | evocation of British society today' | DAILY MIRROR | [new paragraph] [Forest Stewardship Council logo, 8 by 9mm together with ® symbol and text: 'FSC' (all in black) and '[rule, 7mm] | Natural | Renewable | & Recyclable' (all in grey) on white panel, 25 by 12mm] ['visit littlebrown.co.uk' in white on blue panel, 7 by 42mm] | [barcode and 'UK £7.99' in black together with 'FICTION' in grey on white panel, 17 by 30mm]' with e-book logo in light blue (with text 'ebook+audio | also available'), 7 by 13mm, to the right of the three panels and 'Cover design & photography: Duncan Spilling © Little, Brown Book Group Limited 2013' in white at centre foot. Lines 1-11, 15, 21, 25 and 28 in white with lines 12-14, 16-20, 22-24 and 26-27 in black and all on illustration of sky and silhouette of town skyline dominated by steeple.

On inside upper wrapper: extracts from six reviews in black and silver and all on illustration of sky and hill with a bench.

On inside lower wrapper: colour photograph of J.K. Rowling ranged left with text 'J.K. Rowling is the author of the | bestselling Harry Potter series of | seven books, published between | 1997 and 2007, which have sold | over 450 million copies worldwide, | are translated into 74 languages, | and have been turned into eight | blockbuster films. | [new paragraph] *The Casual Vacancy*, her acclaimed | first novel for adults, spent ten | weeks at the top of the *Sunday Times* | bestseller list and was voted the | best novel of the year by users | of Goodreads. | [new paragraph] Author photograph by Debra Hurford Brown | © J.K. Rowling' in white ranged left.

All edges trimmed. Binding measurements: 197 by 126mm (wrappers), 197 by 33mm (spine).

Publication: 18 July 2013

Price: £7.99

Contents:
The Casual Vacancy
    ('Barry Fairbrother did not want to go out to dinner...')

Notes:
On publication date the internet retailer Amazon fulfilled a number of orders with copies of a first reprint.

Copies: private collection (PWE)

Reprints include:
'Reprinted 2013'
'Reprinted 2013 (thirteen times)'

A16(c)   SECOND AMERICAN EDITION   (2013)
(paperback)

J.K.ROWLiNG | [rule, 36mm] | The | Casual | Vacancy | [publisher's device of '175 | YEARS' with 'L' and 'B' in white on black points with circular single ruled borders at centre, 13 by 14mm] | LITTLE, BROWN AND COMPANY | NEW YORK BOSTON LONDON (Lines 1-5 in hand-drawn lettering and all width centred)

Collation: 256 unsigned leaves bound in indeterminate gatherings; 228 by 139mm; [i-vi] [1-2] 3-5 [6] 7-50 [51-52] 53-175 [176-78] 179-255 [256-58] 259-328 [329-30] 331-401 [402-404] 405-465 [466-68] 469-81 [482-84] 485-503 [504-506]

Page contents: [i] half-title: 'The | Casual | Vacancy' (hand-drawn lettering); [ii] '*Also by J.K. Rowling* | [new paragraph] Harry Potter and the Philosopher's Stone | (published in the U.S. as *The Sorcerer's Stone*) | Harry Potter and the Chamber of Secrets | Harry Potter and the Prisoner of Azkaban | Harry Potter and the Goblet of Fire | Harry Potter and the Order of the Phoenix | Harry Potter and the Half-Blood Prince | Harry Potter and the Deathly Hallows | [new paragraph] (in Latin) | Harry Potter and the Philosopher's Stone | Harry Potter and the Chamber of Secrets | [new paragraph] (in Welsh, Ancient Greek and Irish) | Harry

Potter and the Philosopher's Stone | [new paragraph] Fantastic Beasts and Where to Find Them | Quidditch Through the Ages | The Tales of Beedle the Bard'; [iii] title-page; [iv] 'The characters and events in this book are fictitious. Any similarity to real persons, | living or dead, is coincidental and not intended by the author. | [new paragraph] Copyright © 2012 by J.K. Rowling | [new paragraph] All rights reserved. In accordance with the U.S. Copyright Act of 1976, the scanning, | uploading, and electronic sharing of any part of this book without the permission of the | publisher constitute unlawful piracy and theft of the author's intellectual property. If you | would like to use material from the book (other than for review purposes), prior written | permission must be obtained by contacting the publisher at permissions@hbgusa.com. | Thank you for your support of the author's rights | [new paragraph] Little, Brown and Company | Hachette Book Group | 237 Park Avenue, New York, NY 10017 | littlebrown.com | [new paragraph] First Edition: September 2012 | Published simultaneously in Great Britain by Little, Brown Book Group, | September 2012 | [new paragraph] Little, Brown and Company is a division of Hachette Book Group, Inc., and is | celebrating its 175th anniversary in 2012. The Little, Brown name and logo are | trademarks of Hachette Book Group, Inc. | [new paragraph] The publisher is not responsible for websites (or their content) that are not | owned by the publisher. | [new paragraph] The Hachette Speakers Bureau provides a wide range of authors for | speaking events. To find out more, go to hachettespeakersbureau.com or | call (866) 376-6591 | [new paragraph] "Umbrella": Written by Terius Nash, Christopher "Tricky" Stewart, Shawn Carter, | and Thaddis Harrell © 2007 by 2082 Music Publishing (ASCAP)/Songs of Peer Ltd. | (ASCAP)/ March Ninth Music Publishing (ASCAP)/Carter Boys Music (ASCAP)/EMI | Music Publishing Ltd. (PRS)/Sony/ATV Music Publishing (PRS). All rights on behalf | of WB Music Corp. and 2082 Music Publishing Administered by Warner/Chappell | North America Ltd. All rights on behalf of March Ninth Music Publishing Controlled | and Administered by Songs of Peer Ltd. (ASCAP). All rights on behalf of Carter Boys | Music Controlled and Administered by EMI Music Publishing Ltd. All rights on behalf | of Thaddis Harrell Controlled and Administered by Sony/ATV Music Publishing. | "Green, Green Grass of Home": ©1965 Sony/ATV Music Publishing LLC. All rights | administered by Sony/ATV Music Publishing LLC, 8 Music Square West, Nashville, | TN 37203. All rights reserved. Used by permission. | [new paragraph] ISBN 978-0-316-22853-4 (hc) / 978-0-316-22854-1 (large print) | Library of Congress Control Number 2012943788 | [new paragraph] 10 9 8 7 6 5 4 3 2 1 | [new paragraph] RRD-C | [new paragraph] Printed in the United States of America'; [v] 'To Neil'; [vi] blank; [1] 'Part One' together with quotation from Arnold-Baker; [2] blank; 3-5 text; [6] blank; 7-50 text; [51] '(Olden Days)' together with quotation from Arnold-Baker; [52] blank; 53-175 text [176] blank; [177] 'Part Two' together with quotation from Arnold-Baker; [178] blank; 179-255 text; [256] blank; [257] 'Part Three' together with quotation from Arnold-Baker; [258] blank; 259-328 text; [329] 'Part Four' together with quotation from Arnold-Baker; [330] blank; 331-401 text; [402] blank; [403] 'Part Five' together with quotation from Arnold-Baker; [404] blank; 405-465 text; [466] blank; [467] 'Part Six' together with quotation from Arnold-Baker; [468] blank; 469-81 text; [482] blank; [483] 'Part Seven' together with quotation from Arnold-Baker; [484] blank; 485-503 text; [504] blank; [505] 'J.K. ROWLING is the author of the bestselling Harry Potter series | of seven books, published between 1997 and 2007, which have sold | over 450 million copies worldwide, are distributed in more than 200 | territories, have been translated into 73 languages, and have been | turned into 8 blockbuster films. | [new paragraph] As well as an Order of the British Empire for services to children's | literature, J.K. Rowling is the recipient of numerous awards and hon- | orary degrees, including the Prince of Asturias Award for Concord, | France's Légion d'honneur, and the Hans Christian Andersen Award, | and she has been a commencement speaker at Harvard University. | She supports a wide number of causes and is the founder of Lumos, | which works to transform the lives of disadvantaged children.'; [506] blank

Paper: wove paper

Running title: none

Binding: pictorial wrappers.

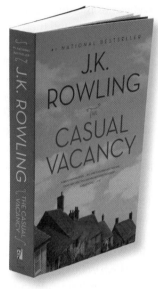

On spine: '[ornate rule] [in orange] | #1 NATIONAL | BESTSELLER | [ornate rule] [in orange]' (horizontally at head) with 'THE CASUAL | J.K. ROWLING | VACANCY' (reading lengthways down spine) with an ornate rule in orange between author and title, together with '[ornate rule] [in orange] | [publisher's device of flaming street lamp, 10 by 6mm] [in light and dark blue] | BACK | BAY | BOOKS' (horizontally at foot). All in light blue on orange red.

On upper wrapper: '#1 NATIONAL BESTSELLER [in black] | J.K. [in blue] | ROWLING [in blue] | THE [in brown] | CASUAL [in brown] | VACANCY [in brown] | "A DEEPLY MOVING BOOK....BIG, AMBITIOUS, BRILLIANT, PROFANE, | FUNNY, VERY UPSETTING, AND MAGNIFICENTLY ELOQUENT.... | A GREAT NOVEL." –*TIME* | [photographic illustration of houses]' (all width centred). All on photographic illustration of a sky with clouds.

On lower wrapper: 'FICTION   A BACK BAY BOOK | [rule] [in black with orange ornate rule at centre] | [new paragraph] "A positively propulsive read." [in blue] | –MEGHAN COX GURDON, *WALL STREET JOURNAL* [in blue] | [new paragraph] The big novel about a small town that became a [in red] | #1 WORLDWIDE BESTSELLER [in red] | [rule] [in black with orange ornate rule at centre] [two columns with 'When Barry Fairbrother dies unexpectedly in | his early forties, the little town of Pagford | is left in shock. Pagford is, seemingly, an English | idyll, with a cobbled market square and an ancient | abbey, but what lies behind the pretty facade is a | town at war. Rich at war with poor, teenagers at | war with their parents, wives at war with their hus- | bands, teachers at war with their pupils...Pagford | is not what it first seems. And the empty seat left | by Barry on the town's council soon becomes the | catalyst for the biggest war the town has yet seen. | Who will triumph in an election fraught with | passion, duplicity, and unexpected revelations? | [new paragraph] Blackly comic, thought-provoking, and | constantly surprising, *The Casual Vacancy* is the | work of a storyteller like no other. | [rule] [in blue] | [new paragraph] "Genuinely moving.... There were sentences I under- [in green] | lined for the sheer purpose of figuring out how [in green] English words could be combined so delightfully." [in green] | –MONICA HESSE, *WASHINGTON POST* [in blue] | [new paragraph] "An insanely compelling page-turner....Rowling [in green] | did not become the world's bestselling author by [in green] | accident. She knows down in her bones how to [in green] | make you keep turning the pages." [in green] | –MALCOLM JONES, *DAILY BEAST* [in blue] | [rule] [in blue] Also available in audio, ebook, and large-print editions | Cover design by Rebecca Lown | Cover photograph by Antony Spencer/iStockphoto | Author photograph by Debra Hurford Brown | Cover © 2013 Hachette Book Group, Inc. | Printed in the U.S.A.' in the first column and '[colour photograph of J.K. Rowling, 30 by 20mm] J.K. ROWLING [in green] | is the author of the | bestselling Harry Potter | series of seven novels, | which have sold more | than 450 million copies | worldwide, are distributed in more | than 200 territories, have been trans- | lated into 73 languages, and have been | turned into eight blockbuster films. | [new paragraph] As well as an Order of the British | Empire for services to children's liter- | ature, J.K. Rowling is the recipient of | numerous awards and honorary degrees. | She supports a wide range of causes | and is the founder of Lumos, a charity | working to transform the lives of | disadvantaged children. *The Casual* | *Vacancy* is her first novel for adult. | jkrowling.com | [new paragraph] littlebrown.com | ['$18.00 US / $20.00 CAN' with barcode with smaller barcode to the right (51800) on white panel, 33 by 61mm]' in the second column]'. All in black on light blue. The initial capital 'W' of 'When' is a drop capital and is printed in red.

    On inside upper wrapper: nine reviews. All in white with source of review in yellow and all on blue.

    On inside lower wrapper: nine reviews. All in white with source of review in yellow and all on blue.

    All edges trimmed. Binding measurements: 228 by 139mm (wrappers), 228 by 30mm (spine). End-papers (free end-papers only): orange wove paper.

Publication: 23 July 2013

Price: $18

Contents:
The Casual Vacancy
    ('Barry Fairbrother did not want to go out to dinner...')

Notes:
The hand-drawn lettering of the title includes 'The' nestled in the top part of the capital 'C' of 'Casual'. This hand-drawn lettering is used on the half-title and title-page. In contrast with the first American edition (see A16(aa)), the hand-drawn lettering is not replicated on the binding.

The setting of the text appears to be the same as for the first American edition. Even the publisher's imprint page is identical with the ISBN cited as that of the first American edition. The correct ISBN is provided on the lower wrapper only.

Copies: private collection (PWE)

THE CUCKOO'S CALLING

A17(a)   **FIRST ENGLISH EDITION**   **(2013)**
(hardback)

The | Cuckoo's | Calling | Robert Galbraith | [curved line] | sphere (All width centred)

Collation: 232 unsigned leaves bound in indeterminate gatherings; 234 by 153mm; [i-viii] [1-2] 3-6 [7-10] 11-53 [54-56] 57-157 [158-60] 161-244 [245-46] 247-414 [415-16] 417-38 [439-40] 441-49 [450-56]

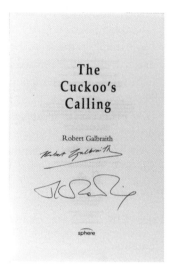

Page contents: [i] half-title: 'The | Cuckoo's | Calling'; [ii] blank; [iii] title-page; [iv] 'SPHERE | [new paragraph] First published in Great Britain in 2013 by Sphere | [new paragraph] Copyright © 2013 Robert Galbraith | [new paragraph] The moral right of the author has been asserted. | [new paragraph] *All characters and events in this publication, other than those | clearly in the public domain, are fictitious and any resemblance | to real persons, living or dead, is purely coincidental.* | [new paragraph] All rights reserved. | No part of this publication may be reproduced, stored in a | retrieval system, or transmitted, in any form or by any means, without | the prior permission in writing of the publisher, nor be otherwise circulated | in any form of binding or cover other than that in which it is published | and without a similar condition including this condition being | imposed on the subsequent purchaser. | [new paragraph] A CIP catalogue record for this book | is available from the British Library. | [new paragraph] Hardback ISBN 978-1-4087-0399-1 | Trade Paperback ISBN 978-1-4087-0400-4 | [new paragraph] Typeset in Bembo by M Rules | Printed and bound in Great Britain by | Clays Ltd, St Ives plc | [new paragraph] Papers used by Sphere are from well-managed forests | and other responsible sources. | [new paragraph] [Forest Stewardship Council logo, 7 by 9mm together with ® symbol and text: 'FSC | www.fsc.org' with 'MIX | Paper from | responsible sources | FSC® C104740' to the right] | [new paragraph] Sphere | An imprint of | Little, Brown Book Group | 100 Victoria Embankment | London EC4Y 0DY | [new paragraph] An Hachette UK Company | www.hachette.co.uk | [new paragraph] www.littlebrown.co.uk'; [v] 'To the real Deeby | with many thanks'; [vi] blank; [vii] two stanzas comprising 'Christina G. Rossetti, 'A Dirge'; [viii] blank; [1] 'Prologue' together with line in Latin and two-line translation from 'Lucius Accius, *Telephus*'; [2] blank; 3-6 text; [7] 'Three Months Later'; [8] blank; [9] 'Part One' together with two lines in Latin and three-line translation from 'Boethius, *De Consolatione Philosophiae*'; [10] blank; 11-53 text; [54] blank; [55] 'Part Two' together with line in Latin and two-line translation from 'Virgil, *Aeneid*, Book 1'; [56] blank; 57-157 text; [158] blank; [159] 'Part Three' together with line in Latin and two-line translation from 'Virgil, *Aeneid*, Book 1'; [160] blank; 161-244 text; [245] 'Part Four' together with line in Latin and two-line translation from 'Pliny the Elder, *Historia Naturalis*'; [246] blank; 247-414 text; [415] 'Part Five' together with line in Latin and two-line translation from 'Virgil, *Georgics*, Book 2'; [416] blank; 417-38 text; [439] 'Epilogue' together with two lines in Latin and one-line translation from 'Horace, *Odes*, Book 2'; [440] blank; 441-49 text; [450-56] blank

Paper: wove paper

Running title: 'ROBERT GALBRAITH' (37mm) on verso and '*The Cuckoo's Calling*' (32mm) on recto, pp. 4-449 (excluding pages on which new chapters commence, part division pages and blank pages)

Binding: navy blue boards.

On spine: 'THE | ROBERT | CUCKOO'S CALLING | GALBRAITH' (reading lengthways down spine) with curved line and 'sphere' (horizontally at foot). All in gilt.

Upper and lower covers: blank.

All edges trimmed. Binding measurements: 240 by 150mm (covers), 240 by 47mm (spine). End-papers: coated wove paper.

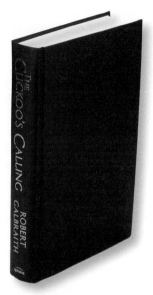

Dust-jacket: coated wove paper, 241 by 561mm

On spine: 'THE | ROBERT [in golden yellow] | CUCKOO'S CALLING | GALBRAITH [in golden yellow]' (reading lengthways down spine) with curved line and 'sphere' (horizontally at foot). All in white on photographic illustration of a sky in various colours and birds.

On upper cover: "*The Cuckoo's Calling* reminds me why I fell in | love with crime fiction in the first place' | VAL MCDERMID [in golden yellow] | ROBERT GALBRAITH [in golden yellow] | THE | CUCKOO'S | CALLING' (all width centred). All in white on photographic illustration of man walking up a street away from ornate fencing with housing on right and ornate street light on left.

On lower cover: 'One of the most unique and compelling | detectives I've come across in years' | MARK BILLINGHAM [in golden yellow] | [new paragraph] 'One of the best crime | novels I have ever read' | ALEX GRAY [in golden yellow] | [new paragraph] [Forest Stewardship Council logo, 8 by 9mm together with ® symbol and text: 'FSC' (all in black) and '[rule, 7mm] | Natural | Renewable | & Recyclable' (all in grey) on white panel, 25 by 12mm] ['visit littlebrown.co.uk' in black on yellow panel, 7 by 30mm] | [barcode in black together with 'CRIME FICTION' in grey on white panel, 17 by 30mm]' with e-book logo in white (with text 'ebook+audio | also

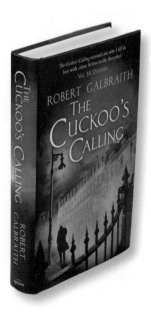

available'), 9 by 18mm, to the right of the three panels. All in white on photographic illustration of an ornate street light and sky in various colours and falling snow.

On upper inside flap: 'When a troubled model falls to her | death from a snow-covered Mayfair | balcony, it is assumed that she has | committed suicide. However, her | brother has his doubts, and calls in | private investigator Cormoran Strike | to look into the case. | [new paragraph] Strike is a war veteran – wounded | both physically and psychologically – | and his life is in disarray. The case gives | him a financial lifeline, but it comes | at a personal cost: the more he delves | into the young model's complex world, | the darker things get and the closer he | gets to terrible danger … | [new paragraph] A gripping, elegant mystery steeped | in the atmosphere of London – from | the hushed streets of Mayfair to the | backstreet pubs of the East End to the | bustle of Soho – *The Cuckoo's Calling* | is a remarkable book. Introducing | Cormoran Strike, this is a classic | crime novel in the tradition of | P.D. James and Ruth Rendell, and | marks the beginning of a unique | series of mysteries. | [new paragraph] UK£16.99'. All in white on photographic illustration of a sky in various colours and birds.

On lower inside flap: 'ROBERT GALBRAITH [in white] is married | with two sons. After several years with the | Royal Military Police, he was attached to | the SIB (Special Investigation Branch), the | plain-clothes branch of the RMP. He left the | military in 2003 and has been working since | then in the civilian security industry. The | idea for protagonist Cormoran Strike grew | directly out of his own experiences and those | of his military friends who have returned to | the civilian world. Robert Galbraith is | a pseudonym. | [new paragraph] sphere | An imprint of Little, Brown Book Group | www.littlebrown.co.uk | [new paragraph] Figure © Arcangel Images. Railing © Trevillion Images. | Street scene & design by LBBG - Sian WIlson [*sic*]'. Lines 1-12 in golden yellow and lines 13-17 in white and all on photographic illustration of a sky in various colours and birds.

Publication: 18 April 2013 (confirmed by the Blair Partnership)

Price: £16.99

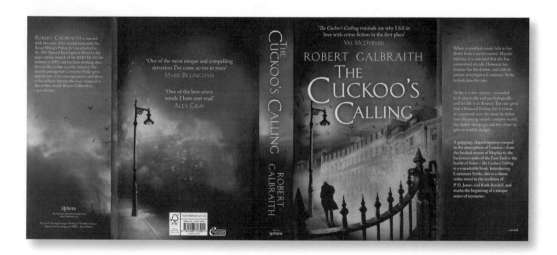

Contents:

The Cuckoo's Calling

('The buzz in the street was like the humming of flies. Photographers stood massed...')

Notes:

Rowling's first pseudonymously published crime novel.

A report in the *Evening Standard* stated that until the weekend of 13/14 July 2013 'the novel... had sold around 500 hardback copies, with total sales rising to 1,500 when ebooks, exports and library copies were counted.' David Shelley, from Little, Brown, commented to me in an email dated 24 June 2014, that the 'sales figures ..., pre-reveal, were a lot higher.' They were accurately recorded in *The Bookseller* on 17 July 2013 where sales were detailed as '1419 print, 822 e-book, more than 2000 export and 3,800 audio download.' The article also noted that the publishers confirmed it was reprinting 140,000 copies. This reprint was to be split 'between hardback and C-format for export and airside.'

The events which led to the revelation of Rowling's authorship started with a tweet from novelist and *Sunday Times* journalist, India Knight, on 9 July 2013. Knight had stated that the work was good for a debut novel. Judith Callegari, a follower of Knight's tweets, responded that it was a novel by an existing author. Knight asked for details and the response was that the author was J.K. Rowling.

The leak had originated from Russells Solicitors. One of its partners, Chris Gossage, had told his wife's best friend, Judith Callegari. The solicitors issued a statement noting that '...while accepting [Gossage's] own culpability, the disclosure was made in confidence to someone he trusted implicitly. On becoming aware of the circumstances, we immediately notified J.K. Rowling's agent...'

India Knight alerted the arts editor of the *Sunday Times*, Richard Brooks, who started investigations. A philosophy tutor at Hertford College, Oxford, Professor Peter Millican, was then approached. Professor Millican had developed computer software that compared and analysed texts. He was asked to compare text from *The Cuckoo's Calling* against *The Casual Vacancy*, *Harry Potter and the Deathly Hallows*, two works by Ruth Rendell, two works by P.D. James and two works by Val McDermid. Millican looked for a variety of word length, sentence length, patterns of punctuation and the frequency of particular words. The result was that, in most tests, *The Cuckoo's Calling* displayed characteristics closest to the other Rowling works. Brooks then played a 'cat-and-mouse game' with the publisher. Eventually, when asked whether the author was Rowling, the publisher admitted the novel's authorship. The news story broke on 14 July 2013.

Rowling stated that she had 'hoped to keep this secret a little longer' and described writing as Robert Galbraith 'such a liberating experience', adding '... it has been wonderful to publish without hype or expectation, and pure pleasure to get feedback under a different name.' She described her editor, David Shelley, as 'a true partner in crime'.

The shock of the pseudonym kept newspapers happy for days. The *Evening Standard* raised the question on 16 July 2013 as to whether *The Cuckoo's Calling* was being offered to publishers before publication of *The Casual Vacancy*. When one editor, Kate Mills of Orion Books, admitted to having turned the book down, it became clear that *The Cuckoo's Calling* had certainly been offered to other publishers before Sphere. Neil Blair and David Shelley are reported as insisting that 'no one at Sphere knew who the author was and the novel was taken on entirely on its own merits' (see Maxine Frith, 'Harry plotter?', *Evening Standard*, 16 July 2013, pp. 20-21).

It appears that 250 copies of the first edition were signed 'Robert Galbraith'. David Headley, owner of Goldsboro Books of Charing Cross Road, a shop which specializes in first editions, requested a book signing session before Rowling was unmasked. The publisher apparently explained that the author was in America but could sign 250 copies for delivery. Before 14 July 130 copies had been sold. Headley apparently sold the remaining stock at the cover price.

On 10 December 2013 the only known copy, to date, signed by both 'Robert Galbraith' and J.K. Rowling was sold at Sotheby's. The copy was sold to benefit EdUKaid, a registered charity, that works with rural communities in Tanzania to improve the teaching and learning environment through building classrooms and ungrading schools. Estimated at £2,000/3,000, the volume sold for £2,500 (including buyer's premium).

With sudden demand, the supply of copies was exhausted and it appears that at least two reprints were ordered by the publisher. This is suggested by a copy ordered from amazon.co.uk during the morning of 14 July. This copy was despatched on 18 July and arrived the following day. It contains the reprint information 'Reprinted 2013 (twice)'. Waterstones in Picaddilly also had stock on 19 July 2013 with identical reprint details. No copies of 'Reprinted 2013' have yet been consulted.

Note a typographical error on the lower side flap with 'Wilson' appearing as 'WIlson'.

Copies: BL (Nov.2014/1105) stamped 11 Apr 2013; private collection (TBP); Sotheby's, 10 December 2013, lot 320

Reprints include:
Reprinted 2013 (twice)

A17(b)   FIRST AMERICAN EDITION   (2013)
(hardback)

The | Cuckoo's | Calling | Robert Galbraith | [publisher's device of a black 'M' with white stitching effect on a grey circle, diameter 16mm] | MULHOLLAND BOOKS | LITTLE, BROWN AND COMPANY | *New York Boston London* (All width centred)

Collation: 232 unsigned leaves bound in indeterminate gatherings; 233 by 145mm; [i-viii] [1-2] 3-6 [7-10] 11-53 [54-56] 57-157 [158-60] 161-245 [246-48] 249-417 [418-20] 421-43 [444-46] 447-55 [456]

Page contents: [i] half-title: 'The Cuckoo's Calling'; [ii] blank; [iii] title-page; [iv] 'The characters and events in this book are fictitious. Any similarity to real | persons, living or dead, is coincidental and not intended by the author. | [new paragraph] Copyright © 2013 by Robert Galbraith | [new paragraph] All rights reserved. In accordance with the U.S. Copyright Act of 1976, the | scanning, uploading, and electronic sharing of any part of this book without the | permission of the publisher constitute unlawful piracy and theft of the author's | intellectual property. If you would like to use material from the book (other than | for review purposes), prior written permission must be obtained by contacting | the publisher at permissions@hbgusa.com. Thank you for your support of the | author's rights. | [new paragraph] Mulholland Books / Little, Brown and Company | Hachette Book Group | 237 Park Avenue, New York, NY 10017 | mulhollandbooks.com | [new paragraph] First North American Edition: April 2013 | Originally published in Great Britain by Sphere, April 2013 | [new paragraph] Mulholland Books is an imprint of Little, Brown and Company, a division of | Hachette Book Group, Inc. The Mulholland Books name and logo are | trademarks of Hachette Book Group, Inc. | [new paragraph] The publisher is not responsible for websites (or their content) that are not | owned by the publisher. | [new paragraph] The Hachette Speakers Bureau provides a wide range of authors for speaking | events. To find out more, go to hachettespeakersbureau.com or call (866) | 376-6591. | [new paragraph] ISBN 978-0-316-20684-6 | LCCN 2013933193 | [new paragraph] 10 9 8 7 6 5 4 3 2 1 | [new paragraph] RRD-C | [new paragraph] Printed in the United States of America'; [v] 'To the real Deeby | with many thanks'; [vi] blank; [vii] two stanzas comprising 'Christina G. Rossetti, "A Dirge"'; [viii] blank; [1] 'Prologue' together with line in Latin and two-line translation from 'Lucius Accius, Telephus'; [2] blank; 3-6 text; [7] 'Three Months Later'; [8] blank; [9] 'Part One' together with two lines in Latin and three-line translation from 'Boethius, De Consolatione Philosophiae'; [10] blank; 11-53 text; [54] blank; [55] 'Part Two' together with line in Latin and two-line translation from 'Virgil, Aeneid, Book 1'; [56] blank; 57-157 text; [158] blank; [159] 'Part Three' together with line in Latin and two-line translation from 'Virgil, Aeneid, Book 1'; [160] blank; 161-245 text; [246] blank; [247] 'Part Four' together with line in Latin and two-line translation from 'Pliny the Elder, Historia Naturalis'; [248] blank; 249-417 text; [418] blank; [419] 'Part Five' together with line in Latin and two-line translation from 'Virgil, Georgics, Book 2'; [420] blank; 421-43 text; [444] blank; [445] 'Epilogue' together with two lines in Latin and one-line translation from 'Horace, Odes, Book 2'; [446] blank; 447-55 text; [456] 'ABOUT THE AUTHOR | [new paragraph] ROBERT GALBRAITH spent several years with the Royal Military Police | before being attached to the SIB (Special Investigative Branch), the | plainclothes branch of the RMP. He left the military in 2003 and | has been working since then in the civilian security industry. The | idea for Cormoran Strike grew directly out of his own experiences | and those of his military friends who returned to the civilian world. | "Robert Galbraith" is a pseudonym.'

Paper: wove paper

Running title: 'ROBERT GALBRAITH' (30mm) on verso and 'The Cuckoo's Calling' (30mm) on recto, pp. 4-455 (excluding pages on which new chapters commence, part division pages and blank pages)

Binding: grey paper-backed spine with black boards.
On spine: 'The Cuckoo's Calling Robert Galbraith' (reading lengthways down spine) and '[publisher's device of a 'm'] | MULHOLLAND | BOOKS | [rule] | LITTLE, BROWN' (horizontally at foot). All in silver.

On upper cover: publisher's device of 'L' and 'B' within circular single ruled borders, 13 by 26mm (all width centred). All in blind.

Lower cover: blank.

All edges trimmed. Binding measurements: 241 by 149mm (covers), 241 by 49mm (spine). The grey paper spine continues onto the covers by 29mm. End-papers: wove paper.

Dust-jacket: coated wove paper, 241 by 537mm

On spine: 'the [hand-drawn lettering] | ROBERT GALBRAITH [in green grey] | cuckoo's calling [hand-drawn lettering]' (reading lengthways down spine) with '[publisher's device of a black 'M' with white stitching effect on a white circle, diameter 9mm] | MULHOLLAND | BOOKS | [rule] | LITTLE, | BROWN' (horizontally at foot). All in white on black.

On upper cover: 'the [hand-drawn lettering] | cuckoo's [hand-drawn lettering] | calling [hand-drawn lettering] | ROBERT GALBRAITH' (title at an angle and with lines 1-2 off-set to the left and lines 3-4 off-set to the right). All in white on photographic illustration of a woman (showing back of the head) with a sea of photographers taking pictures.

On lower cover: '"*The Cuckoo's Calling* reminds me | why I fell in love with crime fiction | in the first piece." —VAL McDERMID, | bestselling author of *The Vanishing Point* | [new paragraph] "The private-eye novel is not dead. | It was merely waiting for Robert | Galbraith to give it a firm squeeze, | goosing it back to bold life. Fans | of hard-boiled crime are going to go | cuckoo for this one. I haven't had | this much fun with a detective novel | in years." —DUANE SWIERCZYNSKI, | Shamus and Anthony Award-winning | author of *Fun & Games*' all in first column together with '"Cormoran Strike is an amazing | creation and I can't wait for his | next outing. Strike is so instantly | compelling that it's hard to believe | this is a debut novel. I hope there | are plenty more Cormoran Strike | adventures to come. A beautifully | written debut introducing one of | the most unique detectives I've come across in years." | —MARK BILLINGHAM, | author of *The Demands* [new paragraph] "Robert Galbraith's debut is as | hard-bitten and hard-driving as its | battered hero. *The Cuckoo's Calling* | scales the glittering heights of | society even as it plumbs the dark | depths of the human heart. | A riveting read from an author | to watch." —MIKE COOPER, | Shamus Award-winning | author of *Clawback* | [new paragraph] [barcode with smaller barcode to the right (52600) all in black on white panel, 25 by 49mm]' all in second column. All in black on photographic illustration of a woman (showing back of the head) with a sea of photographers taking pictures.

On upper inside flap: '$26.00 US | $29.00 CAN | [new paragraph] A BRILLIANT DEBUT MYSTERY | IN A CLASSIC VEIN: | DETECTIVE CORMORAN STRIKE | INVESTIGATES A | SUPERMODEL'S SUICIDE. | [new paragraph] After losing his leg to a land mine in | Afghanistan, Cormoran Strike is barely | scraping by as a private investigator. Strike is | down to one client, and creditors are calling. | He has also just broken up with his longtime | girlfriend and is living in his office. | [new paragraph] Then John Bristow walks through his | door with an amazing story: His sister, the | legendary supermodel Lula Landry, known to | her friends as the Cuckoo, famously fell to | her death a few months earlier. The police | ruled it a suicide, but John refuses to believe | that. The case plunges Strike into the world | of multimillionaire beauties, rock-star boy- | friends, and desperate designers, and it | introduces him to every variety of pleasure, | enticement, seduction, and delusion known | to man. | [new paragraph] You may think you know detectives, but

| you've never met one quite like Strike. You | may think you know about the wealthy and | famous, but you've never seen them under an | investigation like this.' Lines 1-2 and 8-30 in black with lines 3-7 in green and all on white. The initial 'A' of 'After' is a drop capital.

On lower inside flap: 'ROBERT GALBRAITH [in green] spent several years | with the Royal Military Police before being | attached to the SIB (Special Investigation | Branch), the plainclothes division of the RMP. | He left the military in 2003 and has been | working since then in the civilian security | industry. The idea for Cormoran Strike grew | directly out of his own experiences and | those of his military friends who returned to | the civilian world. "Robert Galbraith" is a | pseudonym. | [new paragraph] [publisher's device of a black 'M' with white stitching effect on a grey circle, diameter 7mm all on square with rounded edges, 8 by 8mm] Download the FREE Mulholland Books app. | [new paragraph] mulhollandbooks.com | [new paragraph] [twitter logo on a light blue square with rounded edges, 8 by 8mm] @mulhollandbooks | [new paragraph] [facebook logo with white border on a dark and light blue square with rounded edges, 8 by 8mm] mulhollandbooks | [new paragraph] Also available in audio and e-book editions | Jacket design by Mario J. Pulice | Jacket photography © Robert Daly / Getty Images | Calligraphy by Joel Holland | Jacket © 2013 Hachette Book Group, Inc. | Printed in the U.S.A.' All in black on white.

Publication: 30 April 2013 (confirmed by the Blair Partnership)

Price: $26

Contents:
The Cuckoo's Calling
  ('The buzz in the street was like the humming of flies. Photographers stood massed…')

Notes:
As confirmed by publication dates, the American edition of this novel was published twelve days after the English edition.

The setting of text is not the same as the First English edition. Consistent with American style, single quotation marks in the English edition appear here as double quotation marks, for example.

The publisher's blurb on the dust-jacket has been revised slightly from that which appeared on the American proof (see AA5(b)). The dust-jacket was designed by the same designer who worked on the dust-jacket of *The Casual Vacancy* (see A16(a) and A16(aa)).

An article in *The Bookseller* on 17 July 2013 noted that the 'publisher Mulholland Books has ordered a 300,000-copy reprint.'

Copies: private collection (TBP)

Reprints include:
10 9 8 7 6 5 4 3 2

AA. PROOF COPIES/ADVANCE READER'S COPIES OF BOOKS BY J.K. ROWLING

HARRY POTTER AND THE PHILOSOPHER'S STONE

AA1(a) **ENGLISH PROOF** (1997)

Harry Potter and the | Philosopher's Stone | J. A Rowling | [publisher's device of a house with 'Bloomsbury' above, reading lengthways from head, 25 by 7mm] (Lines 1-3 width centred with line 4 on right margin)

Collation: 112 unsigned leaves bound in indeterminate gatherings; 198 by 129mm; [1-7] 8-18 [19] 20-27 [28] 29-38 [39] 40-48 [49] 50-66 [67] 68-84 [85] 86-97 [98] 99-106 [107] 108-120 [121] 122-32 [133] 134-42 [143] 144-57 [158] 159-66 [167] 168-76 [177] 178-90 [191] 192-208 [209] 210-24

Page contents: [1] half-title: 'Harry Potter and the | Philosopher's Stone'; [2] blank; [3] title-page; [4] 'All rights reserved; no part of this publication may be reproduced or | transmitted by any means, electronic, mechanical, photocopying or otherwise, | without the prior permission of the publisher | [new paragraph] First published in Great Britain in 1997 | Bloomsbury Publishing Plc, 38 Soho Square, London W1V 5DF | [new paragraph] Copyright © Text Joanne Rowling 1997 | Copyright © Cover illustration Thomas Taylor1997 [*sic*] | [new paragraph] The moral right of the author has been asserted | A CIP catalogue record of this book is available from the | British Library | [new paragraph] ISBN 0 7475 3274 5 Paperback | 0 7475 3269 9 Hardback | [new paragraph] Printed and bound by | Caledonian International Book Manufacturing, Glasgow | [new paragraph] 10 9 8 7 6 5 4 3 2 1'; [5] '*for Jessica, who loves stories,* | *for Anne, who loved them too,* | *and for Di, who heard this one first.*'; [6] blank; [7]-224 text

Paper: wove paper

Running title: 'HARRY POTTER' (24mm) on verso, recto title comprises chapter title, pp. 8-224

Binding: white wrappers.

On spine: *'J.K. Rowling* | Harry Potter and the | Philosopher's Stone' (reading lengthways down spine) (all in black on yellow panel, 60 by 14mm) together with publisher's logo of a figure with a bow, 11 by 9mm (horizontally at foot of spine).

On upper wrapper: 'Uncorrected Proof Copy | *J.K. Rowling* | Harry Potter and the | Philosopher's Stone | BLOOMSBURY' (all width centred). All in black with lines 2-4 on yellow panel, 60 by 129mm.

On lower wrapper: 'Publication Date: June 1997 | UK paperback price: £4.50 | UK hardback price: £10.99 | ISBN (pb): 0 7475 3274 5 | ISBN (hb): 0 7475 3269 9 | Trimmed Page Size: 198x129mm | Extent: 224pp | All specifications are provisional. | This is an uncorrected proof copy and is not for sale. It should not be quoted | without comparison to the finally revised text. It does not reflect the quality, | page size or thickness of the finished text.' All in black on yellow panel, 60 by 129mm.

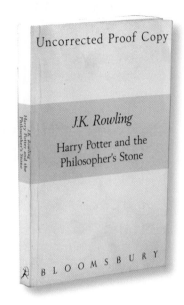

All edges trimmed. Binding measurements: 198 by 129mm (wrappers), 198 by 14mm (spine).

Price: not for sale

Contents:

Harry Potter and the Philosopher's Stone

('Mr and Mrs Dursley, of number four, Privet Drive, were proud to say…')

Notes:

The text was slightly re-set for the first English edition (see A1(a) and A1(aa)). In this proof there is a greater number of words split between lines (and therefore requiring a hypen). The first page reveals 'cran- | ing over garden fences' in paragraph two, 'the Dursleys shud- | dered to think' in paragraph three, and 'the cloudy sky out- | side' in paragraph four, for example.

An unconfirmed print-run of 200 copies is generally accepted for this proof. This is also the figure noted by Bloomsbury.

Several – but not all – copies were distributed with a proof sheet showing the proposed illustrated wrappers. The design would change before publication. The proof of the wrappers is as follows:

On spine: 'HARRY POTTER [in green] *and the Philosopher's Stone* J. K. ROWLING BLOOMSBURY' (reading lengthways down spine). All in black on dark yellow.

On upper wrapper: 'HARRY [in green with crimson outline] | POTTER [in green with crimson outline] | *and the Philosopher's Stone* [in black] | J. K. ROWLING [in white with black outline]' (all width centred). All on colour illustration showing Harry Potter and the Hogwarts Express at Platform 9¾.

458   HARRY POTTER AND THE PHILOSOPHER'S STONE

On *lower wrapper*: 'Harry Potter is an ordinary boy | who lives in the cupboard under | the stairs at his aunt and uncle's | house – until he is | rescued by an owl | and taken to Hogwarts | School of Wizardry | and Witchcraft. | Once there he learns his | true identity, the reason | behind his parents | mysterious death, who is | out to kill him and | finally uncovers the | biggest secret of all, | the fabled Philosopher's stone. | [new paragraph] *This is a magical | and gripping book by a | wonderfully talented author.* | [barcode in black on white panel] | £4.50'. All in black with the exception of the first 'H' in 'Harry' which is in green and all on a dark yellow background with colour illustration on left-hand side of a wizard smoking a pipe, together with nine stars. The initial 'H' of 'Harry' is a drop capital and is printed in green.

The entire design is printed on card with a white border on the left. Printed in black on white is the publication information: 'June 1997 £4.50 224pp 198x129mm 07475 32745'.

On page 53, under the heading, 'Other Equipment', '1 wand' is listed twice. This error was retained in the first edition. Note that the authorship of 'J. A Rowling' from the title-page was corrected.

Copies: Sotheby's, 17 December 2008, lot 214

HARRY POTTER AND THE CHAMBER OF SECRETS

AA2(a)   **ENGLISH PROOF**   **(1998)**

Harry Potter and the | Chamber of Secrets | J. K. Rowling | [publisher's device of a dog, 11 by 19mm] | BLOOMSBURY (All width centred)

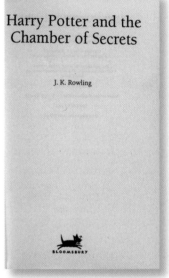

Collation: 128 unsigned leaves bound in indeterminate gatherings; 198 by 127mm; [1-7] 8-14 [15] 16-23 [24] 25-36 [37] 38-52 [53] 54-67 [68] 69-80 [81] 82-93 [94] 95-106 [107] 108-121 [122] 123-36 [137] 138-53 [154] 155-69 [170] 171-85 [186] 187-97 [198] 199-210 [211] 212-26 [227] 228-41 [242] 243-52 [253-56]

Page contents: [1] half-title: 'Harry Potter and the | Chamber of Secrets'; [2] blank; [3] title-page; [4] 'All rights reserved; no part of this publication may be reproduced or | transmitted by any means, electronic, mechanical, photocopying or otherwise, | without the prior permission of the publisher | [new paragraph] First published in Great Britain in 1998 | Bloomsbury Publishing Plc, 38 Soho Square, London W1V 5DF | [new paragraph] Copyright © Text J.K. Rowling 1998 | Copyright © Cover Illustration Cliff Wright 1997 | [new paragraph] The moral right of the author has been asserted | A CIP catalogue record of this book is available from the | British Library | [new paragraph] ISBN 0 7475 3849 2 | [new paragraph] Printed and bound in Great Britain by Clays Ltd, St Ives plc | [new paragraph] 10 9 8 7 6 5 4 3 2 1 | [new paragraph] Cover design by Michelle Radford'; [5] 'DEDICATION'; [6] blank; [7]-252 text; [253-56] blank

Paper: wove paper

Running title: 'HARRY POTTER' (24mm) on verso, recto title comprises chapter title, pp. 8-252

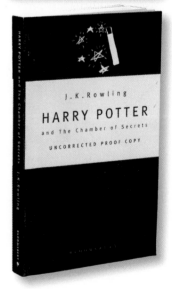

Binding: white wrappers overprinted in blue.

   On spine: 'HARRY POTTER and The Chamber of Secrets J.K.Rowling BLOOMSBURY' (reading lengthways down spine) together with publisher's logo of a dog's head, 3 by 4mm (horizontally at foot of spine). All in white on blue.

On upper wrapper: '[illustration of test tube and six stars, 42 by 44mm] [in white on blue panel, 49 by 127mm] | J.K.Rowling | HARRY POTTER | and The Chamber of Secrets | UNCORRECTED PROOF COPY | BLOOMSBURY [in white on black oval, 13 by 54mm and on blue panel, 80 by 127mm]' (all width centred). Lines 2-5 in black on white panel, 67 by 127mm.

On lower wrapper: '[blue panel, 49 by 127mm] | Publication Date July 1998 | UK Price £10.99 | ISBN 0 7475 3849 2 | Trimmed page size 198x129mm | Extent 256pp | This is an uncorrected proof copy and is not for sale. | All specifications are provisional. | It should not be quoted without comparison | to the finally revised text. | It does not reflect the quality, page size | [blue panel, 82 by 127mm]'. Lines 1-10 all in black on white panel, 67 by 127mm.

All edges trimmed. Binding measurements: 198 by 127mm (wrappers), 198 by 16mm (spine).

Price: not for sale

Contents:
Harry Potter and the Chamber of Secrets
   ('Not for the first time, an argument had broken out over breakfast at number four…')

Notes:
The text was slightly re-set for the first English edition (see A2(a)).

A number of asterisks, which appear in the first edition to create breaks between sections of text, are printed on the left margin. The first English edition has these centred.

An unconfirmed print-run of 300 copies is generally accepted for this proof. Bloomsbury is unable to provide accurate figures and has merely suggested between 200 and 300 copies.

The text on the lower wrapper is incomplete, reading only 'It does not reflect the quality, page size'. The conclusion, as seen on AA4(a) and AA4(b), is 'or thickness of the finished text.'

Copies: Sotheby's, 17 December 2008, lot 215

AA2(b)   AMERICAN ADVANCE READER'S COPY   (1999)

HARRY POTTER | AND THE CHAMBER OF SECRETS | [black and white illustration of Hogwarts castle, in oval, 53 by 91mm] | BY | J. K. ROWLING | ILLUSTRATIONS BY MARY GRANDPRÉ | [publisher's device of a lantern, 12 by 9mm] | ARTHUR A. LEVINE BOOKS | AN IMPRINT OF SCHOLASTIC PRESS (All width centred on a diamond pattern background)

Collation: 176 unsigned leaves bound in indeterminate gatherings; 227 by 151mm; [I-VI] VII-VIII [IX-X] 1-341 [342]

Page contents: [I] Advance publishing information: 'HARRY POTTER | AND THE CHAMBER OF SECRETS | [rule, 84mm] | J. K. ROWLING | [two columns: 'ISBN: | 0-439-06486-4 |

Length: | 352 pages | Classification: | Fantasy | Price: | $17.95
| Ages: | All' on left and 'Scheduled Pub. Date: | September
1999 | Trim: | 6" x 9" | Illustrations: | Pastels | LC: 98-46370'
on right] | [publisher's device of a lantern, 12 by 9mm] |
ARTHUR A. LEVINE BOOKS | *An Imprint of Scholastic Press*
| 555 BROADWAY, NEW YORK, NY 10012' (all within ruled
border with thick rule at head and foot, 167 by 107mm) and, at
foot of page: 'UNCORRECTED PROOFS | If any material is to
be quoted, it should be checked against the bound book. | CIP
information to be included in bound book' (all on a diamond
pattern background); [II] 'PRAISE FOR J. K. ROWLING'S |
HARRY POTTER | AND THE SORCERER'S STONE' (with
device of ten stars at left and right margins) (seven extracts from
reviews listed with sources, the first five extracts are cited within
double inverted commas only whilst the final two extracts are given
a single star before the double inverted commas, the source is noted

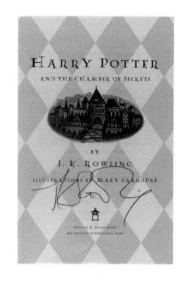

in italics); [III] two extracts from reviews listed with sources, the first extract is given a single star
before the double inverted commas whilst the second extract is cited within double inverted commas
only, the sources are noted in italics, together with '[four-sided device] A *New York Times* Best-seller
| [four-sided device] A *Publisher's Weekly* Best Book of 1998 | [four-sided device] A *Booklist* Editor's
Choice | [four-sided device] Winner of the 1997 National Book Award (UK) | [four-sided device] An
ALA Notable Book | [four-sided device] Winner of the 1997 Gold Medal Smarties Prize | [four-sided
device] A New York Public Library Best Book of the Year 1998 | [four-sided device] *Parenting* Book
of the Year Award-winner 1998'; [IV] 'Also by J. K. ROWLING | [rule, 38mm] | *Harry Potter and
the Sorcerer's Stone*'; [V] title-page; [VI] 'FOR SEÁN P. F. HARRIS, | GETAWAY DRIVER AND
FOUL-WEATHER FRIEND | [device of twelve stars] | Text copyright © 1998 by J. K. Rowling. |
Illustrations copyright © 1999 by Mary Grandpré. | All rights reserved. Published by Scholastic Press,
a division of Scholastic Inc., | *Publishers since 1920.* | SCHOLASTIC, SCHOLASTIC PRESS,
ARTHUR A. LEVINE BOOKS, and associated logos | are trademarks and/or registered trademarks
of Scholastic Inc. | [new paragraph] No part of this publication may be reproduced, or stored in a
retrieval system, or transmitted | in any form or by any means, electronic, mechanical, photocopying,
recording, or otherwise, | without written permission of the publisher. For information regarding
permission, write to | Scholastic Inc., Attention: Permissions Department, 555 Broadway, New York,
NY 10012. | [new paragraph] Library of Congress Cataloging-in-Publication Data | [new paragraph]
Rowling, J. K. | Harry Potter and the Chamber of Secrets / by J. K. Rowling. | p. cm. | Summary:
When the Chamber of Secrets is opened again at the Hogwarts School | for Witchcraft and Wizardry,
second-year student Harry Potter finds himself in danger | from a dark power that has once more
been released on the school. | ISBN 0-439-06486-4 | [square bracket]1. Wizards — Fiction. 2. Magic
— Fiction. 3. Schools — Fiction. | 4. England — Fiction.[square bracket] I. Title. | PZ7.R7968Har
1999 | [square bracket]Fic[square bracket] — dc21 98-46370 | [new paragraph] Book design by David
Saylor | [new paragraph] 10 9 8 7 6 5 4 3 2 1   9/9 0/0 1 2 3 4 | Printed in the U.S.A. 37 | First
American edition, September 1999'; VII-VIII 'CONTENTS' (eighteen chapters listed with titles and

page references); [IX] half-title: 'HARRY POTTER | AND THE CHAMBER OF SECRETS' (all on diamond pattern background); [X] blank; 1-341 text; [342] colophon: '[publisher's device of a lantern, 17 by 13mm] | *This book* | *was art directed by* | *David Saylor. The art for both* | *the jacket and the interior was created* | *using pastels on toned printmaking paper.* | *The text was set in 12-point Adobe Garamond,* | *a typeface based on the sixteenth-century type designs of* | *Claude Garamond, redrawn by Robert Slimbach* | *in 1989. The book was printed and bound at* | *Berryville Graphics in Berryville, Virginia.* | *The production was supervised by* | *Angela Biola and Mike* | *Derevjanik.*'

Paper: wove paper

Running title: 'CHAPTER' and chapter number on verso, recto title comprises chapter title, pp. 1-341 except for pages on which a new chapter commences. On these pages, the running title comprises 'CHAPTER' and chapter number. Each running title (excluding pages on which new chapters commence) begins and ends with a three star device (in mirror image)

Illustrations: title-page vignette, together with nine vignettes at the beginning of chapters 3, 4, 7, 8, 9, 10, 11, 14 and 17 (after chapter and chapter number but before chapter title). Chapters 1, 2, 5, 6, 12, 13, 15, 16 and 18 do not have illustrations in this proof. See notes.

Binding: pictorial wrappers.

On spine: 'ROWLING | [rule]' (horizontally at head) with 'HARRY POTTER | AND THE CHAMBER OF SECRETS' (reading lengthways down spine) and '[publisher's device of a lantern, 15 by 10mm] | ARTHUR A. | LEVINE BOOKS | [rule] | SCHOLASTIC | PRESS' (horizontally at foot). All in grey and all on colour illustration of pillar.

On upper wrapper: 'Harry Potter [hand-drawn lettering] [in grey] | AND THE [hand-drawn lettering in red of illustration] | CHAMBER [hand-drawn lettering in red of illustration] | OF SECRETS [hand-drawn lettering in red of illustration] | J. K. ROWLING [in grey] | ADVANCE READER'S EDITION [in white]' (all width centred). All on colour illustration of Harry Potter holding onto tail of a flying phoenix.

On lower wrapper: 'UNCORRECTED PROOF — NOT FOR SALE | [rule, 104mm] | [four-sided device] Sequel to the extraordinary *New York Times* best-seller, | *Harry Potter and the Sorcerer's Stone* | [four-sided device] Britain's phenomenal #1 best-seller | [four-sided device] Winner of the British National Book Award | [new paragraph] "You don't have to be a wizard or a kid to appreciate the spell cast by Harry | Potter." —*USA Today* | "A charming, imaginative, magical confection of a novel." —*Boston Globe* | "Harry is destined for greatness." —*The New York Times* | [new paragraph] The summer after his first year at Hogwarts is worse than ever for Harry | Potter. The Dursleys of Privet Drive reach new lows of malevolent prissiness. | And just when Harry thinks the endless vacation is over, a neurotic house-elf | named Dobby shows up to warn him against going back to school. Of course, | Harry doesn't listen. But Hogwarts isn't the cure he expects it to be. Almost | immediately a student is found turned to stone, and then another. And some- | how Harry stands accused. Could Harry Potter be the long-feared heir of | Slytherin? | [new paragraph] Harry and his friends are stretched to their limits dealing with the likes of | Moaning Myrtle, a spirit who haunts the girls' bathroom; the outrageously | conceited new professor, Gilderoy Lockheart; and the mysterious Tom Riddle | (a boy from Hogwarts' past), whose diary gives terrifying new meaning to the | phrase "a compelling read." | [new paragraph] | COMING IN SEPTEMBER 1999 | [four-sided device] First Printing 250,000 Copies [four-sided device] Promotional Giveaways | [four-sided device] $150,000 Marketing Campaign [four-sided device] Reservation Board | [four-sided device] National Advertising [four-sided device] Reading Group Guide | [four-sided device] National Publicity Campaign [four-sided device] Featured Online at Scholastic.com | and Author Tour | [four-sided device] 44-Copy Mixed Floor Display with the Paperback of | *Harry Potter and the Sorcerer's Stone* | [four-sided device] ISBN 0-439-06486-4 [four-sided device] 352 pages | [four-sided device] $17.95 US [four-sided device] Black and White Illustrations'. All in black on light green panel within grey rule, 212 by 130mm and all obscuring colour illustration.

All edges trimmed. Binding measurements: 227 by 151mm (wrappers), 227 by 21mm (spine).

Price: not for sale

Contents:
Harry Potter and the Chamber of Secrets
('Not for the first time, an argument had broken out over breakfast at number four…')

Notes:
Note that the title-page vignette is that from *Sorcerer's Stone* (see A4(a)).

The three typographical features present in the first American edition (see A2(c)) are absent in the proof. On page 21 there is a large space for the facsimile of Mafalda Hopkirk's signature. On pages 127-28 (the setting of the text takes more space than the setting in A2(c)) a simple italic font provides the text of the 'Kwikspell' course description and students' endorsements. The newspaper headline on page 221 is provided in italic capitals.

Each chapter commences with a drop capital.

Copies: private collection

HARRY POTTER AND THE SORCERER'S STONE

AA3(a)   AMERICAN ADVANCE READER'S COPY   (1998)

HARRY POTTER | AND THE SORCERER'S STONE | [black and white illustration of Hogwarts castle, in oval, 53 by 90mm] | BY | J.K. ROWLING | ILLUSTRATIONS BY MARY GRANDPRÉ | [publisher's device of a lantern, 12 by 9mm] | ARTHUR A. LEVINE BOOKS | AN IMPRINT OF SCHOLASTIC PRESS (All width centred on a diamond pattern background)

Collation: 160 unsigned leaves bound in indeterminate gatherings; 227 by 153mm; [I-VIII] 1-309 [310-312]

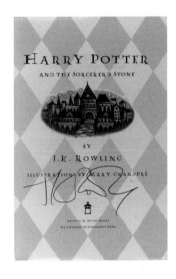

Page contents: [I] 'A Note From the Publisher' ('To be present at the debut of a glorious new talent is one of the great joys…') (facsimile of publisher's signature) with letter head and footer replicating publisher's headed paper and with section of publisher's device of a lantern behind text on right margin in grey; [II] 'PRAISE FOR J.K. ROWLING'S | SMASHING DEBUT | [device of seven stars] | [five extracts from reviews listed with sources]; [III] title-page; [IV] 'FOR JESSICA, WHO LOVES STORIES, | FOR ANNE, WHO LOVED THEM TOO; | AND FOR DI, WHO HEARD THIS ONE FIRST. | [device of twelve stars] | Text copyright © 1998 by J.K. Rowling | Illustrations copyright © 1998 by Mary Grandpré | All rights reserved. Published by Scholastic Press, a division of Scholastic Inc., | *Publishers since 1920*, 555 Broadway, New York, NY 10012 | by arrangement with Bloomsbury Publishing Plc. | SCHOLASTIC, SCHOLASTIC PRESS, ARTHUR A. LEVINE BOOKS and associated logos | are trademarks and/or registered trademarks of Scholastic Inc. | [new paragraph] No part of this publication may be reproduced, or stored in a retrieval system, or transmitted | in any form or by any means, electronic, mechanical, photocopying, recording, or otherwise, | without written permission of the publisher. For information regarding permissions, write | to Bloomsbury Publishing Plc., 38 Soho Square, London W1V 5DF, United Kingdom. | [new paragraph] Library of Congress Cataloging-in-Publication Data | [new paragraph] Rowling, J.K. | Harry Potter and the Sorcerer's Stone / by J.K. Rowling | p. cm. | Summary: Rescued from the outrageous neglect of his aunt and uncle, a young boy | with a great destiny proves his worth while attending Hogwarts School | of Witchcraft and Wizardry. | ISBN 0-590-35340-3 (hc.) — ISBN 0-590-35342-X (pb.) | [square bracket]1. Fantasy — Fiction. 2. Witches — Fiction. 3. Wizards — Fiction. | 4. Schools — Fiction. 5. England — Fiction.[square bracket] I. Title. | PZ7.R79835Har 1998 | [square bracket]Fic[square bracket] — dc21 97-39059 | [new paragraph] 1 3 5 7 9 10 8 6 4 2   8 9/9 0/0 01 02 | Printed in the U.S.A.   23 | First American edition, October 1998'; [V-VI] 'CONTENTS' (seventeen chapters listed with titles and page references); [VII] half-title: 'HARRY POTTER | AND THE SORCERER'S STONE' (all on diamond pattern background); [VIII] blank; 1-309 text; [310] blank; [311] colophon: '[publisher's device of a lantern, 17 by 13mm] | *This book* | *was art directed by* | *David Saylor and designed by Becky* | *Terhune. The art for both the jacket and interior* | *was created on toned printmaking paper. The text was set* | *in 12-point Adobe Garamond, a typeface based on the sixteenth* | *century type designs of Claude Garamond, redrawn by Robert* | *Slimbach in 1989. The book was printed and bound* | *at Berryville Graphics in Berryville, Virginia.* | *The production was supervised by* | *Angela Biola and Mike* | *Derevjanik.*'; [312] blank

Paper: wove paper

Running title: 'CHAPTER' and chapter number on verso, recto title comprises chapter title, pp. 1-309 except for pages on which a new chapter commences. On these pages, the running title comprises 'CHAPTER' and chapter number. Each running title (excluding pages on which new chapters commence)

Illustrations: title-page vignette, together with seventeen vignettes at the beginning of each chapter (after chapter and chapter number but before chapter title). In addition to standard typographical changes (including italics, capitals and small capitals) there are other typographical features, comprising:

    p. 34 'handwritten' envelope address
    p. 42 'handwritten' envelope address
    p. 51 facsimile of Minerva McGonagall's signature
    p. 52 'handwritten' letter
    pp. 135-36 'handwritten' letter
    p. 141 newspaper headline
    p. 164 facsimile of Minerva McGonagall's signature [different from that above]
    p. 202 'handwritten' letter
    p. 261 'handwritten' note

Binding: pictorial wrappers.

    On spine: 'J. K. | ROWLING | [rule]' (horizontally at head) with 'HARRY POTTER | AND THE SORCERER'S STONE' (reading lengthways down spine) and '[publisher's device of a lantern, 15 by 10mm] | ARTHUR A. | LEVINE BOOKS | [rule] | SCHOLASTIC | PRESS' (horizontally at foot). All in yellow and all on colour illustration of archway.

    On upper wrapper: 'Harry Potter [hand-drawn lettering] [in yellow] | AND THE [hand-drawn lettering in brown of illustration] | SORCERER'S STONE [hand-drawn lettering in brown of illustration] | J. K. ROWLING [in yellow] | ADVANCE READER'S EDITION [in white]' (all width centred). All on colour illustration of Harry Potter playing Quidditch.

On lower wrapper: 'UNCORRECTED PROOF — NOT FOR SALE | [rule, 104mm] | [four-sided device] Winner of the British National Book Award, | Children's Book of the Year | [four-sided device] Winner of the Smarties Prize | [new paragraph] "Harry Potter could assume the same near-legendary status as Roald | Dahl's Charlie, of chocolate factory fame." —*The Guardian* | [new paragraph] Harry Potter has never been the star of a Quidditch team, scoring | points while riding a broom far above the ground. He knows no | spells, has never helped to hatch a dragon, and has never worn a | cloak of invisibility. | [new paragraph] All he knows is a miserable life with the Dursleys, his horrible | Aunt and Uncle, and their abominable son Dudley — a great big | swollen spoiled bully. Harry's room is a tiny closet at the foot of the | stairs, and he hasn't had a birthday party in eleven years. | [new paragraph] But all that is about to change when a mysterious letter arrives by | owl messenger; a letter with an invitation to an incredible place that | Harry — and any one who reads about him — will find unforgettable. | [new paragraph] COMING IN SEPTEMBER 1998 | [four-sided device] First Printing 30,000 Copies [four-sided device] Reading Group Guide | [four-sided device] National Advertising [four-sided device] Easel-Back for In-Store Promotion | [four-sided device] National Publicity Campaign [four-sided device] Featured Online at Scholastic.com | [new paragraph] [four-sided device] ISBN 0-590-35340-3 [four-sided device] 320 pages | [four-sided device] $16.95 US [four-sided device] Black and White Illustrations' All in black on purple panel within yellow rule, 170 by 119mm and all obscuring colour illustration.

All edges trimmed. Binding measurements: 227 by 153mm (wrappers), 227 by 19mm (spine).

Price: not for sale

Contents:
Harry Potter and the Sorcerer's Stone
  ('Mr. and Mrs. Dursley, of number four, Privet Drive, were proud to say…')

Notes:
In an interview with me in March 2012 the publisher Arthur A. Levine noted that the publication of the 'Advanced Reader's Copy' was a particularly 'elegant' piece of production. It might have been expected that the publisher would merely distribute a copy of the book in galley-format together with a photocopy of the cover and bind it as a paperback. However, as Levine states, '… we wanted to make a big splash and we actually printed the galleys with Mary GrandPré artwork beautifully printed. I also wrote a letter. I write very few letters because you have to pick and choose – you can't be saying that *every* book is significant.'

The page references in the 'Contents' listing are incomplete. Chapter One is noted as page 1 and all other page references are rendered as '00'.

Each chapter commences with a drop capital.

Copies: private collection

HARRY POTTER AND THE
PRISONER OF AZKABAN

AA4(a) ENGLISH PROOF – PURPLE WRAPPERS (1999)

HARRY | POTTER | *and the Prisoner of Azkaban* | [illustration of Hogwarts crest with legend 'DRAGO DORMIENS NUNQUAM TITILLANDUS' on banner, 67 by 82mm] | J.K.ROWLING | [publisher's device of a dog, 11 by 18mm] | BLOOMSBURY (Lines 1 and 2 justified on left and right margins, and all width centred)

Collation: 158 unsigned leaves bound in indeterminate gatherings; 198 by 129mm; [1-7] 8-17 [18] 19-28 [29] 30-41 [42] 43-55 [56] 57-74 [75] 76-93 [94] 95-106 [107] 108-121 [122] 123-36 [137] 138-55 [156] 157-71 [172] 173-85 [186] 187-97 [198] 199-213 [214] 215-29 [230] 231-42 [243] 244-54 [255] 256-59 [260] 261-74 [275] 276-80 [281] 282-301 [302] 303-315 [316]

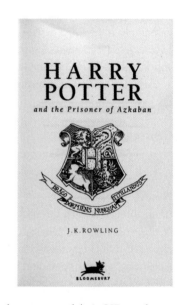

Page contents: [1] half-title: 'HARRY | POTTER | *and the Prisoner of Azkaban* | [illustration of Hogwarts crest with legend 'DRAGO DORMIENS NUNQUAM TITILLANDUS' on banner, 47 by 57mm]'; [2] '*Also available:* | Harry Potter and the Philosopher's Stone | Harry Potter and the Chamber of Secrets'; [3] title-page; [4] 'All rights reserved; no part of this publication may be reproduced or | transmitted by any means, electronic, mechanical, photocopying or otherwise, | without the prior permission of the publisher | [new paragraph] First published in Great Britain in 1999 | Bloomsbury Publishing Plc, 38 Soho Square, London, W1V 5DF | [new paragraph] Copyright © Text Joanne Rowling 1999 | Copyright © Illustrations Cliff Wright 1999 | [new paragraph] The moral right of the author has been asserted | A CIP catalogue record of this book is available from the | British Library | [new paragraph] ISBN 0 7475 4215 5 | [new paragraph] Printed in Great Britain by Clays Ltd, St Ives plc | [new paragraph] 10 9 8 7 6 5 4 3 2 1 | [new paragraph] Cover Design by Nathan Burton'; [5] '? dedication'; [6] blank; [7]-315 text; [316] blank

Paper: wove paper

Running title: 'HARRY POTTER' (24mm) on verso, recto title comprises chapter title, pp. 8-315

Binding: white wrappers overprinted in purple.
  On spine: 'HARRY POTTER AND [in white] | J.K. ROWLING [in white] BLOOMSBURY [in black] | THE PRISONER OF AZKABAN [in white]' (reading lengthways down spine)

together with publisher's logo of a dog's head in black, 3 by 4mm (horizontally at foot of spine). All on purple.

On upper wrapper: '[purple panel, 50 by 129mm] | J.K. Rowling | HARRY POTTER AND THE | PRISONER OF AZKABAN | UNCORRECTED PROOF COPY | BLOOMSBURY [in white on black oval, 13 by 54mm and on purple panel, 84 by 129mm]' (all width centred). Lines 1-4 in black on white panel, 63 by 129mm.

On lower wrapper: '[purple panel, 50 by 129mm] | Publication Date July 1999 | UK Price £10.99 | ISBN 0 7475 4215 5 | Trimmed page size 198x129mm | Extent 256pp | This is an uncorrected proof copy and is not for sale. | All specifications are provisional. | It should not be quoted without comparison | to the finally revised text. | It does not reflect the quality, page size | or thickness of the finished text. | [purple panel, 83 by 129mm]'. Lines 1-11 all in black on white panel, 63 by 129mm.

All edges trimmed. Binding measurements: 198 by 129mm (wrappers), 198 by 20mm (spine).

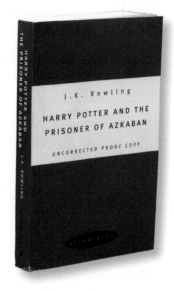

Price: not for sale

Contents:
Harry Potter and the Prisoner of Azkaban
('Harry Potter was a highly unusual boy in many ways…')

Notes:
The text in this proof is in an earlier state than that presented in the green proof (see AA4(b)). The first example occurs on page [7] in the quotation from Harry's essay. In the earlier state Wendelin the Weird 'allowed herself to be caught no less than forty seven times…' This would be revised to 'allowed herself to be caught no fewer than forty-seven times…' Evidently some editorial work has taken place throughout. Contrast text on page 8 detailing Harry's disgrace in the earlier state:

Harry was particularly keen to avoid trouble with his Aunt and Uncle at the moment, because they were already in an especially bad mood with him…

With the later text:

Harry was keen to avoid trouble with his aunt and uncle at the moment, as they were already in a bad mood with him…

On page 13 when Harry observes a photography of Percy Weasley, we learn that:

Percy… was looking particularly smug, with a new silver badge gleaming on the fez he was wearing over his horn-rimmed glasses.

This is expanded in the later version when:

Percy… was looking particularly smug. He had pinned his Head Boy badge to the fez perched jauntily on top his neat hair, his horn-rimmed glasses flashing in the Egyptian sun.

An unconfirmed print-run of 50 copies is generally accepted for this proof. This would suggest that the proof was released to a very select readership, with the publisher expecting to issue the text in a later state to a greater number of readers. Bloomsbury, however, note a print-run of 150 copies.

Copies: Sotheby's, 17 December 2008, lot 216

AA4(b)   ENGLISH PROOF – GREEN WRAPPERS   (1999)

HARRY | POTTER | *and the Prisoner of Azkaban* | [illustration of Hogwarts crest with legend 'DRAGO DORMIENS NUNQUAM TITILLANDUS' on banner, 67 by 82mm] | J.K.ROWLING | [publisher's device of a dog, 11 by 18mm] | BLOOMSBURY (Lines 1 and 2 justified on left and right margins, and all width centred)

Collation: 158 unsigned leaves bound in indeterminate gatherings; 198 by 128mm; [1-7] 8-17 [18] 19-28 [29] 30-41 [42] 43-55 [56] 57-74 [75] 76-93 [94] 95-106 [107] 108-121 [122] 123-36 [137] 138-55 [156] 157-71 [172] 173-85 [186] 187-97 [198] 199-213 [214] 215-29 [230] 231-42 [243] 244-54 [255] 256-61 [262] 263-75 [276] 277-81 [282] 283-302 [303] 304-316

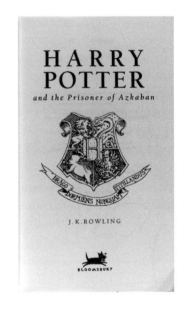

Page contents: [1] half-title: 'HARRY | POTTER | *and the Prisoner of Azkaban* | [illustration of Hogwarts crest with legend 'DRAGO DORMIENS NUNQUAM TITILLANDUS' on banner, 47 by 57mm]'; [2] '*Also available:* | Harry Potter and the Philosopher's Stone | Harry Potter and the Chamber of Secrets'; [3] title-page; [4] 'All rights reserved; no part of this publication may be reproduced or | transmitted by any means, electronic, mechanical, photocopying or otherwise, | without the prior permission of the publisher | [new paragraph] First published in Great Britain in 1999 | Bloomsbury Publishing Plc, 38 Soho Square, London, W1V 5DF | [new paragraph] Copyright © Text Joanne Rowling 1999 | Copyright © Illustrations Cliff Wright 1999 | [new paragraph] The moral right of the author has been asserted | A CIP catalogue record of this book is available from the | British Library | [new paragraph] ISBN 0 7475 4215 5 | [new paragraph] Printed in Great Britain by Clays Ltd, St Ives plc | [new paragraph] 10 9 8 7 6 5 4 3 2 1 | [new paragraph] Cover Design by Nathan Burton'; [5] '? dedication'; [6] blank; [7]-316 text

Paper: wove paper

Running title: 'HARRY POTTER' (24mm) on verso, recto title comprises chapter title, pp. 8-316

Binding: white wrappers overprinted in green.

On spine: 'HARRY POTTER AND [in white] | J.K. ROWLING [in white] BLOOMSBURY [in black] | THE PRISONER OF AZKABAN [in white]' (reading lengthways down spine) together with publisher's logo of a dog's head in black, 3 by 4mm (horizontally at foot of spine). All on green.

On upper wrapper: '[green panel, 52 by 128mm] | J.K. Rowling | HARRY POTTER AND THE | PRISONER OF AZKABAN | UNCORRECTED PROOF COPY | BLOOMSBURY [in white on black oval, 13 by 54mm and on green panel, 83 by 128mm]' (all width centred). Lines 1-4 in black on white panel, 63 by 128mm.

On lower wrapper: '[green panel, 52 by 128mm] | Publication Date July 1999 | UK Price £10.99 | ISBN 0 7475 4215 5 | Trimmed page size 198x129mm | Extent 256pp | This is an uncorrected proof copy and is not for sale. | All specifications are provisional. | It should not be quoted without comparison | to the finally revised text. | It does not reflect the quality, page size | or thickness of the finished text. | [green panel, 83 by 128mm]'. Lines 1-11 all in black on white panel, 63 by 128mm.

All edges trimmed. Binding measurements: 198 by 128mm (wrappers), 198 by 21mm (spine).

Price: not for sale

Contents:

Harry Potter and the Prisoner of Azkaban

('Harry Potter was a highly unusual boy in many ways…')

Notes:

This is a later proof than that issued in purple wrappers. See notes to AA4(a) for a comparison.

An unconfirmed print-run of 250 copies is generally accepted for this proof. Bloomsbury, however, provides a figure of 150 copies.

Copies: Sotheby's, 17 December 2008, lot 216 inscribed 'to Louise, | one of the privileged | few (to have one | of these!) | JKRowling' on p. [5]

AA4(c)   AMERICAN ADVANCE READER'S COPY   (1999)

HARRY POTTER | AND THE PRISONER OF AZKABAN | [black and white illustration of Hogwarts castle, in oval, 53 by 91mm] | BY | J. K. ROWLING | ILLUSTRATIONS BY MARY GRANDPRÉ | [publisher's device of a lantern, 12 by 9mm] | ARTHUR A. LEVINE BOOKS | AN IMPRINT OF SCHOLASTIC PRESS (All width centred on a diamond pattern background)

Collation: 223 unsigned leaves bound in indeterminate gatherings; 227 by 150mm; [I-VI] VII-IX [X-XII] 1-431 [432-34]

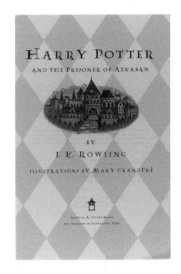

Page contents: [I] 'HARRY POTTER | AND THE PRISONER OF AZKABAN | UNCORRECTED PROOFS | If any material is to be quoted, it should be checked against the bound book. | CIP information to be included in bound book' (all on a diamond pattern background); [II] 'ALSO BY J. K. ROWLING | *Harry Potter and the Sorcerer's Stone* | *Harry Potter and the Chamber of Secrets*'; [III] title-page; [IV] '[device of twelve stars] | Copyright © 1999 by J.K. Rowling. | All rights reserved. Published by Scholastic Press, a division of Scholastic Inc., | *Publishers since 1920.* | SCHOLASTIC, SCHOLASTIC PRESS, ARTHUR A. LEVINE BOOKS, and associated logos | are trademarks and/or registered trademarks of Scholastic Inc. | [new paragraph] No part of this publication may be reproduced, or stored in a retrieval system, or transmitted | in any form or by any means, electronic, mechanical, photocopying, recording, or otherwise, | without written permission of the publisher. For information regarding permission, write | to Scholastic Inc., Attention: Permissions Department, 555 Broadway, New York, NY 10012. | [new paragraph] Library of Congress Cataloging-in-Publication Data | [new paragraph] Rowling, J. K. | Harry Potter and the Prisoner of Azkaban / by J. K. Rowling. | p. cm. | Summary: TK | ISBN 0-439-13635-0 | I. Title. | P | [square bracket]Fic[square bracket] — dc21 | [new paragraph] 10 9 8 7 6 5 4 3 2 1   9/9 0/0 1 2 3 4 | Printed in the U.S.A. 37 | First American edition, September 1999'; [V-VI] blank; VII-IX 'CONTENTS' (twenty-two chapters listed with titles and page references); [X] blank; [XI] half-title: 'HARRY POTTER | AND THE PRISONER OF AZKABAN' (all on diamond pattern background); [XII] blank; 1-431 text; [432] blank; [433] colophon: '[publisher's device of a lantern, 17 by 13mm] | *This* | *book was art* | *directed by David Saylor. The* | *art for both the jacket and the interior was* | *created using pastels on toned printmaking paper. The* | *text was set in 12-point Adobe Garamond, a typeface based on the* | *sixteenth-century type designs of Claude Garamond, redrawn by Robert* | *Slimbach in 1989. The book was printed and bound at* | *Berryville Graphics in Berryville, Virginia. The* | *production was supervised by Angela* | *Biola and Mike* | *Derevjanik.*'; [434] blank;

Paper: wove paper

Running title: 'CHAPTER' and chapter number on verso, recto title comprises chapter title, pp. 1-431 except for pages on which a new chapter commences. On these pages, the running title comprises 'CHAPTER' and chapter number. Each running title (excluding pages on which new chapters commence) begins and ends with a three star device (in mirror image)

Illustrations: title-page vignette. None of the chapters have illustrations in this proof. In addition to standard typographical changes (including italics, capitals and small capitals) there are other typographical features, comprising:

p. 8 newspaper headline

p. 14 'handwritten' letter

p. 14 facsimile of Minerva McGonagall's signature

p. 37 newspaper headline

p. 51 advertisement sign

p. 192 'The Marauder's Map' legend

p. 270 'handwritten' letter

p. 285 four different 'handwritten' comments

p. 289 'handwritten' letter

p. 313 'handwritten' exam schedule

p. 323 'handwritten' letter

Binding: pictorial wrappers.

On spine: 'ROWLING | [rule]' (horizontally at head) with 'HARRY POTTER | AND THE PRISONER OF AZKABAN' (reading lengthways down spine) and '[publisher's device of a lantern, 19 by 14mm] | ARTHUR A. | LEVINE BOOKS | [rule] | SCHOLASTIC PRESS' (horizontally at foot). All in white and all on diamond pattern background in black and red.

On upper wrapper: 'Harry Potter [hand-drawn lettering] | AND THE PRISONER | OF AZKABAN | J. K. ROWLING | ADVANCE READER'S EDITION' (all width centred). All in white and all on diamond pattern background in black and purple.

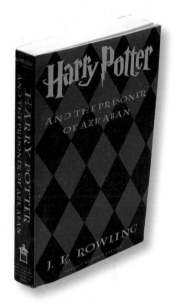

On lower wrapper: 'UNCORRECTED PROOF — NOT FOR SALE | [new paragraph] [four-sided device] HARRY POTTER *AND THE* SORCERER'S STONE | more than 23 weeks on the *New York Times* Best Sellers list | [new paragraph] [four-sided device] HARRY POTTER *AND THE* CHAMBER OF SECRETS | the blockbuster event of the summer | [new paragraph] And now, | we're prouder than ever to bring you Harry Potter's | third year at the Hogwarts School for Witchcraft and Wizardry: | [new paragraph] [four-sided device] HARRY POTTER *AND THE* PRISONER OF AZKABAN | [new paragraph] Due to the unprecedented demand for this book, we have moved the publica- | tion date up a full year. (We understand, we couldn't wait to read it either!) | Accordingly, we have rushed to bring this Advance Reader's Edition to you as | quickly as possible. Please rest assured that the final book will be as elegantly | produced as each of the previous two volumes, and decorated with the delight- | ful artwork of Mary GrandPré. | [new paragraph] And with that said … on to the book! (To be truthful, we doubt anyone will | actually have stopped to read this back cover! We wouldn't!) | [new paragraph] YOURS IN SEPTEMBER 1999! | [four-sided device] First Printing 500,000 Copies [four-sided device] Shelf-talker | [four-sided device] $250,000 Marketing Campaign [four-sided device] Poster | [four-sided device] National Advertising [four-sided device] Reading Group Guide | [four-sided device] National Publicity Campaign [four-sided device] Featured Online at Scholastic. com | and Author Tour | [four-sided device] 44-Copy Mixed Floor Display with the Paperback of

| *Harry Potter and the Sorcerer's Stone* | [new paragraph] [four-sided device] ISBN 0-439-13635-0 [four-sided device] 448 pages | [four-sided device] $19.95 US [four-sided device] Black-and-White Illustrations'. All in black on purple panel within red rule, 190 by 133mm and obscuring diamond pattern background in black and blue.

All edges trimmed. Binding measurements: 227 by 150mm (wrappers), 227 by 26mm (spine).

Price: not for sale

Contents:
Harry Potter and the Prisoner of Azkaban
('Harry Potter was a highly unusual boy in many ways. For one thing, he hated…')

Notes:
Note that the title-page vignette is that from *Sorcerer's Stone* (see A4(a)).

Each chapter commences with a drop capital.

Copies: private collection

THE CUCKOO'S CALLING

AA5(a)   ENGLISH PROOF   (2013)

Copies: no copies have been consulted

AA5(b)   AMERICAN PROOF   (2013)

The | Cuckoo's | Calling | Robert Galbraith | [publisher's device of a black 'M' with white stitching effect on a grey circle, diameter 14mm] | MULHOLLAND BOOKS | Little, Brown and Company | *New York Boston London* (All width centred)

Collation: 234 unsigned leaves bound in indeterminate gatherings; 235 by 152mm; [i-viii] [1-2] 3-6 [7-10] 11-53 [54-56] 57-157 [158-60] 161-244 [245-46] 247-414 [415-16] 417-38 [439-42] 443-51 [452-60]

Page contents: [i] half-title: 'The Cuckoo's Calling | These are uncorrected advance proofs bound for | your reviewing convenience. Please check with the | publisher or refer to the finished book whenever you | are excerpting or quoting in a review.' (lines 4-7 within single ruled border, 25 by 95mm); [ii] blank; [iii] title-page; [iv] 'The characters and events in this book are fictitious. Any similarity to real persons, | living or dead, is coincidental and not intended by the author. | [new paragraph] Copyright © 2013 by Robert Galbraith | [new paragraph] All rights reserved. In accordance with the U.S. Copyright Act of 1976, the scanning, | uploading, and electronic sharing of any part of this book without the permission of | the publisher constitute unlawful piracy and theft of the author's intellectual property. | If you would like to use material from the book (other than for review purposes), prior | written permission must be obtained by contacting the publisher at permissions@ | hbgusa.com. Thank you for your support of the author's rights. | [new paragraph] Mulholland Books / Little, Brown and Company | Hachette Book Group | 237 Park Avenue, New York, NY 10017 | mulhollandbooks.com | [new paragraph] First North American Edition: April 2013 | [new paragraph] Originally published in Great Britain by Sphere, April 2013 | [new paragraph] Mulholland Books is an imprint of Little, Brown and Company, a division of Hachette | Book Group, Inc. The Mulholland Books name and logo are trademarks of Hachette | Book Group, Inc. | [new paragraph] The publisher is not responsible for websites (or their content) that are not owned by | the publisher. | [new paragraph] The Hachette Speakers Bureau provides a wide range of authors for speaking events. | To find out more, go to hachettespeakersbureau.com or call (866) 376-6591. | [new paragraph] [square bracket]CIP or LOC no. tk[square bracket] | [new paragraph] 10 9 8 7 6 5 4 3 2 1 | [new paragraph] RRD-C | [new paragraph] Printed in the United States of America'; [v] 'Dedication'; [vi] blank; [vii] two stanzas comprising 'Christina G. Rossetti, 'A Dirge'';

[viii] blank; [1] 'Prologue' together with line in Latin and two-line translation from 'Lucius Accius, *Telephus*'; [2] blank; 3-6 text; [7] 'Three Months Later'; [8] blank; [9] 'Part One' together with two lines in Latin and three-line translation from 'Boethius, *De Consolatione Philosophiae*'; [10] blank; 11-53 text; [54] blank; [55] 'Part Two' together with line in Latin and two-line translation from 'Virgil, *The Aeneid*, Book 1'; [56] blank; 57-157 text; [158] blank; [159] 'Part Three' together with line in Latin and two-line translation from 'Virgil, *The Aeneid*, Book 1'; [160] blank; 161-244 text; [245] 'Part Four' together with line in Latin and two-line translation from 'Pliny the Elder, *Historia Naturalis*'; [246] blank; 247-414 text; [415] 'Part Five' together with line in Latin and two-line translation from 'Virgil, *Georgics*, Book 2'; [416] blank; 417-38 text; [439] 'Ten Days Later'; [440] blank; [441] 'Epilogue' together with two lines in Latin and one-line translation from 'Horace, *Odes*, Book 2'; [442] blank; 443-51 text; [452] blank; [453] 'About the Author | [new paragraph] Robert Galbraith spent several years with the Royal Military Police be- | fore being attached to the Special Investigative Branch (SIB), the plain- | clothes branch of the RMP. He left the military in 2003 and has been | working since then in the civilian security industry. The idea for Cor- | moran Strike grew directly out of his own experiences and those of his | military friends who returned to the civilian world. "Robert Galbraith" | is a pseudonym.'; [454-60] blank

Paper: wove paper

Running title: 'ROBERT GALBRAITH' (37mm) on verso and '*The Cuckoo's Calling*' (32mm) on recto, pp. 4-451 (excluding pages on which new chapters commence, part division pages and blank pages)

Binding: pictorial wrappers.

On spine: 'Robert Galbraith The Cuckoo's Calling' (reading lengthways down spine) and 'On-sale date: | 4/30/13 | [publisher's device of a black 'M' with white stitching effect on a grey circle, diameter 8mm] | MULHOLLAND | BOOKS' (horizontally at foot). All in black on white.

On upper wrapper: 'the [hand-drawn lettering] | cuckoo's [hand-drawn lettering] | calling [hand-drawn lettering] | ROBERT GALBRAITH' with '[publisher's device of a black 'M' with white stitching effect on a grey circle, diameter 7mm] | MULHOLLAND | BOOKS' all within ruled border, 13 by 19mm and 'COMING IN | APRIL 2013' all within ruled border, 13 by 22mm and both enclosed by ruled border, 15 by 43mm (title at an angle and with lines 1-2 off-set to the left and lines 3-4 off-set to the right, the publication details are off-set to the left). All in white on photographic illustration of a woman (showing back of the head) with a sea of photographers taking pictures.

On lower wrapper: 'COMING IN APRIL 2013 [in white on black panel, 5 by 127mm] | [new paragraph] A brilliant debut mystery in a classic vein: | Detective C. B. Strike investigates a supermodel's suicide. | [new paragraph] After losing his leg to a land mine in Afghanistan, Cormoran Strike is barely | scraping by as a private investigator. Strike is down to one client, and creditors | are calling. He has also just broken up with his longtime girlfriend and is living | in his office. | [new paragraph] Then John Bristow walks through his door with an amazing story: His sister, | the legendary supermodel Lula Landry — known to her friends as the Cuckoo — | fell famously to her death a few months earlier. The police ruled it a suicide, but | John refuses to believe that. The case plunges Strike into the world of | multimillionaire beauties, rock-star boyfriends, and desperate designers, and | introduces him to every variety of pleasure, enticement, seduction, and delusion | known to man. | [new paragraph] You may think you know detectives, but you've never met one quite like | Strike. You may think you know the wealthy and famous, but you've never seen | them investigated by a pro like this one | [new paragraph] Robert Galbraith spent several years with the Royal Military Police before | being attached to the Special Investigative Branch (SIB), the plainclothes branch | of the RMP. He left the military in 2003 and has been working since then in the | civilian security industry. The idea for Cormoran Strike grew directly out of his | own experiences and those of his military friends who returned to the civilian | world. "Robert Galbraith" is a pseudonym. | [new paragraph] MARKETING AND PROMOTION [in white on black panel, 5 by 127mm] | [new paragraph] National media campaign, including print, radio, and online interviews [round point] Web | exclusives, including mulhollandbooks.com feature and imprint e-newsletter, | excerpt posting, contests, and giveaways [round point] Social media campaign | [new paragraph] Follow us @mulhollandbooks on Twitter. | Like us at Facebook.com/mulhollandbooks. | Download the FREE Mulholland Books app. | [new paragraph] 6 x 9¼ [round point] 464 pages [round point] 978-0-316-20684-6 | $25.99 US / $28.99 CAN [round point] On-sale date: April 30, 2013 | Hardcover [round point] Fiction | [new paragraph] Advance Reading Copy [round point] | Uncorrected Proof [round point] Not for Sale | [new paragraph] Mulholland Books / Little, Brown and Company | mulhollandbooks.com'. All in black on white.

All edges trimmed. Binding measurements: 235 by 152mm (wrappers), 235 by 25mm (spine).

Price: not for sale

Contents:
The Cuckoo's Calling
('The buzz in the street was like the humming of flies. Photographers stood massed...')

Notes:
The text was to be reset for the first American edition, hence the difference in pagination between this and A17(b).

The publisher's blurb was to see some minor revisions before publication on the dust-jacket of the first American edition (see A17(b)).

Copies: private collection (TBP)

B. BOOKS AND PAMPHLETS WITH CONTRIBUTIONS BY J.K. ROWLING

B1   *BLOOMSBURY AUTUMN HIGHLIGHTS...*   *JUNE TO DECEMBER 1997*   (1997)

B1(a) First English edition (1997)

BLOOMSBURY | Autumn Highlights | Extracts From | Forthcoming Titles | June to December 1997 | BLOOMSBURY (All width centred)

'First published in 1997 | [new paragraph] Bloomsbury Publishing Plc | 38 Soho Square, London W1V 5DF | [new paragraph] Copyright in order of Contents: [...] © J. K. | Rowling 1997 [...] | [new paragraph] The moral rights of the authors have been asserted | [new paragraph] [...] ISBN 0 7475 3759 3 | [new paragraph] 10 9 8 7 6 5 4 3 2 1 | [new paragraph] Typeset by Hewer Text Composition Services, Edinburgh | Printed in Great Britain by Clays Ltd, St Ives plc' on imprint page

197 by 128mm, [i-iv] [1-2] 3-25 [26] 27-56 [57-58] 59 [60] 61-71 [72] 73-91 [92] 93-105 [106] 107-121 [122] 123-41 [142] 143-61 [162] 163-67 [168] 169-75 [176] 177-84 [185-88] 189-203 [204] 205-217 [218] 219-29 [230] 231 [232-34] 235-51 [252] 253-61 [262] 263-80 [281-84]; wove paper; pictorial wrappers; published early 1997; not for sale

Includes

> [*Harry Potter and the Philosopher's Stone*, Chapter Four]
> ('Boom. They knocked again. Dudley jerked awake...')
> (headed 'J.K. Rowling')

Part of a volume presenting extracts from titles to be published by Bloomsbury from June to December 1997. The contents is presented in four sections: 'Fiction' (four extracts), 'Non-Fiction' (thirteen extracts), 'Children's' (five extracts) and 'Paperbacks' (three extracts).

Textual evidence strongly suggests that this volume pre-dates the English proof.

    The text is closest to that in the English proof (AA1(a)) rather than the first edition (A1(a) and A1(aa)): 'Did yeh never wonder where yer parents learned it all?' (in *Autumn Highlights* and proof) changed to 'Did yeh never wonder where yer parents learnt it all?' (in first edition), 'Term begins on the first of September' (in *Autumn Highlights* and proof) changed to 'Term begins on 1 September' (in first edition), 'turning tea cups into rats' (in *Autumn*

Highlights and proof) changed to 'turning teacups into rats' (in first edition) and 'they were weirdoes' (in *Autumn Highlights* and proof) changed to 'they were weirdos' (in first edition).

Small errors in the setting of text further suggest that *Autumn Highlights* is earlier than the proof: 'Dark days. Harry' (in *Autumn Highlights*) compared to 'Dark days, Harry' (in proof and first) and 'There was somethin' goin' on that night he hadn't counted on –' I dunno what…' (in *Autumn Highlights*) compared to 'There was somethin' goin' on that night he hadn't counted on – I dunno what…' (in proof) and 'There was somethin' goin' on that night he hadn't counted on – *I* dunno what…' (in first edition).

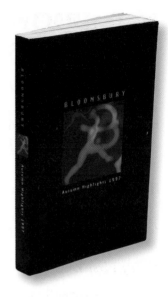

Given that this volume probably pre-dates the English proof it comprises the first appearance of any Harry Potter text in print. A six-line introduction provides a short synopsis:

> Harry Potter is an ordinary boy who lives in the cupboard under the stairs at his aunt and uncle's house – until he is rescued by an owl and taken to Hogwarts School of Wizardry and Witchcraft. Once there he learns his true identity, the reason behind his parents' mysterious death, who is out to kill him, and finally uncovers the biggest secret of all, the fabled Philosopher's Stone.

This is – evidently – an early version of the blurb that would appear on the first English edition (see A1(a) and A1(aa)). 'Advance acclaim for *Harry Potter and the Philosopher's Stone*' is then provided, credited to Wendy Cooling:

> … a terrific read and a stunning first novel. Harry is a really memorable character … This really is one of those books that can't be put down: the story raced along and had me hooked to the last page. Joanne Rowling clearly has a remarkable imagination and this splendid novel leaves me full of anticipation of what she might do next.

Then, after publication date and ISBN, the volume provides, on pages 189-202, the complete text of chapter four.

Nielsen BookData does not record this ISBN or title. The publication date must be assumed to be in the first part of 1997.

Copies: David Cornell, bookseller (bookseller inventory #001353)

B2 BLOOMSBURY [SPRING?] HIGHLIGHTS... JANUARY TO FEBRUARY 1999   (1998)

B2(a) First English edition (1998)

Similar to B1, an extract from *Harry Potter and the Chamber of Secrets* was published within a volume of forthcoming titles from Bloomsbury.

Copies: no copies have been consulted

B3   *WRITERS' AND ARTISTS' YEARBOOK*   (1999)

B3(a) First English edition for 2000 (1999)

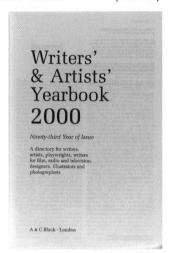

Writers' | & Artists' | Yearbook | 2000 | *Ninety-third Year of Issue* | A directory for writers, | artists, playwrights, writers | for film, radio and television, | designers, illustrators and | photographers | A & C Black [round point] London (All justified on left margin)

'© 2000 A & C Black (Publishers) Limited | 35 Bedford Row, London WC1R 4JH [...] | ISBN 0-7136-5147-4 | Printed and bound in Great Britain | by Biddles Ltd, Guildford and King's Lynn' on imprint page

210 by 148mm; [i-iv] v [vi] vii [viii] [1] 2-150 [151] 152-274 [275] 276-86 [287] 288-330 [331] 332-44 [345] 346-82 [383] 384-404 [405] 406-456 [457] 458-548 [549] 550-94 [595] 596-620 [621] 622-32 [633] 634-58 [659] 660-93 [694-96]; wove paper; printed wrappers; published 2 September 1999 (Nielsen BookData); £11.99

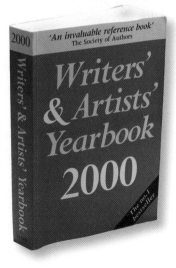

Includes
    'Foreword'
    ('The first time that I ever heard about the *Writers' and Artists' Yearbook* was in a small...')
    (signed and dated 'J.K. Rowling, June 1999')

See also B3(b) (and subsequent years) for a shortened version of this contribution (later entitled 'Notes from a successful children's author'). Note that the *Writers' and Artists' Yearbook* did not include a Rowling contribution for the years 2001, 2002, 2003 and 2004. The publishers would also use the shortened version within *Children's Writers' and Artists' Yearbook* (see B8).

Copies: private collection (PWE)

B3(b) First English edition for 2005 (2004)

Writers' | *& Artists'* | YEARBOOK | 2005 | Ninety-eighth Edition | A directory for writers, artists, playwrights, | writers for film, radio and television, | designers, illustrators and photographers | A & C Black [point] London (All width centred)

'© 2004 A & C Black (Publishers) Ltd | 37 Soho Square, London W1F 0BJ […] | ISBN 0-7136-6936-5 | Printed in Great Britain by | William Clowes Ltd, Beccles, Suffolk' on imprint page

210 by 148mm; [i-v] vi-vii [viii-ix] x [1] 2-126 [127] 128-298 [299] 300-310 [311] 312-74 [375] 376-92 [393] 394-432 [433] 434-52 [453] 454-94 [495] 496-580 [581] 582-98 [599] 600-668 [669] 670-710 [711] 712-39 [740] 741-68 [769] 770-819 [820-22]; wove paper; printed wrappers; published 16 August 2004 (Nielsen BookData); £13.99

Includes
    'Notes from a successful children's author'
    ('I can remember writing *Harry Potter and the Philosopher's Stone* in a café in Oporto…')
    (signed 'J.K. Rowling')

See also B3(a) for the original and longer version of this contribution. This shortened text would also appear within *Children's Writers' and Artists' Yearbook* (see B8).

Copies: private collection (PWE)

B3(c) First English edition for 2006 (2005)

Rowling contribution as for B3(b)

B3(d) First English edition for 2007 (2006)

Rowling contribution as for B3(b)

B3(e) First English edition for 2008 (2007)

Rowling contribution as for B3(b)

B3(f) First English edition for 2009 (2008)

Rowling contribution as for B3(b)

B3(g) First English edition for 2010 (2009)

Rowling contribution as for B3(b)

B3(h) First English edition for 2011 (2010)

Rowling contribution as for B3(b)

B3(i) First English edition for 2012 (2011)

Rowling contribution as for B3(b)

B3(j) First English edition for 2013 (2012)

Rowling contribution as for B3(b)

B3(k) First English edition for 2014 (2013)

Rowling contribution as for B3(b)

B4   LINDSAY FRASER, AN INTERVIEW WITH J.K. ROWLING   (2000)

B4(a) First English edition (2000)

TELLING [in white on black panel] TALES | [photograph of J.K. Rowling, 66 by 66mm] | An interview with | J.K. Rowling | by Lindsay Fraser | [publisher's logo, 9 by 9mm] | Mammoth (All width centred except 'TELLING TALES' and 'An Interview with' which are off-centre to the left)

'[...] Published in Great Britain 2000 by Mammoth, | an imprint of Egmont Children's Books Limited [...] | [new paragraph] Interview questions, design and typesetting © 2000 Egmont Children's Books | Interview answers © 2000 J.K. Rowling | J.K. Rowling's Books © 2000 Lindsay Fraser | [new paragraph] ISBN 0 7497 4394 8 [...] | [new paragraph] Printed and bound in Great Britain | by Cox and Wyman Ltd, Reading, Berks.' on imprint page

198 by 126mm; [i-iv] 1-35 [36] 37-60; wove paper; pictorial wrappers; published 1 August 2000 (Nielsen BookData); £2.99

Includes answers to an interview conducted by Lindsay Fraser in May 2000 ('I was the older of two girls. My earliest memory is of my sister being born...')

The interview is structured under the headings: 'My family and my childhood', My schooldays', 'My career' and 'My career as a writer'.

Page [36] provides two drawings by Rowling of the Sorting Hat and Fawkes the phoenix.

Copies: BL (YK.2001.a.3785) stamped 5 Mar 2001

B4(b) Second English edition (2001)

TELLING [in white on black panel] *TALES* | [photograph of J.K. Rowling, 66 by 66mm] | *An interview with* | J.K. Rowling | by Lindsay Fraser | [publisher's logo, 9 by 9mm] | Mammoth (All width centred except '*TELLING TALES*' and '*An Interview with*' which are off-centre to the left)

'[…] Published in Great Britain 2000 by Mammoth, | an imprint of Egmont Children's Books Limited […] | [new paragraph] This edition first published in 2001 | for The Book People Ltd | Hall Wood Avenue, Haydock, St Helens WA11 9UL | [new paragraph] Interview questions, design and typesetting © 2000 Egmont Children's Books | Interview answers © 2000 J.K. Rowling | J.K. Rowling's Books © 2000 Lindsay Fraser | [new paragraph] ISBN 0 7497 4394 8 […] | [new paragraph] Printed and bound in Great Britain | by Cox and Wyman Ltd, Reading, Berks.' on imprint page

198 by 126mm; [i-iv] 1-35 [36] 37-60; wove paper; pictorial wrappers; published 2001; £2.99 (see note)

An edition identical to B4(a) with the exception of the imprint page. As an edition published by The Book People (see A1(b)), the selling price would, presumably, have been lower than the £2.99 noted on the lower wrapper.

Copies: private collection (PWE)

B4(c) *Third English edition (2002)*

An interview with | J.K. Rowling | EGMONT [photograph of J.K. Rowling, 63 by 47mm] (Line 1 on left margin, line 2 across width of title-page, line 3 centred with photograph on right margin)

'[…] First published in Great Britain 2000 by Mammoth. | This edition published 2002 by Egmont Books Limited […] | [new paragraph] Interview questions, design and typesetting © 2000 Egmont Children's Books Limited | Interview answers © 2000 J.K. Rowling | J.K. Rowling's Books © 2000 Lindsay Fraser | [new paragraph] ISBN 1 4052 0052 9 […] | [new paragraph] Printed and bound in Great Britain | by Cox and Wyman Ltd, Reading, Berks.' on imprint page

198 by 129mm; [i-iv] v-vi [vii-viii] 1-4 [5] 6-18 [19] 20-39 [40] 41-62 [63] 64-68 [69-72]; wove paper; pictorial wrappers; published 24 May 2002 (Nielsen BookData); £2.99

The Rowling content is the same as for B4(a). A foreword by Lindsey Fraser has been added and the bibliography has been expanded.

Copies: BL (YK.2004.a.7763) stamped 21 May 2003; private collection (PWE)

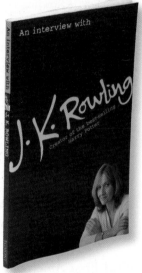

B5 [NATIONAL COUNCIL FOR ONE PARENT FAMILIES], *FAMILIES JUST LIKE US* (2000)

B5(a) *First English edition (2000)*

Upper wrapper:

[two photographs] | [right edge of a photograph] Families [in yellow] [left edge of photograph] | Just Like Us [in yellow] | the One Parent Families good book guide [in black] | with a foreword by J K

Rowling [in white] | [two photographs with Book Trust logo at left margin, 'produced by Young Book Trust and | National Council for One Parent Families' in black at centre and One Parent Families logo at right margin] (Lettering all width centred with photographs at edges)

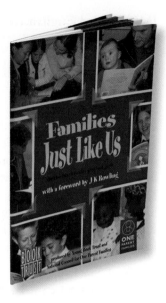

'Copyright © 2000 National Council for One Parent Families | ISBN 1 85199 144 1 Published by National Council for One Parent Families and Book Trust' on imprint page

210 by 148mm; 1-48; glossy wove paper; pictorial wrappers; published 1 November 2000 (Nielsen BookData); £4.99

Includes
   'Foreword by J.K. Rowling'
   ('I still have two early reader books featuring a brother and sister called Peter and Susan…')
   (signed, 'JKRowling')

As noted by the blurb on the lower wrapper, this is a 'guide to books for and about children in one-parent families… from picturebooks for young children to non-fiction titles for teenagers'. It was intended as 'an invaluable resource for parents, teachers, libraries and bookshops'.

A review of *Harry Potter and the Philosopher's Stone* is included on page 34 (within the 8-11 Years category).

Copies: private collection (PWE)

B6 LINDSAY FRASER, CONVERSATIONS WITH J.K. ROWLING (2001)

B6(a) First American edition (2001)

Conversations with | J. K. | ROWLING | [device of six stars] | By Lindsey Fraser | Scholastic Inc. | New York Toronto London Auckland Sydney | Mexico City New Delhi Hong Kong Buenos Aires (Lines 1 and 3 justified on left margin, line 2 towards centre, device of six stars towards right margin, remaining lines justified on right margin)

'Interview questions © 2000 by Egmont Children's Books | Interview answers © 2000 by J. K. Rowling | Overview of J. K. Rowling's Books © 2000 by Lindsey Fraser | The Fourth Book © 2001 by Scholastic Inc. | Illustrations © 2000 by J. K. Rowling | Cover illustrations © 2001 by Mary GrandPré | [new paragraph] *Entertainment Weekly* questions © 2000 Entertainment Weekly Inc. Reprinted by permission, | written by Jeff Jensen [point] O, *The Oprah Magazine* questions appeared in "J. K. Rowling Reads for | the Magic" on O, *The Oprah Magazine*, January 2001. Reprinted by permission of O, *The Oprah | Magazine*. [point] *Larry King Live* questions as seen on CNN's *Larry King Live* October 10, 2000. | Reprinted by permission. [point] *Newsweek* questions from *Newsweek*, July 10, 2000 © 2000 | Newsweek, Inc. All rights reserved. Reprinted by permission. [new paragraph] All rights reserved. Published by Scholastic Press [...] | [...] by arrangement with Mammoth [...] | [...] Original English language edition first published | 2000 under the title *Telling Tales: An Interview with J. K. Rowling* [...] | [new paragraph] [...] ISBN 0-439-31455-0 LC number 2001029392 | 10 9 8 7 6 5 4 3 2 1   01 02 03 04 05 | [new paragraph] Book design by David Saylor | Printed in the U.S.A. | First edition, October 2001' on imprint page

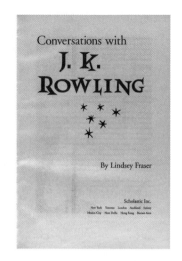

193 by 133mm; [1-10] 11-96; wove paper; pictorial wrappers; published October 2001; $4.99

An enlarged, and differently titled, version of B4. The interview and 'J.K. Rowling's Books' remains unchanged. This title, however, adds a new section entitled 'The Fourth Book'.

'The Fourth Book' provides a brief commentary on *Harry Potter and the Goblet of Fire* before quoting extracts of interviews originally printed within *Newsweek* (10 July 2000), O, *The Oprah Magazine* (January 2001), transcripts of replies and questions on *Larry King Live* (broadcast by CNN on 10 October 2000) and an extract from an interview originally printed within *Entertainment Weekly* (7 September 2000).

Information provided by Nielsen BookData suggests that 'Econo-Clad Books' issued a hardback during October 2001. This was probably a library edition. This edition has the ISBN 0-613-35768-X. No copies have been consulted.

Copies: private collection (PWE)

B7   SARAH BROWN AND GIL MCNEIL, MAGIC   (2002)

B7(a) First English edition (2002)

MAGIC | Edited by Sarah Brown | and Gil McNeil | BLOOMSBURY (All width centred)

'First published 2002 | [new paragraph] This collection copyright ©
2002 by Sarah Brown and Gil McNeil | [new paragraph] Foreword
copyright © 2002 by J.K. Rowling | Introduction copyright
© 20012 by Sarah Brown […] | [new paragraph] Bloomsbury
Publishing Plc, | 38 Soho Square, London W1D 3HB […] | ISBN
0 7475 5746 2 | [new paragraph] 10 9 8 7 6 5 4 3 2 1 | [new
paragraph] Typeset by Hewer Text Ltd, Edinburgh | Printed by
Clays Ltd, St Ives plc' on imprint page

198 by 129mm; [i-vi] 1-312 [313-14]; wove paper; pictorial wrappers;
published 3 June 2002 (Nielsen BookData); £6.99

Includes:
    'Foreword'
    ('My involvement with the National Council for One Parent
    Families…')
    (headed, 'J.K. ROWLING')

A collection of eighteen original short stories by Andrea Ashworth,
Kate Atkinson, Celia Brayfield, Christopher Brookmyre, Lewis Davies,
Isla Dewar, Emma Donoghue, Maeve Haran, Joanne Harris, Jackie Kay,
Gil McNeil, John O'Farrell; Ben Okri; Michèle Roberts, Meera Syal,
Sue Townsend, Arabella Weir and Fay Weldon. The volume was edited
by Sarah Brown and Gil McNeil.

The volume was produced to benefit the National Council for One
Parent Families Magic Million Appeal. As noted on the lower wrapper,
the 'charity's Magic Million Appeal funds services for lone parents so
they can get the help and support they need, when they need it'. £1
from the purchase price of £6.99 was donated to the appeal.

Copies: private collection (PWE)

B8   CHILDREN'S WRITERS' AND
         ARTISTS' YEARBOOK   (2004)

B8(a) English edition for 2005 (2004)

Children's | Writers' | & Artists' | YEARBOOK | 2005 | First Edition | A directory for children's
writers and artists | containing children's media contacts and | practical advice and information |
A & C Black [point] London (All width centred)

'© 2004 A & C Black Publishers Ltd | 37 Soho Square, London W1F 0BJ […] | ISBN 0-7136-6903-9 | Printed in Great Britain by | William Clowes Ltd, Beccles, Suffolk' on imprint page

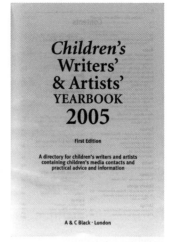

210 by 148mm; [i-iii] iv-v [vi] vii [viii] [1] 2-110 [111] 112-20 [121] 122-39 [140-41] 142-76 [177] 178-98 [199] 200-216 [217] 218-38 [239] 240-42 [243] 244-54 [255] 256-88 [289] 290-328; wove paper; printed wrappers; published 16 August 2004 (Nielsen BookData); £12.99

Includes
'A word from J.K. Rowling'
    ('I can remember writing *Harry Potter and the Philosopher's Stone* in a café in Oporto…')
    (headed, 'J.K. Rowling')

See also B3(a) for the original and longer version of this contribution, originally published within *Writers' and Artists' Yearbook*. This shortened text, as printed here, was first published within B3(b).

Copies: BL (ZC.9.a.7163) stamped 10 Aug 2004; private collection (PWE)

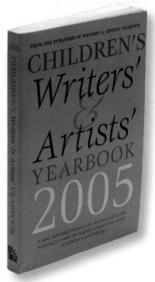

B8(b) *English edition for 2006 (2005)*

Rowling contribution as for B8(a)

B8(c) *English edition for 2007 (2006)*

Rowling contribution as for B8(a)

B8(d) *English edition for 2008 (2007)*

Rowling contribution as for B8(a)

B8(e) *English edition for 2009 (2008)*

Rowling contribution as for B8(a)

B8(f) *English edition for 2010 (2009)*

Rowling contribution as for B8(a)

B8(g) English edition for 2011 (2010)

Rowling contribution as for B8(a)

B8(h) English edition for 2012 (2011)

Rowling contribution as for B8(a)

B8(i) English edition for 2013 (2012)

Rowling contribution as for B8(a)

B8(j) English edition for 2014 (2013)

Rowling contribution as for B8(a)

B9   [ONE CITY TRUST], ONE CITY   (2005)

B9(a) First English edition (2005)

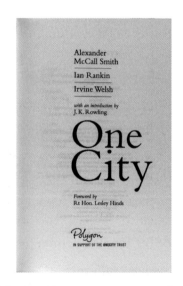

Alexander | McCall Smith | [rule, 29mm] | Ian Rankin | [rule, 29mm] | Irvine Welsh | [rule, 29mm] | *with an introduction by* | J. K. Rowling | One | City | *Foreword by* | Rt Hon. Lesley Hinds | Polygon | IN SUPPORT OF THE ONECITY TRUST (All aligned on left margin)

'First published in | Great Britain in 2005 by | Polygon, an imprint of Birlinn Ltd | West Newington House | 10 Newington Road | Edinburgh | EH9 1QS | [new paragraph] | 9 8 7 6 5 4 3 2 1 | [new paragraph] www.birlinn.co.uk | [new paragraph] Introduction © J. K. Rowling, 2005 […] | [new paragraph] ISBN 10: 1 904598 74 9 | ISBN 13: 978 1 904598 74 9 […] | [new paragraph] Designed by James Hutcheson | in 11/14pt Adobe Bembo | Typeset by Palimpsest Book Production Limited, | Polmont, Stirlingshire | [new paragraph] Printed and bound by | Clays Ltd, St Ives plc, Bungay, Suffolk' on imprint page

197 by 128mm; [1-6] 7-9 [10-12] 13-45 [46-48] 49-79 [80-82] 83-109 [110-112]; wove paper; pictorial wrappers; published 2 January 2006 (Nielsen BookData); £5.99

Includes:

'Introduction'
('When I arrived in Edinburgh in December 1993, the city was snow-covered…')
(signed, 'J. K. Rowling')

All proceeds from the sale of the book were to benefit the OneCity Trust. This charity was created as a result of a report commissioned by Edinburgh's Lord Provost in 1998 to discover the extent of social exclusion in the city. The charity helps communities throughout Edinburgh by supporting educational and social welfare projects.

The legal deposit copy in the British Library (H.2007/956) is a second impression (with the strike-line '9 8 7 6 5 4 3 2' on the imprint page) and is stamped 12 Dec 2006

Copies: private collection (PWE)

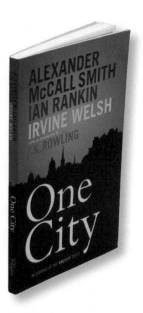

B10   GORDON BROWN (ED. WILF STEVENSON), *GORDON BROWN SPEECHES 1997-2006*   (2006)

B10(a) First English edition (2006)

GORDON BROWN | SPEECHES 1997-2006 | with introductory comments by | Kofi Annan, Helen Clark, Linda Colley, Lord Ralf Dahrendorf, | Al Gore, Alan Greenspan, Wangaari Maathai, Nelson Mandela, | Trevor Phillips, J.K. Rowling, Sir Jonathan Sacks, | Sir Derek Wanless and Sir Magdi Yacoub | *edited by* | WILF STEVENSON | BLOOMSBURY (All width centred)

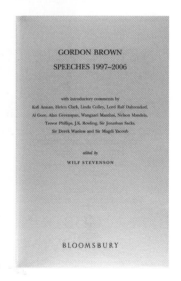

'First published in Great Britain 2006 | [new paragraph] Speeches of Gordon Brown Crown copyright © 2006 | [new paragraph] Selection, introduction and commentary copyright © Wilf Stevenson, 2006 | [new paragraph] Copyright in the introductory comments to each chapter and listed | in the contents page remains with the individual contributors. | [new paragraph] All royalties are being donated to the Jennifer Brown Research Laboratory within | the University of Edinburgh's Research Institute for Medical Cell Biology […] | [new paragraph] ISBN 0747588376 | ISBN-13 9780747588375 | [new paragraph] 10 9 8 7 6 5 4 3 2 1 | [new paragraph] Typeset by Hewer Text UK Ltd, Edinburgh | Printed in Great Britain by Clays Ltd, St Ives plc […]' on imprint page

233 by 150mm; [i-xi] xii [1] 2-4 [5] 6-64 [65] 66-151 [152] 153-83 [184] 185-249 [250] 251-96 [297] 298-335 [336] 337-84 [385] 386-413 [414] 415-36 [437] 438-42 [443] 444 [445] 446-48 [449] 450-62 [463-68]; wove paper; black boards lettered in gilt; dust-jacket; published 25 September 2006 (Nielsen BookData); £30.00

Includes:

> [Introductory Essay to 'Ending Child Poverty']
> ('I met Gordon Brown for the first time in 2000, at a reception for the National…')
> (signed, 'J.K. Rowling')

Publication occurred on the first day of the 2006 Labour party conference. Both this hardback edition and the (differently titled) paperback edition (see B11(a)) were published on the same date. Neither, therefore, has bibliographical priority.

Copies: private collection (PWE)

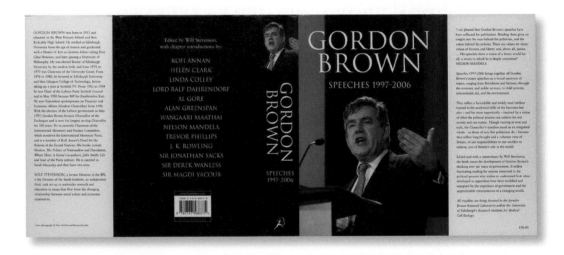

B11 GORDON BROWN (ED. WILF STEVENSON), *MOVING BRITAIN FORWARD: SELECTED SPEECHES 1997-2006* (2006)

B11(a) First English edition (2006)

Gordon Brown | MOVING BRITAIN FORWARD | SELECTED SPEECHES 1997-2006 | with introductory comments by | Kofi Annan, Helen Clark, Linda Colley, | Lord Ralf Dahrendorf, Alan

Greenspan, Al Gore, | Nelson Mandela, Wangaari Maathai, Trevor Phillips, | J.K. Rowling, Sir Jonathan Sacks, Sir Derek Wanless | and Sir Magdi Yacoub | *edited by* | WILF STEVENSON | BLOOMSBURY (All width centred)

'First published in Great Britain 2006 | [new paragraph] Speeches of Gordon Brown Crown copyright © 2006 | [new paragraph] Selection, introduction and commentary copyright © Wilf Stevenson, 2006 | [new paragraph] Copyright in the introductory comments to each chapter and listed | in the contents page remains with the individual contributors. | [new paragraph] All royalties are being donated to the Jennifer Brown Research Laboratory within | the University of Edinburgh's Research Institute for Medical Cell Biology [...] | [new paragraph] ISBN 0747588384 | ISBN-13 9780747588382 | [new paragraph] 10 9 8 7 6 5 4 3 2 1 | [new paragraph] Typeset by Hewer Text UK Ltd, Edinburgh | Printed in Great Britain by Clays Ltd, St Ives plc [...]' on imprint page

215 by 134mm; [i-vii] viii [ix-xi] xii-xiii [xiv] [1] 2-26 [27] 28-45 [46] 47-65 [66] 67-83 [84] 85-135 [136] 137-80 [181] 182-206 [207] 208-222 [223] 224-45 [246] 247-64 [265] 266-68 [269] 270-272 [273]; wove paper; printed wrappers; published 25 September 2006 (Nielsen BookData); £9.99

Includes:
>[Introductory Essay to 'Ending Child Poverty']
>('I met Gordon Brown for the first time in 2000, at a reception for the National...')
>(signed, 'J.K. Rowling')

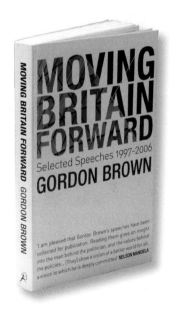

Publication occurred on the first day of the 2006 Labour party conference. Both this paperback edition and the (differently titled) hardback edition (see B10(a)) were published on the same date.

In addition to acquiring a new title, the text appears in a different setting from B10. The order of the speeches is different in the two books. The Appendix and Index included in the hardback edition are omitted here.

Copies: private collection (PWE)

B12(a) First American edition (2006)

Becoming [in grey] | Myself | REFLECTIONS ON | GROWING UP FEMALE | [rule, 60mm] | EDITED BY Willa Shalit | [rule, 60mm] | [publisher's device featuring flower and foliage within ruled border, 5 by 3mm and 'HYPERION' within ruled border, 3 by 21mm] | New York (All width centred)

'Copyright © 2006 Willa Shalit | [...] All rights reserved. No part of this book may be used or reproduced in | any manner whatsoever without the written permission of the Publisher. | Printed in the United States of America. For information address | Hyperion, 77 West 66th Street, New York, New York 10023-6298. | [new paragraph] Library of Congress Cataloging-in-Publication Data | Becoming myself : reflections on growing up female / edited by Willa | Shalit.—1st ed. | p. cm | ISBN 1-4013-0139-8 | 1. Women—Biography. 2. Women in public life—Biography. 3. | Celebrities—Biography. 4. Women authors—Biography. I. Shalit, | Willa. | HQ1123.B43 2006 | 920.720973—dc22 2005045639 | [...] FIRST EDITION | [new paragraph] 1 3 5 7 9 10 8 6 4 2' on imprint page

210 by 137mm; [i-ix] x [xi] xii-xiv [xv-xvi] [1] 2-5 [6-7] 8-12 [13] 14-15 [16-17] 18-21 [22-23] 24-27 [28-29] 30-33 [34-35] 36-38 [39] 40-43 [44-45] 46-49 [50-51] 52-56 [57] 58-61 [62-63] 64-65 [66-67] 68 [69] 70-71 [72-73] 74-76 [77] 78-80 [81] 82 [83] 84-87 [88-89] 90-93 [94-95] 96-97 [98-99] 100 [101] 102-108 [109] 110-14 [115] 116-18 [119] 120-22 [123] 124-26 [127] 128-33 [134-35] 136-39 [140-41] 142-43 [144-45] 146-49 [150-51] 152-53 [154-55] 156-58 [159] 160-64 [165] 166-75 [176-77] 178 [179] 180-83 [184-85] 186-88 [189] 190-94 [195] 196-99 [200-201] 202 [203] 204-207 [208-209] 210 [211] 212-16 [217] 218-20 [221] 222-24 [225] 226-29 [230-31] 232-33 [234-35] 236-40 [241] 242-45 [246-47] 248-52 [253-55] 256-64 [265] 266-69 [270-71] 272-73 [274-75] 276-78 [279] 280-84 [285] 286 [287] 288; wove paper; black cloth-backed spine lettered in silver with white boards; dust-jacket; published 18 April 2006; $22.95

Includes

    [Untitled]

    ('When I was young, I had two teachers whom I found very inspiring...')

    (signed, 'JKRowling' [facsimile])

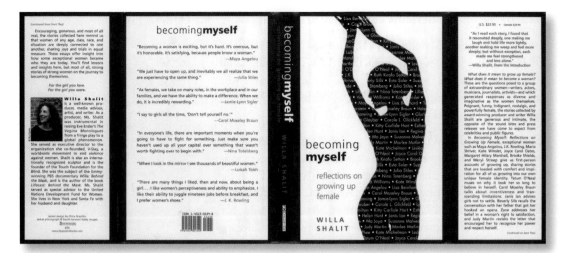

As noted by the dust-jacket, the volume poses the questions 'What does it mean to grow up female?' and 'What does it mean to become a woman?' In the book, 'exceptional women… give us first-person accounts of growing up, sharing stories that are loaded with comfort and inspiration for all of us growing into our unique female identity.'

The volume contains 56 contributions (excluding those of the editor). Each entry concludes with a facsimile of the contributor's signature.

Forty percent of the royalties from the book were given to Equality Now, The Family Violence Prevention Fund, Intersect-Worldwide and V-Day.

Although Nielsen BookData gives a publication date of 2 November 2006, this is incorrect. The same database notes a 'dumpbin – filled' for the title released on 18 April 2006. Moreover, the title is reviewed in *Publisher's Weekly* on 6 February 2006 citing a publication date of 18 April 2006. The title was also reviewed in *Library Journal* on 1 May 2006.

Hyperion Books released a 'dumpbin' display case for this edition at the beginning of April 2006 (Nielsen BookData provides a date of 18 April 2006). The case, presumably filled with nine copies of the book, retailed at $206.55.

It appears that there was no English edition but that copies of the American edition were imported. This would explain the lack of copies in the U.K.'s legal deposit libraries. Imported copies were available in the U.K. from 2 November 2006. Writing in April 2014 a senior customer service representative from Hachette Book Group (which acquired Hyperion in 2013) noted 'we do not have information regarding U.K. publication or import of this title readily available.'

Copies: private collection (PWE)

B12(b) Second American edition (2007)

Becoming [in grey] | Myself | REFLECTIONS ON | GROWING
UP FEMALE | [rule, 60mm] | EDITED BY Willa Shalit | [rule,
60mm] | [publisher's device featuring flower and foliage within
ruled border, 5 by 3mm and 'HYPERION' within ruled border, 3
by 21mm] | New York (All width centred)

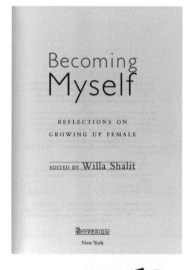

'Copyright © 2006 Willa Shalit | [...] All rights reserved. No
part of this book may be used or reproduced in | any manner
whatsoever without the written permission of the Publisher.
| Printed in the United States of America. For information
address | Hyperion, 77 West 66th Street, New York, New York
10023-6298. | [new paragraph] Library of Congress Cataloging-
in-Publication Data | Becoming myself : reflections on growing
up female / edited by Willa | Shalit.—1st ed. | p. cm | ISBN
1-4013-0139-8 | 1. Women—Biography. 2. Women in public
life—Biography. 3. | Celebrities—Biography. 4. Women authors—
Biography. I. Shalit, | Willa. | HQ1123.B43 2006 | 920.720973—dc22
2005045639 | [...] FIRST EDITION | [new paragraph] 1 3 5 7 9 10 8
6 4 2' on imprint page

202 by 133mm; [i-ix] x [xi] xii-xiv [xv-xvi] [1] 2-5 [6-7] 8-12 [13] 14-15
[16-17] 18-21 [22-23] 24-27 [28-29] 30-33 [34-35] 36-38 [39] 40-43
[44-45] 46-49 [50-51] 52-56 [57] 58-61 [62-63] 64-65 [66-67] 68 [69]
70-71 [72-73] 74-76 [77] 78-80 [81] 82 [83] 84-87 [88-89] 90-93 [94-95]
96-97 [98-99] 100 [101] 102-108 [109] 110-14 [115] 116-18 [119] 120-22
[123] 124-26 [127] 128-33 [134-35] 136-39 [140-41] 142-43 [144-45]
146-49 [150-51] 152-53 [154-55] 156-58 [159] 160-64 [165] 166-75
[176-77] 178 [179] 180-83 [184-85] 186-88 [189] 190-94 [195] 196-99
[200-201] 202 [203] 204-207 [208-209] 210 [211] 212-16 [217] 218-20
[221] 222-24 [225] 226-29 [230-31] 232-33 [234-35] 236-40 [241] 242-45
[246-47] 248-52 [253-55] 256-64 [265] 266-69 [270-71] 272-73 [274-75] 276-78 [279] 280-84 [285]
286 [287] 288; wove paper; pictorial wrappers; published 17 April 2007 (confirmed by Hyperion);
$12.95

Includes
    [Untitled]
    ('When I was young, I had two teachers whom I found very inspiring...')
    (signed, 'JKRowling' [facsimile])

The paperback version of B12(a) includes a front free and rear free endpaper on a higher quality wove
paper than that used for the rest of the book. These endpapers are excluded from the pagination.

As with B12(a), it appears that there was no English edition but that copies of the American edition were imported. Imported copies were available in the UK from 21 June 2007.

Copies: private collection (PWE)

Reprints include:
FIRST EDITION | 3 5 7 9 10 8 6 4 2

B13 *OVER 70 TRIED AND TESTED GREAT BOOKS TO READ ALOUD* (2006)

B13(a) First English edition (2006)

OVER 70 TRIED AND TESTED | GREAT | BOOKS | TO | READ | ALOUD (All width centred in white on red panel, 188 by 148mm, with pink panel, 19 by 148mm, above at head and pink panel, 13 by 148mm, below at foot)

'Published in Great Britain by Corgi Books, | an imprint of Random House Children's Books | This edition published 2006 | 1 3 5 7 9 10 8 6 4 2 | [...] Printed and bound in Denmark by Nørhaven Paperback AS' on imprint page

220 by 148mm; [1-3] 4-19 [20-21] 22-28 [29] 30-35 [36] 37-127 [128]; wove paper; pictorial wrappers; published May 2006; £1

Includes
   [Untitled contribution]
   ('One of my fondest memories of my eldest daughter at age five involved *The Voyage of the*…')

As noted by the blurb on the lower wrapper, this volume is a 'guide to all the best books to read aloud to your child…' and features 'reading tips from experts and sample extracts from brilliantly entertaining stories for all age groups'.

An introduction by Jacqueline Wilson is included together with recommendations from 'celebrity parents' including Cherie Booth, Michael Palin, Philip Pullman and Terry Wogan.

J.K. Rowling's recommendations comprise C.S. Lewis' *The Voyage of the Dawn Treader*, Dr Seuss' *Green Eggs and Ham*, the works of Sandra Boynton, the Hairy Maclary and Slinky Malinki series by

Lynley Dodd and, finally, Julia Donaldson and Axel Scheffler's *The Snail and the Whale* and *The Gruffalo*.

Although the publication date of this volume is mysterious (the title is not recorded by Nielsen BookData and no copies are, apparently, deposited in the UK copyright libraries), a number of online reviews suggest publication around May 2006.

Copies: private collection (PWE)

B14   LINDSAY FRASER AND KATHRYN ROSS, READING ROUND EDINBURGH   (2007)

B14(a) First English edition (2007)

Reading Round Edinburgh | A Guide to Children's Books of the City | Edited by Lindsay Fraser and Kathryn Ross | [coloured vignette of two children reading books, 35 by 30mm] | Floris Books (All width centred)

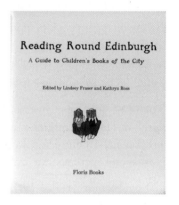

'Illustrations by Adrian B. McMurchie | [new paragraph] First published in 2007 by Floris Books | © Lindsay Fraser and Kathryn Ross | Introduction © J.K. Rowling | Copyright in the texts quoted herein remains | the property of the individual authors who are | listed under the acknowledgments. | [new paragraph] All rights reserved. No part of this book may be | reproduced without the prior permission of | Floris Books, 15 Harrison Gardens, Edinburgh | www.florisbooks.co.uk | [new paragraph] The publisher acknowledges a grant from the | Scottish Arts Council towards this publication. | [...] [new paragraph] ISBN 978-086315-593-2 | [new paragraph] Produced by Polskabook, Poland' on imprint page

190 by 172mm; [1-6] 7-10 [11] 12-13 [14-15] 16-23 [24-25] 26-32 [33-34] 35-39 [40] 41 [42-43] 44-56 [57] 58-61 [62] 63 [64] 65-76 [77] 78-80; glossy wove paper; pictorial wrappers; published 26 April 2007 (Nielsen BookData); £5.99

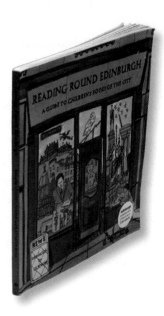

Includes
   'Introduction by J.K. Rowling'
   ('All writers dread the question "where do you get your ideas from?"')
   (signed, '© J.K. Rowling, 2007')

The blurb on the lower wrapper describes this volume as a guide to 'help children and adults to discover Edinburgh through its children's books'.

Copies: BL (YK.2008.a.15520) stamped 3 Aug 2007; private collection (PWE)

B15 SOTHEBY'S CATALOGUE: *THE TALES OF BEEDLE THE BARD* (2007)

B15(a) First English edition (2007)

The Tales of [facsimile] | Beedle the Bard [facsimile] | A COLLECTION OF WIZARDING FAIRY-TALES | BY J.K. ROWLING | The Property of J.K. Rowling, sold on behalf of The Children's Voice | London, Thursday 13 December 2007 | AUCTION EXHIBITION | [two columns with auction information on eight lines in two paragraphs and exhibition information on 11 lines in five paragraphs] | IMPORTANT NOTICES | [single column with important notices on seven lines in three paragraphs] (Lines 1-2 width centred, lines 3-6 justified on left margin, column of auction information and important notices justified on left margin and column of exhibition information justified on a left margin in centre of page)

No publisher's imprint page

180 by 125mm; [1-48]; wove paper; pictorial wrappers; published 16 November 2007 in an edition of 15,927 copies; £6

Includes
  [Statement on *The Tales of Beedle the Bard*]
  ('When I conceived the idea of writing *The Tales of Beedle the Bard* in full…')
  (signed, 'JKRowling' [facsimile])

A souvenir auction catalogue to present the seventh handwritten copy of *The Tales of Beedle the Bard* offered at Sotheby's on 13 December 2007 (see D5).

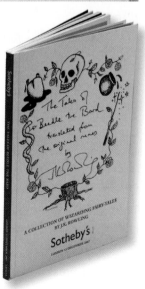

The text was also printed in Sotheby's main auction catalogue (see B16). The souvenir catalogue included a greater number of illustrations and was designed by Jonathan Wills.

The majority of catalogues were sold to purchasers in the United States via the Sotheby's website.

Copies: private collection (PWE)

B16   SOTHEBY'S CATALOGUE: ENGLISH LITERATURE... 13 DECEMBER 2007   (2007)

B16(a) First English edition (2006)

ENGLISH LITERATURE, HISTORY, | PRIVATE PRESS, CHILDREN'S BOOKS | AND ILLUSTRATIONS | LONDON THURSDAY 13 DECEMBER 2007 | AT 10 AM | AUCTION EXHIBITION | [two columns with auction information on three lines in two paragraphs and exhibition information on eight lines in four paragraphs] | Please note that this sale will start at 10 am | in the Main Gallery | IMPORTANT NOTICE | [five lines in two paragraphs] (Justified on left margin with the exception of the two columns of auction and exhibition information which are justified on two separate left margins in centre of page and also off-set to the right, respectively)

No publisher's imprint page

270 by 210mm; [1-9] 10-241 [242-43] 244-58 [259-61] 262-63 [264]; wove paper; pictorial wrappers; published 16 November 2007 in an edition of 2962 copies; £26

Includes
> [Statement on *The Tales of Beedle the Bard*]
> ('When I conceived the idea of writing *The Tales of Beedle the Bard* in full...')
> (signed, 'J.K. Rowling')

This publication was the Sotheby's catalogue for their 'English Literature, History, Private Press, Children's Books and Illustrations' auction on 13 December. The final lot in the sale, lot 311A, was the seventh copy of *The Tales of Beedle the Bard* handwritten by the author. See B15 for the souvenir catalogue devoted to the lot and also D5.

The catalogue notes photography by Wayne Williams. The photographer responsible for images relating to the copy of *The Tales of Beedle the Bard* was Rolant Dafis.

Copies: private collection (PWE)

B17 MICHAEL MORPURGO AND QUENTIN BLAKE, THE BIRTHDAY BOOK (2008)

B17(a) First English edition (2008)

The [hand-drawn lettering] | Birthday Book [hand-drawn lettering] | *In aid of* | The Prince's Foundation for Children & the Arts | *With a foreword by* | HRH The Prince of Wales | [illustration of a birthday present in wrapping paper with a bow, in black, brown, yellow, pink and green] | *Edited by* | Michael Morpurgo & Quentin Blake | JONATHAN CAPE [point] LONDON (All width centred)

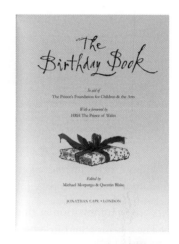

'Published in Great Britain by Jonathan Cape, | an imprint of Random House Children's Books | A Random House Group Company | This edition published 2008 | 1 3 5 7 9 10 8 6 4 2 | This edition copyright © The Prince's Foundation for Children & the Arts, 2008 | [...] Printed and bound in Italy' on imprint page

255 by 192mm, [i-x] 1-4 [5] 6-7 [8] 9 [10-12] 13-17 [18-19] 20-23 [24] 25 [26] 27-31 [32-33] 34-35 [36] 37-38 [39] 40-41 [42] 43-44 [45] 46 [47] 48-53 [54-55] 56-63 [64] 65-68 [69] 70 [71] 72-83 [84] 85-94 [95] 96-98 [99] 100 [101] 102-105 [106] 107-116 [117] 118 [119] 120-21 [122] 123 [124] 125 [126] 127-30 [131-32] 133-35 [136-37] 138-41 [142] 143-49 [150] 151 [152-53] 154-55 [156] 157 [158] 159-60 [161] 162-68 [169] 170 [171] 172 [173] 174-75 [176] 177 [178] 179-90 [191] 192 [193] 194-95 [196] 197 [198] 199 [200] 201 [202] 203 [204] 205 [206] 207-213 [214] 215-19 [220] 221 [222] 223-28 [229] 230-38 [239-40] 241-43 [244] 245 [246] 247 [248-49] 250 [251] 252-55 [256] 257-71 [272] 273-79 [280] 281 [282] 283-85 [286] 287 [288-89] 290 [291] 292-301 [302] 303-306 [307] 308 [309] 310-15 [316-17] 318 [319] 320-21 [322] 323-25 [326]; wove paper; blue boards lettered in gilt; dust-jacket; published 6 November 2008 (Nielsen BookData); £16.99

Includes

[Introduction to an excerpt from *Harry Potter and the Deathly Hallows*]
('I admit that, at first glance, the following might not seem particularly celebratory...')
(signed, 'J.K. Rowling')

'The Forest Again' [excerpt from *Harry Potter and the Deathly Hallows*]
('Finally, the truth. Lying with his face pressed into the dusty carpet...')
(headed, 'Written by J.K. Rowling')

There are two illustrations by Quentin Blake that accompany the Rowling text. A full-page illustration of Harry is on page [302] and a half-page illustration of Voldemort is on page 305.

Copyright information at the end of the volume notes that the excerpt was 'reprinted by permission of The Christopher Little Literary Agency on behalf of the author and by Bloomsbury Publishing plc'. The illustrations were copyrighted to the author.

The collection was published in aid of The Prince's Foundation for Children and the Arts and to celebrate the sixtieth birthday of the Prince of Wales.

Copies: BL (YK.2009.b.9154) stamped 29 Oct 2008; private collection (PWE)

B17(aa) First English deluxe edition (2008)

A deluxe edition of this title was published with a limitation of 500 copies. Copies were signed by both editors Michael Morpurgo and Quentin Blake. No copies have been consulted.

B18   [WATERSTONE'S], WHAT'S YOUR STORY?   (2008)

B18(a) First English edition (2008)

Upper wrapper:

What's your story? | The postcard | collection | Exclusive very short stories | from authors, booksellers | and customers. | ['Dyslexia Action' logo with 'Assessment [point] Education [point] Training'] ['English pen' logo] All profits to charity. (Justified on left margin with illustration of a person reading a book to the right of lines 2-7. The illustration is constructed of words, 'Romance,

Thrills, Adventure, Laugh, Anger' etc. and is printed in red, purple, orange and yellow)

No publisher's imprint page

133 by 198mm; [1-48]; wove cardboard; pictorial wrappers; published 7 August 2008; £5

Includes
　　[Untitled short story]
　　('The speeding motorcycles took the sharp corner so fast in the darkness...')
　　(signed, 'From the prequel I am *not* working on – but that was fun! JK Rowling 2008')

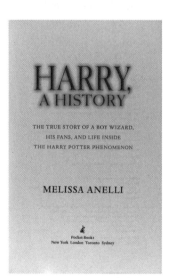

The volume contains 24 postcards with content on the recto. The verso contains authorship and copyright details. There is a perforated line towards the gutter of the book.

The Rowling contribution is the first in the collection and appears over two postcards.

Thirteen original postcards were offered at a charity auction held at Waterstone's Piccadilly store on 10 June 2008. Sale proceeds went to EnglishPEN and Dyslexia Action. See also D6.

Copies: private collection (SHo); private collection (PWE)

B19　　MELISSA ANELLI, *HARRY, A HISTORY*　　(2008)

B19(a) First American edition (2008)

HARRY, | A HISTORY | THE TRUE STORY OF A BOY WIZARD, | HIS FANS, AND LIFE INSIDE | THE HARRY POTTER PHENOMENON | MELISSA ANELLI | [publisher's logo, 6 by 4mm] | Pocket Books | New York London Toronto Sydney (All width centred)

'Pocket Books | A Division of Simon & Schuster, Inc. | 1230 Avenue of the Americas | New York, NY 10020 | [new paragraph] Copyright © 2008 by Melissa Anelli [...] | [new paragraph] First Pocket Books trade paperback edition November 2008 [...] | [new paragraph] Designed by Elliott Beard | [new paragraph] Manufactured in the United States of America | [new paragraph] 10 9 8 7 6 5 4 3 2 1 [...] | [new paragraph] ISBN-13: 978-1-4165-5495-0 | ISBN-10: 1-4165-5495-5' on imprint page

209 by 134mm; [i-vi] vii-xii 1-39 [40] 41-180 [6 illustration pages] 181-201 [202] 203-247 [248] 249-77 [278] 279-309 [310] 311-56; wove paper; pictorial wrappers; published 4 November 2008; $16

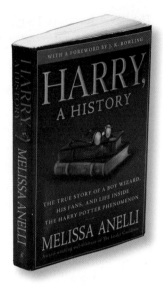

Includes

'Foreword'

('Over and over again they asked me the same question, with tiny variations…')

(headed, 'J.K. Rowling')

The blurb describes this work as 'a personal journey through every aspect of the Harry Potter phenomenon'. The author is the webmistress of the Leaky Cauldron, 'one of the most popular Harry Potter sites on the Internet'.

Melissa Anelli kindly confirmed the publication dates of this and the English edition. The American edition has bibliographical priority.

Copies: private collection (PWE)

B19(b) First English edition (2008)

HARRY, | A HISTORY | THE TRUE STORY OF A BOY WIZARD, | HIS FANS, AND LIFE INSIDE | THE HARRY POTTER PHENOMENON | MELISSA ANELLI | [publisher's logo, 12 by 9mm] | POCKET | BOOKS | LONDON [point] SYDNEY [point] NEW YORK [point] TORONTO (All width centred)

'First published in the USA by Pocket Books, an imprint of | Simon & Schuster, Inc, 2008 | First published in Great Britain by Pocket Books, an imprint of | Simon & Schuster UK Ltd, 2008 | A CBS COMPANY | [new paragraph] Copyright © Melissa Anelli 2008 […] | [new paragraph] Designed by Elliott Beard | [new paragraph] 1 3 5 7 9 10 8 6 4 2 […] | [new paragraph] ISBN: 978-1-84739-458-3 | [new paragraph] Printed by CPI Cox & Wyman, Reading, Berkshire RG1 8EX' on imprint page

198 by 128mm; [i-vi] vii-xii 1-39 [40] 41-180 [8 illustration pages] 181-201 [202] 203-247 [248] 249-77 [278] 279-309 [310] 311-56; wove paper; pictorial wrappers; published 19 November 2008 (Nielsen BookData); £8.99

Includes

'Foreword'

('Over and over again they asked me the same question, with tiny variations…')

(headed, 'J.K. Rowling')

Copies: BL (YK.2010.a.6860) stamped 21 Nov 2008

JOSEPH GALLIANO, *DEAR ME: MORE LETTERS TO MY SIXTEEN-YEAR-OLD SELF* (2011)

B20(a) First English edition (2011)

Dear Me | More Letters to My Sixteen-Year-Old Self | *Edited by* | JOSEPH GALLIANO (All width centred with lines 1 and 4 in dark blue, all within border, 157 by 105mm with a gradual fading effect beyond border)

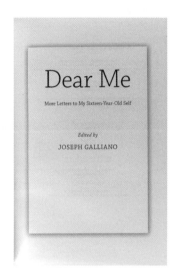

'First published in Great Britain by Simon & Schuster UK Ltd, 2011 | A CBS COMPANY | [new paragraph] Selection copyright © 2011 Joseph Galliano | Foreword copyright © 2011 J. K. Rowling | Copyright of photographs and letters has been retained by the individual contributors, | unless otherwise indicated [...] | [new paragraph] 1 3 5 7 9 10 8 6 4 2 [...] | [new paragraph] ISBN: 978-0-85720-715-9 | [new paragraph] Designed by Kyoko Watanabe | Printed and bound by CPI Group (UK) Ltd, Croydon, CR0 4YY' on imprint page

211 by 138mm; [i-vi] vii-xx [xxi-xxii] [1-128] 129-31 [132] 133-34 [135-38]; wove paper; blue boards lettered in silver; dust-jacket; published 27 October 2011 (Nielsen BookData); £12.99

Includes
  'Foreword'
  ('This is an extraordinary little book, based on a simple but wonderful idea…')
  (signed, 'J. K. Rowling')

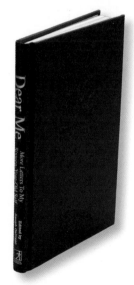

  [Facsimile Letter]
  ('Dear Jo (16), | I'm forty five. We're forty five! And, believe me…')
  (signed, 'Jo' [facsimile signature])

The original *Dear Me*, also edited by Joseph Galliano, was published by Simon and Schuster in 2009. Rowling did not participate. Proceeds from the sale of the earlier title were donated to the Elton John AIDS Foundation.

The dust-jacket notes that 'a portion of the proceeds received by the author from sales of the book will be donated to Doctors Without Borders'.

Copies: BL (YK.2012.a.20107) stamped 28 Nov 2011; private collection (PWE)

C. CONTRIBUTIONS TO NEWSPAPERS AND PERIODICALS BY J.K. ROWLING

C01

'What was the Name of that Nymph Again?', *Pegasus – Journal of the University of Exeter Department of Classics and Ancient History* (University of Exeter, 1998), Issue 41, pp. 25-27

('There is nothing like a pithy quotation to get the ball rolling, so, in the noble…')

(headed, 'by Joanne Rowling')

C02

'J.K. Rowling's Diary', *Sunday Times*, 26 July 1998, 'Ecosse' section [Scottish version of 'News Review' section], p. 3

('Cafe society: At least once a week I go into Nicholsons, the cafe in Edinburgh…')

(headed, 'J.K. Rowling's Diary')

C03

'Let me tell you a story', *Sunday Times*, 21 May 2000, 'News Review' section, p. 8

('I was a squat, bespectacled child who lived mainly in books and daydreams…')

(headed, 'J.K. Rowling reveals…')

C04

'From Mr Darcy to Harry Potter… by way of Lolita', *The Sunday Herald*, 21 May 2000, 'sevendays' supplement, p. 4

('I was a squat, bespectacled child who lived mainly in books and daydreams…')

(headed 'JK Rowling looks back')

C05

'Harry Potter and the Goblet of Fire – Chapter One: The Riddle House', *Newsweek*, volume 136, part 3, 17 July 2000, pp. 57-63

('The villagers of Little Hangleton still called it 'the Riddle House,' even though…')

(headed, 'J.K. Rowling')

C06

'Did they all think I was a scrounger or layabout?', *Sun*, 'SunWoman' section, 4 October 2000, pp. 1 and 4-5

('The words 'penniless single mother' crop up a lot in newspaper stories about…')

(headed, 'J.K. Rowling')

C07

'A Good Scare', *Time*, volume 156, number 19, 6 November 2000, p. 80
('I consciously wanted the first book to be fairly gentle – Harry is very protected...')
(headed, 'A Conversation with J.K. Rowling')

C08

[Reply to the Oration presenting J.K. Rowling for an Honorary Degree], *Pegasus – Journal of the University of Exeter Department of Classics and Ancient History* (University of Exeter, 2001), Issue 44, pp. 19-20
('This is the third honorary degree I've received, and I was feeling quite pleased...')
(headed, 'Joanne Rowling replied...')

C09

'I Miss My Mother Almost Daily', *Scotland on Sunday*, 22 April 2001
('My parents were both 18 when they met on a train going from King's Cross...')
(headed 'By Joanne Rowling')

C10

'I miss my mother so much', *The Observer*, 29 April 2001, 'Review' section, pp. 1-2
('My parents were both 18 when they met on a train going from King's Cross...')
(headed, 'J.K. Rowling's mother died of multiple sclerosis at 45...')

C11

'Once upon a time, when I had no money', *Sunday Times*, 21 October 2001, 'News Review' section, p. 6
('In 1994, when I was 29, I set out to obtain a Postgraduate Certificate...')
(headed, 'J.K. Rowling')

C12

'Multiple Sclerosis Killed My Mother. The NHS Left her to Muddle on Alone...', *Sunday Herald*, 16 November 2003, 'sevendays' supplement, pp. 1-2
('I never liked New Year's Eve in the first place. My friends and I usually...')
(headed, 'By J K Rowling')

C13

'My Fight', *Sunday Times*, 5 February 2006, 'News Review' section, pp. 1-2
('My eldest daughter keeps a pair of rats and I'm quite happy to let them sit...')
(headed, 'By JK Rowling')

C14

'My fight for cage kids', *The Sun*, 9 February 2006, pp. 26-27
    ('My eldest daughter keeps a pair of rats and I'm quite happy to let them sit…')
    (headed, 'JK Rowling appeals…')

C15

'I was so moved by the baby's unexpected smile', *The Sun*, 10 February 2006, pp. 32-33
    ('In Bucharest I met up with Emma Nicholson and the other founding members…')
    (headed, 'By J.K. Rowling')

C16

'Goal Getters', *Personal Excellence*, March 2006, volume 11, issue 3, p. 15
    ('Young ladies 200 years ago weren't allowed to read novels because it would…')
    (signed, 'J.K. Rowling')

C17

'I can't thank you enough… but we need more help to free cage kids', *The Irish Sun*, 26 June 2006, p.22
    ('When I wrote in The Irish Sun about the plight of the children trapped in…')
    (headed, 'JK Rowling writes…')

C18

'The first It Girl: J.K. Rowling reviews Decca: the Letters of Jessica Mitford ed by Peter Y Sussman', *Sunday Telegraph*, 5 November 2006, p. 46
    ('Jessica Mitford has been my heroine since I was 14 years old, when I overheard…')
    (headed, 'J.K. Rowling')

C19

'A Stripping Away of the Inessential', *Harvard Magazine*, July – August 2008, pp. 55-56
    ('On this wonderful day when we are gathered together to celebrate your…')
    (headed, 'from an address by J.K. Rowling')

C20

'Fringe Benefits of Failure and the importance of imagination', *Personal Excellence*, August 2008, volume 13, issue 8, pp. 1-2
    ('I wish to examine the benefit of failure and extol the crucial importance of…')
    (headed, 'by JK Rowling')

C21

'Gordon Brown' [within '100 Leaders & Revolutionaries...'], *Time*, volume 173, issue 19, 11 May 2009, p. 22
  ('Back in the mid-1990s, when he was new labour's brooding, intellectual...')
  (headed, 'by J.K. Rowling')

C22

'The single mother's manifesto', *The Times*, 14 April 2010, p. 20
  ('"I've never voted Tory before, but..." Those much parodied posters, with their...')
  (headed, 'J.K. Rowling')

C23

'By the Book', *New York Times*, 14 October 2012, 'Sunday Book Review' section, p. 8
  ('I loved *The Song of Achilles*, by Medeline Miller...')
  (headed, 'J.K. Rowling')

C24

'I feel duped and angry at David Cameron's reaction to Leveson', *The Guardian*, 30 November 2012 [online version]
  ('I am alarmed and dismayed that the prime minister appears to be backing away...')
  (headed, 'J.K. Rowling')
[This piece appeared only as an online article (at www.theguardian.com/commentisfree/2012/nov/30/jk-rowling-duped-angry-david-cameron-leveson). Although an article appeared in the printed version of *The Guardian* on 1 December 2012 entitled 'Rowling left "duped and angry" at PM's response', this was a piece by the newspaper's political editor, Patrick Wintour, and merely quoted Rowling's statements from C24]

C25

'Inspiration', *Harper's Bazaar* [UK edition], December 2013, pp. 218-221
  ('This is the story of three charm bracelets. I was a plain and freckly five-year-old...')
  (headed, 'JK Rowling')

C26

'This is a Story of Three Charm Bracelets', *Harper's Bazaar* [US edition], December 2013, pp. 250-52
  ('I was a plain and freckly five-year-old when I received the first, and I had never...')
  (headed, 'By J.K. Rowling')

D. ITEMS CREATED BY J.K. ROWLING SPECIFICALLY FOR SALE AT AUCTION

D1

12 December 2002
Autograph card
93 words on autograph card signed
Sotheby's
Sold for £24,000 (estimate £5,000/6,000)

Originally intended to be sold as part of an after-dinner auction at the Society of Authors to benefit Book Aid International, this card was consigned to a specialized sale at Sotheby's in the hope of attracting significant bidding from a wider audience. The card showed the title of the forthcoming *Harry Potter and the Order of the Phoenix* and, in a spiral around this, provided some plot teasers. When the card arrived at Sotheby's I suggested that it be sold, sight unseen, in a sealed envelope.

The item then became a tantalizing statement about the forthcoming book, fuelled by significant anticipation surrounding the book. The 'Leaky Cauldron' website launched a fundraising campaign to secure the item for all those who donated. When the card sold to a private individual in the U.S., the 'Leaky Cauldron' donated the sum it had raised to Book Aid International.

D2

1 November 2004
Miniature Book containing extracts from *Harry Potter and the Philosopher's Stone*
Sotheby's (for 999 Club)
Sold for £11,000 (estimate £4,000/6,000)

Part of an auction of twenty-five miniature books, each approximately one-inch tall, organised by *Tatler* magazine. Rowling provided drawings and short extracts from the first Harry Potter book. The catalogue description noted that the author had 'drawn and written in exquisite detail exactly what Harry Potter needs for his wizardry'. The book ends with 'From *Harry Potter and the Philosopher's Stone* by me'.

The 999 club is a charity based in Deptford, South-East London, which assists the homeless and helpless.

D3

24 March 2005
'The Ballad of Nearly Headless Nick'
Two-page authorial copy of thirty-two line poem in four stanzas cut from *Harry Potter and the Chamber of Secrets*
Lyon and Turnbull (for Scottish Language Dictionaries)
Sold for £2,000

A fair copy in the author's hand of this poem cut from the second Harry Potter novel was contributed to an auction to raise funds for Scottish Language Dictionaries, a research organisation for Scottish lexicography formed in 1992. The manuscript was displayed at the Scottish Poetry Library prior to auction.

In 2010, owned by the book collector and publisher of *Asia Literary Review*, Ilyas Khan, the manuscript was exhibited at the Wigtown Book Festival (24 September–3 October 2010).

D4

21 February 2006
'The Noble and Most Ancient House of Black'
Hand-drawn genealogical tree, framed and glazed
Bloomsbury Book Auctions (for Book Aid International)
Sold for £30,000 (no estimate given)

This genealogical tree of the Black family was titled 'The Noble and Most Ancient House of BLACK (there are many stories between the lines)'. It was offered for sale, as with D1, to benefit Book Aid International.

D5

13 December 2007
The Tales of Beedle the Bard
c. 5,500 words comprising five short stories, one of seven autograph copies
Sotheby's
Sold for £1.95 million (estimate £30,000/50,000)

With the conclusion of the Harry Potter series in July 2007, J.K. Rowling decided that, having made reference to a book of wizarding fairy-tales within *Harry Potter and the Deathly Hallows*, she would write *The Tales of Beedle the Bard* and present individually handwritten copies to six people most closely connected to the series of books.

A seventh copy was created for sale at auction to raise funds for 'The Children's Voice' charity (now Lumos). It consisted of around 160 pages containing a total of approximately 5,500 words and numerous illustrations. The book itself was an Italian hand-made notebook with deckle-edged leaves and bound in brown morocco. The binding was then embellished on the upper cover by Edinburgh jeweller and silversmiths, Hamilton and Inches (see also D8). The embellishments comprised five individually hand-chased hallmarked sterling silver ornaments. Each copy had additional gems mounted and this copy featured moonstones. There was also a separate clasp.

News of the item broke on 1 November 2007 and enjoyed some significant pre-sale coverage. I took the book to the U.S. for exhibition at Sotheby's in New York, 26-28 November (and it featured on *Good Morning America* on 26 November). Back in London an entire gallery at Sotheby's was devoted to the volume for the exhibition, 9-12 December. Badges were made and distributed ('I have seen | Beedle | the Bard | Sotheby's' over a skull), there was an appearance on *This Morning* and then *Blue Peter* on 5 December and, finally, a lavish party on 10 December at which the author read one of the stories.

After a long and protracted bidding war, the successful buyer was
£1.95 million is, currently, a world record for a modern literary man
children's book.

Of the other six copies, two have been exhibited:

Copy belonging to Barry Cunningham (National Library of Scot

Copy belonging to Arthur A. Levine (New York Public Library,

D6

10 June 2008
'What's Your Story?' *Harry Potter* 'Prequel' Story
c. 800 words comprising an episode from a *Potter* 'prequel'
Waterstone's Piccadilly (for Dyslexia Action and EnglishPEN)
Sold for £25,000 (no estimate provided)

Part of an auction of thirteen postcards held at Waterstone's Piccadilly as part of the bookseller's 'Writer's Year' campaign to benefit Dyslexia Action and EnglishPEN. The evening raised £47,150 with work by Lisa Appignanesi, Margaret Atwood, Lauren Child, Sebastian Faulks, Richard Ford, Neil Gaiman, Nick Hornby, Doris Lessing, Michael Rosen, Axel Scheffler, Tom Stoppard and Irvine Welsh.

Rowling's card – later published within B18 – comprised an 800-word double-sided A5 storycard and presented a 'prequel' episode to the Harry Potter series.

D7

21 May 2013
Harry Potter and the Philosopher's Stone. London: Bloomsbury, 1997
First edition, original pictorial boards, annotated on 43 pages, c. 22 illustrations and 1,100 words
Sotheby's (for EnglishPEN)
Sold for £150,000 (no estimate provided)

Lot 39 in EnglishPEN's 'First Editions, Second Thoughts' auction, this was one of fifty lots in which an author was asked to annotate a first edition with 'second thoughts'. Rowling responded with comments on the process of writing, editorial decisions and sources of inspiration together with references to the series as a whole and the film adaptations. There were also twenty-two illustrations, including 'Snape, brooding on the unfairness of life'.

The lot was sold to benefit EnglishPEN and the Lumos Foundation. The buyer was a private individual from the U.K.

D8

10 December 2013
The 'Lumos Maxima' Sterling Silver Charm Bracelet
Sotheby's
Sold for £20,000 (including buyer's premium) (estimate £15,000/20,000)

...s by J.K. Rowling, inspired by the Harry Potter books, a unique sterling silver charm ...rafted by the Edinburgh jeweller and silversmiths, Hamilton and Inches. The bracelet ...e years since the publication of *The Tales of Beedle the Bard*. The charms comprise Harry's ...lighning, glasses and broomstick, alongside a Golden Snitch, Dark Mark skull set with ...hyst eyes, Slytherin locket, winged key, *The Tales of Beedle the Bard* book, sorting hat, Deathly ...allows symbol and the logo of Lumos. The bracelet fastens with a magic wand charm.

The bracelet was sold to benefit Lumos (see also D5). Rowling contributed an article to *Harper's Bazaar* in connection with the bracelet and the charity (see C25 and C26).